RNITÉ OU LA MORT

LE CONSTITUTION

RF

DANTON

ROBESPIERRE

Porte St. Martin

FAUBOURG du TEMPLE

Rue Saint Antoine

Le Bastille

FAUBOURG St. ANTOINE

SEINE

FAUBOURG St. MARCEL

VOLUTION 1789–94

13. Cordeliers Club
14. Café Coraeza
15. Conciergerie
16. St. Sulpice
17. Hôtel Dieu
18. St. Roche
19. La Force
20. Le Châtelet
21. Palais Royal
22. Notre Dame
23. The Sorbonne
24. Les Halles

HELEN McKIE

THE MAN WHO KILLED THE KING

DENNIS WHEATLEY

The Man Who Killed The King

G. P. PUTNAM'S SONS
New York

FIRST AMERICAN EDITION 1965

Library of Congress Catalog
Card Number: 65-13300

MANUFACTURED IN THE UNITED STATES OF AMERICA

For my grand-daughter
ANTONIA
and my step-grand-children
CAROLINE, MAXINE, CHRISTOPHER,
JULIAN AND JAMES
this story which, with its predecessor
THE RISING STORM,
will give them, when they are old enough, the
whole true picture of the French Revolution
in "history without tears".

CONTENTS

PROLOGUE

"MADAM! I would be better served did I live in a hostel."

"Sir! I've not a doubt of it; but there you would have to pay your bills or they would throw you out!"

"Amanda!"

"Roger, I did not mean——"

A long shadow, falling across the entrance of the summer-house in which husband and wife stood, caused her to break off. It was that of the "best man" at their wedding, the clever, eccentric Lord Edward Fitz-Deverel. He had driven out on this sunny Sunday early in June, 1792, to their home in Richmond Park. After an early dinner he had left them, in order to let his groom know the hour at which he proposed to start back for London, and he had rejoined them sooner than they expected. Now, both of them were wondering uneasily if he had overheard their undignified recriminations.

They had been married close on two years, and made a handsome couple. Roger Brook was slimly but strongly built, his good shoulders well set off by a blue cut-away coat that matched the colour of his eyes. Beneath it his double-breasted waistcoat was embroidered with a gay pattern of flowers, and his white twill breeches merged into stockings of the sheerest silk. His brown hair was combed back from a good forehead, and although his mouth had become a trifle hard from the many hazardous experiences of his youth, making him look considerably older than his twenty-four years, his thin face was full of liveliness and charm. Amanda, the same age, was tallish for a woman, with slightly frizzy auburn hair and the flawless skin that often accompanies it. The full skirts of her striped yellow and white taffeta frock accentuated the narrowness of her waist; above it a fichu of snowy lawn fell in graceful folds over her well-rounded breasts. Her lips, as nearly always, were slightly parted, showing a glimpse of fine white teeth, as though about to smile.

"Droopy Ned", as Lord Edward had been nicknamed from his permanent stoop, regarded them in silence for a moment. The pale blue, shortsighted eyes that smiled at them above his beaky nose told them nothing. He was a fop of the first order, and his manners matched his exquisite apparel. After flourishing his lace handkerchief above his heart in a bow to Amanda, he turned to Roger with a lazy shrug, and drawled:

"The dratted fellow must have punished your good ale so heavily that he has gone to sleep it off in a hay-loft, for I failed to find so much as a smell of him."

"I'll go and find him for you," Roger volunteered, glad of the excuse to break up an awkward situation. "I expect my man, Dan, has taken him up to his cottage."

As Roger strode away, Droopy turned, apparently to admire the view out of the window of the summer-house, although he had seen it a hundred times before. Thatched House Lodge, in which the Brooks lived, was a most attractive little mansion that earlier in the century had replaced an old hunting lodge which had once been a favourite retreat of Charles I. It was Crown property, and the Prime Minister, young William Pitt, had given Roger a life tenancy of it as a reward for certain highly secret services. The summer-house, however, was contemporary with the original building. It had been embellished in the '60s with a fine ceiling painted by Angelica Kauffmann, and was lately converted by Roger into a studio, in which he indulged his amateur talent as an artist. Standing on high ground across the lawn from the house, its windows gave a splendid prospect across Richmond Park to the blue haze of the Surrey woods beyond. Suddenly, without looking at Amanda, Droopy spoke:

"M'dear, I have seen this coming for a long time."

"You heard us, then?"

"I could scarce help doing so, though only the deep affection I bear you both excuses me in referring to it."

"Roger has good cause for his annoyance," she defended her husband quickly. "Knowing how fond you are of rich wines, he produced that bottle of Château-Yquem specially for you. As I was aware of his intent I should have provided peaches or white muscats to go with it. But I fear I am an incurably thoughtless creature, so make but a poor housekeeper, and our purse is not long enough to employ a superior woman who would attend to such matters for me."

"So I gathered," rejoined Droopy drily. "And while, m'dear, I count your sweet vagueness about the less important things of life no small part of your charm, it distresses me the more to think that your thoughtlessness on this occasion may have been influenced by a necessary economy."

Amanda shrugged, and with a rustle of her stiff skirts sat down. "God be thanked we are not yet so reduced that the purchase of a bunch of grapes would involve us in a financial crisis. But during the past two years Roger has earned nothing. His allowance from his father and mine from my uncle are barely enough to support us here. Moving in society, as we do, costs more than we can afford, and both of us, alas, have expensive tastes. Were I a better manager we could perhaps make do, but I have a horror of accounts and no head for them, so it was unjust of me to upbraid him over our unpaid bills."

"Nonsense, m'dear, he invited your rebuke," smiled Droopy, taking a seat beside her. "That you should be living beyond your means is as much his fault as yours, but lack of money is not the only reason for the gulf that is opening between you."

"You—you think, then, that our marriage is doomed to end in failure?"

"By no means. He is devoted to you, and his present irritability arises from a natural instinct which it is beyond his power to control. For months past I have watched his increasing restlessness with much concern, and I have no doubt about its cause. To such an active mind painting and gardening can never be more than stop-gaps. Secretly he is eating his heart out from the feeling that he is wasting the best years of his life, and his financial circumstances are now an additional reason why he should seek some employment."

For a few moments Amanda did not reply. The scenes of her married life with Roger were coursing swiftly through her mind. First, there had been their wonderful honeymoon in Italy. A sheaf of introductions from diplomats and others with whom Roger's previous activities had brought him into contact had resulted in a score of invitations to stay in palaces and lovely villas, so that for over six months they had prolonged their carefree wanderings up and down the sunny peninsular. On their return there had been the excitement of settling into Thatched House Lodge, then a brilliant London season in which they were among the most popular newly-weds at innumerable balls and assemblies. In the autumn that followed, Lady Marie Brook's illness had taken a turn for the worse, and as Roger was very devoted to his mother they had removed to his old home at Lymington to cheer her last months. Amanda, too, had loved Lady Marie dearly, and her death in the previous November had sadly distressed them both. A

Christmas visit, carried well into January, to their dearest woman friend, the gay and beautiful Georgina, and her husband, the Earl of St. Ermins, had restored their spirits; but soon after their return to Richmond Amanda had noticed a subtle change in Roger. His painting, instead of improving, had noticeably deteriorated, and although by comparison with most men of that period he was not a heavy drinker, he had formed the habit of consuming a bottle of port every night, even when they were alone. Normally he was easy to please and the most good-tempered of men, but as the spring advanced he had begun to show irritation over trifles and to give way to fits of moodiness, from which she found it increasingly difficult to rouse him. At times she feared that he was tiring of her, but on that cardinal issue, at least, Droopy's denial had sounded convinced and reassuring. At length she said:

"I deem you right. 'Tis some worth-while task on which to engage his good brain that he requires. But what? He has many accomplishments, yet has been trained to nothing. Moreover, he has an inborn hatred of routine. What possible employment could be found for him that would give real scope to his abilities, yet leave him a reasonable independence?"

Even as Amanda asked the question she knew the answer—and feared it. The shrewd Droopy knew well what was in her mind, so he replied as gently as he could, "M'dear, I know of only one thing which would give him satisfaction—to take up again the old work at which he proved so prodigiously successful."

Instinctively Amanda shied away from the thought, and cried, "No, no! Not that! 'Twas so damnably dangerous, and on our honeymoon we agreed that he should give it up for good."

"I know it. Yet travel and excitement have ever been the breath of Roger's life; 'tis that he really needs to make him his own man again. To have held him for two years is a triumph of which any woman could be proud, but I pray you to consider if the time has not now come when you should release him from any promise he may have made to you."

"It is too late!" There was a catch in Amanda's voice as she fought desperately against the thing that she had long been secretly dreading. "Thrice in the past eighteen months Mr. Pitt has sent for him and offered him missions abroad. Each time he has refused them, and after the last occasion the Prime Minister dismissed him almost brutally. Roger told me nothing of these meetings; I learned of them from my Lord Malmesbury. It seems that Mr. Pitt was so incensed by these persistent refusals that he declared that, as Roger would not accept employment when his services were needed, should he ever change his mind he would apply for it in vain. So you see he cannot again play ducks and drakes with his life in the Government's interest, even should I urge him to it."

"In that, m'dear, you are mistaken." Droopy paused a moment, then went on a little hurriedly. "I was with the Prime Minister no longer ago than Friday, and he spoke of Roger's defection far more in sorrow than in anger. Be brave now, and forgive me the hurt I am about to do you. Mr. Pitt formally charged me with endeavouring to persuade Roger to work for him again, and in the event of my succeeding he requests that Roger should wait upon him tomorrow morning."

"Oh, Droopy! How could you become a party to seeking to rob me of him?"

"Much as I dislike the task, I had no option. But would you not sooner that Mr. Pitt, rather than some designing woman, took Roger from you?"

"What a strange question! Pray enlighten me."

Droopy let go the ribbon of his quizzing glass, with which he had been toying, leaned forward and said earnestly, "Surely you are not blind to the alternative that awaits Roger should he refuse this new offer? His nature craves excitement and will secure it one way or another. Given three more months of his present way of life, I vow he'll be as ripe as a September apple to fall for the next attractive minx who sets her cap at him."

Amanda sighed. "As far as any wife can be certain of such things, I'd swear that Roger has been faithful to me; but before we married he was the very devil with the women, and what you suggest is a possibility that has recently caused me heartrending apprehension. Yet, if he goes abroad, there seems an even greater risk of his being unfaithful."

"Mayhap; but I recall your saying to me once yourself that you thought infidelity in a man no serious matter, providing his wife was not humiliated by a public knowledge of it, nor menaced by the loss of first place in her husband's true affections. Here, if Roger entered on an illicit affair, it would fill his mind to the exclusion of all else, and might even prove disastrous to your marriage. Abroad, his mind being mainly occupied with his mission, all the odds are that it would be an infidelity of so temporary a nature that it would detract nothing from his love for you."

Poor Amanda smiled a little wrily. "That, Droopy, is the sort of cynicism with which I used to armour my heart before I married him. Both of us had previously had tragic love affairs, and had vowed never again to allow our inmost being to become vulnerable to the caprice of a member of the opposite sex. Believing then that he was determined to continue in the service of Mr. Pitt, I accepted it quite calmly that while on his travels he would acquire numerous light-o'-loves. Now, having been his constant companion for two years, 'tis a far harder matter to recapture so detached a view. Yet, even so, I doubt not that in time I could bring myself to it . . . if only I could be certain that his heart would remain mine."

As she ceased speaking they both caught sight of Roger approaching across the lawn. He was smiling at them and in his hand he carried a bunch of June roses, that he had evidently just picked as a gesture of contrition for his harsh words to Amanda.

Droopy raised his quizzing glass and twisted it airily, as though he was about to voice some inconsequent witticism, but his whisper came swift and urgent:

"Amanda! If you hold him to his word 'tis a certainty you'll lose him. If you would keep his heart you must let him go."

* * * * *

That Sunday evening, after Droopy had left them, Amanda made Roger add up their bills. To his horror he found that they owed over twelve hundred pounds. Having asked Droopy to leave matters in her hands, she then gave Roger Mr. Pitt's message, declaring as she did so that, as their financial position demanded it and was mainly due to her own mismanagement, she was now fully reconciled to his resuming his old work.

At her self-accusation he protested. It was true that he was by nature much more careful about money matters than herself, but he felt that he was the more to blame for having allowed their liabilities to accumulate unchecked. The frightening total shocked him into a sudden realization that unless he could procure a considerable sum in the very near future they would find themselves in serious trouble, and he knew Amanda was right about there being only one way in which he could earn a large sum quickly.

She clinched the matter by saying sweetly, "Dearest Roger, even if money were not in question I think the time has come when you should leave me for a while. We have been blessed beyond most in having near two years of happy idleness in which to love each other, and it is not right that a man of your parts should spend all his life dancing attendance on a woman. By circumstances beyond our control you became when young a soldier without a uniform. Mr. Pitt's summons means that the country needs you, so you must obey the call of that muffled drum and go forth again to earn new laurels, which though invisible to others make me more than ever proud to be your wife."

A most touching scene ensued, for she was right in her belief that he had been entirely faithful to her since their marriage—a rare thing for those days—and he was most loath to leave her. Yet Droopy had also been right in that another side of him was becoming soured by inactivity, and once the decision had been taken he could not help having a secret feeling of elation.

Next morning, with all his old vigour and eagerness restored, Roger drove up to No. 10, Downing Street. While he waited downstairs in the inner hall for the great man to receive him, he speculated cheerfully on where he would be sent. France, he knew, was ruled out owing to the circumstances in which he had last left it. The missions he had refused had been to Portugal, the Austrian Netherlands and America. As he would have liked to visit the new world he would not have been at all averse to the last project being revived, but he hoped that it would be Austria or Prussia, as they too were countries to which he had not yet been, and either, or any other European court, would offer the prospect that he might later be able to arrange for Amanda to come out and join him there.

His pleasant musings were interrupted by the tinkle of a bell. At its sound a liveried footman led him upstairs and ushered him into the spacious room on the first floor in which the Prime Minister conducted his business. At a glance Roger saw that nothing had been changed since his last visit. On the desk there stood, as usual, a decanter of port and several glasses; behind it, very erect and imperturbable, sat the Prime Minister.

In this year of grace 1792 William Pitt the younger had reached the peak of his magnificent career. He had become Prime Minister at the age of twenty-four, and in the teeth of a powerful Whig opposition, led by such brilliant and experienced politicians as Fox, Burke and Sheridan, he had enforced innumerable wise measures upon a largely reluctant Parliament and nation.

The Peace of Versailles in 1783 had put an end to a desperate war, in which Britain had stood alone against the world and fought it to a standstill. France, Holland and Spain had actively combined against her to aid the American colonists in their War of Independence, while Russia, Denmark, Sweden, Prussia and Austria had ranged themselves with the enemies of the mother country in a pact of Armed Neutrality. It was in the December of that year that young Billy Pitt had assumed the reins of government. Britain lay exhausted, nearly bankrupt and entirely isolated.

With his genius for figures he straightened out the finances, and with incredible industry set about the revival of commerce. Britain was soon selling more goods to her late enemies in the new United States than she had ever done before, and a commercial treaty was entered into with France, which, but for the Revolution, might have for ever buried the hatchet between these two great hereditary enemies. By firmness at the right moment a war over the Dutch Netherlands was averted and that country was, together with Prussia, bound to Britain in a Triple Alliance that once more secured a balance of power in Europe. Again at the risk of war Pitt had curbed the ambitions of Spain and secured the Canadian Pacific coast for future British colonists. By adopting a strong policy at the Convention of Reichenbach he had stopped a war between Austria and Prussia, then by a skilfully conceived blend of inducements and threats he had in turn persuaded Russia and Sweden to make peace at Werelö, Austria and Turkey at Sistova, and Russia and Turkey at Jassy. In eight years of remarkable government he had brought the blessing of peace to all Europe and restored Britain to a marvellous prosperity, making her once again the most powerful and respected nation in the world.

He was still only a little over thirty: a tall, thin, shy, retiring man, who presented to the world a cold, aristocratic mien. No woman played any part in his life, and even those brief periods of relaxation that he permitted himself, when in the company of his few intimates he showed humanity and charm, were becoming rarer as the years went by. Success could not spoil him, because from his earliest youth he had felt a conviction that he would succeed his great father at the helm of the ship of state and that he was born only to rule. Yet his now unassailable position had made him still more dictatorial in manner.

Nevertheless, he greeted Roger courteously, waved him to a chair and, as was his custom, poured him a glass of port. Then he said briskly, "May I take it, Mr. Brook, that your coming here today indicates your willingness to receive my instructions?"

Roger bowed. "I have been too long inactive, sir, and in view of my past refusals am the more grateful to you for the renewed offer to re-enter your service. I am willing to go wherever you may choose to send me."

"Good! We will forget then the disappointments you have caused me in the past two years. Your earlier activities, coupled with a flair for handling difficult situations skilfully, provide a combination peculiarly suited to the matter I have in mind; and to be honest I know of no one else who would stand even a chance of succeeding in this delicate business."

"Indeed, you flatter me, sir."

Mr. Pitt coldly waved the suggestion aside. "I am not given to such practices. Without belittling your courage and resource, I am influenced principally by the fact that in the past you have acquired a personal background which I believe can now be exploited to serve my ends. Your knowledge of the genesis and opening scenes of the Revolution in France is so extensive that I need waste no time in going over old ground. It suffices to state that since you left that country no change has occurred to affect vitally the limited authority that remained vested in the Monarchy, or in the situation of the Royal Family. In October '89 you were a witness to their being forcibly brought from Versailles to Paris by a multitude of their rebellious subjects, to become virtually prisoners in the Palace of the Tuileries. There, for close on three years, they have remained, and by a servile complaisance to the wishes of the National Assembly the King has, to all appearances, succeeded in gradually regaining the affections of his people. I have, however, recently received reliable information that a new and alarming turn of events is expected to take place in Paris towards the end of this month."

Roger's eyes widened with sudden apprehension. With the Prime Minister's next words the bombshell fell.

"Therefore, as soon as your affairs permit, I desire you to proceed to France."

* * * * *

"France!" ejaculated Roger. "Sir, pray allow me to remind you of the circumstances in which I left that country."

"I remember them well," replied the Prime Minister calmly. "You had, a few days previously, denounced to the mob the Spanish Envoy Extraordinary, upon which they hanged him from a lamp-post. A horrible affair, but one that enabled you shortly afterwards to render a signal service to Britain."

"Yes, yes. I know!" Roger's words came tumbling out in a spate of agitation. "But surely you realize that hideous business makes my return impossible?"

"Why so?"

"Because it will have caused all decent people there to regard me as a murderer."

"Then you will find yourself in a great company, since half the public men in France have stained their hands with blood since '89."

"Perhaps, but in the vast majority of cases only indirectly. In any event, the manner in which I brought about the death of Don Diego Sidonia y Ulloa is bound to prove the most appalling handicap in any business I might attempt."

"I judge you mistaken in that. In the two years since he died scores of unfortunate people have been murdered by the Paris mobs. The details of your affair will have been forgotten by now, except by those to whom as a matter of policy you might think fit to recall them deliberately."

"My reappearance in Paris would recall them to everyone. I beg you, sir, to make use of me in some other country—to send me anywhere in the world, but not to France."

The Prime Minister shook his head. "No, Mr. Brook. France it must be, since 'tis there that lies the work for which I cannot find any other man so well qualified as yourself. William Augustus Miles, whom you will recall, still serves me conscientiously with reports of the doings at the Jacobin Club and a Colonel George Munro now furnishes my cousin Grenville with even more lively commentaries on events in France; but you alone have personal contact with the minds that direct both the Royalist and Revolutionary policies."

"But, sir," Roger pleaded, "you speak of the past. Is it not obvious to you that by my act I rendered the greater part of those contacts of no value whatever for the future?"

"In that I do not agree," came the quiet reply. "Unless

marriage has rusted your imagination you will soon think of a story to explain away that old affair to those who may hold it against you. On the other hand it should serve you as a trump card in swiftly gaining the confidence of the extremists. In fact I had this last promising possibility particularly in mind when I sent for you."

Roger shrugged unhappily. "Distasteful as the rôle would be, I could easily present myself as a blood-stained *sans-culotte* if that is all you require of me."

"By no means! In '89 you were *persona grata* with Queen Marie Antoinette. I desire you to see her in secret and urge a certain policy upon her."

"The Queen! God forbid, sir! She must not only know what I did, but must attribute it to the basest personal vengeance. She'd not forgive me in a thousand years, and I'd stand no more chance than a wild beast of being admitted to her presence."

"Again I disagree. Since she left Versailles the pride of that poor Austrian princess has been sadly chastened. In her dire extremity she even formed a secret alliance with Mirabeau, despite the previous horror she had publicly proclaimed at his profligacy and venality."

Momentarily forgetting his distress, Roger gave a quick smile and remarked, "As I had the honour to be the first to inform you, sir—although you refused to credit so astounding a development at the time."

"True! I admit it," the Prime Minister smiled back. "But she has gone further since, in accepting the services of Barnave and the Lameths: men who all participated in hounding on the mob to commit the first excesses of the Revolution. I tell you, much water has flowed under the bridges of the Seine since you brought about Don Diego's death. Marie Antoinette will not have forgotten your past services to her, and she is most desperately in need of friends. I'll warrant you that she'll be quick enough to dismiss all thought of the Spaniard from her mind when you announce yourself to her as my personal emissary."

Roger was now in a frightful quandary. No project could have been more distasteful to him than a return to France, but Mr. Pitt had swept aside what he felt to be his reasonable objections, and ever since he had totted up his bills he had been secretly harassed by his urgent need for money. After a moment's hesitation, he said:

"You remarked, sir, a few moments back, that you wished me to proceed to France as soon as my affairs permit. Unfortunately, the financial side of them is far from healthy. Unless I can shortly lay my hand on a quite considerable sum of money I fear I may find myself in Newgate."

"It is a new departure for you to attempt to drive a bargain with me, Mr. Brook," replied the Prime Minister, giving a tight-lipped smile. "However, I am in the unique position of being able to pay the debts of anyone except myself. As your past record suggests that in this particular business you may accomplish more than any other person known to me, I am willing to buy your services. How much do you require?"

"A thousand pounds would enable me to leave with my mind at rest," murmured Roger rather shamefacedly. Then, in an endeavour to cover his embarrassment, he added with a sudden grin, "But in order to reach the Queen I may have to resort to bribery, and when M. de Talleyrand-Périgord arrived here last January he made no secret of the fact that he had brought with him forty thousand with which to grease the palms of people who might prove useful to him."

"I hardly think," said Mr. Pitt a trifle acidly, "that the National Guards at the Tuileries are likely to prove as avaricious as our Whig politicians. A draft on the secret funds for fifteen hundred pounds should meet your requirements, for the moment at all events. Apart from special activities, your personal reports to me on general matters have always proved valuable, so I am willing to give you a generous credit for them. Should you need more for some particular purpose, you can later apply to Lord Grenville for it through the usual Foreign Office channels."

Roger bowed. "I am deeply grateful to you, sir, and I had no serious intent to compare my situation with that of M. de Talleyrand."

"Have you seen that disreputable friend of yours lately?"

"No, sir. Not since his return to France and his reappearance here on a second mission in April. As you must be aware, he consorts principally with Lord Holland, Lord Lansdowne and others in strong opposition to the Government, and, greatly as I admire him personally, my loyalty to you prevents me from moving happily in such circles."

"I appreciate your delicacy, yet find it difficult to understand how you can admire an apostate priest and renegade noble who has betrayed both his own orders to become the servant of unscrupulous demagogues."

"I owe much to his patronage when I was first in France as a youth, and in his dealings with me since he has always proved both honourable and kind. May I enquire if his present mission here has any bearing on that with which you propose to charge me?"

"It has, so I will inform you of the events that led up to it. The most reactionary of the French nobility, including the King's younger brother, d'Artois, fled abroad in '89. As was not unnatural, they at once attemped to stir up trouble for the new French Government at numerous foreign courts. At first they met with little success, except that King Gustavus of Sweden declared himself the champion of the royal cause and ready to lead a crusade against the revolutionaries if his fellow monarchs would support him. On their refusing, it was he who through his agent, the Comte de Fersan, last summer instigated the attempt of the Royal Family to escape to Metz. The King's other brother, de Provence, succeeded in getting away to Brussels, thereby greatly strengthening the influence of the *émigrés*, but the sovereigns were, as you will know, caught at Varennes, and brought back to Paris in circumstances of the greatest indignity.

"The insults they suffered then did what the *émigrés* had so far failed to achieve. The Queen's brother, Leopold of Austria, felt in honour bound to make at least a show of taking up his sister's cause, and that excitable monarch Frederick William of Prussia also began to threaten France with hostilities. However, Leopold exercised his usual caution, and both of them were anxious to make certain of the attitude of Britain before committing themselves. The British people, having long enjoyed a constitutional monarchy, had shown in no uncertain manner their sympathy with the efforts of the French people to secure a similar liberty, so the German autocrats had some reason to fear that we might declare ourselves as the champions of France's new-won freedom.

"As my highest aspiration has ever been the maintenance of peace in Europe, I would go no further than to reaffirm our reluctance to interfere in French domestic affairs, thus leaving them still in doubt of our attitude in the event of a new situation. That proved sufficient to check their ardour for the moment. Then, on the 1st of September last, King Louis formally accepted the new constitution presented to him by the National Assembly. Leopold, who was much more concerned about Russian and Prussian designs against Poland than about events in France, at once seized on that as an excuse to declare that the King's act having been voluntary, foreign intervention was no longer called for."

The Prime Minister took a drink of port, and went on, "All might then have continued well, but for the attitude of the French themselves. A great part of them, alas, have become drunk on their new-found liberty, and with a missionary zeal send agents to propagate their radical doctrines in other countries. The obvious repercussions ensued. The German monarchs began to fear for their own security. Gustavus again urged them and Spain to combine with him in the forcible suppression of this revolutionary fever that might, if unchecked, destroy the whole fabric of European society—and in that he had a better case. In January preparations for a war began, and it was then that M. de Talleyrand was sent to England on an unofficial mission to make a bid for our support against the Royalist coalition."

"That much I gathered," Roger nodded. "And at least you may count him honest in his endeavours to bring about an alliance between France and Britain, for I know well that such a project has long been his dearest ambition."

"You think so?" Mr. Pitt made a gesture of distaste. "He is an opportunist of the first order and as slippery as an eel; neither my cousin Grenville nor I trusts him an inch. In any case, His Majesty has been profoundly shocked by the indignities the French people have put upon their sovereigns and feels a righteous horror at the atheistic legislation of the Assembly, so nothing would induce him to countenance an alliance with such a Government.

"But to continue; in the spring three events occurred to encourage the bellicose attitude of the French zealots. In Spain, Floridablanca was replaced as First Minister by d'Aranda, who at once made it clear that his country would not join a coalition against France; on the 9th of March the Emperor Leopold quite unexpectedly died, and a week later King Gustavus was assassinated. The National Assembly had already forced King Louis to sanction measures depriving the *émigrés* of their property, and was threatening the Elector of Treves, under whose protection they had set up their headquarters at Coblenz. Both parties sent troops to the frontier. The Elector appealed to Austria for support and Leopold's son, young Francis II, promised it to him. But it seems that with Spain and Sweden out of the ring the hotheads in France were now bent on war in any case, for they declared it on the Princes and their backers on the 20th of April."

"It was then that M. de Talleyrand was sent on his second mission to London, was it not?" Roger commented.

"Yes. Knowing the prime importance that England has always attached to the Low Countries, Talleyrand came with an offer that France would refrain from invading the Austrian Netherlands if we would declare ourselves strictly neutral in the new war."

Having accepted the fact that he was now fully committed, Roger was beginning to enjoy himself. He smiled and said, "I imagine that suited your book admirably, sir?"

"It suited mine," came the prompt reply. "For however regrettable the situation of the French Royal Family may be, I would never consent to plunging this country into war solely on their behalf. Yet a great change has occurred in public opinion here during the past year. Even moderate men feel that the Revolution in France has gone far enough and are disgusted with the excesses which have taken place. They no longer see in it a comparison with our own Great Rebellion, but begin to fear it as a menace to property and the established order in our own land. The violent writings of such radical agitators as Tom Paine have been largely responsible for that, and, as you must know, the country is now swarming with French *émigrés*. Many of them are agents sent by the Princes from Coblenz, and their influence on our aristocracy is considerable; so much pressure has been brought on me by my own party to take up the Royalist cause."

"Yet you are resolved not to do so, sir?"

"I regard war as the antithesis of civilization, and would resort to it only if I were convinced that this country's security was threatened. That being my secret policy, I allowed the Whigs whom de Talleyrand has bribed so lavishly to appear to get the better of me, and he owes far more to me than he is aware. I will admit, though, that no man lacking his brain and charm could have handled his own end of the business so successfully."

About de Talleyrand's qualities Roger needed no telling, and it had always been one of his regrets that Mr. Pitt so greatly distrusted the gifted Frenchman. He made up his mind now to see de Talleyrand at the earliest opportunity, as he felt that there was no one who could better bring him up to date with affairs in France.

In the meantime the Prime Minister was continuing, "However, I am confident in my ability to withstand the war-mongers here in England. 'Tis those in France who fill me with more concern."

"Yet from what you tell me of M. de Talleyrand's mission, it appears that the French Government would be well content with no more than our neutrality."

"That is true of the present Ministry," Mr. Pitt frowned, "but, as I mentioned earlier, I have reason to believe that a fresh upheaval is about to occur in France. If so, it may disrupt all stable government; M. de Talleyrand and those who sent him may find themselves unseated, and a new set of masters might call a very different tune.

"That brings me to your mission. Whatever may occur, one of its principles will be to exert such influence as you can on people of all shades of opinion, with a view to making it easier for me to prevent war breaking out between France and Britain. A second principle will be always to argue that, having brought their present monarch to heel, the French will do far better to keep him than to substitute any other for him."

"I had thought, sir, that since King Louis accepted the Constitution his position was reasonably secure," Roger said with surprise, "and that this year he has enjoyed a popularity greater than at any time since '89."

"That is the general assumption here, but my informants tell me that the Girondins, who are now the most powerful group in France, are not content with having shackled the King; they wish to bring about his death or removal, so that they can replace him with a constitutional monarch more to their own taste."

Roger's eyes narrowed. "I smell that traitor, the Duc d'Orléans, behind this. From the very beginning he has conspired to have his cousin deposed, with the object of replacing him as Regent."

"That is a possibility; although d'Orléans has lost much credit in recent months. I gather the idea of a German prince now finds much more favour in the eyes of Madame Roland and her friends. Again, this has relevance to your mission, for it is a move that I am determined to thwart at any cost."

The Prime Minister paused for a moment, then went on earnestly, "In our desperate need after the late war I entered into an alliance with Prussia, but since then the European situation has undergone a great change. I sought Prussian friendship as a counterweight against the power of France. From the latter we now have little to fear, while the former shows signs of becoming far too powerful for my liking. I still wish to maintain good relations with the Prussians, but in secret everything possible must be done to curb their further aggrandizement. There are two eventualities which might prove disastrous to us: the first is that France should acquire a German puppet for her king, the second that King Louis should allow himself to be rescued from his people by the Prussians; for if that occurred and they reseated him firmly on his throne by force of arms, so weak a man could not escape becoming their cat's-paw afterwards."

"Either would prove calamitous," Roger agreed quickly. "Now that the Prussians are marching to join the Austrians on the Rhine, the Treaty they entered into at Berlin last February is taking concrete form. Should they succeed in imposing their will upon France we might later find the three most powerful nations in Europe combined against us."

"Precisely! However, the danger of Louis XVI being dethroned in favour of a German prince is one which you can do no more than possibly assist in combating, whereas I have hopes that you may succeed in averting the other danger altogether, by taking measures which would eliminate the risk of the King falling into German hands."

"There seems little likelihood of his doing so at present; the war has hardly started. It is a long way from the Rhine to Paris, and the French National forces would first have to be overcome."

"Not necessarily. The King must be aware of this new conspiracy that threatens his throne and life. He may at any time make a second attempt to escape with his Queen, then join his brothers in Coblenz. I desire you to see the Queen and do your utmost to dissuade them from such a step."

Roger pulled a wry face. "To win Marie Antoinette's confidence again will be no easy matter. But that apart, 'tis plaguy unlikely she would heed such counsel, if she believes that in flight lies the only hope of preserving herself and her family."

"You go too fast. I did not say dissuade them from flight, but from throwing themselves into the arms of the Germans. I propose that you should urge upon her the idea of making for Brittany; and there is a good case for that. If King Louis seeks sanctuary with the foreign troops that are about to invade his kingdom he will be playing into the hands of his enemies. It seems beyond doubt that the great majority of the French people are still loyal to the Throne, and by such a move he would instantly sacrifice that last remaining card. On the other hand, if, by retiring to Brittany, he openly demonstrated his disapproval of the attempts of his brothers to overawe his subjects with foreign aid, all the best elements of the nation would rally to him. Of that I am convinced."

"'Tis an inspiration, sir," nodded Roger appreciatively. "So shrewd a stroke would, I believe, both confound his enemies and restore him to favour with nine-tenths of his people."

The Prime Minister picked up the port decanter, refilled their glasses, and said in a kindlier tone than he had so far used during their interview, "That, then, is what I wish you to attempt, although I realize that the task of persuading anyone as pig-headed as Marie Antoinette to take sound advice may prove beyond any man's powers. But nothing venture, nothing gain; touching which I have in mind a still more formidable undertaking which I will present to you only as a possibility."

Roger smiled. "Now that I am again committed I will not shrink from venturing anything in your service, sir; so pray tell me of it."

Mr. Pitt leant forward and answered with a low-voiced question, "What do you consider the prospects to be of detaching the Dauphin from the Queen and bringing him to England?"

"I would be serving both you and myself ill, sir, did I pretend that I thought them anything but exceeding slender," Roger replied with a shake of his head.

"Yet I recall that in '89 Marie Antoinette thought of sending him to her sister, the Queen of Naples, and it was to you she turned to undertake a secret mission for her to the Sovereigns of the Sicilies to enquire if they would receive the child there at the risk of war with France."

"True, and my mission was successful. But on my return the Queen informed me that the King had changed his mind and definitely decided not to be parted from his son; and that on further consideration she was herself convinced that he was right."

"If you can succeed in regaining her confidence, the King, being of such a vacillating nature, might change his mind once again."

"Their circumstances are very different now. I have heard it said that for a long time past the Queen has scarcely allowed the child to leave her side, and that she never appears in public without him, because his presence alone protects her from the violence of the mob. Moreover, I understand that since they were brought back to Paris after their abortive flight to Varennes, the whole Royal Family is far more closely guarded than was formerly the case."

"Both reports are true, and I agree that no higher sacrifice could be asked of the Queen than the surrender of the only shield which still gives her some protection. But the child would no longer be so necessary to her in that capacity if the Royal Family could be removed from Paris, and the problem of outwitting the Palace guard will arise in any case if they decide on an attempt to reach either Brittany or Coblenz. Should they already have settled on the latter course, and you find them unshakable in their determination to adopt it, this project then becomes above all else important. In that case—or should you have reason to believe that the King's life is in imminent peril—you have my permission to stick at nothing which may enable you to remove the Dauphin from his parents."

" 'Tis clear, sir, that you consider the possession of the Dauphin's person would be of great value to us."

"Of inestimable value. King Louis has proved such a weak and unstable monarch that there can be no security for us from war with France as long as he reigns. Should you succeed in persuading him to attempt a flight to Brittany and he reaches there in safety, it will be many months, if not years, before he can finally subdue his kingdom. If the Dauphin were here as our guest meanwhile, during such a lengthy period we should have ample opportunity to treat him with so much kindness that later his friendship for England would prove a most weighty asset in maintaining peace between the two nations. Should King Louis seek sanctuary with the Germans, in the person of the Dauphin we should possess a counterweight to German influence in France. The King would have lost all credit there, so with the French people behind us we might even force him to abdicate in favour of his son. Lastly, should King Louis and his Queen perish at the hands of their enemies, as I fear is only too likely to be the case, and the Dauphin were here, England would then be sheltering the new King of France."

Mr. Pitt sipped his port, set down his glass, and concluded in a clear, firm voice, "As I see it, this child must inevitably become the focus around which the future will take shape. If the Jacobins succeed in bringing about King Louis's death, but can keep the boy, they will be able to rule through him by a Council of Regency. That would ensure them the support of by far the greater part of the French people, and so enable them to proceed with their programme of communism and atheism, which must result in turning France into a festering sore that may later destroy all Europe. If the Germans obtain the little Prince it will prove an evil day for Britain. If we can do so, the Red menace will have been robbed of its stalking-horse, and the thoughts of all decent people in France will turn with hope to this Island. Therefore, he who holds the Dauphin will hold the ace of trumps."

Again the Prime Minister leant forward, and his voice was tense. "Bring me the Dauphin, Mr. Brook, and I will pay you one hundred thousand pounds."

CHAPTER I

A BISHOP BRIEFS A SPY

ON Monday the 18th of June Roger landed at Le Havre. It was nine years since he had first set eyes on its busy port and tall, gabled houses, but the sights, sounds and smells of the French town instantly brought back to him a flood of memories. Round the corner from the Arsenal lay the brothel from which he had fled in horror, and only a few hundred yards along the quay was the spot where, sweating with fright, he had first drawn a sword in earnest, to defend himself against a drunken bravo.[1]

He now wore no sword; times—particularly in France—had changed. The nobility, who in the past alone had been legally entitled to wear swords, had been abolished, and for any well-dressed man now to vaunt that old insignia of rank was to invite immediate trouble; nevertheless, the tall, tasselled Malacca cane that Roger carried concealed a slender, deadly blade. Three-cornered hats, lace jabots and embroidered coats had also gone out of fashion; a hat the shape of an inverted sickle moon was perched far back at a rakish angle on his brown hair, a white linen stock encased his neck, and for the Channel crossing he had worn a long grey riding-coat with a heavy four-layered cape collar.

Had he needed a reminder of those desperate days when as a youngster he had found himself stranded and penniless in Le Havre, the presence of his companion would have sufficed; it was Dan Izzard, once Lymington's local smuggler, who had brought him over when he ran away from home. Dan then had the ill-luck to be captured before they got ashore and had spent six grim years chained to an oar in the French galleys. It was not until '89 that Roger had succeeded in procuring his release through the clemency of Queen Marie Antoinette, and since his return to England Roger had taken him into his personal

[1] See *The Launching of Roger Brook*, which records Mr. Brook's adventures in France from July 1783 to November 1787.

The Shadow of Tyburn Tree records his missions to the Courts of Denmark, Sweden and Catherine the Great of Russia, between November 1787 and April 1789.

The Rising Storm records his missions to France, Italy and Spain between April 1789 and the opening of the present chronicle (June 1792).

service. The years Dan had spent amongst Frenchmen had made him, like his master, bilingual; although when they were alone together he often spoke to Roger in the Hampshire dialect that he had used most of his life. Either of them could pass with ease as a *Français*, and Roger had brought Dan with him now because he felt that, should war between England and France break out and the British Embassy in Paris consequently be closed, the ex-smuggler would prove invaluable as a trusty and resourceful messenger to carry secret reports back to London.

Dan was over fifty, but a big burly fellow, and neither his age nor his long ordeal in the galleys had impaired his physique. His black beard, weather-beaten face and gold ear-rings still proclaimed him a born seaman, and many years as the captain of a lugger had taught him how to handle men. As Roger stood on the quay watching him now, he admired the brusque but jovial way in which his henchman hustled the surly French porters into collecting his baggage and summoning a carriage to take them to an inn.

On their honeymoon Roger and Amanda had travelled to and from Italy by way of Brussels, the Rhine and Switzerland. In consequence, he had not been in France since May 1790, and even the short drive to the inn was sufficient to impress him with the fact that the state of the country must have sadly deteriorated during the two years since he had left it.

After the great upheavals that had followed the calling of the States-General in May 1789, it had seemed that, having at last secured a parliament representative of the nation, France would settle down again. The storming of the Bastille by the mob in the July of that year had marked the end of the days of Louis XVI as an absolute monarch. For a week in August there had raged "The Great Fear", during which apparently spontaneous risings had taken place from end to end of the country, innumerable *châteaux* had been burnt down, thousands of gentry had been murdered and many thousands more compelled to seek safety abroad. Then in October agitators had roused the mobs of Paris to march on Versailles; the King and his family, menaced and insulted for hours on end, had at last been forced by the rioters to accompany them back to the city and take up residence in the Palace of the Tuileries. It had been put about that their permanent presence in Paris would ensure its citizens ample supplies of bread, but the real intent behind the move had been to prevent any possibility of the monarch amassing an army in the provinces and using it to restore his authority in the rebellious capital.

Once the revolutionary leaders had achieved their object they had had nothing more to fear, so had allowed the quite unjustified distrust of the King, with which they had inspired the people, to die down. Indeed, their fears had never had any serious foundation, for the Christian humility which was the outstanding characteristic of Louis XVI fitted him better for a martyr than for a king. At every crisis he had declared emphatically that he would rather die himself than that one drop of the people's blood should be shed in his defence; and, in spite of the vacillation which was second nature to him, from that single determination he had never deviated. Moreover, from the very beginning of his reign, he had conscientiously striven to better the lot of his poorer subjects, and had he not wavered hopelessly between the divided counsels of his ministers he would have introduced many liberal reforms. After being carried to Paris, therefore, instead of resisting the development of the New Order, he had lent himself willingly to its establishment, and regained much of his past popularity by giving a ready assent to all the measures proposed by the National Assembly.

As a result, when Roger had left France the Royal Family, although virtually prisoners in the Tuileries, still lived in considerable state. They continued to hold their Court, even if on a less splendid scale than when at Versailles; they sometimes went to the opera and attended public functions, and not infrequently their appearance was greeted with cheers, which showed that the ordinary citizens of Paris were still mainly loyal to them. Although all legislative power was now vested in the Assembly, the King was still the executive head of the nation, and continued to rule through his Council of Ministers. It had been clear, too, that only a handful of extremists wished to replace the Monarchy with a Republic, so nearly everyone agreed that a satisfactory balance had been achieved between the rights of the People and the powers of the Throne.

The brutalized mobs of the Faubourgs, which had been used by the politicians of the Left to intimidate the old order into submission, could not be expected to return to their dens on a mere announcement that the Revolution was accomplished, so occasional riots of some size, and many acts of individual lawlessness, still occurred; but by the summer of 1790 there had been fair reason to suppose that law and order would soon be fully re-established, and that France might enter on a fine period of prosperity as a constitutional Monarchy.

That these hopes had not been realized Roger saw at once, as he was driven through the streets of Le Havre. Business had been bad when he left France, owing to the great numbers of wealthy aristocrats who had fled abroad, but there had still been plenty of goods for sale in the shops. Now, many of them were closed and the remainder three-parts empty. In 1790 the National Guard had kept their uniforms spick and span; now, most of those he saw wore stained and faded tunics. Most of the bigger houses were either shuttered and empty or had been turned into tenements where ugly festoons of washing half hid the scrolled ironwork of their balconies, while on the street corners lounged little groups of idlers, many of them wearing clothes that had once been good but were now patched and threadbare. Since the years of the great famine in the middle '80s bread had frequently been scarce in Paris, but Normandy had never suffered from any food shortage; yet on this summer day in Le Havre, before each baker's and grocer's shop there waited long queues of dejected women, and as Roger glanced about him nearly every face he saw had a lean and hungry look.

The town was, perhaps, three times the size of his native Lymington—via which he had elected to travel so that he might spend a night *en route* with his father, Rear-Admiral Brook, who was temporarily without a command—but Lymington's port was the busier of the two and its tradesmen were merchant princes compared with the French shopkeepers, who appeared to have been reduced to little better than hucksters.

Nevertheless at the inn—once *Le Roi Soleil* but now re-christened *Les Amis de la Constitution et de l'Egalité*—he secured a very passable meal. It seemed that the French, despite all difficulties, were still capable of producing good omelettes and fine wine for anyone prepared to pay for them, and the sight of Roger's English guineas procured him everything for which he asked; but the inn servants were ill-clad, dirty and offhand. They no longer addressed rich Englishmen as "*milor*", but called Roger "*citoyen*", and eyed him with half-hostile, half-envious looks.

As he ate he ruminated on his mission, and liked the thought of it even less than when he had, with such reluctance, accepted it. The ugly, dangerous decrepitude into which the fabric of

French life had fallen had been brought home to him more vividly by his seven minutes' drive than by a four-hour conversation he had recently had with M. de Talleyrand. All the same, he considered that the conversation had been of great value to him in other ways and he recalled parts of it now.

On his writing to suggest a meeting he had received a prompt and characteristic reply:

Dear friend (had written the profligate nobleman who still styled himself Bishop of Autun), *did you know that I have been excommunicated, so that all men are now forbidden to serve me with fire and water? But come to sup with me tomorrow evening and we will feast on iced paté washed down with good wine.*

So Roger had gone to the French Embassy in Portman Square, not a little flattered by the readiness of so outstanding a personage to devote a whole evening to him. M. de Talleyrand, satin-clad, powdered and exquisitely groomed, had received him with the smile that had seduced some of the loveliest ladies of the *ancien régime* and which in a still distant future was to be sought with nervous eagerness by half the Crowned Heads in Europe.

He was thirty-eight years of age, slim, delicate-looking, serene of brow, and with the indelible stamp of the aristocrat upon his every word and gesture. His limp—the result of an accident in childhood—only added to his grace of movement. His slightly *retroussé* nose gave him an air of boyish impudence, and his blue eyes were capable of either mirroring or concealing thoughts of incredible swiftness.

After they had talked for a few minutes on general topics, Roger said, "May I hope that your Grace regards the secret pact we entered into three years ago as still in force?"

"Ah," smiled the Bishop, "so you are going to France again! I suspected as much."

"Your Grace's deductions are rarely at fault," Roger smiled back. "But may I enquire what led you to this one?"

"The suggestions of urgency in your request for a meeting, coupled with the fact that events in France are once more moving towards a major crisis. Had I believed you to be concerned only with assuring yourself that I continue to enjoy good health I would not have put off attending the Duchess de Mortemar's soirée in order to afford you this private conversation."

"I am both honoured and grateful that your Grace should accord me preference."

"*Mon ami*, knowing the distrust with which your master regards me, it is I who am honoured that by seeking me out you should show that you still have faith in me. Our pact, as I recall it, was that we should pool our information on all matters unprejudicial to the interests of our respective nations, and work together to bring about an alliance between them. In this I am, as ever, unreservedly at your service."

"I thank you," Roger exclaimed heartily, "for I have been set a task that I fear is beyond my powers but which, if achieved, would lead to an almost certain accomplishment of our mutual aspirations."

"That is good news indeed, and I pray that you may succeed better than I have done. I offered a guarantee that the Low Countries should be respected and that the island of Tobago should be ceded, but I have been unable to induce your Government even to consider an alliance with us. Mr. Pitt behaved as though he had swallowed a ramrod with his morning coffee; that bloodless fish, his cousin Grenville, received me so coldly that I feared the Foreign Office chair on which I sat would turn to a block of ice beneath me; His Majesty King George was barely civil, and the Queen turned her back as I made my bow. The story of such slights having been put upon a representative of France is hardly calculated to have improved the reception that an Englishman is now likely to meet with in Paris."

"I should have thought the cordiality with which you have been welcomed by the Whig nobility would have done much to redress the balance," murmured Roger tactfully, "and am I not light in believing that your Grace is not formally accredited here by your Government? If so, the coldness of your official reception, although regrettable, should be accounted no more than personal prejudice."

Talleyrand took a pinch of snuff. " 'Tis true that by a stupid law all persons who were members of the National Assembly are debarred for two years from holding any office under the Crown, so I could not be appointed Ambassador, but your point begs the question. Although that charming scapegrace, the Duc de Biron, was the nominal head of our first mission, and the young Marquis de Chauvelin has since been given formal status as our Ambassador, everyone knows that it was myself who was charged with the real business in hand. Still, no matter; fortunately my back is as waterproof as any duck's. I sought only to prepare you for the fact that Englishmen are no longer acclaimed in Paris as the champions of liberty."

"Yet I understand that your Grace has succeeded in securing a reaffirmation of our intention to remain neutral."

"Ah, but for how long will it remain good? That is what the Jacobins who now control events in Paris will be asking. Their lives depend on maintaining the new order, and they take the attitude that everyone who is not their friend must necessarily be their enemy. You will find that many of them are now convinced that England is only biding her time before joining those who seek to destroy them."

"Provided we continue in our present policy, surely they would not be so crazy as to give deliberate cause for Britain to add her might to the coalition that is forming against France?"

"I would I could be certain of that. Ministries now succeed one another in Paris more swiftly than ever did women's fashions, and each is more fanatical than the last. De Lessart was Minister for Foreign Affairs when I was sent here last January; but he is long since gone, and I received my last instructions from Dumouriez, who, although not a Brissotin himself, is the dominating personality in their Ministry. He is a military man, and one of the few among our new masters who understand even the rudiments of strategy. Much as he desires to maintain peace with England, I know he feels that for our own protection we may have to invade the Austrian Netherlands."

Roger pulled a face. "That would almost certainly result in British intervention."

"I've not a doubt of it. Dumouriez has hopes that we might keep Britain out by a solemn undertaking to give Belgium her independence after the war is over; but how far such a promise could be relied upon I must leave to your own judgment. The Brissotins, or Girondins, as they are now coming to be called, regard the spreading of the new freedom as an almost religious duty. The Belgian lands have for so long been discontented under Austrian rule that they are proving most fertile soil for the doctrines of the Revolution. Dumouriez counts on our troops being acclaimed in their cities as liberators, and if that proves the case I cannot see any French Government of the people ever allowing them again to be separated from France."

"From what you say I fear the odds are that all Europe will become embroiled before this business is over," Roger remarked gloomily. "That makes it more tragic than ever that this war to re-establish the Monarchy should ever have been allowed to start. The *émigrés* were far too few in numbers to do anything on their own, so it was a wanton act on the part of the French Government to have opened hostilities against the Elector of Treves simply because he had given them asylum."

"In that, I fear I must confess myself to have been partly responsible."

Roger lifted his eyebrows. "I am amazed to hear your Grace admit it. When we discussed the matter two years ago you were most firmly of the opinion that a war would prove disastrous to France. Its prevention was the one thing that you and I shared secretly in common with Robespierre and his little group of extremists."

"The circumstances were very different. We feared then that Spain was about to attack Britain and that France would be drawn in as the former's ally. That would have meant a great war, whereas . . ." Talleyrand broke off for a second to give a rueful but disarming smile, ". . . my friends and I intended that this should be only a very little one."

"Surely it was foreseen that the Emperor of Austria would come to his Elector's assistance?"

The Bishop threw up his slender hands. "Leopold was a man of peace, and had shown little inclination to fight a war on his sister's behalf. Moreover, I am personally convinced that both she and the King did their utmost to dissuade him from such a course. His death, and the sequel of his son championing their cause, was entirely unforeseeable. We counted wrongly, alas, on the influence of the King and Queen with their fellow sovereigns to keep the war from spreading."

"Again you amaze me! In 1790 they were quite prepared to plunge France into war solely to honour an old and unpopular treaty. Yet you tell me that this spring you counted on them to oppose a war which had as its object their own rescue and restoration to power."

"For that I consider I had good grounds. King Louis's one and only consistency has been his determination that the blood of his people should not be shed on his account as long as he could in any way prevent it. Robespierre and his *enragés* were also opposed to war, but for very different reasons; they believed that it might unite France and give the Monarchy a new chance to rehabilitate itself in the eyes of the people. Apart from those two minorities, both the Jacobins and those who think as I do wanted war—just a little one—although again for very different reasons."

"Is your Grace inclined to tell me of them?"

"Why not? The Girondins, who now form the majority at the Jacobin Club, must go forward because they dare not go back. It is essential to their continuance in power to press the Revolution further: therefore they are attempting to bring about the dethronement of the King. They reasoned that a war with his brothers was certain to have the desired effect, as it would be easy to convince the people that he and the Queen had incited the *émigrés* to invade France; upon which popular indignation would result in the overthrow of the Monarchy."

"And your reason, your Grace?"

"Exactly the opposite. Early this year I formed the conclusion that the Monarchy was doomed unless its prestige could be resurrected as a result of some new national crisis. The King is still the executive head of France. In the event of war the executive power always becomes of more importance than the legislative. I was convinced that the King would take the side of his people rather than that of his brothers, and like Robespierre, who was shrewd enough to fear it, I believed that the nation would unite behind him. Louis de Narbonne, Madame de Staël, a few others and myself decided that in a short victorious campaign against the *émigrés*, in which the King should personally appear in the rôle of Commander-in-Chief, lay the best, if not the only, hope of restoring his popularity and thwarting the designs of those who seek to destroy him."

Roger remembered Louis de Narbonne well. In the old days this clever, illegitimate nephew of Louis XV had been one of the circle of gifted, liberal nobles—including de Mirabeau, Dupont de Nemours, Mathieu de Montmorency and the brothers Lameth—who had congregated about de Talleyrand. Between them they had done more than any other body of men to bring about the first Revolution, while Madame de Staël had consistently used her bitter wit to defame the Queen. Her father, the vain and pompous Swiss banker Monsieur Necker, foisted as First Minister on the King by popular outcry, had contributed more than any other single individual to the plight into which the Monarchy had fallen.

Sadly Roger shook his head. "I recall that at the time of the fall of the Bastille your Grace took a grave risk, and sank personal prejudices, in a fine endeavour to save the Court from its own folly. But these others that you mention; if they have now become the champions of the Monarchy, times have changed indeed."

The Bishop shrugged. "Before '89 the French cart was being drawn by a sick and weary horse. My friends and I insisted on changing it for a healthy one—too healthy, for it has now run away with the cart. That is the trouble; and in such a case all sane persons must unite in an attempt to avert calamity. But come, my friend, you must be hungry; let us go in to supper."

The meal was no frugal affair, for Talleyrand, as befitted his family name de Périgord, was one of the great gourmets of his age. Roger, however, was much too interested in his host's mind to do full justice to the delicacies of his table. As soon as the servants had withdrawn he reverted to the simile of the runaway horse, and asked:

"How long is it since moderate men first began to be sensible of this danger?"

Talleyrand wiped his lips carefully with a napkin and poured himself another glass of wine. "Soon after you left France a number of the cooler-headed members of the Jacobin Club took alarm at the trend of events. They resigned from the Club, and finding their action met with popular support founded a new one in the ex-convent of the Feuillants. Soon their numbers exceeded those of the Jacobins, and it looked as if there were good hopes that they would be able to check the runaway. They would certainly have succeeded had not the King, as always, allowed himself to be influenced by short-sighted people, and refused to co-operate with them."

"Can that be wondered at in view of their past record as Jacobins?"

"Not in a pudding-head like Louis XVI. But a wise man reviews each new situation on its merits, without giving undue weight to the past. His attitude was the same to Lafayette, when that shallow-pated individual at last saw the red light, and made a tardy but sincere effort to pull him out of his predicament. For all Lafayette's vanity and incompetence, he still had a great following at the time, and might have done the trick if only the King would have let bygones be bygones."

"Doubtless he finds that hard. I certainly should if I were in his situation."

Talleyrand's blue eyes twinkled. "It is inconceivable that you would ever have allowed yourself to get into it. He is, I honestly believe, the stupidest man alive. You would hardly credit it, but by such influence as is left to him he secured the election of that arch-rogue Pétion as Mayor of Paris last November, rather than allow the election of Lafayette, who was the other candidate. And I am convinced that he was not actuated by malice."

"Was it in the capacity of Mayor that Lafayette could have swayed matters in favour of the Monarchy?"

"He might have, but it was not to that I was referring. Having been defeated he took himself off to command the army, but in the spring he returned to Paris and offered to use it to re-establish the King's authority. No man could have offered more or been in a stronger position to rescue the Royal Family, yet that blockhead of a King snubbed the General and sent him packing."

"Do you think Mirabeau might have saved the situation, had he lived?"

"No. He had already lost all credit with the Sovereigns before he died, owing to the forthright manner in which he supported the measures against the Church."

It was Talleyrand himself who had proposed the confiscation of the property of the Church and the sale of its lands for the benefit of the Exchequer. He had also instigated most of the other measures which had led to its severance from Rome and re-creation as a national institution. As the most prominent of the only four bishops who had not refused to take the new oath to the Constitution he had celebrated mass at the altar of the Nation in the Champs de Mars before the grievously distressed Royal Family, the Assembly, and a great concourse of people. Again, as almost the only active prelate who accepted the New Order, he had officiated at the induction of a number of new Bishops, men of dubious piety but prepared to take their orders from the Assembly instead of from Rome.

Curious to learn his true attitude, Roger remarked, "I gather that with regard to Church matters your Grace has not been altogether inactive?"

"And rightly so!" replied the Bishop swiftly. "France has been the milch-cow of Rome for too long, and her priests had become lazy parasites. Your King Henry VIII set me a good example, and I have followed it to the best of my ability. You know well that I have never sought to disguise my own unsuitability for priesthood, and that I was forced into taking Orders when too young to resist. But as a statesman I believe that my measures have laid the foundation in France of a Church that will prove healthier, more honest and less grasping than that which she had before. However, we digress. I was about to tell you that the King, despite his own folly, found himself at the beginning of this year with a Ministry that was mainly Feuillant in character. Louis de Narbonne was at the War Office, and Lafayette in command of the army. The Girondins were by then the most powerful party; they were clamouring for a war against the *émigrés*, because they believed that such a war would both assist the spread of their fanatical doctrines abroad and lead to the destruction of the Monarchy. We believed that by such a war we could save it, so we let ourselves appear to be persuaded by their urgency and hurried forward preparations for hostilities. There you have the true genesis of the present conflict."

"As it happens, it appears that they have come nearer to achieving their object than have you and your friends," Roger remarked with a diffidence that took the sting out of the implied criticism.

"Alas, that is so," confessed the Bishop; "the King's stupidity wrecked all our efforts on his behalf. We had planned to carry him off from Paris in Madame de Staël's carriage to Lafayette's camp, where he could have been made to appear as the champion of the people against their enemies, while de Narbonne, as War Minister, could have suppressed any risings in Paris. But the King refused to allow himself to be rescued and dismissed de Narbonne from office, which led to the fall of the Feuillant ministry. Then, crowning folly of all, the King was persuaded to nominate a new Cabinet composed of Girondins. He could hardly have done worse had he entrusted himself to Danton, Robespierre and Marat."

"Here in England we have been led to believe that the deputies of the Gironde are now the moderates."

"Then you have been misled by the pose they adopt of virtuous idealists who desire only a government of the purest democratic principles. In fact they are vain, self-seeking and treacherous. Like Brutus and Cassius, they are ever mouthing the purity of their intentions while secretly planning to murder Caesar, so that they may usurp his power. They were as radical in their views as the other Jacobins and split from them only early this year because Robespierre and his friends opposed the war."

"Who do you consider to be the most influential among them?"

"Brissot himself is a frothy mediocrity. The King's principal ministers, Roland, Servan and Clavière, are all men of straw. Vergniaud is their best orator, and perhaps the finest the Revolution has produced. Gensonné, Condorcet, Gaudet and Isnard all carry considerable weight in the Assembly, but not one of them is capable of becoming a great leader. 'Tis Madame Roland, with the help of her toady, the despicable Abbé Sieyès, who now governs France from her *salon.* Both of them are clever, unscrupulous and boundlessly ambitious. As a middle-class woman Madame Roland was no more than one of the crowd on her few appearances at Versailles, so she was hardly noticed by the Sovereigns. She considers that she was slighted and has ever since harboured an unappeasable hatred of the Queen. Before the split, and she thought she could do without them, she was hand in glove with the most violent of the *enragés*, and she would stop at nothing to vent her jealous spite on Marie Antoinette."

"You make no mention of Dumouriez."

"As I remarked earlier, he is not a Girondin, although he holds the portfolio for Foreign Affairs in their ministry, and is the strongest man in it."

"It seems, then, that he and Madame Roland are the two people at present best situated to influence future events in France," Roger commented.

Talleyrand helped himself to a hothouse peach, began to peel it with a gold knife, and smiled. "At present, yes; but none other than a fool would hazard how long they will remain so. It would not surprise me if by the time you reach Paris some new turn of events had raised up other rogues to displace them."

In the main the cynical Bishop proved right, as within an hour of Roger's arrival in Le Havre he learned that the King had dismissed Roland and his associates on the 12th of June, and that three days later Dumouriez had resigned to take over command of the Army of the North. No details concerning the reason for the crisis were yet available and the names of the new ministers were so little known that they conveyed no definite impression—except that they were more reactionary than their predecessors, which was already causing the patriots in the port to mutter that the King had betrayed them and that "virtuous Citizen Roland" had fallen a victim to the "Austrian woman's" intrigues.

That afternoon, the 18th, Roger and Dan took the diligence to Paris, and on their journey they had a further opportunity of observing how greatly the state of things in France had deteriorated. Instead of the ostlers at every five-mile post-stage being ready with the relays, so enabling the coach to travel swiftly through the night to its destination, no preparations to speed it onward had been made at any of the halts, and the length of them depended on a number of quite unpredictable factors.

Jean Jacques Rousseau's *Contrat Social* had become the bible of the Revolution. Among the idealistic vapourizings in it, influenced no doubt by the thought of small Swiss cantons in valleys remote from any great centre of population, he had laid it down that democracy thrived best under local government. The French reformers had accepted his principles with the disastrous result that the central government had lost all but a vestige of its former power. Not only each provincial town, but every village, now had its elected representatives who considered themselves to be the supreme authority within their own district.

At every stop the coach had to await the pleasure of some local official, who checked the number of its occupants and the amount of baggage it carried, then demanded a small sum—which varied with each place and appeared to be arrived at quite arbitrarily—in payment for a permit for it to pass through his commune. Often these officials had to be fetched from their homes, some distance away; and even when permission was given to proceed, further delays frequently occurred because the guard had gone off to drink with an acquaintance, or the coachman had decided to have an hour's sleep.

The state of the roads was also against rapid progress. In the old days they had been kept in good condition by the *corvée*, a system by which each peasant had to give a number of days' work every year upon them under the supervision of trained road engineers; but that had been abolished in '89. Labour, paid out of the tolls exacted by each commune, was supposed to take its place, but these funds had a way of disappearing into the pockets of the mayors and their cronies. Accordingly no repairs were done, and the highways had deteriorated to such a degree that in many places they were little better than pot-holed cart-tracks.

In consequence, instead of arriving in Paris soon after dawn as he had expected, it was not until four in the afternoon that Roger, tired, dusty and disgruntled, was set down in the Place Vendôme. About those lost twelve hours he need not have worried; he was destined to more than make up for them in the next twenty-four.

CHAPTER II

THE LADY IN THE BATH

ROGER went straight to *La Belle Étoile*, a big hostelry near the Louvre which he had always made his headquarters when in Paris, and found, to his great pleasure, that his old friends Monsieur and Madame Blanchard were still the proprietors.

The honest Norman couple were greatly surprised, but delighted to see him. They had known him since the days when as a youth he had occupied an attic room in the great Hôtel de Rochambeau near-by. In those days he had been only an under-secretary in the Marquis de Rochambeau's employ, with a modest salary, and no influential friends; but they had seen him blossom into a young exquisite who wore silks and satins; then, after a long absence, he had returned as a rich English *milor* who moved in the very highest society, went frequently to Versailles and was even rumoured to be a member of the Queen's intimate circle.

How that transformation had been achieved they were too discreet ever to have enquired, and now they made no attempt to learn what had brought him back to a dreary and depressing Paris, which all but a handful of English residents had already abandoned. Instead, with much happy fussing, they installed him in a comfortable room that had a smaller one adjacent to it for Dan, took down from the attic a trunkful of clothes that he had left there two years before, and promised him the best supper Paris could provide. Having insisted that they should share it with him in their private parlour, he left Dan to unpack and went out to get a first impression of the city.

Its narrow streets, in which here and there big mansions stood well back behind walled courtyards, were as familiar to him as was the West End of London, and the people in them appeared little changed compared with the poverty-stricken look that had so shocked him about the population of Le Havre. Yet here, in the richest quarter of Paris, there were few provision shops and the hours for queueing were long since over, so he realized that matters might be very different in the Faubourgs. When he had left Paris private equipages with two or more servants clad in bright liveries had already become rare; now, the few that he saw had only coachmen in plain grey, and the coats of arms on their doors had been painted over, as also had the shields that once displayed the arms of the nobility on the gateways of their mansions. But there were still plenty of well-dressed people driving in hired conveyances or walking in the public gardens. However, he soon noticed that everyone without exception was wearing the national colours either in their hat or lapel, so he went into the first mercer's he saw and bought himself a *tricolore* cockade.

From the earliest days of the Revolution the gardens of the Palais Royal had always been the meeting place of the malcontents, as the Duc d'Orléans had set himself up as the patron of the mob and had paid agitators to incite the people to rebellion beneath the windows of his palace; so Roger made his way there as the most likely place to gauge current feeling.

As a result of the King having dismissed his Girondin ministers a week earlier, it was now common knowledge that France was in the throes of a new political crisis, so Roger expected to find the garden packed with excitable people. To his surprise it was three-quarters empty, and although half a dozen orators were declaiming from soap-boxes beneath the chestnut trees, the little groups about them seemed indifferent and apathetic.

Sitting down at one of the tables outside the Café de la Foix, he got into conversation with a respectable-looking man, and, commenting on the lack of enthusiasm shown by the crowd, was told two reasons that accounted for it. Firstly, his new acquaintance gave it as his opinion that after three years of commotions the people of Paris no longer cared a fig for which set of men the King selected as his ministers; all they really wanted was a stable Government that would bring down the high cost of living and reanimate the commerce of the nation. Secondly, on this particular evening, for some unaccountable reason, not one of the mob's favourite orators was there to rouse its temper.

For a while Roger moved round among the crowd and, although he was not yet sufficiently up to date with events to appreciate the full gist of the speakers' tirades, he gathered that they were engaged mainly in inveighing against the King's use of the suspensive veto although it had been accorded him as a right under the new Constitution.

At seven o'clock he returned to *La Belle Étoile* and over an excellent supper of good Normandy dishes learnt from his hosts the reason which had caused the King to dismiss Monsieur Roland and his friends.

On the outbreak of war the Legislative Assembly—which had replaced the original National Assembly when that body had completed the drafting of the new Constitution the preceding September—had called on the whole country to furnish volunteers for the army. In the past two months many thousands of these *fédérés*, as they were called, had collected in the provincial capitals and were soon about to march through Paris on their way to the Front. However, as the war had opened badly for France, the Girondin ministers had proposed that a great camp of 20,000 of them should be formed outside Paris for the city's defence. Secondly, they had proposed that with these patriots to defend him the King would no longer require the bodyguard that he had been granted under the Constitution. Lastly, they had demanded that he should sanction further measures against the priests who had refused to take the oath to the Constitution, and deprive them of their livings.

Still trusting in his old belief, that the people were only misled and would never willingly harm him, the King had agreed to give up his bodyguard; but in the establishment of a camp of 20,000 mostly lawless ruffians outside Paris he had seen great danger to the tranquillity of the capital; and as he was a deeply religious man the idea of debarring nine-tenths of the priesthood of France from practising their office had utterly appalled him. In consequence he had placed his veto on the last two proposals, and dismissed the ministers responsible for them.

The Blanchards, like the great majority of honest Parisians, had greeted the first reforms of the Revolution with enthusiasm, but were strongly in favour of a continuance of the Monarchy in its new constitutional form. They maintained that in the present issue the King had been not only within his rights, but also wise and just in his decision. Like the man with whom Roger had talked at the Café de la Foix, they deplored the constantly changing array of law-makers who, for three years, had disturbed every aspect of life by causing the Assembly to decree a seemingly endless succession of new and often impractical measures; for in those years their lack of experience of governing, their woolly idealism and fanatical desire to change everything simply for the sake of change, had resulted in turning the whole nation topsy-turvy, brought business almost to a standstill, and reduced every respectable family in France to ruin, or very near it. The innkeeper went on to declare that, for all the faults of the *ancien régime*, under it a man at least knew where he stood; but now he could never tell from week to week if he might not find his church closed on Sunday, be out of work on Monday, and on Tuesday wake up in prison as the result of breaking some new regulation of which he had not yet heard.

He added that of all the follies committed by the radicals their attempt to reduce the upper classes to their own level had proved the most disastrous for the country. By it they had killed the goose that laid the golden eggs, for while everyone knew that the nobles who had been driven abroad could not have taken one hundred-thousandth part of their wealth with them, it had not remained in France to be shared out among the people as they had been led to expect. The wholesale abolition of tolls, tithes, rents, dues and other feudal perquisites, the bankruptcy of innumerable commercial undertakings, and the fall of the value of all securities, had caused it to evaporate into thin air. Still worse, this slaughter of the golden goose had had the most appalling repercussions on a great section of the people themselves.

Too late, it was now realized that the nobles had hoarded nothing but a minute portion of their wealth. With few exceptions, what they had taken with one hand they had paid out with the other, and the more extravagant they were, the better for everyone connected with them. At Versailles alone they had supported 40,000 servants, in Paris 100,000, and an even greater number on their estates and at their mansions in provincial cities. Untrained for anything other than private service, by far the greater part of this huge multitude was now jobless and starving. The damage was far from ending there, as it was the wealthy alone who had enabled the luxury trades of France to develop into her foremost industry. The emigration had brought ruin to countless jewellers, furriers, hairdressers, wine merchants, horse-dealers, confectioners, haberdashers, dress-, coach-, cabinet-, hat-, cane-, lace-, harness-, boot- and sword-makers. With the closing down of all these businesses the people they employed had been thrown out of work.

The decline of the silk industry at Lyons had caused 20,000 hands to be stood off, and every city in the country that had catered for fashion, elegance and culture was suffering in proportion. The total bill for the practical application of Jean Jacques

Rousseau's socialist ideals was now being paid for in France by unemployment, which had reached the positively staggering figure for those days of close on three million.

For a further hour, while the little party made heavy inroads into a bottle of fifteen-year-old Calvados that Maître Blanchard had brought up from the cellar, Roger listened to a tale of woe that differed little from that which any other honest bourgeois couple in France would have told him. Knowing that they were typical of their class, he now had little doubt that both Mr. Pitt and M. de Talleyrand had been right in their contention that, if only the King could be made to give his people a lead, nine-tenths of them would support him wholeheartedly in any attempt to re-establish sane and enduring government. That the King was weak and his enemies relentless Roger knew, but he went to bed considerably cheered by what he had learned of general feeling, and next day he hoped to secure a much more intimate picture of the protagonists in this epoch-making struggle than good folk like the Blanchards were in any position to give him.

With this very necessary preliminary to his mission in mind, he had requested M. de Talleyrand to furnish him with an introduction to someone in Paris who could be trusted to give him an unbiassed account of the present situation of the Court and the potentialities of its enemies. The Bishop had responded by furnishing him with a letter to an American gentleman named Gouverneur Morris, and then described him in the following generous terms.

"He is some two years older than myself and my equal, if not my superior, in intellect. His ideals are loftier than my own, and if his outlook is not quite so wide, his talents have brought him riches, success and the respect of all who know him. He is a close friend of General Washington, and the part he played in rescuing the American Army from its desperate situation at Valley Forge during the terrible winter of '78 was of inestimable value to his country. But it is as a lawyer and man of business that he particularly excels. While still a young man he helped to formulate the Federal Constitution. It was he who founded the first bank in the United States and projected their new currency based on a coin called the dollar. As Assistant Superintendent of Finance he came to France in '88 and he has recently been appointed Minister. You will find him astute, remarkably well-informed and as impartial as any decent man can be, since his sympathies with the aristocrats, to whom he is by nature akin, are balanced by his American belief that all peoples should enjoy the blessings of democracy."

"Can I speak freely to him?" Roger had enquired. "I mean, is your Grace sufficiently intimate with him to advise me to trust him completely should the need arise?"

"We are terribly intimate," replied the Bishop with his most cynical smile; "in fact we are almost related. You will recall my dear friend Madame de Flahaut. I tell you nothing that all Paris will not be eager to inform you of when I disclose that Monsieur Morris paid his addresses to that lovely lady with a success that I found it beyond my powers to counter. At first, when the two of us met in her apartment, we behaved like bears with sore heads, and endeavoured to outsit one another; but after a few meetings we found we had so many interests in common that we formed a strong attachment, and settled down quite happily to accept in common too the smiles of our mutual inamorata."

It was therefore with the keenest interest that on the morning of Wednesday the 20th of June Roger set out from *La Belle Étoile* to call upon Gouverneur Morris, but at the American Legation disappointment awaited him. He was informed by a servant that the Minister had already gone out, and that it was unlikely that he would return before nightfall. On Roger's enquiring where he might be met with during the day, the man replied that his master usually waited upon Madame de Flahaut about noon, so Roger decided to do likewise.

To kill time he walked about the streets for a while, then went to have a look at the Tuileries. Its gardens were open to the public, except for a narrow strip along the frontage of the Palace that had been reserved for its inmates and was marked off by a length of *tricolor* ribbon—that method having been found a more effective barrier than any type of fence. A handful of idlers were staring up at the Palace windows, hoping that they might catch a glimpse of some member of the Royal Family; but their chance of that was remote, as during the past three years the spot on which they stood had so often been occupied by riff-raff hurling obscenities at the Queen that she and her relatives now denied themselves the small pleasure of looking out at the gardens rather than risk again being subjected to insult.

Roger then noticed that a quite considerable crowd had assembled on the north side of the gardens near the riding-school, in which the Legislative Assembly held its sittings, so he walked over to find out what had caused it to congregate. A bystander told him that today being the anniversary of that upon which the Third Estate had taken the historic "Oath of the Tennis Court" at Versailles—never to separate until the King granted a Constitution to his people—representatives of the forty-eight Sections of Paris were coming to plant a Tree of Liberty in the Palace garden. In itself that seemed to Roger a harmless enough celebration, and as it was then half-past eleven, he decided to pay his call on Madame de Flahaut.

It had been the practice of the King and Queen to allot all the accommodation not required for their own use in their many palaces to nobles of small fortune who held posts at Court, or to widows and pensioners who could ill afford houses of their own. The Comte de Flahaut belonged to the former category, and on being appointed Superintendent of the Royal Parks he had been given a suite of rooms in the Louvre; so it was to the old palace, from which France had been ruled by the Valois Kings, Henri de Navarre and Cardinal de Richelieu, that Roger now made his way.

He located the de Flahauts' apartment on the second floor, about half-way along the block adjacent to the river, and sent in his name as the Chevalier de Breuc. It was that by which he had always been known at the French Court and he hoped now that it might arouse only memories of pleasant social occasions, but as a precaution against its having an opposite effect, he added that he had just arrived from London with messages from M. de Talleyrand.

The maid to whom he had given his name returned to say that Madame la Comtesse was at the moment in her bath but would nevertheless receive him.

In those days it was still the custom for great ladies to spend much of the day in their bedrooms. During the lengthy process of their elaborate toilettes they both discussed the morning's news with callers and interviewed tradesmen, merely retiring behind a screen to put on their underclothes. However, Roger had never before been received by a lady with whom he had only a slight acquaintance while she was in her bath, so he was quite put to it to hide his surprise as he followed the maid down a short corridor; but as he entered a lofty bedchamber with tall windows that looked out across the Seine he saw that there was no cause for embarrassment. In the middle of the room stood a deep hip bath filled almost to the brim with a milky liquid that was covered with a froth of iridescent bubbles. The only visible parts of the lady were a pair of well-rounded shoulders, a slender neck and her head, now swathed in a turban of towelling. She was twenty-five years of age, and rightly had sufficient confidence in her striking beauty to feel no qualms about receiving a young man with her face unmade-up.

Raising a pretty arm from its submergence, she extended her wet hand for Roger to kiss, and said with a smile, "I positively could not wait a moment to have news of my dear Bishop. Pray tell me how he is enjoying London."

Roger willingly obliged and was much relieved to note, both from her friendly manner and from a reference she made to their having met several times at Versailles three summers ago, that she evidently did not remember the circumstances in which he had left France.

After they had been talking for a few moments Roger's attention was attracted by faint noises coming from behind the silk curtains that rose to a coronet of ostrich feathers above her big bed. Seeing him glance in that direction, the Countess called out, "Charles! Stop playing with your bricks for a moment and come here, so that I may present you to M. le Chevalier."

A remarkably handsome boy of seven emerged from behind the drapes and made his bow, but knowing the child's history Roger was not at all surprised by his good looks. Adèle de Flahaut had been married at fifteen to the Count, who was then over fifty and near impotence from his past dissipations. They had been married by the Abbé de Talleyrand-Périgord and it was to the strikingly handsome Abbé that the beautiful but neglected young bride owed both the cultivation of her excellent mind and her son. They had made no secret of their liaison and she had even named the boy Charles, after her lover.

Like his father he was destined to become a brilliant diplomat and also, by a Queen, to have an illegitimate son, in whom were perpetuated in turn de Talleyrand's great gifts and who, as the Duc de Morny, under the Second Empire, brought pleasure to generations still unborn by the creation of Deauville.

When Roger resumed his conversation with the Countess he commented upon Paris being much quieter than he had expected to find it in view of the recent dismissal of the Girondin ministry.

"I fear appearances are deceptive," she replied. "Everyone is sick to death of these turmoils to which we have so long been subjected, but there are those who are determined to allow us no peace."

With a glance round the luxuriously appointed room he said, "I am happy to observe that these years of political ferment do not seem to have materially affected the comfort in which you live, Madame."

She shrugged her plump shoulders. "No; provided we abstain from ostentation we are rarely molested. The majority of the nobility are gone abroad, of course, but those who remain enjoy comparative peace, and within their own houses live much as before. The *salons* of Mesdames de Staël, de Genlis, and numerous other ladies are still well attended, the boxes at the opera are always full, and the custom of frequently dining at the houses of one's friends has never been more than temporarily interrupted. Cards, literature and music continue to occupy a large place in the lives of people of leisure and among those who refuse to be drawn into politics, of whom there are many. Were it not for the change in fashions and the almost universal topic of how to get money safely transferred abroad, one would scarely know that there had been a Revolution."

"Yet you fear that the present quiet is deceptive?"

"That clever American, Monsieur Gouverneur Morris, is of that opinion, and I find him an exceptionally reliable political barometer."

"So M. de Talleyrand informed me when he very kindly furnished me with a letter of introduction to Monsieur Morris."

She arched her eyebrows and gave him a demure smile. "No doubt then you are aware that Monsieur Morris does me the honour of waiting upon me with some frequency—every morning, in fact—and he should have been here ere this. I cannot think what has detained him."

Roger returned her smile and bowed. "M. de Talleyrand did infer that you, Madame, had performed the remarkable feat of simultaneously making the two most gifted men in Europe your slaves; and now, upon having the privilege of your closer acquaintance, I do not wonder at it."

Her smile deepened and, as many a young woman had done before her, she turned her eyes up to Roger's blue ones with just a hint of invitation. "Since you show such charming sensibility, Monsieur, the privilege is mine. You will always be welcome here while you are in Paris, and I hope that our acquaintance may ripen into friendship."

He would have been only half a man had he not felt his pulses quicken, but he swiftly repressed the impulse to set foot on the slippery slope of a flirtation with the lovely Countess. Having thanked her, he turned the conversation back to impersonal matters by remarking:

"It is most pleasing to learn that social life in Paris has not been seriously disrupted. I had imagined that the streets would prove unsafe for people of quality after nightfall, and that gatherings of the *ci-devant* nobility would have been made an excuse for riots against them."

She shook her head. "Except that they now claim to be our equals, and give themselves absurd airs on that account, the ordinary people are well behaved enough. Occasionally some Deputy who has had the courage to speak against the Jacobins is set upon and murdered, or has his house burnt down. But such acts are the work of scoundrels paid by the extremists, and are part of a deliberate campaign to intimidate the moderates in the Assembly. From time to time, too, those same extremists send their agitators with fresh lies against the King to stir up the poor wretches in the slums. For a few hours gangs of hideous-looking ruffians, and their still more awful females, parade the streets. Sometimes an incident occurs which results in bloodshed, then the mob slinks back to its dens and for a few weeks we enjoy quiet again."

"You think then, Madame, that the present crisis will blow over in the same way?"

"The King has always given way on other matters as soon as the rioting becomes serious; so, in spite of certain fears that Monsieur Morris has recently expressed to me, I find it difficult to suppose that matters will really go differently on this occasion."

It was at that moment that Gouverneur Morris was shown in. He was a fine-looking man with a broad forehead, aquiline nose and somewhat tightly pursed mouth. He had, Roger was somewhat surprised to see, a wooden leg, but it seemed to cause him little inconvenience as he stumped quickly forward to greet his mistress.

After laughingly chiding him for his lateness, the beauty in the bath presented Roger to him, and said, "M. de Breuc has a letter for you from our dear Bishop. Take him into the next room and give him a glass of wine while you read it, then when my woman has dried me and made me presentable you may rejoin me here."

The American led Roger into a small boudoir, opened a cabinet that contained glasses and a variety of bottles, and invited him to choose whatever drink he preferred. Then, when he had read the letter that Roger handed him, he said briskly:

"So you are an Englishman? Well, I'll confess I'd never have known it, and I have been living in Paris for nearly five years."

Roger smiled. "I spent four years of my youth in France and at that time of life one is more impressionable than at any other."

"True, and that no doubt accounts for the French mannerisms that appear so natural in you; but few Anglo-Saxons ever acquire so perfect an accent, and I envy you it."

"You are too kind. Your own fluency leaves nothing to be desired, and one's accent is a matter of luck rather than perseverance. It so happens that I have a good ear for languages and they have always come easily to me."

Mr. Morris pointed at the hand with which Roger was holding his glass. "You would not have had to tell me that had I noticed your hands before. Those exceptionally long little fingers of yours tell their own tale. A long fourth finger, particularly on the right hand, is a sure sign that anyone possessing it enjoys the gift of tongues."

"So I have heard," agreed Roger with a smile, "and I only hope that mine will not cause me to be identified at some time when my work requires that I should remain incognito."

The American tapped de Talleyrand's letter. "Yes, our mutual friend infers that you are here on confidential business. He gives no details of it and I do not ask them; his assurance that you are working in the interests of peace is quite sufficient. In what way can I be of service to you?"

"I should be most grateful for any reliable information you may care to give me about the present situation—I mean information not known to the general public."

"To a banker like myself, plain ignorance can often prove more expensive than underwriting the most crazy speculations, so I spend a lot of money learning what goes on in this city behind closed doors. What particularly do you wish to know?"

"I was informed in London that a fresh upheaval which would menace the continuance of the Monarchy was expected to take place here during the next few days, yet the little I have so far seen of Paris does not support that belief."

"Nevertheless, you were rightly informed. Within a week France will be in the throes of a second Revolution."

"One would not have thought it, seeing the apathy of the people. I was in the gardens of the Palais Royal last evening and the crowd showed not a spark of enthusiasm for the speakers who were attempting to agitate them."

"Do not be deceived by that. The men best qualified to do so—Danton, Marat, Camille Desmoulins and Santerre—were all attending a secret meeting out at Charenton, planning to raise the Faubourgs during the night."

"Indeed!" Roger raised his eyebrows. "It is already one o'clock and there are no signs as yet that they have succeeded."

The American gave a grim smile and waved a hand towards the open window. "Are there not? Listen, Monsieur, and you will hear them."

Only then did Roger become aware of a distant murmur, like the sound of surf rolling in upon a rocky shore. Instinctively they both moved over to the window and looked out. A quarter of a mile or more away to their left they could see the Pont Neuf. Its extremity on the south bank and the open space where it crossed the end of the Isle de la Cité were occupied by a seething mass of people, and the head of a closely packed column was steadily advancing across the river.

After having watched them for a moment, Roger said, "I can only plead my ignorance of affairs here as an excuse for appearing to doubt your alarming prediction, but is it not possible that under pressure from the mob the King will run true to form? He has always succeeded in restoring tranquillity by giving way before, and I see no reason why he should not do so again. He has only to rescind his veto on the two decrees to remove the cause of this fresh hostility towards him."

"That is not its cause: the decrees are no more than a pretext and were put forward as a trap into which he has fallen."

"I pray you then enlighten me as to what lies at the heart of the matter."

"There is no heart to it, but a liver. A woman's liver that distils more bile than other people possess blood. That jaundiced hell-cat, Manon Roland, has sworn to have the Queen's head that she may spit in the eyes that once passed her over with indifference. The King has consistently alienated all those best situated to help him, and still maintains his childish belief that he can trust in the affections of his people. Last March, believing that the Girondins represented the greater part of the nation, he was mad enough to appoint Roland his principal minister; but even that was not sufficient to appease the vanity of Roland's wife, and it is she who has been the directing brain behind the Girondin ministry. Nothing less than the destruction of the Monarchy will satisfy her, and she has worked for that with venomous insistence.

"It was she who jockeyed France into declaring war, hoping that the King might be caught out corresponding with his brothers and so shown up as a traitor to the nation. Since that scheme has so far failed to bear fruit, she conceived the idea of the decrees, knowing that the one concerning the priests would prove so abhorrent to the conscience of the King that he would in desperation resort to the expedient of using his veto. He is constitutionally within his right in having done so, but it has enabled her to raise the mob with the cry that the monarch is defying the will of the people, and that he should therefore now be deprived of the veto altogether. That is the real question at issue. And as the veto is the last remaining remnant of the royal authority, without it there would no longer be any point in having a King at all."

"I see now the true gravity of the situation," Roger nodded. "If the veto goes, the Monarchy must soon follow it. Perhaps then, having been forced into this last ditch, the King for once may make a stand."

"Madame Roland undoubtedly hopes so, as that would crown her vicious intrigues with triumph even more swiftly."

Roger gave a quick glance out of the window. The mutter of the crowd had increased to a roar. The mob was now pouring across the bridge and its leading elements had turned left along the Quai du Louvre below him. Ragged, dirty, fierce-looking, hundreds of men and women, carrying pikes, scythes and muskets, jostled and shouted in a broad living stream as they tramped determinedly towards the Tuileries.

"You mean," he said, "that if the King resists, mobs like this will force the Assembly to decree an end to the Monarchy before the moderates can concert measures by which, given a little time and a quieter atmosphere, they might yet save it?"

"I mean," declared Gouverneur Morris, "that in '89 we witnessed only the rising storm. 'Tis now that we are about to feel the full blast of the tempest. It is my opinion that if the King resists he and his family will be dead before morning."

CHAPTER III

THE TEMPEST BREAKS

ROGER swung round and stared at the American. "You really think that this mob is on its way to murder the King and Queen?"

Gouverneur Morris nodded. "My agents report that they will be incited to do so, as will others like them coming from the eastern Faubourgs."

"I see. They are at present unaware of the purpose for which they are to be used, but later Danton, Marat and their other idols mean to goad them into an attack on the Tuileries?"

"No, no! This horrible business is to be managed much more subtly. Like Madame Roland, Danton and the other brains of the conspiracy will remain behind the scenes, so that should some unforeseen hitch cause their plan to miscarry they cannot afterwards be accused of complicity. They are employing the Duc d'Orléans' old gang of assassins, St. Huruge, Fournier, Rotondo and the rest, to do their devilish work. The excuse by which the mobs are being collected is no more than to plant a Tree of Liberty in the Palace gardens, and to present a petition to the Assembly asking for the withdrawal of the veto on the two decrees and the reinstatement of the Girondin ministers."

"But the Assembly has no power to grant such requests; they are entirely a matter for the King."

"Exactly! And when the Assembly tell that to the mob, Santerre, the big brewer who is the political boss of the St. Antoine district, and that Belgian harlot, Théroigne de Méricourt, who has made herself Queen of the slums, will raise the cry, 'To the Palace, then! To the Palace! Let us convey the will of the People to the King ourselves!' That is the plot, and you can see where it must lead. Once inside the Palace it will need only one shot to start a massacre. Rotondo or one of the others will see to it that during the killing the Royal Family perish."

"*Mon Dieu!* What a ghastly picture you paint! But surely the authorities will intervene? Many members of the Assembly are still loyal to the King; when they see the way things are moving they will take measures to disperse the mob?"

"They may wish to do so, but they will find themselves helpless. Individually they have no authority, and the most powerful party in the Assembly are the Girondins—the very men whom Madame Roland has made the cat's-paw of her hate. It is certain that they will obstruct any attempts to use the authority of the Assembly to restore order."

"Who is responsible for the normal maintenance of it?"

"The Mayor of Paris, Pétion. He is another Girondin, and a smooth-tongued hypocrite. No doubt he will have thought out a way to cover himself for remaining inactive. I'll wager a hundred dollars against a sackful of this worthless paper money the French are printing, that he'll not lift a finger to prevent the mob breaking into the palace."

"Are there no guards or gendarmerie to defend it?"

Mr. Morris pursed up his mouth. "When I passed just now several companies of National Guards were being paraded on the garden side, but they will not act without an order. I greatly doubt if they would fire on the mob, even if one of their officers had the courage to bid them to do so. As part of Manon Roland's plot, the King has already been trapped into dispensing with the constitutional guard which should defend his person. Apart from a few Swiss, the only troops now remaining inside the Palace are the National Guards who act as jailers to the Royal Family."

"Has the King any idea how desperate is his situation?"

"Indeed he has! From the beginning of this month, when the decrees were first mooted, he has been repeatedly warned that they would be made a pretext to bring about his downfall. Since then he has been furnished with full particulars of the plot from a dozen sources."

"But does he realize that it is not only his throne, but also his life, that is now threatened?"

"Yes. On leaving my house this morning I ran into the old Marshal de Malesherbes. He told me that yesterday the King wrote to his confessor asking him to come to him, and saying, 'Never have I had such great need of your consolations. I have done with men, it is towards Heaven that I turn my eyes. Great disasters are announced for tomorrow, but I shall have courage.' Then he came over to the Marshal, who was standing at a window, and as they watched the sun sink behind the trees of the Champs Elyseés, he said, 'Who knows whether I shall see the sun set tomorrow?'

"When I met M. de Malesherbes he was on his way to the Tuileries. He is over seventy, and I did my utmost to persuade the dear old man to return home, but he would not hear of it. He said, 'In happier days His Majesty honoured me by making me one of his ministers. Had I counselled him more wisely he might not now be in such a grievous pass; the least I can do is to go and die with him.' "

"How splendid!" Roger's blue eyes lit up. "It is something to know that at least one of the King's old advisers shows such loyalty, and has the courage to face the consequences of his past actions."

The American shrugged. " 'Tis not his actions nor those of any particular minister that are to blame, but the King's own abysmal stupidity. Your Ambassador, Lord Gower, summed up matters when he said to me last year, after the abortive flight to Varennes, 'If this country ceases to be a Monarchy it will be entirely the fault of Louis XVI. Blunder upon blunder, inconsequence upon inconsequence, a total want of energy of mind accompanied by a personal cowardice, have been the destruction of his reign; and in this last affair he should have either forced his way through those who sought to prevent his reaching the frontier or perished in the attempt.' Should he die today he will do no more than pay the penalty of his folly; the real ghastliness of the tragedy is that by his weakness he has brought ruin and may now bring death to so many others. It is to his poor, courageous Queen and her helpless children that all my prayers go out at this grim moment."

Instantly Mr. Morris's reference to the Queen and her children switched Roger's mind from the alarming general situation to his own mission. Mr. Pitt and Talleyrand had both informed him that in Paris a new crisis of real gravity was imminent, but on his arrival the peaceful aspect of the city and the apathy of its ordinary citizens had caused him to discount such fears.

Now, it was suddenly thrust upon him that events had marched too quickly for him to have the least chance of carrying out his instructions. He had not yet thought out any story to explain away his participation in Don Diego's death. He had intended, when he had done so, to try it out on several of his old acquaintances, before approaching the Princesse de Lamballe with the request that she should secure him a secret interview with the Queen. All attempts at such finesse had now to be abandoned. Before nightfall Marie Antoinette might be dead. Even if some freak of fortune enabled him to reach her, it would be both laughable and cruel calmly to propose that she should plan a flight to Brittany while a mob surrounded the palace howling for her blood.

Yet, even if the onrush of the crisis had cut the ground from beneath his feet for that project, there remained the other that Mr. Pitt had put forward only as a possibility almost too remote to hope for, but pregnant with golden dividends for the man who could accomplish it. Moreover, in speaking of it he had said, "Should you have reason to believe the King's life is in imminent peril you have my permission to stop at nothing which may enable you to remove the Dauphin from his parents." Now, if ever, the King's life *was* in imminent peril.

"I am going to the Tuileries," declared Roger suddenly.

Mr. Morris's plump face showed amazement and his small mouth opened in instant protest. "You must be mad even to think of such a thing! If you did your curiosity would be like to cost you your life. The mob will give short shrift to any *aristos* that it encounters this afternoon, and it could hardly mistake you for aught else."

" 'Tis not curiosity but duty that impels me to attempt to reach the royal apartments."

"Duty be damned!" the American burst out. "Unlike M. de Malesherbes you have no cause to immolate yourself, and it's no part of an Englishman's duty to defend the King of France."

Roger smiled. "I know it, and unless the King is set upon in my presence I have no intention of aiding his defence. My business is with the Queen."

"Still worse! It is popularly believed that she is in constant correspondence with France's enemies. One of the cries that will be raised today is, 'Death to the Austrian woman and the committee of traitors who help her to betray us!' Théroigne de Méricourt has long since sworn to make herself a parasol out of Marie Antoinette's intestines. Your life will not be worth a ducat if they find you with her."

"God knows I have no wish to die! But I have been in tight corners before, and in this matter I feel impelled to take the hazard."

In a last attempt to dissuade Roger, Mr. Morris seized him by the arm and drew him back to the window. "Look!" he cried.

"Look at the hydra-headed monster that you presume to challenge! Once their tempers are aroused those wild beasts down there are capable of tearing limb from limb anyone like yourself."

"I know it," replied Roger, "and for that reason I must ask your help. There is no time for me to go elsewhere and obtain other clothes—old, dirty clothes, the more tattered the better. Yet if I could procure them I could enter the Palace, not as myself but as one of the *canaille*, and thus have little to fear from them. Seeing that my need is so urgent, I pray you ask Madame de Flahaut's aid, and do your utmost to help disguise me."

"Ah!" exclaimed the banker. "That sounds more sensible. Wait here a moment and I will see what can be done."

As he stumped away, his wooden leg tapping sharply on the parquet, Roger endeavoured to co-ordinate his whirling thoughts. A moment's reflection was enough to convince him that an immediate abduction of the Dauphin must enormously increase the chances of the Queen's death. If she were able to remain with the boy at her side while the mob were in the Palace there was a hope that their rough hearts would be touched, and that they would refrain from striking her down in his presence; but if she were deprived of him nothing could save her from their hatred.

Another moment's thought decided Roger that, the fate of the Queen apart, his chances of securing the Dauphin would be far from good. Yet in spite of the obvious dangers and obstacles to the success of such an attempt, he knew that it was his duty to make it; for if he did not Fate might deprive him of all future opportunities. Unless something was done during the present emergency the child might be killed by accident or murdered with his mother, and Mr. Pitt had shown a most positive conviction that the possession of the Dauphin would give England the ace of trumps in future international affairs.

With such a tremendous stake involved Roger would certainly have determined on gambling his luck and wits against all risks, had success meant placing only the life of the futile King in greater jeopardy—but the fate of Marie Antoinette was a very different matter.

Like many another man Roger had first fallen under her spell when she was still a happy woman and in all the glory of her beauty. Later, when he had come to know her personally, his admiration had become veneration; for by that time he had met many royal personages, but none other who combined her kindness, charm, thoughtfulness for others, high ideals and fine courage in adversity. He knew the slanders about her to be infamous lies, and that although married to a gross, unimaginative clot she had proved a model wife and mother. He knew, too, that on coming to France she had accepted it as her own country and done everything in her power to win the love of its people. That she had failed was no fault of hers, but due to the jealous spite of the King's relatives who, over a long period of years, had consistently put an evil interpretation on her every act and deliberately fostered the belief that she was rapacious, extravagant and wanton. Even if it were true that, more recently, driven to despair by insults, threats, humiliations and imprisonment, she had sought help from her own family, who could blame her?

Roger certainly did not; and he realized now that his impulse to go to the Tuileries had really arisen, not from the long chance of swiftly making a hundred thousand pounds or of serving Mr. Pitt, but because he could not have borne to remain inactive while so fine a woman, who had once given him her friendship, stood in peril of her life.

He had barely got the matter clear in his own mind when Mr. Morris came stumping back into the room, holding a pair of old wooden-soled shoes, some dirty blue cotton overalls and a ragged coat.

"Here you are!" he cried. "These should serve your purpose; Madame's maid found them for me in the locker of the man who stokes the furnace. But we'll have to do something about your face and hair. Madame la Comtesse is now out of her bath; when you have put these on, come into her room. I'll go and tell her that she must play the part of barber to you."

Hurriedly Roger stripped off his own things and, with considerable repugnance, put on the smelly garments. Had it been winter he would have shivered from their thinness, but it was a broiling June day, so to exchange his stock for a bare chest, and to feel his naked arms in the loose sleeves of the threadbare jacket, was a relief rather than otherwise. Directly he knocked on the bedroom door Madame de Flahaut called to him to come in.

She was now in a *peignoir* of flowered muslin, and her curly hair, free of its towel but still undressed, made a frame for her face that greatly enhanced its loveliness; yet her manner no longer held any trace of the sophisticated coquettishness with which she had received Roger. Instead, he was given a glimpse of the generous nature and quick, intelligent mind which had enabled her to enslave her gifted lovers.

"Monsieur," she said, "I am overwhelmed at hearing of the plot that Monsieur Morris has just revealed to me; and although I have no cause to feel a personal attachment to either of their Majesties, there is nothing I would not do to aid them at this moment. Whatever may be your intentions, if you succeed in penetrating the Tuileries I cannot think that you mean them evil, so I will do my utmost in helping to disguise you. Sit here, please; I ask your forgiveness in advance for the liberties I shall have to take with your person."

As Roger normally took considerable pride in his appearance, the liberties she took in the next quarter of an hour caused him so much distress that he could have groaned aloud, but he submitted with as good a grace as he could muster. First she chopped off his nice brown hair, until only a bush remained which had ragged ends sticking out in all directions. With a mixture of ashes and soot she dirtied one of her husband's cotton night-caps and set it on top of his head with the tassel dangling over one ear. Using the same ingredients mixed with a little grease, she rubbed it thoroughly into his face, neck, chest and forearms; then she attended to his hands. Having pared his almond-shaped nails jaggedly with a small penknife, she forced grime under what was left of them with an orange stick. Next she mixed a few drops of purple dye with some kohl from her make-up box and used it to give him a glorious black eye. Lastly, she picked up a needle and, before he could guess her intention, gave him a swift, light stroke with its point from ear to chin.

As he started up and clapped his hand to his face in dismay, she smiled at him and said, " 'Tis no more than a scratch, Monsieur, and will be healed in a day or two, but that final touch was necessary to complete the picture. I vow no one would now know you for the handsome Chevalier who waited upon me this morning."

When Roger looked in her mirror he would scarcely have known himself, and amusement at the sight he presented overcoming his distress, he thanked her for her efforts with a laugh. Then, as she staunched the first flow of blood from his long scratch with some cotton wool, he said, "Swift as you have been,

Madame, in your transformation of me, I must not wait a second longer, so permit me to take my leave."

Mr. Morris drew a heavy gold watch from his fob and after a glance at it remarked, "It is not yet two o'clock, and if the National Guards will let you through you should have ample time to get into the Palace before it is attacked by the mob. They will hardly yet have got as far as presenting their petition to the Assembly."

"Thank God for that!" Roger exclaimed. "A little time in which to think may make a world of difference." Then, as they wished him good fortune, he thanked them again and hurried from the apartment.

When he reached the ground floor of the Palace he took the nearest exit he could find on to the Quai du Louvre. The mob was still surging by, although at a much slower pace, and he had only to step forward to be caught up in it as it flowed westward along the river bank.

Now, for the first time, he had an opportunity to observe the marchers at close quarters, and what he saw filled him with the grimmest forebodings. Here again was the lean and hungry look that he had noticed in Le Havre, but added to it in the faces of many of these Paris slum dwellers was something indescribably vicious.

Men and women, old and young, and even lanky children in their teens, were massed shoulder to shoulder in one slowly moving crush, that stank to high heaven beneath the hot sun. Some of the grimy faces within a few feet of his own were gaunt with the markings of years of vice and misery; others were fleshier, darker, and of a foreign cast, and Roger guessed that the latter must be either *fédérés* from the south, or some of the professional Italian cut-throats that d'Orléans had imported in '89 to lead the first riots of the Revolution.

A large part of the men were naked to the waist. Here and there some were hideously crippled or disfigured from accidents, after which they had not received proper medical attention. A great number of them were pockmarked, and the arms of the majority were horribly skinny, which made the knotty biceps they had acquired through years of toil seem abnormally large and ugly. Most of the women looked as wolfish as the men. They ranged from wheezy, toothless old crones, with wispy grey hair, to buxom young viragos whose bold eyes, loose mouths and faces daubed with cheap paint proclaimed their way of living.

Nearly all the marchers of both sexes carried some form of weapon: crowbars, hatchets, knives bound to the end of long poles, billhooks, rusty cutlasses, and ancient firearms bobbed shoulder high or above their heads in an uneven dance as they edged forward. Among this forest of rough and ready arms swayed crudely painted banners bearing such slogans as "Down with the Tyrants", "The Veto Must Go", "Death to the Austrian Woman"; while, scattered between them, one solitary note of fashion stood out incongruously against the background of sordid apparel with which the poverty-stricken multitude covered its nakedness: it was struck by the new red Phrygian caps of Liberty worn by one man or woman in every fifty. Otherwise, the clothes of all but a few, including the prettier of the prostitutes, were grey with age and filth, or were wretched improvised garments made out of threadbare blankets, tattered curtains or sacking.

No normal, uninformed person could have looked on such abundant evidence of utter destitution without pity, and without forming the swift conviction that the workers could not possibly be blamed for attacking a ruling caste so apparently lacking in humanity as to allow such abject poverty to exist side by side with its own wealth.

But Roger was not uninformed, and had he at the moment had the leisure to think about such things he would have reserved his pity for a very small proportion of the crowd into which he was now so tightly wedged. He had known the prosperous France of yesteryear and was well aware that it was not the workers but the bourgeois who, out of jealousy of the nobility, had fermented the Revolution. Both the peasants and the townspeople had been as well off as those in most other countries, and far better off than those in Spain, Italy and many parts of Germany. As with every nation, France had had her very poor in both town and country, whose lots should have been eased by wise legislation, and it was the lack of it that had been seized upon by the radical politicians as an excuse to further their own ends. But those genuine victims of oppression represented only a small fraction of the people and a still tinier fraction of the present crowd.

It was composed almost entirely of hooligans, wastrels and habitual criminals—the lawless dregs of humanity that lurk in the slums of every capital, and are ever ready to join a riot in the hope of a chance to despoil honest citizens. And at this stage of the Revolution more than half the people who formed the Paris mobs were not even *Parisiens*. For years every type of rogue and ne'er-do-well in the provinces had been drawn to the capital by the prospect of loot during disturbances; so it could safely be said that ninety-nine out of every hundred of the demonstrators marching to the Tuileries had no just grievance calling for redress, but were the worst elements of the whole nation, and were as evil in mind as in appearance.

The south wing of the Tuileries was virtually a continuation of the south wing of the Louvre, and separated from it only by a great pair of double gates that led into the Place du Carrousel. As the latter was a public square Roger had hoped to reach it, and proceed from there into the Palace while the bulk of the mob went on to hold their demonstration outside the Assembly; but when he came opposite the gates he saw that they were closed. Too late he realized that he should have left the Louvre by one of the entrances to its courtyard, whence he could have walked straight through to the Place du Carrousel. Now he was caught up in the mob and could only go forward with it.

Again, when he reached the western extremity of the Tuileries, he found it impossible to turn off the quay; the gates of its gardens had been closed, and the tree-lined walks beyond them were occupied by hundreds of National Guards. Pleased as he was to see that someone seemed to be taking precautions for the defence of the Palace, he was more than ever annoyed at his own short-sightedness in having joined the mob on the quay. To reach the riding-school that housed the Assembly it would have to make a long detour right round the huge gardens and approach them via the Rue St. Honoré, and he feared that in the meantime other mobs from the eastern Faubourgs might break into the Palace on its northern side.

Impatiently he began to push his way forward, but, although he took advantage of every opening among the marchers, over an hour elapsed before he managed to get within sight of the riding-school, and then, for a while, he found himself completely stuck. The head of the mob in which he was jammed had met the head of the one approaching from the east, and from end to end the Rue St. Honoré was now one mass of people.

The sun beat down on the heads of the crowd and the stench given out was almost overpowering, yet it was this fierce heat that now came to Roger's assistance. Tough as were the viragos who formed the female element of the mob, here and there one of them fainted. As a hideously pockmarked girl just in front of Roger groaned and sagged, he caught her and hoisted her up over his shoulder. A brawny metalworker near by at once began to bellow for room and use his strength to force a passage for them. Gradually they edged their way forward and after ten minutes of breathless exertion Roger managed to stagger with his burden to the entrance of the Convent des Feuillants, where other women who had fainted were being given attention.

On the west side of the Convent a narrow passage led down to the riding-school, and to its only entrance other than that which gave on to the Tuileries gardens. It was here, two hours earlier, that the leaders of the mob had demanded admittance to the Assembly, and Roger now learned what had transpired.

Several moderate deputies had boldly declared that, since the bearing of arms was illegal, the dignity of the Assembly required it to refuse to receive the insurgents, and others had sought to evade the issue by calling for an immediate suspension of the session; but Vergniaud and his fellow Girondins had insisted that the "people" should be allowed to enter and place their "sufferings and anxieties" before the Assembly. A brothel-keeper named Huguenin had then read the petition, and at its conclusion the Left had carried a vote that the "champions of liberty" should be allowed to march through the hall bearing their arms.

In the meantime, the foremost part of the mob, chafing at the delay while the deputies argued, and half-stifled in the narrow passage, had broken through its exits. Some of the rabble had forced their way into the Convent gardens and there planted the Tree of Liberty; others had broken into the gardens of the Palace where, now leaderless, they had simply dispersed and thrown themselves on the ground to recover from their exhaustion. But the pressure of the crowd behind was so great and the passage so narrow that not a twentieth of the multitude had yet succeeded in getting further than its entrance in the Rue St. Honoré.

Roger's arrival at the door of the Convent occurred within a few minutes of the Assembly having given its consent for the demonstrators to march through its chamber, so he had hardly freed himself of his unsavoury burden when a fresh movement of the crowd again impelled him forward; but on reaching the door of the riding-school he managed to struggle out of the crush and, instead of entering the building, stagger with some other half-fainting people through the broken gates into the Tuileries gardens.

For a few moments he leant panting against a tree, while he swiftly took in the scene about him. Two hundred yards away to his left the National Guards were still drawn up before the west front of the Palace. They were making no move to check the groups of demonstrators that were now infiltrating between their companies, but from what he could see there appeared no urgent reason to do so. Other groups in front of him and to his right were spreading out to seek the welcome shade of the trees in all parts of the gardens. Obviously they were terribly fatigued, and too anxious to rest at the moment even to think of congregating below the Palace windows and hurling their usual insults.

Had Roger not learned from Gouverneur Morris the secret reason for which the demonstrators had been organized he might have believed that this dispersal of the mob could be taken as a sign that there was no more to fear; but he knew they had been told only the first part of the conspirators' programme. They did not yet know that they were to be used for an attack on the Palace. Having planted their tree and presented their petition, they were now quite prepared to rest for a while, then make their way home again. With new hope that he might be able to use this lull to get into the Palace before the leaders of the mob had a chance to reassemble it, Roger set off at a quick pace along the walk beneath the terrace of the Feuillants.

He had not covered sixty yards before he saw that a new movement was in progress. Beyond the riding-school, and up to that moment hidden from him by it, lay a long courtyard parallel to the avenue down which he was walking. The back entrance of the riding-school gave on to this court, and it was now packed with the armed rabble that had just passed through the Assembly. The head of the column had already reached the far end of the court, had turned right and was debouching on to the terrace of the Palace. In an instant Roger saw that, either by accident or design, this approach had outflanked the National Guard. In another few moments the mob would be on the steps of the Palace's great west entrance. Cursing himself for not having foreseen where the still-organized marchers must emerge, he began to run in that direction.

CHAPTER IV

THE VORTEX OF THE CYCLONE

MANY of the groups scattered about the gardens also caught sight of the new move and started to run towards the terrace. Still the National Guard stood at ease with grounded muskets. Although the size of the crowd was increasing every moment, and it now entirely surrounded the militia, the latter was sufficiently numerous to have cleared the gardens by determined action. As Roger raced past a company he saw that most of the men were regarding the demonstrators with open hostility, but no order was given to them. Pétion, the treacherous Mayor, had evidently gone to earth, and the King's mania that no one should ever be harmed on his account being so well known, no lesser official appeared willing to take the responsibility of thwarting the People.

By dodging between the trees at breakneck pace Roger reached the terrace in the van of those now streaming towards it from all directions. The head of the column emerging from the riding-school courtyard had got as far as the main west door of the Palace and halted there, while those behind it overflowed into the swelling crowd. The big doors of the Palace were shut and through the ground-floor windows on either side of them groups of soldiers could be seen. They were the Swiss Guard—the only personal troops of which the Assembly had failed to deprive the King, as the Swiss Government had refused to sanction any alteration in their terms of service—but whether their master would permit them to resist the mob remained doubtful.

Evidently the mob leaders did not think so, as they were yelling at the foremost *sans-culottes* that there was nothing to be afraid of, and urging them to force the doors. Roger caught a glimpse of a small, flamboyantly dressed woman as she ran up the steps and hammered on the doors with her clenched fists; then, as she turned to harangue the crowd, he recognized her.

It was Théroigne de Méricourt. She was dressed in a short scarlet riding habit, jackboots and a three-cornered hat with huge red, white and blue ostrich feathers. Her thin dark face, haggard in repose from years of dissipation, was now lit with a strange demoniacal beauty, and her eyes seemed to flash blue fire as she screamed at her followers that the Palace and all that was in it belonged to the nation—to them, the People—and it was high time they had a look at their own possessions.

On a sudden inspiration Roger hoisted himself upon the parapet and yelled at the top of his voice, "That's right! That's right! But why risk a bullet? Let's go round to the quay entrance. That is not guarded!"

The mob, as ever cowardly by nature and prone to be swayed by any new idea, took up the cry and began to run towards the river. Jumping down from his perch, Roger ran with them and was among the first fifty to reach the great double gates between the Tuileries and the Louvre. As they had been shut when he passed them two hours earlier, he had counted on their making an additional barrier to be broken down before the mob could get into the building. Now, to his consternation, he saw that some traitor's hand had opened them. Another moment, and in the wild rush he was carried through into the Place du Carrousel.

Yet, even as he was borne forward, new hope suddenly came to him that his having diverted the crowd might still prove far from ineffective. In the Place a hundred mounted gendarmes were drawn up, and opposite them another pair of gates, in front of which stood a double row of National Guards, presented a formidable barrier They gave on to the Cour Royale and would have to be forced before the mob could reach the east doors of the Palace.

The gendarmes made no attempt to drive back the insurgents, but the National Guards closed up their ranks and showed that they meant to resist any attack on the gate. At the sight of their firm demeanour the front ranks of the mob halted, wavered and pressed back. Seeing a second chance to play upon their cowardice and hoping at the same time to appeal to their cupidity, Roger shouted:

"Don't be fools and get killed for nothing! The King doesn't keep his gold in the Tuileries! His treasure-chests are stored in the vaults of the Louvre!"

A score of his nearest companions quickly turned about. In another moment he would have drawn the mob after him across the square to the old Palace. But this time his ruse was doomed to failure.

Santerre, the big brewer who had made himself King of the worst slum district in Paris, now took a hand. After leading his contingent from the Faubourg St. Antoine to the Assembly he had since kept in the background, hoping that matters would go as the conspirators had planned without it being necessary for him to compromise himself; but it was already four o'clock, and the real business of the day had not even started. The wrangle in the Assembly had delayed matters and long hours of marching, singing, pushing and shouting under the broiling sun had taken all the ferocity out of the mob. They still had energy enough to bestir themselves at the idea of easy plunder, but clearly were no longer in a mood to fight unless driven to it. As the group facing the gate of the Cour Royale turned away from it to follow Roger, Santerre came running forward and bellowed:

"Halt! Time enough to get the gold afterwards! We have a duty to perform! Have you forgotten, comrades, that we are here to make fat Louis rescind the veto?"

"Citizen Santerre is right!" yelled one of his lieutenants. "We are the People! Everything belongs to us! We'll take it soon enough, but first we must force the King to do our will."

Shouts of agreement greeted this new incitement to force a way into the Tuileries and, the prospect of treasure momentarily forgotten, they began to call on the National Guards to let them through.

"Never!" cried one brave citizen-soldier. "We will die rather than let you enter!" and several of his companions loudly applauded his defiance.

For a few moments the issue hung in the balance, while the mob and the guards hurled insults at each other. Santerre, with shouts of "We must get in! We must get in! It was for that we came here," kept urging the motley crowd to attack, but they still hung back, every man loath to be the first to risk a bullet.

Then above the tumult arose shouts of "Make way! Make way!" followed by the rumble of iron wheels on stone. It was some of Santerre's men dragging two small cannon up from the quay. With a shout of triumph he ordered the pieces to be aimed at the gates, then threatened the guards that if they would not give way he meant to mow them down.

For some inexplicable reason the militia had not a single officer with them. Each man looked at his neighbour, doubting what to do and hoping that one of his comrades would give him a lead. Quite unexpectedly they were relieved of the necessity of taking any final decision. Traitors inside the courtyard, who must have been privy to the conspiracy, had been watching the scene through the grille of the gate. Feeling that there was now sufficient excuse to cover their treachery they raised the big bar that held it closed.

As the gate swung open the mob surged forward, swept the militia aside and poured through into the courtyard. Inside there were more National Guards lined up, but either by an oversight or through further treachery the big doors of the Palace stood wide open. Four officers ran to close them, but standing on the steps were two of Pétion's municipal representatives wearing broad *tricolore* scarves. One shouted to the troops, forbidding them to resist the "sacred people", the other swiftly ordered some of those near him to arrest the four officers. As they were seized and pulled aside Santerre and his men tumbled pell-mell into the hall of the Palace.

Roger, concerned now only with reaching the Queen's side at the earliest possible moment, had remained close behind Santerre, but in the hall the big brewer met with an unexpected check. A group of Palace officials had gathered there. One, bolder than the rest, strode up to him and cried:

"You scoundrel! How dare you incite these good people to force a way into the King's Palace!"

"Yes! Yes!" cried others. "You alone are responsible for this outrage!" "They had no evil intent!" "We saw you urging them on, from the windows!" "They are not to blame!" "It is you alone who are guilty!" "Withdraw at once, or we will testify against you to the Assembly!" "There is still a law in France, and you shall be made to pay for this!"

Santerre's ruddy face paled. It was true that the mob had shown little inclination to attack the Palace until he had hounded them into doing so. Now his companions were looking sheepish and rather scared. Centuries of tradition had made the Royal Palaces almost sacred ground, and as they looked about them at the statues and tapestries in the vast marble-pillared hall they were overawed by such magnificence, the like of which few of them had ever seen. It seemed now as if his earlier fears were to be realized, and that through having placed himself at the head of the mob he would be made the scapegoat of the conspirators.

Nervously, the big bully began to protest that he had been forced against his will into leading the mob, and that he had no intention of invading the King's apartments.

Again, for a moment, everything hung in the balance; but,

knowing nothing of this hold-up, more and more people from outside were forcing their way through the doors. Guards, Palace servants, and even some of the mob's own leaders, were now trying to hold it back with pikes held horizontally and with the pressure of their own bodies.

Suddenly the thin human barrier broke. Like a great tidal wave the close-packed mass burst into the hall and surged up the broad marble staircase. So great was the pressure and the impetus behind it that one of the small cannon was borne on their shoulders right up to the landing of the first floor.

Roger had the advantage of the mob in that he knew the geography of the Palace. The moment he realized that the *sans-culottes* could no longer be held back, instead of attempting to force his way past the officials and up the staircase he turned and dashed off down a side corridor.

His wooden-soled shoes ringing on the marble paving, he ran on until he reached a service staircase that he knew of old. Taking its stairs three at a time, he raced up it to the second floor. There, he turned back in the direction of the grand staircase, but while still some distance from it dived down another corridor, then pulled up before a tall door on which he knocked urgently. It was opened almost at once by a grey-haired woman servant, of whom he asked breathlessly:

"Is Madame de Lamballe here?"

Her reply was a piercing scream and a swift attempt to slam the door in his face. Momentarily he had forgotten that with his cropped hair, black eye, blood-streaked cheek and filthy clothes he must present a terrifying spectacle. Fortunately he was just in time to wedge his foot in the door. With a heave of his shoulder he thrust it open, pushed back the screaming woman and closed it behind him.

He had recognized her immediately as the elderly maid who had admitted him to that suite of apartments on his previous visits to it two years before, but there was no time for explanations. Locking the door, he pocketed the key to prevent any chance of her getting out and calling menservants or National Guards to interfere with him. Her presence seemed to make it certain that the Princess de Lamballe still occupied the apartment, so he called out:

"Madame la Princesse! Please to answer if you are within. Have no fear; I am a friend."

There was no reply, so he swiftly crossed the antechamber and pulled open the door of the *salon*. It was empty, so he crossed that too, and calling out again knocked on the door of the bedroom at its far end. Still there was no reply, but the door opened at his touch. As he had feared would prove the case—since at such a time of crisis the Princess's place was with the Queen—she was not there.

Yet, however helpful her presence might have been, her absence did not invalidate the plan that Roger had in mind, as it was her apartment, not herself, which formed the basis of it. When he had left Madame de Flahaut's he had not had the faintest idea what he meant to do, but during the long interval that he had spent wedged helplessly in the crowd he had had ample time to think out how best he might attempt to rescue Marie Antoinette from the fate that threatened her.

Two years before she had twice granted him secret interviews in Madame de Lamballe's apartments, which lay immediately above her own, and he knew that she must have come up to see him there by a private stairway hidden in the wall of the bedroom. The plan he had formed was to gain entry into the Palace before the mob if possible or, if not, with its leaders, hurry to the Princess's apartment and either send her down the secret staircase, or go himself, to fetch up the Queen. It was, he felt, the one way in which she could leave the royal apartments without the spies who were always lurking about her ante-rooms knowing that she had done so. Once she had been persuaded that her life hung on her immediate use of the secret staircase he did not foresee any great difficulty in transferring her to one of the innumerable attics under the great roof, where she could remain safely hidden until the mob grew tired of searching for her.

Without wasting a moment, he began to hunt for the entrance to the secret stairs. In frantic haste he pulled the principal pieces of furniture from the walls and, rapping on the surfaces they had concealed, listened for a hollow note. Meeting with no success, he rolled back the carpet to see if it hid a trap-door. Again drawing blank, he hurriedly examined a tall, narrow wall-mirror. Half-way up one side of the gilded scrollwork of its frame his glance fell on a boss from which the gilding had been rubbed. Putting his thumb on the place, he pressed it; the mirror swung silently outwards revealing a dark cavity.

His search had cost him a good five minutes, but he felt confident that the faithful Swiss Guards would endeavour to prevent the rioters from entering the rooms below, and make a stand long enough to give him a good chance of smuggling the Queen away before they were overwhelmed. Nevertheless he plunged down the dark, narrow stairs as though his own life depended on his speed.

At the bottom he slid his hands swiftly down the sides of the panel that confronted him. Straight away his right hand found a knob. As he fumbled with it the panel gave and swung outward. Stepping through the opening he found, as he had expected, that he was in the Queen's bedroom.

There was no one there, and its doors were closed. Running to the nearest one, he wrenched it open. It gave on to an ante-room, beyond which was another bedroom. The little boy's clothes, miniature sword and toys scattered about it showed at a glance that it was the Dauphin's room. It contained two other doors and one of them stood half open. From beyond it came the sound of many running feet and a shout of "This way! This way! We'll catch the Austrian woman and make her eat her own dung."

Again, just as in the dawn of the 6th of October at Versailles three years before, some hireling of the Duc d'Orléans who knew the Palace was leading a portion of the mob through a series of little-used side rooms straight to the Queen's apartments.

Springing forward, Roger slammed the door and shot its bolts. Turning, he ran back to the door through which he had come, locked that and pocketed the key. Crossing the Dauphin's room again, he pulled open its third door and looked through. It was the room of Madame de Tourzel, the governess of the royal children. A maid was there, peering from the window at the howling mob below. At the sound of Roger's entry she turned, gave him one look and fled screaming through a further door.

For the second time it was rudely brought home to him that, while his disguise had enabled him to penetrate the Palace with the mob, it was now a serious disadvantage. But he had known that he could not dress to suit both parts he wished to play, so must rely on his accent to reassure the Queen and her friends that he was not the ruffian that he appeared to be. Heedless of the fright he had given the girl, he dashed after her.

The doorway gave on to a long corridor with several other doors along its further side. Hastily he tried one after another, but all of them proved to be locked, until he came to the fourth down the line. As he turned the handle it flew open. An instant later he saw that he was standing in one of the smaller entrances to the great chamber known as the Œil de Bœuf.

At its far end, some eighty feet distant, stood a group of people, all of whom had their backs towards him. It consisted of four Swiss Guards, the King, a woman who was clinging to his arm, and several gentlemen. The whole group was staring at a pair of large gilded double doors, on the far side of which pandemonium was raging. From beyond them came the sounds of shouts, yells and curses, and they were quivering violently under a rain of blows as the mob strove to break them in.

Roger felt sure that the woman holding the King's arm was too short to be the Queen, so must be his sister, Madame Elizabeth. For a moment he paused where he was, debating his next move. In his present fearsome disguise, if he ran forward and asked the whereabouts of the Queen it was quite certain that no one in the group would tell him, but he felt sure that she could not be far off. She had more than once sworn to die at the King's feet if the mob ever attempted to kill him, so it seemed highly probable that she might come hurrying in to take her place by his side at any minute.

Suddenly the lower panel of one of the doors splintered. A second blow on the same spot caused the boards to give with a tearing screech. At a third a large piece of wood flew inward, leaving a gaping hole. A dozen pikes, bayonets and sabres jabbed furiously at it, and in a moment the whole panel had been stove in. Another moment and the muzzle of the little cannon was thrust through the aperture.

Instantly the King's companions threw themselves in front of him, but there was no physically braver man than Louis XVI in his whole kingdom. Thrusting them aside, he lifted up his voice so that it could be heard above the howls of the mob, and cried:

"All defence is useless! The only thing to do is to open the door and meet them calmly!" Then, signing to one of the Swiss Guards, he added, "Unlock the door, Edouard! Open! I have nothing to fear from Frenchmen!"

The soldier obeyed. The great door swung towards him and the mob came tumbling in. Brandishing their weapons and shrieking imprecations, they rushed forward. The Swiss and the few gentlemen with the King drew their swords and prepared to defend him to the death. Madame Elizabeth seized his coat, pulled him round behind her, and shouted, "You shall massacre me before him! Respect your King! Respect your King!"

Although it was the safety of the Queen that dominated Roger's thoughts, it was not in him to stand by and calmly witness such a scene. Having no weapon, he ran to a nearby fireplace, snatched up the poker and came pounding down the long room to aid the brave Princess.

Before he could reach her the ignorant *sans-culottes*, mistaking her for Marie Antoinette, had leapt towards her shouting, "Here is the Austrian! Death to the Austrian!"

Without a second's hesitation she bared her breast to their weapons and cried, "Yes, I am the Queen!"

One ruffian raised his pike to stab her through the throat, another was just about to plunge his bayonet into her heart. But a gentleman beside her shouted, "Stop! Stop! She is not the Queen! She is His Majesty's sister!"

As Roger came racing up he heard her exclaim, "Oh, why undeceive them? Is it not better that they should shed my blood rather than hers?"

Overcome with amazement at the sight of such heroism, her assailants checked their thrusts, but not before the blades of their weapons were only a matter of inches from her body. Putting up her hand, she gently turned the point of the pike aside, and said calmly, "I pray you be careful, Monsieur. You might hurt me, and I am sure you would then be sorry."

Her supreme courage and that of the King produced a remarkable effect on the invaders. They had been told that Louis XVI was a tyrant and was planning to have them massacred by foreign troops, so they had expected to find an ogre who would defend himself with the utmost ferocity. Instead they had come face to face with a placid, benevolent-looking gentleman whose mild blue eyes showed only friendliness.

Santerre had not entered the Œil de Bœuf but had again slunk into the background, and the stupefaction of his now leaderless followers at the King's calm demeanour was so great that they were temporarily robbed of all initiative. As they stood staring at him, now uncertain what to do, he stepped back into the embrasure of a window, ordered his protectors to sheath their swords and beckoned them to range themselves on either side of him.

At that moment Madame Elizabeth again showed great presence of mind. Turning to a gentleman beside her, she said in a swift whisper, "Monsieur Aubier, go quickly to the Queen. Prevent her at all costs from attempting to join His Majesty. If she comes here they will murder her."

Roger, who was just behind her, heard what she said. As M. Aubier turned and ran to deliver her warning, he turned too, waited for a moment to give her messenger a start, then followed him.

The Princess had acted only just in time. The still violent mob out on the landing were clamouring to enter the Œil de Bœuf; those already inside it, who had been subdued by the calmness of the King, were now being forced forward. More and more wild, threatening figures were thrusting their way into the room. And the Queen was already on her way to it.

M. Aubier met her in the corridor and shouted, "Go back, Madame! Go back, or they will kill you!"

"No, no!" she cried distractedly as he barred her passage. "Let me pass! My place is with the King!"

"Please, Madame! Please!" he pleaded. "Madame Elizabeth sent me to prevent you exposing yourself!"

"Only my most cruel enemies could give me such advice!" she retorted hotly. "You attempt to dishonour me by preventing me from dying at my post!"

Then, in a wild endeavour to reach her husband, she threw herself on M. Aubier and tried to push him aside. But Roger had come up behind him. Knowing the one thought that might check her, he cried, "No, Madame! Your post is with your children!"

As she stared past M. Aubier's shoulder at Roger's fearsome visage he saw that her once beautiful blue eyes were now dim and reddened from weeping. There was no trace of recognition in them, or of fear, but it was evident that he intended her no harm. Behind her were a number of her closest friends—the Duc de Choiseul, the Princesses de Lamballe and de Tarente, and the Marquise de la Roche Aymon. They all joined their entreaties to those of M. Aubier and took up Roger's cry. At the thought of her children she had ceased to struggle and now, bursting into fresh tears, she yielded. Taking her by the arms, her ladies led her, half fainting, back along the corridor, away from the Œil de Bœuf.

Hoping that the sight of her children would comfort her, they hurried her towards the Dauphin's bedroom. But Roger, seeing their intention, shouted from the rear, "Not that wav! Take Her Majesty to her own room!"

His shout was ignored, but at that very moment a gentleman came running to head the party off. "Turn back!" he cried. "Turn back! A mob has broken into M. le Dauphin's apartment!"

The Queen gave a piercing scream. "My children! Oh, save my children!"

"They are safe, Madame," panted the man. "Madame de Tourzel has taken them to the Council Chamber, and there are some National Guards of the loyal Filles Saint Thomas Section with them."

"Oh, God be thanked!" breathed the Queen, but this assurance served to turn her frantic thoughts back to the King. Freeing her arms from the grasp of her ladies, she turned about and cried, "Then my place is with His Majesty!"

"For pity's sake, Madame, do not go to the Œil de Bœuf!" exclaimed the Duc de Choiseul.

"But his sister is serving him as a rampart and it should be myself!"

M. Lajard, one of the King's Ministers, had joined the group. As she started forward he barred her path and pointed to the Council Chamber. "Listen, Madame! Listen! Your children are calling for you."

Again the distracted wife and mother hesitated, torn between two equally compelling loyalties. But the cries of the children were an invention of the Minister. The only sound that reached the listening group was the howling of the mob, and it came from both before and behind them.

Seizing on the sudden silence among the group that followed M. Lajard's intervention, Roger thrust his way forward and said quickly, "Take Her Majesty to her bedroom. There lies her only safety. We will bring her children to her. Hurry, now! For God's sake hurry, or it will be too late."

For a moment it looked as if his disguise would cause the wrecking of his plan. Up to then the Queen's friends had been so desperately concerned with preventing her from going to the Œil de Bœuf that they had taken scant notice of the unsavoury-looking stranger in their midst. Now, the faces turned towards him showed doubt, hostility and suspicion. Fearing that he was attempting to lead the Queen into a trap, some of them quickly exclaimed against his proposal, while others demanded his reason for it. But the Princesse de Lamballe gave him one swift stare, then supported him wholeheartedly.

Although she had failed to identify Roger, and the existence of the staircase leading up to her room was a most closely guarded secret, his voice was vaguely familiar to her. She guessed that he must be some friend in disguise who knew of it, and felt he was right in inferring that it was the one hope of getting the Queen away to some safe hiding place.

"Messieurs!" she cried. "Who this man is I do not know, but I regard his suggestion as sensible. As Superintendent of Her Majesty's Household I take full responsibility. M. le Duc, be good enough to bring the royal children to Her Majesty's apartment."

De Choiseul hurried away, the Princess put an arm round the weeping Queen's shoulders to draw her forward, and Roger heaved a sigh of relief. Once inside the bedroom he intended to disclose himself to Madame de Lamballe and take charge of the situation. The courtiers were loyal and brave, but they lacked imagination, and they would rather have died than commit such a horrifying breach of etiquette as to ask the Queen to crawl into a cistern. That was what he meant to do as soon as they could get her up to the attics, and he had good hopes now that within another ten minutes he would have her out of danger.

A minute later he realized that he had been counting his chickens before they were hatched. As they hurried down the corridor the sounds of the mob grew louder. They came from the Dauphin's apartment, which was separated from the Queen's only by a small antechamber, and at any moment the mob might break through. He saw now that they must take a desperate gamble. When the group reached the door of the Queen's boudoir they halted there in consternation. It sounded as if all hell had been let loose in the rooms beyond, but whether the mob was in only one or in all of them it was impossible to tell. Above the din a woman's voice screamed, "We want the Austrian! Search, my friends, search, and we'll get her dead or alive!"

The Queen gave a moan, and murmured, "Oh, why do they hate me so? I have never sought to harm them," then despairingly clasped Madame de Lamballe and let her head fall on the Princess's shoulder.

Pushing past them, Roger ran across the boudoir, eased open the door of the Queen's bedchamber and peered through the crack. The scene he glimpsed made his heart sink. The mob was already there, and behaving like Furies let loose from Hades. Having failed to find the Queen they were venting their hatred on her possessions and sullying her intimate belongings. The curtains had been torn down, the mirrors smashed; clothes, footwear, cosmetics and ornaments lay in an indescribable jumble on the floor. A sailor was slaking his lust with a negress on the bed, a bearded man was urinating on one of the pillows, and a fishwife was senselessly stabbing through one of the Queen's night robes again and again with a large knife.

His hopes of getting the Queen away now shattered, Roger softly closed the door, locked and bolted it. Then, rejoining Madame de Lamballe, he said, "We are too late. If there are reliable troops in the Salle du Conseil our best course now would be to go there."

Again the little group hurried the Queen away, this time through a series of small rooms until they reached the great state apartment. In it they found a dozen guards, who ran to the Queen and assured her of their loyalty; but the royal children were no longer there and the mob from the Œil de Bœuf could now be heard approaching. In a frenzy of anxiety for her little ones the Queen insisted that she must find them, and turned back towards her private apartments.

Fortunately, while her friends were trying to restrain her, the Duc de Choiseul and Madame de Tourzel came running in with the children. But there was not a moment to be lost. As the Queen snatched the Dauphin and his sister to her, the mob began to hammer on the south doors of the Council Chamber.

Momentarily overtaken by panic, the Queen, her ladies, gentlemen and guards all ran towards the north doors. But halfway to them they halted, arrested by the sound of pounding feet and blood-curdling yells coming from that direction. Part of the mob that had invaded the Queen's bedroom had broken out of it and resumed its murderous hunt for her. Some of the guards swiftly shut and bolted the doors, but it now lay in the lap of the gods whether the Queen would live or die in the Council Chamber, for she was trapped in it.

The men hastily shepherded her and her ladies into the bay of one of the big windows, then drew the long council table across it as a barrier. The guards lined up in front of it, and with madly beating hearts the whole party awaited the outcome of their desperate situation.

No one spoke; the guards now stood rigidly to attention; the eyes of the Queen's companions were riveted on the south doors of the Chamber. Under the buffeting of the mob they shivered and vibrated. An axe-blade crashed through an upper panel and remained wedged there. The hinges creaked and groaned as a crowbar was forced in to lever them from their sockets. A rain of blows from pikes, scythes and sabres rattled on the woodwork like a hailstorm. Suddenly there fell a lull. It was followed by a resounding bang. The doors shook from top to bottom. Some of the attackers had picked up a heavy settee and were using it as a battering-ram. Again a lull. Another crash. The doors bulged inwards. For the third time a score of men threw against them their whole weight and that of the settee. With a detonation like the snapping of a bridge carried away by an icefloe, they flew wide open. The blast of air through the opening rocked the great chandeliers hanging from the ceiling. There came a deafening howl of triumph, and the mob surged in.

CHAPTER V

THE QUEEN'S ORDEAL

AFTERWARDS, Roger could not have given a coherent account of the terrible hours that followed. They had seemed an unending nightmare of horror in which every few moments brought a new crisis, and a new apex of ever-mounting fear that a bloody massacre must ensue within a matter of seconds.

He could not have said how they had escaped being overwhelmed in the first mad rush. Perhaps it had been the sight of the little handful of grim-faced guards, so clearly determined to die rather than allow hands to be laid on the Queen. Perhaps it was the barrier of the broad table, which made it impossible for them to reach her without climbing over it and exposing themselves to a sword-thrust from one of her gentlemen. But as these material obstacles to their hate and rage were so flimsy, it seemed more probable that they had been quelled by the mental aura of calm, innocence and dignity that emanated from Marie Antoinette herself.

From the moment that she had regained her children her tears and hysteria had ceased. For a time she had seemed entirely absorbed in quieting their fears; then, when Roger had next glimpsed her, she was standing between them, drawn up to her full height, and facing her enemies with a cold, fearless challenge in her glance.

The group they made was one picture that would for ever remain indelibly imprinted on Roger's mind. She had aged a great deal since he had last seen her. Although she was only thirty-six, her eyes were pouched, her face lined and her hair white; yet in her fine forehead, aquiline nose and Habsburg underlip, she still possessed the lineaments of regal beauty. Madame Royale, her eldest child, was a girl of fourteen, also with Roman features, but of the coarser, Bourbon type. The Dauphin was a beautiful little boy of six and a half. He was her third child, his elder brother having died in '89; but unlike the former heir to France, who had been sickly from his birth, this little chap was healthy, vigorous, intelligent, and had such charm of manner that he was beloved by all who came in contact with him. The girl was standing and the

Dauphin perched on the table, each with one of their mother's arms about them as she faced the mob.

Another picture that Roger would never forget was that of a woman who, nearly four hours later, screamed at the Queen, "It is you, Austrian whore, who is the cause of all the unhappiness in France!"

"So they have told you," replied the Queen sadly, "but you have been deceived. You call me Austrian, but I am the wife of the King of France and the mother of the Dauphin. In all my feelings I am French. Never again shall I see the country of my birth, and I was happy when the French people loved me."

At that the woman suddenly burst into tears and exclaimed, "Pardon, Madame! Pardon! I did not know you before; now I see how good you are."

Between those two clear pictures there was an endless blur of hideous faces that came and went. Unnoticed by Roger, the north doors of the Salle du Conseil had been opened, and a slow-moving procession of Furies, that packed the great room from wall to wall, began to filter through it. The pressure had forced the guards back from the front of the table to its sides, so that the ruffians and viragos leant right across it as they edged past, screaming their insults and obscenities in the very face of the Queen.

Many of them carried ghastly emblems of violence that they waved in front of her eyes—the still-bleeding heart of a calf labelled "Heart of an aristocrat", two saws with a placard "To cut Veto and his wife in half", rough caricatures of the Queen in the nude posturing in obscene attitudes with lovers falsely attributed to her, a model of a gibbet with her effigy suspended from it, and another of the new instrument of death recently invented by Doctor Guillotin.

Again and again some newcomer at the table raised a weapon to strike at her, but either at the critical instant other members of the crowd pulled them back, or the blow was averted by Roger and those who stood with him shouting, "Respect the Law! Do not disgrace the People!"

One hag threw two red caps of Liberty on the table and demanded that the Queen should put one on her own head and one on the Dauphin's. Her eyes suddenly flashing with defiance, she exclaimed, "This is too much!" But the attitude of the crowd became so menacing that De Wittinghoff, a Livonian Field Marshal who was standing near her, placed one of the caps on her white hair, while M. Hue, a faithful *valet de chambre*, put the other on the boy's fair curls.

De Wittinghoff was one of the many loyalists who, like Roger, on learning that the lives of the King and Queen were threatened, had determined to get into the Palace and assist in their defence. Some were nobles who had put on the oldest clothes that they could find in order to mingle with the mob, others simply honest citizens from every walk of life who still believed in and revered their Sovereigns. It was this leaven of brave, decent men, scattered among the crowd, that time and again prevented the criminals from the Faubourgs resorting to violence, either by tactful expostulations, or by bandying rough jokes with them that turned their rancour to coarse laughter.

It was, too, through the gradual infiltration of these secret allies into the invaded rooms that the Queen's protectors now and then obtained whispered news of the King's situation, which they were able to pass on to her. He had been attacked by a *sans-culotte*, but a brave youth of eighteen, named Canolles, who had formerly been nominated to the old *Garde du Corps*, had seized the man, forced him to his knees, and temporarily paralysed the hostility of the other insurgents by the extraordinary feat of making him cry "*Vive le Roi!*" The opera dancer, Joly, and a brewer named Acloque, had been among the first of the mob to break in, and at the earliest opportunity had assured the King that they had done so only with the object of dying in his defence. With quixotic daring, Stephanie de Bourbon-Conti had appeared dressed in a uniform borrowed from a National Guard, and, waving a sabre, had vowed that she would slay anyone who dared to lay a finger on the King.

These occasional tidings that the King was still alive and had loyal friends about him did much to support the Queen in her ordeal, but hour after hour the danger remained very great. The genuine mob still far outnumbered the loyalists, and the ever-present fear remained that some ruffian, half-crazed with drink, would start a massacre, for some mysterious agency was keeping the *sans-culottes* well supplied with free wine.

There could be little doubt that it had been paid for in advance by the conspirators and was being brought into the Palace under Santerre's supervision, in the hope that when drunk the mob would commit excesses from which it still shrank while sober. Within half an hour of the King's ordering the doors of the

Œil de Bœuf to be opened the splendid chamber had become a vast boozing den. Every buhl and marquetry table was loaded with an array of bottles, and groups only paused in their drinking periodically to lurch over, and hector the King. To appease one gang he had to put on a red cap, and to dispel the quarrelsomeness of another he was forced to drink with them from the same bottle.

In both the great rooms, and in those between them, the heat was stifling and the stench appalling. The bizarre scenes enacted were reminiscent of Hogarth's impressions of Hell, and time seemed to stand still; but as twilight began to fall it became apparent that the plot to murder the Sovereigns was going to fail. Even the most bloodthirsty of the *sans-culottes* had ceased to threaten them, and were now regarding them only with curiosity. The ample potations of wine, instead of rousing them to violence, had imbued them with a drunken good humour. Curses and imprecations were replaced with raucous laughter; in wild abandon thieves and prostitutes set to dancing the *carmagnole* and singing the *ça ira*.

This change of feeling in the mob must have been reported to those who were so eagerly waiting to hear that the King and Queen were dead; for, now that it was clear that their instrument had failed them, the men who could have stopped a riot at its inception began to appear in an attempt to save their faces.

At eight o'clock word filtered through to the Queen's protectors that a deputation from the Assembly, headed by the Girondins, Vergniaud and Isnard, had arrived in the Œil de Bœuf, and that close on their heels had come Pétion, who was responsible for maintaining order in the capital. All of them had hypocritically protested their loyalty to the King, and the treacherous Mayor had even had the audacity to declare that he had only just learnt that there was any trouble at the Palace. Then, immediately afterwards, in order to retain favour with the rabble, although he could no longer escape his duty to disperse them, he stood on a chair and addressed them with revolting servility:

"People, you have shown yourselves worthy of yourselves! You have preserved all your dignity amidst acute alarms. No excess has sullied your sublime movements. But night approaches and now you must withdraw yourselves."

Some minutes later Santerre pushed his way into the Salle du Conseil, also anxious now to save his face. As he advanced to the table he noticed that in the foul, overheated atmosphere the little

Dauphin was half stifled by the heavy cap of Liberty that came right down past his ears. Pointing to it, he exclaimed, "Take the cap off that child. See how hot he is!"

Then, leaning across the table, he stared at the Queen and said, "Ah, Madame, have no fear. I do not wish to harm you; I would rather defend you. But remember, it is dangerous to deceive the people."

Drawing herself up she retorted indignantly, "It is not by *you*, Monsieur Santerre, that I judge the French people. It is by these brave men here!" and with a flash of her old impetuosity she reached out to press the hands of the nearest guards on either side of her.

The gesture acted like a spark to a powder-barrel, releasing the feelings of loyalty that had been pent up for so many hours in the breasts of her defenders. The other guards, her gentlemen and a score of people in the crowd, pressed round her to kiss her beautiful hands. Cries of "*Vive la Reine!*" went up, and even a great part of the fickle mob joined in giving her this unexpected ovation.

Disgruntled and now a little frightened on his own behalf, Santerre quickly turned away. Concealing his feelings by a display of bluster, he began to drive the *sans-culottes* from the room.

Roger did not join in the loyal demonstration. He knew that the Queen and the Princesse de Lamballe had witnessed the part he had played that afternoon, so that in his new guise he must have won their confidence. That, he felt, was an ample reward for the comparatively small risk he had run, and, if handled skilfully, might prove a most valuable asset in future plans which he had as yet had no time to formulate. But his disguise had already served him so well that he was anxious to preserve it. Santerre could have noticed him only as one of the foremost among the rabble that he had led in the attack on the Palace, and Roger was quick to realize that if he could confirm this impression of himself in the revolutionary leader's mind it should greatly assist him in the double game he meant to play. So, ignoring a sign from Madame de Lamballe to come to her, he set about helping Santerre to hustle the drunken revellers out of the room towards the grand staircase.

Pétion and his municipal officers were already clearing the rooms ahead of them, so by the time Santerre and Roger reached the staircase they were among the last to go down it. As they walked out to the Cour Royale, Roger gave his companion a sidelong glance and said:

"Well, here we are where we started! Things didn't go as I hoped they would when we first broke in."

"No," muttered the big brewer, "the King got the best of us today, and the affair miscarried. But never mind. We'll come back and settle his hash tomorrow." Then he looked at Roger, and added, "I don't know your face, Citizen. To what Section do you belong?"

"None, as yet. I reached Paris again only this morning after a two years' absence."

"What part do you come from?"

"I am from Strasbourg." The reply was that which Roger had always made to such a question when passing as a Frenchman, since to claim that he hailed from the German-speaking province accounted for any slight fault in his accent. After a moment he went on, "I first came to Paris when I heard of the taking of the Bastille, and I was in the march on Versailles that October. When we brought the fat Baker and his wife, and the little apprentice, back to Paris as prisoners I thought that the Revolution was accomplished, so I went home again. But recently it has seemed to me that you people in Paris have got slack, and have failed to carry matters to their logical conclusion."

"Citizen, you are right!" exclaimed Santerre. "The people of Paris *have* got slack. Look how they let us down today. But there are still some of us who are determined to see matters through."

"So I was told in our local Jacobin club, and it was with the idea of lending the real patriots a hand that I returned here. I want to see France a Republic, like they have in America."

"You may not have so long to wait for that as appearances suggest. What is your name, Citizen?"

"Breuc," replied Roger.

"And where are you lodging?"

"I've had no time to find a place as yet."

"Then go to Citizen Jereau at the sign of the Axe and Fasces. It is in the Section de Montreuil and only a step from what's left of the Bastille. Mention my name and he'll fix you up with a bed. We'll meet tomorrow and I'll find you plenty of work to your taste."

While they were talking they had reached the quay, and there a group of roughs, all armed with pikes, who formed Santerre's personal bodyguard, were awaiting their leader; so, having thanked him and shaken hands, Roger turned in the other direction.

He was elated at having fallen in so quickly with one of the most dangerous revolutionaries in Paris, but he had no intention as yet of using the introduction to Citizen Jereau; neither did he mean to return to Madame de Flahaut's apartment now, as he had intended before his brief conversation with Santerre. One sentence that the brewer had used rang like an alarm bell in his mind—"The King got the best of us today . . . we'll come back and settle his hash tomorrow."

Roger had been on his feet for over ten hours, and had passed the greater part of them in most exhausting circumstances. Moreover, he had had nothing to eat all day. He would have given anything to clean himself up, reclaim his own clothes, and give to M. de Talleyrand's beautiful mistress an account of the attack on the Palace, while eating the good supper with which he felt sure she would willingly provide him. But he knew that such a pleasant ending to this eventful day was not to be his portion. If Santerre meant to lead his ragged legions against the Tuileries again next day there was still work to be done, and work of a most urgent nature.

It was reasonable to assume that the conspirators would profit by the lessons learnt in the failure of their first attack and organize the next one better. When Roger had left the Cour Royale he had noticed that, in their frenzy, the mob had torn from its hinges the half of the gate that had not been opened to them, and many of the doors in the Palace had been battered down. As repairs could not be executed overnight, it would now be much easier to reach the royal apartments. A massed attack by a great mob was no longer necessary; with the complaisance of the treacherous Pétion's officials a small band of determined men would be sufficient to penetrate to them. The King could be counted on to adhere to his policy of non-resistance. It had saved him today by the astonishment it had caused in the ordinary criminals and viragos who had burst in on him without premeditation. It would not have that effect tomorrow, and his attackers would be picked men spurred on by the promise of a big reward if they could succeed in killing him. Clearly, if this new menace were to be averted, drastic steps must be taken, but what steps Roger had very little idea at the moment.

On reaching the Tuileries gardens he turned into them. It was not yet nine o'clock so still half light, and quite a number of people were walking there or standing about describing to one another the parts they had played in the great riot that was only just over. Sitting down on a bench, he began to try to think things out.

At the other end of the bench a middle-aged man was sitting. His hands were resting on a stout cane; he was wearing a high-crowned beaver hat and a well-worn cloak that had once been of good, thick material. His appearance suggested that he was a small tradesman enjoying the cool of the summer evening after the long hot day. Having cogitated for some ten minutes, Roger felt he had the nucleus of a plan, and turning to his neighbour he asked:

"Do you live near here, Citizen?"

The man nodded, so he went on, "I suppose you will soon be going home?"

Again the man nodded. "Yes, Citizen, but why do you ask?"

"Because I am far from home myself, and circumstances compel me to spend the night in the streets. The shops are shut and it is getting chilly. I was wondering if I could persuade you to sell me your hat and cloak for a couple of *louis*."

The man gave him a suspicious but not unfriendly glance; then after a moment he said, "From your voice I judge you to be some gentleman who has got into trouble with the authorities; but in these days it is safer not to ask too many questions. I would like to oblige you and two *louis* is a good price for these old things I am wearing, but times are hard and I can ill afford to part with them. Have you really got the money?"

His speculations and attitude were just what Roger had hoped they would be when he had spoken in a voice that belied the shoddy garments he was wearing. With a smile of thanks he produced his purse and took out two gold pieces.

As they made the exchange the man said softly, "These are evil days for honest folk, Monsieur, and my heart bleeds for that poor King of ours. But these villains who say they represent us have got us in their power now, and there seems nought that we can do about it."

"Yes, we can only hope for better times," Roger nodded, as he tucked his wispy fringe under the beaver and pulled its brim well down to hide his black eye. Then, having thanked the man again, he set off across the gardens towards the riding-school, as he felt sure that at such a time of crisis the Assembly would still be sitting, and it would be the best place to learn where he was most likely to contact a man whom he had decided he must see.

As its galleries were open to the public and always contained a high proportion of *sans-culottes*—who were paid by the extremists to jeer at and intimidate the more moderate speakers—he could quite well have gone there without attempting to hide his disreputable clothes. But he was now both extremely hungry and acutely conscious that he had no time to lose; so he wanted his man to sup with him while they talked, and felt that his invitation would be accepted more readily if he could make himself look a little more respectable.

The man that Roger wanted to see was Antoine Barnave, an old acquaintance of his who had played a great part in the first Revolution. Although only twenty-eight, he had been selected by his native province of Dauphiné to go to Versailles as a deputy of the Third Estate, and had soon made a name for himself by his extreme radicalism. With the single exception of Mirabeau, he had proved the most powerful orator in the National Assembly, and in collaboration with Robespierre, Pétion and other extremists he had founded the Jacobin Club. But Roger knew him to be an honest man, and was aware that he had been one of the first real radicals to appreciate that the Revolution looked like being carried too far. It was, as Roger had learned from Talleyrand, the powerful triumvirate of Barnave, Duport and Alexandre Lameth who had led the secession from the Jacobin Club and founded the Feuillants in opposition to it.

That had occurred over a year ago and Barnave had since, like many of the other leaders of the first Revolution, suffered a partial eclipse as a public figure. This was because Robespierre, the dry, venomous little lawyer from Arras, had, at the dissolution of the old National Assembly, proposed the cunning measure that none of its members should be eligible for re-election to the new Legislative Assembly that was to succeed it.

Too late the moderate members realized the trap into which, by their agreement, their desire not to seem self-seeking had led the nation. Its representatives' experience of parliamentary government had been absolutely nil when they had met in '89, but in two and a half years of intensive application they had learned a great deal. Now, all that was thrown overboard and a fresh set of entirely inexperienced people had to learn from the beginning, while the nation paid the price of their blunders. Worse still, between May '89 and October '91 liberal desire for reform had been replaced by a utopian madness that called for the abolition of the whole existing social order, so that through this ill-considered measure, as Robespierre had foreseen, the deputies elected to the new Assembly proved, on the average, far more radical than their predecessors, with the result that his party increased from a handful of supporters to well over a hundred.

True, he was no longer able to sit himself, and had unseated his ally, Pétion, that waspish monarchy-hater the Abbé Sieyès, the smug Roland, and other Leftist sympathizers; but he had also got rid of the most vigorous Royalist leaders, Cazales and the Abbé Maury; of Bailly, Malouet, Lafayette, Lally-Tollendal, Talleyrand, Clermont-Tonnerre and a score of others who had been the first to advocate liberal reforms; and even of Barnave, Duport and the Lameths, who desired only to retain the Monarchy in a strictly limited form. So the subtle apostle of anarchy had won hands down on points. At one stroke he had deprived all his opponents of the right to speak any further as the elected representatives of the French people.

The practical effects of the law had proved curious, as it had brought about a situation in which France was no longer governed either by a King or by the elected representatives of her people, but by the outcome of a succession of intrigues and incredibly bitter feuds carried on by a few little cliques of private individuals. Naturally the new deputies of all parties, in their ignorance of how best to handle affairs, turned for advice to the old party leaders; the latter, being much more knowledgeable and gifted, had soon dominated both their thoughts and actions. The extreme Left of the Assembly now took its orders from Robespierre at the Cordeliers Club, the Girondins from Madame Roland's *salon* and what remained of the Right from the Feuillants.

Roger thus had no measure by which to gauge Barnave's present influence on political affairs. But at the moment he was much more concerned with the brilliant young orator's personal relationships, for he felt convinced that he was better situated than anyone else in Paris to cope effectively with the danger in which the Royal Family stood.

On reaching the Assembly Hall, Roger made his enquiry of one of the doorkeepers. The man's reply came as a most unexpected and bitter blow.

"Citizen Barnave?" he said with a shake of his head. "You'll have to go a long way to find *him*, Citizen. When the King made Citizen Roland his first minister this spring, Barnave declared that he had had a bellyful of politics, and took himself off to his home at Grenoble to grow cabbages."

For a moment Roger stood there uncertain and dejected, as he did not know sufficiently intimately any other suitable politician whom he could approach with the idea he had in mind. But quite unexpectedly he was rescued from his dilemma. An officer of the National Guard, who was standing near by, turned to the door-keeper and said:

"You are right about his going into retirement, Citizen, but he has come back to Paris; I saw him myself yesterday." With a glance at Roger he added, "The most likely place to find him is the Feuillants Club."

The Club was situated in the ex-convent just round the corner. With a relief corresponding to his previous disappointment, Roger thanked the officer, then walked down the narrow passage in which he had struggled as one of the tightly jammed crowd six hours earlier. To his still greater satisfaction he learned from the porter on the door of the Club that Citizen Barnave was inside; so he asked for a piece of paper, wrote on it *I arrived from England only yesterday, and pray you to spare me a few moments on a most urgent matter*, signed it, and sent it in to the ex-deputy.

Two minutes later Barnave came out into the hall. He was a thin-faced, slightly built man, with a high forehead, fine eyes and a long, sharply-pointed nose. As he looked round his glance passed right through his visitor without recognition, but Roger stepped up to him and said in a low voice:

"Ask me no questions now, I beg, but get your hat and take me to some place where we can sup quietly."

Barnave hesitated a moment. "We are in the middle of a most important debate, and——"

"No debate can be as important as what I have to say to you," Roger cut in quickly.

His urgency prevailed, and shortly afterwards the two old acquaintances left the Club together. It was only then that Roger found himself momentarily at a loss. He had had very little time in which to think out a plan and none at all in which to consider the delicate matter of gaining Barnave's assistance in it. Unlike de Talleyrand, the ex-deputy did not know Roger's true history, and the affair was complicated by the fact that when they had last met he had been posing as a wealthy young Englishman who dabbled in journalism and held extremely revolutionary views. However, they had gone only a few steps when his companion gave him a lead by remarking:

"I never expected to see the elegant Chevalier de Breuc with his hair chopped short and his feet in gaping shoes. Did I hazard a guess, I would say your present attire was prompted by a journalistic urge to be an eye-witness at the happenings in the Tuileries this afternoon."

"In part you are right," Roger nodded. "I donned these rags to gain entry into the Palace with the mob, but my motive was very different from that which you suggest. By chance, I learned in London of a plot to overthrow the Monarchy, and was so concerned that I came over here in the hope of helping to avert it. This afternoon I was among those who aided in protecting the Queen."

Barnave looked at him in surprise. "Then your opinions have undergone a great change since I saw you last. You were then a most furious revolutionary. I well remember your declaring yourself from the rostrum of the Jacobin Club to be the bitter enemy of Monarchy in all its forms."

"True! But I was then striving to avert a war—a war in which the French Sovereigns would have felt themselves in honour bound to engage had not popular opinion been roused to put a check upon them. In yourself, and in other Jacobins who wished to prevent war, lay my one hope of securing action. Therefore, to win the goodwill of such an assembly, I had to pretend extremist opinions."

"I appreciate the point of what you tell me. But that apart, our private conversations never led me to suppose that you were particularly concerned for the Monarchy."

"Nor was I, in its absolute form; but I am now convinced that everything possible should be done to save it from abolition, and I have been given to understand that you had reached that point of view even earlier."

"I reached it this time last year, and for some months did my best to advise the Sovereigns privately."

"But, unfortunately, without success, I gather?"

"The King proved too cowardly to accept my advice," replied Barnave bitterly, "and when he decided to entrust himself to that hypocrite Roland, I retired to the country."

"So I learned only ten minutes ago. But your return to Paris suggests that you found yourself unable to remain indifferent to the future?"

"That is true. Yet news of this new crisis brought me back against my better judgment, for I greatly doubt whether I can do any good here."

"You can do much," declared Roger firmly, "and since we find ourselves once more of the same mind we must again combine our efforts. First though I must eat, as I am starving. Do you know of some place near by where my present filthy state will not disgrace you too greatly?"

Barnave gave a cynical laugh. "Oh, but it is you who are in the fashion, not I. Only the law proclaims us all equals. In practice the *canailles* are now the masters—or they soon will be. Anyway, today's events deprived me also of my dinner, so I should be glad of a meal. Let us go to Minchin's. It is non-political and caters for people of all sorts."

They had already turned into the Rue St. Honoré and gone some distance along it. As they walked on and then down a side turning, Roger explained his long absence from France by speaking of his marriage, and gave it as one of the reasons for his changed political outlook that he had been much influenced by his wife and her relations.

"I too," admitted Barnave, "changed my convictions only partially as the result of pure political thinking. It was getting to know the Queen personally that started my conversion."

Roger was already aware of that, but he made no comment as they had just reached the restaurant. It turned out to be a long, low room divided down the middle by a walk-way, on either side of which were tables fixed between pairs of wooden benches with five-feet-high backs, so that each set of diners had what almost amounted to a private compartment to themselves. When they had made a choice of food and wine, Roger said:

"I saw from the news sheets that you were one of the Commissioners appointed to bring the Royal Family back after their abortive attempt to escape to the frontier last year. Was it then that you became subject to the change of heart to which you referred a few moments ago?'

CHAPTER VI

THE CHANGING OF A HEART

BARNAVE nodded. "Yes, and it was a most extraordinary experience."

"While we are being served, tell me of it," Roger begged. "It would be safer not to broach the matter I have sought you out upon until we are less likely to be interrupted. Why in the world, having safely escaped from Paris, did they ever allow themselves to be halted?"

"Had they taken the Duc de Brissac and the Marquis d'Agoult as their outriders, as was originally planned, they might have got through. To substitute ordinary gentlemen of the bodyguard was a great mistake; they had not the standing to ignore the King in an emergency, and to cut him a way to safety in spite of himself."

"I heard that Their Majesties committed every sort of stupidity before they even started."

"They did. There was the refusal to be separated from their children even for a few hours, and their insistence that Madame Elizabeth and Madame de Tourzel should travel with them. For so large a party no ordinary carriage was large enough, so the Comte de Fersan had a great Berlin built specially for their flight, and during the building of it half Paris guessed the purpose for which it was intended. The Queen dispatched clothes of all sorts to the frontier in advance, and news of that leaked out. Then a Madame Rochereuil, one of the Queen's women who were not in the secret, discovered that she had removed her jewels from their boxes, and laid an information against her."

"It seems a marvel that they ever got away at all."

"They succeeded, I think, only because the venture had been talked of for so long, without maturing, that most people had reached the conclusion that they would never pluck up the courage to attempt it."

"Knowing the habitual vacillation of the King, I can well understand that. How long did it take the poor Queen to bring him to a firm decision?"

"The best part of a year. They were certainly considering it as far back as the late summer of 1790. It would have been easy then, but the delay was at least in part her own fault. She was obsessed with the idea of having her brother, the Emperor Leopold, mass an Austrian army on the frontier before they set out, and months were lost in corresponding about these forces."

"It is really true, then, that she planned the invasion of France?"

"No, no!" Barnave quickly shook his head. "Far from it. She did everything she possibly could to prevent war breaking out; I am convinced of that. She wanted an Austrian army on the frontier only as a security measure. She felt that its presence, coupled with a joint declaration by King Louis's fellow Sovereigns of Austria, Prussia, Sweden, Russia and Spain, would deter the Assembly from taking up arms against him; whereas, lacking such support, the King might find himself forced into a civil war."

Roger smiled. "I see; and as he could never be induced to risk such a commitment, nothing could be done until the Queen had succeeded in eliminating the risk?"

"Yes. The initiative throughout these negotiations was hers, but I incline to think you've put your finger on the truth that underlay the matter. In any case they let the winter months slip by without settling anything; and that, I am sure, was because right up till April '91 they allowed themselves to be lulled into the false belief that they would have no great difficulty in escaping from Paris at any time they liked."

"What caused them to alter their opinion?"

"The King had been ill. His doctor advised him that he needed country air, so it was arranged that the Royal Family should spend Easter at St. Cloud. D'Orléans had it put about that from there they intended flight, so on the morning that they were to leave a mob gathered in the courtyard of the Tuileries. For over two hours the rabble prevented their carriage from moving and shouted insults at them. Bailly, who was then Mayor, and Lafayette did their utmost to disperse the mob, but without avail. Eventually the whole party had to abandon the attempt and go back into the Palace."

"Had they had any sense they would have waited until nightfall, and when the mob had dispersed left Paris for good," remarked Roger.

"You are right; that is just what they should have done. However, the effect of that unhappy episode was to impress upon them that unless they were willing to resign themselves to permanently remaining prisoners, they must make definite plans to escape. The Berlin had been ordered in January by Fersan through a Russian friend of his named Madame de Korff, and was ready. Madame was shortly due to leave France with her two children, so it was settled that the Royal Family should travel as her party. The King finally decided to entrust himself to the Marquis de Bouillé, who was commanding at Metz and reported that he could rely on the troops under him. The destination was fixed as Montmédy and plans made for detachments of de Bouillé's cavalry to protect the royal fugitives from Chalons to that fortress."

"Why, in the name of Heaven, could they not have taken the shorter and less dangerous route through Flanders?"

"That was urged upon the King; but he would not hear of it, because it would have meant leaving France for a few hours while crossing a salient of territory belonging to the Emperor."

"*Mon Dieu!* What a nit-picking!" exclaimed Roger in disgust. "I am at a loss to understand the mind of a monarch who is ready to accept the support of his brother-in-law's troops yet boggles at driving across a corner of his country."

Barnave shrugged. "That is one of his troubles; all his life he has strained at gnats and swallowed camels. His brother, de Provence, was afflicted with no such scruples; he and his wife left the Luxembourg Palace the same night, and made straight for Flanders. When they heard that the King had been captured, instead of going to Montmédy they drove on to Brussels."

"The flight took place on June 20th—just a year ago tonight—did it not?"

"Yes. After the St. Cloud fiasco, they planned to join de Bouillé early in May. But for one reason or another they kept postponing the date, and that, coupled with a most extraordinary series of minor accidents, proved their undoing."

"Who was responsible for planning the actual escape?"

"The Queen and Fersan, as far as Chalons; from there on the King."

"I gathered that they got quite a long way past Chalons."

"They did, but not until several hours after they were expected. To avert suspicion the King had to go ceremonially to bed as was the custom. Bailly and Lafayette who were loyal to the Assembly were both present, so matters could not be hurried, and the *coucher* lasted twenty minutes longer than usual. Each member of the Royal Family left the Palace separately, with only one gentleman of the bodyguard. The Queen and her escort missed their way and for over half an hour were lost in the maze of alleys leading off the Place du Carrousel before they found the rendezvous where Fersan was waiting with a carriage to pick them all up. Fersan was acting as coachman, and in the dark he also missed his way, so another half an hour was lost in reaching the Barrière St. Martin, at which the party was to transfer to the big Berlin. At the end of the first stage, at Bondy, Fersan left them. Although they were two hours behind their time-table, he had succeeded in getting them safely out of Paris, and had every reason to suppose that no further delays or difficulties would arise. But before they reached Chalons the Berlin broke down; a further hour was lost whilst repairing it."

"Heavens, what a series of misfortunes!" exclaimed Roger.

"Yes, each was little enough in itself, but added up they spelled ruin. The Baron de Goguelat, who had acted as courier in carrying all the secret messages between the King and General de Bouillé, had advanced to Pont de Sommeville, the first post past Chalons, with forty hussars, to meet the Royal Party. Had he been any other officer, he would probably have waited there until ordered to retire, but de Goguelat, having been privy to so many preparations and postponements, used his own judgment. The King was due there at three o'clock; at five there was still no sign of him, so de Goguelat concluded that once again the attempt had been put off, and withdrew across country towards Varennes."

"Had not the King already been recognized at Chalons?"

"Yes, by a number of people; but all except the postmaster proved loyal, and no attempt was made to stop the party proceeding. All might yet have been well but for another series of unpredictable misfortunes. Finding no troops at Pont de Sommeville, the King pushed on to St. Ménehould, whither forty dragoons had been despatched under Captain d'Andoins. There, the townsfolk proved revolutionary in sentiment and hostile to the troops. Had the King arrived promptly d'Andoins could have carried off the situation, but during the long wait the people began to demonstrate against his men. To avoid a riot he was compelled to order them to dismount and walk unarmed about the streets. When the Berlin at last appeared there was no way of collecting them without the crowd guessing what was afoot, so d'Andoins could only urge the King to press on, still unescorted, with all speed to Clermont. At Clermont, Colonel Comte de Damas was awaiting him with a hundred dragoons, but there again the unexplained sight of a body of troops hanging about the posting-house for hour after hour had made the townsfolk first suspicious, then hostile. By the time the King arrived a great crowd had collected. It was only with considerable difficulty that Damas forced the Berlin through the town at all, and the majority of his men, by then influenced by the mob's belief that they were being used in some Royalist plot, refused to follow it."

Roger groaned. "What incredible stupidity to post these bodies of troops in the towns! Anyone but a fool would have arranged for them to occupy crossroads in the open country, where they would neither have aroused suspicion nor been liable to be got at."

"The King and de Bouillé must share the blame for that," Barnave replied; "but the chapter of accidents is not yet exhausted. Damas did succeed in getting a quartermaster and a troop of loyal dragoons out of the town shortly after the Berlin had departed, with orders to overtake and escort it; but they took the wrong turning and galloped off along the road to Verdun instead of towards Varennes."

"Ah! The last stage of that ill-fated journey?"

"It need not have proved so but for a final mishap. It is widely believed that Drouet, the postmaster at St. Ménehould, had recognized the King by comparing his face with the profile on a *louis d'or*. That is not true; he invented the story for his own glorification. It was the postmaster at Chalons who recognized the King, and although he had not the courage to prevent the Berlin leaving, he sent a message on to his colleague at St. Ménehould. Drouet did not receive it until an hour after the Royal Party had passed through, but he mounted and set off in pursuit, taking a short cut through some woods.

"The King reached Varennes at eleven o'clock, well ahead of Drouet. The town is situated on the slope of a hill and divided into two parts by a river and bridge. In its lower part, beyond the river, another body of hussars was waiting, with a change of horses for the Berlin. The King had been told that he would find his relays in the upper part of the town and he halted at a house that had been described to him. No one there knew anything about the matter; so, thinking he must have been mistaken in the house, he and the Queen alighted to search for another like it.

"In that action lay Fate's final irony. They had only a further twenty-two miles to go to reach Montmédy and be safe in the heart of de Bouillé's army. Even another half-mile would have brought them to loyal troops and the horses for which they sought in vain. The night was fine but pitch dark. For half an hour the King and Queen roamed the streets and argued with their postillions, who did not know their identity and were averse to driving another stage without a fresh team. In the meantime Drouet passed them, gave the alarm at an inn, and made preparations to barricade the bridge."

Roger sadly shook his head. "It seems as though all the forces of darkness were in league against them."

"Were I a superstitious man I would certainly believe it," Barnave agreed. "Yet, even then, they might have got through had the King shown resolution, or have been rescued but for a further series of most evil mischances. It was getting on for midnight, so nearly everyone at Varennes was asleep and Drouet had had time to collect only a score or so men to hold up the Berlin. The bridge had not yet been barricaded, so if the three gentlemen with the Royal Party had shot down the ringleaders, they could have forced a passage and driven through to safety. Instead, the King's usual horror of bloodshed prevailed and when called on to halt he stopped to parley.

"A grocer named Sauce, who was a Municipal officer, had taken charge. He demanded that the travellers should prove their identity. Madame de Tourzel was travelling as Madame de Korff, the Queen as governess to her two daughters—the little Dauphin having been dressed for his part as a girl. Madame Elizabeth's rôle was that of companion, and the King's that of steward. Sauce refused to accept their declarations and insisted that they alight and remain in his house until further investigations had been made. Meanwhile the tocsin was sounded, the whole town was roused and the bridge was barricaded to prevent the hussars on the far bank from intervening. De Goguelat, still believing that the flight had been postponed, was approaching Varennes across country, but in the dark he lost his way, so did not arrive there with his forty men until it was too late for them to overcome the great crowd that had collected. Meanwhile de Bouillé, who could easily have advanced to the town during the night and had ample troops under him to subdue it, also believed by now that another postponement had taken place, so retired to Stenay."

Again Roger shook his head. "This chapter of accidents seems never-ending."

"Yes; yet one last chance was given them. In the dawn the Duc de Choiseul arrived with de Goguelat and his hussars, and de Damas turned up with another half a dozen troopers from Clermont. By then the King had been definitely identified by a magistrate named Destez, but the three officers drew their troops up outside the house and forced a way in. De Choiseul begged the King to let them charge the mob and cut a way out of the town for him, but he would not hear of it."

"If only he had displayed one-tenth of the courage then that he showed this afternoon," Roger murmured. "I heard it said that when the mob was breaking down the door of the Œil de Bœuf, he made one of the soldiers who were with him place a hand on his heart to prove that it was not beating a fraction faster."

Barnave wrinkled up his thin nose. "Such fearlessness is commendable enough where only one's personal safety is concerned, but he seems oblivious of the fact that others are imperilled by his complete lack of all but passive courage. His mania for preventing a single *sans-culotte* from receiving a scratch may one day cost his children and the Queen their lives."

"You express exactly what I have often thought. But pray continue and tell me of the last scenes of this tragedy."

"There is little more to tell. The King was under the impression that by this time de Bouillé had learned of his flight and must be hastening to his rescue. Four o'clock came, and five, but no de Bouillé. Instead, Lafayette's aide-de-camp Romeuf, and a Commander of the National Guard named Bayon, arrived from Paris, bringing with them a decree of the Assembly ordering the King to return to the capital. Still hoping that de Bouillé would reach Varennes in time to save them, the Royal Party resorted to every possible expedient which might delay their departure. Romeuf secretly hoped for their rescue, so would have aided them; but Bayon proved inexorable, and soon after seven he forced them to set out.

"There followed for them four days of misery and humiliation such as few families can ever have been called on to endure. The Berlin moved only at a foot-pace so that the mob could keep up with it, and the heat, dust and smell were almost beyond bearing. During the whole of the journey back to Paris it was surrounded by a shouting, jeering crowd. As some tired of the spectacle and fell out, others from every village and town through which the cavalcade passed took their places. Anyone who attempted to offer the Royal Family sympathy was set upon and maltreated. A poor old gentleman in St. Ménehould who took off his hat to the Queen was murdered before her eyes, and his head, dripping with blood, was held up at the window of the Berlin for her to see. Later, when Pétion and I had joined them in the Berlin, I only succeeded in saving a village priest from a similar fate by leaning from its window and screaming, 'Tigers, have you ceased to be Frenchmen? From brave men have you become a nation of assassins?' "

Barnave broke off to laugh grimly. "I was so excited that I nearly fell out of the window, and was saved from doing so only by the presence of mind of Madame Elizabeth. How the Queen laughed about that afterwards; and what volumes it speaks for her fortitude that even at such a time she should have preserved her sense of humour. When I came to know her better she told me much of what I have been recounting to you, and it was then that she said it had struck her as incredibly funny to see the saintly Princess saving a revolutionary from breaking his neck, by hanging on to his coat-tails."

"I remember Marie Antoinette when she was always laughing," Roger remarked with a sigh.

"What?" Barnave gave him a surprised look. "I was unaware that you had ever met her."

"Oh yes, I was first presented to her at Fontainebleau, and afterwards went many times to Versailles. Like your friends the de Lameths, the Duc de Laincourt, and a hundred others, I saw no reason why I should allow the fact that I held strongly liberal views to prevent my going to Court. Besides, I have always felt that nobody should allow politics to prejudice their personal relationships, and long ago I formed a most devoted attachment to the Queen."

"You never before made mention of it to me."

Roger smiled. "And with good reason. Had I done so at the time when you could believe nothing but ill of her, it might have wrecked the pleasant friendship that had developed between ourselves. But now, for your private ear, I will admit that it is largely the desire to be of some service to the Queen in her present sad situation that has brought me back to France. We digress though. You were telling me of that terrible return journey. Whereabouts did you join the Royal Party?"

"At Epernay. They spent the first night at Chalons and we should have met them there, but news arrived that the scum of Rheims was advancing in a body with intent to murder them, so they were hurried off on the next stage before we had set out. Pétion and Latour-Maubourg were the other two deputies nominated by the Assembly to escort the fugitives back to the capital. The former travelled with the Queen's two waiting-women in a carriage that had followed the party, Pétion and I in the Berlin. I would it had been otherwise, as Latour Maubourg is a decent fellow, and Pétion's behaviour was abominable. Even now, it makes me go hot when I think of it."

As Roger had met Pétion at the Jacobin Club two years earlier, he could imagine the scene. The ex-deputy, now Mayor of Paris, was vain, stupid and brutal. His coarse good looks were spoiled by corpulence and by a receding forehead that sloped back to a fringe of thick, frizzy hair. He was a friend of Robespierre's and was just as pitiless, so it was easy to imagine his taking every advantage of his situation to show malice and rudeness to the prisoners. Barnave, his thin face flushing, added a few touches to the picture:

"Except at night, we took our meals in the Berlin. Every time we ate he belched in the faces of the ladies, and he frequently spat on the floor of the carriage. Once he took the Dauphin on his knee and amused himself with winding the child's curls round his finger so tightly that the little boy cried out in pain. The Queen snatched her son from him; had she not, I would have struck him for his cruelty and insolence."

"And this ordeal lasted four days?"

"Yes; for three of which I was the unhappy witness of their torment. The nearer we came to Paris the bigger and more menacing became the mob. On more than one occasion I feared that we would never get our prisoners to the capital alive. The heat and dust were terrible, and the Royal Family were already half dead from exhaustion. When we did reach the Champs Elysée it was a sea of people, and the Berlin could move only at a snail's pace owing to the additional weight of a score of *sans-culottes* who had clambered on to its roof and boot. When at last we reached the Tuileries the three *Gardes du Corps* were dragged from the box and it required my utmost efforts to prevent their being massacred. From start to finish the journey was a nightmare impossible to describe, and the conduct of the people for whose liberties I had fought was so utterly disgusting that I was within an ace of abandoning public life for good, there and then. I should have done so but for my sympathy with those two brave royal women, with whom a duty for which I was selected by chance had so unexpectedly brought me into such close and prolonged contact."

Roger nodded. "Three days' confinement in a travelling coach gives ample opportunity to get to know one's companions."

"It certainly did in my case. When Pétion and I entered the Berlin our feelings were, I imagine, somewhat similar. I felt that the King had betrayed his people by attempting to fly abroad; that he had been incited to the attempt by his scheming, unscrupulous wife; that they had earned contempt and deserved public reprimand; and that it was for us to maintain a frigid dignity throughout the journey, thereby displaying our disapproval of their act and at the same time armouring ourselves against the hatred of us that it seemed certain they would not seek to hide. But they displayed no animosity whatsoever. Instead, with the same natural politeness as if it had been a social occasion, they readily made room for us, apologized for the Berlin being so crowded, gave us cushions to make us more comfortable, and insisted on sharing their food and wine with us because we had none ourselves. No one but a baboon like Pétion could possibly have remained churlish in the face of such civilities, and when Madame Elizabeth began to talk politics with me it was only natural that I should put to her the Assembly's point of view."

"I was under the impression that she occupied herself almost entirely with religion," Roger remarked, "and knew little of mundane affairs."

"You are right in supposing that the teachings of Christianity dominate all her thoughts. She is a saint if ever there was one, and purity actually seems to radiate from her. But she is far from lacking a sense of humour, and has a shrewd mind and wide knowledge. She argued well that her brother, having given liberty to his people, should at least be free to go from place to place about his kingdom as he wished. It was only later that the Queen joined in our conversation.

"In due course she told me of her coming to France, of the

difficulties she had met with at the old King's Court, of the appalling ignorance of herself and her husband when they came to the throne as two very young people, and of how badly advised the King had been by his Ministers. She said how hard they had striven to meet the wishes of the people by giving way to every fresh demand, even at times against their better judgment, and cited many examples. She complained of nothing, except that an unreasonable restraint had been placed upon their liberty; then sadly remarked how greatly in the past two years she had missed her garden and model farm out at the Trianon. And I had only to witness the way in which her children, her husband, and the few retainers who still remained with them behaved towards her to see how greatly she was beloved by them all."

Barnave paused for a moment, then shrugged his shoulders. "Well, I fell in love with her; I could not help myself. To my dying day nothing will now convince me that she was ever guilty of any evil intent. Her dignity, her sweetness, her courage and her forbearance won me completely. There is nothing I would not do for her."

Roger had worked hard to get his companion's mind into a condition specially receptive to certain ideas, and he now felt that he had achieved his object. Fascinated as he had been by this first-hand account of the Royal Family's abortive attempt to escape, he would never have given up a precious hour to listening to it in the present circumstances had he not had a definite purpose in so doing. While they were eating their meal he had deliberately led Barnave on to talk of it, in order to arouse his memories of that unique experience and to revive the emotions he had felt at the time. In addition, during the telling of the tale Roger had succeeded in most skilfully reorienting Barnave's ideas about his own past, and had provided a logical reason for now presenting himself as a champion of the Queen.

Pushing aside the empty plate that lay in front of him, he leaned forward and said, "What of the King? Did you succeed in winning his trust while you were privately advising him?"

"I think so. It was certainly not personal distrust that caused him to reject my advice; he failed to follow it only because he lacked the courage to resist the popular pressure that was being brought upon him."

"And the Queen?"

"She knows my devotion to her, and that nothing could ever

induce me to advise her against what I believed to be her best interests."

"You said just now that there is nothing you would not do for her. Does that mean that you would be prepared to risk your life on her behalf?"

"It does."

Roger leaned still further forward, and said in a whisper, "That is all I wish to know. I require your help in getting her and her family out of Paris tonight."

CHAPTER VII

"TOUJOURS L'AUDACE"

"You cannot be serious!" Barnave exclaimed, jerking himself back from the table.

"I was never more serious in my life," Roger assured him.

"You tell me that you arrived in Paris only yesterday. How can you possibly have found time to concoct a plan and make all the elaborate arrangements necessary to such an attempt?"

"As yet I have made no arrangements, and so far my plan is based only on an idea."

"Then you are mad, *mon ami*! Like many of your countrymen, you are quite mad!"

Roger grinned. "That is a tradition I am not averse to living up to, as apparent madness often pays high dividends. And such a mental attitude is no monopoly of the English, as you seem to think. Many Frenchmen have it too, only here you term it *l'Audace*."

"Well, yes; and I admit that by audacity many great coups have been pulled off. But alone, in such an affair as this, it is not enough. Without the most careful planning in advance, what you propose is quite impossible."

"Last night, perhaps; tomorrow night, perhaps; but not tonight."

"What leads you to think that?"

"Today's events. A short while ago you were telling me how the mob prevented the Royal Family from going to St. Cloud the Easter before last. I remarked then that had they had the sense to make a second attempt that night after the mob had dispersed, they would have got away without difficulty. And you agreed with me."

"Ah! I see your line of thought. But that was very different; St. Cloud is only on the far side of the Bois de Boulogne, so almost a suburb of Paris. The Sovereigns had been permitted to go there for a change of air in the previous summer, ten months after the mob had brought them as prisoners from Versailles. Again on this occasion the consent of the Assembly had been obtained; it was the mob alone that prevented their departure.

Had they set out again that night the Municipal officers and National Guards in the Tuileries would not have attempted to stop them, whereas now they would certainly do so."

"You are still thinking of the situation at the Tuileries as it was yesterday, and will probably be again tomorrow," Roger said earnestly. "But throughout tonight everything there is bound to remain in the utmost confusion, and it is that on which I counts The gates to the Cour Royale cannot be shut, nearly all the doors. of the royal apartments have been broken down, and the bedrooms of the Queen and the Dauphin wrecked. The Royal Family will have to sleep in rooms which the guards are unaccustomed to watching, and will have been deprived of their usual means of communication. Therefore, on the excuse of wishing to see one another, they will be able to move about the Palace comparatively freely without exciting suspicion. I know a way by which we can communicate with them, and also one by which they can be secretly smuggled to the upper floors of the Palace. Could we but provide them with adequate disguises, I am convinced that on this one night they stand an excellent chance of making their escape."

"*Mon Dieu!* I believe you are right! But the risk is an appalling one. Should they be caught it may cost them their lives when the people get to hear of it."

"The risk is no greater than if they remain where they are. The plot to kill them failed today, but the Palace is to be attacked again tomorrow."

"How do you know that?"

"I was close to Santerre when the mob broke into the Palace and again when they left it. He believes me to be a good patriot from Alsace. It was he who told me that the attack is to be renewed, and you may be certain that his second attempt on the lives of the Sovereigns will be better organized."

"Then you had sounder reasons than I thought for wishing to take this desperate gamble tonight."

"I do not regard it as so very desperate," Roger said quickly, "because even if they are caught all will not be lost. The frightful ordeal through which they passed today may now stand them in good stead. The National Guards and many of the Municipal officers are decent men; they were clearly horrified by the excesses of the mob, and would have prevented them if they could. Those very excesses give the King a reason for attempting to escape, which he did not possess before. Should he be caught he can plead that, since they were unable to protect him today, there is no reason to suppose that they will be able to do so tomorrow, and that by remaining in Paris he is now endangering the lives of himself and his family. He could say that he intended to go only to St. Cloud, and might even urge them to accompany him. To that they might well consent. If so, we should at least temporarily have got the Royal Family out of danger."

Barnave's brown eyes lit up. "That is indeed a thought! In fact, it makes the venture very far from being the forlorn hope that I at first believed it. In what way do you require my help?"

Roger's blue eyes lit up in turn. Without Barnave his plan was doomed to almost certain failure; with him, and a little luck, Mr. Pitt's wish that the Royal Family should reach Brittany might be fulfilled much more speedily than that gentleman had any grounds to expect. Leaning forward again, he said quickly:

"First in the matter of disguises. As a family they are so damnably easy to recognize. We must split them up, of course; but, even so, all of them will have to come out through the Cour Royale. Can you suggest any means by which we could render them less easy of identification at a casual glance as they cross the court?"

For a few moments Barnave sat pulling nervously at the lobe of his right ear, then he said: "The Tuileries still houses scores of pensioners who had been given apartments there before the Sovereigns were brought to Paris. A member of one such family might easily have fallen ill, and although priests and nuns are often jeered at by the mob in these days, they still go about their duties of attending on the sick. They always work in pairs, so the Queen and Madame Elizabeth would be very unlikely to arouse suspicion if they left the Palace dressed as two nursing sisters."

"Excellent! Nothing could be better, as their coifs would hide their faces; but where the devil can we lay our hands on such garments within the next hour or two?"

"That is simple; in fact the robes gave me the idea. The Convent of the Feuillants was used as a depot for their Order and they were given little time to remove their possessions. Only yesterday I happened to notice that a small room off the hall of the Club is still half-filled with religious habiliments; I have only to take a portmanteau there and collect such garments as we require."

"Could you also find something suitable for the King?"

"I will borrow a porter's blouse from the *concierge* at my apartment. Wearing that, he could follow the two ladies as though he was their servant."

Roger nodded quickly. "That would serve the purpose well, and still better if you can find him something to carry. It should be a medium-sized box or small, round-lidded trunk, that he can carry on his shoulder. By transferring it from side to side as the situation demanded, he could conceal his face from anyone who was approaching him."

"For that he can use the portmanteau in which we furnish them with their disguises. But what of the two children?"

"I have already devised a plan to cover them." Roger glanced at his dirty hands with their broken nails, and added, "It needs only a little soot to give me the appearance of a chimney-sweep. The landlord at my inn is a trusty fellow, and will get me a few brushes without asking questions. All sweeps have their boys for going up big chimneys. The young Madame Royale must submit to having her face and arms blackened, her hair pushed under an old cap, and dressing herself in any dirty rags we can find for her; then I'll take her out as my apprentice."

"The idea is a good one, except for the fact that a chimney-sweep would hardly be likely to be working at the Palace in the middle of the night."

"It is getting on for eleven o'clock already. We shall need at least a couple of hours to make our preparations, then the King and Queen have to be roused and persuaded to make the attempt. After that those who are to escape will require further time to disguise themselves, so I doubt if at the earliest we could get them away before three in the morning. That is not a good hour, as there will still be so few people about that they would run a maximum risk of being challenged. Moreover, in the dark it would be much more difficult for the various parties to find one another outside the Palace. I suggest that we should aim to leave at six o'clock. It will be light then and there will be enough people beginning to go about their ordinary business for the presence of nuns and chimney-sweeps not to arouse unwelcome comment."

Barnave smiled. "You reason extremely well for a madman. But how about the Dauphin? He is too young to play the rôle of a second assistant to you, and a child of that age is not often seen accompanying grown-ups in the street soon after dawn."

Roger's blue eyes sparkled with amusement. "I know him to

be a brave and intelligent child; he will do whatever his mother tells him. I mean to carry him out as if he was a hundredweight of soot—in a sack on my back."

"Bravo!" exclaimed Barnave. "I am really beginning to feel now that only ill-luck can rob us of success; providing, of course, that you can convince the King and Queen that their best hope of living through tomorrow lies in entrusting themselves to you."

Slowly Roger shook his head. "No, not to me. It is to you that they must be persuaded to entrust themselves."

"To me! But why? From what you have said I gather that you have known the Queen far longer than I have. This plan is yours and you tell me you have secret means of communicating with her; therefore, it is obviously for you to get in touch with her and convince her of its soundness."

It was in this very matter that Barnave was essential to the carrying out of Roger's plan, so he sighed, and making his voice deliberately emotional, said:

"Alas, *mon ami*; time was when Marie Antoinette would, I think, have trusted me even in the most delicate affairs, but 'tis so no longer. On our way here you recalled my anti-war speech in the Jacobin Club, which of necessity was also strongly anti-monarchical. You must, then, also remember how I succeeded in securing such a favourable hearing there—it was because I had incited the mob to murder the Spanish Envoy, Don Diego Sidonia y Ulloa. The Queen must know of both that and my speech, and so must believe that formerly she was entirely deceived about my character. If in these past two years she has ever thought of me at all, it must have been as a hypocrite who once curried favour with her but was all the time secretly a *sans-culotte* at heart. For me to approach her now would spell certain ruin to our intentions; but she still has faith in you, so will be favourably disposed to listen to your counsel."

"I see," murmured Barnave; "then there seems no alternative but for me to make all arrangements with her. How do you propose that I should set about that?"

"You must go to the Tuileries. Do you happen to know the Princesse de Lamballe's apartment? It is immediately above that of the Queen."

It was Barnave's turn to smile. "Yes, I know it well; and the staircase in the wall that connects the two. When I was secretly advising the Queen she often used it to come up and give me a private audience in Madame de Lamballe's *salon*."

"That you should know it is all to the good," nodded Roger. "Tonight the Queen will not be sleeping in her old room, but Madame de Lamballe will know where to find her. I suggest that you see Madame de Lamballe and explain to her all we have in mind, then ask her to collect the Royal Family and bring them up to her apartment. In the meantime I will provide a hackney coach, and the driver of it will be my own servant, who is entirely trustworthy. I will give you an hour's start, which should be long enough for your *pourparler* with Madame de Lamballe, and for her to assemble the five people we propose to carry off. I shall then join you in her suite. In my rôle of sweep I will lead the way with the two children down to the street; I shall take them past the coach and along to the quay, where you can pick us up later. You will follow me at a distance with the two nuns and their servant. At that hour it is most unlikely that there will be any other coaches about, but should there be, you will easily be able to identify the right one from the fact that its coachman will be a middle-aged, bearded man of seafaring appearance, with gold rings in his ears. Does such a programme seem sound to you, or can you improve upon it?"

"It seems sound enough; but what if we succeed so far? Whither do you propose to convey them? That problem alarms me greatly, now we have come to it. To get out of Paris we must pass through one of its gates. There, and beyond, the party will be subjected to the scrutiny of innumerable enemies. Every village in France now has its Commune, a busybody member of which examines all travellers. Alas! I fear that this great coup is still no more than a dream. We would not cover a dozen leagues before our passengers were recognized and arrested."

"You may set your mind at rest on that score," Roger replied cheerfully. "At that hour the gates of Paris will be open, and to proceed less than a league beyond them will be enough to serve our purpose. I have already realized the dangers of an immediate flight to the frontier or the coast, and do not propose to attempt it. We will take them to a little house at Passy that has been placed at my disposal; they can lay low there until we can make arrangements to take them further afield in safety."

"*Sacré bleu!* You seem to have thought of everything! When the escape becomes known every post-house for a hundred miles around Paris will be in a ferment, but nobody will suspect that the fugitives have gone no further than one of its suburbs. This house, though—we dare not trust the servants, and what excuse can you make to turn them out without warning? And its owner—he might return unexpectedly; is he to be trusted?"

"At present it is occupied only by an old butler, who is well known to me, and his wife. My friend is abroad, and he told me that except for these two and his valet, who is with him, he paid off his other servants before leaving."

The friend to whom Roger referred was M. de Talleyrand. In offering the house the gallant Bishop had remarked lightly that it might serve as a discreet rendezvous to entertain ladies who combined a charming frailty with a desire to protect their reputations; but Roger had no doubt at all that the offer had been intended also to cover the use of the house for more serious purposes.

Barnave nodded. "Then it sounds most suitable. However, one final point: I realize that it is essential that you should remain incognito, lest the Queen's confidence in the whole venture be shaken. But you propose to take charge of her children, and she is hardly likely to relinquish them, even for half an hour, unless it is to a person whom she feels that she can trust. How do you propose to get over that?"

"You can vouch for me to her; since we are now about to risk our necks together in this matter, I take it you would be prepared to do so?"

"Yes, readily; but she sets a higher value on her children than on her life, so it is certain that she will ask for particulars about you."

For a moment Roger stared at the table, then he looked up. "Tell her that I am your foster-brother, and came with you from Grenoble. Then add that I was the man with the black eye who stood near her while the mob were threatening her this afternoon. I actually spoke to the Princesse de Lamballe, and I am certain the Queen noticed me. My conduct at that time will be sufficient guarantee of my loyalty."

So the basis of the matter was settled. For a further half hour they discussed details, then paid their bill and went out into the night.

It had been agreed that Barnave should go straight to the Tuileries as soon as he had collected a portmanteau from his lodging and picked up in it the nuns' garments from the Feuillants. By so doing he would be able to get into the Palace before its inmates had all settled down for the night, and so run less risk of being questioned than if he left his entry until the quieter hour of four o'clock. Roger, on the other hand, was not to make his entry until five, at which hour the servants would be rising and the arrival of a sweep would appear quite normal.

He considered going out to Passy to prepare de Talleyrand's butler but decided against it. Old Antoine Velot was, he felt certain, entirely to be relied upon. It would take over an hour to get there, and to have roused him in the middle of the night in that quiet neighbourhood might have stirred up an interest in the house which it was of the utmost importance to avoid.

Owing to the intense excitement caused by the attack on the Palace the streets were much more crowded than usual and, although the half hour before midnight was chiming from the tower of St. Germain l'Auxerrois as he reached *La Belle Étoile*, the inn was still doing a roaring business. In all the lower rooms little groups, mainly composed of tradesmen and honest artisans, were heatedly denouncing the conduct of the mob, or relating experiences they had met with during the day; so it proved easier than Roger had expected to evade the eyes of the busy potmen and slip up the private staircase without being noticed.

Much relieved at having escaped recognition in his present squalid attire by any of the servants, and having thus preserved the secret of his present rôle, he reached his rooms to find Dan about to go to bed.

That worthy grinned from ear to ear at the sight of his master's villainous appearance, but soon became serious when he was told the reason for it and of what was afoot. After setting forth the whole matter very fully and explaining the risk that would have to be run, Roger asked him if he was prepared to face another spell in the galleys, or worse, in an attempt to rescue the Royal Family.

"Why, blood me, Cap'n," Dan said quickly, " 'twas the Queen as gotten me out o' they damned galleys, so I's game to risk bein' sent back to 'en, if so be there's a chance to save the good lady from the likes o' they villains what behaved so atrocious to Her Highness today."

Roger slapped him on the shoulder. "Thou art a good fellow, Dan, and I am mightily pleased to have thee with me. Go now and fetch up our landlord. But mark me, not a word to him, or to anyone, of what we intend."

"Aye, aye, Cap'n!" Dan clattered away down the stairs, and returned a few moments later with Maître Blanchard. As the honest Norman entered the room his fair eyebrows shot up, but Roger said at once:

"*Mon vieux*, I counsel you to forget that you have ever seen me in this unsavoury condition, or in the even more repulsive state which I shall assume in a few hours' time. Enough that my present urgent affairs necessitate it; but the less you know about them the better. Then, should you be questioned, you can honestly affirm that you know nothing of the business I am engaged upon. I need your help, though, and will pledge you my word that no one shall ever learn that you gave it me."

Maître Blanchard bowed. "I appreciate Monsieur le Chevalier's reasons for not confiding in me and, being a cautious man, prefer that matters should be left that way. As for my help, I will give it willingly. Monsieur has but to ask and anything it is in my power to do for him shall be done."

Roger knew that the landlord kept in his stables several vehicles for hire, so he said he wanted a closed carriage—preferably a shabby one, provided it was sound—to be made ready with a good strong horse between its shafts at half-past four in the morning. He proposed that Dan should go down with Maître Blanchard now to see the horse and carriage selected, so that in the morning he could harness them up and drive the carriage straight out of the yard, thus avoiding the need for one of the stablemen to bring it round to the door. Then he asked for the loan of the brushes with which the inn's chimneys were swept, and a couple of large soot sacks. Lastly, as he was anxious that both Dan and himself should get some sleep before setting out, he asked the landlord to be good enough to call them in person at four o'clock.

All his requests having been readily agreed to, as soon as he was alone he undressed and, without attempting to wash, got into bed. A quarter of an hour later Dan reappeared with the chimney-sweep's things, and reported that he was perfectly satisfied about the horse and carriage; then he too turned in and they snuffed the candles.

At four o'clock the landlord woke them and Dan, after pulling on his clothes and sluicing his face in cold water, went down to the stables. Meanwhile, Roger, feeling much refreshed from four hours of sound sleep, was indulging in a little amateur chimney-sweeping. Having put the clothes and hat he had worn the previous day in the grate, he fetched down enough soot to thoroughly dirty them, then used some of it to blacken his face and hands.

As he did not wish to get to the Palace too early, he had told Dan not to bring the carriage round until a quarter to five. A couple of minutes before it was due he gave a last glance in the mirror, grinned at his coon-like reflection and was pleasurably surprised to see how white his teeth looked, then went quietly downstairs.

Maître Blanchard had already unbolted the door, and opened it a crack to peer out. As the church clock chimed the quarter Dan drove up. The landlord whispered, "*Bonne chance, Monsieur*!" and Roger slipped past him into the street. Paris was already waking to another sunny day, but few people were about as yet, and there was nobody near enough to take particular notice of him. Instead of entering the carriage, he clambered up on to its box as though he had cadged a lift, and murmured:

"Give way, Dan! It's true we're on a foreign shore, but all the same we'll be pulling today for England, Home and Beauty!"

"Aye, aye, Cap'n!" replied the old salt, and as he tickled the horse with his whip they set off at a steady rumble down the cobbled street.

They approached the Tuileries by way of the Rue St. Nicaise, and just before they came in sight of the Palace, at a word from Roger, Dan pulled up. Before getting down from the box Roger described to his henchman exactly where he wished the carriage to wait, then he watched it drive away across the Place du Carrousel.

As soon as it had disappeared he put his brushes and sacks over his shoulder and slouched round the corner. Looking neither to right nor left he walked across the open space straight for the gates of the Cour Royale. With relief he saw that the broken half was still open and hanging twisted from its hinges. Just as he reached it, he gave a swift glance to his left to assure himself that Dan had carried out his instructions. The carriage was drawn up as he had planned, only thirty yards from the gate and facing the river. Whistling the *ça ira* with cheerful nonchalance, Roger slouched into the courtyard.

He had expected that three or four National Guards would be sitting about a brazier inside it, and his worst fear was that, having seen him go in, one of them would remember that he had been alone, so start asking awkward questions when he reappeared on his way out accompanied by a little apprentice. But, to his delight, he saw that the nearest guards were a good sixty yards away, lounging in the main doorway of the Palace. They gave the impression of being tired and bored, and were not even looking in his direction.

One glance round the court showed him that the Palace servants were already setting about their daily tasks. Three men with brooms were sweeping up the litter that the mob had left there the previous night. At the far end of it big earthenware crocks of milk were being delivered through a basement entrance from a country cart. A buxom woman was approaching with a string bag on her arm, evidently on her way to market.

As Roger turned towards the entrance at which the milk was being delivered, the woman smiled at him and blew him a kiss. For a second he was dumbfounded, then he remembered that he was posing as a sweep. Quickly recovering himself, he grinned at her and wished her good morning.

Resuming his whistling of the *ça ira*, he nodded to the milk-man and entered the Palace. In the corridors on the lower floors he met several cleaners, a footman and one National Guard, but nobody questioned him. As he mounted the stairs he found that the upper floors appeared deserted; evidently the occupants of most of the rooms were still sleeping, and cleaning was not permitted there until a later hour. When he reached the door of the Princesse de Lamballe's apartment he suddenly became conscious that his heart was beating with excitement like a sledge-hammer. He waited there for a moment in an attempt to still it, then rapped gently.

The door was instantly opened a crack, and someone peered at him through it. A second later Barnave pulled it open. Roger slipped past him into the ante-room and saw that it was empty. By the early morning light he noticed at once that his fellow conspirator's thin face looked incredibly tired and haggard. His heart seemed to miss a beat as he asked in swift apprehension:

"Where are they? Did you fail to persuade them?"

Barnave shook his head. "No, but it was the very devil of a job. The King fears that if they are caught again they will all be murdered out of hand, instead of being brought back here. The Queen said that she was prepared to face any risk for a chance to get away; but that nothing would induce her to go without the King, and that it was her duty to leave the matter entirely to his judgment. I prevailed upon him to make the attempt only with the argument that if they remained here and the mob broke in again the Queen's assassination was certain."

Roger nodded towards the farther door. "Are they up here?"

"Yes, they are all in there, dressed in their disguises. They found some old clothes belonging to one of the pages for Madame Royale. We tore them to rags, and blacked them and her with soot from one of the chimneys. What are our prospects like outside?"

"There is many a slip, but they could hardly be better. There are no guards on the courtyard gate, below stairs the servants are moving about, and there are tradespeople coming and going freely."

"God be thanked! All that remains to be done then is to get the Dauphin into one of your sacks."

"Then let us get on with it. Our chances are as good as they ever will be at this moment, so there is nothing to be gained by waiting."

With a quick intake of his breath, Barnave tiptoed across to the further door and disappeared through it for a moment. When he reappeared there were seven people with him—two women in nuns' robes with white coifs that hid their faces from all but a direct glance; a burly man wearing a short cape with a hood, and across his big stomach a porter's apron, who looked as if he must be a lay-brother in some religious institution; a ragged boyish figure with soot-streaked face and hands; the little Dauphin undisguised; and Mesdames de Lamballe and de Tourzel in ordinary morning robes.

Roger, as was fitting to his character as the son of Barnave's nurse, made an awkward bow and touched his forelock as they came in.

The taller of the two nuns walked quickly up to him and said, "Monsieur, we are already greatly in your debt for having stood by us so bravely yesterday afternoon; and now I understand that we are to owe you a debt so great that it will be beyond our power to repay. But you may be certain that you will always enjoy our friendship and that we shall never forget you in our prayers."

At the gracious words, the melodious voice now so near to

tears, and the trusting glance, Roger's impulse was to go down on one knee and exclaim, "Madame, I have never ceased to be your humble, obedient servant, and I would willingly shed the last drop of my blood for you."

But he managed to keep control of himself, touched his forelock again, and muttered gruffly, "God bless Your Majesty; the little chap will be safe enough with me."

She beckoned the Dauphin forward and said, "My son, this is our friend who is going to give you a piggy-back in his sack. You will not be frightened or cry out, will you?"

"No, mama," came the childish treble in an amazingly adult reply. "I cannot think why the people hate us so much, but I understand the danger we are in, and could not shame you by being afraid."

"That is well said, my son. Now thank our friend in advance for what he is about to do for us."

The handsome little boy smiled at Roger and said, "I thank you, Monsieur. Some day I will make you a sergeant in my regiment." It was the highest honour that his young but already well-formed mind could bestow.

"And I'll make Your Highness a good one," murmured Roger with a smile. "But we must be getting along to have a bite of breakfast. Step in now and I'll give you your ride."

As he spoke he spread out one of his sacks and held its mouth wide open, low down. The Dauphin had already put one foot into it when the King started forward and exclaimed:

"That man! I know him! He is not Barnave's foster-brother, as we have been told!" Grasping the Queen's arm with one hand he pointed accusingly at Roger with the other, and went on in an agitated voice, "He was often at Versailles! I would recognize those over-long little fingers of his anywhere. His name. . . . His name. . . . He is the Chevalier de Breuc!"

"De Breuc!" cried the Queen, snatching up the Dauphin in her arms. "That traitor and murderer! This is a trap! Oh, God, we are betrayed! I would not trust my son to him were he the last man on earth!"

CHAPTER VIII

A NEW IDENTITY

ROGER sat in the bath in which, nineteen hours earlier, he had first seen the beautiful Adèle de Flahaut. The warm, scented water in which he was immersed up to the neck brought balm to his body, but his soul was still a tumult of rage and disappointment.

For half an hour he had fought his case with the most dogged tenacity, using every argument he could think of which might retrieve the situation. He had told the whole truth about himself and produced a Letter of Marque that he carried from Mr. Pitt; but, as he had feared, that testimonial failed to shake the Queen, because he had already disclosed to her that he was a British agent before he had brought about Don Diego's death. To his plea that, had she two years ago given him her co-operation when he requested it, there would have been no necessity for him to seek help from the Jacobins, she replied that, while her course had been the only one she could take with honour, his had been that of a vile intriguer. Then the King, who for all his shortcomings was no fool, had pointed out that had Roger in the present case been open with them, whatever their views of his past conduct they would have known where they stood, whereas he had attempted to deceive them by posing as Barnave's foster-brother; and since Barnave had been a party to that deceit, it could only be assumed that they had combined to lead the Royal Family into a trap.

Barnave had protested his own loyalty most vehemently, but had had to admit that he knew nothing about his confederate except what Roger had told him; and his own past record as one of the most fiery extremists during the first Revolution now told heavily against him.

As a last resort Roger had urged that since Barnave and himself had both at one time enjoyed the confidence of the Sovereigns, they at least deserved that they should now be given the benefit of the doubt, and that the King and Queen would do better to give it to them than to remain where they were and patiently wait to be murdered. To that the Queen seemed inclined to agree, but a moment later his hopes were dashed. The King, running true to form as ever, took the wrong decision and declared:

"I still have faith in the French people. I am convinced that they will never harm me."

Then Roger had lost his temper. Ignoring the respect due to Royalty, he had spoken to King Louis of France as man to man. He told the kind, weak, ineffectual monarch that his own irresolution was entirely to blame for the miserable plight in which he found himself and the state of anarchy to which his country had been reduced; that his death would mean no great loss to anyone, and if he chose to get himself killed that was entirely his own affair, but that at least he might show some concern for the lives of those supposedly dear to him.

The King had taken it all with his usual placidity; his protuberant eyes did not even show a gleam of anger as he said only a trifle sharply, "Monsieur, I am the best judge of my own affairs."

But the Queen had gone white to the lips. Almost choking with fury she cried, "How dare you! How dare you so insult His Majesty! Leave us this instant! Go, and never let me see your face again!"

So when Roger had shut the door of the Princesse de Lamballe's apartment behind him he knew that once and for all he had cooked his goose with Marie Antoinette. He had proved himself right and Mr. Pitt wrong about her present lack of friends inducing her to turn a blind eye on the past and receive him back into her good graces; she was far too proud and courageous a woman to stoop to such a cheating of her conscience. Had he had the time and opportunity he might perhaps have won her round by some carefully-thought-out explanation, but by his outburst he had now robbed himself of even that possibility; for in rounding on the King he had struck her in her most tender spot. She knew better than anyone her husband's hopeless inability to make up his mind, and the awful consequences it had brought upon them, upon their dearest friends, and upon hundreds of thousands of their loyal subjects. In openly declaring it in front of her children and her ladies, Roger could have done no worse for himself had he slapped her face. Too late he realized that by his act he had opened up a gulf between himself and the Queen that could never be bridged in a lifetime.

As he drew up his knees a little of the water splashed over the edge of the tub, but he was much too preoccupied with his gloomy thoughts to notice it. It occurred to him that as he had said his piece to the King after producing Mr. Pitt's letter he had, at the moment of his outburst, been to some degree an official representative of His Britannic Majesty's Government. That highly prized line, *Mr. Roger Brook knows my mind upon this matter, and is commissioned by me to speak upon it*, now took on a new and horrifying significance.

It was possible that, if the Queen survived the present crisis, she might speak of the incident to the British Ambassador and require him to report it to the Prime Minister. But no! From that final catastrophe at least he would be spared. He had spoken the truth, and the Queen knew it; shame would restrain her from repeating to anyone what he had said. But she might simply say that he had been insolent to the King without specifying in what way. If she did, when Mr. Pitt heard that Roger had used his name as a passport, then given offence to the very people whose confidence he had been sent to win, he was going to be extremely angry.

That thought did not worry Roger unduly. There had been previous occasions on which the Prime Minister had been extremely angry with him, but all had been forgiven and forgotten when he had eventually returned home triumphant. The thing that *did* worry him was that on this occasion there now seemed no possible chance left of his achieving even a partial success. The central themes of his mission—to induce the Royal Family to go to Brittany, then to persuade the Queen to let him take the Dauphin to England—now appeared about as likely of achievement as if he had wanted to get them to the moon.

For a moment he wondered if he ought to go back to England and confess defeat, but swiftly dismissed the thought. In an initial report he must admit that there was no longer any prospect of his succeeding in the main object of his mission, in case Mr. Pitt did find somebody else whom he thought suitable to attempt it. Meanwhile there was the fifteen hundred pounds' advance to be worked off, which could now only be done by purveying ordinary routine intelligence. That seemed a sad come-down after his spectacular hopes of a few hours ago, but, in the hotbed of trouble that constituted Paris at present, there was always the possibility that he might uncover some potent new development of which it would be valuable for the Prime Minister to know.

He began to consider in what rôle it was likely to repay him best to take up this more nebulous work of general investigator, and it suddenly struck him as extraordinarily appropriate that, having been confronted with this crossroads in his affairs, he should, at the moment, be as naked as God made him.

On leaving the Tuileries numerous reasons had decided him to walk straight round to Madame de Flahaut's: he was itching to get himself clean and that was the nearest place at which to do it; he did not want any of the servants at *La Belle Étoile* to see him disguised as a sweep, so was loath to return there in broad daylight; Madame de Flahaut's maid had seen him arrive the day before dressed as a gentleman and depart looking like a *sans-culotte*, so she would not be unduly surprised if he returned only a few shades grimier than when he had left, and lastly he felt sure that Madame de Flahaut would do her best to repair the damage she had done to his appearance.

In the event, the maid had burst out laughing at his blackened face, then demurely apologized for being "disrespectful to the gentleman". To consolidate her good will, Roger had grinned, offered to kiss her for luck, then slapped her bottom and sent her off laughing again to rouse her mistress. The lovely Adèle had appeared, still dewy eyed and languorous from sleep; but she had quickly shaken herself into wakefulness, ordered a bath to be prepared for Roger in her dressing-room, and promised him that when he had finished his ablutions her maid should manicure his nails while she turned his short hair into a cluster of curls, which would make him look quite respectable.

So a wide choice lay before him—he could leave Madame de Flahaut's apartment in his own well-made clothes and with his hair in the new style termed *à la Romaine*, which many better-class Frenchmen with democratic views were now affecting; he could go out once more as a *sans-culotte* of villainous appearance; or he could strike a mean between the two, by having his hair plastered down and wearing the old hat and cape he had bought from the man in the *Jardin des Tuileries* to offset his own coat, shirt, breeches and boots.

His natural inclination was to adopt the first course, and by posing once more as a Whig journalist endeavour to win the confidence of some of the more respectable deputies. But the memory of his recent parting with Barnave gave him pause. Before going downstairs they had decided that it would be better if they left the Palace separately, and after they had commiserated with one another on the failure of their plot, Roger had asked his fellow conspirator where they could meet again. Barnave, still greatly agitated, had replied:

"It is useless for us to do so. Three days in Paris have been enough to convince me that I was a fool to return at all. The control of affairs has already passed out of the hands of men who are even moderately intelligent and honest. Narrow-minded bigots, sly, unsuccessful lawyers, empty-headed windbags, vain, pompous pedants and crazy fanatics have succeeded in ousting the men of '89 who were of solid worth. And it will not stop there; evil ever makes a stalking-horse of folly. In a year, or less, you will see these people ousted in their turn by the Marats, the Dantons and the Santerres—the men who are by instinct criminals, but know their own minds and will stick at nothing to achieve their personal ambitions. Knowing that I have not the power to stop this awful thing I can at least spare myself the agony of witnessing it; so I intend to return to Grenoble tomorrow."

If Barnave was right—and Roger feared he was—the future lay in the hands of the men who controlled the mob. He had already scraped an acquaintance with Santerre, so his best prospects now appeared to lie in following it up. Besides, another attack on the Palace might develop at any hour, and the fury with which Marie Antoinette had dismissed Roger had not lessened his desire to serve her. Perhaps, as a *sans-culotte*, he might repeat his rôle of the previous day, and even find some pretext at the last moment by which to divert the mob from its intended victims. There was, too, a possibility that if the King and Queen were assassinated their children might be spared. In that case it was of the first importance that he should be on hand to learn at once what was to be done with the Dauphin. By swift action in the confusion that was certain to follow the murder of the Sovereigns there might even be a chance of spiriting the boy away, so, after all, drawing the Ace of Trumps from the pack for Mr. Pitt. The more he thought about it the more certain he became that, whatever might happen that day, his best course now was to develop the rôle of a fanatical revolutionary from Alsace.

Much refreshed by his bath, he dried himself, put on a morning robe that had been laid out for him, and joined Adèle de Flahaut in her boudoir. Feeling certain that he must be hungry, she had had a meal prepared for him. While he did justice to the tempting array of good things on the tray that her maid brought in, he told her that he believed there would be another attack on the Palace, and had decided to go there again dressed as a *sans-culotte*, but that he thought on this occasion he need not assume quite such a villainous appearance as on the previous day.

He felt that Santerre could have formed only a vague impression of him, and his object was not merely to get himself taken on as one of the big brewer's trusty bullies, but also to win his confidence. His chances of quickly doing so would obviously be better if he were to represent himself as having at least a rudimentary education; but the whole problem was immensely complicated by the fact that if he succeeded he was certain to come into contact with other revolutionary leaders who might remember him as the Whig journalist.

As he gave Adèle an account of the storming of the Tuileries, one half of his mind was revolving around this new conundrum. Barnave and Camille Desmoulins were the only Jacobins he had known at all well. The one was no longer a danger but the other was still in the front rank of the extremists, and there were also quite a number of moderate and Royalist ex-deputies who were almost certain to recognize him if he appeared again in the political arena. Fortunately, he had always deliberately kept his background as nebulous as possible, and most of these acquaintances believed him to be a Frenchman by birth who had adopted English nationality only because he had been taken to England when quite young and educated there. When it had appeared necessary, he had made vague allusions to his relatives in Strasbourg or to an English godmother who had brought him up, and there was no reason to suppose that any of the deputies he had known in '89 had any idea where he had been living during the past two years. It was, therefore, most unlikely that anyone would challenge the statement he had made to Santerre, that he had recently arrived from Alsace. But there remained the tricky business of bridging the gap between his former social status and that of a *sans-culotte*.

Obviously he would have to make up for Santerre some history of himself which would not seriously conflict with what his old acquaintances in the Jacobin Club believed about him, and it seemed that this could best be served by a hard-luck story. There would be some nasty fences to get over, but the first would be the worst; and, prompted once more by his belief that audacity pays, he decided that he would slough off the hideous chrysalis of a *sans-culotte* before Santerre had it firmly in mind that he had ever been one.

As soon as he had finished his breakfast he told Adèle that he had still further modified his ideas about his dress, and that his purpose could best be served by assuming the appearance of a professional man who for some time had been roughing it. She agreed that he would certainly be more comfortable in such a guise and left him to hunt through a wardrobe of clothes that her husband kept there for use on his occasional visits to her apartment.

The final result was that when Roger took leave of her he was wearing his own boots, which had been roughened with emery paper to make them look ill-cared for, woollen stockings, an old cloth country suit of the Count's, which fitted him nowhere and had had the moth in it, and the well-worn beaver hat that he had bought the previous evening. The stain Adèle had used the day before to give him a black eye had not yet entirely washed off, although it was fainter, and he had decided against shaving, and against having his short hair curled; so she had plastered it down flat for him with a dressing of macassar oil.

On leaving the Tuileries he had paused for a moment to rid himself of his sweep's brushes by slipping them into the waiting carriage, and to have a word with Dan. Being still uncertain then of his future plans, he had told his henchman to return to *La Belle Étoile* and not to worry if he did not hear from him for a day or two, and there were no other commitments to prevent him from setting about establishing his new identity at once by taking up residence in the St. Antoine quarter.

As it would have been out of character to arrive in the slums in a hackney coach, Roger walked the mile and a quarter eastwards to the great open space where the eight mighty towers of the Bastille had once frowned down on a rabbit warren of filthy courts and tenements. For weeks after the storming of the fortress the mob had amused itself by attempting to demolish this ancient symbol of tyranny, but it was so vast that little impression had been made upon it until the municipality of Paris had put the work into the hands of a qualified contractor. Months of systematic demolition had at length reduced it to scores of pitted mounds of rubble from which masses of weeds and even small trees were now sprouting. On reaching its western edge Roger enquired for the Axe and Facies, and received directions which ten minutes later brought him to the inn. It was a rambling building, situated on a corner, and was a considerably larger place than he had expected. Entering the taproom, he asked a potman for Citizen Jereau.

The man slouched off and returned a few minutes later with a short, thick-set, middle-aged fellow who had a shock of red hair and a slight cast in one eye. When Roger had stated his business, Jereau said:

"Citizen Santerre told me to expect you last night, but he described you as a *sans-culotte.* I meant to give you a bed in my doss-house at the back, but you seem a cut above that. I can find you a room to yourself if you can afford to pay."

"Ah," laughed Roger, "borrowed plumage makes fine birds of us all; although as a matter of fact I look more like my normal self this morning than when he saw me. As to terms, I am in pretty low water at the moment, but I could run to a franc a night if that would suit you."

Jereau nodded, and took him up to a back room on the second floor. It was a dim and squalid place. Instead of glass, the panes of its solitary window were made of oiled paper, the iron truckle bed had on it a straw-filled palliasse; for bedding there were no blankets, let alone sheets, but only a soiled coverlet. Some hooks in a corner screened off by a tattered curtain did duty for a wardrobe, and an old sea chest with a cracked mirror on top sufficed for a dressing-table; one rush-seated chair and a pail completed its furniture.

Mentally, Roger shuddered at the thought that for several weeks he might have to make his home there, but he showed no sign of disgust. Producing some small silver, he carefully counted a week's rent in advance into the dirty palm that his landlord extended, then asked where he could find Santerre.

"He makes this his headquarters; so he will be here presently," replied the red-headed Jereau. "In the meantime, how about taking a glass of something for the good of the house?"

It was barely nine o'clock and not much over an hour since Roger had finished breakfast, but he felt it would be tactless to reject the suggestion; so they went downstairs and the landlord produced a jug of wine newly drawn from a cask in his cellar. It was a *vin rosé* and, although inexpensive, fresh and palatable. Jereau said that it came from the Rhône Valley, where he had a relative who sent him several casks of it each year, which gave

Roger a lead to mention mythical relatives of his own in Alsace who also produced a good wine. Their talk then turned to the events of the previous day, and they were still discussing the invasion of the Tuileries when Santerre came in accompanied by several other men.

After calling greetings to the company now scattered about the long, low taproom, they all trooped upstairs. As Santerre had failed to recognize Roger, Jereau ran after him. A few minutes later the landlord returned and took Roger up to a room on the first floor. There, the Slum King and his cronies had settled themselves round a big table, and were being served with drinks by a potman.

They were a queer-looking crew and Roger judged at a glance that if they discovered him to be a spy he would stand very little chance of leaving the place alive. There were less than a dozen of them, but every face in the group betrayed brutality, viciousness or fanaticism. Only two displayed bare, hairy chests and arms, and could truly be termed *sans-culottes*; the others looked as if they might be professional card-sharpers, small tradesmen ruined by vice, pimps, or deserters from the army. Later Roger learned that every one of them had either actually been in prison or had committed some crime which would have landed him therein but for the Revolution.

Santerre gave him a searching stare and said, "So you found your way here, Comrade, but not till this morning; and during the night you seem to have taken a step up the social ladder."

With the boyish grin that had disarmed so many people, Roger replied, "After I left you, Citizen, I had a bit of luck. I ran into a young woman I knew when I was in Paris two years ago. Like a sensible girl she prefers fellows of my age to her doting old husband, and as he was away on business I helped keep his bed warm for him. What is more, I exacted payment for my services this morning by making her give me his second-best suit."

A general guffaw greeted his bawdy innuendo, but Santerre remarked, "Yesterday I thought you a *sans-culotte*, but you no longer have the air of one."

Roger shrugged. "That's hardly surprising, as I've never worn clothes like those in which you saw me yesterday except during the past week."

Santerre motioned to a vacant place on one of the wooden

benches that surrounded the table and said non-committally, "Sit down, Citizen, and tell us about yourself."

A foxy-faced man moved up a little to make room, filled an earthenware mug from a pitcher of the Rhône wine that stood on the table, and pushed the mug towards Roger as he stepped over the bench. After taking a drink, Roger said:

"I come from Strasbourg and my name is Rojé Breuc, but my parents died when I was still a youngster and my godmother had done well for herself by marrying an English merchant; so she took charge of me and brought me up in England."

Suddenly he received a most unexpected challenge. A man in the middle thirties, with a head as round as a cannon-ball and with close-cropped fair hair, shot at him in German:

"When were you last in Strasburg?"

As that language was used almost universally in Alsace, ignorance of it might easily have spelled Roger's death warrant. Fortunately he spoke fairly good German, and the varieties of its *patois* were so numerous that when he answered the Prussian who had questioned him his accent was accepted without comment as that of a native of the Upper Rhine.

Nevertheless, he found the stare of the expressionless china-blue eyes that bored into his most disconcerting, and it was not long before he learned that they were those of Anacharsis Clootz, a most dangerous criminal maniac. A Prussian Baron of Dutch descent, Clootz had stumped Europe from the age of twenty preaching revolution and atheism, describing himself as the personal enemy of Jesus Christ. The outbreak of the French Revolution had brought him hurrying to Paris, and in 1790 he had led thirty-six other foreigners to the bar of the Assembly to declare that the world adhered to the Declaration of the Rights of Man. This had earned for him the title of "the orator of the human race", which he had adopted instead of Baron; and he had since spent his time fermenting violence, destruction and murder by every means in his power.

Santerre recalled Roger's attention by saying abruptly, "Well! Let's hear some more about you."

"I received a good education at Ringwood Grammar School in Dorset," replied Roger, "and on completing it I took up journalism as a career; but it does not pay well, so I continued to be dependent on an allowance from my godmother. As I had never ceased to regard myself as a Frenchman I was thrilled by the news that the tyrant Louis had at last been compelled to summon the Three Estates, and I returned to France. For some time I contributed newsletters from Paris to several English Whig journals that were in sympathy with our efforts to gain freedom. In those days, as you know, most of the English were heart and soul with us, so I was paid well for my articles and lived very comfortably; but that did not last, because my views were greatly in advance of those of my paymasters. I chanced to learn that the Spanish Envoy was plotting to drag France into a war with England as an excuse to march a Spanish army into France and restore the power of the Monarchy, so I incited a body of patriots to hang him from a lamp-post."

"Ah," exclaimed a keen-eyed, elderly man with the bridgeless nose of a syphilitic, "I now recall where I have seen you before; I remember you speaking against the war in the *Club des Jacobins.*"

Roger now thanked his stars that he had taken the bull by the horns instead of attempting to conceal his past activities. He nodded. "I am glad, Citizen, that you should recall that great moment in my life; but my act cost me dear. My bourgeois editors refused to accept further articles from me, and my rich godmother cut me off with a shilling. Being able no longer to support myself in Paris I returned to London; there I found the English becoming more and more reactionary. My story was known; I was regarded as a dangerous firebrand, and as I refused to alter my opinions I was soon reduced to such straits that I could not even find the money to get back to France, where patriots such as yourselves might have found a use for me."

"How did you manage to do so after all?" enquired Santerre.

Roger smiled. "Some weeks ago, Citizen, I had a windfall. An uncle of mine died this spring in Strasbourg, and I was informed that he had left me a small legacy. On the strength of this information I raised enough money to go and collect the principal. When I arrived, my rascal of a cousin, who is a lawyer, told me that the money could not yet be paid over, and provided me only with a weekly pittance to keep me from starvation. I joined the local Jacobin Club and, learning how badly the Revolution had hung fire, determined to get back to Paris. I am a Republican, and hoped to aid those who think like myself that we should finish with the tyrant once and for all. My cousin is one of those servile creatures who has always been content to earn his living as a parasite on the nobility. Naturally we quarrelled violently, but at length I obtained the money, and I arrived in Paris yesterday."

"Since you are a man of some standing, Citizen, and possessed money, why did you arrive begrimed with dirt and dressed in rags?"

Roger smiled again, slyly this time, and his glance took in all the intent faces round the table. "We are all friends here," he said slowly. "We serve the same cause, and in order that we may continue to do so it is sometimes necessary for us to put personal scruples aside. I said that I obtained the money—not that it was paid over to me."

An ex-sergeant of the *Garde Française* burst out laughing. "So you had to get out of Strasbourg in a hurry, eh, Citizen? Well, you're not the only patriot the tyrant's police would have laid by the heels if they could. It was a good ruse to put them off the scent by making your journey disguised as a *sans-culotte*."

Big Santerre and all the others were smiling now. The jugs of wine were passed again, then Roger's health was drunk as a Comrade who had suffered for liberty, and had earned their regard by showing resource in outwitting both his bourgeois relative and the authorities.

Roger knew that Amanda always visualized him as doing his secret work in the Cabinets of Ministers and the boudoirs of Queens. He wondered what she would say if she could see him now.

CHAPTER IX

THE GREAT CONSPIRACY

When Santerre's crew of blackguards had emptied their mugs to Roger's health, he asked, "And now, Citizens, when do we march against the Palace?"

Santerre shook his head. "Yesterday's fiasco has had more serious repercussions than I expected. The tyrant's lack of resistance surprised those who know nothing of him, and it is reported to me that in the taverns last night some of our thickheads were even saying that he seemed quite a good fellow. We'll need a new pretext before we can work them up again. You had best leave us now, Citizen, as we have private matters to discuss, but keep hereabouts as there are plenty of ways in which I can employ you."

Surprised but greatly relieved to hear that the conspirators had received even a temporary check to their murderous intentions, Roger gave the company a fraternal salutation, then swaggered out of the room. As he went downstairs he sighed with relief at having survived so well such a dangerous ordeal, then smiled at the thought that his luck had proved even better than the best he could have expected. Not only had his life-story been accepted, but the elderly man having publicly identified him as an old member of the Jacobin Club had provided, without further trouble, the bridge with his past, the establishment of which was so essential to his safety. When he now ran across old acquaintances he would have nothing to fear. Royalists and respectable moderates might speak of him with the same repulsion as had the Queen, but that would now be all to the good. What really mattered was that he had succeeded in consolidating his position with the extremists, among whom henceforth lay his only prospect of carrying on his secret work in a way that might prove valuable.

It soon became evident that Santerre, and those who gave him his instructions, had been right in their decision not to attempt another attack on the Palace for the time being. On the day after Roger's arrival at the Axe and Facies the King made a dignified protest to the Assembly and followed it by a proclamation to the nation. The result was a strong reaction in his favour. Many of the Sections of Paris dissociated themselves with the insurrection, an enquiry was instituted, and on the 1st of July a petition was presented signed by 20,000 people condemning the attitude of the Municipality and the inaction of the Commandant of the National Guard. Clearly an overwhelming majority of the people of Paris deeply sympathized with the Royal Family and wished to see all possible measures taken to prevent further outbreaks of lawlessness.

In the summer of 1790, with the object of destroying the *esprit de corps* which was still a source of strength to the Monarchy in the old Provincial Governments, the Assembly had decreed the abolition of these Governments and a new division of France into eighty-three Departments. The affairs of each Department were managed by a Directory, that of Paris being dominated by a majority of liberal, *ci-devant* nobles, including such men as the Duc de la Rochefoucauld and de Talleyrand. The powers of the Directory were ill-defined, but it now endeavoured to assert itself, and became the rallying point of all moderate opinion in opposition to the Municipality, which was elected from the forty-eight Sections of Paris and was strongly radical. On the 7th of July the struggle between the two factions was brought to a head by the Directory suspending Pétion and his right-hand man, the *procureur* Manuel, for failing to use their powers to suppress the insurrection of the 20th of June; and for a few days it looked as if this definite bid to gain control of the situation might result in a permanent restoration of law and order.

Roger, meanwhile, found plenty to occupy him. Philosophically, he made the best of his bug-ridden, uncomfortable quarters, and, until June was out, he left the Faubourg St. Antoine only once, in order to arrange with Dan a weekly rendezvous at a small café near the Arsenal. As he was always on hand he quickly dropped into the position of one of Santerre's unofficial *aides-de-camp* and attended to a score of small matters for him. His willingness and intelligence soon made their mark and although he was not yet trusted with any of the conspirators' secrets, he had ample opportunity to gain a general comprehension of the local organization.

As an outsider, he watched the struggle between the Directory and the Municipality with intense interest, and included all the details he could secure about it in a first report to Mr. Pitt—which he sent by Dan to Lord Gower for safe transmission to London in the Embassy bag—but he ended his report by stating that in his opinion the Directory would not succeed for long in checking the development of the Revolution.

After dismissing the Girondin Ministers and accepting the resignation of Dumouriez, the King had replaced them with non-party men of little standing; but de Monciel, his new Minister of the Interior, fearing that the arrival in Paris of thousands of war volunteers was certain to add to the disturbances, had courageously ordered the Departments to keep these *fédérés* at home. Yet at the instigation of the Jacobin Club, which had branches in all the principal cities of France, this order was being ignored in many instances, and Roger knew that the conspirators were only awaiting the arrival of these reinforcements before recommencing hostilities.

Even so, now that the King had the majority of the people behind him, and the active support of the Directory, he might, once and for all, have crushed those who planned his destruction, for into his hand was given the one weapon with which he could have done so. On learning of the insurrection of the 20th of June, General Lafayette had hastened to Paris. He was in a sense the Father of the Revolution; few men had done more to bring it about and his passionate admiration for American institutions had made him a convinced Republican from the very beginning. Being a vain and not very clever man, he had persistently courted the favour of the mob at the expense of the King, and had contributed largely to the humiliations that the Royal Family had suffered. But in the preceding spring he had at last realized that while a republican government might suit a young country like the United States, it could not be achieved without anarchy in a society, such as that in France, based on ancient traditions. He had, as de Talleyrand had told Roger, then sought a *rapprochement* with the King, but when his advances were repulsed he had taken himself off to the army. Now, he appeared again, determined to gamble everything on an attempt to save the Monarchy.

His prestige with the people was still immense; he possessed a curious ability to win over to his views all but the extremists whenever he spoke in the Assembly, and having commanded the Paris National Guard for over two years from its inception there was little doubt that it would accept his orders in preference to those of any of its temporary commanders, who were now appointed monthly. On his arrival at the bar of the Assembly the extremists endeavoured to spike his guns by moving a vote of censure against him for having deserted his post in the face of the enemy; but the vote was defeated by a large majority, and he succeeded in arousing the deputies to the danger in which they stood of being coerced by the mob into passing measures which were against the true interests of the people. He then went to the King and offered to take over the control of the city.

Had he been allowed to do so the *fédérés* could have been turned back outside its gates by the National Guard, further insurrection in it could have been suppressed by them, and the Constitutional Monarchy could at last have been established on a firm basis to the great relief of nine-tenths of the nation. But the King once more refused to grasp the lifeline that had been thrown to him. With that hopeless lack of judgment which had caused him to overlook the sly and treacherous Pétion's past record and back him for Mayor, he now decided against trusting the honest, if misguided, Lafayette. The General's repentance had come too late, and on the 30th of June he left Paris for his headquarters, having failed in his sincere effort to repair the worst of the damage he had caused.

It was the King himself too who, by his crass stupidity, gave the deathblow to the attempts of the Directory to save him. Instead of endorsing the suspension of Pétion and Manuel, and using all the authority that remained to him to support it, he tamely referred the matter to the Assembly. For a week they refused to take a decision, then, on the 13th of July, they decreed that the two revolutionaries should be reinstated; and followed that, at the instigation of the Rolands, by offering all the *fédérés* who were advancing on the capital free quarters therein from the 14th to the 18th of the month to celebrate the anniversary of the fall of the Bastille.

After the life of near-luxury that Roger had led for so long, he found conditions at the Axe and Facies trying in the extreme. To have left the inn for better lodgings near by would have deprived him of many opportunities for casual chats with Santerre and the other leaders of the Section, and while he remained there he felt that, however distasteful, he must accept its normal life as his portion. Having established himself as an educated man who in the past had made good money, he could have brought in some comforts and taken some of his meals at better-class restaurants without exciting suspicion, but he knew that in the long run it would pay him infinitely better to go the whole hog and practise the doctrines of equality and fraternity that he now preached. In consequence it was only by concentrating entirely on his work that he was able to keep his mind off his physical miseries.

As it was high summer he was at least spared the additional discomfort of acute cold under the sparse coverings of his bed, and as he was young and healthy the lumpy straw of his palliasse did not prevent his sleeping soundly when he threw himself upon it after a long and tiring day. But at other times the fleas and bed bugs drove him nearly crazy, and the food that he had to eat along with his rough companions sometimes made him actually sick after a meal. All of these ruffians had been reared in hunger, so to refuse a dish suggested a faddiness that was certain to be taken as a sign of an aristocratic upbringing, and to invite any such inference about himself was the one thing above all others he was determined to avoid. Fortunately, the usual fare in the common-room was vegetable stew followed by a good variety of cheeses, but sometimes a platter of meat was dumped in front of him, and to get it down with apparent relish always proved a horrible ordeal; vinegar was poison to him, and in the summer heat the meat that the poor ate, when they could get it, always had to be soused in vinegar because it had gone bad long before it reached Paris.

He forced himself to endure these trials only with difficulty, but was encouraged to bear them by the fact that he was steadily consolidating his position as a "true patriot" and that towards the middle of July Santerre began to give him more confidential tasks which brought him into touch with many of the revolutionary leaders in other Sections.

Towards the end of the month it became clear to him that the situation was rapidly deteriorating. He had learned that a permanent Committee of Insurrection had been established under the direction of Marat and Danton, which included Santerre, Carra, the Pole Lazowski, Fournier the American, and an Alsatian officer named Westermann. Owing to de Monciel's effort to stop the *fédérés*, only 3,000 of them had arrived in Paris by the 14th in time for the Feast of the Federation, and consequently the King and Queen during their public appearance at the feast met with no worse than a very mixed reception; but many thousands more *fédérés* were now approaching the capital. The news from the front was bad and on the 22nd the Assembly had a black flag hoisted over the Hôtel de Ville, launched a great recruiting campaign, and officially declared the country to be in a "State of Danger". That provided a ready pretext for fresh demonstrations against the Tuileries, in which, the people were led to believe, the Queen daily took the chair at an "Austrian Committee", where her friends planned the betrayal of France and drafted letters containing valuable military information for secret despatch to the enemy. On the 21st of July and again on the 26th spontaneous insurrections took place, showing that the mob had once more become ripe to be used as a tool by the conspirators, and on the 30th, amid scenes of wild enthusiasm, the long-awaited bands of *sans-culottes* from Marseilles at last entered Paris by the Porte St. Antoine.

Roger felt that against the force of such a tide there was little he could do, but he still had hopes that when the crisis came he would be able to find some means of taking advantage of it. Having now appeared on the scene once more as a revolutionary, it was obvious that he could expect no help from lesser men of Barnave's stamp, much less from old friends of his among the Royalists; but he knew that there were many thousands of honest working men in Paris who were still loyal to the Monarchy, and he decided to enlist secretly a little group of them upon whose aid he might call in an emergency.

To have attempted such a business himself would have been fraught with the utmost danger; so towards the end of the month he made a rendezvous with Dan and instructed him how to proceed. The ex-smuggler had a head like a rock and Roger believed in the truth of the saying '*in vino veritas*'. He told Dan to frequent some of the taverns in the Filles St. Thomas Section, in which the National Guard were known to pride themselves on their loyalty. He was to listen to their conversation, pick men who expressed antirevolutionary sentiments when still sober, scrape acquaintance with them, make them as drunk as he could and argue against them. If they showed an inclination to fight him that could be taken as reasonable proof that they really meant what they said; he could then calm them down by admitting that he had only been leading them on, and arrange another meeting. When he had got to know them well, but not before, he was to sound them cautiously as to their willingness to carry their words into deeds and strike a blow for the King. By these means he hoped that Dan would be able to collect eight or ten really trusty fellows, already possessing uniforms and able to appear as a squad of National Guards ready to accept his orders when called on to do so.

The war fever that now held Paris in its grip was being taken utmost advantage of by the extremists. On the country having been declared to be in a "State of Danger", the Assembly, and all other legally constituted bodies, began to sit "*en permanence*", which frequently enabled the nominees of the conspirators to rush measures through on occasions when the majority of the moderates were absent. The Sections were not official bodies, as they were merely groups of electors who had been called together solely for the purpose of nominating deputies from their district to the Assembly, but, quite illegally, they had continued their sessions and claimed the right of dictating the policy of the deputies they had elected. Now, the conspirators set in motion an agitation for the Sections also to sit "*en permanence*", and the Assembly weakly gave way, thus strengthening still further the power of the Committee of Insurrection.

The next step was to undermine the stability of the National Guard, and on the 1st of August Carnot initiated the passing of a decree by the Assembly ordering its reorganization. Formerly, it had been recruited entirely from citizens who paid not less than one silver mark tax per annum; now its ranks were thrown open to the proletariat, its *compagnies d'élite* were suppressed and many of the most ruffianly *fédérés* were incorporated in it. On the 20th of June the National Guard would have fired on the mob had they been ordered to do so, but after these new measures they could be counted on to remain passive. To make certain of matters Pétion reorganized the staff on democratic lines and issued an instruction that no officer might give an order that had not been sanctioned by the Municipality.

Between the 14th of July and the 30th some 5,000 *fédérés* left for the front; but they were the genuine volunteers who had joined up with the intention of fighting for their country, and there remained behind all those who had come to the capital in search of free keep and plunder. Each day fresh bands of brigands were arriving, accompanied by hordes of slatternly women armed with knives and pitchforks. Drunk, quarrelsome, fierce and filthy, they swarmed in the streets, insulting respectable people by day and robbing them by night.

Half the criminals in France were now concentrated in Paris, and their attitude to property of all kinds became so menacing that even the original authors of this state of affairs took alarm. Santerre told Roger that the "lily-livered" Girondins had panicked and, abandoning their plans for the overthrow of the Monarchy, were preparing to combine with the remnants of the Royalists as the only means of maintaining a government strong enough to avert anarchy.

He added gruffly that it would make no difference, as the control of the Committee of Insurrection had already passed out of their hands, and that its new chiefs, Danton and Marat, were not the men to give up the game so tamely; but Roger could see that he was much upset, and knew that he now had good cause for anxiety. All but a minute fraction of the two hundred thousand householders in Paris, its Directory, and the Section Councils in all the better districts, were intensely worried and were most anxious that order should be restored. The Girondins were by far the most powerful body in the Assembly; if they threw their weight into the Royalists' scale strong measures might be taken for the dispersal of the *fédérés* and the suppression of the Committee. In fact, Roger began to wonder if his six weeks' association with Santerre had not already brought him into sufficient prominence for his own name to be included on any list of arrests to be made, should the Assembly suddenly order the rounding-up of Danton's committee and of all its principal agents.

He need not have worried. On the 2nd of August there occurred an event which prevented the Girondins from exerting any influence on the situation. Although war had been declared in April, owing to the delays of mobilization it was not until mid-July that the Allies had succeeded in concentrating a considerable army on the French frontier. Now that hostilities were about to commence in earnest, the Duke of Brunswick, who commanded the Prussian Army, issued a manifesto to the French people before launching the attack.

He disclaimed therein all desire for territorial conquest or any intention of interfering in the internal affairs of France. *But*, after calling on the French people to rise against their "oppressors"—by which he meant their legally elected representatives—he threatened any who dared to defend themselves against his invading troops with "the rigour of the laws of war", and declared that in the event of a further violation of the Tuileries he would inflict on the citizens of Paris an "exemplary and never-to-be-forgotten vengeance" by giving the city over to his troops to sack and by executing all who had borne arms against him.

The moment Roger saw the text of this incredibly tactless

document he knew what Londoners would have done had it been addressed to them; and he had little doubt that the reactions of the *Parisiens* would be exactly the same. He proved right; great as the menace of the professional armies of the Germanic Monarchies then appeared, rich and poor alike joined in defiance of them. The shallow, self-seeking Girondins, although now frightened by the result of their own acts, no longer had the courage even to hedge and to attempt to forestall a new attack upon the Monarchy. Even had they done so, their long-winded hypocritical orations in its defence would have fallen on deaf ears, as nearly everybody believed that the weak King, dominated by the "infamous Austrian woman", had secretly inspired and approved the Duke's manifesto. Rather than risk their future prospects by committing themselves either way, Roland and these other self-styled "Fathers of the Country" hurried home and hid, leaving the majority of the deputies in the Assembly leaderless, and an easy prey to the machinations of the extremists.

The Committee of Insurrection instantly grasped this golden opportunity to carry out its plans for seizing power. On the day following the issue of the manifesto Santerre called Roger into the room he used as an office, and said:

"Citizen Breuc, our chance has come! The withdrawal of the Girondin leaders has left the Assembly little more than a collection of honest fools, windy idealists and nonentities. Apart from Manuel and a few others, the Municipality is little better. We propose to create a new body consisting of real patriots, which will oust the Municipality and menace the Assembly into doing its will.

"The permission granted to the Sections to sit *en permanence* has created for us conditions which will enable us to carry out this plan. The majority of the electors have long since tired of attending the sessions of their Sectional assemblies; only those with strong political convictions now do so regularly. In many Sections the majority of these are our enemies, the bourgeois who favour a continuance of the Monarchy; but they must sleep some time. By skilful organization we can so arrange matters that a time will occur when, the Section halls being almost deserted, our trusties can force through a resolution that will be legally binding on the Section in which they are operating.

"The resolution will consist of a vote of non-confidence in the

Municipals previously elected to represent the Section, and it will be followed immediately by the election of three *new* Commissioners in each Section to replace them in the Communal Council of Paris. You see the idea?"

Roger nodded. "Yes; and it is a clever one. Even if we fail to get our nominees elected in the more reactionary Sections, we should succeed in creating a legal body far more patriotic in character than any which exists at present."

The burly brewer pulled on his short clay pipe for a moment, then said, "That's right enough. But for us to reap the maximum benefit from our plan we must have an overwhelming majority in this new Chamber, and that is not going to be easy to secure. If we attempted to do the job piecemeal, the moderates would take alarm and pack the Sections where the resolution had not been put, in order to prevent its being passed; so it will have to be done in all forty-eight Sections on the same night. Local events in some of them may cause well-attended meetings on the chosen night and so present an unexpected obstacle in forcing the resolution through. We can count on the Faubourgs, but much is going to depend on the skill with which each situation in the inner Sections is handled."

He took another puff at his foul pipe, then went on, "I am giving you the Section des Granvilliers to look after. It is up by the Porte St. Martin. Nearly opposite the gate you will find the sign of *Le Coussin et les Clefs*. The landlord, Citizen Oysé, is one of us. He will furnish you with papers as an elector of the Section and give you full particulars about its Council. Without giving away what's in the wind, use the names of Citizen Danton and myself to secure the obedience of the patriots that Oysé will make known to you. Arrange with them to be ready to vote at a snap division whenever you call upon them. On the day I send you word have everything ready to pack the Council at midnight; then get yourself, and the two other men in that Section selected by the Committee, elected as Commissioners."

"That's clear, Citizen," replied Roger promptly, "and you may depend upon me."

They discussed details of the plan for a further half hour; then Roger collected the few belongings he had acquired during his stay at the Axe and Facies, paid his bill, shook Citizen Jereau warmly by the hand and, with a feeling of unutterable thankfulness, left its stench and squalor behind him.

The Section to which he had been appointed being a better-class district, he could look forward to more comfortable accommodation and decent food there; but he had far more important things to think of at the moment. As soon as he was well outside the Faubourg St. Antoine he went into a quiet café and, calling for pen and paper with his drink, wrote a letter to Lord Gower. In it he gave full particulars of the plot and urged the Ambassador to warn not only the King, but also such ministers and deputies as might be able to frustrate it. He then walked to within a stone's throw of *La Belle Étoile* and tipped a small boy to go in, ask for Dan and, if he was there, bring him outside.

Fortunately Dan was in, so they repaired to a nearby café. There Roger passed Dan the letter for immediate delivery, learned that he had succeeded in making friends with seven National Guards who could be fully relied on, and gave him new instructions. As Danton's *coup d'état* might occur any day he now wanted Dan to keep in close touch, so it was arranged that he should drop into the Cushion and Keys the following noon, and that they would greet one another as old acquaintances who had met by chance. This public renewal of friendship would be excuse enough for Dan to become a regular frequenter of the inn if he also gave it out casually that he had recently obtained work in the district.

After they had parted Roger decided to do some shopping, as he felt that policy now coincided with his own inclination to smarten himself up a little. He was still wearing the Comte de Flahaut's old and ill-fitting country suit and, for the moment, had no intention of changing it for anything better; but he thought that the electors of the des Granvilliers Section were likely to regard him with more confidence if he took to wearing reasonably clean linen, shaved every day and had his hair washed and dressed by a barber.

Three hours later, still seedily attired but clean in appearance, he arrived in a hackney coach at the Cushion and Keys, carrying a second-hand portmanteau containing his new belongings. Citizen Oysé, a swarthy little Provençal, had been notified in advance of his coming by Santerre, and received him with fraternal cordiality. After showing him to a rather shabby room which, nevertheless, seemed the very height of comfort compared with the dreadful attic he had occupied for so long, the landlord invited him to dine in his parlour; and over a meal, the very sight of which made Roger's mouth water, he was initiated into the affairs of the Section.

Oysé said that to pull off their proposed coup would not be easy, because if even a moderate number of the electors were present at the voting the revolutionary proposals would be defeated by a large majority; and that their greatest danger lay in a young Doctor Guilhermy, who watched the transactions of the Section like a hawk, and who, if he got wind of their intentions, would do everything in his power to thwart them. He was also an excellent orator, and the weakness of the Left in the Section lay not only in their small numbers, but in their lack of a good speaker; so Roger gathered that it was largely on account of his own ability to talk with fluency and conviction that Santerre had sent him to Oysé's assistance.

Towards the end of the meal a rough, morose-looking man named Bichot joined them; he was a tinworker, and the leader of the comparatively few *sans-culottes* who enjoyed the status of electors in the Section. It then transpired that he, together with Oysé and Roger, had been nominated by the Committee of Insurrection as the three potential Commissioners. After drinking a glass of wine to the success of the plot, all three of them went round to the Section hall.

In order to provide Roger with legal qualifications as an elector, Oysé had already arranged the bogus sale of a small piece of property in the neighbourhood, and had had Roger's name inserted in the conveyance as the purchaser. On the production of the deeds his name was duly entered on the electoral register, then they went in to the sitting. Only about thirty people were present and a rather dreary debate was in progress on the subject of whose responsibility it was to pay for the restoration of a church porch, which had become dangerous and threatened to fall in the street, now that the Church had been deprived of its funds and all its property taken over by the nation. There followed a more spirited discussion about providing additional free quarters for the *fédérés*, and both Oysé and Bichot, wishing to see how Roger shaped as a speaker, urged him to join in; but he declined.

Later, when they had left the hall, he told them his reason for refusing. He said that the most dangerous thing he could do would be to alarm their enemies prematurely by a display of revolutionary fireworks, and, now that he had been registered, he did not even mean to go to the hall again until the night of the coup.

Instead, they must provide him with lists of electors who inclined to the Left but were at present only half-hearted, then he would employ himself by seeking them out individually and endeavouring to convert them into trusties. This evidence that he possessed a more subtle mind than themselves impressed his two simple companions most favourably, and they readily promised him their assistance.

When he woke next morning, in the surprising comfort of a comparatively well-sprung bed, he took serious stock of his position. It had already occurred to him that by double-crossing Santerre he could ensure the failure of the coup in the des Granvilliers Section; but it was only one out of the forty-eight into which Paris was divided, and if he did so it would spell his own ruin with the revolutionary leaders. He would be throwing away the status he had won for himself, by enduring six weeks of incredibly hard apprenticeship, for an issue that could have little effect on the general situation; and gone would be all further chance of learning the secrets of those who were about to make a ruthless bid to become the new masters of France. He soon decided that by having warned Lord Gower of what was afoot he had made the only useful contribution that he could to checkmate the conspiracy, and that he must now go all out to secure a good future position, if the coup succeeded, by acting in every way as if an invisible Santerre was constantly at his elbow.

At noon he enacted his little comedy with Dan and, in the hearing of Oysé, asked him to dinner the following day; then, as it was a Sunday and therefore a good opportunity for catching a number of the working-class electors in their homes, he set off with his lists to canvass the district. Santerre had told him that for the purpose of bribery ample funds were available, and that he could draw what money he required from Oysé. So, after a general talk on the burning questions of the day with each elector on whom he called, he sounded them carefully on their willingness to put an antireactionary measure through on a snap vote, without disclosing to them what it would concern. Then, if he formed the impression that they were to be trusted, he ticked their names off on his list and promised them five *louis* apiece, as a strong inducement to turn up when sent for.

For the next four days he followed the same procedure, by which time he had secured about eighty doubtfuls upon whom he felt he could depend, in addition to some fifty dyed-in-the-wool radicals that Oysé and Bichot promised to bring along. The total was only a small fraction of the electorate, but the vast majority had long since wearied of attending political meetings out of which no good seemed to come, and the conspirators counted on a continuance of this apathy unless the plot should be betrayed. Then, on the afternoon of Thursday the 9th, a runner arrived from Santerre with a sealed message to say that the coup was fixed for that night; the measure was to be put to the vote in all Sections between twelve and half-past, and the newly elected Commissioners were to report to the Hôtel de Ville as soon as possible afterwards.

The intervening hours passed swiftly while Roger and Oysé were making a round of visits to give their supporters verbal warning. It was half-past nine before they had finished and met again at the inn for supper. Dan was there, sitting in a quiet corner of the taproom enjoying a noggin of cognac, and Roger went over for a quick word with him. There seemed no point in assembling his loyal squad until there was a definite part for them to play, but after they had greeted one another with their usual heartiness Roger lowered his voice and said:

"It is tonight! Just write that on a slip of paper and take it at once to the person to whom you took my letter."

Dan nodded, finished his cognac, stood up and, leaning towards his master, asked in a hoarse whisper, "Any order for my lot?"

"No," Roger whispered back, "but from now on remain at the *Étoile* till you hear from me."

Bichot came in at that moment; so Roger went up with him to Oysé, and the three of them supped together. As soon as the meal was finished the others wanted to go round to the hall, but Roger would not let them. He had given orders that none of his people was to arrive there before midnight, foreseeing that directly they started to crowd in the unexpected influx of radicals would alarm the moderates; and the later matters could be left the better, as a larger number of regular attendants would have gone home to bed—with luck Doctor Guilhermy among them.

At last the moment came. Downstairs some forty of their supporters were enjoying free drinks while waiting; Oysé leading, they all trooped out into the hot, sultry night. At the hall there were more people than Roger had expected, but a glance round reassured him. The young Doctor, who had been pointed out to him on his previous visit, was present, but the extra numbers were accounted for by most of Bichot's men having arrived early. Singly and in couples more radicals were coming in every moment, but the session was still proceeding in a quiet, orderly manner.

An elderly man with steel-rimmed spectacles was speaking about soup kitchens. Roger let him continue for a few minutes, then stood up and said firmly:

"Citizens, we have heard enough on this matter. Let it be put to the vote."

Suddenly, in the smoky atmosphere and dim light cast by the candles, the peaceful scene changed to one of violent drama. The President rapped on his desk with his gavel, and called him to order. A roar of voices supported his intervention. The moderates, already uneasy at the numbers and appearance of the new arrivals, cried out in alarm, "A plot! A plot!", and jumping to their feet joined the President in his calls for silence.

As soon as the babble had died down a little, Roger went on in a loud voice, "Citizen President! Citizens Electors! Our Liberties are in danger! I have just been sent word of a new conspiracy by those wretches in the Tuileries! They have planned to install a powder magazine under the Assembly and blow up the People's representatives. All other business must be suspended so that——"

"It's a lie!" shouted Doctor Guilhermy, cutting him short. "I challenge you to prove it."

He was howled down by the radical *claque*, and Roger went on: "In concert with the other Sections of Paris, tonight we must take immediate measures to protect our representatives and our rights!"

With "Hurrahs!" and "Bravos!" were mingled cries from the moderates of "Who is this man?"—"He doesn't belong to the Section"—"Turn him out!"

Oysé sprang up and yelled, "He is a registered elector of des Granvilliers! I have seen his papers! I demand that he be heard!"

Evidence of legality always seemed to have a curiously hypnotic effect on honest men in such assemblies; so Roger was allowed to proceed and, with comparatively few interruptions, he spoke for about five minutes. Broadly, his theme was that the members of the Legislative Assembly and their own representatives in the Municipality of Paris were too naïve and kindhearted to deal effectively with the menace emanating from the Tuileries. Stronger measures must be taken and citizens of proved patriotism must be elected to replace their present representatives in the Commune if the People's liberties were to be preserved.

Immediately he had finished, the young Doctor heatedly denounced him as an agitator and declared the measures he proposed to be illegal.

He was cheered by his friends but was booed and hissed by the majority, until a friend of Oysé's rose to speak in Roger's support. While he was speaking, Roger saw Guilhermy scribble a note, pass it up to the President, then push through the crowd, evidently meaning to leave the hall.

Guessing his intention, Roger whispered to Oysé to keep things going, then slipped out after Guilhermy. He knew that no decision could be taken legally until the President had put the matter to the vote. The young Doctor had evidently asked that a vote should not be taken until he had had time to rouse his friends in the neighbourhood and bring them running to the rescue.

Just inside the door Roger caught up with Guilhermy and tapped him on the shoulder. They were of about the same age, and for a moment stood eyeing one another coldly. Then Roger said:

"I do not wish to force a quarrel upon you, Citizen Doctor, but I should like you to know that I am a fencing-master. If you leave this hall I shall have no alternative but to call you out."

It was an old way of dealing with troublesome political opponents, and on many occasions had been carried to its logical conclusion. The nobles had started it in the early days of the National Assembly and, being the better swordsmen, had, in this manner, rid themselves of a number of the most revolutionary deputies. The Left had retaliated by hiring professional fencing-masters to challenge the most dangerous nobles; and, much as Roger secretly hated having to do so, he felt that by posing as one of these he might intimidate Guilhermy into abandoning his intention.

Guilhermy was a mentally courageous man of forceful character, but he knew only the barest rudiments of swordplay, and his flesh shrank at the almost certain prospect of having six inches of cold steel thrust into it on the following morning. His face went white with anger, but he fought down the suicidal impulse to strike Roger and, with a muttered curse, turned back into the hall.

After that the conspirators met with little resistance. In vain the President protested that the proposed measure was illegal, and endeavoured to postpone the issue. He was howled down by Bichot's *sans-culottes* and by the men whom Roger had bribed. On the President being forced to put the matter to the vote, Roger, Oysé and Bichot were elected as Commissioners for the des Granvilliers Section to the Commune of Paris with a mandate to replace those previously elected. At twenty-five minutes to one they left the hall, to the ringing cheers of their supporters, on their way to the Hôtel de Ville.

Within ten minutes of their leaving, the bells of Paris suddenly began to clang out, sounding the louder for the silence of the night. The Committee of Insurrection had ordered the tocsin to be rung at 12.45 in order to rouse the mobs of the Faubourgs and the *fédérés* to action while the bulk of the National Guard was still separated and in bed at home, as the plan was to attempt to take the Tuileries by storm before dawn. Lights began to appear in the upstairs windows, and heads were thrust out of them as the three new Commissars marched down the hill, but few people came out into the street.

Soon after one o'clock they reached the Hôtel de Ville. In its public Council Chamber the legally elected Commune was sitting *en permanence*, but only a handful of its members were present. Outside in the main hall stood a little group of newcomers. Roger and his companions joined them; the group gradually increased, but it took no action as no prominent leader had yet appeared to issue any orders.

After a while Huguenin, the brothel-keeper, suggested that they ought to constitute themselves, so they took possession of a side hall that was furnished with a dais and benches. Huguenin was elected chairman and a printer-journalist, named Tallien, secretary. There being nothing further they could do, they sat about wondering uneasily what was delaying matters, and why more than half the expected number of Commissioners had so far failed to arrive at the rendezvous.

As they waited, a trickle of late-comers began to bring in news that all was not going well with the insurrection. Many Sections had refused to elect new Commissioners. In other cases, where revolutionaries of the first rank like Robespierre, Chaumette, Farbe d'Églantine and Billaud-Varennes had been elected, they had made some excuse to go home, after promising their followers that they would take their seats in the new Commune next day; and the caution of these experienced politicians seemed to indicate a grave lack of confidence in the whole venture. Then it was learned that the Faubourgs, now become blasé about insurrections, had refused to rise. A young *apache* named Rossignol, whom Roger had come to know well as one of Santerre's principal lieutenants, arrived as a Commissioner for their old Section, and told him gloomily that their chief had succeeded in getting together only some few score trusties.

At three o'clock in the morning, Danton—big, burly, and brutal-faced, looked in and checked the new Commissars. It was found that only nineteen out of the forty-eight Sections were represented. Blustering and cursing he hurried away, but, as Roger learned afterwards, only to hide himself in his own cellar.

Now acutely nervous, the conspirators began to talk among themselves of abandoning the attempt and going into hiding before they could be arrested. Only the persuasion of Tallien and Hébert, a theatre cloakroom attendant who had been discharged for stealing, and now edited a scurrilous rag called *le Père Duchesne*, succeeded in keeping them together.

Shortly after four, Santerre arrived. He was in a furious rage, and declared that they had been betrayed. Sixteen battalions of National Guards had been called out to defend the Palace, and strong bodies of troops had been posted on the bridges over the Seine to prevent the *fédérés* quartered on the south bank from joining up with his contingent from the Faubourg St. Antoine.

Roger knew that in a conspiracy necessitating concerted action in every quarter of the city there must have been many leakages, but he felt a glow of satisfaction from the knowledge that the warnings he had sent must have played some part in initiating these strong measures to render the insurrection abortive. But his satisfaction was swiftly tempered by the thought that he might soon be called upon to pay the penalty of all unsuccessful revolutionaries and, within a few hours, find himself in prison.

CHAPTER X

THE GREAT BETRAYAL

THE news that Santerre brought threw the meeting into a panic, but Marat arrived close on his heels. Diseased in mind and body, the erstwhile Doctor had, for over two years, never ceased to incite the mob to violence. His paper, *L'Ami du Peuple*, was the most inflammatory of all revolutionary journals, and even his fellow extremists feared to cross him lest he should charge them with half-heartedness in one of his venomous articles. Hunch-backed and stooping, the festering sores on his head only partially covered by a dirty cloth, he clambered on to the dais and began to castigate the would-be deserters for their lack of courage.

Their terror of him being greater than that of being called to account for their illegal action, they began a noisy wrangle as to how best they could save the situation. Someone suggested that Pétion, as Mayor, had the power to order the National Guards back to their homes, and that he should be sent for. He was fetched from the Council Chamber, and some of the ringleaders cornered him.

White-faced and trembling, the hypocritical Girondin protested that he was entirely on their side and had done what he could to aid them. He had prevented the Swiss Guard from receiving more than thirty rounds of ammunition per man, and had limited the issue for the National Guards to three rounds each, while on the other hand he had caused five thousand rounds to be distributed among the Marseillais. His official duty required his presence at the Palace, but so that he should not be called on to order resistance to an attack he had sent himself a message saying that he was urgently required at the Hôtel de Ville. He now begged them to arrest him, so that he could not be accused later by the Assembly of having failed in the duty entrusted to him.

They insisted that he should return to the Palace and dismiss the National Guards. He protested that they would not obey him, and that the root of the trouble lay in the fact that the *ci-devant* Marquis de Mandat had chanced to be top of the roster, so had automatically become Commandant General of the National Guard for that month. Mandat, he said, was popular with the men as well as being able and determined. It was he who had secured the bridges and called out the extra battalions of Guards; only about a quarter of their number had obeyed the summons, but those who had were loyal, and Mandat had made his dispositions of them for the defence of the Palace very skilfully.

It was then decided that Mandat must be sent for and either intimidated or disposed of. There was another anxious wait while Pétion sent some of his Municipals to fetch the Commandant. At length they returned to report that he refused to leave the Palace.

Dawn had now come, and by its pale light Roger saw new fear in the haggard faces about him. Santerre declared that he intended to disband his contingent, but Westermann called him a traitor and swore he would kill him if he did. The Alsatian then made Pétion sign an order that the troops on the bridges should allow the *fédérés* to pass, and Santerre reluctantly set off with it; but as long as the Marquis de Mandat remained in command it seemed unlikely that his men would obey the order. Now, more than ever, the insurrection looked like being a failure. No one could offer any new suggestion. Again there were murmurs of "The game is up! Let us disperse and save ourselves!" Again they were kept together only through fear of being branded as traitors in *L'Ami du Peuple*, while, as a forlorn hope, a second attempt was made to secure Mandat.

This time the affair was managed with more cunning. A message was sent to Pétion's colleague, the Attorney-General Roederer, who was known to be at the Palace, asking him to persuade Mandat that as he commanded citizen troops he was legally bound to obey the summons of the Commune. The plan worked and, at seven o'clock, the Commandant reported himself to the rump of the old Municipality, which was still sitting in the Council Chamber. Like Pétion, they had no idea how matters would end and were desperately anxious not to compromise themselves; so they asked him only a few questions, then let him go; but on leaving the Chamber he was seized and dragged into the room where the new Commissioners had established themselves.

There, his examination was very different. Crowding about him with weapons in their hands, they thrust their brutal faces into his and demanded that he should give them particulars of the garrison of the Tuileries. In the hope of preventing an attack, he gave it as far stronger than it was. They then required him to sign an order directing one half of it to withdraw; heroically he declined.

Huguenin, as President, ordered his arrest; then, as the Marquis was led away, he made a significant horizontal gesture with the flat of his hand across his throat. Rossignol drew a pistol from his belt and followed Mandat out. A few minutes later there came the sound of a shot. There was a moment's silence, then a white-faced doorkeeper ran in to say that, as the prisoner was being taken down the steps to the street, the young *sans-culotte* had put a bullet through the back of his head.

This foul deed produced an instant reaction among Roger's companions. Without a shadow of real authority they had seized the principal officer of the "People's Army"—the man who had been legally appointed, not by the King, but by their own Municipality, to be responsible for the maintenance of law and order in Paris. Their President had, in their name, ordered his detention and had indicated that as a defender of royalty he ought to be liquidated. Now, he was dead—and one of their number had murdered him. From that moment onwards there could be no drawing back.

With the spontaneous movement of a herd, they crowded out into the main hall. Running and shouting, they dashed up the stairs and into the vast Council Chamber which occupied the whole of the first floor. The Municipals there had just learned of Mandat's arrest and were about to order his release. In vain a few of them stuck to their guns and insisted that they were the legally elected representatives of the Communes of Paris. The insurrectionists flung them out, retaining only Pétion and Manuel, now under arrest for their own protection, as members *ex officio* of the new Commune.

There followed an orgy of destruction. The walls of the great Chamber were decorated with the portraits and busts not only of past Kings, but also of such Fathers of the Revolution as Necker, Bailly and Lafayette. All were torn down, ripped and smashed. Then, amidst the dust and debris, they voted themselves the *Conseil Général de la Revolution*, with supreme powers to carry out the "Will of the People".

News now came in that the troops on the Pont Neuf, having failed to receive instructions from Mandat to ignore the order from the Commune, had surrendered the bridge, and that the head of the mob streaming over it had penetrated the Place du

Carrousel. In spite of that, Roger remained very hopeful that the insurrection would yet fizzle out. From what he had heard it was clear that, in addition to the 950 Swiss, there were 2,500 trustworthy National Guards prepared to defend the Palace, and, on top of that, several hundred gentlemen who had congregated there during the night, ready to give their lives rather than allow the Royal Family to be killed or taken prisoners.

Knowing that the instigators of the insurrection had proved too cowardly to take a hand themselves, and having witnessed for himself the irresolution and lack of organization among the subordinates whom they had left to carry out their business, he could not believe that the ill-led mob would prove a serious menace. Four thousand armed and resolute men should have no difficulty at all in dealing with the sort of lukewarm rabble that it had taken Santerre and his friends all night to collect. If they had the guts to attack at all, a couple of volleys fired over their heads should be sufficient to send the whole lot running.

Yet, with dramatic suddenness, the crisis was resolved. Shortly after 8.30 a.m. a report came in that the King and his family had left the Tuileries, crossed its gardens to the riding-school, and placed themselves under the protection of the Assembly.

Roger could hardly believe his ears, but the news was soon confirmed. The new Commissioners who, ten minutes before, had been glancing over their shoulders expecting loyal National Guards to burst in and arrest them all on the orders of the men they had just turned out, broke into a riot of cheers and rejoicing. Without a single shot being fired at the Palace, the day was theirs.

Later Roger learned the tragic tale of weakness which had led to the surrender. No longer having the brave Mandat at his side, the King had lost his nerve. At the urging of his friends, he had gone out to inspect the National Guard; but miserable and uncertain of himself, he could not find a single brave or cheerful word to say to them. It did not seem to occur to him that they, far more than the half-foreign mob leavened with cut-throats—black, white and brown—from every port in the Mediterranean, were truly representative of his people. Barely acknowledging their cries of "*Vive le Roi*!", he had shambled back into the Palace to await events. When the mob had entered the Place du Carrousel he had shown no trace of the fortitude he had displayed on the

20th of June; his eyes wet with tears, his hair disordered and his coat awry, he had looked round helplessly for guidance. Roederer and other officials who were present, and who were secretly in sympathy with the insurrection, advised him to seek safety with the Assembly. The Queen cried out indignantly that she would "rather be nailed to the walls of the Palace than leave it", upon which Roederer had said to her:

"You wish then, Madame, to make yourself responsible for the death of the King, of your own son, of your daughter, of yourself and of all those who would defend you?"

Silenced by this blackmail, the Queen could only turn again to her husband. Looking out of the window he remarked, "It does not seem to be a very big mob." Yet, without a shot being fired and with four thousand men to defend him, he added, "Let us go, then," and turning to his nobles took leave of them with the words, "Messieurs, there is nothing more to be done here, either for you or for me."

Between a double line of National and Swiss Guards, the Royal Family and their immediate entourage then crossed the gardens of the Tuileries. As they did so the King remarked, "The leaves are falling early this year," but when they reached the Porte des Feuillants he was at last shaken out of his hapless lethargy. The mob from the Faubourg St. Antoine had congregated there; thrusting the guards aside, they shook their fists in his face and in the Queen's, spat at them and jostled them. The Queen's purse and watch were snatched from her and, to her horror, a bearded giant wrenched the Dauphin from her arms; but he proved to be a loyal workman who was anxious only to protect the boy, and he carried him safely into the Assembly hall.

To the uneasy and dour-faced deputies, the King said: "Messieurs, I have come here to prevent a great crime."

No one with whom Roger spoke doubted that the King believed what he said, but the fact remained that he did not prevent the crime to which he referred, although he might have done so by showing a little firmness. Instead, by his premature and abject surrender he had encouraged the mob to attack his loyal soldiers and subjects. Within a few minutes of his giving himself into the keeping of the politicians who had so consistently betrayed and humiliated him, the first shots were being fired against those who still thought him worth defending—those who, now that he had deprived them of their high inspiration to face death, were doomed to die with the bitter knowledge that they were giving their lives for no useful purpose whatsoever.

So, at nine o'clock on the morning of the 10th of August, 1792, that poor, well-meaning, befuddled man, in whose veins the blood of *Henri Quatre* and *Le Grand Monarque* had turned to water, betrayed and brought to an end the eight-hundred-years-old Monarchy of France.

As soon as the shooting started Roger decided to go out and see what was happening. Now that victory seemed so unexpectedly and unwarrantably to have crowned the nervous bungling of the conspirators, it was no longer imperative that he should remain with them to maintain his new status; and he had a momentary flicker of hope that the firing might be caused by some resolute Royalists making a belated attempt to rescue the King from his own folly.

At the door of the Chamber a Municipal employee, anxious to toady to his new masters, had produced some rolls of broad *tricolore* ribbon, and was snipping off lengths of it for any of the new Commissars who approached him. Roger availed himself of two yards, threw one end over his left shoulder and tied it to the other end in a big bow on his right hip. It was the symbol of authority which had been worn by the members of the old Municipal Council, and which meant far more in Paris than did the laced hat of a General. Running down the steps on which the heroic Marquis de Mandat had so recently been done to death, Roger emerged into the sunshine of the August morning as Citizen Commissioner Breuc.

The Hôtel de Ville faced on to the Place de Grève—the Tyburn of Paris, in which great crowds collected whenever there was a public execution; but it was almost empty now, as the centre of the disturbance lay nearly three-quarters of a mile away. The southern end of the Place opened on to the river, so Roger hurried across it and along the quay. When he reached the end of the Pont Neuf he was slowed down by the crowd that was still streaming across it from the south bank, but by half-past nine he was near enough to see for himself the cause of the shooting. It was no attempt to rescue the Royal Family—the *fédérés* and the National Guards were attacking the Tuileries.

Having penetrated with difficulty as far as one of the entrances to the Place du Carrousel he found that the attackers were shooting up at the windows of the Palace and that the soldiers at them were returning their fire. Retreating into cover, he came upon an officer of the National Guard who was staunching the blood from a slight wound in his arm, and asked him why, as the King had gone to the Assembly, fighting had broken out.

With a respectful glance at Roger's *tricolore* sash the officer replied, "It was the Marseillais, Citizen Commissioner; they have marched all the way to Paris not on account of the war, but in the hope of plunder. As soon as it was known that the King had left the Palace, General Westermann led them to the great gates over there; someone opened them and the main doors of the Palace as well. My men were in the Cour Royale, but as the King had gone they offered no resistance. The Swiss had retreated inside the building and a number of them were massed on the grand staircase. General Westermann called on them to lay down their arms, but they refused to do so, then some of the Marseillais used their long pikes with hooks at the end to pull the foremost Swiss from the staircase. Five of them were dragged out that way into the courtyard and butchered there. Who fired the first shot I don't know, but if it was a Swiss one could not blame him. For a few moments the fighting became general, then the Swiss fired a couple of volleys and the *fédérés* took to their heels. The Swiss promptly cleared the court, and the situation became as you see it. That was half an hour ago."

"But why," asked Roger, "have your men now joined the *fédérés* in shooting at the Swiss, instead of trying to keep order?"

The officer shrugged. "They were in quite good heart early this morning, and were prepared to defend the Palace; but when the King came out to inspect us he made a very bad impression on them. His sneaking off to the Assembly finished him as far as they were concerned. When General Westermann's crowd entered the Cour Royale the women among the mob began to get at them, and persuade them to fraternize with the Marseillais. My brother officers and I did what we could to stop them, but when the Swiss fired their volleys into the courtyard several women were killed; after that there was no stopping my men from going over to the mob."

For a further quarter of an hour desultory firing continued on both sides, then a sudden cry went up, "Save yourselves! Save yourselves!"

Peering round his corner, Roger saw that a body of Swiss had made a sally from the Cour Royale. With well-disciplined precision they were driving the *fédérés* before them, winkling them from the cover of doorways and from some low buildings in the middle of the square as they advanced. Meanwhile the crowd was stampeding towards the river, and Roger was carried back with it on to the quay. In less than three minutes the Place du Carrousel had been completely cleared of the attackers; and the Swiss, taking their time, collected some small cannon that the Marseillais had abandoned in their flight, before returning unmolested to the Palace.

The episode made Roger more than ever disgusted with the King, as it gave incontestable proof that he could have stayed with complete safety in the Tuileries. The building had been broken into only because, Mandat being dead, no order to resist had been given; yet, even then, the 750 Swiss that the King had left there had not only ousted the attackers but had also cleared its courts and approaches. With the full battalion, together with several hundred gentlemen and over 2,000 National Guards, he could not only have defied the mob, but used the riots as a legitimate excuse to deprive the treacherous Municipality of its power and to arrest the Committee of Insurrection. But, as it soon emerged, Louis XVI was that day to be guilty of something far worse than folly.

When the Swiss had retired into the Palace the Marseillais edged cautiously forward again and resumed their sporadic firing at its windows. The fire was returned, but only for a few minutes; then, quite inexplicably, it ceased. Suspecting a trap, the attackers were most chary of advancing, but at length, goaded into action by the taunts of their women, a few of the boldest crept along the sides of the Place du Carrousel and into the Cour Royale. Still not a shot was fired at them, so greater numbers began to follow. The first group entered the doors of the Palace and, a moment later, emerged again to stand cheering wildly on its steps. The crowd surged forward and Roger, leaving his observation post, moved forward too. Another moment, and the reason for this bloodless victory was being passed excitedly from mouth to mouth. From the Assembly the King had sent a personally signed order to the Swiss that they were to cease fire and retire to their barracks.

He had been told that the shots he had been hearing for upwards of an hour were those of his Swiss "massacring the people"; but a single thought for his devoted troops would have told him that, after a fight had been raging that long, to order them to cease fire without any guarantee that their opponents would reciprocate was to hand them over to the mercy of their enemies. Still worse, by ordering them to retire to their barracks he deprived them even of the shelter of his Palace, as in order to obey him they had to leave it and cross the Tuileries gardens, which meant running the gauntlet between strong bands of armed insurgents. Neither did he spare a thought for the several hundred gentlemen who had come to the Palace during the night prepared to die for him; it was as certain as the sun would set that the very sight of these *aristos* would arouse the bloodlust of the mob. Scarcely an hour earlier, just as he was about to enter the Assembly, three of their class had been butchered before his eyes. By ordering the Swiss to evacuate the Palace he was also depriving them of the help necessary to defend it, and so by this horrible betrayal he was abandoning many of his personal friends to massacre. Had he sat down and signed a thousand death warrants he could not have better ensured the deaths of these loyal troops and subjects.

By the time Roger had pushed his way into the Palace the shooting had already started on its far side. Making his way upstairs, he reached a window that looked out on the gardens; below him was a spectacle that made tears of rage and frustration spring to his eyes. With incredible courage and iron discipline two long columns of Swiss were marching steadily down the main avenue. From behind the trees the *fédérés* were shooting at them, yet not one of them made a movement to disobey the King's order and return the murderous fire to which they were subjected. As the columns advanced their wounded and dying fell and were left behind. Like human hyenas the *canaille* of the Faubourgs then rushed upon them, stripped them naked and hacked them to pieces with cutlasses and knives. Near the statue of Louis XV one column, now ragged and leaving a ghastly trail of blood from the hundreds of wounds it had sustained, faltered to a halt and attempted to form a square. But most of the survivors were already dying on their feet and were no longer capable of resistance. Like a tidal wave the mob engulfed them. Sick and shaken, Roger turned away to avoid witnessing the final massacre.

In spite of the heat of the day a cold sweat had broken out on his forehead. He felt ill, dizzy and temporarily incapable of coordinating his thoughts. In the distance he could now hear shots being fired inside the Palace, and from the embrasure of the window in which he stood he gazed helplessly upon a ghastly scene.

The *fédérés* from Marseilles and from the Breton ports had been the first to burst into the Palace. At least half of the former were sea-rovers—Genoese, Moors, Sicilians and Arabs. Among the latter were many negroes and mulattos, taken from the plantations to man the ships that traded between the French West Indies and Brest and Nantes. From these brutal corsairs and ex-slaves Roger's scarf of office served to protect him personally, but he knew that his immunity would last only so long as he refrained from interfering with them.

Detachments of them had lost no time in breaking into the cellars, and were now bringing up baskets stacked high with bottles to share with their comrades. Regardless of whether the bottles contained wine or spirits, they were knocking off their tops and gulping the liquor from their necks. In an incredibly short time they were reeling drunk and seized with a senseless urge for destruction. They shattered the great mirrors with blows from their weapons, hurled priceless china and clocks to the floor, smashed the lovely furniture to matchwood and threw the pieces from the windows.

Had Roger had any plan, or any definite task to perform, he would have done his utmost to execute it; as it was he could think only of escaping from this hellish imbroglio. The door by which he had entered was now blocked by a seething mass of people, forced forward by the horde that was still pouring up the grand staircase. Turning in the other direction, he managed to elbow his way out through the far door.

The crowd was less dense in the *salon* beyond it, but the scene more horrifying. Three gentlemen lay huddled in a corner more dead than alive with bleeding heads and faces, and a score of ruffians were finishing them off by pelting them with ornaments and empty bottles.

Reaching a corridor, Roger saw that one end of it was blocked by a group committing another murder. In the other direction he glimpsed a side staircase and ran towards it. The sounds of shots, screams and curses were louder now. One company of the Swiss had failed to receive the order to retire and, on the incursion by the mob, had scattered about that end of the Palace; in groups and individually they were now being hunted to their deaths.

As Roger reached the staircase one of them came plunging down it, tripped and fell on the landing. Instantly his pursuers leapt upon him, dragged him to his feet and thrust him backwards across the banisters. With a demoniacal screech a tousle-headed harridan sprang forward and drew her knife across his throat.

Roger had shed his own blood and that of numerous other people without turning a hair, but at the sight of the poor wretch's gore spurting from the ghastly wound his stomach turned over. Swerving away, he pushed open a nearby door, staggered across a little ante-chamber and vomited in a corner.

When his nausea had eased a little, he went out by another door and found himself in a bedroom. Some women there had pulled the clothes from the wardrobes and, having half-stripped themselves of their rags, were arraying themselves in a court lady's finery. On seeing Roger one of them flung her arms round his neck, kissed him and belched in his face, while the others roared with drunken laughter.

Thrusting her off, he dashed into the next room, but he had now lost his bearings. At every turn he took he came upon some fresh scene of horror. The mob had become human tigers, intent upon butchering every inmate of the Palace—Swiss, nobles, officials, servants; none was spared. Their weapons dripping with blood, the *fédérés* and the *sans-culottes* hauled their victims from cupboards and from under beds, chased them up to the attics and down to the cellars. When Roger at length succeeded in finding another stairway and reached the ground floor, he could hear the shrieks coming up from the basement. There, these fiends, whose immunity from harm the imbecile King had placed above all other interests, were breaking his scullions' heads in with their dishes and roasting his cooks in their own ovens.

At last Roger stumbled out through a small door that gave on to the terrace. Sick, faint, bewildered, he crossed it in a daze, staggered down into the garden and collapsed upon a bench. He had been up all night and had eaten nothing since the previous evening. Physically and mentally he was exhausted.

Gradually, he began to take in the scene in front of him—it was almost as horrifying as those from which he had just escaped. During the night Santerre and his friends had found great difficulty in rousing the Faubourgs, but as the morning advanced their efforts were no longer needed. The sound of the firing, together with the news of the King's surrender and of the

Tuileries being sacked, had emptied every den and kennel in the slums of Paris. By their thousands, the criminals, the harlots, the destitute, the hungry, the diseased in mind, and the crippled in body, had swarmed from east, south and north to participate in the overthrow of the Monarchy.

In the half-mile-long garden there were now twenty *Parisiens* for every *fédéré*, and they had become infected with the furious lust of the assassins from the ports. A great part of the contents of the Palace cellars had now found its way out into the gardens; everywhere men and women were drinking from the necks of bottles, and the empties littered the ground in all directions. It was afterwards assessed that over 10,000 bottles were consumed in the course of the morning, and that at least 200 people died from the effects of the quantity of neat spirits they had drunk.

A saturnalia of the most ghastly description was taking place, as drunkenness and lechery were combined with the defiling of the bodies of the dead Swiss. Their corpses had been stripped and hung from the branches of trees, or arranged in revolting postures; while with raucous laughter and indecent jests rings of intoxicated furies of both sexes bellowed the *ça ira* and danced the *carmagnole* round them.

For a time Roger watched the hellish orgy with lacklustre eyes, scarcely taking in its horrifying details any more. Never in his life before had he felt so utterly helpless. There was nothing whatever he could do, and he was tired—most terribly tired. The exertion of getting himself elected as a Commissioner the previous night had been considerable, the long, anxious hours of waiting at the Hôtel de Ville had been an appalling strain, and the soul-shattering sights he had seen in the Palace had burned up all that had remained of his nervous energy. Matter triumphed over mind; his head nodded once or twice, then fell forward on his chest, and he slept.

CHAPTER XI

IN THE NAME OF THE LAW

WHEN Roger awoke it was late afternoon. There were still hundreds of people in the gardens, but in the majority of them the frenzy had burnt itself out. Those who were on their feet were mainly newcomers who had arrived belatedly from the more distant suburbs; most of the others were either sitting, maudlin drunk, singing unmelodiously, or sprawled out, full length, asleep. Almost at Roger's feet lay one of the scores of tightly embraced couples who were to be seen under almost every tree. The pair were dead drunk and snoring; a half-empty bottle was still clutched in the woman's outstretched hand.

Reaching down, Roger took the bottle from her, wiped its neck, and drank. It contained noyeau, a sweet liqueur made from almonds. He threw it away, got up, and hunted round until he found a nearly-full bottle of white wine. The noyeau had done nothing to make his mouth feel less gummy and parched; he rinsed it out several times and gargled with the white wine, then drained the bottle. After that he felt slightly better. Adjusting his sash and the big cockade in his hat, he set off towards the Assembly.

The doorkeepers greeted him with respect and one of them led him to a low box in the body of the hall reserved for members of the Municipality. Looking up, he saw that the public galleries were packed to suffocation, but the Chamber itself was half empty. Since his arrival in Paris, errands for Santerre had taken him to the Assembly on several occasions, and he knew that the attendance of deputies at important sittings was usually over six hundred. Now, less than half that number were present; evidently a very high proportion of the more respectable had remained at home for fear of their lives.

The Royal Party had been put in the Press box. Half a dozen nobles, who had risked their lives to join them, stood near it. They had dressed themselves up as National Guards, but among them Roger recognized the Ducs de Choiseul and de Brézé, the Comte François de la Rochefoucauld, and Talleyrand's friend, Comte Louis de Narbonne. The fleshy face of the King, with its big hook nose, was quite impassive; the Dauphin, lying across the laps of the Queen and his governess, Madame de Tourzel, was asleep; little Madame Royale was quietly crying; Madame Elizabeth and the Princesse de Lamballe looked utterly worn out. Only the Queen showed any animation; she was following the debate with keen interest, but turned every now and then to comfort her daughter, or to smile and say a cheerful word to one of her companions. Roger's heart bled for her.

For eight hours the Assembly had been debating what was to be done next. Various proposals had been put forward—that the King should be deposed, temporarily suspended from his functions, held as a hostage, or reinstated with new Ministers selected for him by the Assembly. But among the deputies there was not a single man of real vigour; they seemed bewildered, uncertain of themselves and quite incapable of handling the crisis; so nothing had yet been decided. After an hour listening to their windy vapourings Roger felt that he was wasting his time, and that he would do better to go and take his own seat in the new Commune.

When he reached the Hôtel de Ville he found a very different state of affairs. All the *enragés*—as the dyed-in-the-wool revolutionaries of the old National Assembly were termed—had been debarred from election to the Legislative Assembly, but most of them had seized on this opportunity to emerge into public life again as "the People's Commissars". To them had been added half a hundred of the most violent Jacobins and Cordeliers, the whole body being controlled by the Committee of Insurrection; so the Commune had now become the weapon of the most forceful, cunning and ruthless men in Paris. It did not take Roger long to realize that here lay the real power that would soon dominate the situation.

Although the meeting had been in session since dawn, no one appeared to think of leaving it. Some of the members had fallen asleep on the benches, but most of them were on their feet a good part of the time, either declaiming, interrupting or cheering; and to prevent hunger interfering with their long and violent debate a buffet had been set up at one end of the chamber.

Going over to it, Roger helped himself to a meal and, while he was still eating, Santerre joined him. When they had last met the big bully had been in a dither from fear of everything going wrong, and that even if he were not called to account by the authorities for his part in the insurrection, he might lose his status as a leader through Westermann reporting his cowardice to the

Committee. But now he was boisterous and boastful again; the coup had succeeded after all, and he had forestalled the Alsatian. Immediately on hearing that the King had surrendered, he had returned to the Hôtel de Ville and got himself appointed *Commandant Général* of the National Guard, in Mandat's place. The post made him practically unassailable, and he had promptly made use of it to remain well out of danger all day, at the Hôtel de Ville, on the pretext that a Commander's place was at his headquarters.

He greeted Roger effusively, and heaped congratulations on him for his work of the previous night. Apart from the wealthiest Sections of the city, that of des Granvilliers had been regarded as one of the most difficult to handle. Oysé had given a glowing report of Roger's skilful and resolute tactics, and there had been so many delays or complete failures in the other doubtful Sections that his swift coup was regarded as an outstanding success. During the course of the day, after seeing how things were going, nearly all the other Sections had elected Commissioners to the new Commune, but Roger, with his colleagues, had been among the few to arrive when this momentous day was barely an hour old, so he now found himself acclaimed as one of the heroes of the hour by Santerre and the group of men at the buffet.

When asked why, having taken his seat, he had absented himself for the rest of the day, he stated unblushingly that on hearing the shooting he had felt that matters still hung in the balance, so had gone out to use his new authority in encouraging the insurgents. He described his entry into the Palace among the first of the Marseillais, then added that he had later gone to the Assembly to see how matters were progressing there, and had only just left it.

This provoked fresh applause and great interest, as everyone wanted to hear the latest report of the way in which the deputies were reacting to the situation. Santerre jumped upon a chair, cut in on the harangue of the man who was speaking, and bellowed in his stentorian voice:

"Silence! Silence for Citizen Commissioner Breuc, the patriot who led the Marseillais in their attack on the Tuileries! He comes from the Assembly and can tell us what those useless windbags are up to there."

Roger had already realized that his new rôle would entail public speaking, and that he would defeat his own ends if the sentiments he expressed were the least half-hearted. On the other hand, the very last thing he wished to do was to use his talents to forward the aims of the Revolution; so he had decided that when he had to speak he would express the sentiments that were expected of him boldly, but very briefly, and speak as seldom as possible, relying rather upon his private contacts than upon oratory to maintain his reputation as a full-blooded patriot.

Therefore, when he had been pushed up by eager hands on to the tribune, he shouted: "Today is a great day! The People have conquered the Tyrant! To defeat his foreign slaves in uniform they gave freely of their blood. I was there! I saw them! They fought like heroes. And why did they shed their sacred blood upon those marble floors polluted by vice and idleness? It was to achieve Liberty! Equality! Fraternity!"

That was the sort of meaningless claptrap they liked, and it brought him a great ovation. Then, as it would have been both pointless and dangerous to deceive them, he gave a short but truthful account of the proceedings in the Assembly. He ended by quoting one of the well-worn tags from Rousseau's *Contrat Social*—the Bible of the Revolution, without some reference to which no such speech was complete—cried, "*Vive la Commune!*" and jumped down.

He had scarcely got the last word out before a dozen members began to speak at once, each trying to shout down his competitors. For a few minutes the chamber was a babel, but at length the speakers were reduced to two, both saying much the same thing: "Now is the moment to dethrone the King. If it is lost all may have to be done again."

Other speakers followed in rapid succession. Ignoring the fact that their election had been shamelessly framed, and that even if it had been legal they represented only Paris, whereas all but 24 out of the 700-odd deputies who made up the Assembly represented other parts of France, they declared that the Assembly no longer spoke for the nation. They alone, they now told one another, were true patriots, capable of giving expression to the wishes of the tillers of the soil and the workers in the towns, who formed the vast bulk of the population. The Assembly was a nest of reactionaries and bourgeois, who would betray the People unless they, the Commune, acted to protect the People's rights. At length a motion was put and passed with acclamation that a deputation be sent to the Assembly to inform it that the "Will of the People" was that the King should be deposed.

Twelve members, Roger among them, were chosen to form the deputation, and a little before ten o'clock they set off, packed into two hackney coaches. At the Assembly a body of obviously frightened deputies received with nervous flattery this embassy from the new and terrible Power that had come into being overnight. Roger's only contribution to the proceedings was a stern face and unbending air; several of his companions were eager enough to do the talking, and he was glad enough to be able to leave it to them.

The scene had not altered since his last visit, except that the Royal Party looked still more woebegone and weary; but they roused themselves a little at personal insults with which the Commissioners interlarded their speeches. When three of the deputation had delivered themselves of their personal remarks, and had conveyed the message from the Commune in much the same terms, Vergniaud, who had been whispering with Brissot in a corner, mounted the tribune and proposed the following plan:

That the King should be, not deposed, but suspended, while a Convention was summoned to replace the present Assembly and produce a new Constitution. In the meantime the King was to be lodged in the Palace of the Luxembourg and the government of the country carried on by a Provisional Executive Council.

This did not fit in at all with the deputation's ideas, or with those of their friends among the deputies, so the latter took up the cudgels on the Commune's behalf and an acrimonious debate ensued that went on until nearly three o'clock in the morning. By that time the unfortunate Sovereigns, with their family and friends, had been sitting in the Press box for close on seventeen hours. No decision as to their final fate having yet been arrived at, it was then agreed to accommodate them for the rest of the night in some of the cells at the ex-convent of the Feuillants; and, this much having been settled, the deputation returned to the Commune.

The negative result of their mission was far outweighed by two facts of immense significance. By admitting the right of the new Commune to have a say in matters at all, the Assembly had tacitly acknowledged it a legally constituted body, and had not yet dared to take a decision in defiance of its wishes.

Members who had been active all day were now falling asleep

where they sat, but others who had been sleeping woke up again and took part in the new arguments—as was the custom during a crisis at these *en permanence* sessions. However, Roger, now feeling his position to be assured, and like the sensible fellow he was, saw no reason why he should sleep on a bench when he could do so in a bed; so at a quarter past four he went back to the Cushion and Keys.

It was past midday when he awoke, but he lay in bed for some time thinking over the situation. Vergniaud's proposals clearly indicated that the Girondins did not want a Republic, but were probably aiming at a change of King. Whom they had in mind had not yet emerged and the odds were that upon that point they were still divided. Nearly all of them had originally been Orléanists; later the Duke of Brunswick had been named, but now the Duke had put himself out of the running by his manifesto there were rumours that they favoured King George's second son, the Duke of York.

Contemptuously as Roger regarded King Louis, he knew that he was at least honest, which was much more than could be said for the boorish, dissipated Duke, and as the Duke had always been one of Mr. Pitt's most inveterate enemies, it seemed unlikely that the Prime Minister would be at all pleased to see him on the throne of France. However that might be, Mr. Pitt's instructions to Roger had been to contribute in any way he could to keeping King Louis on his own throne.

That he was two-thirds off it already was fully apparent, and only one way presented itself of putting him back again—to kidnap him and carry him off to one of his still loyal Provinces. After the fiasco of his last attempt Roger had been left no illusions that he might yet persuade the King and Queen to entrust themselves to him, but there remained the possibility that he might rescue them against their will.

From the moment the idea first occurred to him he had realized that the chances of pulling off such a coup would be far greater if he could gain for himself a position of authority which would give him ready access to the Sovereigns, and it was largely the determination to do so that had enabled him to stick out the hideous six weeks he had spent at the Axe and Facies. Now, that horribly unpleasant experience had paid an extraordinarily handsome dividend. He was a recognized revolutionary leader and a powerful official of the Municipality; he could demand admission to the King at any time he liked, and he did not believe that anyone would dare to refuse it to him. But it was one thing merely to go and speak to the King, and quite another to spirit him away with his wife and children without anyone attempting to prevent it. He could but keep his wits about him and hope that the uncertainties of the crisis might suggest to him a more detailed plan and provide him with an opportunity to execute it.

Having dressed, he ate a hearty meal and immediately afterwards went straight to the Hôtel de Ville. Quite a number of his colleagues had, like himself, gone home for a few hours' sleep, but the *Conseil Général de la Commune*, as it styled itself, was now setting about its business in earnest. The cautious Robespierre had taken his seat that morning, and a *Comité de Surveillance*—which replaced the old Committee of Insurrection—was formed to guide the Commune in its struggle with the Assembly. Robespierre now came to the fore as its directing brain and, mainly at his instance, a number of decrees to strengthen the Commune's powers were rapidly being put through.

The 20,000 signatories of the petition to the King, asking him to oppose the establishment of a great camp for the *fédérés* outside Paris, were prohibited from holding any public office as "enemies of the People". By a new measure, the policing of Paris was secured to the Commune, while all active citizens were empowered to drag anybody suspected of a crime against the State in front of the Sectional Tribunals, and unlimited powers of imprisonment were accorded to the Communal Commissars.

While all this was going on, the dispute with the Assembly regarding the future of the King was continued by a number of deputations. The Commune accepted the proposal for a Conventional Assembly to replace the Legislative, but rejected the suggestion that the King should be lodged in the Luxembourg, on the grounds that it had secret passages leading from its cellars which might be used for his escape. Further, it boldly asserted that the Commune was the proper body to be given the custody of the Royal Family.

At nine o'clock in the evening, having spent the intervening hours in cheering at the right times and voting by raising his hand whenever a majority did so, Roger went to the Assembly.

There, he learned that the Girondins Roland, Clavière and Servan had been recalled to serve as Ministers in a Provisional Government, with Dumouriez's late subordinate, Lebrun, at the

Foreign Office, and that, as a sop to the extremists, Danton had been made Minister of Justice. With a mirthless grin Roger thought of the old saying about the tail wagging the dog, as he had no doubt at all that the voracious Danton would eat up his crooked but timorous colleagues in no time at all.

The Royal Family had spent another awful day in the reporters' box, and were still there listening to the dispute about what should be done with them. It had just been proposed that they should be lodged at the Hôtel de la Chancellerie in the Place Vendôme, but the Commune had not yet given its views on this, and it was now unlikely that the matter would be settled until the following day; so they were led off to spend another night in the Feuillants.

After waiting for a quarter of an hour, Roger left the Assembly and walked round the corner to the convent. His sash proved the passport he had expected, and no one attempted to stop him as he entered. He told a National Guard officer whom he met in the hall that he wished to assure himself that the Royal Family could not escape. The officer deferentially explained to him the system of guards that had been arranged, then led him to the end of a corridor and pointed down it to four cells that had been allotted to his charges. The corridor, however, was not empty: it was occupied by the gentlemen who had managed to remain with the King, and by several of the royal servants, who were making up shakedowns for themselves on the floor for the night.

Roger had been toying with the idea of asking Dan to collect his squad and a coach and returning with them in the early hours of the morning, but he saw now that any attempt to carry off the Royal Family in their present circumstances must prove hopeless. All their loyal retainers would clamour to accompany them, then, unless they had been officially informed that they were to be entirely deprived of attendants, they would probably refuse to leave until the matter had been referred to a higher authority; and that would be the end of Citizen Commissioner Breuc.

From the Feuillants he went back to the Hôtel de Ville and put in a couple of hours at a midnight sitting, during which the proposal to lodge the Royal Family in the Hôtel de la Chancellerie was rejected and a counter-proposal carried that they should be taken to the Temple, an ancient building in northern Paris not far from Roger's Section, which belonged to the Comte d'Artois.

The next day was a Sunday, but that did not mean any break in the sittings of public bodies; so, after sleeping again at the Cushion and Keys, Roger attended the Commune, arriving about ten o'clock in the morning. The Assembly had rejected the suggestion regarding the Temple, so the matter had now been referred to a Commission; but the point at issue had emerged more clearly—the Assembly wished to save the prestige of the Throne by interning the King in a palace, whereas the Commune wished to put him in a prison.

During the day the Commune pressed on with its now quasi-legal seizure of power and measures to crush any resistance to its will. By its decree all reactionary journals were suppressed; and, as the Assembly had sent Commissioners to the armies requiring them to take an oath of fidelity to the new Provisional Government, the Commune now despatched Commissioners to the Jacobin cells among the troops, to inform them that Louis XVI was overthrown and that there was no fear of treachery at home because the Commune of Paris was watching over the Assembly.

In the late afternoon Roger felt like stretching his legs, so he took the slightly longer route to the Assembly by way of the quays and the Tuileries gardens. The Sunday crowds were entirely pacific and were mainly composed of people who had come in from the country out of curiosity. Those who were morbid-minded had ample opportunity to satisfy their ghoulishness, as no attempt had been made to clear away the evidence of Friday's horrible excesses. Every tree was surrounded by piles of empty bottles, and within fifty yards of where the new Government of France was sitting still lay the naked bodies of the murdered Swiss, now covered with flies and stinking with putrefaction after three days in the hot sun.

In the Press box at the Assembly the Royal Family were enduring their third long day of suspense, but the Commission had not yet given its recommendation on their fate, and was rumoured to be quarrelling violently. Roger had reached the conclusion that his only chance of spiriting the prisoners away would occur when a definite decision had been reached. Then, when everybody was expecting their removal, he might be able to forestall the officials charged with escorting them to their new domicile, and whisk them off into hiding.

It now seemed unlikely that they would be removed until next day, as, wherever they were to be taken, a few hours would be needed to make arrangements for their reception; but a decision might be reached that night, so he felt that he ought to have the preparations for his attempt completed by dawn.

After only a short visit to the Assembly he left again. Outside, in the Passage des Feuillants, he slipped behind an outjutting wall, removed his *tricolore* sash and stuffed it in his pocket. Then, in the Rue St. Honoré, he hailed a cab and was driven out to M. de Talleyrand's charming little house at Passy.

As he had expected, the grey-haired butler, Antoine Velot, and his plump, elderly wife, Marie, who for many years had been the Bishop's cook, were its only occupants. The pink-cheeked old man was delighted to see Roger again and said that he had been expecting a visit from him for some weeks, as his master had written in June to say that M. le Chevalier was returning to Paris and might make use of the house.

Roger sent him to find his wife, then asked the couple if they would be willing to risk very grave trouble, and possibly their lives, by hiding in the house a noble family who stood in danger of death from the revolutionary authorities. Velot smiled at his wife, who nodded, then he replied:

"M. le Chevalier, Marie and I have had our lives, and we have passed them happily in the service of gracious people. I see no future for old folks like ourselves now that the *canaille* have become the masters; so if we should lose them that would not be too much to pay for the many kindnesses we have received from our good nobility."

"Well said, *mon vieux*," Roger smiled back; "I felt sure I could rely on you. I hope to bring my friends here tomorrow night, and we shall be a party of five or maybe six; so please have beds made up and get in food for that number. We shall be here a week at least, perhaps longer, as it will take me some time to make arrangements to get these unfortunate people to the coast. Do you think they could remain here for that length of time without their presence being suspected?"

Old Marie waved a hand towards the window that looked on to a leafy garden. "Why not, Monsieur? All our best rooms are at the back of the house: provided they occupy only those, no one will see them through the windows. No one ever calls on us now that Monseigneur l'Évêque is abroad. One of our next-door neighbours has already emigrated, and on the other side we have an elderly couple who live very quietly."

"What you tell me is most reassuring," Roger nodded. Then for a while they chatted of the good days, when the house had always been filled with merry people, and of the Bishop's famous buffet breakfasts, which had been such a feature of the old intellectual life of Paris. Before leaving he gave them some money, with a caution to buy the food required at shops some distance off where they were not known, then he drove back to Paris.

From the café near *La Belle Étoile*, in which he had made arrangements with Dan before moving to the Cushion and Keys, he sent a message to him; and when Dan joined him there they discussed matters in low voices over a bottle of Anjou.

Dan reported that during the past week he had secured three more adherents and could, had he wished, have sounded many others with good prospects, as all the better men in the National Guard were openly resentful of the insults put upon the King; but he had thought it wiser not to increase the number further, as every extra man meant an additional risk of betrayal. With Roger and himself they would now be a round dozen, including two sergeants and a corporal, and he went on to describe each man's background.

When he had finished, Roger praised him for his zeal and caution, then gave him his instructions. He said that they would need a coach with two fast horses, which could be obtained from Blanchard's yard. Dan was to ask for a volunteer to drive it, making it clear that the risk involved in this particular job would be much greater than that for the others. The driver was to wear civilian clothes and bring the coach to the cul-de-sac behind the Church of St. Roche soon after dawn next day; the others, in uniform, were to join him there. Dan was to check their arrival, then come round to the porch of the church and wait for Roger; and, as Dan was to play the part of a second Commissar, he was to get himself a piece of broad *tricolore* ribbon and make a sash of it for use when required.

They talked for a while of the crisis, finished their wine, then impulsively shook hands—as the silent English way of expressing their trust in one another for the dangerous venture to which they were now committed—and parted. By ten o'clock Roger, once more wearing his scarf of office, was back at the Commune.

During his absence the session had been notified by the Assembly that its Commission could not reach agreement about the disposal of the King; so the Commune, now feeling itself strong enough to take the law into its own hands, had replied with a peremptory message to the effect that it would stand for no further evasions, and had decided that the Royal Family must be surrendered to it next day for transfer to the Temple.

Everyone realized that this would provoke a real test of strength between the two bodies; so the occupants of the Chamber were in a state of voluble excitement that prevented the introduction of any other serious business. Santerre was there talking to Rossignol and, taking them aside for a drink, Roger put out the suggestion that the best way to deal with the Assembly was to ignore it, and to go and collect the King themselves.

As he had felt sure would prove the case, they were much too cowardly to engage themselves in such a risky undertaking. They hurriedly shelved the proposal by replying that they thought the idea an excellent one, but that before carrying it out it would be better to wait until the Assembly had shown the attitude it meant to take to the note sent it that evening.

Having planted the idea in their minds, Roger talked to them on other matters; then, finding that his own mind now refused to concentrate for any length of time on anything other than nervous speculations connected with his proposed coup, he used the temporary suspension of the debate as an excuse to go home early.

Half an hour before dawn next day he was up and dressed. He went first to the Commune, where he learned that no reply had yet been received to the challenge it had sent the Assembly; next he kept his appointment with Dan in the porch of St. Roche. He told him that as nothing had been settled they might have to hang about all day; so he should prepare his men accordingly, and send two of them straight off to buy a good supply of food and drink so that it would not be necessary for them to leave the vicinity of the coach later. Then he crossed the Rue St. Honoré, walked the two hundred yards along it to the entrance of the Passage des Feuillants, and so to the Assembly.

There, only routine business was being dealt with; no more than a hundred members were present and many of them were sound asleep. Gradually the Chamber and the public galleries began to fill up. At eight o'clock the Royal Party was brought in and, for the fourth day, installed in the box on the dais behind the President's desk; shortly afterwards the debate on their future was resumed.

To Roger, now almost jittery with nerves at the thought of the self-appointed task that lay before him, the long, windy speeches of the deputies were positive torture. They quoted Rousseau by the yard, spoke of the purity of their own intentions, of the virtues of the People, of the wickedness of the King in using the veto they had given him, and openly accused the Queen of conspiring with France's enemies, but few of them would commit themselves on the point at issue, further than to assert half-heartedly that it was for them and not the Commune to decide the matter.

At midday a strong deputation from the Commune appeared and was received at the bar of the house. Several of its members also spoke of the People's virtues, and of their own, but they also showed a grim determination to carry through the mission they had been sent upon. At half-past one the Assembly, cowed by the menacing demeanour and open threats of the Commissars, gave way. It was agreed that the Sovereigns should be lodged in the Temple and that the Commune of Paris be given the responsibility for their safe-keeping.

The Royal Party was then led from their box, but Roger knew that a considerable time must elapse before arrangements could be made to convey them to their new quarters, and he dared not be too precipitate.

While he waited one thought came to cheer him a little. His chance of being allowed to remove the Royal Family from the Feuillants in the middle of the day was much greater than it would have been during the night or very early in the morning, as the audacity of making the attempt when the maximum number of people were about would render it less likely to be suspected.

On the other hand he would be deprived of the friendly darkness, under cover of which the coach might have vanished without trace before a hue and cry started; and in daylight it would be much too risky to drive straight out to Passy, as scores of people might notice the coach *en route* and afterwards inform pursuers which way it had gone. But those factors would have had to be faced had he had no alternative but to make the attempt at dawn, so he had already decided on a plan which he hoped would fox the pursuers if only he could manage a clear quarter of an hour's start.

For the first few hundred yards the coach would have to proceed at a walking pace so that Dan's squad, marching on either side, could keep up with it; and he meant it to set off northwards, across the Place Vendôme, as though going to the Temple. But as soon as it got through the square it would turn west instead of east and, once round the corner, break into a smart trot, leaving the guards behind. By turning down the Boulevard de la Madeleine, it should be able to reach the quiet streets to the north of the Champs Elysées within five minutes. Thence he meant to head for the Bois de Boulogne, and if he could reach it without being overtaken he reckoned they would be fairly safe. At a quiet spot his companions would leave the coach and hide with him in one of the dense thickets there for the rest of the day, while it was driven on out into the country. With luck it might get clear away, but if caught the driver was to say that his passengers had transferred to a six-horse coach that had been waiting for them at the Place de Neuilly. No one would ever suppose that the Royal Family had alighted in order to walk, but that was what he was determined they should do for the last couple of miles of their journey; and he felt confident that once he had convinced the brave Queen of the honesty of his intentions she would make no bones about it. Thus, by bringing them through the Bois to the quiet village of Passy, which lay on its south-eastern outskirts, after darkness had fallen, he hoped to get them safely to their hiding-place without anyone having the faintest idea where to look for them.

At two o'clock Roger left the Assembly, and five minutes later was in the church porch giving Dan his final instructions. He explained his whole plan, then said, "You can now join your squad and tell them that we are about to rescue the Royal Family. Make the coachman repeat twice the route he is to take; but you are not to tell any of them about the house at Passy. When the church clock strikes the half hour, you are to put on your sash, get in the coach and drive down the street to the entrance of the Feuillants Passage; the guard will escort you on foot. There the coach will halt, you will get out, and the squad will march behind you down the passage to the main door of the convent. I shall be there waiting for you. The men will line up on either side of the door, and we shall go inside. While they are waiting for us they are not to enter into conversation with anybody. If they are asked what they are doing there, the senior sergeant is to reply that they form part of General Santerre's headquarters guard and were sent with you from the Hôtel de Ville. When we appear with our prisoners it is of the utmost importance that the squad should remain absolutely wooden and show no mark of respect for the King. They will form up on either side of the Party, escort it to the coach, and escort the coach until it has passed out of the Place Vendôme; then they should disperse as quickly as possible. Finally, you must impress upon them that the success of the plan depends almost entirely on their adhering absolutely to their orders. If anything does go wrong while we are inside the convent I shall make some remark to you, addressing you as Citizen Commissioner. If I do that your job is to get out as quickly as you can, march the men to the coach, pile them into it, drive off, and disperse them as soon as you are at a safe distance. Is that all clear?"

"Aye, aye, Cap'n." Dan touched his forelock, grinned and turned away.

As soon as he had disappeared round the corner, Roger went back into the Rue St. Honoré and entered a café. He knew that he might not have a meal for hours, so ought to eat something, but he was much too wrought up to tackle more than a ham roll, and that he got down only with the aid of a double cognac.

At twenty-five-past two he crossed the road and walked down the Feuillants Passage. Now that the moment for action had arrived the nervous fear from which he had been suffering all the morning had vanished. His blue eyes were hard and cold; his chin, covered with two days' stubble, stuck out aggressively. With his seedy, ill-fitting clothes, but determined bearing and bright sash of authority, he looked every inch the earnest young revolutionary.

As he entered the hall of the convent two National Guard officers saluted him, and the senior, a captain, came forward to ask what he required. Halting just inside the door, he replied, "I am waiting for my colleague and the escort."

"You are here to remove the King, then," said the Captain.

"Of course." Roger nodded.

"May I see your authority?"

Roger's eyebrows went up. "The Assembly has decreed that the Commune should assume responsibility for the safe-keeping of the Royal Family. My presence is authority enough, but if you wish I will sign a receipt for the Party before we leave."

The tramp of feet was already audible; Dan appeared outside with his squad of National Guards. He and Roger exchanged a formal greeting. The squad formed two lines in accordance with its orders. Dan entered the hall; Roger turned to the officer beside him and said, "Citizen Captain, lead us to the King."

The Captain looked at his lieutenant and gave the order, "Turn out the guard!"

"Stop!" snapped Roger, holding up his hand. "By the order of the Commune no honours are to be paid to Monsieur and Madame Veto."

"Very well, Citizen Commissioner," murmured the Captain. "This way, if you please."

With Roger and Dan following, he led them to the corridor where the Royal Family had its quarters. Several of the King's retainers were standing there talking together in low voices. At the sight of the two Commissars they made way, eyeing them gloomily but without hostility. The Captain rapped on the door of one of the cells. A voice from within cried "*Entrez!*"

Roger pushed the door open and, followed by Dan, stepped into the cell. The King was standing with his head outlined against the square of a small barred window set in the thick stone wall. The Queen was sitting on the hard, narrow, nun's bed that she had occupied for the last three nights. She had aged greatly in the past week, and her cheeks were furrowed with tears. They were alone there.

Without removing his hat, or even inclining his head, Roger said in a harsh voice: "Monsieur, you have heard the decision of the Assembly. Arrangements will be made for a limited number of your attendants to follow. In the name of the Law, I require you and your immediate family to come with me."

CHAPTER XII

THE BEGINNING OF THE TERROR

"*Mon Dieu!*" exclaimed the Queen; "it is Monsieur de Breuc!"

Roger had expected them to recognize him. He knew that the worst risk he ran was that, in the presence of their guards, one of them might make some reference to the past which would arouse suspicion about his present intentions. In the hope of silencing her, he replied insolently:

"Like the Monarchy, Madame, and much else that is useless in France, prefixes have been abolished. When you have cause to address me it should be as Breuc—or, if you prefer it, by my new rank as Citizen Commissioner."

"Ah!" she cried impulsively, springing to her feet. "Since the trap you laid for us failed you now reveal yourself in your true colours! But your ribbon should be entirely red, Monsieur, for you are indeed a man of blood. When no more than a youth, you slew M. de Caylus. I realized that I must have been mad to pardon you for that, when I heard how you had had the Spanish Envoy strung up to a lantern. And now you are come to murder us!"

Her attitude now was much what Roger had hoped it would be. He shrugged, and retorted with an icy smile, "If the People charged me with your execution, Madame, I would carry it out. As it is, you need have no fear; I am charged only with conveying you safely to the place appointed as your prison."

"Prison?" repeated the King, who was so literal-minded that for months past he had carried a copy of the Constitution in his pocket in order to be able to show his Ministers that he knew it better than they did. "Nothing was said about prison, Monsieur. And you are incorrect in saying that the Monarchy has been abolished; I have only been suspended from my functions."

Suddenly Roger felt sorry for that awkward, unlovely, pathetic figure. But he dared not show it, and every moment was precious. "I have no time to split hairs with you," he said roughly. "Call your sister and the children, and we will set off."

"But we cannot leave entirely unattended," protested the King.

"I have already told you that arrangements will be made for your attendants to follow."

"You mentioned a limited number. What did you mean by that, Monsieur?"

Feeling certain that the Royal Family would be allowed only a very small establishment at their new abode, Roger had automatically used the word "limited". Now he mentally cursed his thoughtlessness, and said hurriedly, "I meant only that an extravagant horde of retainers would not be tolerated."

With maddening slowness the King began to name the most important members of his household, ticking them off on his thick fingers. The Queen joined in and they began to discuss which of these should be regarded as essential.

Having listened for a few minutes, Roger could bear it no longer, and broke in:

"Monsieur! Madame! All this can be settled later. Where are your children?"

"I will fetch them," said the Queen in a low voice, and Dan made way for her to go out into the corridor. She was absent for over ten minutes—minutes that seemed like hours to Roger. He dared not show too much haste, yet knew that every moment lost decreased their chances of getting away safely. He was about to follow the Queen when the King suddenly reverted to the matter of his attendants by saying:

"Even in my new circumstances it would not be fitting for me to have less than a dozen gentlemen, besides my valets and other servants; and the Queen——"

"Yes, yes, Monsieur!" Roger rudely cut him short, and pointed to the door. "All that will be arranged. Be good enough to precede me."

At that moment the Queen appeared in the corridor with her children, accompanied by Mesdames Elizabeth, de Tourzel and de Lamballe. It was evident that she expected to take them all with her, so Roger said quickly:

"My colleague and I have to ride with you, Madame. We can take Madame Elizabeth, but your ladies will have to remain behind."

The Marquise de Tourzel stepped forward, blocking the doorway, and cried in a high, excited voice, "I am the *gouvernante* to Monseigneur le Dauphin! It is my right to accompany him wherever he goes. I insist upon it!"

"Madame," snapped Roger, "you have no rights! And we have only one coach: nine persons is too many for it."

"Then," said the King, with the stolid common sense that he displayed only in everyday matters, "since you are the master here, give orders for another to be brought."

Roger was now in an agony of apprehension. By this time the news that the Royal Family were about to be taken away must have run through the convent and reached the Assembly. At any moment someone with more authority than himself might appear on the scene, bringing ruin to his plan and exposing him and his confederates as plotters, liable to the death penalty. His blue eyes ablaze, he stormed at Madame de Tourzel:

"Get out of the way, woman! I will not allow your absurd pretensions to interfere with my duty. My orders are to remove the King and his family, and for that one coach is sufficient."

The Marquise retreated into the corridor, but Marie Antoinette was not the woman to be intimidated by anybody. Stepping forward, she said haughtily:

"Monsieur, I refuse to leave without my ladies. I understand that M. Pétion is still Mayor of Paris, and is therefore your superior. He has always shown us a reasonable consideration, and I demand that this matter should be referred to him."

Roger's impulse was to cry, "Oh God! If only I had some way to make you realize the truth and trust me, instead of talking of appealing to that hypocrite!" But he was not even given time to formulate an answer. Above the noise of footsteps a few yards along the corridor an oily voice came clearly:

"Madame, I heard you mention my name. Be pleased to inform me what is going on here, and in what way I can serve you." A second later there came into Roger's view the heavy profile, high, bald forehead and frizzed hair of the treacherous Pétion.

Behind the Mayor were his *Procureur*, Manuel, and another Commissioner whom Roger did not know. In an instant he realized that they must be the real nominees sent by the Commune to remove the Royal Family. They had arrived earlier than he had expected. Even so, had the King and Queen not held matters up for twenty minutes by attempting to preserve a remnant of their prestige, he might have saved them. It seemed as if there was a curse upon them which made of themselves the instrument to wreck every plan devised for their salvation. Now, there was no alternative but to abandon them to their fate. He could only hope that by swift action he might yet save Dan and his friends, and himself.

Before the Queen had a chance to answer, Roger forestalled her by himself appealing to Pétion. "Citizen Mayor," he cried, "my colleague and I are here to remove the Veto Family to the Temple. They want to take a score of intriguers with them. Why should they be allowed to keep their parasites at the expense of the People?"

Pétion gave him a surprised look. "But how do you come to be mixed up in this matter? It is I, and those with me, who have been charged by the Commune to undertake it."

Like all good commanders Roger had provided himself with a line of retreat. It was far from being a certain bridge to safety, but he now put it to the test. "I discussed this business with General Santerre last night, and he agreed with me that whatever view the Assembly might take it must be done."

At Santerre's name Pétion's shifty glance faltered a trifle, then he frowned. "To anticipate the Assembly's decision was a bold step, Citizen, and you may find yourself in trouble for displaying this excess of zeal."

"With the Commune?" asked Roger sharply.

"No, no!" replied Pétion hastily. "And I have no wish to criticize any orders General Santerre may have given you."

Seizing on this admission, Roger boldly followed it up. "I am glad to hear it, Citizen Mayor. I felt certain you could not really mean that it is a bad thing to show zeal in the cause of the Revolution."

Experience had already shown him that discipline was almost unknown in the ranks of the revolutionaries. The crowds in the galleries at every meeting-place where government business was carried on bullied their own representatives; the privates in the National Guard often dictated to their officers; and under the new régime every "patriot" considered that he had a right to poke his nose into other people's business. So, having momentarily averted suspicion from his real intent, he felt that his best chance of killing it altogether lay in maintaining the rôle of a self-important busybody; and he added aggressively, "Your presence now relieves me of any responsibility, but I shall remain to assist you in the duty we both came upon."

Pétion, obviously anxious not to make a gratuitous enemy of such a fiery young Commissar, replied in an unctuous voice,

"We shall be pleased to associate you with us, Citizen. We brought two coaches and it will be just as well to have two or more Commissioners riding in each, as the news of the move has spread abroad and there is now a mob collecting outside."

"Then if you have ample coach room we can dispose of ours," said Roger promptly. It was the very opportunity he had been praying for, and with a swift glance at Dan, he said:

"Do you wish to accompany us, Citizen Commissioner?"

Dan looked as big a pirate as any of the Marseillais, yet cleaner than many of the Commissars who had been sent to the Commune by the slum Sections. He shrugged his broad shoulders, tilted his beard with a slight toss of the head, and muttered:

"Too many cooks spoil the broth, Citizen. I'll dismiss our escort and get back to the Hôtel de Ville."

As he shouldered his way out, Manuel looked at Roger with a frown and asked, "Who is that Commissioner? I don't recall his face."

The *Procureur* was a thin, dark, middle-aged man. Before the Revolution he had earned his living as a tutor; so he was well educated, and possessed a quick intelligence. Roger, now greatly relieved that all his fellow conspirators would soon be out of danger, met Manuel's glance squarely, and shook his head:

"I think his name is Durand, but I am not certain. I know nothing more of him than that he was elected by one of the south bank Sections. He was with several of us last night when we were discussing this business, and later volunteered to accompany me."

Again Roger was aware that he was treading on terribly thin ice; but the explanation was plausible. No member of the new Commune had yet had time to get to know all his colleagues, even by sight. At least a third of them were hitherto unknown outside their own localities—workers like Bichot, who had been pushed in to make certain of the *sans-culottes'* vote. Some of them had already been withdrawn by their Sections, in order that more able men might be substituted. During the crisis everything had remained in a state of flux; no official list of the members of the Commune had yet been compiled and Roger had chosen Durand for Dan as one of the commonest names in France. If Dan never appeared again it would be difficult to prove that he had never been elected; but if any enquiry were set on foot about this little conspiracy that Santerre was supposed to have fathered the previous night, things might become very awkward.

Suddenly the Queen spoke: "Messieurs, when you have settled your own affairs, perhaps you would be good enough to attend to ours."

They were still all crowded together; the King and Roger in the cell, Pétion, Manuel, the other Commissioner and Madame de Tourzel in the corridor, the Queen and her children in the doorway. Naturally, now that a move was about to take place, she was anxious to get away to more spacious and comfortable quarters as soon as possible. Her impatient outburst distracted the attention of Manuel and Pétion from Roger, for which he was profoundly grateful. From that point on he put in a truculent word only now and again.

Over an hour elapsed before a start was made. The Royal Family had arrived there only with the things in which they stood, and had since received only some clothes for the Dauphin from Lady Gower, who had a small boy of his age, and some linen for the Queen sent by the Duchess de Grammont; so it was no business of packing that caused the delay. But Roger had been right in his supposition that they would be allowed to take only a limited retinue. The Commune had ordered that the King was to be deprived of his gentlemen, and it took him quite a long time to persuade Pétion to agree that the two valets, Chamilly and Hue, were not included in this order; then there was further argument about who should be allowed to accompany the Queen. At length it was agreed that she might take three of her women, as well as Mesdames de Lamballe and de Tourzel and the latter's daughter, Pauline, who happened to be with them.

Soon after four o'clock they set out; the Royal Party with Pétion and Manuel in the first big coach, the waiting women and valets with Roger and the other Commissar in the second. The latter seemed such a nonentity that Roger could not imagine why he should have been chosen as a representative of the Commune on an important occasion like this. His name was Simon; he was a shoemaker by trade, a scruffy little man who reeked of garlic. His nose was large and flat, his eyes small and squinting, and above them his eyebrows formed two circumflex accents. He was wearing a felt pudding-basin hat, the battered brim of which was turned up all round; and below it, on either side, protruded tufts of straight, shaggy hair about five inches in length.

The journey gave Roger a very good idea of what the last stages of the Royal Family's compulsory return from Varennes must have been like. Into each of the great coaches were crowded eight or more people and each was drawn by only two horses; so the pace was a slow walk, and there had to be frequent halts. The crowd that had collected in the Rue St. Honoré accompanied them the whole way, booing and shouting; and there were moments when it looked as if their hatred of the Queen would no longer be satisfied by thrusting their heads through the coach windows to cry obscene abuse in her face, but that they would overturn the vehicle and tear her limb from limb.

Before the coaches had proceeded a quarter of a mile they were held up by a mob in the Place Vendôme, which insisted that the Sovereigns should be given ample leisure to contemplate "the People's honourable activities" there. They had overthrown the great equestrian statue of Louis XIV and were smashing it to pieces while crying again and again in chorus, "Thus are tyrants treated! Thus are tyrants treated!"

Roger wondered grimly if, had he arrived there with the prisoners an hour and a quarter earlier, he would have been able to get them safely through the Place; but such speculation was now futile. The sight of a mob attacking a statue was no new one to him, as for several days past the rabble had been amusing itself by eliminating all symbols of royalty from Paris, and even by attacking shops whose owners had not had the sense to take down from over their doorways coats of arms with the once-prized announcement that they had the honour to supply some Prince of the Blood. At last the coaches were allowed to proceed, but, with other hold-ups and halts to rest the horses, it took them over three hours to cover the two miles to their destination.

The Temple was a relic of mediæval Paris. It had been the headquarters of the Knights Templars until the suppression of the Order by Philippe le Bel, and the property consisted of a big walled garden, in which were set the Palace of the Grand Prior and a tall donjon tower some distance from it. The King and Queen were misled into believing that they were to be lodged in the Palace, by finding that the Commune had prepared an official reception for them there; but, as Roger soon learned, this hastily-planned party was really only to give the Commissars an opportunity of celebrating their triumph and of gloating over their royal prisoners. Instead of being allowed to retire, the Sovereigns and their unhappy children were compelled to stand about from seven-thirty till ten, then endure a public banquet that went on until one in the morning.

During the journey from the Feuillants, Roger had been consumed by anxiety to return to the Hôtel de Ville, so that he might endeavour to put a good light on his unauthorized activities; but the reception rendered it unnecessary. Santerre, Hébert, Tallien, Marat, Chaumette and Robespierre were all present, and, realizing that his only hope of averting the suspicion that Pétion and Manuel might entertain about him lay in showing a fanatical patriotism, he went about openly boasting that before the Assembly had been brought to heel he had taken the law into his own hands. No one questioned his right, as one of themselves, to have done so; and after an hour he could breathe freely again from the knowledge that, although his attempt at rescue had failed, it had made his position with the extremists even stronger.

Meanwhile, the great tower having been found utterly unsuitable for habitation, a smaller tower that jutted out from one of its sides was commandeered. M. Berthélemy, a scholarly bachelor who occupied it in his capacity of archivist, was evicted into the street, and into its three floors were crowded the fourteen people who made up the Royal Party, together with a score or more Commissars and guards who sat up drinking and singing for the rest of the night in rooms adjacent to the prisoners'.

Having seen them installed, and realizing the hopelessness of any further attempt at rescue for the present, Roger made his way back to the Cushion and Keys. It was nearly three o'clock when he flopped into bed, and he did so with heartfelt thanks at having had such a narrow escape from arrest, imprisonment and probable execution.

In the fortnight that followed, a state of alarm and semi-anarchy continued. The Commune's hold on the power it had usurped was still tenuous and was threatened both from outside Paris and from within.

Once more Lafayette could have saved the situation had he possessed the necessary resolution. His prestige was still enormous; the Prussians were far away on the Moselle, and he was no great distance from Paris. Had he marched upon the capital, both the Provinces and the National Guard would have supported him, and a majority in the Assembly would have thanked him for saving them from the Commune. As it was he refused to take an oath of fidelity to the Provisional Government, arrested the Commissioners it had sent to him, and entered into various measures aimed at saving the King and the Constitution. But these moves were too slow and too half-hearted. While he was still weighing his theories about the "Rights of Man" against the now obvious fact that the capital had become the prey of a gang of brigands, Danton succeeded in having him superseded in his command. He was forced to flee the country, and fell into the hands of the Austrians, paying for this, the last of his many fatal hesitations, by spending the following five years as a prisoner.

Thus relieved of the most serious menace to its continued existence, the Commune felt itself strong enough to hector the Assembly and terrorize the many thousands of honest citizens who made up the great bulk of the electorate of Paris. On the 11th of August the Assembly had appointed a court martial to try the King's ex-Ministers and a number of important civil and military prisoners who had been arrested during the riots of the previous day. On the 15th, Robespierre appeared at the bar of the House and insisted that instead of being court martialled these prisoners should be handed over for trial by the Sections, which was equivalent to ensuring their deaths. For two days the Assembly resisted the Commune's demand, then with criminal weakness sacrificed these innocent men who had done no more than carry out their duties.

The terrorization of Paris was then undertaken as a deliberate policy. On the 10th the Assembly had decreed its own dissolution as soon as a Convention could be elected to replace it. This offered a chance for the firebrands of the Commune to gain control of the National Chamber, but they knew they could count on only a small minority of votes; so they decided that their best hope lay in making the moderates believe that to attend the polls would be to risk their lives.

It was decided to spread the belief among the mob that the Royalists were plotting a *coup d'état* to release the King and murder the representatives of the People. A story was circulated that the reactionaries had 80,000 muskets concealed in their houses, and were only waiting for a few thousand more *fédérés* to leave for the front before opening the prisons and, with the help of the nobles and officers confined in them, capturing Paris for the Austrians.

Most unfortunately, events played into the hands of the plotters. On the 26th, after only a light skirmish, the frontier town of Longwy was captured by the enemy. This was made to appear the opening of a great Austro-Prussian offensive aimed at Paris, and Danton demanded the right to subject the city to domiciliary visits in search of arms.

No measure could have been better calculated to intimidate middle-class families. During the days that followed every house, office and apartment owned by people of means was searched by gangs of *sans-culottes*, who took the opportunity of threatening to return and break it up if its owner was later reported to them as being on the "wrong" side. And it did not end there. The searchers had been furnished with lists of Royalists, and the possession of a sword, a pistol, or even a sporting gun was made sufficient excuse to drag these opponents of mob law off to prison. In the course of the week thousands of arrests were made and the prisons of Paris were filled to overflowing.

Roger found himself forced to lead many of these domiciliary visits in his own Section. It was a hateful task, but vital to the maintenance of his official status, which not only enabled him to secure reliable information about the extremists' plans, but also gave him access to the Temple.

The Commune displayed a most lively fear that, somehow or other, its Royal hostages would vanish from its grasp; so hardly a day passed without some further measure designed to make their rescue more difficult. On the 19th, in the middle of the night, their remaining friends were taken from them, the Princesse de Lamballe and the de Tourzels being carted off to the prison of La Force. On the following day the King's two valets were allowed to return to him, but thereafter neither he nor the Queen was allowed to communicate with any other of their old friends or servants. By night and day 200 National Guards, equipped with cannon, guarded the Temple from attack; nobody without a pass was allowed to enter its precincts, the number of Commissars charged with acting as jailers was increased from four to eight, and instructions were issued that they were never to allow the Sovereigns out of their sight.

As a pass-holder Roger was able to witness the state of affairs at the Temple for himself, but although he saw the Royal Family taking their exercise in a railed-off part of the garden, under the personal supervision of "General" Santerre, he was not allowed to approach them. However, he knew that he could arrange to act as one of their guardians in due course, and he hoped that during his tour of duty he would be able to devise some means by which communication could be established between them and the outside world. He was well aware that they would not trust him personally; but waiters, cleaners, and carriers of wood for their fires were regularly in their immediate vicinity, and if one of these could be induced to play the rôle of messenger it seemed possible that, when the Commune's first acute apprehension had died down, their rescue might yet be accomplished.

By way of protest at the imprisonment of their Most Christian Majesties, the British Ambassador was recalled; but he left Mr. William Lindsay as *Chargé d'Affaires*, and, through the latter, Roger sent another report to his master, giving detailed particulars of the situation of the prisoners and forecasting that when the Convention met it would be dominated by the Communists. In one paragraph of the report he wrote of Danton as follows:

"The most potent personality on the political scene at the moment is the Minister of Justice. He is a little over thirty, comes from Arcis-sur-Aube and has been a moderately successful barrister. He is coarse, cruel, unscrupulous, corrupt, and owes his power largely to his unquestionable gifts as an orator. He has a foot in both camps, having intrigued his way into office with the aid of Madame Roland, while being secretly hand in glove with the most violent extremists, whom he represents in the Ministry. I have it on good authority that early this year, through the ex-Minister, M. le Comte de Montmorin, Danton accepted a considerable sum from the King as a bribe to counter certain revolutionary motions in that hotbed of communism, the Cordeliers Club. As is customary among these demagogues, he kept the money and failed to honour his promise. Recently he has seized on the war as a means of increasing his own popularity. With Gallic abandon he declaims about the honour of France and the sacred duty of all Frenchmen to defend her soil; but in secret he sees to it that call-up papers are issued only to the young men of the upper and middle classes, while exemption is given to his political supporters, the *sans-culottes*. He has deliberately prevented the Marseillais from being despatched to the front, because he wishes to make them his instrument in another Saint Bartholomew, for the destruction of her enemies *en masse*, of which plot I shall have the honour of informing you in a later portion of this despatch. Therefore, should your attention be drawn to reports in the *Monitor* of glowing orations made by M. Danton, while you should not discount their effects on the masses here, you would be well advised to disabuse your mind of any idea that he is inspired by genuine patriotism. He is governed only by a voracious appetite for power, money and women."

The plot to which Roger referred was the peak in the Communists' campaign to terrify the great mass of moderate electors. On the pretext that "honest patriots" could not be expected to go to the front while thousands of reactionaries, now in the prisons, were conspiring to break out when they had gone and murder their wives and families, the *fédérés* were to be instigated to massacre the inmates of the prisons.

Appalled as Roger was by the prospect of this heinous crime, there seemed nothing he could do to prevent it; but it did occur to him that if he informed Gouverneur Morris of the plot the rich American might find ways of procuring the release of a certain number of the intended victims before the massacre started.

It was now ten weeks since those first hectic thirty-six hours after his arrival in Paris, during which time he had met the American and had twice availed himself of Madame de Flahaut's aid in disguising himself; but he had seen neither of them since, as to have pursued his acquaintance with either might have led to unwelcome complications. The servants of the rich were by no means all trustworthy, and had one of them reported to some of his colleagues in the Commune that he was in the habit of visiting *aristos*, his whole position would have been endangered. For that reason he was loath now to seek out the banker-diplomat personally, or even to send a letter to him; so, after some thought, he sent a note to the beautiful Adèle, on the afternoon of the 29th, simply saying that he wished Mr. Morris to meet him regarding a very urgent matter on the Quai du Louvre at nine o'clock that night, and signed it *The Chimney-Sweep*.

Dusk had fallen when he reached the place of appointment; but there were few people about, so he was soon able to identify a portly figure, stumping slowly along with a wooden leg. The night was warm; so, after exchanging greetings, they went over to sit on the stone parapet, and while the river gurgled below them Roger gave a brief account of his own doings, then revealed the hideous plot.

After a few shrewd questions, the American said, "Owing to

the state of terror to which all moderate men have been reduced, I see no hope of being able to prevent this horrible business through such friends as I have in the Assembly; but, as you suggest, we might buy the release of a certain number of prisoners. The devil of it is, who among these rogues can one trust not to take the money and do nothing to earn it?"

Roger nodded. "That is the trouble. It is useless to approach any but the few at the top, who are sufficiently powerful to do as we wish without endangering their own position; and they are all either fanatics or thieves. Danton would certainly betray us; Robespierre is, I believe, both heartless and incorruptible; Marat is a criminal lunatic whose lust for blood is greater than for gold; Roland and his friends would be too frightened to interfere."

"What of Pétion?" Gouverneur Morris asked. "He is greedy and unscrupulous, and I know that in the past he took big bribes from the Court to ease its situation."

"No. He has intrigued with both sides so often already that his own position is no longer any too secure. He would take the money, but he dare not risk liberating any of the prisoners. Still, that gives me an idea. His *Procureur*, Manuel, might be your man. He is, I know, considered to be one of the reddest of the red, but I have formed the impression that he is not altogether heartless or without principles. His official position would make it easy for him to arrange releases, and if his better instincts were stimulated by a handsome compensation for the awkward business of explaining matters to his colleagues afterwards, he would, I think, observe his part of the bargain honourably."

The American slid off the parapet and stood up. "Then I will try him first; and there is no time to lose, lest he refuse and I have to try some of the lesser men. I will go at once and send one of my agents to sound him."

They shook hands, and Mr. Morris stumped away in the direction of the Tuileries gardens. As Roger watched him go, he noticed another figure emerge from the heavy shadows cast by one of the buttresses of the old Palace and limp towards its nearest entrance. In a few swift strides he crossed the road, caught up with the figure, and tapped it on the shoulder.

With amazing swiftness, the man he had followed swivelled round with his back against the wall, threw open his cloak, and drew a thin, glittering blade from a sword-cane.

CHAPTER XIII

PARIS RUNS WITH BLOOD

"COME, come, Your Grace!" said Roger in English. "Surely you would not stick that dangerous toy through the ribs of an old friend?" He would have gambled on knowing that elegant limp anywhere, and seeing it in the vicinity of Adèle de Flahaut's apartment had made him certain of the limper's identity.

M. de Talleyrand sighed with relief and put up his weapon. "So 'tis you! God be thanked! I thought myself caught by one of these cut-throats who are after me to throw me into prison."

Roger stared at him in surprise. "Do you really mean to say that you, one of the Fathers of the Revolution—a legislator who has introduced more sensible reforms into France than any other—have actually been proscribed as a reactionary?"

"Yes; and if they catch me they will like as not parade my head on a pike without further argument." The handsome Bishop laughed cynically. "Let my case be a lesson to you. The nobilty who really ground down the poor have fled abroad and are safe. It is liberals like myself who must now pay the penalty for their own folly in having undermined authority. I must have been mad to return to Paris."

"I had no idea you were back. When did you return, and why?"

"I have been back a week. I came to report the appalling repercussions that the events of the 10th of August have had in England. Till then, in spite of the publication of Edmund Burke's *Reflections on the Revolution in France*, we had managed to retain the goodwill of a strong liberal minority; but the tales of massacre and of the imprisoning of the King that have been pouring across the Channel are doing us untold damage. Charles James Fox alone has dared to defend the actions of the French mob. Even his friends among the Whig nobility criticize him severely for it; practically the only pro-French element left in Britain are the voteless people who form the radical Corresponding Societies and an out-at-elbows religious sect who call themselves Methodists. I returned to impress upon our new Government the danger they are in of uniting the whole of the English nation against us; to implore them to retrieve the situation by announcing a programme of moderation while there is still a chance of keeping

England from joining our enemies. And do you know what they said to me?"

Roger shook his head.

"Lebrun, that miserable clerk they have made Foreign Minister, had the insolence to tell me that as I put forward the English point of view so strongly it was evident that I could no longer be in sympathy with the Revolution, so I had better go back to England and he would have me listed as an *émigré*."

"Strap me! That's a fine way to reward a man for his services! There is a law by which the property of all *émigrés* is subject to confiscation."

"I know it! But one's property is a small matter compared with one's life; and it is that I am now liable to lose if I stay here. I learned this afternoon that the Commune has ordered the arrest of all the Directors of the Department of Paris, and I am one of them."

"Why do you not leave, then?"

"I cannot. I have no passport."

"But surely Lebrun——"

"No, no! The issue of passports has now been taken over by the Ministry of Justice, so that before an applicant is granted one it can be ascertained that he is in what is called a state of 'civic virtue'."

"Dare you not apply?"

"I had been to Danton already; and listen to what happened. That stinking brute welcomed me with open arms. 'What a delightful surprise, my dear Bishop,' said he; 'I could not be better pleased to see anyone at this moment. You, so talented, so clever, so subtle, are the very man to help me, and help France. Do you know that the tyrants of other countries are complaining of the way we have treated our King, and have the insolence to threaten us on that account? If I had my way I would tell them to mind their own business, or we will march upon them and aid their subjects to treat them in a like manner. But my fellow Ministers are of the opinion that the soft answer turneth away wrath; so they are anxious that a pacific reply should be framed. In fact, they want a few thousand words outlining the wicked manner in which the good, honest people of Paris had been provoked by the Sovereigns, and explaining how fully justified the People were in acting as they did on the 10th of August. Now, who better than yourself—understanding as you do the mind of despots—could perform the patriotic duty of writing this memorandum? I am told, too, that you want a passport.' "

"The blackmailing blackguard!" muttered Roger. "Naturally you refused?"

"Certainly not!" snapped de Talleyrand, rapping the point of his sword-stick sharply on the cobbles. "Had you been in my shoes and done so you are more of a fool than I take you for. Of course, they will publish the damned thing under my name now, and I shall never live it down; but nobody will believe a word of it. How could they when thousands of people saw the corpses of those poor Swiss, and when the Royal Family continue to be kept under lock and key as though they were a gang of coiners? It will do the King no harm; for to my mind he has dug his own grave and is already as good as dead. I wanted my passport; and you must admit, *mon ami*, that a live Bishop is very much more a matter for consideration than is a dead King, particularly when one happens to be the Bishop. But would you believe it, when all was done that son of a harlot, begotten on a dung-heap, said that before giving such an important person as myself a passport he must consult his colleagues. That was three days ago; each time I have called at his office since he has put me off with some excuse, and to go there again now is to risk arrest."

Had his friend's situation not been so serious, Roger would have roared with laughter. The logical de Talleyrand had run true to form in his quick realization that it was silly to have scruples about flogging a dead donkey; but Danton had also run true to form in first using him, then adopting an attitude which would secure his death. To Roger it was clear that now the *enragés* regarded the Bishop as a reactionary they had never had any intention of allowing him to leave France. Being so truly devoted to his country, he had taken it for granted that no one would ever suppose him capable of assisting its enemies; but, being venal and treacherous themselves, they had jumped to the conclusion that he would at once place his brilliant gifts at the disposal of the *émigrés* and the Austrians. So Danton had deliberately delayed his departure, knowing that he was certain to be arrested in the course of the next few days and that, once in prison, he could be liquidated among the victims of the proposed massacre. After a moment, Roger asked:

"Are you living out at Passy?"

"I was until this morning," came the quick reply; "but I am

wondering whether I dare return there, lest I find a reception committee of *sans-culottes* waiting for me."

"It would be safer not to; doubtless old Antoine told you of my visit?"

"Yes, and of the family you intended to hide; but you never turned up with them after all."

"Alas, things went wrong, and they are now in prison."

"I am sorry; but do not hesitate to use the house for such a purpose in the future, if you consider it safe to do so."

"Thank you; it might yet prove of great use to me. I fear, though, that if Lebrun has put your name on the list of *émigrés* it will sooner or later be taken over by the Government."

Talleyrand chuckled. "No; at least I can get the better of them there. I propose to make it over, with all its contents, to Gouverneur Morris on a pre-dated bill of sale. These rogues no longer respect God or the King, but they still make a parade of treating Americans as though they had invented all the virtues. I will tell him you may wish to make use of the house. No one will interfere with you there while it is in his name, and if I am still alive when my poor country does come to its senses, I will at least get my property back intact."

"That is an excellent thought," Roger agreed; then, glancing towards the dark entrance-way, he added, "I take it you were on your way to Madame de Flahaut?"

"Yes. I have been hanging about for the past two hours, from fear that if I approached her apartment before darkness had fallen some enemy of mine might recognize me on my way up to it. But I am most anxious to persuade her to leave Paris. The way things are going it looks as if at any time now the Commune might make the bare fact of having been born an aristocrat sufficient excuse to put her, and every one like her, in prison. I hope, too, that she will find me an attic in which I shall be safe, for the night at least; for I have not the devil of an idea where else to go."

Roger shook his head. "Should a committee of the Section pick on this block for a round of domiciliary visits tonight it is hardly likely they would overlook an attic. No; I have a better plan. Go to *La Belle Étoile*. The landlord, M. Blanchard, is an old friend of mine, and for the past ten weeks I have kept a room there. Tell him that I sent you and wish you to have the use of it; then ask for my servant, Dan Izzard, and tell him to be at the

Cushion and Keys at midnight. What I can do to help you get away I don't yet know, but at all events you will be safe enough for the time being if you lie low in my room."

Talleyrand took his hand and pressed it. "Chevalier, I see from the broad ribbon you wear how skilfully you have managed your own affairs, and it is most generous of you to risk your position on my behalf. *La Belle Étoile*—Dan Izzard—the Cushion and Keys—I will follow your instructions to the letter; but first I must see Madame la Comtesse and urge her to leave Paris before it is too late."

"By all means," Roger smiled. "Present my compliments to her, please; and if it would not be asking too much of a Bishop to carry a parcel for a Commissar, I should be grateful if you would collect the clothes I left with her, and take them to *La Belle Étoile*."

"*Mon ami*, I would carry a jerry-pot for you, if by so doing I could render you a service," laughed the Bishop; and with a wave of his hand he limped into the side-entrance to the Palace.

Roger walked slowly off in the direction of the Tuileries gardens. In the desperate game he was playing situations occurred every day, and often several times a day, in which he was tempted to take risks in order to save some unfortunate person from arrest, but he knew that if he did so with any frequency he would soon be deprived of the authority he had worked so hard to win—then it would be good-bye to any prospect of being able to make some really telling use of it on behalf of Mr. Pitt. Now, however, he was beset by no uncomfortable hesitation. Charles Maurice de Talleyrand was his personal friend, and, come what may, he must be saved from his enemies. The only question was how best to set about it.

It was not yet ten o'clock and the night was a warm one; so on reaching the gardens he sat down to think things out on the same bench he had shared on the evening of the 20th of June with the man from whom he had bought a cloak and hat. Twenty minutes later he rose, crossed the gardens, went through the Passage des Feuillants and so to the Place Vendôme, in which the Ministry of Justice was situated.

There, he asked for Citizen Danton and learned to his satisfaction that the Minister was at work in his room upstairs. After a short wait Roger was shown up. Since the 10th of August his work had brought him into contact with Danton on several occasions; so he gave him a hearty, fraternal greeting, and said without hesitation:

"Citizen Minister, I've come to ask you a favour."

Danton had just returned from supping with some of his cronies. He belched loudly, then replied with a grin, "Well, what is it? They tell me you're a great fire-eater; but if you've come to demand Antoinette-Medici's head on a charger I'm afraid I can't oblige you just yet."

Roger grinned back. "No; I want the body of a live girl on a well-sprung bed; and only you, Citizen Minister, can give it me."

With a roar of laughter, Danton sat back. "Go on, Citizen Commissioner; tell me about her."

"I found her during a domiciliary visit. Her family are *ci-devants*, of course. She looks like a piece of Dresden china; I'd probably be bored with her in a week, but I've got to have her. I've got to have her once, just to find out what these *aristo* girls are like when they are stripped of the dignity that their clothes gives them."

Danton shrugged. "You'll probably find her poor fare. But you don't look to be lacking in muscle. If you want her, why the hell don't you get some of your fellows to keep her family quiet while you pull her clothes off and give her a tumble?"

"No." Roger shook his head. "I could easily rape her, but that would not be the same thing at all; I want her to undress in front of me and go through the whole business as if she were not compelled to it. I have had several talks with her and the first time she fainted, or pretended to; but like everyone else she has her price. This evening I got it out of her. She wants to get her brother and her uncle, who is an abbé, to England. If I can produce three passports, she is ready to pay me in her own coin for them."

"Why bother about the passports? If she is willing to give herself at all, you have only to threaten to have her brother and the abbé arrested to induce her to do so."

"Citizen Minister!" Roger said with sudden firmness. "Such a meanness would not be compatible with the high principles of our glorious Revolution."

Danton did not laugh; he did not even allow a cynical smile to twist his thick lips, for such absurd illogicalities were uttered quite frequently, even, at times, by his most unscrupulous colleagues, either with deliberate hypocrisy or through plain muddled thinking. Pulling open a drawer of his desk he took out a file of blank passports, counted off six, handed them to Roger, and said:

"I am selling these at one hundred *louis* a time. I make you a gift of three, but you can dispose of the other three for me, and let me have three hundred *louis* by the end of the week."

"That is easily done," Roger smiled as he took the precious pasteboards, "and I am greatly indebted to you, Citizen Minister."

He turned away and had just reached the door when Danton's voice boomed after him, "Did you know, Citizen Commissioner, that you are liable to be deprived of your rank and sash tomorrow?"

Those words jerked Roger to a halt as promptly as if he had been shot in the back. He was momentarily stunned by the awful thought that Danton had only been playing with him—that he had counted too far on his lecherous inventions to gain the good-will of a man noted for his own immoralities—and that the wily demagogue meant to denounce him as a helper of aristocrats to escape from Paris.

He caught his breath. For a moment the blood seemed to have ceased from coursing through his veins. Suddenly his heart began to hammer violently and he could feel his face go scarlet. Desperately he strove for control of his alarm. The room was lit only from a three-branched candlestick on Danton's desk; so, as he turned, the shadows by the door hid the signs of his agitation, but there were beads of perspiration on his forehead as he stared at the heavy figure with the brutal, pockmarked face.

"Yes," went on the Jacobin, "you may even find yourself in jail by this time tomorrow. The Assembly has got wind of the use we mean to make of our brave Marseillais, and they don't like the idea of their paying a social visit to the prisons. Quite a number of the leading deputies are holding a secret meeting tonight. They are trying to work their courage up to put a decree through the Assembly dissolving the Commune."

Roger suppressed an audible sigh of relief only with the greatest difficulty. Slowly he bared his teeth in a sort of snarling grin, which he had found very effective on occasions when it had been necessary for him to play the terrorist, then he said:

"They had best beware how they trifle with the People's representatives or it is they who will find themselves in prison. Good night to you, Citizen Minister."

He had expected to have to give detailed particulars of the

people for whom he had begged the passports, and had meant to give descriptions near enough to cover Adèle de Flahaut, de Talleyrand as her uncle the abbé, and himself as her brother. His idea had been that as the Bishop had for many years past never worn clerical clothes, except on the very rare occasions when he had to perform a religious ceremony, an abbé's gown would be the best possible disguise for him; and the thought that three passports should prove no more difficult to secure than two had prompted him to ask for a third to put by for himself in case it later became necessary for him to leave Paris in a hurry. But his luck had been in, as he had not even had to run the risk of giving false names; and he now had six, all blank except for the all-important signature.

When Dan arrived at the Cushion and Keys, Roger gave him four—two for de Talleyrand to fill in as he wished and two to hide at *La Belle Étoile* in case of an emergency—and kept the remaining two himself. He then told Dan to obtain from the Bishop the names under which the fugitives decided to travel, and to book two seats for them in the diligence leaving for Calais the following afternoon and, if the Bishop approved the idea of travelling as an abbé, to buy him a second-hand cassock in the morning. Then, very pleased at having been able to do so well for his friends, and praying that no hitch would occur to prevent their departure, he went to bed.

No hitch did occur. For four years Talleyrand was to pass into impecunious and unhappy exile, and it was to be still longer before Roger learned how he had filled in the blank passport. With great courage and extraordinary far-sightedness, he had used his own name and written under it "*En mission diplomatique en Angleterre*". Thus, after Danton's head had fallen beneath the knife of the guillotine, Talleyrand was able to produce his pass and assert that he had never fled from France as an *émigré* but had left it on government business, which enabled his friends to arrange for his return to the country that he loved so dearly very much sooner than could otherwise have taken place.

Years later, in a lofty, luxurious room, curtained with royal blue satin bearing the golden bees and eagles of the Emperor Napoleon, Roger was to see again that flimsy piece of pasteboard. It was to prove his own passport to liberty at the order of his friend, Monseigneur le Prince de Talleyrand, Prince de Bénévent, Arch-Chancellor of Europe.

But on the 30th of August Roger was given other things to think of besides the nocturnal flight of the man whose liberal mind and true patriotism had brought upon him the hatred of his fellow nobles, his fellow priests and now even of his fellow revolutionaries. Danton's forecast proved correct; in a sudden spate of bravery induced by terror of their own future, the moderates in the Assembly put through a decree dissolving the Commune.

The excitement at the Hôtel de Ville was intense. Robespierre drafted a long memorandum on the services to "liberty" that the Commune had rendered and forced Pétion to read it at the bar of the Assembly. All through that day and the next the deputies stood firm; but on the 1st of September Danton came to the rescue and briefed Thuriot in a cunning speech. The Assembly gave way and the Commune was reinstated. Its *Comité de Surveillance*, now the legal masters of Paris again, issued their secret instructions that night. It had been planned to use the fall of Verdun as an excuse to launch the massacre. The city had not yet fallen, but it was given out that it had, that the Prussians were marching on Paris, and that the prisons were full of conspirators who were about to break out and murder the People's representatives. On Sunday the 2nd the massacres began.

In the last days of August the domiciliary visits had resulted in the arrest of over 3,000 suspects, and a number of these had been temporarily confined in the Hôtel de Ville until they could be allocated to various prisons. Among those removed at midday, twenty-four priests were ordered to be transferred to the prison of the Abbaye. The brigands from Marseilles were waiting for them: surrounding the coaches into which the prisoners were crammed they accompanied them, yelling threats and imprecations. When the cortège arrived outside the prison a cut-throat leader named Maillard gave the signal; the priests were hauled out of the coaches and butchered.

Billaud-Varennes, wearing his Municipal scarf, then arrived on the scene as the representative of the Commune. Standing among the dead bodies, he cried, "Patriots! You have executed justice on scoundrels! For having done this duty you shall each receive twenty-four *livres*."

With this official encouragement, the roaring mob streamed off to the Convent des Carmes, in the church of which it was known that some 180 other priests were incarcerated. Behind the convent lay a big, high-walled garden with extensive shrubberies and an oratory at its far end. Breaking into the church the assassins ordered the prisoners out into the garden. A number of these saintly men, under the leadership of the venerable Archbishop of Arles, went straight to the oratory and, kneeling before the altar, offered themselves up to martyrdom. They were slaughtered as they knelt, until the flagstones were awash with blood. Others, less saintly, made a bid for life, and a terrible manhunt ensued as they were pursued through the bushes, the quiet of the September evening being shattered for a mile around by their hideous screams as they were caught and murdered.

With the blood-lust of the killers now at fever heat, Maillard led them back to the Abbaye, and at seven o'clock they broke in there. The building contained several hundred prisoners, including sixty-nine Swiss who had managed to escape on the 10th of August. They were the first to be killed, but now the massacre was to be made a travesty of justice. In one of the corridors a tribunal was set up, the prison register was produced, and each prisoner was given a brief mockery of an examination. A few, by their own wit or through the freakish humour of the mob, escaped the fate that awaited the great majority. The rest were told in turn, "You are to be transferred to La Force," and hustled down a passage. It led to the courtyard where the *sans-culottes* were waiting, their pikes, sabres and bayonets dripping blood.

The coming of night did not stop the dreadful carnage. It was continued by the ruddy glow of torches, which turned the shambles into a scene from Dante's Inferno, and later by the even more sinister silver light of a beautiful September moon.

Meanwhile, the tocsin had been rung and the Faubourgs roused. Those fiends who had perpetrated such horrors at the sack of the Tuileries, three weeks before, again issued from their dens. The scum of Paris joined the *fédérés* and directed by Marat—the chief organizer of the massacre—attacked other prisons, the Châtelet, the Conciergerie, St. Fermin and La Force.

It was to La Force that most of the Queen's ladies had been taken after her removal from the Feuillants, and a few days later, when she was deprived of the Princesse de Lamballe and the de Tourzels, they too had been confined there. The Princess's father-in-law, the Duc de Penthièvre, had—at the suggestion of Gouverneur Morris, as Roger learned from him afterwards—paid

Manuel 50,000 *écus* to save her and her companions. Manuel now did his utmost to honour his bond. He succeeded in saving Madame de Tourzel, her daughter, the Princesse de Tarente and the four other ladies, but his attempt to save Madame de Lamballe was foiled. Her brother-in-law, the unscrupulous Duc d'Orléans, had both a personal spite against her and wished to get her huge dowry back into the family coffers to restore his waning fortune; so had determined to make certain of her death. He caused a message to be got to her that her life depended on her remaining in her cell, and when Manuel came for her she refused to go with him.

At eight o'clock in the morning, after a night spent listening to the dying screams of earlier victims, she was dragged before a tribunal of which the sadist, Hébert, had made himself President. They demanded that she should take the "oath of liberty, of equality, of hatred for the King, the Queen, and Royalty".

She replied, "I will willingly swear to the first two, but not the last; it is not in my heart."

A man near her whispered, "Swear; if you do not you are as good as dead."

Normally she was of such a nervous disposition that her fears over trifles were often commented on with kindly amusement by her friends; but now she heroically refused to swear. A door was thrown open and she was pushed out, to stumble over the bodies of the dead and dying.

The band of assassins hired by d'Orléans to commit so many crimes during the Revolution were waiting for her there. Like demons they fell upon her. A mulatto got in the first blow. Their leader, the Italian Rotondo, grasped her bodice and tore it open, but her head fell forward and, for a moment, the cascade of her wonderful golden hair hid her breasts. Dragging her forward, they thrust their daggers into her sides, then stripped her naked. At the sight of her beautiful white body they became possessed with a fury of lust, satiated it upon her still warm corpse, then mutilated it most horribly and cut off its head.

Throughout this terrible night and day Roger remained in the precincts of the Temple. He felt that this opportunity was certain to be seized upon to attack the prison of the Royal Family and murder its inmates; so both duty and inclination impelled him to a post where he might at least make an attempt to save the Dauphin.

In the dawn Santerre arrived with an additional company of National Guards, and told him privately that now the *Comité* had the Sovereigns in its clutches it considered them more valuable as hostages than as corpses, so they were to be defended; but, having given an order that they were not to be allowed out in the garden for exercise that day, he quickly made himself scarce.

Knowing, as Santerre obviously feared, that one of the mobs might get out of hand and beyond the control of the *Comité*, Roger stayed and dozed through the morning in one of the downstairs rooms of the old Palace. Then, at three o'clock in the afternoon, distant shouting announced the approach of a great crowd.

Soon it came in sight, and its leaders proved to be the cannibals who had murdered the Princesse de Lamballe. They had taken her head to a barber, had the blood washed from the face and the hair dressed, curled and powdered. Now they had it stuck on the end of a long pole, and had brought it to show to her dearest friend, the Queen.

After bobbing the head up and down in front of the windows of the tower, they demanded admittance to the prisoners. The Commissioners on duty refused and ordered them to retire, but they would not go. They began a raucous shouting, "Bring out Veto and his wife!" "We want the head of the Austrian!" and things began to look ugly.

To make the prison more secure the Commune had given orders for a number of old houses near by to be pulled down and for an eighteen-feet high wall to be built right round the Temple. This work was still incomplete; so the mob were able to approach right up to the door of the tower, and now looked like forcing their way in. But a Commissioner named Daujon climbed up on a heap of rubble and called out to them, "The head of Antoinette does not belong to you. It is the property of all France and has been entrusted to Paris until national justice decides what is to be done with it."

Roger supported Daujon with his utmost vigour, and for nearly two hours they argued with the mob before the greater part of it got bored and melted away in search of easier game. But the ringleaders were men of d'Orléans's gang and proved persistent in their murderous intent. About five o'clock some of them went off and, having raised another mob, returned with it an hour later.

Many of the newcomers were drunk, and threatened to storm the tower unless the Sovereigns were given up to them. Again Daujon and Roger argued and pleaded, through what seemed a never-ending evening. They were far from confident that the National Guard would fire on the mob if ordered to do so, and knew that if the order was given and not obeyed the mob would then murder them for having given it.

The crisis came soon after eight. The rabble tried to drag Roger and his companion away from the door; a hand-to-hand struggle ensued and the door was partially forced open. Fortunately no shot was fired, and several other Commissars, who had been lurking in the background, now plucked up the courage to come to their assistance. After rescuing Daujon and Roger they tied three of their *tricolore* sashes together across the entrance. Even d'Orléans's cut-throats did not dare to risk the mob turning on them as a result of laying impious hands on the nation's colours. For a while they remained there, cursing and sullen; then, at about nine o'clock, they at last withdrew.

During that night, and the following two days and nights, the massacres continued. When the executioners tired, the *Comité* supplied them with wine to give them new strength. No longer caring who they killed or why, gangs of drink-maddened *canaille* broke into the prisons of the poor—the Tour Saint Bernard, where they killed seventy-five convicted criminals awaiting transfer to the galleys; Bicêtre, where they slit the throats of pickpocket street urchins scarcely in their teens; and the Salpetrière, the women's prison, where they raped the inmates before disembowelling them.

At last, on Thursday the 6th, the exhausted slayers were permitted by the *Comité* to relax. Four days and nights of ghastly carnage had had the desired result; Paris lay silent, stricken numb with terror; and few moderates would now risk death to attend the polls. To clinch matters, the Sections demanded that they should be allowed to manage the elections in their own way. Robespierre set an example in his own Section of des Piques, by abolishing the secret ballot and making each elector give his vote by word of mouth to a committee; the other Sections followed suit. In consequence all twenty-four deputies returned to the new Convention by the City of Paris were extremists. Among them were Danton, Marat, Collot d'Herbois, Billaud-Varennes, Camille Desmoulins and, not least infamous, Philippe, Duc d'Orléans, who, by decree, was permitted to change his name to Philippe Égalité.

While the elections were in progress Paris was given over to pillage. Between the 2nd and the 16th of September many hundreds of houses were broken into and many thousands of pounds' worth of valuables stolen. But the depredations of the Municipality made those of the mobs, by comparison, only petty pilfering. The Commune asserted its right to the property of all the murdered prisoners, and arbitrarily confiscated, taxed and fined, when, where and how it would. Gold and jewels to the value of millions poured into the Hôtel de Ville, and every Commissar helped himself to a share of the loot. Roger, with a logical cynicism that de Talleyrand would have applauded, took the opportunity of financing himself in no half-hearted manner for his private war against the Revolution. In Dan's care he lodged diamonds worth several thousand pounds, and took for immediate needs as much gold as he could conveniently carry after paying Danton 300 *louis* for the passports.

However, on the night of the 16th the Garde-Meuble was broken into and property estimated at 24,000,000 *livres*, including the Crown jewels, was stolen. At last the robber barons of the Commune were roused to the necessity of putting an end to private pillage, and on the 17th a number of decrees were passed for the suppression of further rioting and looting. In addition, strong measures were taken to remove the *fédérés*—who had now served the dreadful purpose for which they had been brought to Paris—out of the capital and to the front.

On the 4th Verdun had fallen to the Prussians, and it was now apparent that the Duke of Brunswick had at last launched his long-delayed offensive against Paris. A fever of genuine patriotism seized on all classes. Danton's formerly insincere oratory now lit a torch from the spirit of the people; they flung themselves heart and soul into preparations to resist the invader.

Up to the end of the massacre Roger had remained with the dozen or so Commissars who had congregated at the Temple. Other attempts were made upon it, but none so serious as the one that had lasted for six hours on the first day. Then, when things quietened down a little, he had once more had to occupy himself with his many duties at his Section, and to show himself frequently at the sittings of the Commune. Now that order had been restored he again began to consider the possibility of rescuing the Royal prisoners.

For such an attempt he believed that two entirely opposite sets of circumstances provided the best opportunities. Firstly, during the excitement and disorganization brought about by a time of crisis; secondly, when the jailers had been lulled into a sense of false security by a reasonable period of uneventful routine. It was now over five weeks since the Royal Family had been lodged in the Temple; so it seemed to him that the time was approaching when the second set of circumstances might be fulfilled.

Already some weeks had elapsed since the Commune had reduced to three the number of Commissioners responsible for the prisoners, and had instituted a regular procedure for them. They went on duty for twenty-four hours, took their meals on the ground floor of the little tower and, between them, kept the prisoners under constant surveillance. This duty was carried out by volunteers, and any Commissioner who wished could put his name down for it. At first there had been a great scramble for the chance to sit staring at the prisoners, but the curiosity of the most morbid having been satisfied, there was now less competition to spend twenty-four hours without sleep. For Roger, it offered the perfect opportunity for a preliminary investigation, during which he could assess the lie of the land at his leisure, but he had been content to bide his time. Now, he put his name down to go on duty at the Temple on the night of Friday the 21st of September.

But it was not to be. While he was having dinner at the Cushion and Keys on the evening of the 18th a note was brought to him. It was written in a thin, neat, legal hand, and read:

In the present emergency the Comité *are much concerned as to the purity of the revolutionary sentiments and patriotism of the Army. All reactionary elements must be eradicated and any manifestation of treachery ruthlessly suppressed. You have been selected as* Citoyen Représentant en mission *to the army of General Dumouriez, with full powers of life and death. You will proceed to his headquarters with the least possible delay.*

It was signed *Maximilien Robespierre*, and from that order to leave Paris Roger knew there was no appeal.

CHAPTER XIV

"CITOYEN REPRÉSENTANT EN MISSION"

THE war which France had declared against Austria on the 20th of April, 1792, was destined to continue, apart from two brief intervals, for twenty-three years. All the great Powers of Europe and many smaller ones were to be involved. Most of them were to be vanquished—some more than once—and for a time forced to fight for their conquerors against their late allies. Armies, on a scale hitherto unknown, waged their campaigns in the mud of Flanders, the snows of Russia and the torrid heats of Spain. Naval blockades were maintained day in, day out, for years at a stretch, and naval actions fought in every sea from the Baltic to the Nile and from the Caribbean to Trafalgar. Millions of men were killed; the drain upon France's manpower was so terrible that it crippled her for a hundred years and reduced the average height of her population by two inches. Sea power alone saved Britain and enabled her to persevere in her determination to destroy the aggressor, but sea power was not enough to overthrow the military might of the French Empire and liberate the enslaved peoples of Europe; so she too had to become a land power, and with dogged persistence through the long years sent army after army overseas, until at last final victory was achieved in 1815 on the field of Waterloo.

But when Roger Brook rode out of Paris on the morning of the 20th of September, the names of Nelson, Wellington and Napoleon were known only to a few hundred people, and the dreadful slaughters of the future mercifully veiled. Moreover, although the war had been on for five months, active hostilities had only just begun.

The Austrians and their Prussian allies had been slow to mobilize, as both were looking uneasily over their shoulders towards Poland. The first partition of that country had taken place in 1775 and it now looked as if there might soon be another; so the Germanic Powers were most loath to commit armies against France. In May, 1791, King Stanislaus had granted to his people a democratic Constitution—the first of its kind on the continent of Europe—and this had been viewed with grave disapproval by Poland's autocratic neighbours. Catherine of Russia, ever greedy to extend her Empire, had put it to her fellow monarchs that the Poles were going the same way as the French and might soon prove a similar menace to the old order in other kingdoms, so their radical tendencies should be curbed in good time. It was clear that she contemplated marching in, and, if the unfortunate Poles were to be deprived of more territory, Austria and Prussia wanted to retain adequate forces in the north to ensure her not having it all her own way. Only so could they make certain of obtaining a share of the loot, and they were much more interested in adding to their own territories at the expense of Poland than in waging a profitless war to put Louis XVI back firmly on his throne.

The French were even less ready to attack, as three years of revolutionary agitation had played havoc with the fine army built up by the old Monarchy. The mutinies of the *Garde Française* in Paris in '89 had started the riot, and it had soon spread to many regiments in the provinces. Jacobin clubs had been formed among the troops, and these "Soldiers' Councils" had put an end to the maintenance of discipline. Many of the most unpopular officers had been murdered, a still greater number had fled abroad, and as time went on most of the regiments had deteriorated to little better than an armed rabble entirely unfitted for active service, as at once became apparent on the first engagements of the war.

In May, General Count Dillon, who was commanding in the north, had been surprised by the enemy near Lille. His army had fled after an exchange of only a few shots, and his troops, accusing him of treachery, had promptly liquidated him and his staff in a most barbarous manner. The Duc de Biron's troops had also decamped at the first sight of the enemy at Mons, crying out that they were betrayed; and he had narrowly escaped a similar fate to that which had overtaken Dillon.

The Austrians could then have marched to Paris almost unopposed, but they preferred to wait until their Prussian allies were also actively committed, and both still hoped that the French might yet be overawed by threats. King Frederick William had chosen the Duke of Brunswick as his field commander; by mid-July Brunswick had marched his army up to the French frontier, and on the 24th Prussia declared war on France. The declaration was followed by Brunswick's manifesto. Actually the Duke had strongly disapproved of its contents, as he was a mild and elderly prince who ruled his own dominions in a most enlightened manner, and had openly shown his sympathy for the French reformers of '89; but it expressed the views of his King and had to be issued as it stood. As Brunswick had foreseen, its only effect was to arouse the patriotism of the French nation and stiffen the morale of the better elements in the French army, for what little that might be worth.

In the meantime, three new Commanders—Rochambeau, Lafayette and the elderly General Luckner—had attempted to instill some sort of order into the armies of the north, centre and east; but the downfall of King Louis had been followed by a further weakening of their commands through most of the remaining trained officers going over to the Austrians. Lafayette had surrendered himself to them, and the three armies had been merged into two under Dumouriez and Kellermann.

Dumouriez had been in the saddle hardly a week when at long last Brunswick opened his campaign in earnest. On the 19th of August he had crossed the French frontier and captured Longwy, and on the 3rd of September Verdun had fallen an easy prey to him owing to the cowardice of its garrison. He had then begun his march on Paris by a slow but methodical advance through the defiles of the Argonne; so it was hardly to be wondered at that Robespierre and his colleagues were intensely worried. Against the well-disciplined regular forces of Austria and Prussia they could oppose only untried Generals with ill-fed, poorly equipped and semi-mutinous troops. The enemy were only a little over eighty miles from Paris, so might be at its gates in a fortnight, and if the city fell that would be the end of the Revolution and of themselves.

Roger naturally hoped that would prove the case, and that within a month he might see the gang of murderers who were terrorizing France lined up and shot; but in the meantime he had an extremely difficult and unwelcome rôle to play. He was one of several Special Commissioners who had been hurriedly despatched to various parts of France, some to strengthen the resistance of the armies of the north and east, others to those opposing the Piedmontese—who had now joined the Allies and were invading the south of France—and others again to the larger centres of population where fresh levies were being raised. All were charged with weeding out the men with whom Roger was secretly in sympathy and having them shot, and he was most uncomfortably aware that unless he had a considerable number of people killed in the near future he would stand a very good chance of being executed as a reactionary himself.

For company he had the congenial and trusty Dan as, although it was not *de rigueur* for Revolutionary officials to go about attended by private servants, the more intelligent of them employed secretaries; and Dan was now filling that rôle. The fact that his writing was slow and awkward mattered little, as his post was that of personal assistant rather than scribe; and for the former no man could have been suited better than the shrewd, capable ex-captain of smugglers. In the past three months he had had ample opportunity to acquire all the revolutionary jargon; and while his hatred of the terrorists, equalled Roger's no one could possibly have guessed it. In fact, Roger was counting on him to lend the authentic touch to their mission when they had to deal with the Soldiers' Councils.

During the past month Roger had noted with interest that, with the one exception of Marat, the most violent of his colleagues in the Commune were by no means the dirtiest. Hébert, who vomited obscenities under the name of Père Duchesne in a paper he edited specially designed to pander to the lusts of the *sans-culottes*, was actually a fashionably-dressed young man of deceptively mild appearance; Billaud-Varennes, who had egged on the mob with money and wine to its worst atrocities in the September massacres, habitually wore a carefully-curled black wig and a lace-edged coat of puce satin; Robespierre, the most ruthless of them all, was always impeccably clad and was notorious for the spotlessness of his linen. So Roger had felt that the time was coming when he could afford once more to modify his appearance without any risk of losing revolutionary caste. He disliked the inconvenience of shaving only twice a week, and ill-fitting clothes; and this change of employment provided him with an excellent opportunity to shed the last traces of the personality he had assumed for his grim apprenticeship to Santerre.

He was, therefore, once again wearing his own well-cut garments and, apart from his *tricolore* sash, his only concession to revolutionary fashion was a huge, violently-coloured, red, white and blue woollen cockade that he wore in his hat. The moderates usually wore only small cockades made of silk or cotton and dyed in pale colours. It should, however, be added that his return to cleanliness, and even to a degree of elegance, was not entirely governed by his own inclination. He was convinced that a man like Dumouriez was much more likely to be impressed by a representative having the appearance of a coldly ruthless intellectual than by an out-at-elbows demagogue. Dan, on the other hand, with his burly figure, black beard, and gold earrings, could, when he chose, look as formidable as any *fédérés'* leader.

When they took the road for Châlons, side by side on two excellent mounts commandeered from the Royal stables, they presented a strange contrast; but Roger had good hopes that their very diversity of appearance, coupled with obvious common aims, would prove the strongest possible card in the difficult task of instilling fear and obedience in a half-mutinous army.

As they did not leave Paris until midday, they contented themselves with a thirty-mile stage and slept at La Férte that night. Next morning they were off early, and reached Montmirail by ten o'clock, to learn the most surprising news: a major battle had taken place the previous day in which the French had proved victorious. Roger could hardly credit it, but the news was confirmed at other towns along the road, and when they arrived at Châlons that evening they were able to secure eye-witness accounts of the battle.

Châlons was the headquarters of a reserve army that was forming; and the sight of the ragged, ill-armed and totally undisciplined *fédérés* with which the town was swarming made it more difficult than ever to believe that an army largely composed of similar raw material could possibly have defeated crack troops, the bulk of whom must have served under Frederick the Great. However, it soon became clear to Roger that it was not a battle in the real sense of the word that had taken place. It had, in fact, been almost entirely an artillery action, and was to go down in history as "the Cannonade of Valmy"; but its effect was out of all proportion to the casualties sustained, as it was the first clash of major forces in the war, and this success of the Army of the Revolution both enormously strengthened French morale and filled every crowned head in Europe with sudden fears for the future.

The credit for the victory lay equally with Dumouriez's good generalship and an element in the French army which had escaped the undermining influence of the Revolution. When Brunswick began to penetrate the Argonne, Dumouriez had been at Valenciennes. By a rapid and daring flank march he had deployed his army in front of the invaders, at the same time calling Kellermann's army from Metz to his assistance; he had thus succeeded in blocking the road to Paris with forces superior to those of the enemy. Even so, victory would almost certainly have gone to the Prussians had the columns and squadrons come into serious conflict; that they did not was due to the excellence of the French artillery—an arm in which France had long been counted superior to all other nations. This corps, and the engineers, unlike the French cavalry and infantry, had always been officered by men mainly of bourgeois birth; so they had not been driven into seeking refuge abroad, but had remained with their batteries, maintaining in them the old high standard of discipline and training. In consequence, the slaughter caused by the guns at Valmy against the massed ranks of the Prussians had appeared so formidable to Brunswick that he had broken off the battle and fallen back.

At Châlons, Roger learned that Dumouriez's headquarters were situated in a village a few miles to the north-east of the town; so on the morning of the 22nd he and Dan set out for it. As they rode he thought over what little he knew of the General, and recalled de Talleyrand saying of him, when speaking of the Girondin Ministry in which Dumouriez had held the portfolio for Foreign Affairs:

"He has more personality and energy than the rest of them put together, but I neither like nor trust him. Both as a soldier and secret agent he has travelled considerably; so he knows far more than his colleagues about international affairs, and is capable of acting the great man in a manner that deceives most people into believing him to be one; but he does not deceive me. He is a clever little upstart; an adventurer lacking both principles and ideals, who sees in the Revolution only a God-sent opportunity to feather his own nest. His singleness of purpose, audacity and talent for intrigue have already carried him a long way; but he is not a member of any political party, and playing a lone hand is a dangerous game; so whether he will prove equal to staying the course remains to be seen."

To the shrewd Bishop's assessment Roger was now able to add certain particulars gleaned during his three months in Paris. Dumouriez was fifty-three years old, and had been greatly attached to Mirabeau; but he was much more of a radical and, to curry favour with the *enragés*, had appeared in the Jacobin Club wearing the *bonnet rouge* of a *sans-culotte* whilst a Minister of the

Crown; yet, in spite of that, he had won the personal liking of Louis XVI—firstly because he spoke to the King with complete freedom, as if they were friends and equals; secondly because he had enlivened the dreary meetings of the Royal Council by producing an endless fund of amusing stories.

On the evidence to hand, Roger decided that the General might prove very dangerous, as he was evidently in the habit of concealing his real designs under the appearance of being "all things to all men"; but Roger was well practised in playing that game too, and he hoped that his host would be much too involved in military matters to take more than a cursory interest in his own activities.

When he arrived at the small *château* that Dumouriez had made his headquarters, he found that the General was out; but on his return at midday their first interview passed off very satisfactorily. Dumouriez proved to be a small, wiry man with a square face and big, lively eyes under heavy brows that nearly met over the bridge of a fleshy nose. As soon as he had seen Roger's credentials he treated him with the same breezy cordiality that had so fascinated the King, declared himself the loyal servant of the Assembly, and asked his visitor to join him for dinner.

During the meal Roger gave him the latest news from Paris and, tactfully but firmly, spoke of the implications of his mission. He added that although he had received his orders before the General's brilliant victory at Valmy, that did not relieve him of his responsibility to investigate the political soundness of the army; but he hoped nevertheless that his work would prove a help rather than a hindrance to its Commander.

The General replied with apparent candour that he welcomed the investigation, and would give the Citizen Representative every facility to make it. He then attached to Roger one of his *aides-de-camp*, a tall, thin young man named Vebord, with orders to take him to every regiment in turn; but after the meal he drew his guest into a corner and said with a sudden intenseness that suggested genuine concern:

"I trust, Citizen, that when exercising your powers you will discriminate between the liberty of action that any individual is entitled to claim while a civilian, and the obligations into which he enters when he becomes a serving soldier. Cases will be brought before you of men who have abused the doctrines of equality in order to set themselves up in opposition to their superiors in military rank. To encourage such conduct would be disastrous, whereas to make an example of them would contribute greatly to the general effectiveness of the army. Again, I trust that you will not unduly molest my officers who happen to be of gentle birth. If you find evidence that some are likely to prove traitors, I should be the last to defend such people; but remember that I am desperately short of men trained to leadership, and that by weakening the army from purely political motives you may bring the Revolution itself into danger."

No policy could have suited Roger's book better; but he was too cautious to show it, and replied with a sanctimonious air, "The purity of political convictions can become the most deadly blade in your armoury, Citizen General, and I have been sent to sharpen it for you. Nevertheless, your signal success at Valmy entitles you to make these requests, and I will observe them in so far as they do not conflict with my duty."

Next morning the news came through that on the 21st the National Convention had held its first sitting; all parties had united in voting for the abolition of the Monarchy, and France had been proclaimed a Republic. By the same courier there arrived official congratulations from the Convention to the Army and its General on their victory of the 20th. As Citizen Representative *en mission* it fell to Roger to make these announcements to the troops, so he spent the day with Dumouriez, riding from camp to camp and proclaiming again and again, until his voice was hoarse, these epoch-making despatches. The news soon spread before them like wildfire; wherever they appeared bands played, flags flew, and the hollow squares of hastily-paraded men showed by their cheers that few of them had any regrets for the final passing of the old Order.

This semi-regal progress gave Roger an opportunity to appreciate the garrulous little General's extraordinary energy and immense capacity for tackling swiftly every kind of problem that his subordinates put to him. It also served as a perfect means of introducing Roger to the army, and during it he made his arrangements with the colonel of each regiment. He gave orders that they should bring before him at a drumhead court martial all officers, N.C.O.s and men against whom they had a complaint of any kind; then during the days that followed he left General Headquarters every morning with Dan and Vebord to conduct so bloody an assize that it would have made even Judge Jeffreys pale.

On receiving the instruction of the all-powerful *Comité de Surveillance* he had realized at once that he must either accept the mission or abandon for good the identity which he had built up with such care; and it was that alone which was enabling him to supply Mr. Pitt with really valuable information about the personalities and probable developments of the Revolution. Repugnant as the task might be, it was clear where his duty lay, and he was comforted somewhat by the thought that there were plenty of men in the army whose crimes would have sent them to the scaffold during any period of normal law and order. His problem was, on scant evidence and a few minutes' questioning, to sort the wheat from the chaff, so that only those who deserved death should be condemned; but he had thought out a way of dealing with this awful responsibility that greatly eased his conscience.

Nearly all the men brought before him by the colonels were charged either with cowardice in the face of the enemy, fomenting mutiny or using threats against their officers. Most of the cowards Roger let off with a reprimand, as he had no desire at all to strengthen the morale of the revolutionary army, and secretly hoped that the same men would start other panics among their comrades in the future. Of each man in the other two categories, having heard what he had to say, he asked the question, "What service have you rendered to the Revolution?"

Almost invariably the prisoners fell into the trap, and boasted of horrible crimes they had committed in the past three years during outbreaks of violence in their home towns. He was then able to shake his head and say, "That is not enough to excuse your recent conduct. You have imperilled the safety of the nation by weakening the efficiency of the army; I condemn you to be shot."

Against his verdict there was no appeal; the wretches were immediately dragged away behind a barn or haystack and executed by a firing squad that had been provided for the purpose. In a week Roger had exacted vengeance on over 150 self-confessed murderers, and his ruthlessness—in what Dumouriez considered to be the right direction—had earned him the esteem and confidence of the General.

During the ten days that had elapsed since Valmy the opposing armies had lain sullenly confronting one another, owing to a temporary armistice which had been arranged between their commanders to allow for the burial of the dead and the exchange of prisoners; but now hostilities recommenced. Dumouriez told Roger that, in spite of the greatly improved morale of his troops on account of their recent victory, he did not yet consider them sufficiently reliable to risk a general battle; so he intended to train and season them in a constant series of small engagements. Brunswick, too, was evidently averse to again risking his columns against the French artillery, for the Prussians began a slow withdrawal.

As the French moved forward at an equally discreet pace, Roger became daily more conscious that he must do something about a problem that had worried him from the beginning. He was dealing with the troops in a manner satisfactory both to himself and to Dumouriez; but what of the officers? If he could not report on his return to Paris that he had weeded out the reactionaries, Robespierre would charge him with being one himself, and he already stood in some danger of being denounced in a letter to Paris from one of the Jacobin cells. Dan, who kept him well informed on such matters, had warned him more than once that the *sans-culotte* element among the soldiery was raging against him in secret for his drastic treatment of mutineers, and that only the fact of his having had so many of their leaders executed kept them from organizing a revolt with the object of bringing about his death.

By the 5th of October he felt that he dared not delay longer in taking some form of drastic action; so that night he wrote out an order informing the Jacobin cells that, having dealt with indiscipline throughout the army, he was now prepared to hear all complaints that the men had to make against their officers.

Dumouriez flew into a passion and refused to circulate the order; but Roger told him that if he did not, and it came to the ears of the *Comité*, they would deprive him of his command. As the voluble little General's dominant characteristic was ambition, he gave way, and next morning Roger set about his uncongenial task.

By that time they had reached St. Ménehould, so he commandeered an office in the Town Hall, and summoned the Soldiers' Councils, one by one, to attend there. As they were in no position to arrest the officers of whom they complained, he was spared the necessity of pronouncing any immediate judgments; he simply greeted each group of visitors with revolutionary sentiments of a violence which surprised and delighted them, then had their depositions taken down and promised a full investigation of each case.

Actually, he had no intention of making further investigations into any of the cases, as the only thing which really concerned him was that the Jacobins must be appeased by the removal of the officers whom they hated most. Instead, he judged each case as he heard it, decided then and there what he would have done had he really been a dyed-in-the-wool revolutionary, and marked his list with ticks, crosses, and circles accordingly.

By the 14th he had finished his enquiry, and moved on to join Dumouriez, who had advanced his headquarters to Varennes. That evening, after dinner, Roger showed the General his list of 255 officers denounced by the Soldiers' Councils. The little man's pop-eyes bulged and he went purple in the face at the thought of what the loss of so many would mean to his forces; but Roger checked his rage by saying:

"The charges against many of these people are vague and unsubstantiated, and it would give the Councils the whip hand over every officer in the army if we cashiered all whom they chose to denounce; but examples must be made of those who have spoken against the Revolution. In the case of one hundred and twenty I propose to take no action; I suggest that you should transfer eighty-eight to other regiments as being the best means of dissipating the friction between them and their men; the remaining forty-seven I require to be arrested and handed over to me tomorrow night."

In his relief at learning that he was to lose only about a fifth of the number he had feared, the General gave way to Gallic abandon and kissed Roger on both cheeks; then, over another bottle of wine, they went through the list in detail and agreed on a slight rearrangement which would exempt a few officers whose services Dumouriez considered particularly valuable.

Next morning, after having paid a visit of curiosity to the house of Citizen Sauce the grocer, at which the Royal Family had been held captive, Roger rode out with Dan on a reconnaissance of the country to the north of the town. At the village of Châtel he found what he was seeking—a huge old tithe barn. Returning, he told Dumouriez of his find and the use to which he intended to put it. He said that if half a hundred officers accused of having Royalist sympathies were brought into the town, it was certain that attempts to lynch them would be made; so he wished his prisoners to be taken to the barn at Châtel, where he could question them at his leisure without fear of intervention by a mob. Dumouriez praised his perspicacity and gave the necessary orders; so that night forty-two officers were collected from their respective regiments and put in the barn under guard.

The following day Roger spent some hours at the barn questioning a number of his prisoners, while Dan laboriously took notes; but at three o'clock he announced in front of the officer in charge of the guard that he must return to Varennes to dine with the General, then told Dan that he was to carry on with the questioning. Secretly, he had already given Dan instructions that at five o'clock he was to get himself quarters in the village for the night, then buy a small barrel of wine from the local *estaminet*, and do his utmost to make the guard dead drunk. As the terrible Citizen Representative's assistant, Dan was regarded with respectful awe by the troops; moreover he could tell most hair-raising stories of the sack of the Tuileries and of the September massacres; so Roger was quite confident that, from the officer down, the guard would be eager to drink with him, and that well before midnight he would have the whole lot reeling.

At midnight Roger rode back to within half a mile of Châtel, tethered his horse to a tree, then walked the remaining distance across a field. No sounds came from the village and no lights were showing in it; evidently the greater part of the guard was sunk in a drunken slumber. Cautiously he tiptoed round the end of the barn. The starlight showed a solitary sentry, but he was sitting on the ground, his back against its doors, his head fallen forward on his chest, snoring. Going round to the rear of the barn again, Roger produced flint and tinder and lit the thatch in four places. Recrossing the field, he stood by his horse until he was certain that the great barn was so well alight that no normal effort could put the fire out, then he returned to Varennes and slept with his usual soundness.

In the morning Dan reported. The great barn had been burnt to the ground. The guard, when roused, had proved incapable of taking any effective action, either to put out the fire or to stop the prisoners escaping from the blazing building.

Everything had gone as Roger had planned. The walls of the

barn being made of mud and straw, it had been a foregone conclusion that the prisoners would break a way through them, and risk a bullet from the sentries rather than remain inside to be roasted alive. He had made as certain as he could that there should be no bullets. By this time the forty-two Royalist sympathizers must be beyond pursuit and probably already within the enemy lines. No one could blame him for that; and he smiled to himself at the thought that he had saved his own bacon with Robespierre and the Soldiers' Council by making the arrests, yet had succeeded in saving honest men from the danger in which they had placed themselves by openly expressing their beliefs; in addition, he had made a most useful present to the forces that had taken up arms against the Revolution.

The weather was exceptionally bad that autumn and there had hardly been a day since mid-September on which it had not rained; so the Prussian army had been severely stricken with illness, and seemed less inclined than ever to put up a fight. Dumouriez's troops appeared to be hardier and they pushed on up the Meuse, reaching Sedan on the 21st of October, while Kellermann, fifty miles away on the right, had recaptured Verdun and despatched his subordinate, General Custine, with a flying column, on a daring foray into the Principalities of the Rhine. On the 23rd, salvoes of blanks were joyfully fired all along the frontier to announce that the enemy had been driven from the soil of France.

This first great achievement of the armies of the Republic naturally called for celebration; so the civic authorities of Sedan invited Dumouriez and all his principal officers to the Town Hall that night, a number of the prettiest local girls were asked in for dancing, and wines of all kinds were provided in abundance. The little General had a head like a rock; so when Roger came upon him in one of the ante-rooms at about three in the morning he showed no outward signs of the number of toasts he had been called on to drink, but he was nevertheless distinctly mellow. Roger, too, as the guest only second in importance to the General, had been lavishly wined; so there was little to choose between them as they smiled at one another and, almost instinctively, sat down together on a comfortable settee.

During the past month they had spent a considerable amount of time in one another's company, and although they both continued to maintain a cautious reserve on certain questions, they had fallen into the habit of discussing army matters with complete frankness; so it was quite a natural question for Roger to ask his companion's intentions now that he had cleared France of the invaders.

The General replied without hesitation, "We must press on into Belgium. Old Brunswick has so many sick on his hands that he is in no state to stop us, and the Austrian Netherlands are ripe for the picking. For years past they have been in semi-revolt against the rule of Vienna, and from every town our agents report that the people are ready to hail us as deliverers."

Roger nodded. He knew that the Jacobin Club had sent hundreds of agitators into the Belgian cities to incite the workers to revolution; so he had expected some such answer. He remarked now with no ulterior motive, "I judge you right that we have good prospects of overrunning the country; but, if we do, the Government would be well advised to give guarantees to England that we mean to withdraw when the war is over, otherwise we'll run a grave risk of her being added to our enemies."

"That may be unavoidable," Dumouriez said thoughtfully. "I have a great admiration for the English and no desire at all to fight them; so I think we should endeavour to buy them off with concessions in the West Indies and elsewhere, if that be possible. But if I conquer Belgium nothing will induce me to give it up; and when I was in Paris the Government agreed to back me in that, even if it does mean war with England. All my life I have dreamed of expanding France to her natural frontiers. Now is my chance, and I do not mean to lose it."

Suddenly, beneath the fumes of alcohol, something clicked in Roger's brain, and he realized that this conversation, begun so casually, was of the first importance. Without altering his tone he asked, "What do you consider to be the natural frontiers of France?"

Dumouriez lifted a slightly shaky hand, and a little ponderously counted them off on his fingers. "The Alps, the Mediterranean, the Pyrenees, the Western Ocean, and the Rhine from the mouth of the Scheldt to the Alps. In the south our people have taken Nice from those lousy Piedmontese, so let's hope that it won't be long before they reach Monaco, which should be our natural frontier down there. Here in the north we've far more to do, but we'll do it. We'll chase those lousy Austrians out of Belgium and turn the country into French

Departments. I was born in Cambrai, you know, and my native town has been the victim of far too many invasions. It is essential that the industrial towns of northern France should be properly protected, and the only way to ensure that is to push our frontier forward to the Scheldt and Rhine."

They talked on for a while, had a final drink together, then made their way, just a shade unsteadily, to a mansion round the corner in which they had been given comfortable lodgings.

When Roger awoke a few hours later the conversation was still fresh in his mind, and he was more than ever convinced of its importance. Dumouriez had been lucky in many things—at Valmy, in being opposed only to a nervous mediocrity like Brunswick, and even in the weather—but the fact remained that he had saved Paris and driven the invader from the soil of France. His stock with the Convention must stand very high, and the zealots who dominated it would undoubtedly back his project for incorporating Belgium into the Republic. Moreover, he was shrewd, capable, immensely energetic, and rapidly converting an armed rabble into a reliable military machine. He was a realist, and although he had been most circumspect in all his conversations with Roger he had not entirely succeeded in concealing the contempt he felt for the revolutionary doctrines. With a powerful army behind him he might easily become another General Monk, marching on Paris and reinstating the King, or even proclaiming himself Dictator. In any case, there was now every reason to suppose that he would exercise an immense influence on the future policy of France; so Mr. Pitt must be informed of his personal views with a minimum of delay.

Dressing as quickly as he could, Roger went downstairs and waited until the General appeared. Having wished him good morning, he said: "I have been thinking of our conversation last night. Since you intend to invade Belgium, I consider it important that steps should be taken to strengthen the morale in the fortress towns between your army and the coast; otherwise there will be a risk of the Austrians up there turning your left flank. Having purged the army in the field, I propose to continue my mission by visiting the garrisons along the frontier right up to Dunkirk."

"You could not render me a greater service," replied the General quickly, "and the sooner you set about it, the better. We may not see eye to eye in everything, and I'll not conceal from you now that on your arrival at my headquarters I feared that your interference in army matters was going to cause me a lot of trouble. But for all your extremist views, you are a sound, sensible fellow; and during the past month you have proved a great help to me. I've made that clear in my despatches to Paris, and when you have completed your circuit I'll be glad to see you back here."

As Roger thanked the little man he could not help wondering just how much he had contributed to the better morale of the revolutionary army; but he felt that his own part had been a small one compared with the General's own ubiquitous activities, and the basic fact that from Valmy on it had not sustained a single setback. In any case he believed that in a very difficult situation he had succeeded in doing more good than harm to the cause he secretly served; and it was most satisfactory to know that Dumouriez's despatches must have still further strengthened his own position with the men who ruled in Paris.

An hour later he and Dan were on the dreary rainswept road to Meziers. They slept at Cambrai that night, and the following day pushed on through Douai and St. Omar to Calais. Before arriving in the port Roger removed his scarf of office, and, having filled in two of Danton's blank passports, they boarded the packet boat for Dover. At ten o'clock on the evening of the 26th of October they arrived in London; but late as it was, Roger hired a post-chaise to take them on to Richmond.

He found Amanda already in bed. They had been separated for eighteen weeks, and their reunion was rapturous. Later, they put on dressing-gowns and went down to the larder to collect a picnic meal, which they carried up to eat in front of the bright fire in her bedroom. He had been able to write to her from time to time, but only to assure her of his well-being; and he had not dared allow her to write to him at all, in case one of her letters fell into wrong hands and gave him away; so both of them had a thousand questions to ask. But soon all serious enquiries were answered and they became as gay as the bubbles in their glasses of champagne. With the glorious appetite of youth they laughed, loved and drank the night away; so daylight was seeping through the chinks of the drawn curtains before they finally fell asleep in each other's arms.

The day was Saturday, and Roger knew that Mr. Pitt almost invariably spent the week-end at his country house near Bromley. He could have ridden over to see the Prime Minister there that afternoon, but he dared not stay long in England, from fear that his disappearance from the scene of his mission would be discovered. The news he brought was important, but of no special urgency, and he saw no reason why he should spoil by interruption the very limited time that he could give to being with Amanda; so he decided to remain with her till Monday morning, then see his master, and set out again for France as soon as he had done so.

That evening, for fun, they put on their best silks and satins, powdered their hair, and dined in state. As the last dish of the meal, he had arranged a surprise for her with their cook's help; it was an ice pudding *à la tutti-frutti*, but instead of pieces of candied fruit and glacé cherries the rich ice cream was larded with diamonds.

Laughing like children, they sucked the precious stones clean, as though they were coins found in a Christmas pudding, and piled them on a plate; but Amanda's fair face became clouded with distress when he had to tell her how he had procured them.

He pointed out that there was no possible way of returning the gems to their owners, most of whom were undoubtedly dead; and that in gambling his life, as he did, he felt that they were fully entitled to such perquisites, which, had he not taken them himself, would have gone to some murderous revolutionary. But he added that, if she were agreeable, it had occurred to him that they might give half the value of the stones to the fund which had been raised to help destitute French *émigrés* in England.

To that she agreed at once; but after a moment she said thoughtfully, "If you have no objection, dearest, I would prefer that the half we give away should go to Lady Atkyns."

He raised his eyebrows. "And who, my sweet, may Lady Atkyns be, that we should endow her with several thousand pounds?"

Amanda smiled. "She is a new neighbour of ours; I find her most sympathetic and have come to know her intimately while you have been away. She is elderly and quite rich but would, I feel sure, welcome further funds to assist her plans. And we could hardly put the money to better use, as she has vowed to rescue poor Queen Marie Antoinette."

Roger's eyes nearly popped out of his head; then he sat back and roared with laughter. "Strap me!" he chuckled. "What a picture! No, my poppet, you cannot be serious."

"Indeed I am," replied Amanda a trifle stiffly.

"Come, come," he admonished her with a mocking smile. "Has this elderly lady ever been within the precincts of the Temple, let alone inside its donjon? How does she propose to set about the business, pray? Perhaps by fishing the Queen out of the tower by a hook on the end of a rope and hauling her up into a balloon?"

"Mr. Brook, I think you are being quite horrid," said Amanda, tears starting to her eyes.

Immediately Roger was all contrition, and running round the table kissed her back to happiness; but although she assured him that Lady Atkyns was a very intelligent woman and already had several agents working for her in France, he could not be persuaded to finance her schemes with a part of their windfall. Instead, as he had originally intended, he made Amanda choose twelve of the best stones for making up into a necklet, then said he would dispose of the others and that later they could discuss how best to deal with the money they fetched.

Sunday passed all too quickly, and on Monday morning Amanda bravely waved farewell again to him and Dan.

Their first call was at No. 10, Downing Street, where Roger left his name, with a message that he would be at Amesbury House until he learned from the Prime Minister at what hour it would be convenient to wait upon him. They then drove on to the Marquess of Amesbury's mansion in Arlington Street, where his second son, Roger's old friend Droopy Ned, lived when in London.

Droopy was at home, although still yawning in his great four-poster bed; but he was delighted to see Roger and, wrapping himself in a Roman toga, ordered breakfast to be brought up to the small dining-room of his private suite. While they ate their way through two Dover soles, a porterhouse steak and a brace of cold grouse, with a quart of claret apiece to wash them down, Roger gave his host the news out of France and listened with interest to his shrewd comments. Then, when the table had been cleared, he produced the fat little packet of diamonds.

Lord Edward Fitz-Deverel was considered eccentric because he held blood-sports in abhorrence, and instead pursued the hobbies of studying ancient religions, trying out dangerous drugs on himself, and collecting antique jewellery; so as he flicked the stones over with a long thin forefinger his pale-blue, short-sighted eyes peered at them with the knowledge of a connoisseur.

"I would I had been at your elbow, Roger, when you had your pick of the Commune's looted treasure," he murmured with a smile. "More than half of these are paste, and I doubt if a goldsmith would give you more than two thousand guineas for the lot. But leave it to me, and I'll squeeze three-five for you out of one of those rogues in Hatton Garden."

Roger was grievously disappointed, as he had believed his haul to be worth between eight and ten thousand pounds, and had, in any case, decided to settle five hundred of it on Dan as a reward for his loyal service. However, it consoled him a little to think that he was lucky to have a friend like Droopy, who could obtain for him nearly double what he would have had to take himself, and that he was after all under no compulsion to give half the money away to the fund for French *émigrés*.

Soon after midday a running footman arrived from Downing Street with a message that the Prime Minister would receive Roger at five o'clock, so he sent Dan round to the coach office at the White Bear in Piccadilly to book inside seats on the Dover mail for that night. In the afternoon Droopy fulfilled a long-standing promise by taking him to see the Duke of Richmond's superb Canalettos. They took a dish of tea with the Duchess, then Roger said good-bye to Droopy on the steps of Richmond House, and walked across Whitehall to keep his appointment with the Prime Minister.

Mr. Pitt gave more than two hours of his time to Roger, listening to all he said with keen interest and asking him many questions. He was greatly perturbed when he heard about Dumouriez's ambitions and, standing up, began to pace the room as he said angrily:

"Such people drive one to distraction! Is there not trouble and poverty enough in the world without whole nations setting about cutting one another's throats for an ideal? By stupendous exertions I had all Europe pacified at the beginning of the year; yet look how these madmen in France have since destroyed my work. Austria, Prussia and Sardinia are already involved, and now they would draw Spain, Holland and ourselves in against them. But I'll not have it; this nation is today more prosperous than she has ever been in all her history, and I'll not see her wealth squandered senselessly while there remains the least possibility of preventing it."

"If Dumouriez overruns Belgium we'll have to fight," said

Roger quietly. "Antwerp in the hands of the French would be a loaded pistol at our heads."

"Yes, yes!" muttered the Prime Minister. "I know it. But they are very far from being in Antwerp yet; and even if they get there we may find ways of getting them out again without resorting to war."

Roger shrugged. "Perhaps I have failed to make it sufficiently clear to you, sir, that the new leaders of the Revolution are not men, but tigers—and tigers who have already tasted blood. In the south their troops have taken Nice from the Sardinians and are beginning to overrun Savoy. In the north General Custine has already reached the Rhine; Speier and Worms have fallen to him, and when I left Sedan he was advancing on Mainz in response to a call from the German Jacobins there that they were ready to murder their magistrates and hand over their city to him. Who can say now where this will stop? If they get Belgium, what of Holland? It is scarce four years since many of the Dutch cities revolted against their *Stadtholder*. They will prove fertile ground for agitators, and the zealots in Paris will not need much pressing to order their troops to continue their advance across the Low Countries."

"You may be right," Mr. Pitt sighed. "If that occurred we should be bound to honour our treaty with the Dutch; but time will show, and I think you over-pessimistic."

It was quite clear that he hated the thought of war so intensely that he was determined to shut its possibility out of his mind, unless further events positively forced it upon him; so Roger broached another subject.

"A while back, sir, you expressed great distress at my account of the appalling scenes I witnessed in Paris. In France today there are thousands of unfortunate people who have been forced into hiding from fear of their lives; can nothing be done to help them?"

Mr. Pitt's face softened, but he shook his head. "Even if I were willing to reverse my decision to refrain from interference in the internal affairs of France, I cannot think that a note to the French Government would have the least effect; and I am determined to do nothing which will worsen our relations with them."

"I was not thinking of any official step, sir; but that as a matter of Christian humanity you might consider authorizing certain unorthodox measures by which at least a proportion of these victims of the terror might be saved."

"What have you in mind, Mr. Brook?"

"The establishment of a secret escape route for them. A few resolute Englishmen could do much, if you were prepared to make them a grant from the secret funds and place at their disposal one or more naval sloops laid up from the last war."

The Prime Minister smiled. "You are evidently not aware that such an organization exists already."

"Indeed, sir!" Roger's eyes widened. "No; I have come across no traces of its activities, but I am much pleased to hear that. To undertake rescue work myself would interfere seriously with my activities on your behalf, and would be next to impossible so long as I remained tied to certain duties as a Commissioner of the Commune; but it would be a great comfort to me if I were able to pass on the names of people whom I knew to be in desperate straits to someone who could get them safely away to England. There is, too, the matter of my future despatches to yourself."

"Yes. Although we recalled my Lord Gower, to mark our disapproval of the events of the 10th of August, we had hoped to keep Mr. William Lindsay on in Paris as *Chargé d'Affaires*; but the September massacres were so alarming that they drove nearly every diplomat left there into asking for his passport, and on Mr. Lindsay's departure our Embassy was closed."

Roger nodded. "So I learned just before I set out for General Dumouriez's headquarters. I can, of course, send reports to you by the hand of my servant; but I am loath to spare him if you consider these people of whom you speak trustworthy, and will put me in touch with them."

"Are you perchance acquainted with Sir Percy Blakeney?"

"I know him by name, but have never met him. Has he an agent in Paris with whom I could get in touch?"

"I imagine so. I will take an early opportunity to have a word with him on the matter."

For a moment Roger sat silent, then he said, "I would greatly prefer that Sir Percy and his friends should know nothing of myself; therefore I suggest, sir, that we should use Gouverneur Morris, the American Minister in Paris, as a go-between. He is to be entirely trusted."

"Very well, then. I will ask Sir Percy to make contact with

Mr. Morris, and when you require the help of Sir Percy's League you can do the same. Is there anything else?"

"No, sir," replied Roger, finishing his third glass of port. "I leave tonight. Have you any further instructions for me?"

"I think not. All good fortune to you." They shook hands and Roger turned towards the door. As he reached it the Prime Minister's voice came again. "Oh, there is just one thing: not an instruction but a reminder. Although your two attempts to rescue the Royal Family failed, they did you great credit. I hope, though, that since then other interests have not caused you to forget them—particularly the Dauphin?"

Roger had certainly not forgotten the Dauphin. He was simply biding his time, and he replied with a laugh, "Gracious me, no, sir! I count on him to make my fortune."

CHAPTER XV

"I VOTE FOR DEATH"

On the 4th of November Roger and Dan quite unexpectedly found themselves back at Dumouriez's headquarters. They had crossed on the night of the 30th of October and spent three days carrying out a whirlwind assize in the garrisons of Dunkirk and Lille. Then, on moving to Valenciennes, they learned that, instead of advancing straight into Belgium, the wily little General had carried out an eighty-mile flank march behind the French frontier and established himself there, opposite Brussels. He was, fortunately, far too busy now preparing his offensive to show the least interest in Roger's activities during the past ten days; and the following morning he launched his army into Austrian territory near Mons.

The result, on the 6th, was the battle of Jemappes. At Valmy seven future Marshals of France and over twenty future Imperial Generals of Division had been present, but few of them had even drawn their swords; now for the first time they, and scores of young officers like them who were destined to die before reaching high rank, led their men into battle. Made confident by a six weeks' advance, fired by the new ideals of democracy, and burning with the desire to liberate the people of the Belgian lands, they flung themselves pell-mell upon the slow-moving, cumbersome, parade-ground formations of the Monarchies. The Austrians fought well, but were hopelessly outnumbered; so, although many regiments of *fédérés* broke and ran at the first exchange of shots, Dumouriez's regular troops alone were sufficient to outflank and overwhelm the enemy.

As the French advanced the Belgians threw open the gates of their cities to them, set up Trees of Liberty, sang the *ça ira* and danced the *carmagnole*. It was no longer a campaign but a triumphal progress. Flying columns received the surrender of Ypres, Bruges, Tournai, Ghent, Namur and Antwerp; with incredible swiftness the danger to which, barely a fortnight before, Roger had drawn Mr. Pitt's attention as a possibility that should not be ignored, had become a *fait accompli*. The Austrian Government fled; their forces evacuated the Netherlands. On the 14th of

November Dumouriez entered Brussels to the cheers of the multitude, and, in all but name, Belgium had already become a French province.

Roger now felt that he had every excuse to consider his mission at an end and, as he had long wished to do, return to Paris. He and Dan left on the 16th and arrived on the 19th. That night he made his report to the *Comité*, and could not have chosen a more appropriate moment for his return. For ten days tidings of victory had been preceding him, and he was able to announce the culminating triumph of the campaign. The thanks of the nation were voted to him for his services; Danton embraced him, and even Robespierre, with a pale, cat-like smile, offered him a limp hand to shake.

It so happened that on that same night a measure which later was to have enormous repercussions was passed by the Convention. A member arose to announce that the citizens of the Duchy of Limburg had adopted the *tricolore* cockade and wished to become French, and that those of Mayence had asked for the protection of France against despots. With little thought, but much enthusiasm, the Convention voted that the French nation would grant fraternity and assistance to all people who wished to recover their liberty, and would order its Generals to give effect to their decree. Eight days later the declaration that France desired no territorial conquests was rescinded, by the Convention formally incorporating the captured territory of Savoy into the Republic. Then, on the 15th of December, another motion was passed that France would regard as hostile any nation that dared preserve its Sovereign and privileged Orders.

No steps could have been better calculated to increase the hatred and fear with which all established Governments regarded the new France, and even the most pacific monarchs now felt themselves threatened. Moreover, the decrees had the effect of stirring up serious troubles for them in their own dominions. All over Europe, ever since '89, secret societies in correspondence with the Jacobins of Paris had been spreading their networks, increasing their membership, and working for the overthrow of the old order. Even democratic England was not exempt; Revolutionary clubs in London and the provinces had distributed many thousands of subversive pamphlets, and one of the leading authors of these, the honest but violent Tom Paine, had recently been elected to the Convention as deputy for Calais. The workers of a dozen British cities had sent addresses of congratulation to the Republic on its victory at Jemappes; the news of it had been received with wild enthusiasm by the weavers of Spitalfields, while in Sheffield 10,000 ironworkers had celebrated it by roasting an ox whole, then parading the streets behind a French *tricolore* flag.

Roger expected any day to hear that Britain had declared war on France; particularly after the French had opened Antwerp and the Scheldt to international commerce, as this was both a contravention of guarantees that France had herself repeatedly given to Britain, and a deliberate challenge to the Dutch, whom, in this matter, Britain was under a solemn obligation to support. But it seemed that Mr. Pitt was still turning a blind eye to the "writing on the wall", and continued to be unwilling to take a realistic view of all that was implied by the aggressions of the young Republic.

The elected representatives of that Republic were a matter of professional interest to Roger; so as soon as he had settled down again at the Cushion and Keys, and made certain that all was well in his own Section, he paid several visits to the Convention. Of its 782 members, only 183 had sat in the recently dissolved Legislative Assembly, and 75 in the original National Assembly of '89; so more than two-thirds of the deputies were newcomers to the political arena of Paris.

It would have been a hopeless task to endeavour to memorize such a multitude of new faces; so Roger contented himself with noting the names of any who showed eagerness to speak, and letting his glance rove over the crowded benches in search of features that promised an unusual personality. After he had been conducting his scrutiny for some time one of the new deputies came in and took his seat among the Moderates. He was a tall, thin, abnormally pale-faced man in the early thirties, and catching sight of him gave Roger a most unpleasant shock. His name was Joseph Fouché: he had been a lay teacher of the Oratorian Order, and occupied himself at times with amateur crime investigation. It was in the last rôle that Roger had crossed his path, and each had good cause to hate the other.

Fouché had robbed and killed a friend of Roger's; moreover, he knew both that Roger was the son of a British Admiral and that he had made off with some vitally important French State papers. A reward of 500 *louis d'or* had been offered for their return; the ex-Oratorian had been to very great trouble to earn that reward, and had been deprived of it only when he thought the money was as good as in his pocket, so on that old score he had strong grounds for resentment.

They had met only during a night and day in '83, and again for a few moments in '87. Since they had last been face to face Roger had grown from youth to manhood and changed considerably in appearance; so he had fair reason to hope that Fouché would not recognize him; but he knew that his mind would never be at rest until he had put the matter to the test, otherwise he would always go in fear of some unexpected meeting placing him in sudden acute danger.

In consequence, during the next week he took such opportunities as he could to place himself casually in the way of the new deputy on his entering or leaving the chamber. As Fouché had a habit of never looking anyone straight in the face, it was not easy to obtain a reaction from him; but after Roger had passed within a yard of him on several occasions he came to the reassuring conclusion that the passage of years had altered his features too much for his old enemy to recall them.

In the meantime, the thoughts of nearly everyone in Paris were mainly occupied with the question of bringing the King to trial. As he had already been deposed and imprisoned, even his most violent enemies had no particular desire to try him, and the project had been mooted by the *enragés* only as a cunning move which might enable them to get the better of their political opponents.

A strong reaction had now set in against the violence of August and September, and when the Convention met its composition had proved to be very far from what Robespierre and his friends would like to have seen it. By terrorization they had swept the board in Paris and secured all its 24 seats, yet in the whole of the rest of France their nominees had won less than 30, so they controlled only some 50 votes out of 782. The Girondins mustered some 120, thus leaving a huge nebulous majority of 600 independents owing allegiance to neither Party.

From these results there could be no doubt whatever that the French nation as a whole considered that the Revolution had gone far enough, and desired only to be given a reasonable security to enjoy the reforms of real value that had been secured in '89; but the extremists were now so deeply committed that they had to go forward or face impeachment for the crimes they had already instigated, while the Girondins, who had until recently been their allies, were little better situated. So it had become a question of which of these two small parties could either win or terrorize the greater number of independents into giving it their support.

The extremist group included the most forceful men in the chamber—among the Paris deputies Danton, Robespierre, Marat, Collot d'Herbois, Billaud-Varennes, Camille Desmoulins, Fréron and David; among those from the Provinces Couthon, Saint-Just, Carrier, Carnot, Tallien and Le Bas. As they took their seats high up on the extreme Left, they became known as the Mountain or *Montagnards*. The Girondins, somewhat reluctantly, occupied the benches on which the Feuillants had once sat; so now, despite themselves, they became associated with the Right—but a Right that had deteriorated into a rabid socialism as opposed to the outright communism of the Mountain. In the body of the hall sat the independents, which caused them to be referred to as the Plain; the majority of them were small traders and professional people who were really much more conservative than the Girondins, but had little experience as legislators and no leaders, while almost all of them were much too scared for their own safety to risk drawing attention to themselves by challenging any measure put forward by the political giants who had brought about the overthrow of the Monarchy.

The Montagnards were quick to realize that the King's life was the key to the position. If the Girondins were brave enough to protect him, they could be accused of being reactionaries. If, on the other hand, they could be frightened into contributing to his death, they would, at one stroke, be deprived of their greatest potential asset—the support of the overwhelming majority of the electors, who would still have preferred a constitutional monarchy, but had faith in the Spartan republican ideals that the Girondins so persistently proclaimed as cover for their own unscrupulous ambitions.

In consequence the Gironde did not dare to oppose the Mountain in its proposals that the King should be dealt with as a criminal; they sought only to give to his trial some semblance of legality. Saint-Just, a pale, handsome young man, who was a newcomer to the ranks of the extremists, argued the case for the Mountain. With icy logic, he maintained that proceedings against Louis XVI could not be legally justified but were redundant, since the King had already been condemned on the 10th of August, and should now be executed without further argument. Roland and his followers lacked the courage either to defend the King or to frankly agree that it would be a good move to kill him simply as a matter of political expediency. Instead, they took refuge in legal chicanery, half-hearted accusations based on papers found in an iron coffer that had been brought to light from a secret cupboard in the Tuileries, and equally half-hearted attempts to have the issue as to whether the King should be tried or not referred to the nation. After more than a month of shifty, ineffective fumbling on their part, the King was, on the 11th of December, brought to the bar of the House and charged with complicity in a number of matters contrary to the interests of his people.

For Roger the choice of date was unfortunate. Soon after his return to Paris he had volunteered for duty at the Temple, but had been told that the list was full up until the 2nd of December, and that no further names were being taken, as Municipal elections were being held on that day which might disqualify any of the present Commissioners from continuing to hold office. The backing of the *Comité* secured Roger's re-election as President of his Sectional Committee without difficulty, but the elections brought many newcomers to the Commune, and most of them were eager for a sight of the Royal prisoners; so in the ballot that ensued Roger drew Monday the 10th, and the normal routine of which he had hoped to take advantage to establish some form of communication with the prisoners was turned topsy-turvy by the crisis in the Royal affairs already decreed for the following day.

He found, too, that since he had last been in the precincts of the Temple the confinement of the prisoners had become much more rigorous, and that the Commune had instituted many additional measures to guard against their escape. They had then been living in the small tower and had taken their meals in the Prior's Palace; but Palloy, the contractor who pulled down the Bastille, had made the great tower habitable by the 25th of October, since when the prisoners had been entirely confined there, except for daily visits to a small part of the garden now enclosed by a high board fence.

The number of Commissioners on duty had been increased to eight, doing forty-eight-hour shifts, four of whom were relieved daily. No other Commissioners were now even allowed to see the prisoners except by special authority, and an elaborate system of iron doors and turnkeys had been organized. In addition, since the 29th of September, Simon, the ex-shoemaker, and another Commissioner named Charbonnier, had been installed as permanent custodians.

Formerly the Commissioners had their headquarters in the Council chamber of the Palace; now they occupied the huge ground-floor room of the tower. Its first floor was a permanent guardroom for forty-eight National Guards, who slept there on camp beds. The second floor had been partitioned off into four rooms—a big ante-room in which two of the Commissioners were always on duty; a dining-room separated from it only by a glass screen; the King's bedroom, in which the Dauphin also slept; and a room for Cléry, who had formerly been the Dauphin's valet and was now the only attendant the Royal Family had been allowed to retain. The third floor was similarly partitioned off—into an ante-room, occupied day and night by two Commissioners; the Queen's bedroom, which she shared with her daughter; a room for Madame Elizabeth; and another in which lived a surly couple named Tison, who had been appointed by the Commune to do the rough work of the household.

The great square tower had a small round tower, surmounted by a pepper-pot turret, at each of its corners, and the interior of these formed small additional rooms. On the two upper floors those on the south were water-closets, those on the east were used to store wood for the stoves, and those on the west were the King's Oratory and the Queen's toilet-room. The fourth tower contained a spiral staircase which was the only means of access to the prisoners' apartments, on which no fewer than eight doors had to be unlocked when going up to the Queen's floor.

The four new Commissioners came on duty about eight o'clock, dined with the officers of the National Guard, then drew lots to decide which of them should occupy the King's ante-room and which the Queen's for the night, going to their posts about midnight. During the following day they shared duties with their four colleagues. The instructions of all were never to lose sight of the prisoners for an instant, to speak to them only when answering questions, to give them no information of any kind, to address them only as Monsieur and Madame, and always to keep hats on in their presence.

Over dinner Roger learned the usual routine of the day. The King rose between six and seven, the ladies an hour later. At nine o'clock he and the Dauphin went down to breakfast in the Queen's apartment; then they separated again, and the King gave his son lessons until midday, after which came recreation and a walk in the boarded-off piece of garden, if the weather permitted. At two o'clock they dined on the King's floor, and when the meal was finished played games till four. The King then rested, while the Queen continued the education of both her children until supper-time, at nine o'clock. After the meal the Dauphin was put to bed, and the rest of the family retired at eleven o'clock.

The prisoners were treated with an extraordinary mixture of meanness and generosity. They were made to talk all the time in raised voices, so that the Commissioners with them could hear every word they said; and they had been deprived of pens, ink, pencils, paper, and all cutting implements, even to the Queen's embroidery scissors. On the other hand, they were allowed to have any clothes made that they wished, to order any games they liked for the children, and to feed almost luxuriously. A chef, scullions and three waiters from the old staff of the Tuileries had been installed in the kitchen of the Prior's Palace, and the King, who alone among them drank with his meals, was offered four kinds of wine every day. However, this excellent table was not provided solely for their benefit; the Commissars shared the dishes, and at night often made heavy inroads on the cellar.

It was after the lights had been put out in the Commissars' room, and a flaming bowl of brandy-punch put on the table, that Roger was able to glean from loosened tongues the real attitude of his companions to their charges. In such circles it was the fashion to speak of the "Capets", as the Royal Family were beginning to be called, with austere disapproval, if not actual abuse; but as the evening advanced it became clear that most of those who had been in contact with them found it difficult to hide the pity and respect they felt at the dignified bearing of the prisoners. They were, apparently, not only always good-tempered and polite to their guards, but often showed thought for them by suggesting that they bring their chairs nearer the fire or the lamp, while they rarely allowed the great anxieties from which they must be suffering to prevent them entering into noisy games to amuse the children. Their simple manners evidently never ceased to astonish the semi-educated artisans and small shopkeepers who made up the larger part of the Commune, and the Dauphin won the hearts of all by the gay, talkative way in which he made friends with even the most frightening-looking of the Commissars.

When lots were drawn it fell to Roger to doss down on a truckle bed drawn across the doorway of the King's bedroom, while a Commissar named Verdier occupied another across the doorway of Cléry's room. At six-thirty the following morning they moved their beds, and Cléry led them into the King's room. Louis XVI pulled aside the curtains of his bed and, recognizing both Verdier and Roger, wished them good morning by name. Having been helped into his chamber-robe and shoes, the King shaved himself while Cléry lit the fires. The valet then assisted his master to finish dressing in the pale maroon-coloured suit with gilded buttons that he always wore whilst a prisoner. Next the Dauphin was awakened, said his prayers at his father's knee, and was dressed by Cléry while the King went into his Oratory to read his breviary.

Meanwhile, on the floor above, there was considerably more activity. The woman Tison, cunning and suspicious, was pottering about while the Queen and the two princesses dressed; her husband was laying the breakfast in the ante-room under the eye of the two Commissars who had spent the night there; two men employed for the purpose were refuelling the wood stoves; a water-carrier was refilling the jugs and filters, and a fourth man trimming the lamps. But by nine o'clock the hubbub had subsided, and the family met for breakfast.

The meal was brought from the distant kitchen by three waiters, under the supervision of the four Commissars who had been on duty the previous day. Their responsibility included the examination of every utensil used and all the food served to ensure that no message was smuggled by these means to any of the prisoners. Normally, now, Roger and his team would have been free to spend the morning downstairs; but, after having breakfasted there, knowing that the King was to be taken before the Convention, curiosity drove them upstairs again.

They found the King, with admirable unconcern, giving the Dauphin his usual reading lesson; but at eleven o'clock two Special Commissioners arrived from the Commune with an order that Louis XVI was now to be separated from his son. The King, greatly distressed, embraced the boy for a long time, then reluctantly allowed him to be taken up to his mother.

A depressing interval of two hours ensued, during which Roger was given a good opportunity to realize the exceptional gloominess of the prisoners' quarters. On the pretext of preventing them from communicating by signals with anyone outside, all the windows had been fitted with a type of shutter called a *soufflet*, which consisted of wooden boards fixed at an outward sloping angle from the window-sills, so that nothing but a patch of sky was visible beyond their tops. No sun could penetrate the rooms, even in the summer months, and on this grey December morning they were still semi-dark at midday. Even so, normally at this hour the children would have been romping in the rooms above while their elders enjoyed games of piquet, draughts or backgammon; but today all was silent while they prayed that the father of the family might be strengthened for his coming ordeal, and afterwards brought safely back to them.

At length, at one o'clock, Chambon, the new Mayor of Paris, Santerre, Chaumette and other officials of the Commune arrived and took charge of the King. Below, a coach was waiting to convey him through the wind and rain to the Convention, and in the chilly drizzle thousands of troops lined the streets to guard against any attempt to rescue him. After his departure Roger and his companions went down to dine, and spent the afternoon speculating on the outcome of the session.

The King was absent for five and a half hours; then, on his return, the poor man was informed that arrangements had been made for his son to sleep in the Queen's room, and that in future he was not to be permitted to see any members of his family. This new affliction plunged all those concerned into such depths of grief that during that evening and the next day they did little but weep and pray in their bedrooms.

The Queen was so absorbed by her distress that Roger felt certain she did not even recognize him during his attendance at mealtimes; and Princess Elizabeth, who was reported to be much the more talkative of the two, did not address a single word to anybody. On completion of his tour of duty, at 8 p.m. on the 12th, he left the Temple without having made a useful contact of any kind, and fully convinced that as long as the present arrangements for guarding the Royal Family continued, their rescue would be rendered next to impossible.

In discussions with his acquaintances he learned that the King's appearance at the bar of the Convention had confounded his enemies. Although he had had no warning whatsoever of the questions which would be put to him, he had answered them all promptly and convincingly. The fact was that he was entirely innocent, and that not a single piece of evidence could be produced to show that he had ever acted tyrannically, opposed reforms, violated the Constitution or encouraged foreign invasion. Nevertheless, his accusers were determined to proceed with the trial, and for its further stages agreed to his employing counsel for his defence.

He chose two lawyers named Target and Tronchet. The former refused to defend him, but the latter accepted. There then occurred an extraordinary manifestation of the feelings of the common people; the fishwives of Paris proceeded to chase Target with a bundle of birchrods because of his cowardice, whereas to Tronchet they carried flowers and a laurel wreath. Roman Desèze took Target's place, and the King's old Minister, Malesherbes, came forward begging to be allowed to assist in co-ordinating the defence.

As Roger could see no prospect of getting any members of the Royal Family out of the Temple, he now began to develop his plans for other rescue work.

The guillotine was no new instrument of death, as in various forms it had been used in Italy, Scotland and Germany from the thirteenth century; but Doctor Guillotin had, as a deputy of the National Assembly, proposed its official adoption in France, and, after satisfactory trials on dead bodies, one had been set up in the Place de Grève in the previous April. It was simply a device for eliminating the degree of human error which sometimes made two or more strokes of an axe necessary in beheading; as the sharp, sloping blade of the instrument was heavily weighted, and, when released by the pull of a cord, fell between the grooves in two posts with a force no human neck could resist; in addition the victim, instead of kneeling, was strapped to an upright board, which had a waist-high axle on its far side for tipping him face downwards horizontally beneath the blade, thus preventing him from flinching at the last moment. The first person to die by the new machine had been a highwayman named Pelletier, and since April it had been in fairly constant use; but the great majority of the condemned had, so far, been common criminals, as the time had not yet come when people were sentenced to death merely for their political opinions. In consequence, Roger was not so much concerned with getting people rescued from the prisons as in aiding others who might be arrested at any time to escape being thrown into them.

His position was now very different from what it had been when he had last seen Gouverneur Morris. It might then have proved very dangerous to his newly-established reputation as a revolutionary for him to associate openly with the rich and aristocratic American Minister; but since that time he had climbed high in the nefarious company that now had France at its mercy. Gradually, it had become almost like belonging to an exclusive Order to be known as "one of the men of the 10th of August", who had formed the original Commune. He had served the *Comité* well as Citizen Representative *en mission*, and had received much favourable publicity from being present with Dumouriez at the great victory of Jemappes. He still lived at the Cushion and Keys, and had resumed control of the des Grandvilliers Section; so he was firmly established as the political dictator of a forty-eighth part of Paris. In addition, as a member of the Cordeliers as well as of the Jacobins, he was now personally known to all the leading men of the Left. All this combined to make him one of the privileged few who, like Robespierre, could afford to dress well without fear of criticism, and be seen talking to anyone without arousing suspicion.

He therefore went openly one morning to the American Legation and spent over an hour closeted with his old acquaintance. Mr. Morris had already received an intimation from London regarding the business on which he called, and said that, while his own official position debarred him from personal participation in the work of Sir Percy Blakeney's rescue League, in the interests of humanity he was willing to allow the Legation to be used as a secret clearing-house for information.

That was all Roger required. Dan was again living at *La Belle Étoile*, but keeping in close touch with him; so now, whenever he learned that some unfortunate Royalist was to be arrested on a trumped-up charge, he could send Dan to the Legation with particulars for transmission to Sir Percy's agent. If the number of cases warranted it, Dan could later make direct contact with the agent and arrange a series of regular rendezvous; and it was with this possibility in mind that Roger had decided to employ his henchman in the matter, for thus he could continue to protect the all-important secret of his own double identity.

When he had explained about Dan and his intention to use him as a go-between, they began to talk of the war; and after a while the American said, "I fear it is bound to spread, particularly if they kill the King; and most of these crazy demagogues don't seem to give a damn if they have to fight all Europe."

"I know," Roger agreed. "If England comes in it will be only because they have forced her to. Mr. Pitt is most anxious to avoid war, and I am sure he would do practically anything consistent with honour to keep Britain out."

"That's just what Maret was telling me the other day," nodded Morris. "Do you know him? I don't mean that leprous spawn of hell, Jean Paul Marat, but Hugues Bernard Maret. He is an advocate who took up journalism, started the *Bulletin de l'Assemblée* in '89, then became editor of the *Moniteur*; but he has since been employed in the Foreign Office."

"Yes, I know him slightly. Dumouriez has great faith in him. It was he who put him into the Foreign Office; and, as a matter of fact, it was when he was visiting the General at his headquarters in November that I met him."

"Did you know that he has since been on a secret mission to London, and has had several important conversations with Mr. Pitt?"

Roger raised his eyebrows. "Are the French then endeavouring to negotiate behind their Ambassador's back?"

"That's what it amounts to. All the intelligent people here favour peace, and they've no faith in M. de Chauvelin; he is too young and inexperienced, and every time he remembers that he is a *ci-devant* marquis the thought sends cold shivers down his back. From fear that they'll bring him home and chop off his head he now spends all his time hobnobbing with people like Horne Tooke, and encouraging the English revolutionaries to make trouble for their Government. That is no way for a diplomat to behave; still . . ." Gouverneur Morris broke off to smile, "I will say he held his own with that stiff-necked Foreign Secretary of yours."

"Pray tell me about it," Roger smiled back. "My Lord Grenville is no fool, and is an indefatigable worker, yet so prim and unsympathetic a man that I'd pay a guinea any day to hear how he had been scored off."

" 'Twas on one of the few interviews granted to Chauvelin at the Foreign Office. My lord received his visitor with the most frigid air, then motioned to the hardest-bottomed and stiffest-backed chair in the room for him to sit upon; the Frenchman merely bowed, walked a few paces away and settled himself comfortably in a large armchair on the far side of the apartment. But reverting to Maret; I think it might prove worth your while to develop his acquaintance. Since most of my friends have been driven from Paris I endeavour to amuse myself by entertaining the more civilized and interesting of these new history-makers. Maret and some others are coming to dine with me on Tuesday. If it would not compromise you to do so, I should be delighted if you would join us."

Roger accepted, and, when Tuesday came, enjoyed his evening most thoroughly. After six months, broken only by his few days in England, of exclusion from all social amenities, it was a great joy to dine again in really civilized surroundings; and he found Maret both likeable and highly intelligent—which was by no means surprising, as the diplomat was later to become one of Napoleon's most trusted Foreign Ministers and to be created by him Duc de Bassano.

As a lead, Roger told his old story of having been educated in England by his stepmother, and Maret at once began to talk about his recent stay in London. He was convinced that England could be kept out of the war if only their mutual friend Dumouriez could be deterred from reaping a cheap triumph by the invasion of Holland, and since his return he had done his utmost to impress upon the Ministry the necessity for restraining the General. Apparently he had got on so well with Mr. Pitt that the Prime Minister had suggested he should ask his Government to replace the obnoxious Chauvelin by himself, and that possibility was at present under consideration.

To work for peace being one of Roger's instructions, he went to considerable pains to encourage Maret in his ideas by giving him what passed as the views of a French journalist who had mixed with all classes in England. He spoke of the colourful orations of Charles James Fox in praise of the French Revolution, and said, as he knew to be the fact, that they were simply the outcome of political venom, and must not be regarded as having any serious weight of opinion behind them which might hamper Britain if she once engaged in a war with France; then he went on to speak of the immense wealth, solidarity and determination of the English in comparison with any Continental people, which made them such formidable antagonists once they had made up their mind to fight.

Maret was much impressed; and they parted on the best of terms, having agreed to keep in touch with each other.

On the 26th of December the King was again brought before the Convention. This time Roger was able to be present, and he happened to pass through the ante-chamber of the great hall as the King and his counsel were walking up and down there waiting to be summoned. One of them, in speaking, addressed the King as "Sire". A scruffy little deputy named Treilhard was standing near by, and shouted angrily:

"What makes you so bold as to use a term here that has been forbidden by the Convention?"

Old Malesherbes turned and withered him with the reply, "Contempt for you and contempt for life!"

Afterwards, to Roger, that swift exchange seemed to have typified the whole of the proceedings. The King's counsel showed a splendid fearlessness and spoke with irresistible logic, but the great majority of the deputies entirely ignored their arguments and the fact that they were supposed to be trying a human being for his life. Their mean minds were concerned only with humiliating the simple-hearted man who had had the misfortune to be born heir to all the trappings of supreme power.

When his counsel had concluded, the King spoke very briefly, merely giving his personal testimony to the truth of all they had said. Only one thing seemed to distress him, and that greatly—the accusation that he had been responsible for the shedding of the blood of his people. Roger had never before felt any sympathy for Louis XVI, but, as he sat a silent spectator in the tribune reserved for the Municipality of Paris, his ire rose at the monstrous injustice of the charge.

The King was not allowed to hear the debate that followed, and immediately after his removal pandemonium broke loose. One deputy demanded that his defence should be ignored and that he should be sentenced there and then; another, Lanjuinais, a Breton deputy, courageously invoked Article One of the Constitution as incontestable proof that the Convention had no legal right to try the King at all. Shouts and curses rent the air; the mob in the galleries yelled and hissed. Several of the deputies began to exchange blows, and at one time over sixty of them were engaged in a scrimmage on the floor.

At length order was partially restored, and on the motion of Couthon, Robespierre's lame, embittered shadow, the Convention rendered the trial a farce by ruling that the arguments of the King's counsel should be given no consideration.

For days on end the acrimonious arguments continued with unabated fury. The Mountain was much the smallest party in the House, but it had the backing of the *sans-culottes*; its violence and the manner in which its deputies showed themselves prepared to ride roughshod over every law to gain their ends began to terrify the Girondins. They were the men who had brought their King and country to this sorry pass, and, too late, they saw that by allowing the Monarch to be brought to trial they had fallen into Robespierre's trap. They dared not defend the King openly, yet realized that if he were condemned they themselves might soon become victims of the illegal methods that were being used to secure a verdict against him. In a weak attempt to save him, yet evade the odium of appearing in the guise of Royalists, they advocated referring the whole question to the nation; but they were overruled.

On the 6th of January Dumouriez appeared in Paris, to protest about many grave difficulties with which he was now meeting. The *fédérés* had been mobilized under the old conception that war was not waged seriously during the worst months of the winter, and had signed on with a proviso that from the 1st of December they could go home if they wished until the end of January; the measure had in a few weeks reduced his army to half its former size. At the War Office, Pache, an incompetent nominee of Robespierre, had succeeded the competent Girondin Servan. Pache added to his incompetence a personal hate for the General, and was deliberately reducing his army to a state of helplessness by denying him all but a trickle of supplies. The Belgian cities had welcomed the troops of Republican France with open arms, but had soon become disillusioned about the invaders; wherever Dumouriez's men went they looted and raped, and commandeered every form of property to make good the breakdown of their own commissariat. Then the decree of the 15th of December, by which Belgium was ordered to accept all the new French institutions, had driven the Belgians into open revolt; and Dumouriez was now only able to hold down his conquests by a reign of terror, which Danton himself as Citizen Representative *en mission* had left Paris to institute.

On Dumouriez's arrival, his old colleagues of the Girondin Ministry urged him to use his great influence as the victor of Jemappes in an effort to save the King. He agreed; but once more the majority of the liberals continued blind to the future they were preparing for themselves, and supported the Mountain when a cry was raised that the General meant to threaten the chosen representatives of the People, and that to allow him to intervene in the debate might prove to be the thin end of the wedge to a military dictatorship. So, in spite of repeated endeavours to address the House, Dumouriez was refused a hearing.

At length, on the 14th of January, the Convention decided that three questions should be put to the vote: (1) Is Louis guilty? (2) If guilty, what should be his punishment? (3) Should your decision be ratified by an appeal to the People?

Again desperate efforts were made by the more clear-sighted to have the last question taken first; but Barère, an extraordinarily astute politician and persuasive talker, although a deputy of the Plain, sensing that the Mountain would triumph in the end, decided to curry favour with it, and played into its hands by arguing his associates into voting that the question of guilt should be given priority.

Voting began the following day and was carried out under the grossest intimidation. The men of the Plain, who formed the vast majority, were, almost without exception, opposed to the King's condemnation; but they were harassed, bewildered, leaderless, and utterly incapable of standing up to Marat, Robespierre, Couthon, St. Just and a dozen others who declared that anyone maintaining the King's innocence was a traitor, and deserved to die with him. All Paris was in an uproar, with mobs parading the streets and threatening another massacre like that of September if the King was declared innocent. As the deputies entered the hall, *sans-culottes* waved daggers and pikes before their faces, yelling that unless they voted for death they should themselves die; and within the hall itself the *canaille* in the galleries screamed further threats at them as each rose, trembling, to his feet to give his vote.

A final mockery of justice was resorted to by each deputy being required, contrary to the law, to declare the King "guilty" or "not guilty" *en bloc* of all the thirty-four charges which had been brought against him. Some of the lesser ones were items such as having continued to pay his old bodyguard after their dismissal, of which he was certainly guilty; in consequence not a single deputy could, or did, declare him innocent. Then, under the menace of the mob, the appeal to the People was quashed by 424 votes to 284.

On the evening of the 16th the brave Lanjuinais rose, before the final voting began, to demand reassurance that in accordance with the penal code a majority of two-thirds should be necessary to carry the death penalty. Howls of execration greeted this plea that the King should at least receive the same justice as that meted out to the meanest criminals; and Danton, just returned from Belgium, used his brutal bellow to secure a decision that a majority of a single vote should suffice.

The voting on the supreme question occupied thirty-seven consecutive hours. It took place amidst scenes of unparalleled disorder and disgusting licence. The extremists had filled a private gallery with their women friends, many of whom were the new *poules de luxe* of the Revolution. Wearing the immodest garments made fashionable by "liberty" and decked out in jewels looted by the men who kept them, these women behaved as if they were at a cabaret—drinking champagne, eating ices, sucking oranges and throwing the half-consumed fruit at the deputies who voted only for imprisonment. Innumerable fights took place in the body of the hall, and uproar constantly interrupted the proceedings. With magnificent courage the Spanish Ambassador fought his way in and endeavoured to appeal to those better instincts that had made the French a great nation; but he was thrown out. Manuel, who had attempted to save the Princesse de Lamballe, now tried to save the King by making off with some of the slips on the President's desk on which votes for death were recorded; he was caught, savagely manhandled, and escaped death himself only by swearing that he had taken the slips in mistake for some other papers.

The culminating moment of these frightful two nights and a day was reached when Philippe Égalité, *ci-devant* Duc d'Orléans, was called on to record his vote. Through unscrupulous use of his millions to hoard grain, pay agitators and supply free liquor to the mobs, he had done more than any other single individual to bring about the Revolution; yet many people still believed that he had been more misguided than wicked, and that the worst crimes connected with his name had been committed by his associates without his knowledge. Now was the moment when his true character was to be revealed. Pale as a ghost, with every eye in the vast, dimly-lit hall upon him, he mounted the tribune and said clearly, "I vote for death."

A terrible hush fell on the assembly. Men rose slowly from their seats; women recoiled with nausea. Even to the regicides who had already cast their votes for the extreme penalty, and the *sans-culottes* of the galleries, it seemed too horrible that a man should voluntarily aid the sending of his own cousin to the scaffold. A low murmur ran round the hall. A voice cried, "Oh, the monster!" Then suddenly a great wave of booing surged over Egalité's bent head.

As though to stress more fully the ghastliness of his crime, when all was done it transpired that Louis of France was condemned to death by a clear majority of that one vote only.

Among the minority were a number who had also voted for death, but demanded a debate on the postponement of the sentence, and it was agreed that this should take place next day; so when Roger left the chamber in the cold light of dawn, amongst a crowd of exhausted deputies and spectators, there still remained a hope that the King's life might be spared. But Roger was in no position to attend that final debate, as a most unexpected turn in his affairs had carried him post-haste out of Paris.

CHAPTER XVI

"MADAME LA GUILLOTINE"

DURING the latter part of December and early January Roger had had several meetings with Maret and, also, with Dumouriez, since the latter's return to Paris. Before midday on the 19th of January, after only a few hours' sleep, he was woken with an urgent summons to come at once to the Foreign Office. There he found them both closeted with the Foreign Minister, Lebrun; all three were intensely worried, and the garrulous little General explained the reason for their anxiety.

"My army is falling to pieces," he declared angrily, "and it's now all I can do to hold down Belgium. Two months ago I wouldn't have given a damn for the English; but if they come in now it will prove our ruin. Now that the vote has gone against the King he may be dead within the week. If he is executed that may prove the last straw with the Monarchies. England, Holland and Spain may all declare against us; but England is the key to the situation. You speak English and were educated among those stiff-necked islanders, so must understand them; moreover you have a far better grasp of international affairs than most men of your standing in the Republic. We want you to leave for London immediately, and do your utmost to prevent the war spreading."

Roger suppressed a gasp of amazement and dismay; to be sent as a diplomatic representative of revolutionary France to his own country was the very last thing he had ever expected or desired. Scores of people in London knew him as the son of a British Admiral and he would have to pose there as a Frenchman; it needed only one person to greet him as an old friend in front of some other member of the French Embassy and his return to France to continue the valuable work he was doing would be rendered impossible. Yet this was clearly a great emergency. Peace or war apparently hung upon it; and, above all things, his master desired that peace should be maintained. For that, he must risk everything. After a second, he said:

"Of course I will go if you wish me to, Citizen General; but if Capet should be sent to the scaffold, what can you enable me to offer the English that may serve to counter the intense feeling his execution is certain to arouse among them?"

It was Maret who replied. "That is our great difficulty; the Citizen Minister, the Citizen General and I all feel that every possible concession must be made. We are agreed that as the price of peace we should renounce the Scheldt and, if need be, withdraw our troops from Belgium."

"Then I think you have little to worry about," said Roger in some surprise; "such a gesture should certainly satisfy them."

"Ah!" cut in Lebrun, "but the trouble is that as yet I have no power to make it. All my colleagues are so occupied with the trial that I cannot get them to spare me even a moment, and without the consent of the Council no such proposals can be put forward. I am even far from certain that they will agree with my ideas, as several of them have no conception of the gravity of our situation. They might even insist on our issuing a wanton challenge to England, should they feel that she has given us grounds for provocation. Such grounds would be given did England presume to threaten us in the matter of Louis's life or death, as the Council consider that entirely a question for the French people. Should he be executed, tempers in London will run high, and the object of your mission will be to pacify them as far as possible by a promise of conciliation."

"How can I, if I have nothing to offer?" asked Roger.

"Our idea is that your arrival on the scene, as an earnest that we intend to open fresh negotiations, may gain us a little time. I have decided to recall Citizen Chauvelin and replace him by Citizen Maret, who has already succeeded in making a favourable impression on Mr. Pitt; but it would be futile for Maret to leave until we have won the Council round to consenting to these concessions. You can tell the English that we mean to remove Chauvelin because he has proved so obnoxious to them, and that we now hope to send proposals to them very shortly. You can also calm their fears regarding the decrees of November 19th and December 15th, to which they have taken such strong exception. Tell them that those decrees were intended to apply only to territories adjacent to France in which a majority of the population invited us to intervene, not as a promise that we would give armed support to any group of malcontents who wish to set themselves up in the place of an established government."

"Tell them too," added Dumouriez, "that should Maret's

negotiations proceed favourably, I will come to London myself later and discuss the possibility of a general peace."

Maret looked grave and raised his eyebrows. "Dare we contemplate that? Do you realize that it would mean those forty thousand desperate ruffians of yours returning to our cities?"

The General shrugged. "I consider that a lesser danger than allowing them to be cut to pieces as an army and seeing France invaded. Believe me, we should still be striking a good bargain did we give up Mayence, Nice and Savoy as well as Belgium, if by so doing we could secure a lasting peace. No one can accuse me of being a defeatist, but no General can wage even a defensive campaign without some reliable troops; and looting the flesh-pots of Belgium has turned all mine into a drunken, dissolute, mutinous mob."

"Then Maret's fears are all the better founded," remarked Lebrun glumly. "Better to rely on a renewal of patriotic fervour to hold back the invader again, than have peace at the risk of the Revolution perishing in a reign of anarchy. That would cost us our own necks. 'Tis clear that we must do everything possible to prevent any addition to our present enemies, whilst keeping the war going; and the best service you can render the nation, Citizen General, is to shoot a few hundred of your ruffians, then march the rest as far away as their legs will carry them."

An hour later Roger was on his way to England. It was bitterly cold and in the January frosts the neglected roads were more than ever appalling; but he travelled with all the speed that fear and the ingenuity of man could provide. When from the muddled Councils of the Revolution a clear order did emanate, it was now executed with ruthless swiftness; Roger carried in his pocket a warrant of arrest for anyone who failed to expedite his passage to the utmost of their ability. Four hussars acted as his outriders, and he had only to show his order to make the lazy, and normally arrogant, Municipals of little townships run to do his bidding. His horses were changed every few miles with amazing celerity, and he reached Calais the following afternoon. There, he did not wait for the packet, but ordered out a naval sloop to carry him across the Channel. The wind was contrary and the sea running high; so, being an indifferent sailor, he was horribly sick, and the delayed crossing caused him to miss the morning coach out of Dover; but he hired a post-chaise and reached London on the evening of the 21st.

Leaving his post-chaise in Piccadilly, he walked round the corner to Amesbury House, where he was lucky enough to catch Droopy Ned on the point of going out. Having explained his anomalous position, he asked his friend to get in touch with Mr. Pitt and inform him of the peculiar circumstances that required an urgent meeting at some secret rendezvous, in case No. 10, Downing Street was kept under observation by a French agent; then to invite Amanda up to Amesbury House for a few days, so that he could see as much as possible of her while he was in London. In order to meet again in a place where it was unlikely that Roger would run into anyone he knew, they arranged to lunch together the following day at the Cheshire Cheese in Fleet Street. Muffling himself up against the bitter wind, Roger then walked back to his post-chaise and was driven to the French Embassy.

The *ci-devant* Marquis de Chauvelin received him politely, but with evident uneasiness; and, having perused his credentials, expressed his willingness to do everything possible to aid him. Roger had decided that the less he had to do with the diplomat the less danger he would run; so he adopted the haughty attitude of a fiery young revolutionary who felt contempt for old-fashioned diplomatic methods, made no mention of Chauvelin's imminent recall, gave only the barest outline of his mission, and said that all he required was that an appointment should be made for him to see either Mr. Pitt or Lord Grenville as soon as possible.

Chauvelin replied that such interviews were far from easy to obtain, and as they went in to a meal that he had ordered for his guest he proceeded to explain the difficulties of his position. The British Government had not yet recognized France as a Republic, so they persistently refused to accord him diplomatic status. When he had last requested Lord Grenville to see him, the Foreign Secretary had replied that he should put what he had to say in writing; and on his urging the greater benefits likely to accrue from a personal conversation, Grenville had only consented to receive him a week later.

Roger then gave an account of the King's trial, and remarked that in view of it his business was most urgent; so the *Conseil Général* in Paris would hold his host responsible if an interview could not be obtained promptly. The wretched Chauvelin promised to do his utmost, and swiftly launched out on an account of his many activities to aid the Revolution in England.

For an hour Roger listened to his stories of the operations of Lord Stanhope, Lord Semphill, Doctor Priestly, the "Reformation Society of Manchester", the "Revolution Society of Norwich", the "Friends of the People" and other persons and groups who were fomenting trouble, as he felt that such information might be useful to Mr. Pitt; after which he went to bed.

Next day, at the Cheshire Cheese, Droopy told him that Mr. Pitt would see him at Mr. Dundas's house out at Wimbledon that night, and would have a plain carriage to take him there waiting on the south-east corner of Portman Square at ten o'clock; and that Amanda would be joyfully awaiting him at Amesbury House on his return.

Naturally Roger was most anxious to spend the night with her; so, later that afternoon, he casually informed Chauvelin that when walking down the Haymarket he had run into a pretty baggage whom he had known when he had previously been in England, and meant to stay the night at her apartment in Jermyn Street.

Henry Dundas, the Home Secretary, was as near an opposite to William Pitt as it would have been possible to find—apart from the fact that they both had an immense capacity for work and drinking port—for the former was a big, bluff, foul-mouthed Scot with no pretensions to culture or aristocratic lineage; yet the two were the closest of boon companions, and when Roger arrived at Wimbledon he found them still at table, now well into their second bottle.

Dundas thought Roger's appearance in London as a French envoy a huge joke; he roared with laughter, slapped him on the back, then in his rich Scots accent bade him help himself to the port. Pitt, too, now in his most genial mood, was much amused; but soon both became grave when Roger gave them an account of Louis XVI's trial.

"Think ye they'll send the puer footlin' mon to the scaffold?" Dundas asked.

"Aye," Roger replied, lasping quite unconsciously into an idiom he had caught when very young from his Scottish mother; "there may be a postponement for a few weeks, but 'tis more likely that his execution will take place within the next few days; it may even have taken place already."

The Prime Minister glanced at his friend. "This means war, Hal; I have long dreaded it, and have in recent weeks come with the utmost reluctance to regard it as inevitable."

"You have always said, sir," Roger remarked deferentially, "that you would never embroil England on account of any French domestic matter; and surely this is one?"

"That is true enough, Mr. Brook, and I stand by what I said; but there are other matters, such as the decrees. By them all England saw the formal declaration of a design to extend universally the new principles adopted in France, and to encourage revolt and disorder in all countries; even in those which are neutral. Again, there is the question of the Scheldt and of the security of Holland; this nation will never look on with indifference while France makes herself, either directly or indirectly, the Sovereign of the Low Countries, or general arbiter of the rights and liberties of Europe. Should the French murder their King, His Majesty's Government could not allow such a crime to pass without marking in some signal manner their horror at so barbarous an act. If fight we must, what more suitable opportunity will ever be afforded me to make the break, and allow the nation to enter upon the war which so large a part of it now desires, and which I myself am compelled to agree has become essential to our future safety?"

"Personally, sir, I have no desire to argue the opposite case," Roger replied, "for I am convinced that sooner or later we must fight these devils, or be undone; and there could be no better time to do so than now, because their army has practically disintegrated. But my duty to you demands that I should inform you of the circumstances which, to my mind, make it feasible to postpone the issue if you wish." He then gave his listeners a full account of his meeting with Lebrun, Dumouriez and Maret at the French Foreign Office.

When he had finished, the Prime Minister looked at him doubtfully and said, "If France is really desirous of maintaining peace and friendship with England, she must show herself disposed to renounce her views of aggression and aggrandizement, and to confine herself within her own territory, without insulting other governments, without disturbing their tranquillity, and without violating their rights. Are you fully convinced that those are her honest intentions?"

Roger shook his head. "I could not say that. When I left Paris Lebrun himself could not even guarantee that the Council would support his efforts to maintain peace. But of one thing I am convinced: the wisest men that France has left to guide her now consider her to be in dire peril; therefore they are prepared to make every reasonable concession rather than see England added to her enemies."

Mr. Pitt's eyes lit up. "If that be so, you give me new hope."

"Billy, ha' regard to the facts!" Dundas cried, bringing his great fist smashing down on the table. Then he went on to recall how Lord Auckland, their Ambassador at The Hague, had furnished them with a copy, taken by a Dutch secret agent at Dumouriez's headquarters, of a letter written by the General in which he had made enthusiastic mention of his plans for invading Holland.

"That was before Christmas," the Prime Minister shrugged, "and I believe Mr. Brook right in his contention that they have had ample cause since to modify their views. In any case, the news he brings decides me to refrain from slamming the door in their faces. Should they send King Louis to the scaffold we must make plain how gravely such a step has prejudiced their interests with us; but I'll not make it a cause for war, as I had intended. Monsieur Maret seemed to me an honest and capable man; we will wait to hear what he has to say, and pray that between us we may yet find a way to avert a final rupture."

Roger, having now said all that his duty made it incumbent on him to say, was anxious to get back to London; but his superiors continued to circulate the port and meanwhile ply him with innumerable questions about life in the Paris of the Revolution. It was three in the morning before he managed to get away, and past four when he kissed a drowsy Amanda into joyful wakefulness; but at least he had the compensating thought to set against their sadly abbreviated night together that he had never stood higher in the estimation of the Prime Minister.

That he had done exactly what those who had sent him had desired, more swiftly and efficiently than anyone else they could have sent, seemed extraordinarily ironic; but it had just happened that their wishes coincided with his master's fixed determination to snatch at any straw that might avert war. He did not approve of Mr. Pitt's ostrich-like attitude, as he believed that it was only putting off the evil day, and to no ultimate advantage; but having said so he could do no more about it.

By nine o'clock he was back at Portman Square. Over breakfast with Chauvelin it gave him considerable amusement, having spent most of the night with Mr. Pitt, to harry the Frenchman for the interview which it was beyond his powers to secure for several days at least. Then, that afternoon, a despatch arrived which made the diplomat's inability to be of use more galling for himself than ever; it contained the news that at 10.20 a.m. on the 21st Louis XVI had been executed.

The guillotine had been specially set up in the great open space between the west end of the Tuileries gardens and the entrance to the Champs Élysées. The arrangements had been so perfect that no incident had occurred. The Convention had made the generous concession of allowing a non-juring priest, the Abbé Edgeworth, to accompany the tyrant to the scaffold. Having mounted it, Capet had endeavoured to address the people, but his voice had been effectively drowned by General Santerre promptly ordering the troops to beat a tattoo on their drums. When Citizen Executioner Samson had held up the head of the tyrant for the multitude to see they had shown unbounded joy.

That was the gist of the despatch. On reading it, Roger, having for so long been accustomed to act a part, gave a cynical laugh, then announced that he was going out to celebrate with his English *chère amie*, and would not be back before morning.

That night, when he discussed the news with Amanda, she again put forward Lady Atkyns as a most suitable candidate for such part of the money from the sale of the French jewels as they meant to give away. For a moment he was impatient at her suggestion, then grateful for it; because the comical conception of this elderly widow carrying off Marie Antoinette from under the eyes of Citizen Simon, the eight Commissars on duty, and 240 National Guards, helped to dispel from his mind the tragic picture of the hapless, martyred King.

After attempting to convey to Amanda the hopelessness of any such attempt, he told her that he had found a much better use for the money, as a secret League existed for the rescue of less exalted people, which was a really practical undertaking, and that he proposed to ask Droopy to send a thousand pounds anonymously to the man who was running it. With a sigh Amanda agreed; but she was soon laughing again, and, the sad state of France temporarily forgotten, they made up for the time of which Mr. Pitt had unwittingly robbed them the night before. It was as well they did, as, after they parted next morning, they were not destined to meet again for a long time, and then only in far from happy circumstances.

When Roger reached Portman Square he found that a small mob had already collected outside the Embassy, and they booed him as he went into it. The news of Louis XVI's murder was now all over London, and Londoners were showing their disapproval in no uncertain manner. As the day wore on the crowd increased; stones were thrown, windows broken and insults shouted at anyone who appeared at them. Pale, helpless and frightened, Chauvelin kept well out of sight, while Roger taunted him, enquiring sarcastically where all his English Jacobins and radical Corresponding Societies were now. For Chauvelin he had only pitiless contempt and, given the opportunity, would have had him shot far more readily than most of the *sans-culottes* that he had sent to their deaths while with Dumouriez's army, for the Marquis had betrayed his own Order. Roger secretly hoped that the mob would break in, as he would willingly have risked a severe manhandling himself for the chance of seeing Chauvelin hanged from a lamp-post. Instead, all that happened was that the Embassy continued to be the focal centre of an angry crowd till late at night; and, much to Roger's annoyance, he felt compelled to abandon any thought of going to Amesbury House, as to leave the building in such circumstances would have been so entirely out of keeping with his rôle of a French diplomat.

Then first thing next morning there arrived an Order in Council, peremptorily commanding Chauvelin and his staff to quit the country immediately. It was the gesture that the Prime Minister had told Roger he would have to make to satisfy public opinion in England, should the French send their King to the scaffold. There could be no argument or delay in the face of such an order. It would not prevent Maret coming to England as a private person and opening secret negotiations with Mr. Pitt later, but Roger had been officially accredited to Chauvelin's staff; so he had no option but to leave with him, and by midday they were on the road to Dover.

At Blackheath they met a messenger from Paris, who, recognizing the French liveries, pulled up and handed Chauvelin a despatch. It was the order for his recall. The sight of the consternation and fear with which it filled him were Roger's only consolation for having had to leave without saying good-bye to Amanda.

A few miles outside Calais they passed a coach, but failed to recognize its occupants in the darkness. Later they learned that it contained Maret, on his way to England with the new proposals. He, Dumouriez and Lebrun had won round the Council to agreeing to every possible concession being made which might prevent Britain entering the war; but the dismissed Ambassador's arrival in Paris on the 29th again threw everything into the melting-pot.

Roger dared take no other line with Lebrun than to say that his mission had proved abortive owing to Chauvelin's having failed to secure him an interview with a member of the British Cabinet; while Chauvelin, to cover his own failure, reported to the Council that the English were bellicose, intractable, steeped in reaction and only awaiting the completion of their preparations before striking at the young Republic. The zealots overruled the diplomats and insisted that the dismissal of their Envoy should be made a *casus belli*. On the 1st of February, 1793, the Republic of France declared war on both Holland and Britain, and early in March declared war on Spain.

Meanwhile Dumouriez's fears were being realized; the tide of battle began to turn against France, both on the Rhine and in the Low Countries. An expedition, under Dumouriez himself, across the mouth of the Scheldt against southern Holland, was partially successful; but General Miranda failed to take Maestricht, and Custine was forced back from Mayence. On the 18th of March, at Neerwinden, the main French Army suffered a severe defeat, and Dumouriez, now convinced that the reign of the Convention could only lead to anarchy, began to contemplate playing the part of a General Monk.

In Paris all was disorder. The Girondins and the Montagnards had entered into a desperate struggle for power, and fought, impeached and intrigued against each other incessantly, while the Plain looked on in terror. Another Committee of Insurrection was formed. A plan was hatched at the Cordeliers to break into the Convention on the 9th of March, arrest the Girondins and begin a general massacre of the moderates. It failed because the Girondin leaders were warned to keep away from the evening sitting; but the riots that ensued were put down only with difficulty.

In Brittany insurrections of a different kind had broken out. The peasants there had been better treated by their landlords than in other parts of France, and they were also deeply religious. They had accepted the measures against feudalism without active opposition, but the persecution of their priests and the murder of the King filled them with savage resentment, and the call-up for the army proved the last straw. In the Bocage, the Marais, and other districts of La Vendée, great numbers of them had now risen spontaneously, murdered the republican Municipals and taken up arms under the white and gold banner of the *Fleur-de-lys*, to fight for Monarchy and Church.

This alarming news from the west coincided with rumours that Dumouriez intended to betray the Republic. On the 30th of March the *Comité de Défense Générale*, which had replaced the Executive Council, despatched five Commissioners to investigate and, if necessary, suspend him. On the 1st of April he denounced the Convention as "300 scoundrels and 400 imbeciles", arrested the Commissioners and handed them over to the Austrians. During the next four days he did his utmost to persuade his Army to abandon the Republic; a great part of the regular troops were ready to follow him, but the *fédérés* prevailed upon them to refrain. On the 5th of April he gave up the attempt, and, with a few score officers, including eleven Generals, went over to the enemy. Already the French had been driven from the soil of Belgium, and were falling back on all fronts; so this defection by the high command was a matter of the utmost gravity.

From mid-March the cry had again arisen in Paris, "The country is in danger! To arms, Citizens! To arms, or the Revolution will perish!" There was heard again, too, that other sinister cry, "We are betrayed!" "There are still traitors in our midst! Death to the traitors!"

The Girondins had with their usual cowardice, although still numerically the strongest party in the Convention, allowed a new form of legalized massacre to begin. The inmates of the prisons who had shown any prominence as reactionaries were now being hauled from their cells and, on quite minor political charges, sent to the guillotine. In the new emergency, the extremists had their chance to accelerate the movement. A special Revolutionary Tribunal was set up for the swifter liquidation of the "enemies of the Republic"; and on the 6th of April Danton succeeded in establishing the first "Committee of Public Safety" with powers to deliberate in secret, to override Ministers, and with 100,000 *livres* to pay its agents. The word "suspect" began to take on a terrible significance.

Throughout February and March Roger had overtly continued to rule with a rod of iron in the des Granvilliers Section, whilst secretly using Dan as his liaison with the Rescue League to get many people whose lives were in jeopardy smuggled out of Paris. On the 25th of March the *Comité de Défense Générale* had decreed the levy of a further 300,000 men for the army, and had despatched representatives to every Department of France to speed up their raising. Roger had not been chosen for this work, but in April he was sent for by the Committee of Public Safety and charged with a far more dangerous and disagreeable task. It had been decided that the Royalist risings in the Vendée must be suppressed at all costs, and he had been selected as one of the small band of Commissioners which was to be despatched with absolute powers to crush the rebels.

On the 10th of April he again left Paris as *Représentant en mission*, but this time he was escorted by a troop of cavalry, while in his wake lumbered a heavy wagon containing a portable guillotine and a squad of executioners.

The heart of the Royalist rebellion lay to the south of the river Loire, in territory where the towns were few and small. This had enabled the fanatical peasants under their audacious leaders—Cathelineau, a poor hawker of woollen goods, and Gaston, a barber—swiftly to overcome the local Municipals and seize control of a large area. Regular troops were now being sent against them, but Roger's instructions showed that he was not one of the Commissioners detailed to operate with the army. He and several others had been given areas outside that in which the actual fighting was taking place, with orders to liquidate all reactionary elements in them, and thus prevent the revolt spreading.

He had been allotted three out of the five new Departments that made up the old Duchy of Brittany—Ille et Vilaine, Le Morbihan and Côte du Nord. That of Finistère, in the extreme west, was already being purged by the Jacobins of Brest, while the fifth, Basse Loire, to the south, with Nantes in its centre, was the Department in which civil war had flared up. Rennes was the largest town in Roger's area, and he had been told to leave a visit to it as the last on his circuit, as it was the smaller places that called more urgently for "cleansing".

On being charged with this mission, he had had to face the awful choice of either accepting it or abandoning the position which enabled him to supply Mr. Pitt with invaluable first-hand information. Had it entailed the slaughter of hundreds of loyalist peasants as they were captured by the Reds, he would have felt it too terrible a price for any man to pay in serving his country; but he determined to carry on as long as his conscience would allow, and left Paris hoping that in the still peaceful parts of Brittany to which he was sent he would find this new ordeal no worse than that which he had gone through whilst with the Army of Dumouriez. In that hope, however, he proved mistaken.

During the latter part of April, and in May and early June, he was called on to face more shattering experiences than any he had previously encountered in his whole life. Week after week he moved through the villages and townships of the west, bringing death in his train. In all those he came to that were of any size he stopped for several days. His first duty was to purge the local Municipality. Almost invariably, this meant listening to a series of the foullest accusations and meanest betrayals, as the local "patriots" strove to save their own necks at the expense of those of colleagues whom they hated or envied. As there were comparatively few of them who were not guilty to some degree of crimes committed in the name of the Revolution, Roger did not find it too repugnant a task to send one or two of them to his guillotine at every place at which it was set up. It was after this preliminary that the real horror of his task began. The list of the prisoners in the local jail was brought to him, with the charges on which they had been imprisoned; then, supported by the Municipals whom he had spared, he had to try all those accused of crimes against the new Order, while a crowd of local *sans-culottes* looked on and broke into angry murmurs whenever they considered that he was being too merciful.

Day after day, and often far into the night by the light of smoky lanterns, he had to sit stern-faced and impassive while terrified men and women were dragged before him. Very few among them were aristocrats or people who in the past had enjoyed wealth. Some were of the professional classes, and there were quite a number of priests; but the majority were tradespeople, small farmers, teachers, servants who had been loyal to their employers, and ex-N.C.O.'s of the old army. As a temporary relief to his feelings he could acquit some of them and so secure their release from prison; but in every place where his guillotine was set up he had to send four or five to the scaffold.

There were times when he thought he would go mad; and the strain might well have proved too much for him had he not had the rugged, faithful Dan to whom he could pour out his overwrought mind when they were alone. Only one thing enabled him to keep going with this ghastly routine instead of throwing his hand in and returning to England—the knowledge that he was saving life as well as taking it. He could save only a small proportion of those proved to be counter-Revolutionaries; but every one of them would have been sent to the guillotine had he abandoned his mission, with the inevitable result that some genuinely blood-lusting Jacobin fanatic would have been despatched to replace him.

Dan was once more acting as his secretary; so, wherever they halted, exercised an authority second only to his own; and before leaving Paris Dan had secured full particulars of the Rescue League's network in Brittany. After a preliminary investigation at each place, Roger went through the lists of accused and suspects with him; and they held a secret court of their own, which was almost as great a strain as sitting on the Revolutionary tribunal, for they had to decide there and then who could be saved and who must be left to die.

Roger could have had no better man than Dan for such a job. His old trade of smuggler had taught him cunning and resource. As an ex-galley slave he could talk the filthy argot of Marseilles, Toulon and Finistère as well as could any cut-throat who hailed from those ports. Even his presence as Roger's *alter ego* appeared to the *sans-culottes* a guarantee that Roger's own patriotism was irreproachable, despite his cleanliness and well-cut clothes. Dan's memory, too, was marvellous; he needed to write nothing down; his great physical strength enabled him to work day and night with little sleep; and he was as brave as a lion.

So, week in, week out, the awful work went on, and the knife of Roger's guillotine clanked and crashed, severing heads from bodies. But night after night brave Englishmen in strange disguises haunted the streets of the towns in which the guillotine was set up. By some mysterious means they knew the weak spots of the jails, sometimes possessed the keys to them, and knew the hours at which the guards were changed. Again and again, in pitch darkness or under a fitful moon, the people whose names Roger had given to Dan disappeared from their homes a few hours before the Municipals arrived to arrest them, or were spirited away from the prisons to lightless luggers that lay concealed in unfrequented coves along the coast.

Roger had entered Brittany from the north, his first stay of more than twenty-four hours being at St. Malo; from there he zigzagged about the country, staying for several days at Dinan, St. Brieux, Lorient and Vannes in turn. Most of the larger places were well under the thumb of their Red Municipalities, but in the country districts the peasants were sullen and sometimes openly hostile. On three occasions he was shot at and twice members of his escort were wounded; but Citizen Captain Labord, their commander, was a tough, capable ex-N.C.O., and whenever they moved from village to village he had vedettes out on either flank, which prevented snipers getting near enough to aim with any accuracy.

During most of this time Roger learned only belatedly what was going on in the rest of France; but towards the end of May it became clear to him that the Revolution was moving swiftly towards a new crisis. Austrian, Prussian, British and Dutch armies were now taking the offensive in the north, from the coast right down to Alsace; Piedmontese and Sardinians were again attacking in the east and south; the Spaniards had opened a new front in the south-west from across the Pyrenees, and the Royalists of La Vendée were rapidly gaining ground in the west. But foreign enemies and the Royalists were no longer the only threats to the extremists in Paris; their control of the country was now menaced by the possibility of a second civil war tearing it apart.

The more ground the Girondins and their associates lost in the Convention, the more strongly the provincial cities that had sent them there resented the tyranny of Paris and clamoured for a new Constitution under which France should be federalized on the model of the United States, thus enabling them to administer the Departments adjacent to them under laws made by themselves. They had no desire whatever to restore the Monarchy, but they were set on preventing further inroads on property and on the rights of the individual, and aimed to destroy the communist minority which was seeking to crush all opposition by instituting a reign of terror. The three great cities of Bordeaux, Lyons and Marseilles all declared against the Jacobins; Toulouse, Rouen, Nîmes, Grenoble and Caen were reported ripe for insurrection, and revolts had already broken out in the mountainous districts of eastern France.

In Paris, from mid-May onward, the Girondins had made a belated attempt to suppress the forces of disorder. As a precaution against a successful repetition of the 9th of March, in which they might all be killed, they proposed the creation of a Reserve Convention at Bourges which was automatically to assume power in the event of their arbitrary arrest. But the treacherous Barère persuaded them to abandon the measure in favour of the appointment of a Committee of Twelve to investigate subversive activities.

The new Committee made numerous recommendations for curbing the power of the Commune, the Sections and various unorthodox bodies, all intent on stirring up insurrection; but the only active steps it took were the arrest of Hébert for publishing an incendiary article in *Le Père Duchesne*, and of Dobson, the Commissar-President of the Cité Section, for refusing to disclose the minutes of his Sectional Committee.

These arrests on the 24th led to the final clash, as the Commune, backed by the *sans-culottes*, made violent demands for the release of its two members. On the 25th the Girondin Isnard attempted to quell the mob by a speech in which he threatened that the Provinces would annihilate Paris unless order was restored, but, like Brunwick's manifesto, this only added fuel to the fire. The Committee of Insurrection now collected 500 extremists from the Sections at the Archbishop's Palace and these, on the lines of the 10th of August, declared themselves the true representatives of the People; but instead of turning out the old Commune they merged themselves with it, thereby enormously strengthening the communist element in the already radical Municipality.

Hébert and Dobson were released. Hanriot, a bloodthirsty drunkard, was appointed Commandant of the National Guard, and on the 31st of May a mob of 30,000 people surrounded the Convention. The Girondins, now in terror of their lives, were forced to give way and dissolve the Committee of Twelve. Madame Roland was arrested that night, and by morning the Insurrectionaries were well on the way to winning their battle.

June the 1st passed comparatively quietly, but on the morning of Sunday the 2nd great crowds began to collect again outside the Tuileries, to which the Convention had recently moved from its old quarters in the riding-school. Hanriot, reeling drunk and egged on by his friends, brought up several batteries of guns and threatened to bombard the Palace unless the leading Girondins were arrested.

A number of deputies came out and argued with him in vain; so Barère as usual stepped into the breach and proposed that since the Convention was powerless to resist force the threatened

Girondins should save their colleagues' faces by proscribing themselves. This absurd and cowardly expedient was adopted by the majority and at 11 p.m. the session broke up, the twenty-two leading Girondins having been suspended from further participation in the government of the country by the orders of the Commune backed by the mob.

It now became clear that the very principle of government by democracy, which the Revolution had been launched to secure, was being challenged by the Commune of Paris and the little group of extremists led by Danton and Robespierre, and that France was about to fall under a new type of tyranny far worse than the old—unless Paris could be subdued by the Federalists. Some seventy of the most moderate deputies left Paris in secret to raise the provinces, and their arrival at the cities they represented proved the signal for war to be declared on the Convention.

Between the 8th and the 12th of June rumours reached Roger that armies were being raised in Lyons and Bordeaux to march upon the capital; that in Marseilles the Municipality had been overthrown and a Tribunal set up to try "patriots" accused of revolutionary excesses, and that an insurrection had broken out in Normandy; while the Bretons, as he could see for himself, were ready to rise at any moment. So he began to contemplate seizing on this new situation as an excuse to abandon his grim task.

He hesitated from doing so at once only because his information was so scanty, and his men were all full-blooded revolutionaries. If he took them back to Paris prematurely, and the Dantonists came out on top, it would be the end of his hard-won credit with the Committee of Public Safety. After some thought he decided that, as he had been definitely ordered to "cleanse" Rennes, he had better take it next on his itinerary. He would learn there whether the Federal movement looked like dominating the province and, if so, would be able to justify a retirement from it by reporting that disaffection had increased to such a degree that it was no longer possible for him to overawe the reactionaries with the limited number of troops at his disposal. In consequence, on the 13th of June, with some hope that the sinister wood and steel "Madame" who trundled behind him might remain packed in her wagon, he led his cavalcade of death into the Breton capital.

The sight of the narrow streets of the old town filled him with nostalgia, as it was here that, after running away from home, he had spent nearly two years of his boyhood working in Maître Léger's office; and although he had at first been made miserable by the bullying of the eldest apprentice, he had received much kindness from the lawyer and his family, and had known times of ecstatic happiness while living with them. Those joyous hours, which now recurred to him so vividly, had been occasioned by his love affair with the beautiful Athénaïs de Rochambeau. She had been scarcely more than a child when he had first met her, but to him, with her lovely blue eyes, delicate aquiline profile, milk and roses complexion and halo of golden hair, she had seemed like a fairy princess become mortal. She had been his first and, therefore, most desperate passion. From the beginning he had known that nothing could ever come of their romance, for, although well born, he was only a penniless youth who had cut himself adrift from his family, and had then but the poorest prospects of making his fortune; whereas she was the only daughter of a rich and powerful noble. But, in spite of that, in the end she had confessed her love for him, and married another only for reasons that were beyond the control of either of them.

To his disappointment, Roger found Rennes still firmly in the grip of the Jacobins, and of the gangs of *sans-culottes* from the river wharfs who acted as their bullies. There were plenty of rumours that smaller towns in the province had declared against the Convention, but the Red Municipality was confident that troops sent from Paris would soon suppress the deviationists; so Roger had no option but to order his guillotine to be set up in the Champs de Mars, and the usual arrangements were made for him to hold his Special Tribunal.

When the lists of prisoners were submitted to him he went through them with particular care, in case any of his old friends happened to be on them. A third of the way down one list he came on the names of Maître and Madame Léger, the very couple in whose house he had lived and who had been so kind to him. On others appeared the names of a girl with whom he had once had a passing affair, of her brother, of his old fencing master, and of a dear old gentleman who had been a neighbour of the Légers.

At the first opportunity he consulted with Dan, and put in hand the preliminary measures for saving them, which included ensuring that they were not brought before him for the next few days, in order to give time to make arrangements for their rescue. As they discussed the matter he wondered a shade uneasily if other citizens of Rennes, who had known him in his boyhood, might not recognize him during his stay there and involve him in an undesirable tissue of lies and possibly dangerous explanations; but he decided that it was unlikely.

It was eight years since he had left Rennes, and in the meantime he had not only grown up, but altered greatly, particularly during the past two months. His ghastly work had played havoc with both his appetite and his sleep; his height was now accentuated by his thinness, his face was pale, lean and bony, his mouth a hard grim line, and his eyes bright but with heavy shadows beneath them. How could anyone associate the jolly boy of sixteen with the tall, sinister figure of the dreaded Citizen Representative in the new plumage which had recently been designed to distinguish that rank—a blue tail coat, red waistcoat, white breeches, broad *tricolore* sash of silk worn as a cummerbund round the waist, with gold fringe dangling on the hip, and a tricorne hat with three great ostrich feathers of red, white and blue rising above its crown?

After holding his first day's session in the court, he took an evening walk round the city. Boyhood's memories are strong; he saw a dozen people that he could definitely identify, because they were still occupying the same shops, and a number of others whose faces he knew yet could not place. All of them looked at him with curiosity and fear, then swiftly averted their glance; but in the eyes of none was there a flicker of recognition.

As he passed the Church of St. Malaine he recalled how he used to wait each Sunday with swiftly-beating heart near its font, to offer Athénaïs Holy water as she came out, and the almost unbearable thrill of joy that the light touch of her fingers on his had given him as she took it. Near by lay the Jardin des Plantes, in which, during midday recesses at the lawyer's office, he had laboriously taught himself German, and where, on summer evenings, he had endeavoured to console himself with the embraces of half a dozen pretty light-o'-loves when Athénaïs had left Rennes and he had given up hope of ever seeing her again.

At the other end of the town he crossed the Champs de Mars to look at the *Hôtel de Guesclin*, to which he had come with old Doctor Aristotle Fénelon on his first night in the city. The hostelry looked much smaller than he remembered it, but it had not altered. Up in an attic there the poor old quack had been murdered, and he had fled from it in terror with Fouché pounding after him down the stairs shouting that he was a murderer. Half-a-mile away, behind the barracks, were the crossroads near which Athénaïs's coach had been standing in the semi-darkness. Like a hunted hare going to earth he had leapt into it; and it was she who had saved him. She had then been only fourteen; so although that night seemed a whole lifetime away, she could now be only twenty-four. But how much had happened since! His travels had taken him to Holland, Denmark, Sweden, Russia, Italy and Spain, and he had married twice. He wondered about her marriage, and if it had proved the success that he had hoped. In order to enable her to marry the Vicomte de la Tour d'Auvergne, whom she liked, instead of being forced to wed an immensely wealthy but repulsive noble of her father's choice, he had, at the age of nineteen, fought and killed one of the finest swordsmen in all France. He had loved her terribly—more than life itself—and he could still never think of her without a stirring of the pulses.

On taking his seat in court on the second day of his session he received an unpleasant shock. Although he had not been told of it, the lawyer who had acted as Public Prosecutor the day before now transpired to have been deputizing for his chief, owing to that official having been absent in Nantes. With a sudden catch of his breath Roger instantly recognized the new man as Hutot, the great, stupid, brutal oaf who, while senior apprentice at Maître Léger's, had bullied him so savagely during his first months as a member of the lawyer's household. That such a man should have secured such a post was typical of the Revolution. Knowing that any attempt to evade Hutot's eyes for the whole of several days' sittings must prove futile, Roger stared at him with a cold impassive gaze, as he ingratiatingly smirked his apologies for his previous day's absence. During the morning Roger kept a covert watch on him, but by midday he was quite satisfied that Hutot had no idea that they had ever met before.

For two more days Roger held his bloody assize. To his great relief, Dan's secret associates had succeeded in rescuing the Légers and his other old friends, so that worry was off his shoulders; and as he took a final look through the cases he was to try on his last day in Rennes, he could see no name that even faintly rang any bell in his memory.

Shortly before the midday recess, the name Marie Tourney was called, and a slim, black-haired young woman was led into court. Roger glanced at her only casually, and turned to Hutot, who had jumped to his feet and was now crying with revolting eagerness:

"Here, Citizen Representative, we have a case of the very type of lice of which you have been sent from Paris to rid us. This bitch you see before you is a scheming aristocrat. Under a false name, as we have just discovered, she has been concealing the enemies of the Republic and caused an honest patriot to be done to death. No special pleading by me is needed to ensure her receiving justice; the bare facts are enough. The penalty is death, and I demand it!"

Roger looked again at the thin, proud face of the girl. It was her jet-black hair that had temporarily blinded him to her identity. He was staring at his beloved Athénaïs.

CHAPTER XVII

THE "QUESTIONING" OF ATHÉNAÏS

As Roger stared at Athénaïs he saw recognition dawn in her eyes. Love had imprinted his features too firmly on her mind for her to be deceived, as others had been, by his revolutionary plumage. Her oval face, hitherto impassive and resigned, had suddenly become alive, and he could see the emotions chasing one another across it—amazement at seeing him in such a guise, hope where there had been none before, then elation and relief at the certainty that her old lover would never send her to the scaffold.

Swiftly he averted his gaze, praying that she would have the sense to say nothing which might compromise him and make it more difficult to aid her. His heart was hammering wildly and he had to clasp his hands to keep them from trembling. As though from a long way off he heard Hutot giving particulars of the crime of which she was accused.

For some weeks she had been living in a small house on the outskirts of the town under the name of Madame Tourney, but that morning she had been identified as the *ci-devant* Vicomtesse de la Tour d'Auvergne. Suspicion had been aroused by the frequency with which people had been seen entering and leaving her house either late at night or very early in the morning. A domiciliary visit had been ordered, and a man discovered in one of the upstairs rooms; he had been recognized as M. de Charette, a retired naval lieutenant who owned property in the Marais and had become one of the leaders of the rebels. Athénaïs had managed to delay the search party long enough for Charette to dress, but not long enough for him to get away. As they entered the room he was about to climb out of the window; turning, he had shot one of them with his pistol, then leapt into the branches of a tree, scrambled to the ground and escaped.

It was a case in which Roger dared show no mercy; even to have postponed sentence would have provoked unwelcome comment. He could only pray that condemnation by him would not shock her into some violent plea or protest which would reveal to the crowd in court that in the past he had been the lover of this high-born beauty. In the hope of preventing any such outburst by rendering doubtful her recognition of him, he looked straight at her again; but this time he narrowed his eyes and bared his teeth in a ferocious grin. Then, without even referring to his colleagues on the bench, which he usually did as a matter of courtesy, he drew the side of his hand across his throat and said hoarsely:

"*Madame la Guillotine* is ever thirsty, and best of all she loves to drink so-called blue blood. I am happy to provide her with this treat on behalf of the Sovereign People."

Athénaïs's blue eyes opened wide. He read in them a flash of incredulity, then horror, but lastly doubt. She half opened her mouth to say something, but, evidently shaken by uncertainty, closed it again. His cruel jibe brought forth coarse laughter and a murmur of approbation from the onlookers. Before it subsided Athénaïs had been seized by the arms and hurried from the court.

Roger put his hand up to his mouth to conceal the intake of a sharp, painful breath. He could feel the perspiration that had started out on his forehead, and with a quick sweep of his red silk handkerchief brushed it away: he felt sick almost to fainting point and knew that he must be deathly pale, but his past eight weeks' work had made such a death's head of his face that no one seemed to notice how ill he was feeling. With a stupendous effort he pulled himself together and managed to focus his attention on the next case.

At the midday interval he refused the meal provided for him at the Town Hall, and went at once to his lodgings at the *Hôtel de France* to find Dan. It was not until he arrived there that he remembered Dan had told him first thing that morning that he was going to Dinan that day to tie up loose ends with the League before their return to Paris.

Fortunately only four cases had been left over for the afternoon session, and those were swiftly dealt with; so by three o'clock Roger was free to give unchecked rein to his frantic anxiety in the privacy of his own room at the hotel. He knew that, unless he took steps to prevent it, Athénaïs would be executed at nine o'clock the following morning. Dan could not be expected back before eight that evening; so they would have only a bare twelve hours to work in, and that was desperately little time in which to plan and carry out an escape. His agitation was further increased by the awful fear that, as they were about to leave Brittany, Dan might already have broken off contact with their secret friends there, and be unable to arrange a rescue. It was bad enough that Athénaïs should now be in a condemned cell, imagining that the man she had once loved, or someone extraordinarily like him, had deliberately sent her there; to allow her to die was utterly unthinkable. But if Dan could not help, how was he to effect her escape without making himself glaringly suspect to the Jacobin-controlled Municipality of Rennes? Given actual proof that he was betraying the Revolution, they would be within their rights in arresting and executing him, fully confident that the Committee of Public Safety in Paris would afterwards approve their act. As he paced restlessly up and down his room, he could not rid his mind of the horrid thought that the attempt he was determined to make to save Athénaïs might not only fail, but result in his head following hers into the basket.

Soon after eight Dan got back, and Roger at once ordered a meal to be brought for him to their private sitting-room on the ground floor. While it was being fetched he could hardly disguise his impatience; the moment they were alone he poured himself a glass of wine from Dan's bottle and gulped it down, then in a low voice gave a swift account of what had happened. Within a minute his worst fears had been confirmed.

Dan gravely shook his head, and whispered, "This be bad, Cap'n. Had I but knowed the lady's plight this forenoon I could 'a' fixed summat; but there b'aint none o' they gentry ye wot of nearer than Dinan, an' the Devil hisself 'ud be hard put to it t'ride there an' bring 'en back here much afore dawn. 'Sides, what then? Prison breaks take a mint o' thought an' plannin'. Specially since the night afore last, when they other friends o' yourn were gotten away. I'se told they bloody varmints has doubled the guards, an' the sentries be ordered to shoot anyone suspicious-seemin'."

"I feared as much," Roger exclaimed; "all the same, an attempt must be made. There was a time, Dan, when I loved this lady more than my life, and risked it for her; coming upon her in this desperate strait has aroused in me all those old feelings. Cost what it may, I'll not let these swine take her to the guillotine."

With a shrug of his broad shoulders, Dan helped himself to another big wedge of rich Brittany butter. As he began to spread it on the crusty bread, he said resignedly, "That bein' the way o' it, Cap'n, I'll get she out for thee somehow. A bold bluff be our best hope, an' I could say——"

"No, no!" Roger cut him short. "I had hoped that there might still be time for you to arrange something with your friends, but since that is impossible I'll not let you imperil yourself; this is my affair."

"Best let I make first cast, Cap'n; I'se more knowin' wi' the ways o' prisons than you be. Should I take a tumble I know ye'll be there t' throw me a line an' haul me aboard agin."

Roger placed a hand affectionately on his henchman's shoulder. "A thousand thanks, old friend, but I am resolved that you shall remain above suspicion. While waiting for you I've had ample time to think of a plan should your friends be unable to help, and this is what I propose. Normally, at midday tomorrow the whole of our hellish circus should take the road back to Paris. In the morning you will tell Captain Labord that having completed my mission I had no mind to travel at the slow pace of the death wagon, so I set off at dawn, leaving you in charge. That will explain my disappearance both to the Municipals here and to our own people. In an hour or two I will go to the prison; my authority is sufficient to demand that Madame should be surrendered to me for private questioning."

" 'Twas summat o' the kind I had in mind," Dan mumbled, his mouth full of chicken. "I'd need a signed order o' yourn, tho', to get she."

"Yes, they would not hand her over without one," Roger nodded, "but what then?"

" 'Twixt the prison an' here I'd tell she to take to her heels, then wi' a mighty long face tell ye she give me the slip."

"No, Dan, that's no good. If we failed to report her escape at once we would both be suspect, and if we allowed a hue and cry after her to start so soon, all the odds are that she would be recaptured before morning. We have got to get her clear away to your friends at Dinan; that means one of us disappearing for at least ten hours. If you took her there after having got her out on my order I'd either have to raise the alarm when you failed to bring her here and have you hunted, or become suspect myself. As I have planned matters, no one can accuse you of knowing anything about it, and my own disappearance will be accounted for by the story that I am on my way to Paris."

"Aye, but ye'll have taken she from prison, an' what'll they Devil's spawn be sayin' when 'tis found that the pair o' ye's gone in the morn?"

"They can say what they damn' well choose; I'll be fifty miles away by then."

"S'pose they send after ye to Paris?"

Roger shrugged, then his worried expression gave place to a smile. "You had best pretend to be greatly puzzled, then reluctantly suspicious of my motives, and offer to take the report yourself. But I'm not greatly troubled on that score. I'll have plenty of time to think up some explanation, and if any account of the affair does get through to Paris you may be sure that the *Comité* will accept my word rather than the tittle-tattle of these little provincial Jacobins. I'll probably say she bought her freedom by giving me valuable information about the rebels. Wait, though! Why should we not meet trouble half-way by using a story of that kind now? Gad, yes! That could be made even better cover for my disappearance. I'll leave a note to the effect that I promised to spare her life in exchange for information, but do not mean to let her go until I've checked it; so I've taken her with me post-haste down to Nantes and mean to return to Paris independently from there."

"Aye"; Dan nodded quick approval; "an' meanwhile ye'll have gone north to Dinan. That be a good trick to play 'en. 'Twill also save me an awkward bit o' play-acting come mornin'. How do 'e plan to get she to Dinan, though, wi'out risk that a coachman or postil'on will betray ye arterwards?"

"We shall ride. She is, thank God, a first-class horsewoman, although not dressed for the part at the moment; but you can help me in that. Put out a spare pair of my riding breeches and boots, and half-stuff the boots with some soft material, so that her small feet will not slop about in them. Better have ready for her, too, a light cloak in case the night turns chilly, and make a bundle of things she may find useful—a brush and comb, a flannel, a couple of my soft shirts, a scarf, some handkerchiefs; and put in my flask of cognac and a slab of chocolate. Tell me, now—when we reach Dinan, where shall I find your friends?"

Dan gave careful directions to an inn called *Le Homard Rouge* on a by-road about a mile beyond the town, and described the recognition signs that Roger should make to its landlord, who would conceal Athénaïs until one of the English *milors* appeared again and could take her to the coast. Then he asked at what hour Roger intended to go to the prison.

It was nearly half-past nine, but the light of the July day still lingered. Now that Roger knew for certain that he must rescue Athénaïs himself, he was more impatient than ever to get on with the business; but the streak of caution which had saved him from disaster many times decided him against rushing matters; so he replied:

"I had best wait until it is fully dark. Should anyone who saw her in court today recognize us together in the street it would set tongues wagging; and I am loath to risk doing that unnecessarily."

Dan grinned. "They'll do so tomorrow, Cap'n. These sewer-rats'll nair believe a Citizen Representative asked nought but information o' so pretty a lady for her life. 'Twould be agin' nature as they unnerstan' it."

"That's true, and must be accepted. I am concerned only with reducing to a minimum the chance of the Municipality's learning that I have removed her from prison until we have had time to get well clear of the town. It is most unlikely that it would ever occur to them that I was rescuing her; but these accursed Reds have such a passion for poking a finger into every pie that they would be certain to come running to enquire what I was at, did a report reach them that she had been seen in my company."

After a glance out of the low window, Dan said, " 'Twill not be full dark for an hour yet. I'll hail the potman for another flagon, then ye can drink a glass while ye wait. Meantime I'll set to packin'. Should I take all your things to Paris, or do ye wish aught for use on t' road?"

"My trunk must go in the wagon, with you; but stuff as many of my things as you can into my saddle-bags. I don't want you to saddle up yet, though. That must wait until I have Madame here, otherwise it might be said later that I had planned to make off with her. It should be believed that I decided to take her to Nantes only after questioning."

Another bottle of wine was brought and Roger drank part of it while restlessly pacing up and down the room. The minutes seemed to drag by, and the street outside became only very slowly a little darker; but at twenty-past ten he felt that he could control his impatience to be off no longer. Pulling-to the curtains over the window, he had a last word with Dan, set his tricorne hat with the three great feathers on his head, and went out into the street.

The prison was barely half a mile away, yet his mental agitation seemed to make it double that distance. He thought it improbable that the jailers would refuse to surrender Athénaïs to him, but there was always the chance that they might insist on first consulting some local authority. If that proved to be the case, things would become very awkward. He would probably be asked why he could not interrogate Athénaïs in her cell; a committee might be formed to assist him in questioning her; in the last event he might be compelled to exert his overriding authority and cow with dire threats any Municipals who opposed him in order to get Athénaïs out and carry her off. Should he be forced to employ such strong measures and fail to return her to the prison in the morning, it would take a lot of explaining away to the Committee of Public Safety when he returned to Paris. Finally, there remained the grim possibility that Athénaïs might give away the fact that he was her old lover; his intent to betray the Republic for her sake would then be clear, and he would be lucky if he escaped accompanying her to the scaffold in a few hours' time.

On reaching the gateway of the grim stone building he pulled the hanging handle of the bell; it was still jangling hollowly within when a small door in the great arched wooden gate was pulled open and a slovenly sentry peered out. The light of a lantern suspended from a bracket in the wall shone on Roger's gaudy sash and feathered hat; at the sight of them the man drew back, bade him enter, and asked what he wanted.

Stepping inside to a broad stone-flagged passage, Roger closed the door, and told the man to fetch the head turnkey. Three more unshaven, surly-looking ruffians appeared from a nearby guardroom, and with a muttered oath one of them shambled off along the dimly-lit passageway. A few minutes later he returned, bringing with him a huge barrel of a man who limped, and who seemed to roll rather than to walk; from the belt that encircled his gargantuan paunch there dangled a bunch of heavy keys.

"Citizen jailer," Roger addressed him, in an even, almost casual, voice, "I require the woman de la Tour d'Auvergne for private questioning. I will, of course, give you a receipt for her. Bring her here without delay."

The monstrous turnkey stared at him for a moment, then suddenly began to wheeze with laughter; one of the soldiers tittered, and the others guffawed.

"Silence!" snarled Roger, "or by God I'll wipe the laughter from your faces with my crop! Now, what do you find in my demand to give you such cause for mirth?"

His outburst quelled them in a moment, but a sly grin still twitched the corners of the fat turnkey's mouth as he replied:

"You come too late, Citizen Representative."

For a second an awful fear caused Roger's heart to contract. At times, when his circus was due to move on the next morning, afternoon sessions with the guillotine had been held. That had never occurred except on his personal order; but it was possible that his executioner, anxious to get early on the road to Paris and home, had taken the law into his own hands. The ghastly thought that Athénaïs's lovely head might already have tumbled into that blood-soaked basket made his own blood drain from his face. He could only gasp:

"Too late! What—what the hell d'you mean?"

The fat jailer was grinning openly again, and he wheezed, "Another was before you, Citizen Representative. You're not the only one who thinks it worth losing a night's sleep to question a pretty *aristo* in bed. Were I younger I'd envy the man who took her off, and I'll wager he won't bring her back much afore it's time to push her into the death-cart."

Roger's relief was almost instantly overcome by a wave of rage and horror. He knew quite well that revolutionary officials often used their powers to make good-looking women prisoners the victims of their lust. Private questioning was always the excuse. The woman was promised her life if she submitted willingly; in most cases she did, if not she was raped. In either case she rarely secured a permanent reprieve. Sometimes she was kept on ice for a few weeks to provide further enjoyment, while praying that each new degradation to which she submitted would prove the final payment; but as soon as the man tired of her it was a hundred to one that he would send her to the guillotine.

Now Roger cursed himself for not having foreseen such a possibility, and for his excessive caution in not having come to the prison earlier. The thought of Athénaïs, forcibly stripped, beaten half-senseless, and in the grip of some swinish Municipal, filled him with demoniacal fury. Only by clenching his teeth like a vice for a full minute could he keep control of himself; then he snapped out:

"To whom did you hand her over?"

The turnkey was no longer grinning; he could see the blinding rage in Roger's blue eyes. In an effort to excuse himself, he stammered, "To a man who had the right to question her, Citizen

Representative—one I could not refuse. 'Twas the Citizen Public Prosecutor Hutot."

Of all the Revolutionary officials in France, the man could not have named one better calculated to add fuel to Roger's blazing anger. Hutot was not, as were so many of them, a pervert or a sadist; he was quite normal, but with the normality of a rutting hog. Years before, Roger had shared a room with him and four other apprentices for several months. In an instant of time a series of mental pictures of those days flashed through his brain—Hutot at nineteen, a great rawboned lout guzzling the lion's share of the food in the kitchen where the apprentices fed—Hutot dead drunk and vomiting on the bedroom floor, which meant that Roger had to clear up the disgusting mess—Hutot climbing back through the dormer window in the early hours by a rope that Roger had let down for him, after a night spent with some slut down at the river docks—Hutot sneaking back into the bedroom, still red-faced and perspiring from having tumbled the fat cook in the little room under the stairs where she slept. Almost choking with fury, Roger blurted out:

"How long is it since he took her away?"

The fat man shrugged. "Twenty minutes—no, it must be half an hour or more, Citizen Representative."

"Half an hour!" Roger knew his hands were trembling. He could not stop them. Hutot was not the type of man to savour his dishes with the sauce of refinement. He would have plenty of liquor handy, but it would not even occur to him to provide a tempting supper and during it endeavour to woo Athénaïs into some degree of complacency. No—having got her to his room he would set about her without delay. By a supreme effort Roger shut out from his mind the picture of what might be happening at that very moment, and snapped:

"Where does the Citizen Prosecutor live?"

To his horror, the jailer shook his head. "I have no idea, Citizen Representative; I have had only official dealings with him."

It was the last straw; Roger could have screamed aloud in his dismay at being faced with this awful impasse. He could run to the Town Hall. They would know there, but at this hour it would be closed for the night. The custodian was probably already in bed and would have to be roused. It was quite possible that he would not know Hutot's address either, and more precious time would be lost—half an hour, or an hour perhaps—before someone could be found who did.

Unexpectedly, one of the National Guards came to Roger's rescue. After spitting on the floor, he said, "The Citizen Prosecutor installed himself some weeks ago in the house of a lawyer who was arrested—the one who escaped from prison the night before last. I know the house, but forget his name."

"Léger!" exclaimed Roger. "Was it Maître Léger?"

The man nodded. "That's the one."

Almost before the words were out of his mouth Roger had turned, wrenched open the door, and sprung through it. Next moment he was pelting as fast as his long legs would carry him down the deserted street. The moon had not yet risen and the starlight hardly percolated to the narrow cobbled ways, but Roger had known them in boyhood so well that he could have found the right turnings without hesitation even in pitch darkness. Within six minutes he had entered the Rue d'Antrain; panting, he halted before a well-remembered door, and began to pound upon it with the head of his riding-crop.

After a moment there was a stir inside. A bolt was shot back and the door swung open to reveal a slovenly-looking young woman. She was holding aloft a lighted candle. Roger could see that she was blonde, about twenty-five and coarsely good-looking; but one side of her face was now red and swollen. It looked as though she had recently received a blow there. She was just the type of gutter-bred dance-hall queen that Hutot had pursued so avidly in the past, and Roger guessed at once that she was for the time being his permanent mistress.

Still struggling to retrieve his breath, he gasped, "Where is the Citizen Prosecutor?"

Fear, at first sight of the trappings that showed Roger to be one of the all-powerful Commissars of the Revolution, swiftly gave place in the woman's pale blue eyes to malicious pleasure. Standing aside for him to enter, she jerked her blonde head back towards the stairs.

"He's up there with an *aristo* girl he brought home." Putting a hand up to the bruise on her face, she added angrily, "The lecherous swine! I've told him before I wouldn't stand for his having women in the house, and when I gave him the rough side of my tongue he knocked me down. I'll leave him! I swear I will!"

Unheeding her complaint, Roger sprang past her and took the stairs three at a time. To his left, as he reached the first landing, lay a room that Maître Léger had used as a private office; to his right lay the family sitting-room; beyond them were the main bedrooms of the house. Just as he was about to dash on down the corridor he heard a groan. It seemed to have come from the sitting-room. Halting in his tracks, he swung round in that direction. Another groan came and the sound of heavy breathing.

A shudder of horror shook him. White to the lips, he seized the door handle. It turned loosely in his grasp. The door was locked.

Raising his clenched fist, he beat frantically upon it, and shouted, "Open! In the name of the Law, I command you to open!"

There was no reply. There came a fainter groan, then again that awful sobbing for breath.

Stepping back, Roger ran at the door, lifted his right foot and brought the sole of his boot crashing flat against the lock. With a tearing of wood the lock gave and the door flew open. Drawing a pistol from his sash, he cocked the weapon and strode into the room. The scene within was utterly different from that which he had feared and expected.

The groans and laboured breathing were not coming from Athénaïs, but from Hutot. The great brute lay sprawled in a corner. She stood a few feet away from him, the neck of a broken bottle clutched in her hand. A trickle of blood was running down from his wiry hair on to his fleshy nose, and tears were oozing from the corners of his eyes. Why a knock on the top of the head should cause him to be gasping like a fish out of water, and how, considering their respective heights, Athénaïs had succeeded in administering such a blow without standing on a chair, provided a puzzle which Roger did not attempt to solve for the moment.

The main facts were clear. Two nearly empty glasses were standing on the table and Athénaïs's dress had been ripped open; the curve of her right shoulder showed pink and naked above her left hand, with which she was holding up the torn dress to conceal her breast. Evidently Hutot had made her drink two or three glasses of wine with him, then assaulted her; but she had been too quick for him, and using the empty bottle as a weapon had got the best of the encounter. Her eyes round with excitement, she was now staring at Roger. She broke the brief silence by exclaiming:

"Rojé! So it *is* you! When I saw you in court I would have taken an oath that it could be no other."

In his relief at finding her unharmed, his impulse was to run forward and take her in his arms. But Hutot, although in bad shape, was not unconscious. He was lying with his back propped up against a press and he looked dazed, but might still be capable of making sense of all he heard or saw. Swiftly Roger assumed his most severe expression, and was on the point of silencing Athénaïs, when she hurried on:

"When I was told in my cell that I was to be taken from the prison for questioning I felt certain it must be you who——"

"*Citoyenne!*" he cut her short; "you mistake me for someone else." Then, waving a hand towards Hutot, he added, "This man has exceeded his authority. That you appear to have given him cause to rue it does not concern me. As a Public Prosecutor he had no right to remove for questioning a prisoner who had already been condemned; but, as the representative of the Committee of Public Safety, I have that right."

Athénaïs was greatly overwrought by the ordeal she had just been through. Still convinced that she was face to face with her old lover, she gave an hysterical laugh, and cried, "Do you then mean to risk my serving you as I have served him? I warn you, Monsieur, that it can be prodigiously painful."

"Silence!" roared Roger, "or I'll use my crop on those bare shoulders of yours! Now! Take that Indian shawl from the settee to cover them, hold your tongue, and accompany me hence."

Jolted out of her hysteria, Athénaïs threw down the bottle-neck that she was still holding, picked up the shawl and draped it about her. At that moment a low wail caused Roger to swing round towards the door. The blonde girl had followed him upstairs. She was standing in the doorway regarding Hutot with a half-angry, half-pitying, look.

Hutot's breathing was becoming easier, but had he given a last gasp and died Roger would have considered it no more than his deserts. Now, he thought only of what would suit his own plans best, as he said to the girl:

"Put him to bed and give him something to make him sleep. When he wakes you may tell him that, in view of his having caught such a tartar in this little *aristo*, I'll institute no disciplinary action against him for removing her from prison, and that I make myself responsible for returning her there."

With a mutter of thanks, she knelt down beside her stricken man and began to mop the blood from his face. Roger grasped Athénaïs firmly by the arm and hurried her downstairs; as soon as they were out in the street she said in a swift whisper:

"Oh, Rojé! No words can express my amazement and gratitude that God should have sent you, of all people, to rescue me! But how comes it that you are dressed in this livery of the Devil?"

He smiled a little grimly, but gave her arm a reassuring squeeze. "This is no time to talk of that, m'dear. Let it suffice that unless we are monstrous unlucky within the next hour I'll have you safe out of Rennes. I've not yet forgiven myself, though, for arriving so late upon the scene. That you should have succeeded in turning defence into attack so effectively fills me with astonishment and admiration. How in the world did you manage to overcome that swine?"

Athénaïs, still intensely excited at having been rescued by him, gave a nervous laugh. "When he grabbed my dress I drew back and kicked him with all my strength in—in a certain place. As he doubled up with pain I seized the chance to snatch up the empty bottle and break it over his head."

It was just on six years since Roger had seen Athénaïs. They had parted at the time of her elopement with the good-looking young Vicomte de la Tour d'Auvergne, which he had made possible. She had then been a girl of eighteen, and too innocent to even imagine such a method of rendering a man *hors de combat*; her disclosure of it, with only the barest hesitation, brought home to Roger more swiftly than anything else could have done that marriage and the years had matured her as much as they had himself. After a moment absorbing the fact, he felt that he must risk a question of the type that no one in France any longer put casually to an aristocrat, and asked:

"M. le Vicomte? I trust that he is . . . safe, and that I may have the happiness of restoring you to him?"

"Alas! he has been dead nearly a year," she replied. "Our marriage brought us more happiness than most couples enjoy, and I still miss him greatly. As you may remember, he held most liberal views, so he became an officer in the National Guard; but during a riot in Brest he was treacherously shot by one of his own men."

The news saddened Roger, as M. de la Tour d'Auvergne had been one of the earliest friends he had made among the French nobility. His mind swiftly jumped to the two children he had heard that Athénaïs had borne; but before he could bring himself to ask about them, she went on bitterly:

"My children also are dead. While I was absent in Brest with M. le Vicomte, our *château* in the country was burnt down at the instigation of some agitators from Paris. The . . . the children perished in it. Now that I have told you this, please do not refer to it again. It is a subject which I endeavour to banish from my mind, except when an opportunity occurs for me to revenge myself on the *canaille.*"

The positively venomous hatred that Athénaïs put into her last few words again revealed to Roger how greatly she had changed. He had known her as a lovely romantic girl, spoilt by her riches and high station to a degree that at times had made her petulant, but at heart sweet-natured and idealistic. At twenty-four she was even more beautiful than she had been at eighteen, but grim experiences had clearly tempered her into a violent and dangerous woman.

Another twenty paces brought them to the *Hôtel de France.* Without a word, Roger led her into the courtyard and through the side entrance to his private sitting-room. Dan was there with the riding things all laid out, and Roger asked her to change into them at once, so that they could be off with a minimum of delay; then he took Dan out into the corridor and told him what had happened.

After a short whispered conference they decided that there was no necessity to alter their plan because it had been Hutot who had removed Athénaïs from prison. The story that, after questioning her himself, Roger had decided to take her to Nantes to check her information was still perfectly plausible. Even if Hutot had taken in Athénaïs's claim of recognizing him as an old friend who had come to rescue her, he might equally have swallowed Roger's repudiation of it. If his suspicions had been aroused the worst he could do would be to send a Municipal after them to Nantes to verify that they had really gone there. But by the time it was discovered that they had not they would have disappeared without trace; and if the story ever reached Paris, Roger felt confident that he would have no difficulty in quashing it.

Leaving Dan on guard outside the door of the sitting-room, Roger went out and saddled his own charger and a spare horse that he and Dan shared between them. On his return he found

Athénaïs ready. Quickly he wrote one note for Captain Labord, placing Dan in charge of the death circus on its return to Paris, and another about Athénaïs for Dan to show the Rennes Municipals in the morning; then they collected their bundles, said good-bye to Dan, and left the hotel without being seen by anyone. Roger's visit to the prison had occupied no more than a few minutes, and his removal of Athénaïs from Maître Léger's house little longer, so it was only just past eleven when they mounted and turned out of the yard.

As they entered the main square of the town, she asked, "Where do you intend to take me, Rojé?"

"To an inn near Dinan, where I have friends who will hide you until you can be got away to England," he replied. Then, having made up his mind what he would tell her about himself, he went on, "Just over a year ago I returned to France as an unofficial observer for my Government. Naturally they are anxious to be kept well informed on the progress of the Revolution, and it seemed to me that the best way to carry out my mission was to pose as a revolutionary myself."

"You must have played your part exceeding well to have become a Citizen Representative," she remarked coldly; "but having seen you as President of the Tribunal this morning I can hardly wonder at the high standing you have achieved among these satanists."

" 'Twas all or nothing. I'd have learned no secrets worth having had I remained one of the mob."

"True; and you were ever ruthless, Rojé, where anything you had set your heart upon was concerned. Even so, in the past twelve hours I have done little but marvel that you could bring yourself to send innocent people to the guillotine."

"Had I not, some genuine terrorist would have done so in my stead, and my position enables me to save at least a proportion of those who would otherwise be sent to die. 'Tis the thought of that alone which has given me sufficient resolution to continue with the ghastly task the Committee of Public Safety thrust upon me. Long before I left Paris I was in touch with a League of gallant Englishmen who smuggle suspects and escaped prisoners across the Channel. Since carrying out my assize in Brittany I have been able to work much more closely with them, so have been the means of having scores of victims of the terror rescued and conveyed to safety. It is to a member of the League that I am now taking you."

She lifted a hand and laid it on his arm. "Oh, Rojé, how could I ever have doubted that you were on the side of the angels, and I have not even thanked you yet for rescuing myself; but seeing you acknowledged by all as one of these terrible Citizen Representatives seemed so utterly inexplicable."

When they reached the Dinan road they trotted and cantered for a time, then while they gave the horses a breather at a walk, he spoke of the terrible strain he had been under in going from town to town with his guillotine, and sitting day after day in judgment. But now she praised him for having borne it, and when he told her something of the way in which he had used the excuse of purging the Municipal Councils to send some of the worst criminals to the scaffold, she eagerly asked on how many he had exacted vengeance.

"I've kept no count," he replied, "but since joining Dumouriez's Army on a similar mission last September I should say that I have ordered the execution of not less than two hundred self-confessed murderers."

"Oh, Rojé, how marvellous!" Her voice thrilled with admiration. "Had I my life to live over again I'd willingly give half my happy years could I buy with them the satisfaction of having killed even a hundred. But I have not been idle; I too belong to a secret organization—not for rescue, but to further revolt and revenge. For that reason I do not intend to accept your kind offer to take me to your friends at Dinan; while the Revolution lasts I will never desert the cause I serve by leaving France."

Remembering how she had been arrested for sheltering M. de Charette, Roger was not at all surprised to learn that she was actively engaged in assisting the Royalists of La Vendée. In view of the fact that such a high proportion of the men of her caste had fled abroad, he felt that, for a woman, her attitude was a particularly brave one. But this sudden announcement of hers clearly called for an alteration in his plans, so he said:

"Why, then, did you let me bring you so far along the Dinan road? We must have covered three miles of it already."

"Because it is the road I would have chosen for myself," she laughed. "Surely you have not forgotten that my father's Château of Bécherel lies only a mile or two off it?"

"That I would never forget, since it was there you first confessed that you loved me. But when I enquired in Rennes about the *château*, I was told that it had been burnt down."

"Indeed it was, and is now no more than a gutted shell; but I have a secret hiding-place among the ruins which is moderately comfortable. It will not be the first time that I have taken refuge there, as Bécherel is the very last place in which those fiends would look for me."

Her reasoning seemed sound to Roger, particularly as he had lain a false trail behind them to Nantes; so they again let their mounts have their heads in a canter. The night was fine and warm, with a myriad stars shining overhead; so they had no difficulty in seeing their way, and at intervals when they walked their horses they asked and answered innumerable questions. Roger learned that Athénaïs's father had died in '91, and that her brother Lucien, the present Marquis de Rochambeau, was with the *émigré* army on the Rhine. He told her of his own marriage and, when pressed, endeavoured to describe Amanda; but he did not feel that he had succeeded very well, and they did not pursue the subject further. They talked of the murder of the King and of what the poor brave Queen must be suffering as a prisoner; of people they had known in their youth; of the iniquities of the Convention and of the prospects of the revolt in La Vendée.

Bécherel was little more than half-way to Dinan, so they reached it half an hour after midnight. Roger had lived for many months at the *château* whilst employed by the late Marquis as an additional secretary to conduct exhaustive researches among old title deeds, so he well remembered the splendid mansion with its great marble entrance-hall and staircase, its scores of rooms furnished with rich carpets, hangings and tapestries, its cabinets filled with precious china, and its library of rare books. On occasions when the family had been in residence the huge house had swarmed with people—old Aldegone, the major-domo, pompous in his black and silver; Chenou, the chief huntsman, resplendent in his green and gold; chaplains, musicians, chefs, wine-butlers, coachmen, gardeners, grooms, housemaids, footmen, scullions, and laundry-hands had made the place as busy as a township.

Now it was as silent as the grave; the spacious forecourt was waist-high in weeds, the gaunt and blackened walls of the ruin towered up against the star-spangled sky, while here and there a row of frameless windows gaped, making lighter rectangles in the dark patches of still-standing masonry.

One end of the long stables had escaped destruction; so having watered their horses at the trough in the yard, they put them into two loose-boxes. While Roger unsaddled, Athénaïs prised up a board in the floor of a nearby shed and fetched a feed for them from a secret store of corn that she kept there; then, side by side, they made their way round to the back of the main building.

When they had mounted the broken steps to the terrace and crossed it, she took his hand and led him in among the heavy shadows of the ruin. Picking their way through the debris, they advanced for about thirty feet until they reached a gaping black hole; it was the entrance to a stone stairway, which they descended into pitch darkness. At the bottom of the stairs she let go his hand and fumbled for a minute with some loose stones in the wall; from a hiding-place there she took a big key, a flint and tinder-box and a piece of candle. As the candle flickered into flame, Roger saw that they were in a broad, stone-flagged passage. Along either side of it was a row of heavy wooden doors; leading the way over to the third on the left, she unlocked it, then turned to him with a cynical little smile, and said, "Monsieur le Chevalier, I bid you welcome to my home."

As Roger followed her inside she began to light some more candles, and he saw that it was a fair-sized room, warm, dry and fully furnished. It contained a table, chairs, three chests of drawers, a big divan, at one side of which there was a *prie-dieu*, and at the far end from them two cupboards and a charcoal stove with a pipe to carry off the fumes. The carpet and most of the furniture was badly singed, so had evidently been salvaged after the fire; but in summer, if not in winter, anyone could have lived concealed there for weeks without suffering any discomfort. All the same, recalling Athénaïs as she had been when living two floors above where they now stood, surrounded with every conceivable luxury, it seemed quite extraordinary to Roger to think of her sleeping, cooking, eating and washing in this dungeon, entirely alone, unserved and unprotected; and his admiration for her courage was further increased at the thought that few women would have been brave enough to live alone in this grim and eerie ruin.

The contrast with the past was all the more striking when she threw off her borrowed cloak, as she still had the Indian shawl knotted about her shoulders and, below it, was wearing Roger's breeches and boots, which were much too large for her. But she seemed quite unconscious of her appearance, and even those unbecoming garments could not disguise her grace of movement as she quickly fetched from one of the cupboards a bottle of wine and two glasses.

Roger pulled the cork and poured the wine; silent but smiling they drank to one another. Now, for the first time, they had the leisure to study one another's faces. She thought him as handsome as ever, but pitifully thin and worn-looking; he thought her bright-blue eyes even bigger than he remembered them, and her imperious features even more perfectly chiselled. Her mouth was harder, and tiny lines were forming round the corners of her eyes; but her figure had filled out, and she looked marvellously healthy in spite of the harassing life she must have led.

"You've altered only for the better," he said, after a moment, "except that I cannot help regretting that to disguise yourself you committed the sacrilege of dyeing your wonderful golden hair."

"My dear," she smiled, "tragedy had robbed it of its lustre. Although I am only twenty-four it was already turning grey; I assure you that it was no loss."

"Do you remember . . ." he began, and for an hour that sped swiftly they recalled the high spots of their old love *affaire*. At length they touched upon the desperate day on which Roger had gone out to waylay and kill the fiancé whom she feared and loathed, so that her father would not be able to force her into that hateful marriage. Smiling at him across the table, she murmured:

"Oh, Rojé, in that time long ago you must have loved me very dearly."

"Indeed I did!" he assured her quickly, "and I think with a greater passion than I have ever felt for any other woman, because you were my first real love."

"I loved you that way too, Rojé; and since we knew that we could never marry, it is all the more remarkable that we never consummated our love. It was certainly not for lack of opportunity, and I cannot believe that many young men would have behaved towards me with such chivalry."

"In that belief I think you wrong the young," he smiled. "When a youth is truly smitten in the heart it brings out all the best in him. By some strange alchemy he can be ravished to distraction by the kisses of his beloved, yet have no thought of tempting her from the seventh heaven to which she has lifted him and turning her to common clay. 'Tis age and experience that make men unscrupulous and cynical."

They fell silent for a moment, then he said, "Talking to you of old times has made me selfishly forget that you woke this morning in prison. After the terrible experiences you have been through today you must be quite exhausted; I ought not to keep you up any longer."

She shrugged. "It was the third time I had been in prison, so I have become armoured against the barbarous conditions one meets with in such places."

"Perhaps; but I imagine you have never before been condemned to death. I dared take no other course, from fear that if I publicly reprieved you there would be such an outcry that I might be greatly hampered in any attempt to effect your rescue later."

"I guessed as much; but my mind was so fully engaged by wondering how you could conceivably have become the President of a Revolutionary Tribunal that I thought little of the possibility that you might not rescue me after all, and that I would have to mount the scaffold. In any case, I am not afraid of death. My only really bad moments were when, instead of yourself, that man Hutot took me from prison and began to 'question' me."

"I was in half a mind to finish what you had begun, and pistol him where he lay; but I am still a trifle squeamish about killing a helpless man. Thank God you got the best of him; but that half hour must have been a ghastly strain, and then there was our long ride on top of it. Really, it is time for you to get some sleep."

Athénaïs nodded, stood up and stretched herself, then walked over to the *prie-dieu* and knelt down at it. While she was saying her prayers, Roger quietly collected the cloaks, some rugs and a couple of cushions, and made himself a shakedown on the floor. When she had finished her prayers she came back to the table and snuffed out the candles until only one remained, a little pool of light which cast their shadows on the walls. Then, her eyes still fixed upon the flame, she said softly:

"Rojé, do you remember my favourite fairy story?"

"Yes," he smiled; "you were the beautiful princess and I was the miller's penniless youngest son."

"Times have changed, have they not?" she murmured. "And a different story is now more suited to us. In it, I am reduced to the poor beggar maid, while you have become, in appearance at least, a prince of this new bloody era."

Suddenly she lifted her eyes to his. They were wide and shining. A mocking smile twitched the corners of her mouth, and she went on, "Yet we are the same people, and only a few years older. Now that the terrible Citizen Representative has me alone and in his power, does he not wish to 'question' me?"

Only a pace separated them. In an instant he had taken it. His pulses throbbing with excitement and delight, he drew her to him.

So, at last, the years between forgotten, these two, who in their youth had loved one another so desperately, gave, in their maturity, free reign to passion; and spent the remaining hours of the night locked in each other's arms.

For them the night had no morning, as no ray of daylight penetrated to Athénaïs's secret retreat. When they awoke they made love again, laughing and teasing like a honeymoon couple who had not a care in the world on the first morning of their marriage.

Roger had no qualms of conscience at having been unfaithful to Amanda. Men were not expected to be faithful to their wives in those times and he had been so to her for longer than most husbands would have been. His love for her was not lessened by his newly-aroused passion for Athénaïs, as he thought of his marriage as a thing apart, and an enduring bond which could be severed only by wanton neglect and cruelty. He knew that on his return to England Amanda would be far too wise to question him, and he counted his honour involved in protecting her from any knowledge that he had entered on a clandestine love affair. In the meantime he considered himself free to enjoy to the uttermost the glorious gift that a strange fate had sent him.

It was Athénaïs who, with a woman's natural curiosity, brought up the subject of his marriage, and he told her his views about it; upon which she said, "Your attitude is, then, the same as that adopted by most women of quality in France. After marriage we consider ourselves free to take lovers, provided that we do not bring shame upon our husbands; and I will confess to you that, deeply attached as I was to M. le Vicomte, I was more than once persuaded to let another find happiness in my bed, although I exercised the greatest care that my lord should know nothing of it. Yet, had I married you, Rojé, after our four-year courtship my love had grown so intense that I believe I would have remained completely faithful."

"And I to you," he replied; then added on an impulse to be entirely honest, "That is, as long as I had stayed in France. But had I been called upon to go to England, or elsewhere abroad, for long periods, and met, shall we say, Amanda I'll not say that what has happened between you and me would not have happened between her and me."

Athénaïs withdrew her arm from beneath his neck and half-rolled over on to him. Looking down into his face she said with sudden intensity, "I hate her! Thank God she is in England, or I would fight her for possession of you. As things are, I shall endeavour to put her existence from my mind. Rojé, while you are in France I want you to think of me as though we *had* married, and that it was with her, while staying in England, that you had no more than an *affaire*. I have never truly loved anyone but you, and in these years I have thought of you and longed for you so often. Will you give me a greater happiness than I have ever known by promising to think of me like that?"

He smiled. "Now that fate has restored you to me, that will be no hard thing to do. Yes, as long as I remain in France I promise that I will think of you and regard you in all things as my wife."

They sealed their pact with a long sweet kiss.

It was afternoon before they rose and set about preparing a meal. In an iron chest, for protection from mice, Athénaïs kept a store of pickled eggs, pork in brine, dried fruits, wheaten biscuits, sugar and other things which would not seriously deteriorate when she was absent for several weeks.

As she lit the stove she told Roger how she had managed to establish herself there. On first being proscribed she had fled to Bécherel in the hope of finding a hiding-place with one of the tenant families that she had befriended in her youth. At a keeper's lodge in the forest she had pulled up to beg a meal, and found that Chenou, the ex-chief huntsman, had moved in there after his quarters at the *château* had been burnt out. He was completely loyal, and it was he who had helped her organize her hide-out, dug its furnishings out of the rubble, fixed the stove and generally made it habitable. Whenever she returned to it she went over to his lodge to let him know that she was back, and he then kept her supplied with game, butter, fresh milk and vegetables.

Roger well remembered the big, jolly, black-bearded chief huntsman, who had sired half the prettiest peasant wenches for miles around; and was delighted at the prospect of seeing him again, as it was Chenou who had provided nearly all his relaxation during the months he had spent wading through the Marquis's musty documents. But Athénaïs said that as Chenou's cottage was nearly two miles away, it would be best to put off a visit to him until next day, and make do for the time being with the food in her emergency larder.

Having noticed a fowling-piece in one corner of the room, Roger remarked that, while he would be happy with anything she could provide, he might take the gun out for an hour after they had eaten and see if he could bag something for the pot to garnish their evening meal.

"Yes, do," she smiled. "Despite the new laws which make the game free to all, the place abounds with it, as the village is a good mile away. I have several times shot hares and partridges in what used to be the garden. While you see what you can get, I will tidy up and replenish our water supply."

When they had finished eating she took from one of her chests of drawers riding breeches, boots and a cloth coat of her own, and began to dress in them; so he said in some surprise, "Why the choice of those unimaginative garments, my sweet? Have you nothing here more graceful with which to adorn your lovely figure?"

"Indeed I have," came the quick reply; "not much, but enough for me to dress for you tonight, if you wish, in satin and brocade. But at the moment I am about to groom and feed the horses."

Roger was so accustomed to having his mounts tended for him that he had to confess he had forgotten all about them. Now, he quickly offered to see to them himself, but she laughed and shook her head.

"Nay! It is a compliment that my kisses should have driven the poor beasts from your mind; but I have become used to such menial tasks and am now clad for it. Hunting has ever been the husband's part, so go to it, and leave all else to me."

Above ground the sun was shining, the air clear and invigorating. Crossing the open park, Roger entered the nearest belt of woodland and strolled down an overgrown covert. For over an hour he renewed his acquaintance with half-forgotten beauty spots, then shot a hare and returned with it to the *château*.

The entrance to Athénaïs's underground retreat was not conspicuous, but quite easy to find, as a rough path had been trodden to it through the rubble. It occurred to Roger as he followed it that she ought to take better precautions against its discovery by some casual visitor to the ruin, but he supposed that its isolation had made her careless. When he reached the stone stairs he ran gaily down them; he was half-way to the bottom of the flight when, out of the darkness, Athénaïs's voice came in a sudden desperate cry:

"*Garde-toi*, Rojé! We are discovered!"

His impetus carried him down two more steps. As he pulled up a tall form sprang out from the deep shadows. The light from above showed a brace of pistols levelled at him; behind them the white blob of a face. Next second his eyes adjusted themselves to the semi-darkness. The face of the man who had him at his mercy assumed features. It was Hutot.

CHAPTER XVIII

A GRIM BUSINESS

ROGER was standing a little above Hutot, and near enough to have kicked aside one of his pistols—but not both. For a moment they glared at each other in silence, then Hutot's bloated face broke into a smile and he sneered:

"So I've caught you, Citizen Representative, and your *aristo* bitch as well. I felt sure we'd met before when I saw you in court, but I couldn't place you. The moment you entered the Légers' sitting-room I knew you, though. Seeing you in that old screw's house where we devilled together rang the bell. Then your bitch gave you away entirely. I remember hearing how you'd become secretary to her father and gone to live here. I'll bet you seduced her then. Anyhow, it was a thousand francs to a rotten apple that the two of you would make for Bécherel, counting on finding a hide-out for her among the reactionary peasants. So many of them are still fools enough to think that they owe something to the gilded lice that battened on them in the past. But you shouldn't have left your horses in the stable. Finding them told us you couldn't be far off."

He paused for a second, then went on with relish, "I wonder what the Committee of Public Safety would have to say to you if they learnt that you had made off with a *ci-devant* Vicomtesse condemned to death for harbouring a rebel leader. There's nothing against a patriot making such bitches provide him with a bit of fun, but saving their dirty necks is a very different matter. It is the act of a traitor to the Revolution, and punishable by death. I don't think we'll have to bother to send you to Paris, though, because the case against you is such a clear one. You have used your official position in an endeavour to save a condemned aristocrat to whose family you are known to have been indebted. My men and I can form a tribunal competent to deal with that. Drop that fowling-piece and put your hands up! If you resist I'll put a brace of bullets through your guts!"

Roger needed no telling that he was face to face with an enemy who would show him no mercy, and that his life hung by a thread; but Hutot's wordy savouring of his triumph had at least given him a few seconds in which to think. Nearly a hundred feet away, at the far end of the broad passage, two shadowy figures were moving with a lighted candle. At about half that distance a streak of light showed that the door of Athénaïs's room was ajar, and sounds of movement came from it. His brain racing wildly, he strove to reconstruct the dire misfortune that had occurred during his absence. It looked as if Hutot had surprised Athénaïs in her room and that some of his men still held her there. She must have been listening intently for his footsteps, but had been too far from the stairs to hear them and give her shout of warning in time to prevent his walking into the trap. Had it been a trap, though? Probably not, otherwise Hutot would have had one or more of his men hiding with him to strengthen the ambush. Roger decided that they could have arrived only a few minutes before himself, and were still hunting for him in the cellars along the passage. Hutot must have been at the bottom of the steps just then by pure accident; but that did not alter the fact that Hutot's two pistols were now pointing at his stomach.

Desperately he strove to assess his chances. If he moved he was liable to die there on the stairs in the next few moments. His mouth went dry at the thought of what Hutot and his bullies would then do to Athénaïs. Yet if he surrendered, would she be any better off? The tribunal that Hutot had spoken of would be a farce. He meant to settle matters before he left Bécherel. There was murder in his eyes. Yet he was the type of brute who would prefer to take his time over a killing. More than half his pleasure in it would be lost if he were deprived of the opportunity of taunting his victim first. Those small evil eyes of his seemed to be already gloating over the prospect of forcing Athénaïs to witness her lover's trial and execution as a preliminary to her own immolation. Or, no less soul-shattering for his victims, perhaps he intended to reverse the proceedings.

Swiftly Roger made up his mind that in this present extremity time must prove an enemy rather than a friend. He knew that the shadow of death was on both Athénaïs and himself, and that their last slender hope lay in his forcing an immediate decision.

"Drop those things and put your hands up!" snarled Hutot for the second time.

The fowling-piece was under Roger's right arm, the dead hare dangled from his left hand. As though about to obey, he let go of the gun, but at such an angle that it clattered down the last few steps on to Hutot's feet. In order to kick it away, Hutot looked down for the fraction of a second. At that instant Roger flung the hare into his enemy's face. As the hare left his hand he threw himself backward and slithered down the remaining stairs.

Both pistols exploded simultaneously; the bullets sang over Roger's head and smacked into the stone stairway. Hutot recoiled under the impact of the hare and was momentarily thrown off his balance. Next second the soles of Roger's flying feet struck him on the knees. They landed with the full weight of Roger's slithering body behind them. Hutot's legs were struck from under him, his pistols flew from his grasp and he pitched forward. As he fell Roger attempted to jerk himself aside, but failed, and his enemy came crashing down on top of him. Grabbing wildly at one another, each strove to get a grip upon the other's throat.

Hutot was taller, weightier, and much stronger than Roger, but years of dissipation had played havoc with his constitution, and in a moment he was blowing like a grampus. As they rolled over and over Roger's heart bounded from the sudden conviction that within a few minutes he would get the better of his adversary. Then, in a flash, he realized that those minutes were unlikely to be granted him.

At the sound of the shots the underground passage had become a babel of sound. Men began to run from the far end of it, and others dashed out of Athénaïs's room. The opening of the door drove back the darkness. As Roger heaved himself up on top of Hutot, he glimpsed in the half-light four shouting figures rushing towards him.

That very instant, from somewhere unseen, a pistol cracked. The rearmost figure gave a cry, threw up its arms and fell. Another pistol cracked; a second man lurched sideways, recovered, and staggered back through Athénaïs's open doorway. The other two men halted, turned about, lost their nerve, bolted for cover after him, and swung the door to.

Darkness descended again upon the passage like a pall; only a glimmer of daylight now lit the end of it nearest to the stairs. Ten feet away Hutot and Roger were still locked in a desperate tussle, but Hutot was tiring fast. Roger suddenly exerted all his strength and succeeded in breaking his adversary's grip. Kneeling astride Hutot's body, he clenched his fist and smashed it with all his force, again and again, down into the prostrate man's face. Hutot, his nose broken, his thick lips streaming blood, squirmed, groaned and cried for mercy; but he cried for it in vain. Even had he been deserving of it, Roger would not have dared to grant it to him while the men he had brought with him remained unaccounted for. The odds were still far too heavily against Athénaïs and himself escaping from this ghastly trap. Drawing his poniard from his belt, Roger drove the sharp blade under Hutot's ribs. His victim let out a piercing scream. Roger turned the weapon in the wound to free it, drew it out and drove it in again a few inches nearer to the heart. Hutot retched and gave an awful groan, then his body began to quiver violently.

Staggering up, Roger sheathed the poniard, ran to the bottom of the steps and recovered his fowling-piece. The little canister of shot and the powder-horn with which he had gone out were still dangling from his belt. Swiftly loading the gun, he primed it carefully, then stole on tip toe towards the door of Athénaïs's room. He had almost reached it when he tripped, and nearly fell, over the dead body of the man who had been shot while he was still struggling with Hutot. He had only glimpsed the episode in the semi-darkness. In the wild excitement of the last few moments he had not had a second to wonder how it had occurred. Now, he jumped to the conclusion that in the confusion two of Hutot's men must have shot each other.

As he recovered from his stumble and stepped over the body, light flooded upon him. The door had been flung open; a man stood framed in it, covering him with a pistol. Roger dropped to one knee and, knowing how the shot of his fowling-piece would scatter, fired from his hip. Struck in the face and body at close range by half a hundred pellets, the man gave a roar of agony, dropped his pistol and stumbled backwards. Clubbing his gun, Roger leapt forward and felled him by a smashing blow on the head.

While the man was still falling two others rushed at Roger. As he swerved to meet them his glance took in the room. Athénaïs was not there, a prisoner, tied to a chair, as he had expected; but a third man was standing back by the divan, clasping an arm from which blood was dripping. One of Roger's attackers was armed with a sword, the other with a sabre. The first lunged at him. With an awkward swing of the clubbed gun, he knocked the thrust aside. The sabre came slashing down, but he flung himself sideways just in time. Regaining his balance, he dodged another thrust. The movement brought him round with his back to the two cupboards and the stove.

All he could do now was use his unwieldy weapon to parry the cuts and thrusts that his attackers made at him. He dared not lift the butt of the gun to aim a blow from fear of exposing himself to a lunge that might prove fatal. The sweat was pouring from him, his eyes were staring, and his mouth was gaping open.

Suddenly, to his utter consternation, he saw that the wounded man in the rear had drawn a pistol and was seeking an opening to shoot him. Hard pressed as he was, he could do nothing to avoid the shot. It seemed that another few moments must see him crippled by a bullet, then hacked to pieces.

Like a bolt from the blue, help came to him when he had no earthly reason to expect it. One of the cupboards behind him swung open; an explosion almost wrecked his left eardrum. As his attackers sprang back he threw a swift glance over his shoulder. Athénaïs was standing between the doors of the cupboard holding a brace of pistols. From the barrel of one a spiral of blue smoke was issuing. She had just fired it at the man who had been seeking a chance to shoot him. The man had dropped his pistol and, wounded a second time, had collapsed across the table. Her second pistol banged. The man with the sabre jerked like a puppet on wires, clapped his hand to his side, reeled against the wall, then toppled over. Lifting his fowling-piece, Roger rushed upon the third man, beat down his sword and bashed sideways at his head. In an endeavour to avoid the blow the man jerked back, but the butt of the gun caught him on the chin. With a loud grunt, he swivelled half round and crashed to the floor.

Athénaïs had thrown her pistols down on to a chair and snatched up a kitchen knife. Like a tigress she attacked, one after another, the *sans-culottes* that Hutot had brought with him. Three out of the five were still alive, but incapable of resistance. Her face chalk-white with hate, her blue eyes blazing, she slashed and stabbed at them in turn until their groans and whimpering had ceased and all five lay dead.

Roger, gasping and temporarily exhausted from his fight for life, made no effort to stop her. It was men such as these who had burned her children alive, so who could contest her right to exact vengeance? The whole ferocious encounter had taken place in an incredibly short space of time. Barely six minutes had elapsed since Roger had started down the stairs, fowling-piece and hare in hand, suspecting nothing; now Athénaïs's retreat was a bloody shambles.

Leaving the knife sticking in the last of her victims, she turned, with staring eyes, to look at Roger. Her steps now faltering and uncertain, she staggered towards him. Suddenly she half lifted her arms and burst into a passion of tears. He caught her to him as she fell and held her in a tight embrace, while she sobbed out her heart upon his chest.

It took him a long time to calm her, but during the process he got from her enough coherent scraps of speech to learn how it was she had been able to aid him in such a decisive fashion. The hanging cupboard from which she had emerged contained only some of her clothes and it backed on to a doorway opening into the next cellar. Chenou had removed the back of the cupboard so that she could pass through it in an emergency. His idea had been that if at any time while occupying her retreat she heard steps approaching she could enter the cupboard, close it behind her and watch through its keyhole whoever entered her room. If it proved to be Chenou, well and good; but if it was an enemy, she would have a chance to escape through the door of the further cellar. Hutot and his men had nearly caught her, as she had at first taken the sounds of their approach for Roger's returning; but the noise of so many footsteps outside had warned her in time. She had gone through into the empty cellar, but by the time she had loaded her pistols and reached its far door she found that her escape was cut off by men exploring other cellars between her and the steps. A moment later, as she peered along the passage to the square of daylight that lit the stone stairs, she had seen Roger's boots as he came down them, and given her shout of warning.

Her shout had brought the two men who were exploring her end of the passage running towards her; so she had had to crouch back against the wall, holding her breath to save herself from discovery. At one moment they had been fumbling about within a yard of her, but their running forward had blown their candle out, and the pitch darkness had mercifully hidden her from them.

Then, as Hutot's pistols had gone off, they had turned and raced off towards him. She had stepped out into the passage and shot them in their backs. One, as it transpired, she had shot dead; the second, wounded, had staggered into her room with two others who had just emerged from it. She was still reloading her pistols when the door of her room had opened again, there had come the flash of Roger's fowling-piece and she had seen him dash inside. Instantly the idea had come to her of taking in the rear the men he was attacking. She had recrossed the empty cellar and scrambled through the cupboard to find him, unexpectedly, with his back to her; so she had had to fire over his shoulder.

As her sobbing eased, he carried her to the divan, laid her on it, gave her a tot of brandy from his flask, and covered her up. Then he set about the gruesome task of disposing of the bodies. There were the four inside the room, that of the man whom Athénaïs had shot through the back just outside it, and Hutot's. One by one Roger dragged them to the far end of the passage, where its roof had fallen in and it was blocked by a mass of debris. There, he laid them out side by side, as close together as possible, then piled rubble upon them until they were completely hidden and unlikely to be discovered unless a deliberate search was made for them.

When he had finished, he came back to look at Athénaïs and found that, overcome by mental and physical exhaustion, she had dropped into a sound sleep. As quietly as he could, he fetched water from the well, mopped up the spilt blood, put the room to rights, then collected his hare, skinned it and set it on the stove to boil.

His labours occupied the best part of two hours. It had been about three o'clock when he had gone out with the fowling-piece, so it was now a little after six. Sitting down at last for a badly-needed rest, he began to think about the future. As soon as he had realized that none of Hutot's men had got away, he had felt confident that there was nothing more to fear until the next day, at the earliest. Hutot might or might not have told his *confrères* in Rennes where he was going. Even if he had, it was most unlikely that his failure to return would result in a search party being sent out to see what had become of him before he had been absent for twenty-four hours; but after that, to remain in Athénaïs's hide-out would be dangerous. They must leave the neighbourhood while they had the chance. It would be best, he felt, to do so during the hours of darkness, to avoid any chance of being seen by someone who might afterwards report which way they had gone; but whether they should make a start soon after dusk, or sleep there most of the night, then set out an hour before dawn, must depend on how Athénaïs was feeling later in the evening.

He waited until the hare was cooked before rousing her with a kiss. For a second she peered at him through half-closed lids, then smiled and threw her arms round his neck; but she was very silent while they ate their meal, and he noticed that every now and then she could not stop her hands from trembling. When he put the position to her she remarked very sensibly that if they remained there the night there would be a risk of their oversleeping; so it was better that they should leave soon after dusk, and that she was quite prepared to do so. Then she added:

"I feel much shamed at having broken down. I would not have you think, though, that it was remorse at having killed those men: it was relief at finding you had come through unharmed. That, and reaction from having gone mad for a few moments; but it is men such as those who have brought endless misery upon France, and I am glad now that the sight of them drove me into a frenzy. We could never have brought ourselves to kill wounded men in cold blood, yet having disposed of them so completely will give us a far better chance of evading capture."

Roger nodded. "If some of them had escaped, or been found wounded, 'tis a certainty that troops would have been put on to hunt us down; but, even if it is known that they left in pursuit of us, when they fail to return it is most unlikely anyone will suggest that the two of us accounted for all six of them. The odds are on it being assumed that they met with a band of Royalist peasants in the woods who killed them and buried their bodies—a thing quite likely to happen with the country in its present state. As for ourselves, no one can be certain yet whether I really made off with you or took you down to Nantes, as I gave out that I meant to do. Hutot alone had grounds to suspect us and reason to seek a private vengeance. Should a search party be sent out and find no trace of either him or us, it is hardly likely that they will bother their heads further about us. The question now is whither shall we proceed tonight?"

"Wherever you wish to go, I will willingly go with you, Rojé."

He shook his head sadly. "My love, I thank you, and God knows the grief it will be to me to lose you after having found you again; but, for a time at least, our ways lie apart. The road which I have no option but to pursue is a difficult and dangerous one."

"I am grown used to danger, and would be all the more ready to face it at your side."

"After this afternoon no one could doubt your bravery; but, loving you as I do, how can you possibly expect me deliberately to bring you into jeopardy? I will go further: when I am gone the thought that you are still here in Brittany, in constant peril of your life from a continuance of your secret activities with the Royalists, will be positive torture to me. Can I not prevail upon you to let me have you conveyed to England and safety?"

"Nay! To that I will never consent!" she cried, her eyes flashing. "I'll seek no security for myself until once more a King reigns in France!"

To her outburst he could find no reply, and she hurried on, "Your original intent was to see me safely to an inn near Dinan, then proceed to Paris, was it not? Oh, Rojé, I beg you to take me with you; I vow that I will be no burden, and I might prove of help."

"I'll make no promise for the moment," he smiled, "but I never had it in mind to thrust you from my life again quite so swiftly as you suggest. Batches of fugitives can be smuggled away to England only at intervals, so the odds are that you would have had to remain at the inn for some days at least. I am long overdue for a respite from the grim duties I perform, and had thought to bear you company until you sailed."

"Is there no urgency in your reaching Paris, then?"

"From my own point of view, none; and for the Jacobins to whom I must report, the unsettled state of the country will provide an ample pretext of delays upon the road. In fact, I have been considering if it would not be prudent for me to keep out of Paris until the situation clarifies a little. If the half of what I have heard in the past few days be true, this Federal movement is spreading with great rapidity. Once back in Paris I'll have no option but to support the Committee of Public Safety. Should it fail to maintain itself against the Federalists I should be involved in its destruction; and, Heaven knows, I tread a slippery enough path without courting the additional risk of being guillotined as a terrorist."

"Then why should we not go to this inn, where we know we shall be safe, and stay there together for a while?"

Roger's smile deepened. "I had not previously envisaged our staying there as man and wife; but since last night I can think of no more joyous prospect."

They had ample time in which to make their preparations. While it was still light, Roger went out to look for the horses that had brought Hutot and his men from Rennes. He found them, as he had expected, in the stables, and watered and fed them with the other two. Athénaïs, meanwhile, made up most of her clothes into bundles, ready to go on one of the spare mounts that they proposed to use as a pack-horse. After locking the door of her retreat and hiding the key, they spent half an hour heaving lumps of stone and brick on to the steps and across the path that had been trodden to them, so that the entrance should remain unnoticed if anyone came to the *château* next day in search of Hutot.

A little before eleven o'clock they set off, taking the string of six horses with them. When they had covered about six miles Roger dismounted, unsaddled the five spare horses, hid their saddlery and bridles well off the track among some thick undergrowth, then turned the animals loose in the forest. No longer being encumbered by the string, they were able to maintain a quicker pace on the remaining six miles to Dinan, but it was well after midnight when they passed through it, so the streets were deserted and only a few chinks of light were to be seen in upper casements.

Dan had said that *Le Homard Rouge* was some way along the road to the village of Plancoet and stood on high ground; so they had no difficulty in identifying it, even before they pulled up to peer through the semi-darkness of the summer night at its sign. It was a rambling building with several barns attached; so it appeared to be more a farm than an inn, and its size, coupled with its isolated situation, made it admirably suited for a number of people to lie hidden there. Roger estimated that it could not be much more than five miles from St. Briac Bay, and he had little doubt that refugees were only a new commodity among the secret cargoes that had long been smuggled to and from it by night.

With the handle of his riding-crop he gave a series of irregular taps, as he had been directed, on the door. After a few moments an upper window was opened, and a nightcapped head thrust out. Roger asked for accommodation, but used the word "berth" instead of bed. This preliminary password brought a stout, red-faced man, who was obviously the landlord, down to the door. His eyes narrowed slightly as he saw how his visitor was dressed, for although Roger had packed the feathers from his hat and his *tricolore* scarf in one of Athénaïs's bundles, his clothes still gave him away as a Revolutionary official; but it was not the first time that fugitives had arrived there in disguise, and Roger soon reassured the man by completing the recognition signs, then addressing him in English.

Using his second name, of McElfic, he said that he and his

wife had come from Paris, where they had lived since their marriage; but a warning that he was about to be arrested had caused them to abandon everything; and having reached the coast they now hoped to escape safely to his relatives in Scotland. As they had no real intention of crossing the Channel with the next batch of refugees, he added that a faithful maid would be bringing their children to them, but might not be able to do so before the end of the month; so he hoped it would be convenient for them to remain there that length of time.

Mine host of the Red Lobster said there would be no difficulty about that, and remarked that his house was empty at the moment; but he wished it to be understood that while staying there they must never go out, except into the orchard behind the big barn. He then roused a youth from a cubby-hole under the stairs to take the horses, shouldered Athénaïs's bundles himself, and led them up to a low-raftered room on the first floor, which was plainly but comfortably furnished. Very tired now, but greatly relieved to have found such a pleasant haven, they undressed and slipped into bed.

During the past year these two had lived in constant contact with fear, with death, and with horror; now for a blissful three weeks fortune made up to them for much that they had gone through by granting them all the joys of a honeymoon. Forgetting everything else, they lived only for each other, lazing away the sunny summer days and putting all thought of the uncertain future from them. Neither of them was capable of ever again quite recapturing the carefree attitude of youth, but they came near to it; and there were compensations which outweighed that minor loss. Both were experienced lovers, so they could give each other far more pleasure than they would have known had they married as boy and girl. The minds of both had broadened immeasurably since they had parted six years before, and dangers and difficulties had taught them not only restraint, tolerance and understanding, but how to count their blessings.

They rose late and fed simply but well. The inn was named from the succulent lobsters caught down in the bay; there were home-baked bread and rich Brittany butter, fresh-killed veal, cheeses of many kinds, and wood strawberries, with red sweet-scented sparkling cider to wash them down. The big orchard was surrounded by a high mud wall, and they idled there for hours every day with no desire ever to leave it, except when appetite called them to another good meal, or the lengthening shadows of evening told them that it would soon be time to again find joy in a passionate embrace. After a few days the weary, hunted look had faded from Athénaïs's eyes, while Roger's face filled out and he began to put on some of his lost weight.

They talked mostly of the past and of the years during which they had been separated, referring only rarely to the Revolution; but she told him something of the heroic exploits of the Royalists in La Vendée. He had not previously credited the statement that the early successes there were due solely to the courage and initiative of an unorganized peasantry, but she assured him that it was so, and that only after a score of spontaneous risings had taken place and some 30,000 men were under arms had they called upon their old *seigneurs* to lead them.

In the Bocage, Messieurs de Lescure, de Bonchamps, d'Eblée and Henri de la Rochejaquelein had swiftly emerged as bold and audacious commanders of quite considerable forces; while M. de Charette, operating in the Marais, had made himself master of a great area of fenland near the coast. Nevertheless, when the insurrection had succeeded to a degree that called for a commander-in-chief to co-ordinate operations, the local commanders had unanimously selected the brave wool-vendor, Cathelineau, who had initiated the revolt; and his aristocrat officers were now serving him with as much willingness as if he were a Marshal of France.

In the Vendéens' favour was the fact that with foreign enemies on all the frontiers the Convention could spare few seasoned troops to send against them, so they were opposed mainly to a rabble of unwilling conscripts and *sans-culottes* as little trained to war as they themselves. As against that they were greatly handicapped by lack of arms and ammunition. The capture of the fortified towns of Thouars and Fontenay had brought them much-needed supplies, including some artillery; but they were still pitifully short of weapons, and it was to arrange for a consignment of muskets to be smuggled from central Brittany that M. de Charette had been in Rennes when he had so narrowly escaped capture in the secret Royalist intelligence post of which Athénaïs had been in charge there.

The greatest achievement of the Vendéens, so far, had been the capture, on the 10th of June, of Saumur, and their main army was now reported to be moving down the Loire on Nantes, while

M. de Charette with his smaller force was moving up to the city from the south. If they succeeded in taking this great Revolutionary stronghold it would open for them the glittering prospect of being able to advance almost unopposed into central Brittany, Maine and Normandy; and, as these provinces contained large numbers of Royalist sympathizers, of rousing the whole of north-western France to march in a great crusade against the godless terrorists of Paris.

Roger was by no means so sanguine as Athénaïs about their chances. Although many of the big towns were now openly hostile to the Convention, he felt certain that they would resist any attempt to restore feudalism and the thraldom of the Church with as much, if not more, vigour than they were beginning to show against communism and anarchy. Moreover, many of the Convention's best officers were brave and experienced leaders, and the dyed-in-the-wool Revolutionaries were capable of fighting with as much fanaticism as the Royalists.

That proved the case at Nantes, as they learned on the 1st of July. To Roger's sorrow and Athénaïs's acute distress, the news reached them that three days earlier a full-scale assault had been launched against the city and a battle of unexampled ferocity had raged for nine consecutive hours. During this time innumerable feats of valour had been performed by both attackers and attacked, but at four o'clock in the afternoon Cathelineau had received a mortal wound while leading a last desperate onslaught, and the terribly-mauled Vendéens had then fallen back in despair. For the time being, at least, all hope was gone of their inciting other provinces to rebellion by carrying their white and gold banners across the Loire.

That the news was authentic there could be no doubt, as it was brought by an elderly Nantes shipowner who had succeeded in escaping from prison there owing to the confusion that had reigned in the city during the battle. He was the fifth guest to arrive at *Le Homard Rouge* after the "McElfics", the others being two priests who were anxious to reach Ireland and an ex-Councillor of the Parliament of Rennes with his wife. The company was further augmented the following day by a Comte and Comtesse de Bourlainvilliers, their three children and governess, and a banker named de Kock.

It so happened that Roger witnessed the interesting manner of the arrival of this last party, a touch of collywobbles having sent him down to the yard exceptionally early in the morning. As he was about to cross it a covered wagon entered the gate and drew up. Its smock-clad driver got down from his seat, walked round to the back with long lazy strides, and called in excellent French, "You can come out now"; upon which the seven dishevelled and woebegone-looking people crawled out from a hollow space cunningly masked by bales of hay. When his charges were assembled the driver pushed his battered hat on to the back of his head, began to whistle cheerfully, and led them towards the back door of the inn. As he did so he passed within a few feet of Roger and touched his forelock politely, but in that second their glances met. Both remained poker-faced, but each had recognized the other. The last time Roger had seen that smock-clad lout he had been exquisitely dressed in satin, gambling 50 guineas a time on the turn of a single card at White's.

So far, the presence of other guests at the inn had bothered Roger and Athénaïs very little. They exchanged civilities whenever they met in the dining-room or about the farm; but the fugitives appeared much depressed by their experiences, and had evidently formed the habit of reticence, as they showed no inclination to talk about their affairs. M. de Kock, however, proved an exception, and to the "McElfics'" annoyance displayed a strong inclination to attach himself to them.

He was a dapper little man of middle age, with a sharp nose and very bright eyes under beetling brows; and their only consolation for the infliction of his company was that he was extremely well-informed. As he had done the greater part of the journey from Paris on horseback and joined the de Bourlainvilliers in the covered wagon only at a secret rendeavous in Dol—which was all that had been disclosed to him on setting out—he was pretty well up to date with events in the capital. He described it as a den in which a thousand loose tigers had been driven mad by having Chinese crackers attached to their tails.

The Mountain now completely dominated the Convention, but was menaced by enemies on all sides. Mayence and Valenciennes, the two bastions of the north, were cut off and besieged; the Piedmontese were attacking in the east, and the Spaniards in the south; Lyons, Bordeaux and Marseilles were firmly in the grip of the Federalists; there were insurrections in La Vendée, the Jura and the Rhône Valley; the Departments of Normandy had formed a federation of their own; Félix Wimpffen, the Convention's

General Commanding-in-the-West, had gone over to them and was now marching his army on Paris. It could hardly be wondered at that Danton, Robespierre and their associates were striking out right and left like wild beasts at bay, since, should they fail to ride the whirlwind, their lives would not be worth a month's purchase.

But M. de Kock was much more interested in finance than in the fate of France, and constantly reverted to it. Even before he had made the cynical remark, "Governments come and go, but money goes on for ever!", it had become apparent to Roger that, although he gave himself out to be a banker, he was really a speculator. His trouble was that for a long time past the currency of France had been behaving very trickily, and looked like increasing its trickiness soon to such a degree that even the clever M. de Kock would not be able to see a trick ahead.

The abolition of the feudal system had automatically destroyed the wealth of the nation and rendered inoperative the old means of collecting all but a fraction of the former taxes, with the result that the new masters of France had soon found themselves at their wits' end for money. In this dilemma they had hit upon the expedient of assessing the value of the property confiscated from the Church and the *émigrés*, and issuing a new paper money, termed *assignats*, to that amount. The theory was that as these confiscated lands were sold to smallholders, *assignats* to the amount of each purchase would be called in to be burnt, and in this manner sufficient funds would accrue to carry on the Government and finance the upkeep of the fighting services.

From the beginning the cautious French tradespeople and peasants had looked askance at this revolutionary type of cash, and shown the greatest possible reluctance to accept it in payment for their wares; with the result that the *assignats* had soon fallen to a discount. In normal times that might, in due course, have rectified itself; but as the Government became more and more socialist in character fewer and fewer people felt inclined to put their money into property. In consequence the *assignats* were not being taken up, and their value was becoming ever more dubious.

Yet they had become a factor which could not be disregarded in the life of the nation, because the Government no longer paid its contractors, its officials, or its troops with anything but paper. Nobody wanted them, but everybody who was obliged to earn a living had to take them, then passed them on to someone else for the best value they could get. Widespread speculation in them had resulted and, although the Convention had decreed a six-year prison sentence for anyone convicted of selling *assignats* below their face value, and a similar penalty for any shopkeeper caught giving better value for coin than for paper, the illicit traffic in them had grown to alarming proportions. Gentlemen like M. de Kock had been buying them for as low as four paper *francs* to one silver one, then swiftly converting them into good stocks, such as those of the French East India Company, or Bills of Exchange on London, Vienna and Amsterdam. His present trouble was that he had been compelled to fly from Paris with half a million *francs*' worth of *assignats* still unloaded; and, although he had bought them advantageously, he feared the civil war which now threatened between the Convention and the Federalists might cause the bottom of the market for them to drop out altogether.

In the nightmare world of death, persecution and poverty that France had become, Roger and Athénaïs could feel little sympathy for the speculator; and they were glad when, a few days later, they were relieved of his presence. One evening two Breton sailors came to the inn and took a glass of cognac with the landlord in a small room at the back of the house. Roger would not have known of their visit had he not chanced to be passing and caught sight of them through the window; one was a bearded giant of a man, the other of medium height with a thin face that had deep laughter-wrinkles round the mouth, and bore a decided likeness to that of King Charles II. The resemblance was not surprising, as he was, in fact, the Earl of St. Ermins, a direct descendant of that monarch. In spite of the stubble on his chin and a woollen stocking-cap that dangled over one ear, Roger recognized him instantly. As His Lordship's wife, the beautiful Georgina, had played so great a part in Roger's life, he was greatly tempted to go in and enquire news of her; but he needed no telling how important it was that everyone engaged in these secret operations, including himself, should keep their real identities concealed; so he walked on to join Athénaïs in the orchard. Next morning he was not surprised to find that the inn was once more empty of guests except for themselves.

For three more days it remained so, then on the 9th of July a newcomer appeared in the dining-room. He was an elderly man with a big paunch, a gentle expression and kind, pale blue eyes. He told them that his name was Jean Poussaye, and that he had been one of the Queen's musicians. Later that afternoon they learned that he was one of the many people in whom Marie Antoinette's kindness had inspired a humble love and lifelong devotion, and that it was on that account that he had got into trouble.

He had been sitting in a café that he had long frequented near the Hôtel de Ville, when two men at an adjoining table had begun to repeat the most infamous slanders about the Queen. Such stories were not new to him; but on this occasion, for some reason for which he could not account, something had seemed to snap in his brain. He had rounded on the men, called them liars, gone on to denounce the Revolution, and ended up by shouting "*Vive le Roi! Vive la Reine!*"

The two men had endeavoured to seize him, but a big fellow at another table had intervened, knocked them down, hustled him round a corner and carried him off in a hackney coach that happened to be passing at the moment. On learning that his name and address were known at the café, his new friend had said that unless he left Paris that night he would certainly be arrested, and probably lose his head. The mysterious stranger had then provided him with a permit to leave the city, secured him a place in the St. Malo coach, and given him instructions on how to reach *Le Homard Rouge* from there. He was greatly saddened at the thought of having to go into exile, but knew that only a freak of fortune had saved his life by sending his unknown rescuer to the café at that hour. He was a bachelor, so he had no immediate family to cause him anxiety; but had had to abandon all his possessions and was now almost penniless.

Roger pressed some money upon him for immediate necessities when he reached England, and Athénaïs strove to comfort him with the assurance that a good musician would find no difficulty in earning a living there; then their talk turned to the prisoners in the Temple.

On account of his devotion to the Queen, M. Poussaye had kept himself well informed about the progress of the martyrdom of the Royal Family, and had fallen into the habit of going to a café near the Temple two or three times a week. There, he had developed an acquaintance with some of the kitchen staff and others whose duties enabled them to give him news of the prisoners. He said that they were well, but that the Queen was reported to have aged greatly since the death of the King, and that the poor lady had recently been dealt a new and savage blow.

On the 3rd of July the Dauphin—as he was still called, although by the death of his father he had become Louis XVII—had been taken from her to live on the upper floor, in the apartments previously occupied by the King, with the uncouth Citizen Commissioner Simon and his squalid wife.

After they had been discussing the prisoners for some time, Athénaïs remarked how extraordinary it was that, considering the many thousands of brave and loyal men there were in France, no attempt had been made to rescue them.

Roger laughed a little bitterly, and said, "M'dear, had you been in the Temple, as I have, and seen the horde of guards with which they are surrounded, you would realize the hopelessness of such a task."

M. Poussaye looked at him with his kind blue eyes for a moment, then announced, "Nevertheless, an attempt has been made—and quite recently. The authorities are apparently anxious that nothing should be known of it, but I had it in confidence from one of my friends at the café only a few days before I was compelled to flee from Paris. A woman posing as a dressmaker to the Queen was caught smuggling a note to her. It concerned a plan for her rescue hatched by the Baron de Batz and an English woman named Lady Atkyns. The woman they caught was also English and her name was Mrs. Brook."

CHAPTER XIX

THE GOOD ASSASSIN

THAT night Roger set out for Paris. M. Poussaye would give no further information about the abortive attempt to rescue the Queen; but his positiveness that a Lady Atkyns had been concerned in the plot placed it beyond reasonable doubt that the Mrs. Brook, who had been caught smuggling in a note while posing as a dressmaker, could be no other than Amanda.

As Roger rode through the summer darkness he was torn by a tempest of conflicting emotions. Uppermost was dire distress at the thought of his dear Amanda being subjected to the humiliations and filth of a Paris prison and, worse, in imminent danger of being guillotined. Yet he was furious with her for having got herself into such a situation, and was filled with passionate regret at having had to tear himself away from Athénaïs. But with Athénaïs he was also intensely angry, as he felt that she had behaved extremely ill; for, instead of accepting the fact that it was his duty to go instantly to his wife's rescue, she had made a terrible scene about his leaving her.

Then, on top of all this, there was the highly annoying knowledge that in being forced to return to Paris at this particular juncture he was doing the very thing that caution had counselled him to avoid. The issue between the Federalists and the Convention now had all France in a ferment, but it was still impossible to guess which side would come out on top. "Out of sight, out of mind" was, in this instance, a sound old proverb, and if he had been able to keep out of the political scene for another few weeks he could then have re-emerged in his old rôle or that of one who had "seen the light" and become a moderate. As it was, his only hope of rescuing Amanda lay in his being able to make use of his status as a Commissar. That meant nailing his flag to the mast at the height of the crisis—a commitment which, should the Federalists triumph, might easily entail his finding himself in one of a string of carts carrying Danton, Robespierre and their friends to the scaffold.

The one and only positive attraction offered by his enforced return to Paris was the knowledge that he would once more be in the vortex of the cyclone. During the past three months he had given a very great deal of thought to saving all sorts of people from a premature death, but very little to the affairs of Mr. Pitt. Apart from the three weeks' holiday, to which he felt he had been amply entitled, this was through no fault of his own, as he had had to accept the mission or throw in his hand altogether. But while he was in Brittany he had been in no position to secure information that would be of any use in Whitehall, and, knowing that the Prime Minister set a considerable value on his reports, his inability to continue them had, when he had had the leisure to think about it, worried him considerably. It was, therefore, some small comfort to know that he would soon be in a position to send his master an appreciation of the new crisis as seen from its centre.

To speculate upon its possible outcome at the moment was pointless, as he had so little up-to-date information to go upon, while to worry himself sick about Amanda was equally futile, so his thoughts reverted to Athénaïs.

She had taken the line that since Amanda had mixed herself up with a group of conspirators, and they had escaped while she had not, it was for them to get her out of her mess, and that since they possessed sufficient resources and daring to contemplate rescuing the Queen, they should be perfectly competent to rescue Amanda. She had recalled to Roger the vow he had made her in her cellar at Bécherel to regard *her* as his wife while in France, and Amanda as a mistress acquired while in England. So firmly had she established this idea in her own mind that she went to the length of asserting that Amanda had poached on her preserve by coming to France at all, and that although she had done so in ignorance, that was no reason why he should sacrifice his French marriage for his English one. Finally she had burst into a storm of tears and implored him not to leave her, insisting that if he once did so she would never see him again.

When he could get a word in he had put forward the argument that, even had she been his wife in the sight of God, and Amanda no more than a relative of his who was in dire peril, surely she would not stand in the way of his going to that relative's assistance. To that she had perforce to agree, but she then proposed that she should go to Paris with him. Feeling that she could only prove a serious embarrassment to him there, he had flatly refused to let her; but he had compromised by suggesting that she should join him there as soon as he had had a reasonable time to rescue Amanda from trouble.

As he had put that idea forward, he had shuddered at the thought that Amanda might already be dead by the time he reached Paris; but he could only hope for the best, and felt that if she was still alive he should, somehow, be able to arrange for her escape within a fortnight, and have her out of the country in well under three weeks. In consequence, it had been settled that Athénaïs should join him a month hence—at the end of the first week in August; and as he was most averse to saddling himself with any entanglement, however entrancing, at the Cushion and Keys or *La Belle Étoile*, he had given her particulars of Talleyrand's house out at Passy.

It was many months since he had visited it himself, but during the past year he had, on four occasions, sent Dan out there with sums of money, so that old Antoine and his wife should want for nothing. The last time he had done so had been just before leaving Paris, and Dan had then reported that they were well and had suffered no molestation; so it was reasonable to hope that matters continued unchanged there. It had, therefore, been agreed that only in the event of Athénaïs finding the house at Passy unoccupied, or in other hands, should she communicate with him through Dan at *La Belle Étoile*, and that he would warn old Antoine to expect her between the 7th and 10th of the coming month.

At the time, he had thought her behaviour unbelievably callous; but now he began to make allowances. The French, as he had had ample opportunity to observe, were much greater realists than the English. They were, as a rule, more selfish, but, notwithstanding, they were not subject to the unconscious hypocrisy with which English people so often muddled the issues in which they were concerned. French people generally knew what they wanted and saw no reason why they should disguise their feelings; Athénaïs wanted him, and felt that she had an extra-legal claim to him as long as he was in France. Obviously, it had never even occurred to her to pretend otherwise. At the root of her attitude lay the unusual circumstances of their union. Had they met only for the first time three weeks before in Rennes, they might quite well have become lovers after he had rescued her, but then her mental attitude to him would have been entirely different. It was the fact that she had built a romance about him when young, been married to a man for whom she had felt only deep affection, had lovers who had appealed to her senses but not her mind, then found in him, when they met again, all her old dreams realized. He could not but feel both forgiving and a little humble as he recalled how the once-proud and intolerant Mademoiselle de Rochambeau had knelt clasping his knees, while she declared that he was now the only person left in the world that she had to live for, and begged him not to desert her. Now that he was calmer himself, he felt that few things said during an emotional crisis could not be excused by such a deep and desperate attachment.

His journey to Brittany, with *Madame la Guillotine* trundling behind him, had taken him over a fortnight; but he made the return trip, riding all-out, in under four days. On entering the capital late on the evening of the 13th of July he found it in a ferment, and was not long in learning the reason—Jean Paul Marat had just been assassinated.

It transpired that the assassin was a young woman named Charlotte Corday, who had come from Caen. She had succeeded in securing an interview with Marat on the pretext of giving him details of the activities of those moderate deputies who had fled to Normandy and were organizing the Federalist forces there. Marat's loathsome disease made it necessary for him to spend a good part of his day in a hip-bath containing an infusion of medicinal herbs. While seated in it he wrote the leading articles for *Les Amis du Peuple* on a board placed across its top, and often received visitors between periods of work. Mademoiselle Corday had been shown in to him while he was so situated; she had talked to him quite calmly for some moments, then produced a dagger from her bosom and, with unerring aim, plunged it in his heart up to the hilt.

The *sans-culottes* crowded the narrow streets howling for vengeance, screaming that they had been betrayed, and wildly asserting that this was another plot of the *aristos* to murder them and their wives and children. But Roger had other things to think of than the sudden demise of the blood-lusting maniac who had been their chief patron. Pulling up outside the first large café he came to, he gave a lounger his horse to hold and, going in, asked to see the issues of the *Moniteur* for the past fortnight.

The Revolutionary Tribunal had not been long established and, as yet, was sending to the scaffold only people convicted of serious crimes against the New Order; so the lists of executions were not lengthy. Roger swiftly opened up one paper after another, glanced at it and pushed it aside. As he reached the last he was able to throw off the nightmare forebodings that had haunted him for the past four days—Amanda had not been executed. Having lavishly tipped the waiter and his horse-holder, he rode on to *La Belle Étoile*.

It was over a year since he had been to this old haunt of his, although during the whole of that period he had kept his rooms there, and for most of that time Dan had occupied them. His neglect of the inn had been deliberate. He knew that, in spite of the fact that the Blanchards must disapprove of his apparent politics, they were entirely to be relied upon, and that by his never being seen at their hostelry, no one would think of looking for him there should he wish to use it as a hiding-place in an emergency. Now, he had decided to spend the night there, because he wanted to see Dan—firstly, about Amanda and, secondly, to learn if there had been adverse comment on his failure to return to Paris—before exposing himself to possible questioning by his Revolutionary associates. For the latter reason he had sought to make himself less conspicuous and liable to recognition by removing his plumage and sash before entering Paris.

To Maître Blanchard it had long been obvious that Roger would not have continued to pay for the best suite in the house simply as a lodging for his servant, and he was shrewd enough to guess the real reason. Moreover, as he knew Roger to be an Englishman, and one who, in the past, had been on intimate terms with many of the nobility, he also guessed that more than met the eye lay behind all he had heard of his activities as a Commissar. He therefore greeted him with some surprise, but with no less friendliness than of old.

Dan, Roger learnt to his relief, had arrived back four days before, but was out at present; so he asked Blanchard to provide him with a cold meal and a bottle of wine in his private parlour. As he sat down to it, he asked his old friend what he thought of the present situation, adding with a grin that he could speak his mind without fear of being denounced as an *aristo*.

The landlord replied that it was pleasant for once to be able to say freely what one thought, as in these days all honest folk had to be extremely careful; he then launched out on a bitter tirade against the Revolution. Business had never been so bad; supplies could now be got only by lavish bribery; the city swarmed with petty officials who made life intolerable; these little masters of the new régime were stupid, arrogant, dishonest and would have been incapable of earning a living in the old days; in order to buy, sell, take on a new hand, or leave the city, even for a walk in the country on a Sunday, permits now had to be obtained; endless time was wasted filling up forms and answering stupid questions; still more time was wasted standing in queues to buy food, clothes and every other necessity; gold and silver had almost disappeared, so one was forced to accept payment in *assignats*, which everyone knew had no permanent value and of which from day to day more and more were required to purchase anything of solid worth; the genuine poor could not possibly earn enough of them to feed and clothe themselves; thousands were starving and being forced willy-nilly into the ranks of the *sans-culottes*, who were now being paid forty *sous* a day by the Convention to idle in the streets until required to demonstrate against anyone opposing the measures of the Mountain. In the previous week Danton, as the head of a Committee seeking ways to establish a more equal distribution of goods, had put through a new law termed the "Maximum"; it placed a price control on all commodities, making it a prison offence for any trader to ask a price for his wares higher than that fixed by the Government, and compelled traders to unload their stocks whether they wished to or not, with the result that everything was being bought up for a few almost worthless bits of paper. This new law of the Maximum meant inevitable bankruptcy for thousands of shopkeepers, and when their stocks were exhausted what then? The only ray of daylight that the honest Norman could see was the rising in his own and other Provinces; so he was praying fervently that the Federalists would soon arrive in Paris, to execute the maniacs in the Convention and save the capital from complete anarchy and starvation.

Soon after eleven a potman looked in to say that Dan was back; so Roger excused himself from listening further to Maître Blanchard's tale of woe, and went upstairs to join his henchman.

Dan reported that his party had had an uneventful journey and that he did not think Roger need fear finding himself in hot water on account of the delay in his own arrival. As he had taken considerable pains to see that his escort and execution squad were well cared for, Citizen Captain Labord and the rest had all spoken well of him on their return. Nothing had come out before they left Rennes of his having taken Athénaïs from Hutot, and

Dan was of the opinion that the Committee of Public Safety must be far too occupied with the crisis to worry themselves over the temporary disappearance of one of their Citizen Representatives.

When Roger told Dan about Amanda he was absolutely dumbfounded at the idea of his vague and impractical mistress attempting to rescue the Queen; but he promptly swore with many violent seafaring oaths that he would "get she out o' the clutches o' they Devil's pimps", even if he died doing it. Nevertheless, when they got down to brass tacks, the only help he could offer lay in his own courage, brute strength and ability to make any Frenchman believe that he was a dyed-in-the-wool *sans-culotte*. As Roger had feared, the League could smuggle suspects out of Paris, but had no means of penetrating the prisons, and had only on a few rare occasions succeeded in snatching captives from their guards when they were being taken for trial or were being transferred from one prison to another.

As there was nothing they could do until the following morning, they went to bed; but Roger woke early and went over in his mind the plans he had made on his journey, on the assumption that he would have to get Amanda out of prison himself. In doing so he knew that he would have to risk both the status he had acquired through many months of hard, repugnant work, and his head; and he was determined to protect both to the utmost of his ability. If he were to retain his reputation as an irreproachable "patriot", it was important that he should not appear to have any personal interest in Amanda, so that he should not later be suspected of having had a hand in her escape—except, as seemed unavoidable, by one key-man to whom the affair could be put as a matter of business.

Therefore it must be for Dan to make all the necessary enquiries and, when Amanda had been located, get messages smuggled in to her if necessary. People were constantly enquiring at the prisons for lost relatives, and for a small bribe any of the jailers was willing to take food or clothing in to the prisoners from their friends outside; so no danger normally attached to such activities. In this case there was just a chance that some official might get the idea that anyone asking about Amanda was possibly implicated in her plot; but if Dan were held for questioning he could say that he had chanced to learn of her arrest from one of the guards at the Temple, and was solicitous about her because it was she who had induced the Queen to have him reprieved from the galleys four years ago. No one could prove that he had seen her since, whereas it could be proved that he had only just returned from three months in Brittany on the Revolution's business; and the latter fact would clear him entirely.

When Dan woke, Roger asked him to make a round of the prisons until he found out in which Amanda was confined, then visit the office of the Public Prosecutor and bribe one of the clerks to find out for him if her name had yet been put down for trial. They agreed to meet at the Cushion and Keys as soon after midday as possible. Roger then decked himself out in his feathers and sash, ate a good breakfast at a café, and spent the next two hours writing a report of his mission to Brittany. When it was finished he took it along to the office of the Committee of Public Safety and boldly demanded an immediate interview with Citizen Danton.

A secretary informed him that, owing to the crisis, the Committee had recently been "strengthened"—which meant that it had become a still deeper shade of red—and that Danton was no longer on it. Danton was still represented by two of his friends, but all the moderate men had been pushed out and replaced by Couthon, Saint-Just, Prieur de la Marne, and other Robespierrists. The little lawyer from Arras was not on it himself, but now controlled the votes of seven out of its nine members, and came every day to its office to consult with his nominees.

Roger decided that it would be more proper to hand his report personally to one of the members of the Committee than to leave it with a clerk; so he sat down to wait. Presently Saint-Just came in, and on being informed of his business invited him into a small committee room. As it was the first time that Roger had met this new power in the land he was glad of the opportunity to form an opinion of him. He was twenty-five—the same age as Roger—dark, and good-looking except for an enormously over-developed jaw which he did his best to hide by wearing a high, stiffly-goffered cravat of muslin. Reports had it that he was a visionary who dreamed of turning France into a Utopian State where all men should be really equal, and that he was a fanatic who would stick at nothing to achieve his ends. His large, dark, burning eyes gave colour to the latter belief; but Roger found him practical, quick-minded and decisive in his views.

They had not been talking long when Robespierre joined them. Roger had known him since '89, although he had talked with him on only a few occasions. He was now thirty-four, a very little man of no more than five feet three inches in height, but eaten up with a consuming vanity. This morning he was in a particularly good humour because he had found in a smuggled English paper a passage which, instead of referring to the enemy as the armies of France, or of the Republic, spoke of them as "the armies of Robespierre".

He was quick in all his movements, but suffered from a convulsive twitching of the neck and shoulders. The same twitch caused him constantly to blink his eyelids and, like Roger's old enemy Fouché, he never looked anyone straight in the face. His eyes were dull and sunken, his complexion bilious; and although his nose was sharply-pointed there was something curiously cat-like about his features. Having heard him speak in public scores of times, Roger was convinced that he was in no way a great man, but that he had had power thrust upon him, and was frightened by it. The fact that he never initiated a new move himself, but always set the ball rolling through some committee or one of his nominees, bore that out. He had never given a lead in any single crisis, but always lurked in the background waiting for a chance to spring out upon people he thought might prove a menace to himself, when he had them at a disadvantage. In his speeches he was a past-master at the art of converting errors into crimes and crimes into errors; and by sudden vindictive attack, or skilful palliation, he had succeeded on innumerable occasions in striking down his enemies, or protecting colleagues whom he thought might still prove useful to him.

Now, as usual, instead of listening to what Roger had to say, he did nine-tenths of the talking himself, making constant references to his struggle, the great burden he bore almost alone, his acceptance of responsibility only at the desire of the French people, and the irreproachable purity of his intentions. As Roger had put in his report that the reason for his delay in returning to Paris was that he had been held for nearly three weeks as a hostage by Breton Federalists, from whom he had succeeded in escaping only with great difficulty, he was naturally much averse to being closely questioned on that invention. He therefore blessed the loquacity of this small, vain, evil creature, with the nervous twitch and dandified manner of taking snuff; as it enabled him to plant his story and, by making the appropriate grimaces and adulatory remarks, take his leave in as good favour as anyone might hope to stand with "the Incorruptible".

Repairing at once to the Cushion and Keys, Roger spent an hour with Citizen Oysé, gave him a suitably expurgated account of his tour of Brittany, and learned what had been going on in the Granvilliers Section. Soon after midday Dan joined him there with the news that Amanda was in La Force, and the most welcome tidings that her case had not been set down for trial. He had, on his own initiative, given one of the warders money to buy comforts for her, and made the man a handsome present, so that he would be well disposed to perform further mildly illegal, but generally winked-at, services.

As soon as Roger had eaten he went in search of Manuel, the one-time Procurator of the Commune. This notable Revolutionary was one of the few living people who had seen the inside of the Bastille as a captive. He had been imprisoned there in '83 for publishing an anti-monarchical historical essay, and it was largely this that had made him such a fervid apostle of Republicanism when, six years later, the Revolution had broken out. In its early years he had been regarded as one of the most dangerous of the extremists; but his sense of justice had by no means deserted him, and after being elected a deputy to the Convention he had taken the quite extraordinary step of resigning from it in protest at the King's condemnation. As against that, in the preceding November he had, by a brilliant speech at the Jacobins, virtually saved Robespierre from ostracism; so nobody knew quite what to make of him. Had he ever expressed the least sympathy for the Girondins he would have been proscribed with them; but, as it was, he had been left in a sort of political limbo. It was not until late in the afternoon, after considerable difficulty, that Roger succeeded in running him to earth at a comfortable apartment on the south side of the river.

Feigning a detached cynicism, Roger put his case quite frankly. He said that he had been offered 50,000 *francs* to procure the release of an Englishwoman named Madame Brook, who, he gathered, had been involved in an attempt to rescue the Queen; and he asked Manuel how he should set about earning the reward.

Manuel's eyes narrowed slightly, and he said, "Why should you imagine that I can help you in such a matter?"

"Because," replied Roger, "it was you who arranged the escape of Madame de Tourzel, la Princesse de Tarente and others, at the time of the September massacres."

"You are quite wrong!" exclaimed the other hastily. "I deny it!"

Roger saw that he had Manuel rattled, but he had no intention of disclosing the fact that it was he who had suggested him to Gouverneur Morris for that undertaking. Instead, he shrugged his shoulders and said with a smile:

"Why should we waste time going into the past, Citizen? All I desire is to make some quick money, and I am prepared to give you half the reward if you can pull this chestnut out of the fire for me."

"How am I to know that this is not a trap? I have many enemies these days."

"Did I wish to make trouble for you I should have no need to embroil you in a fresh affair: I have only to tell the *Comité* what I know of your activities last September."

For a moment Manuel stroked his brown cheek thoughtfully, then he said, "Michonis, the Inspector of Prisons, is still a good friend of mine; I spent an evening with him a few nights ago, and he told me of this plot to rescue the Widow Capet. The Convention are anxious that it should not get out, but he seemed to think the whole thing a mare's nest. Nevertheless, it is a grave charge, and it would create a fine rumpus if a prisoner involved in such an affair was allowed to escape."

"What reason has Michonis for thinking it a mare's nest?" Roger asked.

"The letter that this Madame Brook was caught passing to the Queen was written in her own hand; it mentioned the Baron de Batz and a Lady Atkyns, but the one is known to have been in Brussels at the time, and the other in England. No date was suggested for the attempt and the letter was mainly a questionnaire —saying if this, if that, if the other thing, could be arranged, would the Queen agree to place herself in these people's hands. One of the ifs was 'if de Batz could get into the Temple with a company of National Guards all loyal to him'. That alone makes the whole thing sound preposterous."

With a flash of inspiration Roger said, "Since this Madame Brook is English, perhaps she is mad."

"Perhaps; anyway, it looks as if she is no genuine conspirator, but a woman whose head has been turned by romantic ideas of becoming the Queen's rescuer."

"Then could we not do the trick by getting her certified as a harmless lunatic?"

"Ah!" exclaimed Manuel, "there you have certainly hit upon something. If we made it worth Michonis's while, a message could be passed to her telling her to show signs of madness, and later he could get the prison doctor to order her transfer to the Hôtel Dieu. Once she is in the madhouse there her name will be struck off the Public Prosecutor's books. There would then be nothing to prevent our getting her moved to a private asylum, and after that . . ." He ended by snapping his fingers.

They discussed the project in detail, and it was agreed that for a payment of 30,000 *francs*, half of which was to go to Michonis, Manuel would arrange matters; then Roger departed with a very much lighter heart.

On thinking matters over, he felt that, although the plan had a good prospect of success, it could be marred by Amanda ignoring a tip from some prison official to feign madness, as she might get the idea that they were trying to lead her into some kind of trap. So, as soon as he got back to the Cushion and Keys, he began to draft a note to be sent in to her, letting her know that her friends outside wished her to play a madwoman's part, and cheering her with the knowledge that those friends were Dan and himself.

The message had to be thought out with some care, as to smuggle it in would be to risk her not receiving it; it had therefore to be an apparently harmless missive which could be shown to a jailer and passed on by him without his appreciating its hidden significance. After some cogitating, Roger drafted a short letter which might have come from a grateful servant to a lady who had once befriended him, and he included the following sentence:

. . . and having seen the inside of French prisons myself, I know, kind Madame, what you must be suffering. I was once locked up for a while in Bedlam, and found it better by far to be there, as I am sure you would. . . .

Roger felt confident that no ordinary French jailer would ever have heard of Bedlam, and if Dan were questioned he could simply say it was an English prison which he had found much less unpleasant than French ones; whereas Amanda would know that Bedlam was the London madhouse and would, he hoped, react accordingly. That evening he told Dan to rewrite the note in his laborious scrawl and put his own signature to it; but they decided that it would be better not to send it in for forty-eight hours, in order to give Michonis, or one of his trusted agents, a chance to first put the idea of feigning madness into Amanda's mind.

That day, Charlotte Corday had been tried by the Revolutionary Tribunal. In all history there was no precedent for a case like hers. She was twenty-four years of age, in good health, unmarried and agreed by all to be a girl of unusual beauty. She was well-educated, intelligent and quite normal, as she had had a love affair with an officer and been prevented from marrying him only by his premature death. She came from a good, upper-middle-class family—being a descendant of the gifted playwright Pierre Corneille—had a comfortable home, many friends of both sexes, and every reasonable prospect of a happy life before her. Yet she had deliberately sacrificed all this in order to make the maximum contribution of which she was capable to the destruction of evil.

At her trial she had displayed no trace of fear, remorse or hysterical self-glorification; serene, dignified and completely mistress of her emotions, she had calmly admitted to killing Marat, and gone on in unruffled tones to state why she had done so. After deep thought she had formed the conviction that the Revolution had brought the most hideous ills on her country, and that those who had encouraged its worse excesses were criminals deserving of death. She indignantly repudiated the suggestion that any other person had instigated her act, and claimed that she had long been resolved upon it as the only means by which she could help to restore sane, responsible government to France. On being asked if she thought she had killed all the Marats, she had sorrowfully replied "No"; but it transpired that she had at first thought of killing Robespierre, and only later decided on Marat as the more evil of the two. Clearly she would have killed both, and doubtless a number of their associates as well, had she had the power to do so; and she was going to her death with the hope that her example would be followed by others with the same convictions as herself.

After she had been condemned, she wrote letters to her father and friends full of grace of mind and lofty sentiments, describing what she had done and asking forgiveness only for any trouble that her act might bring upon them. Next day, calm and smiling to the end, she was taken to the guillotine; and so powerful had been the effect of the purity of her motives on the mob that, despite all the efforts of the terrorists to blacken those motives, hundreds of people acclaimed her as a heroine while on the way to the scaffold.

Her deed, and the attitude of the people towards her as she was taken to her death, gave Roger food for deep thought, and he came to the conclusion that, as a weapon against a minority that sought to force its will upon a nation, assassination was fully justified. The pity of it was that in all France there did not appear to be even one other person with the singleness of purpose, clear vision, and high courage to ignore the man-made law, and face death in a bid to save countless thousands of human beings from the suffering they had brought upon themselves by their own muddled thinking, weakness and folly.

During the next few days Roger was a constant prey to anxiety about Amanda. Dan had had the message passed to her; so they could only hope that she would act on it. But time had to be allowed for Manuel to arrange matters, and there was always the awful possibility that before Michonis could have her transferred to the Hôtel Dieu her name might be put on the list for an early trial.

As there was nothing more that Roger could do for the moment to aid her, he endeavoured to occupy his mind by collecting all the information he could for another despatch to Mr. Pitt. His wide acquaintance among members of the Convention, the Commune, the Jacobins and the Cordeliers stood him in good stead. They spoke freely to him of their fears, and through these sources it soon became clear that the extremists were faced with a much more desperate situation than most people in Paris were aware of, or than he himself had supposed.

The best troops of the Revolutionary army were locked up in Mayence, which was being besieged by the King of Prussia, and in Valenciennes, which was being besieged by the Austrians and English. The whole of Brittany, Maine and Normandy had gone over to the Federalists, and General Wimpffen was advancing on Paris from the latter province; the Piedmontese were thrusting into south-eastern France and the Spaniards were at the gates of Roussillon. English fleets were blockading the Channel and Mediterranean, and it was feared that at any moment they might land an army in the west to support the Vendéens. On the day that Charlotte Corday had been guillotined, the reactionaries of Lyons had executed Chalier and Picard, the two leaders of the extremists there; and the city was in open rebellion. Grenoble and the upper valley of the Rhône were in the hands of the Federalists. In both Marseilles and Bordeaux armies had been mobilized and were marching on the capital. In short, apart from isolated areas, the Convention's writ ran only in Paris and northern France; and the latter might soon be overrun by the invading armies of the Allies.

Knowing that they had their backs to the wall, the extremists were making the most desperate efforts to counter the many dangers that threatened to overwhelm them. Special Commissioners were being sent north, south, east and west to rally the "patriots". Not only, as in the past, were deputies and members of the Commune being despatched, but also scores of Jacobins who had no official position. All were being given the status of Citizen Representatives *en mission*, with instructions to stamp out reaction at any cost. Terror was to be spread from end to end of the country, and wherever opposition to the will of the *Comité* was encountered, townships were to be handed over to pillaging by the mobs.

On the 19th of July Roger learned to his immense relief that Amanda had been transferred to the Hôtel Dieu; and Manuel gave him the name of one Doctor Despard, who ran a private asylum upon the heights of Clichy, to which she could be moved in the course of the next few days. The Doctor was well known at the public madhouse, and was making a nice thing out of occasionally lending himself to such transactions as that upon which they were engaged. For 5,000 *francs* he would see his friends in the Hôtel Dieu and have Amanda handed over to his care; so Roger sent Dan off to make arrangements with the Doctor, while he set about preparing for Amanda's reception when she was freed.

To have her at the Cushion and Keys was out of the question, and he was very loath to bring his friends the Blanchards into possible danger by hiding an escaped prisoner at *La Belle Étoile*. In fact, as she would be liable to re-arrest if recognized, he felt that it would be a considerable risk to find her even temporary accommodation anywhere in central Paris; so his thoughts had already turned to Talleyrand's house at Passy. Athénaïs was not due to arrive for another two and a half weeks, and long before that he expected to have Amanda safely back in England; so that evening he rode out to the sleepy suburb.

On his arrival he found to his satisfaction that nothing was changed. Antoine Velot welcomed him in, said how grateful he was for the money which had enabled him and his wife to carry on without selling any of their master's things, and expressed himself ready to help in any way. Roger told him that he wished to hide an English lady there for a few nights, until arrangements could be made to get her safely to the coast; but so accustomed had he become to pursuing all his ends with the greatest possible secrecy that, instinctively, he refrained from disclosing the fact that the lady was his wife. Instead, he gave her the name of Godfrey, which she had borne before her marriage, when telling the old butler that Dan would bring her out to Passy in two, or it might be three, days' time. Antoine assured him that everything possible would be done to make her comfortable; then, on his master's behalf, he offered his visitor wine. Roger accepted, but when a cobweb-festooned bottle had been decanted, he insisted on the white-haired retainer sharing it with him while they talked of the terrible times in which they were living.

It was on the evening of the 22nd that Amanda was removed from Doctor Despard's home by Dan, and taken to Passy under the name of Madame Godfrey. Intentionally, Roger was not there to welcome her. Now that his harrowing anxiety about her was at an end a reaction of feeling had set in. For over a year he had been walking a tight-rope with the knowledge that any day some unforeseen incident might pitch him from it into the abyss. He had, by skill and good fortune, managed Amanda's rescue without compromising himself. Had he not known about Manuel's past transactions he might, in order to free her, have had to risk both his unrivalled position for supplying Mr. Pitt with accurate information and his life. Amanda had, in fact, come very near to giving his rope just the sort of jerk that would have overbalanced him, and might easily have pitched him head first on to the plank of the guillotine. Even as it was, the bribes he had had to pay out to Manuel and Despard in order to free her had cost him the nominal amount of £1,400 in English money—the bulk of what he had been able to make as a Revolutionary since the previous September; and all because the foolish, romantic-minded girl had got the fantastic idea into her head that she and some old woman could rescue Marie Antoinette from the most jealously guarded prison in Europe. He felt entitled to be angry, and intended to have a first-class row with her. But he decided that, after what she must have been through, he ought in decency to allow her a good night's sleep in security and comfort first; so it was not until the morning of the 23rd that he went out to see her.

He found her up, dressed, and looking little the worse for her harrowing experience. At the sight of him her face lit up, but its expression swiftly changed to amazement when he did not rush forward and kiss her. Instead, having said that he was pleased to see her in such good health, he told her he had always known that her mind was not a very practical one but that, all the same, he had not supposed her to be an outright fool, let alone a dangerous one who, for a whimsy, would place both her own life and his in jeopardy.

Apparently quite astonished at the attack, she protested that she might have risked her own life, but certainly not his.

"For what," he asked, "do you suppose Mr. Pitt pays me to live in France, if not to keep myself informed of what goes on here? You believed me to be in Paris. Had I been I should have learnt within a few hours of the peril in which your absurd antics had landed you. Do you suggest that I should have looked calmly on while you were guillotined?"

"Oh no, m'dear." She waved a hand in airy protest. "I knew that the second you heard of my plight you would come to my rescue. It was mainly that which emboldened me to play the part I did, and kept me cheerful while in prison."

He almost choked with rage. "You—you actually mean to tell me that you went into this crazy plot relying on me, should it fail, to pull you out?"

"Why, yes! Since you must pose as one of these horrible Commissars to earn a living, and thus have acquired the power to decree life or death for anyone in Paris, it would have been stupid of me not to have counted on you as a sheet anchor did things go awry."

"Strap me!" he exclaimed, and sitting down began to mop his face.

"Of course," she went on in rather a hurt tone, "I realized that you might be a little annoyed at being diverted from your work; but I had no reason to suppose that, in an emergency, you would grudge me this slight service."

"Diverted from my work! Slight service! God in Heaven, Madame! Let me tell you the facts. Neither I nor any other Revolutionary official, apart from the members of the Committee of Public Safety, has the power to order a prisoner's release without trial. To get you out of prison has cost us in bribes well over a thousand pounds."

Her eyes widened. "Oh, Roger, I am sorry! I had no idea."

"And that," he stormed on, "although representing nearly a year's earnings of mine here, could have been but a bagatelle compared with what it might have cost in other ways. For thirteen months I have submitted to much physical discomfort and a degree of mental agony that few people are called on to bear, in order to create an unassailable position for myself in which I can render valuable services to our country. Then, without warning, you prance upon my stage, and confront me with a *fait accompli* which calls for the risking of all that I have been through so much to attain. Still worse, this irresponsible caprice of yours might easily have placed Dan and myself with you on the death list. Such utter lack of comprehension of realities as you have shown leads me to wonder if the Hôtel Dieu would not have proved a suitable permanent residence for you."

Amanda drew herself up to her full, considerable height. "Lud, sir! I see no occasion why you should forget your manners."

"Manners be damned!" he cried. "We are talking of life and death. Do you not think I run risk enough of losing my head without your coming here and causing me to become suspect?"

"I gather that, in spite of all the excitement you display, I have not done so?"

"No; yet had you deliberately planned to bring me into danger, you could hardly have devised a trap better calculated to induce me to stick my head into a noose."

"Roger, you are unfair! I knew that I was taking a certain risk myself, but I had no intention of involving you in my undertaking. It was for that reason I made no attempt to seek you out when I arrived in Paris. It lay only in the back of my mind that, should I prove unfortunate, you would be sure to learn of it and come to my rescue. Honestly I had no idea that it would need more than a stroke of the pen from anyone in your position to have me out of prison. Had I had the least suspicion that it would cost so much, and possibly bring calamity upon you, I would have endeavoured to send a message out to Dan, asking you to refrain from further efforts on my behalf."

"What! And remained there until they took you to the guillotine?"

"Nay. Had you not got me out, I am confident that the friends with whom I have been working would have done so."

He gave a short sarcastic laugh. "Really, Amanda! Your simplicity has to be witnessed to be believed. To find the money for the bribes was but a small part of the business. Ninety-nine out of a hundred of these blackguards will take cash in return for empty promises. It was knowing who to trust that counted. How can you possibly suppose that these amateur adventurers with whom you are mixed up would have known how to handle such a matter successfully?"

"You do not know my friends, and your scorn of them is quite unjustified."

"Indeed! How else can one regard two women who come to Revolutionary Paris as though it were Cloud Cuckoo Land, and this precious Baron who proposes to introduce a whole company of loyal National Guards into the Temple at one time, as if that were as simple as producing the Devil out of a trap-door in a pantomime? The utter fantasy of such a proposal shows that none of you can have the faintest idea what you are about."

"In that you are entirely wrong; and I much resent your contemptuous reference to women. It is Lady Atkyns who has inspired us all, and at least we can claim that to date we have done far better than yourself."

Roger gaped at her for a second, then he shrugged. "I meant no rudeness, only to infer that by nature women excel in qualities very different from men, and that this is clearly a man's affair. But inform me, pray, in what way you consider you have succeeded where I have failed?"

"After making two unsuccessful attempts to rescue the Royal Family last summer, you abandoned the project altogether; at least, so you told me when I saw you in November. You said that, having been inside the Temple, you decided that they were too closely guarded for there to be any hope at all of getting them out, and that it would not even be possible to devise a means of regular communication with them. This nut that the great professional considered too hard for him we amateurs have all but cracked. My own capture was a misfortune, but I was only one string of a bow that has many. At least half a dozen inmates of the Temple are in our pay. Several of your fellow Commissioners are working with us. General Jarjayes and Lady Atkyns have both visited the Queen, and the Baron de Batz has actually once already introduced a whole company of loyal National Guards into the precincts of the prison. That my friends could have rescued me and will soon succeed in rescuing the Queen I have not the slightest doubt."

"Amanda! Are you really serious in this?"

"I am indeed, m'dear." Amanda's partly-opened lips widened into a smile. "But I think you in no suitable state of mind to discuss such matters with me at present. You had best leave me now in order to give your choler time to cool. Come back this evening to sup with me, and I will prove to you that women can do as well as men in these dangerous affairs."

Twelve hours later Roger found himself in bed with his wife, and committed in a new attempt to rescue Marie Antoinette.

CHAPTER XX

THE OATH

WHEN Roger rode out to Passy that evening he had not had the least intention of making love to Amanda or embroiling himself in Lady Atkyns' attempts to rescue the Queen; but in the first matter circumstances proved too much for him, and in the second he, for once, allowed himself to be cajoled into an undertaking against his better judgment.

Few men of that day felt any qualms of conscience about exchanging their wife's bed for that of a mistress, then exchanging back again; and had Roger rejoined Amanda in the familiar surroundings of their home at Richmond he would have taken their reunion as a matter of course. But the reawakening of his old tempestuous passion for Athénaïs, and their blissful three weeks together, was too fresh in his mind for him to contemplate an immediate *volte-face* with equanimity. His feeling for her was very much deeper than anything that could have arisen out of a casual love affair; so he realized that he had been mentally as well as physically unfaithful to Amanda, and while in that state felt that there would be something rather shameful about taking advantage of her love for him.

In consequence, he had, that morning, intended to give Amanda a good wigging for running herself into such danger, then soften his strictures by confessing how desperately anxious he had been about her while she was in prison, but add that he was making arrangements for Dan to take her back to England in a few days' time, and that, greatly as he regretted it, most urgent work would prevent his seeing her again before she left. This programme had been completely upset by Amanda's staggering assertion about her friends' activities in the Temple, and her offer to prove how far he had been left behind in his own highly specialized business.

That she was inclined to be hopelessly vague about some matters and to make the most sweeping assertions about others he knew well enough; but he also knew that she would never tell him a string of deliberate lies. Not only curiosity prompted him to hear what she had to say—it was his clear duty to learn every possible detail from her; and as she had refused to give any further information then, he had felt compelled to accept her suggestion that he should return to sup with her.

Although old Antoine knew Amanda only as Madame Godfrey, having been in M. de Talleyrand's service for twenty years he did not expect to be given detailed instructions on how to prepare for such an occasion. When Roger arrived he found the room adjacent to Amanda's arranged for his reception, one of the gallant Bishop's most elegant brocaded chamber-robes laid out for him to change into, and everything else made ready to ensure a gentleman at least a couple of hours' pleasure before returning to Paris, even if he did not intend to remain all night.

Madame Velot had done her share by providing just the right kind of supper, with light but well-spiced dishes; and when Amanda and Roger had eaten, to the accompaniment of Montrachet, Champagne and several glasses of Imperial Tokay, he knew quite well what was going to happen next.

To jump up and make sudden excuses about urgent affairs requiring his immediate presence in Paris was impossible; it could only have been interpreted by Amanda as a declaration that he had an assignation for that night with another woman. To tell her the truth would have been an act of no less wanton cruelty, and he was certainly not prepared to ease his own mind at such a price. Besides, passionately as he was attracted to Athénaïs, he found that Amanda had lost nothing of her capacity to stir him. Therefore, as he peeled a peach for her, he decided that to fake some reason for depriving both her and himself of the natural conclusion to their evening—simply because they happened to be in Passy, France, instead of in Richmond, England—would be the height of unkind and hypocritical idiocy.

A few hours later, as he lay in the Bishop's broad, comfortable bed with Amanda now curled up happily asleep beside him, he went over in his mind all that she had told him about the prisoners in the Temple.

Apparently the dolt-like King, happy at last to have been relieved of all responsibility, and the saintly Madame Elizabeth, whose temperament suited her better for life in a nunnery than in a palace, had both settled down quite contentedly to prison routine; but this was far from being the case with Marie Antoinette. From the very beginning her lively, courageous mind had rejected all thought of finality and surrender. Forced against her sunny nature to hate, she now did so with all her might. No longer compelled, out of deference to the King's muddled thinking, to make herself agreeable to woolly-headed Liberals and treacherous place-seekers, she prayed that her nephew's Austrian legions would swiftly descend on Paris and wipe out in blood the humiliations she had suffered at the hands of the French Revolutionaries. With the hope of rescue ever present in her mind, her worst torment had been lack of news, as the Commune forbade all tidings of events in the outside world being given to the prisoners.

To appease her craving, she had at first turned to the valets, Hue and Cléry, and both, until their dismissal, had done their best for her; but the real genius at this dangerous game had proved to be one François Turgy, an ex-waiter from the Tuileries, who, out of loyalty to the Royal Family, had followed them to the Temple and managed to have himself taken on for similar duties there.

Between them they had derived a sign language, and daily, as Turgy waited at table, he scratched his left or right ear, fumbled a fork, filled a glass overfull, dropped his napkin, brushed an imaginary speck of dust off his coat, and by a score of other natural movements conveyed to his Royal mistress, under the eyes of the watching Commissars, the principal news of Paris and the battle fronts. Then this intrepid man began to smuggle notes to the Queen, engaged a paper-seller to cry out the news aloud every evening under her window, and was soon acting as her messenger on many dangerous commissions.

Through him, loyalists outside had sent in proposals for attempts to escape; but here, as ever, the addlepated King proved the stumbling-block. He was fully resigned to death himself, but did not believe that "his beloved people" would ever harm his family; so he could not be persuaded even to consider any project which, if it went wrong, might lead to a more rigorous captivity; and with phlegmatic unconcern he spent his time reading and praying. On a hundred occasions he had heard the mob screaming for his wife's blood; to her he was kind, affectionate and considerate, but with the irresolution and cowardice that had marked his whole life he deliberately shut his eyes to the peril which she would have to face alone once he had been taken from her. And she had loyally refused to leave without him.

Towards the end of January, Louis XVI's execution had

relieved the Queen of this self-imposed but most formidable barrier to attempting an escape, and after she had recovered from the first shock of her clod-like husband's death, she showed a more eager interest than ever in such projects. It was then that a new ally had appeared upon the scene.

Very sensibly, Marie Antoinette reserved her hatred for the woolly-minded intellectuals whose policies had led to anarchy and for the criminal maniacs who had murdered her friends. To all members of the Temple staff—guards, servants, soldiers and Commissars—who treated her with even reasonable respect, she continued to show her natural affability. Two of the turnkeys delighted to puff foul tobacco smoke in her face every time she went downstairs to take a little exercise in the strip of garden; some of the Commissars who took turns at duty, like the ex-priest Jacques Roux, sang filthy songs all night outside her bedroom door, while others got drunk and spewed upon the floors. But the majority of the Revolutionary officials were fundamentally decent men, who had for years heard the most frightful stories of "the Austrian whore"; yet, when they came into actual contact with her, were quick to realize that they had been completely misled about her character.

Even now, prematurely-aged and grey-haired as she had become through anxieties and sorrows, with no particle of the former glamour that had surrounded her left to dazzle new acquaintances, she still retained much of that devastating sweetness and charm that had enslaved cultured, famous and brilliant men of all nations. To a number of the Commissars it now proved irresistible; they could not find it in their hearts to hate her, and showed her such little kindnesses as they could.

Among them was a bookseller named Toulan, a scruffy-looking little fellow who, as one of the "men of the 10th of August", was regarded as above suspicion by his colleagues. He was shrewd, daring and intelligent and had, after a few turns of duty at the Temple, conceived a chivalrous desire to serve the Queen. As a means of making this known to her he had done her a signal service. Before leaving prison for the scaffold, Louis XVI had given his signet-ring and a packet containing lockets of hair of his children to Cléry, his faithful valet, for transmission to the Queen; but the Municipals had refused to allow them to be given to her, and locked them up under seal. Toulan had broken the seal and taken the things, then put it about that they must have been stolen by some souvenir hunter; but a few days later he had secretly passed them on to the widow.

Having won her confidence, he proposed that he should arrange her escape, but told her that to do so he would require the help of another Commissioner. He had sounded a colleague named Lepître who was willing to co-operate; but he was the head of a prosperous school and, since he would have to abandon it as a result of participation in the enterprise, he required compensation. Toulan asked nothing for himself, but Lepître would have to be indemnified by a payment of 200,000 *francs*. Could the Queen raise such a sum?

She had sent him with a letter to General de Jarjayes, who, out of devotion for her, had remained on in Paris at the War Office; Toulan had then, on two occasions, smuggled de Jarjayes into the Temple disguised as the lamplighter who visited all the rooms every evening, and at these secret conferences the Queen and the General had agreed that Toulan's proposals for escape were perfectly practical. But de Jarjayes could procure only half the money needed to satisfy Lepître; so the Queen had put him in touch with the Baron de Batz, who, before the Revolution, had acted as her personal banker.

De Batz possessed brains, ability and extraordinary daring, and was a millionaire. Although he was known to be a fanatical loyalist his immense riches enabled him to bribe scores of corrupt officials, and he continued to move freely about Paris under a dozen different aliases. He was secretly fighting the Revolution tooth and nail, and had already made an abortive attempt to rescue Louis XVI on the way to execution. Considerable time had been lost in these negotiations, but as soon as De Batz was informed of the plot he immediately put up the money.

After the death of the King, the number of Commissioners appointed daily for duty at the Temple had been reduced from four to three; but the conspirators still had to eliminate the third man. Toulan, however, had hit upon an ingenious method for doing this. The custom was for the three newcomers to draw lots out of a hat on their arrival, two of the lots being marked "night" and the third "day"; he simply wrote "day" on all three pieces of paper and offered the hat first to the Commissioner who was not in the plot. The dupe, pleased at having got off night duty, never bothered to notice that Toulan then threw the other two papers into the fire unopened. In this manner Toulan and Lepître were, on numerous occasions, able to confer at night at their leisure with the Queen.

It was arranged that Toulan should smuggle two Municipal officers' uniforms up to the Queen's room, and that she and Madame Elizabeth should walk out dressed in them; while the Dauphin and his sister were to leave disguised as the lamp-lighter's two children, whom he often brought with him in the evening when making his rounds. De Jarjayes was to have three light carriages waiting outside the prison to carry off the whole party, and a number of Royalists with pistols were to be stationed in the street near the outer gate, ready to overcome the guard, should the escapers have the misfortune to be held up at this final barrier.

The plan had been wrecked at the last minute by Lepître's suffering a fit of nerves and refusing further co-operation unless it was modified. The reverses of the Republican armies had led to a stricter supervision of suspects attempting to leave Paris, and the Commune had issued an order that in future all vehicles were to be searched at the gates of the city. Lepître maintained that three carriages could not possibly pass through without something going wrong, therefore the risk must be minimized to smuggling out the Queen alone. On hearing this, despite the utmost efforts of Toulan and de Jarjayes to persuade her, Marie Antoinette had refused to proceed further with the matter. She wrote to the General, thanking him for all he had done, but saying that nothing would induce her to abandon her children, and requesting him to now place himself out of danger by leaving Paris at once.

De Jarjayes had lingered for a while, still hoping that he might help to save her; but anxiety for this devoted friend had caused her to deprive herself of him by a commission which he could not refuse. She sent him the late King's ring, the packet of hair he had always carried, and a wax impression of a signet-ring that she herself always wore, with the request that he would take the first two items to the late King's brothers, and the last to Count Axel Fersan; for it was his crest upon her ring, and although she had played the part of a most devoted wife, few who knew her intimately had ever doubted that it was the Swedish nobleman to whom she had given her heart.

The General departed, but there remained others ready to run all risks; and now that the resourceful Baron de Batz had taken a hand in the game, he at once began to concert measures with

Toulan for a new attempt to rescue the whole Royal Family. Through his underground channels, he let it be known among the corrupt Revolutionary officials that he was offering a million to be divided among those who would help him save the Queen and her children. Tempted by the idea of earning a major share of this huge reward, that same Michonis who had arranged Amanda's release had offered to play a leading rôle. This ex-lemonade seller, as Inspector of Prisons, could enter or leave the Temple at any hour of the day or night he liked, so his aid promised to be invaluable; and in the meantime de Batz had been working with cautious energy on a project of his own. He had had the same idea as occurred to Roger the preceding summer, when he had set Dan to form a squad of secretly loyal National Guards; but gone about it in a more ambitious manner. In a few weeks he had succeeded in enrolling thirty reliable men and a Captain Cortey, who on certain nights commanded the garrison of the Temple.

Everything was proceeding well when an unforeseen misfortune prevented matters being brought to a head. The Tison couple, who lived on the Queen's floor of the tower and did the rough work there, were one day arbitrarily refused permission by an officious Municipal to receive their daughter up in their room on a visit. Tison promptly flew into a rage and declared that if the prisoners could receive visitors he did not see why he should be forbidden them.

On being formally questioned, he asserted that when certain Commissars thought themselves unobserved they showed great friendliness to the Queen, and allowed her friends to come in various disguises to see her. He then made his wife confirm his statement and add that she knew such forbidden articles as pencils and sealing-wax were in the possession of the prisoners. Among the six Commissars that they denounced were Lepître and Toulan.

The result was a midnight raid led by the terrorist Hébert; the prisoners were hauled out of bed and six Commissioners spent five hours searching the rooms from floor to ceiling. Fortunately only a few wafers for sealing letters were found, which, together with all lack of evidence supporting the Tisons' statements, saved the accused Commissars from arrest; but it had been touch and go, and the conspirators decided that they must postpone further operations until a period of complete inactivity had again lulled suspicions that a plot might be afoot.

After a time it was considered safe to go ahead again. Michonis and Toulan had got themselves appointed for duty on a night when Captain Cortey would be in charge of the guard. The plan was that uniforms should be smuggled in for the Queen, Madame Elizabeth and Madame Royal. Dressed in them, and shouldering muskets, they were to march out with a squad of loyal troops for whom Cortey would have the gates opened at midnight, and under cover of darkness the little King was to be smuggled out in their midst. De Batz, dressed in the ragged uniform of a National Guard, was to go in himself to supervise the operation; and he had made all preparations to convey the prisoners swiftly to a small *château* he owned at Neuilly just outside Paris.

The great night came; but the ill-starred Queen was doomed to suffer yet another bitter disappointment, and it was brought about by the evil genius of the Temple. All the conspirators were at their posts, Cortey had placed loyal men as sentinels in all the key positions, Michonis had smuggled the uniforms up to the prisoners, Toulan was keeping watch with him, and de Batz was counting the minutes until he could give the signal. Then, well after eleven o'clock, there came a loud knocking on the outer gates. It was Simon, the ex-cobbler, the stupid, brutish but incorruptible man whom Chaumette and Hébert, the responsible officials of the Commune, had given access to the prisoners at all hours so that he might act as watchdog.

Late that night he had received an anonymous message saying that Michonis intended to betray the Revolution and release the Queen. He had run to the Commune, where he had been laughed at as the victim of a hoax; but, owing to his fanatical zeal, he had succeeded in obtaining authority to replace Michonis for that night.

On seeing Cortey he had expressed great relief, thinking all to be well; and while they were talking de Batz had hurried off to warn Michonis.

There were 280 National Guards in the Temple, only a small proportion of whom were in the plot. To have killed Simon might have saved the situation, but had he first succeeded in raising an alarm the conspirators would have been overwhelmed, and the prisoners, through their anxiety to escape, been held responsible for Simon's murder. It was hurriedly decided that the attempt must be abandoned. Michonis succeeded in disposing of the disguises and showed remarkable calm in dealing with Simon, but he could not ignore the Commune's order to hand over his duty to him; Cortey meanwhile smuggled de Batz out into the street, and the routine returned to normal.

In the enquiry that followed, the Commune continued to maintain its view that Simon had been hoaxed; so Michonis got out of the affair without suspicion attaching to him. But it was noted that Toulan. who had already been denounced by Tison, was on duty on this night, and had in recent weeks volunteered for duty at the Temple with exceptional frequency; so, as a precautionary measure, he was suspended from his functions.

Disappointed but undismayed, de Batz had determined on a further attempt as soon as things had settled down again; but the loss of Toulan was a serious blow to the conspirators. By this time Lady Atkyns and Amanda had come on the scene, and their rôles had been to receive the Royal Family at de Batz's house at Neuilly. As nothing further could be attempted until Toulan had been replaced by another trustworthy inside man, it had been decided to find out from the Queen which of the other Commissioners she considered best disposed towards her, and therefore most amenable to de Batz's bribes or persuasion, and Amanda had volunteered for this task. The letter with which she had been caught had made no mention of this all-important question, which she was to ask verbally, and had contained only an enquiry as to whether, could matters be arranged on more or less the same lines as before, the Queen was still willing to place herself in the hands of the conspirators.

Most unfortunately, as Roger knew, Amanda's capture had excited considerable alarm in the Commune. They had suppressed all public mention of the affair, just as they had suppressed Simon's suspicions of Michonis and the Tisons' denunciations, because, as a matter of policy, they were most strongly averse to putting the idea into people's heads that it was even remotely possible to rescue the Royal prisoners. Luckily, too, the majority believed that the Tisons were liars, that Simon had been fooled, and that the contents of Amanda's letter were fantastic to a degree which suggested her to be a crazy romanticist without serious backing. But the more suspicious-minded had insisted that precautions against an escape from the Temple should be redoubled. As a result, on the 3rd of July, the little King had been separated from his female relatives and taken to live in the late King's apartments with the watchful and incorruptible Simon as his jailer.

In spite of this new difficulty, Amanda declared herself

confident that the rescue of the whole Royal Family could yet be effected, if only de Batz had at his disposal another Commissioner to take Toulan's place and go on duty with Michonis. She had deliberately refrained from suggesting Roger, as she had realized how important it was to preserve, even from her closest friends, the secret that her husband was a British agent holding a high position under the Revolutionary Government; but now that her dangerous mishap had thrown them together without her fellow-conspirators knowing anything about it, she acclaimed the fact as a direct act of Providence. Who in all Paris, she insisted, was better qualified to fill the gap that Toulan had left? Clearly God, in His wisdom, had guided Roger's every step through the labyrinth of the Revolution in order to fit him for a key rôle in this all-important undertaking—the rescue of the prisoners in the Temple.

The moment Roger had seen which way the wind was blowing he had been conscious of a still, small voice within his mind urging him to keep out of the affair. No one could accuse him of lack of courage or of desire to see the brave Queen restored to liberty, but he did not at all like the idea of getting himself mixed up with so many people. If he went into it, de Batz, Lady Atkyns, Michonis and Cortey would all have to be informed of the part he was to play some days before the *coup* took place. Toulan, although now deprived of a major rôle, would still be standing by to render such help as he could, and no doubt the avarice of Lepître would keep him lurking somewhere in the offing; then there was the lamp-lighter in the Temple, whom it was proposed to make use of again, and a Royalist who had apparently taken his place to pass messages in to the Queen on several occasions. Many of these were acting solely from the highest motives and could be regarded as trustworthy, but the co-operation of others was being bought; and if the latter lost their nerve they might at any time endeavour to save their necks by giving away all their associates.

For a time during his long conversation with Amanda he had had a very guilty feeling that he could have, and ought to have, played Toulan's part, and that his failure to do so had been culpable neglect of the most vital task with which Mr. Pitt had charged him; but on reflection he had decided that to play such a rôle had been placed beyond his powers by circumstances.

It was not until precautions had been relaxed after the King's death that Toulan had felt able to make the first proposals to the

Queen about arranging her escape, and it was clear that all the time the conspirators had been at work conditions in the Temple had been very different from those which had maintained during the early months of the captivity. Over 700 passes for admission to the precincts of the prison were being issued every week, so they could now be obtained without much difficulty. The sentries no longer examined them closely; for visitors simply to hold them up at a distance was deemed sufficient. The majority of the Commissioners had become bored with doing duty at the Temple, and now its novelty had worn off they regarded it as a fatigue; so those with an ulterior motive could have themselves put on more or less whenever they wished, thus making it easy for them to co-ordinate their turns of duty with arrangements outside. Apparently, too, discipline among the National guards had so deteriorated that many of the men detailed for a twenty-four hour duty failed to parade for the changing of the guard at eight in the morning, and often did not bother to turn up until midday or later.

In fact, the slackness, almost inevitable after many months of changeless routine, had permeated the whole organization, just as Roger had foreseen that in due course it would; but that he had been unable to keep a look-out for it setting in, and take advantage of it when it had, was not altogether his fault, as for the greater part of the past four months his duties as a Commissioner had kept him out of Paris.

Even had he been able to remain in the capital, he would have been faced with a special difficulty that Toulan had not had to surmount—his past relations with the Queen. She still regarded him as a murderer and a traitor, and would not have forgotten the way in which he had insulted her husband on the morning following the mob's invasion of the Tuileries. That obstacle might now be surmounted by these friends she trusted vouching for him and informing her that his participation in their plot was essential to its success; but had he been acting alone it was highly probable that she would have feared that he was trying to lead her into a trap, and refused to have anything to do with him.

His final conclusions were that he had no real grounds for reproaching himself, but that he would have if he now refused to aid the conspiracy and it failed on that account. That he would have to disclose his true colours to a number of people, some of whom were untrustworthy, was a most disturbing thought; but no personal risk could be allowed to weigh against the chance to accomplish this greatest of all anti-Revolutionary projects.

Amanda had told him that the Commune had been fooled into the belief that Lady Atkyns had returned to England, and that de Batz had retired to Brussels. Those stories had been prearranged for circulation by the Baron's agents among the Revolutionary police in the event of her being caught whilst in the Temple. Lady Atkyns was still at Neuilly, and he was still living in the city; so before Roger finally drifted off to sleep he decided that, now he had committed himself, the sooner he got into touch with de Batz the better.

In consequence, on the following morning, Amanda wrote a letter in code, briefly informing the Baron that she had regained her freedom, introducing Roger to him, and stating that he was prepared to take the place of "the faithful", as Toulan had been christened by the Queen and was known among the conspirators. In accordance with her instructions, he took it to a grocer's shop south of the river in the rabidly Revolutionary Théâtre Français Section, and, while buying a packet of biscuits, slipped it across the counter to an elderly man who had been described to him. He then crossed the river to the Hôtel de Ville, took his seat in the Council Chamber of the Commune, and passed most of the day there participating in its business.

On leaving the Commune, a little after six o'clock, he had not walked far before he was accosted by an orange-seller. With a smile he shook his head, but the girl said in a swift whisper, "I come from the grocer you visited this morning."

Stopping at once, he bought a couple of oranges from her, and as she handed him his change she slipped a screw of paper into his palm. After walking a quarter of a mile, he turned into an alley and opened the slip; written on it was simply, *Café Coraeza, 10 o'clock.*

Of all places in Paris, the café would have seemed the most unlikely for a hunted Royalist plotter to arrange a rendezvous. It was also in the Théâtre Français Section, hard by the Cordeliers, the Club of the extremists, and with many of them it was a favourite haunt. Yet, as Roger thought the matter over, he mentally saluted the Baron for his perspicacity and courage. Had a number of the well-known terrorists who were accepting his bribes come to see him at a private address, their visits might have been noticed, commented on, and reported by the spies of the Sectional *Comités de Surveillance* which now infested Paris; whereas these crooked Revolutionaries could drop into the *Café Coraeza* at any time without arousing the least suspicion, and, provided the Baron was adequately disguised, no one would dream of suspecting his presence there.

When Roger entered the café four hours later he saw a number of people whom he knew—Camille Desmoulins, one of the first of the Revolutionaries with whom he had become acquainted; Billaud-Varennes; Tallien; the ex-actor Collot d'Herbois; and the incompetent lawyer, Fouquier-Tinville, who, solely owing to his ferocity, had got himself appointed Public Prosecutor to the Revolutionary Tribunal. Nodding a greeting to them, Roger sat down at an unoccupied table, ordered a glass of the cold punch for which the place was famous, then picked up a news-sheet and pretended to become absorbed in it.

Some ten minutes elapsed, then the proprietor came over to his table and asked him if he would care for a game of billiards. Taking this lead, Roger agreed, finished his drink, then followed the man through the back of the premises and upstairs to the first floor. To the left, across the landing, was a door from behind which came the sound of voices and the click of billiard balls; but the landlord turned right, led him down a short passage, and showed him into a room at its far end.

Seated there at a table was a medium-sized, round-faced, rather plumpish man. His eyes were extraordinarily piercing and his movements quick. As the door closed behind Roger he came swiftly to his feet, bowed, and said, "I am de Batz. You have no need to identify yourself, as I have often seen you in the Commune; I am pleased to make your acquaintance."

He was much younger than Roger had expected, and, he judged, not much over thirty. Apart from the fact that his clothes were those of a *bourgeois*, and somewhat faded, he appeared to be using no disguise at the moment. Having made a suitable reply, Roger took the chair the Baron offered him, and they began their talk.

Roger had seen no alternative to allowing Amanda to let it be known, in her letter to the Baron, that he was her husband, as that had seemed the only way of entering on this business without telling a string of lies that might later lead to awkward complications; but he had no intention of disclosing one atom more of his private concerns than proved absolutely necessary. He was, therefore, extremely pleased when, after some preliminary conversation regarding Amanda's capture and release, de Batz said:

"It is natural for one in my position to know a considerable amount about you, Monsieur, as you are a Revolutionary of some prominence; and I keep files recording the principal activities of all those who have ever been Ministers, Deputies, Members of the Commune, or have held any important public office. When looking through yours this evening, I noted that, although you have always assiduously carried out the duties assigned to you, and are regarded as a thoroughly sound 'patriot', you have never committed any act of terrorism yourself, or initiated any measure in the Commune which would actively further the progress of the Revolution. That interested me very much; but, believe me, I have no intention of prying into your motives for exercising this somewhat unusual restraint. On the contrary, I wish you to understand that I make it a rule never to discuss politics with my associates. Experience has shown me that it is a great mistake to do so, as valuable help may be lost through attempting to convert others to one's own point of view. All I require is that I should be able to rely upon them to perform certain agreed services, either voluntarily or on a purely business basis. In which of these categories do you wish me to place you?"

Nothing could have suited Roger better than this frank approach, and he replied at once, "On a business basis, M. le Baron."

De Batz raised a pair of sandy eyebrows. "Really! From what your wife inferred in her letter . . . But no matter; everyone must live! She tells me she had informed you of our activities. As a Commissioner of the Commune you have it in your power to carry on where Citizen Toulan was compelled to leave off. How much do you ask for your services?"

"I fear I have misled you a little," Roger smiled. "I will willingly give you my aid without payment, but I have a considerable interest in the disposal of the Royal Family after they are freed. Our views may be the same. If so that would be excellent, but if not I may find it necessary to drive a bargain with you, or, if you cannot see your way to meet my terms, refuse you my aid altogether."

For a full moment the Baron made no reply. In the sudden silence the ticking of a small clock on the mantelpiece could be heard distinctly, and a distant murmuring from the billiard-room. Then he said, "This is not a matter that I would normally be prepared to discuss with anyone; but since you press me to it, I had Normandy in mind, mainly because it affords the shortest route by which they could be removed from the clutches of the Convention."

"Given certain guarantees, I would be prepared to compromise on that," said Roger thoughtfully.

"May I ask to which place you would definitely be opposed?"

"To Brussels, Coblenz, or any place where they would be liable to fall into the hands of the Germanic powers."

"Should I adhere to my plans to get them to Normandy, what are the guarantees that you would require?"

"That they should remain in hiding there with a reliable Royalist family, and in no circumstances be handed over to the Federalists."

It was the Baron's turn to smile. "I see, Monsieur, that we are at one in believing the Federalists to be basically Republicans, even if a shade less Red in their opinions than the Jacobins. No doubt they would be glad enough to welcome the little King at the moment, in order to use him as a pawn in their game; but later, should they overcome the Convention, I fear he might find himself back in the Temple. No, you need have no fear that I mean to give him and his mother to the Girondins."

"That being the case, why stop at Normandy?" asked Roger. "Unlike the Vendée, no considerable area of the Province is truly Royalist, and although many Royalist households might be found there in which they could lie hidden, there would be the ever-present danger of their being betrayed."

De Batz nodded. "I am fully conscious of that risk; more, I think I see the way your mind is working. As long as they remain under cover they would be of no value to the Royalist cause, and that they should become so is important. Lady Atkyns put it to me most strongly that Normandy should be used only as a temporary asylum, and that as soon as possible they should be sent to England; in that, after much thought, I agreed with her. Would such a programme meet your requirements?"

"Entirely," said Roger, "and with that as our final objective, I am fully prepared to risk my life with you."

For some time they discussed the situation in the Temple, and the new difficulty which had arisen through the little King having been separated from his mother; then Roger agreed to return to the café at the same hour on the following night, when de Batz promised to have Michonis there so that the three of them could confer on possible ways and means.

It was midnight before Roger got back to Passy, but he found Amanda still up, and waiting for him with a cold supper. Over it, he told her, to her delight, about his interview with de Batz, and how well the audacious Baron's plans fitted in with his own.

The following night, soon after ten, Roger was closeted in the upstairs room of the *Café Coraeza* with de Batz and Michonis. He already had a nodding acquaintance with the broad-shouldered, ruddy-faced Inspector of Prisons, and now that they found themselves together in the Baron's company they laughed—although the laugh was on Roger—over Amanda's release from prison. As she was a member of the Baron's organization, Michonis had intended to rescue her anyhow; so had not Roger been so anxious and impatient, he could have saved himself 30,000 *francs*, but the Inspector did not offer to return his share of the plunder.

When they had settled down, Roger said, "Having thought over the matter, it seems to me that this operation must necessarily be performed in two entirely separate parts: firstly, the rescue of the Queen and the two Princesses; secondly, that of the little King."

"I fear it is beyond anyone's powers to persuade Her Majesty to leave the prison without her son," commented de Batz.

"Might she not be persuaded to do so if she received our promise that the boy should be rescued on the same night?"

"That far she might go; but what have you in mind?"

"Simply this. If the original plan is adhered to, and I can think of none better, the Queen and the Princesses will march out in the midst of a squad of National Guards, dressed similarly to them. If they are to pass from the tower to the street without risk of recognition, that part of the programme must be carried out during darkness; but, as long as darkness lasts during these short summer nights, the little King will be in bed in the Simons' apartment. To secure his person, Simon and his wife must either be temporarily got out of the way, or surprised and overcome. Simon is a queer creature, almost a moron in most respects; but with a fanatic zeal which gives him the cunning of an animal he devotes himself to this one task of plugging every loophole that might enable the prisoners to escape. He is suspicious of everyone, and has already had occasion to suspect Michonis. Alone, I could not hope to overcome Simon and his wife and get the child out of their room without their raising an alarm; and should Michonis accompany me, if I rouse them on some pretext after they have gone to bed, Simon might at the first sight of him well suspect our intentions and yell for the turnkeys. If, on the other hand, we make our visit in daylight, Simon will be off his guard. It should then be possible for us to take him and his wife by surprise, hold them up, bind and gag them, and make off with the boy. So my proposal is that the Queen and the Princesses should be smuggled out as soon as the garrison has settled down for the night, but that Michonis and I should remain behind and, from dawn onwards, wait outside the Simons' door until we hear sounds of movement. Then, having given them time to dress, we should pay our visit, and afterwards, by some means or other, smuggle the little King out of the prison."

The other two considered this in silence for a moment, then de Batz said, "I think your reasoning sound. The Simons never let him out of their sight, so at whatever hour the attempt is made one or both of them will have to be overcome. The chances of surprising them successfully in the daytime would be much greater than during the night; yet only at night can we get the three ladies out dressed as National Guards. Yes, you are right. The Queen must be persuaded to agree to our carrying out the business in two separate movements."

Michonis nodded his agreement, and Roger went on, "There remains the problem of how we are to smuggle the boy out in broad daylight; and that, I confess, so far entirely defeats me."

All three of them stared, deep in thought, at the table, for quite a time. Suddenly the red-faced Inspector sat back, banged his fist upon it, and cried, "I have it! We'll smuggle him out inside the birdcage!"

"What the devil are you talking about?" exclaimed de Batz. "How could one possibly get a well-grown child of eight into a birdcage?"

"Ah," laughed Michonis, "this birdcage is very different from the usual run of such things. It is said to have been made for the Prince de Conti. In any case Simon found it in the Temple Palace and had it moved up to his floor of the tower as a plaything for little Capet. It is a huge affair made of silver wire and decorated with gold, crystal-encrusted garlands. It is large enough to contain a score of birds and is one mass of ingenious devices. Its foot-thick base contains a complicated musical-box which plays different tunes in turn as springs are released by the birds alighting on the perches. Once the Simon couple are trussed and gagged, why should we not put the boy into it and cover it up with a sheet or tablecloth? We could say that it was being taken away to be repaired. Two of our trusties dressed as workmen could collect it and wheel it away on a hand trolley. Cortey could be standing near the main gate and could lift a corner of the wrapping, as though to inspect it before it went out; and that would forestall any of the guard making a closer examination of it."

The Baron and Roger both agreed that Michonis's idea was an excellent one; so they went on to discuss a date for the attempt. As the Queen's consent would have to be obtained to the new plan, in which she was to leave her prison some six hours in advance of her son, it was essential that the matter should be discussed with her before any orders were given for outside preparations. To effect this, Roger suggested that he and Michonis should arrange for themselves to be appointed for duty on the earliest date possible; but the wily Inspector shook his head.

"No, no!" he said. "Since you have not done a turn there for many months, no one will think anything of it should you now act twice in a fortnight; but for me to do so might re-arouse Simon's suspicions, and it is essential that I should be there with you on the night of the actual *coup*. You must manage this preliminary business on your own."

"But," objected Roger, "should I be landed with a conscientious and watchful colleague, I may not be able to exchange so much as a whisper with the Queen."

"That difficulty can be overcome," said the Baron quickly. "We know of several Commissioners who would not go to the length of risking their heads in aiding the prisoners to escape; but who are, nonetheless, sympathetic towards them, and who for a consideration would keep watch on the stairs while you talk to the Queen for as long as you like. Goret would, I think, be the most suitable man. I will make him an offer and let you know a day that suits him for you to go on duty together. Should there be any difficulty about securing him, I will approach some other. If you will call at the grocer's round the corner tomorrow, any time after four in the afternoon, I will have a note there for you to pick up, informing you of the date for which to put your name down."

The main lines on which the new attempt was to be made having been settled, the conspirators separated, and Roger again returned to Passy to sup with Amanda. Next day he spent the morning with Citizen Oysé dealing with the business of their Section, then shortly after four he collected de Batz's note from the grocer's. It said only *G.29th*, but that was enough.

Recrossing the river, he went to the office of the Commune and put his name down for that date, noting as he did so that Goret had already entered his, and that the third place was still blank; but that did not matter, as the lots could be fixed so that whoever served with them would draw the day-duty slip. Just as he was about to leave, Chaumette came in and, seeing that Roger had signed the book, remarked:

"I'm glad, Citizen, that now you're back in Paris you're prepared to take a turn in guarding the she-wolf and her whelp. During the last few months we've been finding it quite a job to get enough volunteers, and unless our colleagues show a bit more willingness, we'll have to put them on a roster to serve, whether they like it or not."

It was a matter that naturally gave Chaumette concern, as since the previous December he had been *Procureur* of the Commune; and, with his deputy, the frail, effeminate-looking sadist, Hébert, he was responsible for the safe-keeping of the Royal prisoners. He was a little man with a broad, heavy face, widely-spaced blue eyes, big nose and thick, sensual lips. Although only thirty, he had crammed an immense variety of experiences into his life, having started as a cabin-boy at the age of thirteen. He was a jack-of-all-trades and master of none, but was prepared to speak on any subject; and his volubility, coupled with an apparent good nature, had made him the dominant personality in the Commune.

From the beginning, the Commune of Paris had been much more radical than the National Chamber; but it had lost much of its power when a number of its most prominent members had been elected to the Convention, and its influence was declining still further now that the extremists had gained control of the Committee of Public Safety, as they could do without it. But it still held a trump card as the custodian of the Queen and the little King. Chaumette and Hébert were well aware of that, and regarded the prisoners as a ransom for their own lives in the event of a counter-Revolution; therefore the guardianship of the captives was the thing always uppermost in both their minds. It was they who had chosen the stupid but earnest Simon as watch-dog, and Chaumette spoke of him now:

"You will find the little Capet much changed since you last saw him. We removed him from his family in order to make him lose the idea of his rank, and Citizen Simon is turning him into a good *sans-culotte.*"

Roger laughed and made an appropriate comment, but he was greatly shocked when he saw the boy three nights later.

After the Commissars and officers of the guard had dined in the ground-floor room of the tower, Simon invited several of them, including Roger, up to the second floor for a game of pool. The whole of the late King's apartments there were now occupied by the Simons and the child; all three of them slept in the main bedroom, and Cléry's room now contained a billiard table. When Simon and his visitors came in the little King was there playing with a model guillotine.

Everyone now called him Charles, which was his second name, and within a few minutes Roger saw that he appeared perfectly happy in his new environment. He had always been precocious and talkative, and although he had been ill for some weeks in May he now seemed fully recovered. It was the things he said and did that horrified Roger. There was something peculiarly disgusting about hearing the prattle of a child of eight constantly interspersed with the most filthy and obscene words, and in seeing him become tipsy on sweetened brandy.

Whilst in the care of his mother he had been made to spend a good part of his day doing lessons, and had been put to bed at a proper hour for his age. Having as companions only a sister seven years older than himself and two women both terribly saddened and depressed by their misfortunes, he must have found life very gloomy. It was, therefore, understandable that he should be enjoying this new freedom, in which there were no lessons, no tedious devotions with Aunt Elizabeth, no tears and no furtive whispered conferences; but, instead, men who applauded all his antics, taught him bawdy songs, and encouraged him to drink potent cordials like a grown-up. But the extraordinary thing about it was that less than a month had elapsed since the boy had been taken from his mother.

Formerly he had been gay and, if a little wilful at times, on the whole obedient, most affectionate, very carefully brought up and had charming manners; now he swore, spat and kicked people who teased him, as if he had always been a slum child. It seemed incredible that Simon should have succeeded in changing the boy's whole nature in such a short time; but he undoubtedly had, and to an extent that was even greater than appeared on the surface, as Roger learned through a revolting episode which took place about half an hour after they had started their game of pool.

They all heard the sound of something heavy, perhaps an armchair, being dragged across the floor above, where the Queen and Princesses were now retiring for the night. The little King looked up, jerked his thumb towards the ceiling, and said:

"It's time those noisy bitches up there had a taste of this," and pointed with his other hand at his toy guillotine.

Roger could hardly believe his ears, but he forced himself to join in the laugh that the child's terrible jest raised among the others.

An hour later the party broke up; Roger and Goret relieved the two Commissars who had spent the evening in the Queen's ante-room, and the others went downstairs. Once they were alone Goret sighed and said:

"It makes me almost physically sick to see what Simon is doing to that boy. Fancy teaching a child of eight to chop off the heads of his dolls in a guillotine; and did you hear the awful thing he said about these poor women here?"

"I did." Roger nodded. "The whole thing is monstrous, and I only pray the time may come when Simon's own head rolls into the basket."

They drew the two truckle beds across the doors of the two bedrooms and, as they could hear the Queen still moving about, they stood talking for a while. Then, when complete silence had fallen in the tower, Goret lit his pipe and went out to sit on the top step of the stairs, while Roger walked over to the door of the Queen's room and gently scratched upon it in a certain manner that he had been told Toulan had always used as a prearranged signal.

After a few moments the door opened a crack. The only light came from an oil lamp that was burning dimly on the far side of the ante-room; so the shadow was too deep for the Queen to recognize Roger, and her voice came in a whisper, "Who is there?"

"Madame," he whispered back, "I am an old friend and a true

one. In more recent times, alas, circumstances have caused you to form a prejudice against me; but this note will inform you that those you still count their friends are satisfied of my fidelity."

Without a word, she took the folded paper he held out and drew back. A faint light came through the crack, showing that she had lit her bedside lamp; then, momentarily, a brighter glow, which told Roger that having read the note she had burnt it. Again the crack went dark, and her whisper came:

"Monsieur de Breuc, I know not what to say. It may be that you come here at the peril of your life; but it may be that you have deceived my friends, just as you deceived me a year ago, when I told you never to let me see your face again."

As Roger had feared, the note alone had proved insufficient to remove her doubts of him, so he replied in an earnest whisper, "I deceived you then, Madame, solely because time was precious, and I was desirous not to waste it in a discussion such as this. Had you but placed your trust in me then, you would not be here now."

"Perhaps; yet how could you expect me to trust you, knowing as I did that you were twice a murderer?"

"Madame, 'tis true that I slew the Comte de Caylus and caused Don Diego Sidonia y Ulloa to be killed; yet in neither case did I stand to gain for myself either love or money by their deaths. I killed de Caylus in fair fight, and then only that Athénaïs de Rochambeau might marry a man more suited to her age and tastes. As for the Don, he had already had my poor Isabella d'Aranda done to death, and I did no more than execute justice upon him, which he would have otherwise escaped."

The Queen sighed. "Those names! Those names! How strange they sound in this grim place, recalling as they do memories of those happy days when I thought only of beauty, grace and laughter. But is it indeed the truth, Chevalier, that in these awful deeds you had no ulterior motive? Would you take an oath on that?"

"I swear it, Madame! I vow, too, that I had your best interests at heart that morning when, dressed as a sweep, I endeavoured to take you out of the Tuileries; and again, when I attempted to forestall the Commissioners who brought you here. I beg you, Madame—nay, I implore you—to give me back your confidence, and help me in this new attempt to save you from your enemies."

For a moment the Queen was silent, then she whispered, "Very well, Monsieur, I will listen to what you have to say."

"God be thanked!" breathed Roger; then, in a low voice, he told her what was proposed. But when he came to the necessity for the rescue of the little King to take place some hours later than her own, she instantly took alarm, and exclaimed:

"No, no! I will not hear of it! Either my son comes with me or I will not go. This is a trap to separate me from him."

"Madame," Roger reasoned, "is he not separated from you already?"

"Yes, oh yes! How could they be so cruel!" She gave a sob. "That brutal Simon now has charge of him, and treats him abominably."

"Nay, that is not true; Simon is uncouth, but not unkind," he strove to reassure her. "That your son should have been taken from you is hard indeed, but I promise you he is not ill-treated."

She sobbed again. "I—I spend most of my days now peering through a slit in the wall of the turret at the top of the stairs. Some days Simon takes him up to the leads to stretch his little legs, and once in a while I see a glimpse of him. It is my only joy—all that is left to me." At the thought she broke down and burst into tears.

"Courage, Madame! Courage!" Roger urged her. "I beg you not to let your thoughts dwell on that now, but to give me your attention."

Beyond the dark crack the sobs were gradually stifled, then the Queen murmured, "Forgive me, Monsieur, but I can think of little else. They are doing terrible things to him, terrible things. He sings the *ça ira*, and he would never do that unless he were forced to."

"He cannot understand the meaning of the song, Madame."

"I would I could believe you. But it is not only that. Sometimes he uses the most frightful words, and the terrible thing is that he uses them in their right context. I would sooner be placed upon the rack than know their intentions towards him; yet I cannot escape it. There is a worse crime than the murder of the body, Monsieur: it is the murder of the mind. And it is that these wretches are plotting against my poor child."

Again the distraught mother's grief temporarily overcame her, and Roger could not wonder at it. From what he had seen that evening, he knew that a kernel of awful truth lay at the heart of her accusations; and he decided to use it in an attempt to persuade her to accept the plan. When her weeping had eased a little, he whispered:

"I believe you right, Madame; but how can this devilish crime be prevented? Only by His Majesty being restored to your care; and what hope can you have of that as long as you and he remain in the hands of your enemies? You have been separated from him for near a month, so why should you baulk at the thought of leaving here a few hours in advance of him, when that offers a good prospect of your retrieving him for good?"

"Ah; but while I remain here we are still in the same building. As I have told you, I can still catch a glimpse of him now and then. That means so much to me. What if you succeeded in rescuing me but failed to rescue him? Can I trust you? Can I really trust you?"

"Madame, as we have planned matters, his rescue should prove much easier than your own. If we succeed with yourself and the Princesses, I am confident that we shall succeed with him."

"You swear it? You give me your solemn oath that this is no trick to separate me from him permanently?"

Roger realized that something more than a ready assent was needed; otherwise she would think matters over later, become plagued with renewed doubts, and perhaps back out after all on the night of the attempt. In an effort to convince her absolutely of his integrity, he said in a low, tense whisper:

"I, Roger Brook, swear to you, Marie Antoinette, that naught but God's intervention shall prevent my restoring your son to you."

CHAPTER XXI

THE PRICE OF INFIDELITY

TWO nights later, as soon as Roger came off duty, he went to the *Café Coraeza* and reported to de Batz. Michonis, having been warned by the Baron that he expected Roger, was already there. Now that the Queen's consent to the plan had been obtained, it remained only to settle on a date and make the final preparations.

The ruddy-faced Inspector said that he was averse to rushing things. He thought that an interval of a week ought to be allowed to lapse before Roger again put his name down for duty, and he suggested that they should make it the 8th of August.

De Batz, however, announced himself in favour of the 5th, because Captain Cortey was already on the roster for duty with his company at the Temple on that date; and, although he might be able to exchange duties with another officer, such a complication should be avoided if possible.

Roger supported the Baron, and disposed of Michonis's doubts by reporting the conversation he had had with Chaumette; so they agreed that it should be the 5th. He was to tell Amanda to rejoin Lady Atkyns at the Baron's house at Neuilly on the afternoon of the 4th; otherwise all that Michonis and himself had to do was to put their names down for duty. It was de Batz's province to co-ordinate all other arrangements, including those for getting the prisoners safely out of Paris; so, having drunk a glass of wine to the success of their great venture, and agreed that it was unnecessary for them to meet again until "the night", they separated.

In a matter of such importance as the Queen's escape, Roger would never have allowed his private affairs to bias his contribution to the making of a decision; but, all the same, he was extremely relieved that the earlier date had been chosen, as the later one would have landed him with a major worry. He was far from having forgotten that the beautiful and passionate Athénaïs was due to arrive at Passy any day from the 7th of August on. When he had made the arrangement with her he had hoped to have Amanda out of prison and on her way to England with Dan within a fortnight. The first part of that programme had been accomplished with a day to spare, but the second had been entirely upset by her winning him over to commit himself with de Batz. Athénaïs had said, as he was about to leave her, that she would be bored if she remained on alone at the Red Lobster; so she meant to make her way to Paris by easy stages, and, as he had not the faintest idea how far she had progressed, he could not write and ask her to postpone her arrival. Therefore, once he had committed himself, he had realized that, should the Queen not have been rescued and Amanda have left Paris with her by the end of the first week in August, he would be faced with the knotty problem of how to prevent his adored mistress from running into his beloved wife.

The choice of the 5th had spared him this anxiety, but he now began to consider how best to arrange his affairs after the escape of the Royal Family. One thing was clear—his participation in the escape would put an end for good and all to his activities as a Commissar, and never again would he be able to come face to face with any prominent Revolutionary without risk of recognition, arrest and death. Therefore the *coup* would also put an end to his usefulness to Mr. Pitt in France; but it would, if successful, more than compensate for that. He had, with some skill, led de Batz to disclose his views on the disposal of the Royal Family before giving his own; and, since the Baron had already settled with Lady Atkyns on England as their final destination, there was no reason at all to suppose that he would go back on his word. Mr. Pitt had stated in no uncertain manner that the greatest service Roger could possibly render him was to get the little King to England; so he certainly would not complain if his agent sacrificed all else to achieve that one great triumph. Furthermore, Roger felt that, as he was to play a principal part in the affair, he would be entitled to claim the magnificent reward.

Had the plans for the escape been entirely to Roger's liking, they would have ensured that he would never have to leave the little King until they were both safely across the Channel. But the overruling objection was that, whereas he was to be removed in the birdcage at seven o'clock by two Royalists disguised as workmen —this being considered the earliest hour at which it would be plausible for them to appear—Roger and Michonis, being on night duty, could not leave the tower until a few minutes before eight, when anyone seeing them walk out would assume that they had just been relieved.

While they remained holding the fort for this anxious hour, the trolley on which the birdcage had been taken away was to be wheeled half a mile to a house where de Batz and Lady Atkyns would be waiting. There, the boy's clothes were to be changed for those of a girl, then Lady Atkyns was to take him out of Paris as her daughter, the Baron acting as their coachman.

It was hoped that they would be going through the St. Honoré barrier at about the time that Roger and Michonis left the Temple, but for them the margin was going to be dangerously short. It could only be a matter of minutes between their coming out through the gates and a hue and cry starting after them. Both were well known to hundreds of people, and their descriptions would be swiftly circulated. Any attempt by either of them to catch up with the little King would therefore be the height of folly, as that might lead their pursuers to him. Obviously they must disappear as soon as possible, disguise themselves, and make their way separately out of Paris.

Even then, for Roger to go to the house at Neuilly, where the Baron meant temporarily to conceal the Royal Family, would, de Batz considered, entail a certain unnecessary risk, as he intended them to remain there for a week or more, and was most averse to making the party bigger than it need be. So Roger had had to content himself with an understanding that he should join them in Normandy, and accompany them only on the last lap of their journey to England.

For nearly fourteen months his work had entailed his participation in the Revolution and tacit approval while innumerable crimes were committed in its name. He was sick to death of the life he had been compelled to lead; and the idea of settling down at home on a handsome fortune seemed, at times, the most desirable of all possible visions—but only at times. There was Athénaïs; there were, too, the thousands of unfortunate people who so desperately needed the help that he could give them to escape, and in his heart of hearts he knew that he would never be really content to settle down for very long.

His three weeks with Athénaïs had not even blunted the edge of his passion for her; on the contrary, it had been just the right length of time for her to get into his blood and, now that he was separated from her, to appear more desirable than ever before. Only when he was with Amanda, or engaged in some important affair, could he shut his mind to her; at no other time could he do so completely. Mentally he could re-create her image in a score of attitudes, and hear again her provocative laughter; so the idea of going home and abandoning her for good was unthinkable.

Had the attempt to rescue the prisoners in the Temple been fixed for any date later than the 7th, he had intended, somehow or other, to persuade Amanda to rejoin Lady Atkyns. Since he could not stop Athénaïs coming to Passy, he had not seen how else he could prevent their meeting, distasteful as the thought was, of deceiving his wife so flagrantly; but now the plan, as finally agreed, would spare him this embarrassment.

On the 5th, Amanda would go to Neuilly, in order to be there to receive the Queen the following night, and remain with her while the Baron and Lady Atkyns returned to bring the little King out to them in the morning. Although the Queen had not yet been informed of the decision, de Batz intended to split the party into four for their journey to Normandy, in order to minimize the chances of their being recognized. He meant to take the Queen himself, with Amanda as her companion, while three other Royalist gentlemen separately escorted the two Princesses and Lady Atkyns, who would have charge of the little King. Amanda, therefore, would be in constant attendance on the Queen from the night of the 5th until they reached the coast, and would not expect to see anything of Roger until he joined them there; so after the escape he would be free of all responsibility for ten days or more.

Since he had to go into hiding for that time, where could he do so better than at Passy? Athénaïs should join him there after he had been lying low for three or four days, and they would still have the best part of a week together in which to make future plans. As to what those plans were to be he was still a little vague; but he knew that Athénaïs would never consent to leave France, and that her dearest wish was to continue fighting the Revolution. In the back of his mind lay the thought that she should accompany him to Normandy, and remain there while he delivered the little King to Mr. Pitt; after which he would return to her, and they would then both take a hand in rescuing the refugees, of whom an ever greater number stood in need of succour as the Terror mounted in ferocity.

July '93 had been a desperate month for the Convention, and it had won a breathing space only by the extraordinary energy and ruthlessness of its *Citoyens Représentants en mission*. Their strongest weapon with which to confuse and divide their internal enemies had been the argument that, while invasion threatened on every frontier, it was the basest treachery to France to take up arms against the central Government. Such reasoning made no appeal to the Royalists of La Vendée, but it had a great effect on the Federalists in all parts of the Republic. It enabled Fabre to subdue 30,000 insurgents in the Eastern Pyrenees, Dubois-Crancé to bring Grenoble back to its allegiance, other Representatives to be equally successful in Bordeaux and manage to prevent the Federalists of Lyons from openly declaring war on the Convention. In other areas, where the Commissars found negotiation useless, they stamped out revolt with terror, and inspired or menaced the Generals of the Revolutionary forces to unceasing efforts.

In Normandy, after a brief, muddled, half-hearted campaign, the Federalists under General Wimpffen had been defeated and dispersed. In the Jura 15,000 equally ill-led Federalists had been broken up by 15,000 fanatical "patriots". The Revolutionary General, Cateaux, had cut off Lyons from Marseilles, and the Terrorist, Westermann, had made a daring penetration with his Alsatian Legion into the heart of La Vendée.

Had the Allies, during this month of desperate internecine strife, chosen to concentrate their efforts on invasion, they could easily have conquered the whole country; but the opportunity was lost through divided counsels, the sloth of their generals and the selfish aims of their respective Governments. The Spaniards wanted Roussillon, the Sardinians wanted Nice, the Piedmontese wanted Chambéry, the Prussians wanted Mayence, the Austrians wanted Valenciennes, and the English wanted Dunkirk; so, instead of by-passing these fortresses, they tied up the bulk of their forces by besieging them.

Here, again, the fanatic ardour of the Citizen Representatives with the armies proved the deciding factor. Knowing that their own lives were at stake, they worked ruthlessly, tirelessly and with great bravery to animate the defenders of these cities. On the 17th of July, Dagobert and Brabantane won a victory over the Spaniards which relieved Roussillon, and restored the morale of the Revolutionary troops in the south; Dubois-Crancé assumed the command of the army of the east, and held off the Piedmontese; Cochon and Briest defeated all the endeavours of the Prince of Coburg and the Duke of York to take Valenciennes, and Rewbell and Merlin performed prodigies of valour in holding Mayence against the King of Prussia.

Yet the fate of these last two cities temporarily brought to naught the plans upon which Roger was engaged. After being reduced to living on horseflesh, cats and rats, the garrisons of both surrendered—Mayence on the 25th of July and Valenciennes on the 28th. Now that there was no longer anything to keep the two Allied armies from marching on Paris, the Convention was again rendered desperate. In this extremity the Committee of Public Safety decided to use the Queen. To threaten her with death was at once a gesture of defiance and at the same time a possible means of making the Allies halt their offensive while bargaining for her release. At midnight on the 2nd of August she was removed from the Temple to the Conciergerie.

From La Force, L'Abbaye and other prisons in which aristocrats were confined, there was always some hope of release, but from the Conciergerie there was none, and for that reason it had become known as "the ante-chamber of Death"; so without any announcement being made, the intentions of the *Comité* were plain both to their friends and to their enemies.

Roger learned what was afoot on the 1st of August; and having told Amanda to write a note in the code she used with de Batz, he took it to the grocer's shop. Next morning, as he approached the Hôtel de Ville to attend a session of the Commune, the orange-seller handed him a reply; it read *To-night: 10 o'clock.*

In the upstairs room at the *Café Coraeza* he found Michonis already with the Baron, and they at once went into anxious consultation. The Inspector of Prisons had known of the contemplated move even before Roger, and said at once that it was beyond his power either to stop or delay it, so, although the two of them would still have to go on duty at the Temple on the 5th, the job was definitely off.

Roger at once pointed out that since the rescues of the Queen and the little King had been planned as entirely separate operations, there was nothing to stop their going ahead with the latter, but de Batz shook his head.

"That is so; but at a price which I consider it too high to pay. To get the boy out, you and Michonis would have to overcome the Simons. Such an act entails official suicide, and both of you would have to seek safety in immediate flight. Deprived of the invaluable help you two can give me, what hope should I have left of rescuing Her Majesty?"

Loath as Roger was to sacrifice the Queen, he had already

made up his mind that, for reasons of State, the boy must be given priority over his mother; so he replied, "I admit that once Michonis and I have shot our bolt it will be impossible for either of us to play a similar part in another rescue; but better half a loaf than no bread. Now that the Queen and her son are in separate buildings it is obvious that any attempt to combine their escapes, as we had hoped to do, is out of the question. The Queen's removal to the Conciergerie confronts us with an entirely new problem, and one which may prove impossible of solution; whereas everything connected with the rescue of the little King is in hand, down to the last detail; so surely common sense dictates that we should make certain of him while we have the chance?"

Again de Batz shook his head. "No; I consider that Her Majesty's removal to the Conciergerie makes it incumbent on us to redouble our efforts on her behalf. It would be little short of criminal were I to prejudice our chances of saving her by depriving myself of my two most valuable allies through going ahead with this other venture."

"But would you be prejudicing your chances?" Roger argued. "Remember, the Queen's situation will be such that totally different measures will have to be adopted. On her leaving the Temple tonight the Commune will cease to be responsible for her and the Minister of Justice will become so. She will no longer be guarded by Commissioners, but by the professional jailers at the Conciergerie. It is with them that any new project for her rescue will have to be arranged, not with Michonis and myself. I doubt if either of us would even be allowed inside the prison."

"I shall be," Michonis put in. "As Inspector of Prisons I can enter any one of them at any time, and I have the right to demand to see and speak to any prisoner."

Although Roger had an extremely strong financial interest in the little King's rescue, he was really fighting Mr. Pitt's battle rather than pressing his own inclinations as he replied, "Perhaps; but for how long? And how far will that get you? It is one thing for a pair of us who are of the same mind to have her in our care for a whole night, but quite another for you to slip in and merely exchange a few whispered words with her."

"Nevertheless, the fact that Michonis can get in and speak with her at any time is a very great deal," persisted de Batz, "and as long as you remain in Paris with your rank of Commissioner you also may prove useful to us in due course."

"I quite see that; but if we abandon the little King in order to concentrate on the Queen, are we not liable to fail on both counts? What of the guard at the Conciergerie? At the Temple we have Cortey and his loyal company already primed to turn a blind eye at the right moment; they cannot be transferred to duty at a different prison."

"No; but men might gradually be infiltrated into the battalion which supplies the Conciergerie guard, and a suitable officer found in it to play Cortey's rôle."

"That will take time."

"All the more reason that we should not deprive ourselves of Michonis by proceeding with the latter half of our old plan for the 5th. With him to aid us we need not lose a moment in resuming communication with the Queen, and ascertaining the exact conditions of her new confinement. No one has threatened the little King with death, nor is anyone likely to do so. Chaumette and Hébert mean to keep him as a hostage for their own necks. But, having him, they do not need Her Majesty; and Hébert has already promised the *sans-culottes* her head. In the matter of the boy there is no great urgency; but if we are to save his mother we must now work fast and use every single asset we possess to that end."

The Baron's last argument was unanswerable, and Roger felt no personal reluctance in giving way to it; but on his ride out to Passy he had ample cause to cudgel his wits. Athénaïs was due to turn up there in five days' time.

After telling Amanda of de Batz's decision, he gave her his own honest view about the Queen's chances. Incarceration in the Conciergerie always meant a fairly quick trial, and anyone who was condemned by the Revolutionary Tribunal was invariably executed the following day. He said that in the Queen's case a special indictment would undoubtedly be prepared and this might take a week or two; but he did not believe that even a delay of a month would be enough to enable the Baron to complete all the complicated arrangements necessary for a rescue. There was, therefore, little point now in Amanda remaining near Paris, and he suggested that Dan should escort her back to England.

Amanda would not hear of this. She at once declared that as long as there was any chance at all of the Queen being rescued she intended to remain where she was.

Roger then pointed out, quite truthfully, that her own position was none too secure, and therefore a source of anxiety to him. Under a medical instruction, she had been transferred to Doctor Despard's private asylum, and was officially supposed still to be there. Should some officious little representative of Authority decide at any time to check up, he would be shown a young woman in a padded cell; so that side of the business was all right. But, should Amanda chance to be recognized by any "patriot" who had seen her while she was in Paris and knew of her arrest, she would promptly be rearrested, and it would prove very difficult indeed to effect her release from prison a second time.

She countered that by saying that she rarely ventured more than a mile from the house, and that the chances of her being recognized in a village like Passy were infinitesimal; but she offered to give up her afternoon walks if Roger so wished.

Temporarily defeated, he did not press the matter; but he returned to it next evening by suggesting that she must find it very lonely with no one to talk to day after day, and that it would surely be better if she joined her friend, Lady Atkyns, at Neuilly, if only for a while.

Amanda promptly replied that, although he could not get out to Passy every night, and it was often late when he did, she infinitely preferred even a few hours of his company to whole days with Lady Atkyns; or, for that matter, to moving in the most amusing society.

Her answer made Roger mentally squirm, but he was determined if he possibly could to save her the distress she would feel if she found out about Athénaïs; so the following day he put on a worried look and told her that the *Comité* was thinking of shortly sending him on another mission. But even that did not shift her. She appeared much concerned at the thought that if Roger had to leave Paris he would no longer be able to assist de Batz in any further plans for the Queen's rescue, but said that he must not worry about her, as she had developed a great fondness for old Antoine and his wife, and would be quite content to remain with them until Roger's return.

Actually, as far as he knew, there was little likelihood of his being sent by the *Comité* on another journey. In view of the great number of Commissioners who had been despatched to all parts of the country during July, he had daily dreaded being nominated himself; but he had recently learned through the tittle-tattle at the Cordeliers that, although his work in Brittany had been considered satisfactory, he was not deemed to possess the ruthlessness necessary to cope with emergencies. That piece of intelligence had afforded him great relief, but it neither helped nor hindered him in the matter of Amanda.

As she was digging her toes in about remaining at Passy only because it was easy for him to come out there as long as he remained in Paris, he had no doubt that she would be willing enough to move if he suggested a place where it would be as easy or easier for him to be with her; but he dared not expose her to danger by bringing her into the capital itself. On the other hand, Athénaïs would run no special danger if she was installed at *La Belle Étoile*; so, now at his wits' end, he decided that, somehow or other, he must head her off from meeting Amanda, and take her there.

It was now the 4th of August, and next day he was due to go on duty at the Temple at 8 p.m. for forty-eight hours. He would not be free again until the evening of the 7th; so there was the unpleasant possibility that Athénaïs might turn up in his absence, and that next time he went out to Passy he would find that the fat was already in the fire. Almost hourly from the beginning of the month his secret agitation had been increasing, and now that the collision of his two beauties seemed imminent, he could hardly take his mind for a moment off the unhappy *contretemps* that it conjured up.

Athénaïs, arriving without being warned that Amanda was his wife, could hardly be expected to hide her annoyance at finding another pretty woman already in the house. Amanda was much too quick-witted not to smell a rat. Inevitably something would be said on one side or another to spill the whole bag of beans. Both would be furious. Athénaïs would have every right to be intensely indignant at his having placed her in such a humiliating situation, and Amanda, although in a much stronger position, would also feel humiliated and be most terribly upset.

With a heavy sigh, he recalled that line of Gay's in the 'Beggar's Opera', "How happy could I be with either, were t'other dear charmer away," for that exactly expressed his own feelings; but he had a horrid foreboding that in the event of an encounter he would be given no option, and no happiness at all. The probability was that his entrancing mistress would disappear in a cloud of black anger, never to be seen again; and his charming wife would prove anything but charming to him for a long time to come.

Greatly depressed, but still determined to leave no step untaken which might save the situation, he sought out Dan early on the morning of the 5th and informed him exactly how matters stood. As Dan had seen Athénaïs in Rennes, and knew that after rescuing her his master had disappeared for three weeks, the story he was now told did not surprise him in the least; but to Roger's annoyance he seemed to find it very funny. However, he gradually suppressed his mirth, and with a more suitable gravity took his instructions.

He was to go out to Passy and tell Amanda that on leaving the house that morning his master had seen some suspicious characters loitering about; so for the next few days he was to remain there and act as watchdog. It was unlikely that Athénaïs would arrive before the 7th, but she might be a day early. In any case, should she turn up, Dan was to tackle her before she reached the front door, tell her the house was no longer a safe hideout, use the conveyance in which she had come to take her to *La Belle Étoile*, then report to Roger at the Temple. Should Amanda witness this little scene from one of the windows, she could be told afterwards that Athénaïs was an escaping suspect who had been sent out there by mistake, but fortunately Dan had recognized her, and been able to put matters right.

Only very slightly easier in his mind, Roger went on duty at the Temple. Dinner there with the other Commissioners served to distract him a little; and later that night he heard from Michonis his first news of how the Queen was situated in her new prison, as the Inspector had paid her an official visit there the preceding day.

General Custine, who was shortly to be guillotined for having failed to relieve Mayence, had been transferred to a common dungeon so that his private cell could be used for Marie Antoinette. It was a gloomy little room with barred windows that gave on to a court in which over 300 prisoners had been butchered during the September massacres. It contained no political prisoners now, but during the daytime was used as a *buvette* where common criminals were allowed to receive visitors, and to smoke and drink with them. The window of the cell was too high up for them to see into it; but the noise, stench and filthy language arising from this thieves' kitchen were an infliction which the Royal prisoner was forced to bear for most of her waking hours. The stonewalled cell itself was divided by a wooden partition with a gap in its centre only partially closed by a battered screen, and in the outer half of the cell two gendarmes were on duty day and night; so the Queen was under constant supervision.

As against this, Michonis said, sympathy for her, coupled with her own dignity and charm, had already gained her some friends inside the prison. Madame Richard, the wife of the chief turnkey, had done all she dared without risking a reprimand to make the cell comfortable; and a beautiful peasant girl named Rosalie Lamorlière, who was employed as a cook, was taking special pains to find out what the Queen liked to eat, in order to tempt her poor appetite with specially prepared dishes. But the Inspector added that he thought it was going to be very difficult to arrange an escape.

Next day Roger saw the little King again, and was shocked afresh by the boy's disgusting behaviour. He also saw the two Princesses, but as nothing was to be gained by contravening standing orders he did not attempt to hold any private conversation with them. From the morning of the 7th he was too absorbed in his own worries to think of much else, and as soon as he could leave in the evening he hastened back to Passy in a turmoil of apprehension that the worst might be happening at that very moment.

As he approached the house, the sight of Dan standing in the lane made his heart contract more violently than it would have done had a footpad suddenly jumped out of the hedge and levelled a pistol at him; but his faithful henchman was waiting there only to let him know that Athénaïs had not yet put in an appearance. In consequence, over supper, he made a final effort to move Amanda by telling her that Michonis considered the rescue of the Queen to be hopeless; so that there was no longer any reason why she should postpone her return to England.

For a moment she remained silent, then gave him a queer look, and said, "You seem very anxious to be rid of me, Roger; and I cannot see why, as long as I remain quietly here, you should be so concerned for my safety. Your persistence in this matter might almost lead one to suppose that you wanted me out of the way because you are having an affair with another woman."

Roger hoped that his laugh was not as hollow as it sounded to himself; but he promptly pooh-poohed the idea, and only afterwards began to wonder if he had been really wise to do so. To have told the truth and shamed the devil would certainly have relieved him of the awful strain he had been under for the past week; but he swiftly rejected the idea. That would have been relieving his feelings at Amanda's expense; so most unfair to her. He knew that he had got himself into this mess, and was now paying the price of his infidelity. Clearly he must continue to do so as long as that would serve to spare her unhappiness.

For the next three days he lived in perpetual torment. Every morning he went off to his work as usual, leaving Dan on guard, but he could settle to nothing and returned each evening expecting to find Amanda in tears and Athénaïs gone out of his life for ever. The last thought harrowed him intensely. Amanda, he felt sure, would forgive him after making both him and herself thoroughly miserable for a while, but he had convinced himself that the proud Athénaïs would not; and, since the Revolution compelled her to live under false names anyhow, it would be impossible for him to trace her and make his peace. The more he thought about her, the more desirable she became; and the idea of losing her for good seemed as bad as a threat of never knowing another summer.

By the 11th his anxieties had taken a new turn. Dan vowed that he had never been off duty for more than a few moments at a time, and Amanda's unruffled contentment was ample evidence that Athénaïs had not arrived during one of the brief spells when he had ceased to be on the look-out for her. What, then, could have happened to prevent her keeping to their arrangement? Roger felt certain that nothing would have stopped her reaching Passy between the dates agreed had she been in a position to do so. Was she ill? Was she in prison? Was she dead?

Day and night such grim speculations now plagued him like an aching tooth, and in a few more days he was praying that she would arrive even if she ran slap into Amanda. Surely, had she been detained only by illness, she would have written to him? It must be that she was either dead or once more in the clutches of the Revolutionaries. To have known that she was safe he would now have faced any sort of upset willingly; but still there was no sign of her, and there was nothing whatever he could do to trace her whereabouts.

Meanwhile his duties had been particularly onerous. Since 1790, a national feast day had been held on the 14th of July to commemorate the fall of the Bastille; but this year the 10th of August had been selected as more appropriate to celebrate the termination of the *ancien régime*. Thousands of Municipals from all parts of France had come to participate, and, as a member of the Commune of Paris, Roger was one of their official hosts.

From four in the morning till late at night there were marches, receptions, speeches, blaring bands and displays of symbolism. David, the bloodthirsty painter, acted as master of ceremonies; the eighty-six senior members of the Convention played the part of the Departments, carrying spears to represent the rods of the National Fasces; the other deputies bore sheaves of corn; there was an Ark containing a scroll bearing the Rights of Man, and an Urn containing the ashes of an Unknown Soldier; every trade was represented in the long procession, and at its end came several tumbrels filled with crowns, sceptres, coats of arms and *fleur-de-lis*-spangled banners, which in due course were formally burnt. There was a huge statue of Regeneration, with water, of which everyone drank, spurting from her breasts; and an even vaster one of the French people striking down Federalism and stifling it in the mud of a marsh.

The excitement was intense; and, in a lesser degree, so it continued for many days afterwards, as the hordes of official guests were all eager to take a hand in running the country. Their deputations besieged the Convention, the Commune and the Jacobins, and had to be listened to patiently, then fêted afterwards. The state of the country made their representations more urgent, as it was still menaced on all sides, and torn by three major internal revolts.

The Federalists of Marseilles had been forced to abandon Aix, but were still in control of a large part of the south. In Lyons an army of 40,000 men with 300 guns had been assembled; the Royalist Comte de Précy had been nominated as its Commander, and on the 8th the city had declared war on the Convention. Meanwhile La Vendée continued to be a festering sore in the side of the Republic. Down there, men, women and even children had taken up arms, and were fighting for Church and King with the utmost ferocity. Their fanatical priests were promising them resurrection in three days if they died in battle, and the superstitious peasants were hurling themselves in hordes upon the levies of *sans-culottes* sent from the cities to quell them.

The *ci-devant* Duc de Biron had been transferred from his command on the Rhine and given the uncongenial task of suppressing the rebellion, but he was not a strong enough man to compel his subordinates to co-operate; so Westermann, Santerre and

Rossignol were all raging through the country independently, burning whole villages and committing the most appalling atrocities, but unable to make any permanent headway against the equally ferocious Royalists.

It was these threats to the Revolution from without and within that caused the visiting Municipals to demand that the Convention should decree a *levée en masse*, and on the 23rd of August a law was passed to the following effect:

"From this moment till the enemy shall be driven from the territory of the Republic, all the French shall be in permanent requisition for the armies. The young men shall go forth to fight; the married men shall forge the arms and transport the supplies; the women shall make tents and clothes and serve in the hospitals; the children shall make lint out of rags; the old men shall cause themselves to be carried to the public places, to excite the courage of the warriors, to preach hatred of Kings and love of the Republic."

It was a magnificent declaration; and the brave common people of France hailed it with enthusiasm, although it bore with great severity upon them. Danton, keeping his head during this orgy of patriotism, pointed out that to conscript the whole nation simultaneously must kill it from famine within a month; and he succeeded in modifying the immediate application of the law, which also applied to grain, horses and every type of vehicle. The whole population was called up at once only in the danger areas of La Vendée, Lyons, Toulon and the Rhine; elsewhere the Convention contented itself temporarily with a first requisition, embodying all unmarried men and widowers without children, between the ages of eighteen and twenty-five. Yet even these measures resulted in providing another 450,000 for the armies.

It was not until the 28th that Roger heard further from de Batz. That morning the orange-girl passed him a slip, and in the evening he went to the *Café Coraeza* at the time appointed. On this occasion the Baron was alone, and with his irrepressible optimism at once launched into particulars of a new plot he had been hatching to save the Queen.

He said that unofficial negotiations were proceeding between the Convention and the Court of Vienna, in which the former were using the Queen as a bargaining counter in an endeavour to stop the war, and that it was for this reason she had not yet been brought to trial; but the Allies now showed no inclination at all to abandon their campaign against communism and atheism as the price of the life of a single woman. On the other hand, they showed an equal reluctance to gamble everything on a forced march on Paris, as every King and Commander among them was being implored to do in a spate of letters from de Fersan and de Mercy-Argenteau, and other personal friends of the Queen. She could, therefore, hope neither to be ransomed as one of the terms of peace, nor rescued by the swift advance of an allied army; so everything must now be risked on another attempt to snatch her from prison.

Only the sadist Hébert and the fanatics whom he led were now endeavouring to hound her to her death; the common people felt that she had been made to suffer more than enough already, and thought of her with sympathy. There was strong evidence of this from the markets. Madame Richard had gone out to buy her a melon; the woman behind the stall had said, "I am sure you want it for our poor Queen. You shall have the best one I've got, and I refuse to take any money for it." Her brave words had met with applause and been carried to the other markets; now, every day, women who had screamed "Austrian whore" at Marie Antoinette in the days of her prosperity came to the gates of the Conciergerie bringing her presents of the choicest fruit, fish and flowers. Many of them had husbands and brothers among the soldiers who formed the prison guard, and, de Batz argued, under the influence of their womenfolk they might tacitly abet an escape.

Michonis had been in to see the Queen on several occasions and had won over the Richards. He had also introduced into her cell a new associate of the conspirators. This was an old friend of the Queen's, named the Chevalier de Rougeville. He had approached Michonis independently, and the Inspector, convinced of his good faith, had passed him on to de Batz. It had been agreed that the Queen needed the sight of someone she had known well in the old days to give her confidence in a new attempt; so on the previous evening Michonis had taken de Rougeville in to her. Even in the dim light of the cell she had recognized him at once, but they had not dared to exchange more than a fragment of conversation. While Michonis engaged the attention of the guards, the Chevalier had said:

"Take courage, Madame; we have arms and money." Then, seeing how frail-looking she had become, he asked, "Does your heart fail you?"

To that she had replied, "It never fails me, but it is deeply afflicted," and, placing her hand on her heart, had added, "If I am weak and downcast, this is not."

As one of the guards had poked his head through the opening at that moment, de Rougeville had dropped at her feet a red carnation that he held ready for the purpose. A note had been concealed in it, asking her if she would trust herself to him a week from that night, which would be the coming Friday, the 2nd of September.

The new plan was that de Rougeville, disguised as an officer of the National Guards, and a squad of trusted Royalists, dressed as soldiers, should accompany Michonis and Roger to the Conciergerie in the middle of the night. The two Commissioners would produce a forged order instructing them to convey the Queen back to the Temple. Richard would accept it as genuine and ask no questions. When they had taken the Queen outside they would drive her to a prearranged rendezvous, where she would transfer to the Baron's carriage, and he would drive her out of Paris to Lady Atkyns.

The scheme seemed as sound as any that could be hoped for, and Roger saw that it might be thought suspicious if only one Commissioner was sent on such an important undertaking; so he at once agreed to give Michonis his support. It was settled that he should come again to the *Café Coraeza* on the night before the attempt for a final conference with Michonis, de Rougeville and the Baron, and that he should also warn Amanda to be ready to play, on the night of the 2nd of September, the original rôle assigned to her. On leaving the café he went out to Passy, and when he had told her the plan they agreed that she should leave there to rejoin Lady Atkyns at Neuilly on the afternoon of the 1st.

Athénaïs was now three weeks overdue. After that first week of extreme tension, Roger had reached the stage of fearing that little hope remained of her making a belated appearance; so he had relieved Dan of his tedious watch for her. During the fortnight that followed he had continued to worry himself sick at the thought that some evil fate must have befallen her, but now the first effects of the blow had had time to become a little dulled, and for a few days after his meeting with de Batz anxieties connected with the new plot helped to lessen the periods he spent brooding about her. Then, on the 1st of September, an event occurred that temporarily drove her image completely from his mind.

On entering the Hôtel de Ville at midday he learnt that Michonis had been arrested.

CHAPTER XXII

THE ANTE-CHAMBER OF DEATH

THE precincts of the Council Chamber were buzzing with rumours. A plot had been discovered to rescue the Queen. As yet no details were known, but the chief turnkey, Richard, his wife, a gendarme named Gilbert, and Michonis had all been arrested and taken to the Abbaye. The complicity of the Inspector of Prisons, who had always been regarded as such a good "patriot", filled many of the Commissars with amazement; but others sagely shook their heads and recalled honest Citizen Simon's unheeded denunciation of him while the Queen was still confined in the Temple. It was said that the police were already on the track of the *aristos* who had suborned Michonis, and that all Paris was being combed for them.

Outwardly calm, but inwardly a prey to the most fearful apprehensions, Roger listened to all this; and as he did so one alarming thought after another flashed through his mind. Would the trail of discovery lead to de Batz? If so, would it lead through him to Lady Atkyns? At all costs he must stop Amanda setting out that afternoon to join her at the Baron's country house. Thank God there was still time to do so—if he was not arrested before he could reach her. Thank God, too, he had had the foresight to keep it from everyone that he used the house at Passy. Amanda would be safe there if he could stop her leaving. But what of himself? Should he disappear and go into hiding with her? If he did, and there was the least suspicion against him, his disappearance would be taken as a certain sign of guilt. As long as he remained ignorant of how much the police knew, to reappear and resume his duties would be to risk his head; so if he once abandoned ship it would be the end of his activities as a Commissar. It seemed unlikely that police enquiries would have led as far as himself yet. But what of Michonis? Would the ex-lemonade-seller break down under examination? Would he try to save his own life by giving his confederates away?

Only one thought kept recurring in the back of Roger's mind —he must do nothing on impulse; in keeping his head while he still had it on his shoulders lay his only chance of preventing it from rolling into the basket under the knife of the guillotine. So, fighting down the urge to dash off to Passy at once, he walked into the Council Chamber and took his usual place there.

With his brain still whirling, but with praiseworthy self-control, he remained there for an hour; then, after a vote had been taken on some minor measure about which not one word had penetrated to his mind, he left the building. Outside in the street the orange-seller accosted him and slipped him a note, which read, *Fear nothing. Tonight, north door St. Sulpice, 9 o'clock.*

The Baron's optimism did little to reassure him, since the worst danger lay in what Michonis might give away; and over that de Batz could not possibly exercise any control. However, during Roger's hour in the Council Chamber one thought had encouraged him to believe that his own chances might not be too bad—the Inspector of Prisons was a brave fellow, and on the occasion when Simon had so very nearly caught him out he had shown an exceptionally cool head. Moreover, he and Roger had formed a definite liking for one another; so it seemed reasonable to assume that he would protect his colleagues if he possibly could. It was this estimate of Michonis's character that had decided Roger not to go into hiding, but to play the game out and gamble his head against retaining his status as a Commissioner.

He had also decided not to go out to Passy himself, but to send Dan, as by doing so he could eliminate the risk of being traced there should the police already be watching him. There was the further point that, during the many months they had been in Paris together, Dan must inevitably have become known to a number of people at the Cushion and Keys as his *alter ego;* so if he were arrested Dan might be hauled in as well on suspicion.

To guard against this possibility, when Roger ran Dan to earth half an hour later, after giving him the message for Amanda that all arrangements were cancelled and in no circumstances was she to leave the house, he added, "Things look atrocious black, and you can serve me best by keeping yourself out of trouble—at any rate for the present. I wish you to remain with Mrs. Brook at Passy for a week. If by the end of that time I have not come out there, you can return to Paris, but must do so in disguise. First contact the League and arrange with them to convey Mrs. Brook safely to England. Only after that should you, if you wish, run the risk of trying to find out which prison I am in and doing what you can to get me out."

"Should I wish!" muttered Dan angrily. "As though I'd be like to leave 'e marooned here; I'd burn they's bloody city down first."

Roger had known well enough that if anything could be done to save him Dan would do it; so he gave him a friendly grin and they shook hands surreptitiously. Having watched him hurry off, he went into a restaurant and ordered himself a meal, although he found that he could do scant justice to the food when it was placed before him. The rest of the afternoon and early evening he spent at his Section, endeavouring to concentrate on business, while fearing at any moment that the agents of the *Comité de Sûreté Générale* would arrive to arrest him; but nothing unusual happened and, as far as he could judge, he was not followed in the street on his way to meet the Baron.

When he reached the north door of the now deserted church he could see no one in the deep shadow thrown by the great building; but after a moment the figure of a woman, draped in a dark cloak, emerged from the angle of a buttress. For a second he stared at her uncertainly, and it was only when she spoke that he realized that the roundish blur of features beneath the poke-bonnet were those of de Batz.

"Give me your arm," said the Baron in a low voice, "and we will walk a little way. My time is short; so say nothing unnecessary. Leave me to do the talking." Then, as they set off, he continued:

"They have caught only those on the inside. All else is secure for the moment, but unfortunately I am compromised. M.'s sister is the wife of the man who owns the café. She cleans my room there and knows where to find me in two of my other haunts. From those I might be traced to others; so, you see, she has it in her power to make Paris too hot to hold me. Had it not been M. who has been caught she would still be one hundred per cent reliable, but she is greatly attached to him. This morning she held a pistol to my head, and threatened to denounce me unless I can save him. Could I see my way to, I would do so without being blackmailed, for M. is a good fellow and deserving of all possible help. But the devil of it is that I can do nothing without a group to work with me; and men like C. and de R. would not be willing to risk their necks for M. Not unnaturally, perhaps, they do not regard him as one of themselves, but as a man who betrays his own side for money. Therefore I have no alternative but to get away while I can. But before leaving I wished to assure you that there is nothing among my papers which could throw suspicion on you, and to ask your intentions. I should add, too, that to the best of my knowledge M.'s sister has never been about at the times when you visited my room; so you have nothing to fear from her."

"Then for me everything hangs on whether M. endeavours to save himself at our expense?" murmured Roger.

"Yes. No harm can come to you from any other quarter; and, personally, I believe he is the type of man who will hold his tongue."

"That is my impression; and what you have told me confirms my inclination to remain."

"My felicitations on your courage," said the Baron. "I was greatly hoping that you might so decide, as for one in your position there may yet occur a chance to aid the widow." Then, producing a piece of paper from the bosom of his dress, he pressed it into Roger's hand and added, "Here, take this; it is a draft on Thellusson's Bank for a hundred thousand *francs* to be paid in gold. Should you find the opportunity, I wish you to use it for bribes."

"Thank you," smiled Roger in the darkness. "I promise nothing, but if I escape arrest I will do what I can. Tell me now, will Lady A. also have to leave, or is her retreat safe and are you about to join her there?"

"My country properties are not involved," replied de Batz, "but I detest inactivity, and should be bored to desperation did I have to go into hiding with that good, earnest woman. I propose to stay in Brussels for a while, as there I have many interests."

For a moment Roger wondered if the slippery Baron was putting out the same sort of cover as he had used so successfully at the time of Amanda's arrest, but in a few more paces they reached a street corner. De Batz halted there, wished him a whispered "Good fortune" and, turning, minced away with a woman's short steps into the shadows.

It was only by the exercise of considerable resolution that Roger made his way back to the Cushion and Keys. He needed no telling that it was the common practice of the terrorists to make their arrests in the middle of the night, but cold logic told him that there was little point in evading capture during the dark hours if he meant to expose himself to it when daylight came. Nevertheless, when he reached his room he did not undress, but lay down fully-clothed to doze upon his bed. That precaution would, he felt, at least give him a sporting chance, as by the time his locked door had been broken in he could be out of the window and attempting a perilous get-away over the neighbouring roofs.

Morning seemed terribly long in coming; but it came at last, and with its coming he permitted himself a few hours' proper sleep. He awoke with a violent start at a banging on his door and, for a second, stared at it in terror; but it was only Citizen Oysé's sister come to rouse him, thinking that he had overslept. After tidying himself up, he breakfasted, then went out to face the hazards of the day.

At the Commune, he found that all interest in the attempt to rescue the Queen had been submerged in excitement, fear and indignation caused by a new menace to the survival of the Revolution. That morning a courier had arrived from Toulon. The Federalists who controlled the port, fearing that they alone would not be able to hold it against the Revolutionary Army, had appealed for help to the British Squadron cruising in the Mediterranean, offering to hand the city over to Admiral Lord Hood; and on the 29th he had signed an agreement with them. The English had promptly landed sailors and marines; they were now the masters of France's most important naval base, and with it had taken no less than thirty-six French ships of the line.

It was a major disaster, and no one to whom Roger spoke had a thought for anything else; but he knew that it would not hold up police enquiries; so he spent most of the day trying to check himself from giving furtive glances over his shoulder.

Again he passed a miserable night, but the dreaded visitation did not mature; and next day a new topic was uppermost in the minds of everyone in Paris. The Convention had issued decrees which would have the most drastic effect on the nation's finances.

Cambon had already introduced a well-conceived, if far-reaching, measure, by which the scrips of all national loans, irrespective of date of issue or rate of interest, had to be surrendered within a given period. The amount of those cashed-in was to be credited in one Great Book, and new scrips issued bearing a uniform rate of interest. This he called "Republicanizing the National Debt", as it placed the dubious new issue on a par with the gilt-edged old ones. It also prevented stock-jobbing in Government securities; so on two counts it was a serious blow at the monied classes.

The new measure was, however, far more drastic. The Convention required of the nation a Forced Loan of one thousand million to be secured only on the unsalable confiscated lands of the Church and *émigrés*. From the income of each family only 1,000 francs for each of its members was to be regarded as untaxable; on the next 10,000 a tax of ten per cent was to be paid; and above that the entire income for the year was to be taken away in exchange for practically worthless paper.

The idle, pampered nobility and worldly, indolent priests, who had been the original cause of discontent in France, had long since left the country, taking with them what they could in gold and jewels; so this savage attack on capital was aimed at the middle classes, its object being to make the thrifty surrender their hard-earned savings and eventually to drag them down to the level of the most improvident workers.

Naturally the law did not affect the Communist officials, as they were all admirably placed to look after themselves and make handsome incomes which were not subject to taxation. The small fry, corrupt to a man, levied their unofficial tolls for passing every one of the innumerable forms that had to be filled up, and without which existence in Revolutionary France was no longer possible. The big fish, with the exception of perhaps half a dozen incorruptible fanatics like Robespierre, were making fortunes. The Convention had voted to the Commune a million a week for the upkeep of Paris; five-sixths of that huge sum, as was later shown in the accounts, disappeared into the Commissars' pockets. Roger had no scruples about taking his share, and in less than a month he had recovered more than he had had to pay out to ransom Amanda.

On the 6th of September there was a further reshuffle in the Committee of Public Safety. Since Danton had left it his influence had declined still further, and now the last of his friends on it, Thuriot and Hérault, were replaced by two Hébertists, the gloomy fanatic Billaud-Varennes and the dissolute cut-throat Collot d'Herbois; while the shifty Barère had gone over to Robespierre, who, since the end of July, had come out into the open and taken a seat on it himself.

The original *Comité* had been Danton's idea. He had realized that the Revolution could not possibly survive if every measure to fight enemies without and within had to be argued by the ignorant, the visionaries, the fools, the spiteful, and the timid, who made up the madhouse of the Convention; so he had sought to form a small, strong, executive body that could take the most urgent decisions without reference to any other. He had succeeded in forging the weapon, but it had been prised from his hand by terrorists even more bloody-minded than himself.

The work of the *Comité* divided itself into two parts—the organization and supply of the armies, and the enforcement of Revolutionary measures upon the civil population. Of its eleven members, five devoted themselves to the first task, and by far the most outstanding of these was Carnot, a forty-year-old officer of the regular army, who had been one of the earliest to go over to the Revolution and had first come to public notice as a member of the Legislative Assembly. He was a man of high principles and a genuine patriot, who elected to close his eyes to the crimes of his colleagues rather than allow the War Office to fall into incompetent hands and see his country overrun by foreign soldiery. Clear-headed, tireless and with a genius for picking men, he took over the incredible muddle that had been left him by his predecessors and soon made himself so indispensable that his colleagues dared not interfere with any decisions he took in his own field. In a large measure he succeeded in restoring discipline, and protected his best Generals, Kléber, Hoche, Kellermann, Pichegru and Jourdan, from the jealous accusations of their *sans-culotte* subordinates; while he also brought forward many promising younger men, such as Berthier and Davoust, who were later to become Napoleon's greatest marshals. He raised, equipped and supplied fourteen armies, and unquestionably saved France.

The remaining six members of the *Comité*, Robespierre, Couthon, Saint-Just, Billaud-Varennes, Collot d'Herbois and Barère, were henceforth to form the *camarilla* that bathed France in blood; for they now instituted a Terror which made all that had gone before seem, by comparison, no more than a mild persecution.

To achieve this they had at their disposal a body that had now become the second most powerful in France—the *Comité de Sûreté Générale*. This had originated as a directorate for the control of the Police, but the detection of crime soon became the least of its activities. Its moderate members were replaced by men such as David, Vadier, Amer and Vouland, all ferocious terrorists who had been nominated either by Hébert or Robespierre. Under it worked the 48 *Comités de Surveillance* in the Sections, which, in conjunction with its innumerable agents, formed a vast espionage system for the suppression of all resistance to the will of the Committee of Public Safety.

By the 7th, Roger was breathing a little more easily. For some days and nights he had lived in a state of ghastly suspense, but he felt that if the police had any information leading to him they would have acted by now. Michonis had not been brought to trial, and until he found himself actually faced with death there must remain the unnerving possibility that he would then endeavour to buy his life by disclosing the names of his accomplices. It was the very "Sword of Damocles" that Roger had feared he might at any time find suspended over his head when he had so reluctantly allowed Amanda to involve him in Lady Atkyn's plots. As long as he had been working alone, only personal ill-luck or his own stupidity could have brought him to grief; now he must pay the price which was so often demanded of those who become enmeshed in a widespread conspiracy, and always go with fear at the back of his mind that through no fault of his own he might suddenly be struck down by a bolt from the blue.

That night he went out to Passy to relieve the anxieties of Amanda and Dan. All was tranquil there, and after he had told her that de Batz had been forced to leave Paris, with the result that his organization had collapsed, he put it to her very strongly that she should now go home.

After a moment's thought she replied, "I am most unwilling to leave you, Roger, while you are in such peril, but I know that my presence in France adds greatly to your anxieties; so, were no one else concerned in the matter, I would agree to do as you wish. But I came here with Lady Atkyns and am pledged to her. It would not be honourable in me to return to England while the Queen still lives, unless Lady Atkyns agreed that we should now abandon all hope of her rescue."

Silently, Roger "damned" Lady Atkyns, but he replied kindly, 'M'dear, I am deeply sensible of your love for me, and also of your feelings in this matter; but now that de Batz's associates are either in prison or scattered, what possible hope can Lady Atkyns and yourself have of rescuing the Queen? In the circumstances, I suggest that you should pay a visit to Lady Atkyns, put the matter to her, and do your utmost to persuade her to return to England with you."

To that Amanda consented; and it was agreed that next day

she should hire a carriage to take her to de Batz's little *château* at Neuilly, where Lady Atkyns had been living ever since she and Amanda had arrived in France towards the end of June.

In this new move to send Amanda home Roger had no thought of Athénaïs. At odd, unexpected times he still caught himself thinking about her with desperate longing; but he knew that all he could hope for now was that she was still alive, and that they might meet again in the unforeseeable future. He was pressing Amanda to leave him only because he knew that, although she was comparatively safe at Passy, as long as she remained in France she was in some peril herself; and that, should misfortune overtake him, it was far better that she should be in England and know nothing of it until she heard of his death, than remain just outside Paris and suffer the agony of being unable to help him while waiting for him to be executed.

However, like its predecessors, this new attempt proved in vain. On the following night, Amanda broke it to him as gently as she could that, contrary to his wishes, she felt she must remain. Lady Atkyns had released her from her obligation, but refused to leave France herself until the Queen was either dead or free. She had been into Paris several times since de Batz's disappearance and had hopes of soon being in communication with the prisoner; so Amanda had decided that she could not desert her friend as long as a possibility remained that her help might be required in a new bid to rescue the Queen. Then, to Roger's intense annoyance, she confessed that she had given Lady Atkyns her address at Passy, so that if she were needed her friend could communicate with her there.

When thinking of Lady Atkyns dispassionately, Roger had conceded to himself that she must be a very brave woman and also an intelligent one, or de Batz would not have trusted her; but from the beginning he had been prejudiced against her because it was through her that his dear, courageous, romantic Amanda had become embroiled, and had actually fallen under the shadow of the guillotine. It was owing to her, too, that he had involved himself with Michonis, so that he now went about in fear of his life. And, to crown all, Amanda had given to this meddling widow the secret of the retreat that he had guarded so jealously all these months. He felt that he had a right to be angry, and, slamming the door, stamped out of the house.

On his way back to Paris he wondered how far Lady Atkyns

had progressed in her approaches at the Conciergerie. In the matter of the Queen he had not been idle himself, but the last thing he wanted was any interference, and he was glad now that he had told Amanda nothing of his activities. In view of the fact that during the past fifteen months he had risked his life on four separate occasions either to protect, or attempt to save, Marie Antoinette, it irked him that his wife should appear to consider him lukewarm and far less to be counted on than her comparatively inactive friend; yet he had to admit to himself that his own hopes of being able to get the Queen out of prison were exceedingly slender.

In pursuance of their policy, the *Comité* had suppressed all public mention of the last attempt, but Roger had picked up the details from his well-informed acquaintances of how things had gone wrong. The Queen, having no pen or pencil, had pricked out with a pin on a piece of paper a reply to the note de Rougeville had left for her hidden among the petals of the red carnation. Believing the gendarme Gilbert to be trustworthy, she had given him her pricked-out message to pass on to Madame Richard. Both, presumably, had been bribed by de Batz to assist, but had then suffered a fit of nerves. For three days they had argued and dithered, and only then decided to ask Michonis if he thought they were all really justified in aiding the Queen to escape. Had they stopped at that all might yet have been well; but unfortunately they brought several other people, whom they believed to be in sympathy with the attempt, into the discussion. Michonis, realizing that the matter had got too far out of control for him to hush up, had had the sense to make the Queen's message indecipherable by pricking a lot more holes in the paper; and his instinct had proved right, for an hour later the plot had been denounced by one of the people Madame Richard had consulted.

The following day the Queen had been put through a long interrogation, but had protected her friends to the best of her ability by flatly denying all knowledge of the matter. Naturally she had not been believed, and in a pitiless determination to prevent any further attempt the authorities had added with savage severity to the strictness of her confinement. She had been removed to a smaller cell, the walls of which were running with damp, and which had only a slit for a window; the sole furnishings were a bed with a straw mattress, a broken rush-bottomed chair, a chamber-pot and a small screen. The last was the only modicum of privacy allowed her, as two gendarmes, who had been told that they would have to pay for it with their lives if she escaped, were stationed in her cell to keep a constant watch on all she did. She had been deprived of everything she possessed, except the clothes in which she stood up. Even her watch, a locket containing her children's hair, and her rings had been taken from her. She was not even allowed a light, and the slit window only gave on to an interior court; so she was compelled to remain in total darkness for fourteen or more hours out of every twenty-four.

Rarely were malefactors guilty of the most heinous crimes treated with such atrocious barbarity, and no political prisoner had been made to suffer so brutal a confinement since the Middle Ages. The thought of the delicately-nurtured, and once gay and beautiful, mistress of Versailles, Fontainebleau and the Petite Trianon in that slimy, foetid cell made Roger's blood boil; but he was convinced that, at present, only a miracle could get her out of it.

Nevertheless, he was laying his lines, for he still believed that the same principle would apply as had so nearly enabled de Batz to rescue the Royal Family from the Temple. With time, any standardized routine was bound to become slack and improve the chances of would-be rescuers; the vital question was, would enough time elapse to make conditions favourable for an attempt before the Queen was brought to trial? No preparations had been made for that as yet, as the *Comité's* agents were still haggling in secret with Vienna; but if those negotiations broke down within the next month or two, this last hope would be gone.

Roger's new approach had been facilitated by the fact that after the arrest of Michonis it had been decided to reconstruct the Prison Committee. Merely as a precaution, the old members, who, it was assumed, must have been on intimate terms with him, had been relieved of their duties, and new ones appointed. The competition for these appointments was fierce, as they offered ways of making big money. Firstly, the Commissioners who held them had sufficient power over the prison officials to make them connive at the escape of the less-important prisoners, if bribed sufficiently heavily by the prisoners' friends to make it worth their while to do so; secondly, condemned prisoners were always stripped of their valuables before being taken to execution, and it was an understood thing that the lion's share of these jewels and trinkets should be reserved for the Commissioners.

Roger, having de Batz's fund at his disposal, had been able to bid high, and by placing 20,000 gold *francs* in the right quarter, gold now being ten times the face value of paper, he had ensured his election. Further, knowing that to be of any service to the Queen he would need at least one other member of the Committee to act with him, he had approached Goret, who had turned a deaf ear while he had talked to her in the Temple. Goret had been delighted at the prospect of such a lucrative post, providing Roger put up the money for him; so for a further 20,000 gold *francs* his election also had been secured, and he had been promised big payments for himself on any occasions that his help might be required.

Only that morning the reconstructed Prison Committee had received its instructions from the Committee of Public Safety. Its members were empowered to inspect all prisons at any hour of the day or night, and question all jailers, turnkeys, guards and prisoners, either in public or in private. In the Queen's case, however, as Roger had expected, an exception was made, and she was never to be questioned unless two or more Commissioners were present. He was, therefore, now in a position to go and see her at any time, but he had no intention of jeopardizing this privilege by making premature use of it.

For another week he went about in considerable apprehension and concerned himself only with his official duties. At the end of that time he was feeling considerably more confident that he now had little to fear unless Michonis was brought to trial. But a new gloom and fear had fallen on the people of Paris.

On the 17th of September the *Comité* decreed the terrible "Law of the Suspect". This infamous measure, which came to be known as "the procuress of the guillotine", defined as suspects all who had either befriended tyranny, were related to *émigrés* and had not consistently proved their "patriotism", could not give proof of their means of subsistence, had not paid their taxes, or could not produce their civic cards of identity. All such persons could be arrested by anybody, tried by any tribunal of "patriots" and, if their answers were unsatisfactory, thrown into prison at once. The Sections of all cities and the Communes throughout France were urged to form reliable tribunals and purge their populations forthwith. At the same time the right was given for any "patriot" to enter and search any dwelling at any hour of the day or night.

It was an open licence for gangs of *sans-culottes* to break in and plunder wherever they wished. It laid every decent person in the country open to intimidation, blackmail, malice and revenge. Within a few weeks every village in France had a tribunal manned by the most mean, vicious and criminal elements in the community. Over 50,000 tribunals were established, and day by day thousands of innocent people were dragged before them, mostly on false accusations, to be robbed, maltreated, imprisoned and later done to death. The Great Terror had begun.

Roger waited until the 25th of the month, then, taking Goret with him, went to see the Queen. He had no intention of trying to open communications with her, but wished simply to see how the prison was arranged and the number of gates and guards that would have to be passed in any attempt to get her out; so they hung their visit on a general inspection of the Conciergerie.

In its vaulted crypts and interior courts many hundreds of prisoners of both sexes were confined. The squalor and stench in most of them were nauseating, but in the great hall where the politicals were segregated conditions were better. Those who had money, or friends outside to send things in, were permitted to alleviate their sad lot with small comforts. Some of the prisoners were lying comatose upon their straw palliasses, but most were idling away the time in an apparently congenial manner. Among the men there were several games of cards and dice in progress, and numbers of the women had formed little circles where they were talking quietly while they mended their clothes. Everyone there must have known that they had not long to live, but there was no sign of fear or hysteria: the atmosphere was one of subdued decorum.

When at length they reached the Queen's cell Roger could have wept at the sight of her. She was only thirty-seven, but she might have been seventy. Her body had become thin and frail, her cheeks had fallen in so that her aquiline nose stood out bony and prominent, her once bright blue eyes had become pale and lustreless, her once rich, generous mouth was now a pale, hard line, her once luxuriant golden hair had been cut short and the strands of it that showed under her cap were snow-white. She was dressed in an old black gown, the hem and cuffs of which were frayed with wear. Her hands were folded in her lap and she was sitting quite motionless, like a wax figure, on the solitary chair. Roger turned quickly away, and drew Goret after him.

On the way out Roger counted the gates and guards between the Queen's cell and the street; then, before leaving, he used his official position to ask the chief turnkey if the same number of guards were kept on duty at night. The hairy ruffian who had replaced Richard replied with a grin that there were double the number, and the men were never drawn from the same battalion two nights running. His reply confirmed Roger's belief that any attempt at rescue must prove hopeless until these extraordinary precautions had been relaxed.

Three days later he learned that Fouquier-Tinville had been instructed to prepare an indictment against the Queen. Apparently her Austrian relatives would make no worthwhile offer to ransom her, and Hébert was pressing for her death. He still held the little King, so could afford to sacrifice the "Tyrant's Widow" to win a greater popularity with his cut-throat following. The obscene-minded journalist had raved at the *Comité*, "I demand the head of Antoinette. I have promised it to the *sans-culottes*, and you must give it to them, for without them you are nothing. If you refuse, I will go and hack it off myself." And Hébert was now a power to be reckoned with, as he had taken Danton's place as the idol of the scum of Paris. The *Comité* had wanted to keep their pawn in the diplomatic game for a while longer, but gave way because they considered that Hébert's help in a new move they were contemplating would be more valuable.

On the 3rd of October they struck. The doors of the Convention were suddenly locked and Amar, on Robespierre's instructions, impeached the proscribed Girondins. No less than 129 deputies were charged with being "enemies of the Revolution"; 43 were at once handed over to the Revolutionary Tribunal, 65 more arrested and the remaining 21, who had already escaped from Paris, outlawed. A week later Saint-Just put it to the cowed and mutilated Convention that "the Government shall remain Revolutionary until peace". The measure was passed without a protest, although at one stroke it abolished the Constitution and all pretence of democracy. Henceforth the eleven men of the Policy Bureau, officially called the Committee of Public Safety, could rule unchallenged with absolute powers to dictate the way of life of every Frenchman from the cradle to the grave.

This final seizure of supreme power was well timed as, simultaneously with it, the fall of Lyons was announced. Dubois-

Crancé had both prevented the relief of the city by the Piedmontese and invested it, with considerable military skill. After well-directed attacks early in the month on several key positions, he had reached the conclusion that it would soon fall without any further considerable expenditure of troops; but Couthon had then arrived upon the scene. This semi-paralysed lawyer had raised 25,000 peasants in the Auvergne and brought them to reinforce the besieging army. He would listen to no arguments about tactics, but insisted that a mass attack should be delivered immediately. As a member of the *Comité* his word was law. Some 2,000 Royalists and leading Federalists managed to cut their way out under the Comte de Précy, and a number of them succeeded in reaching Switzerland, but the remainder of the garrison was overwhelmed.

This attack *en masse* of Couthon's succeeded only because the garrison was already enfeebled by starvation and knew that surrender would soon be inevitable, but it had far-reaching effects. Barère presented a report to the Convention showing that the reverses of the armies on the frontier had been caused by combats in detail, and urging that new tactics should be imposed upon the Generals. Nine-tenths of the troops of the Republic were raw, untrained and ill-equipped levies, totally unsuited for the old type of military operations, but when used in great hordes had courage, and in a fierce onslaught, could overwhelm their less numerous enemies; so the attack *en masse* was adopted and henceforth became a salient feature in the battles of the Revolutionary Wars.

Roger, meanwhile, had been keeping his ears open for news of the Queen's approaching trial; but all he could gather was that, although the lean, cadaverous Fouquier-Tinville had had a fortnight in which to prepare the indictment, he was finding great difficulty in formulating suitable charges. The old accusations about Marie Antoinette's extravagance, her correspondence with the enemies of France, and her instigation of the flight to Varennes had been dug up; but there was practically no solid evidence which could be produced about any of them, and even if it were faked it would be hardly sufficient to convince the nation that she deserved death. Yet the *Comité* were determined that she should die, and, quite unexpectedly, just the type of thing they required to hold her up to the people as a monster fell into their hands.

It was in conversation with a Commissioner named Daujon

that Roger learned of it, and he had great difficulty in hiding his rage and disgust. Apparently, on the 6th, the ever-busy Simon had come running to his masters, Hébert and Chaumette, with a piece of news that had filled them with revolting glee. He had caught the little King indulging in a habit not uncommon in small boys, but calculated to undermine their health; and on being asked where he had learnt this bad practice he declared that his mother had taught it to him.

Hébert, Chaumette and the Mayor, Pache, had at once hurried to the Temple, taking with them several of their cronies, including Daujon. Under examination the boy had, without prompting, reiterated his statement, also involving his aunt, and adding that his mother had taken him into bed with her for the purpose of teaching him other games, which he described.

On the following day Chaumette, Daujon, the painter David, and others had held another obscene Tribunal at the Temple. This time the little Capet had been confronted in turn with his sister and his aunt, neither of whom he had seen for three months; both had been compelled to listen to these shameful accusations, and, although both denied them with horror, he had stuck firmly to what he had said. Still worse, he had taken the part of the Commissars against them and, when questioned on other matters, had disclosed all he knew of the prisoners' secret dealings with Turgy, Toulan and Michonis.

Daujon said frankly that he had found these scenes, and particularly the questioning of the young Madame Royale on such a subject, degrading to a degree, and would not have believed them possible had he not witnessed them with his own eyes; but when questioned by Roger he insisted that little Capet had been neither browbeaten nor drunk. He had sat in an armchair cheerfully swinging his legs and appeared to have all his wits about him, as he had several times intervened to contradict his sister.

It seemed quite probable that Simon had put these ideas into the child's head, and he had spouted them out simply from the habit he had formed of saying anything he thought would please or amuse his brutish tutor. Yet it was only three months since he had been removed from his mother, towards whom he had always shown the greatest affection; and to anyone who knew the way in which she adored him the whole thing was utterly preposterous. There could be no question of the boy having been exchanged for another primed to play that revolting part, as his aunt and sister would have instantly declared the child with whom they were confronted to be an impostor. Roger decided that the only possible explanation lay in the little King's mind having become diseased, and that he must now be regarded as a pathological case; but he knew that that would not prevent Hébert from bringing these dreadful accusations against the poor Queen, and that they would hurt her in a way that no other outrage inflicted upon her could have done.

On the evening of the 12th of October, Marie Antoinette was taken upstairs at the Conciergerie to go before the Revolutionary Tribunal. Although greatly debilitated by the rigours of her last five weeks' confinement in a cold, damp, semi-dark cell, she rallied her faculties magnificently. Shrewdly and with dignity she answered every question put to her, showing remarkable quickness in evading the traps set to catch her, and great subtlety in avoiding the incrimination of her friends. After this preliminary hearing, the Tribunal adjourned until 9 a.m. on the 14th; it then continued to sit for most of that and the following day, the final session lasting from 5 p.m. on the 15th to 4 a.m. on the 16th.

Forty-one witnesses were called; but to the consternation of the judges many of them refused to testify against the Queen and some, with great courage, spoke in her favour. One of the latter was that Father of the Revolution, Bailly. Stranger still, Manuel, the one-time *Procureur* of the Commune and noted terrorist, refused to incriminate her.

At length Hébert's infamous charge of incest was hurled at her by Fouquier-Tinville. She was then accused of having deliberately sought to weaken her son's health so that in the event of a Restoration she might rule through him.

For a moment she made no answer; then when Hermann, the President, ordered her to do so, she rose from the chair she had been given, turned away from the Tribunal towards the spectators, and cried:

"If I did not reply, it was because nature refuses such an inculpation made to a mother. I appeal to all those mothers who may be present."

The public galleries were packed with fishwives and market women. For years they had been told that Marie Antoinette was a squandermaniac and a nymphomaniac. The fact that her husband had proved incapable of consummating their marriage during its first eight years had given ample grounds for malicious tongues at Versailles to circulate stories that she had both consoled herself with unnatural vice and taken lovers. Her enemies had spread those stories broadcast, printed them on secret presses in pamphlet form by the hundred thousand, and even issued beautiful editions of them with illustrations portraying her in every imaginable erotic scene. So, through the years, the whole nation, except for the comparative few who knew her personally, had gradually come to believe that she was a Messalina. It was with that background in mind that Hébert and his friends had counted on the people believing this last infamy of her.

But they did not believe it. A swift murmur of pity and indignation ran round the court. Hissing broke out, and it was not directed at Marie Antoinette, but at Fouquier-Tinville.

Hastily he shuffled away under his other papers the signed statement of the little King that he had been about to read aloud, and began to rant on another absurd charge—that she had sent 200 millions in French gold to her brother, the Emperor of Austria.

Roger did not attend the trial. He knew that he would be terribly harrowed by it, and that it could have only one ending; moreover, from its second day on he was engaged upon another matter. It had suddenly occurred to him that, although he could not save the Queen, he might be able to render her a great service. She had never pretended special piety, but she was God-fearing, devout, and all her life had gone regularly to confession; now, in her extremity, her greatest need must be a true priest, and it was certain that the fiends who were martyring her would deny her that last consolation. With the cynicism that they displayed in such matters, they might send her one of the renegade priests who had broken his own oath to the Roman Church and accepted the doctrines of the Revolution; but she would never make a last confession to such a man, as for her he would have forfeited the power to give absolution.

The more Roger thought about the matter, the more decided he became that, somehow or other, he must find a non-juring priest and smuggle him in to her. That was no easy matter. Great numbers of priests had been killed in the September massacres, many thousands had fled abroad and, apart from those who had become renegades, only a handful now remained, all of whom were in hiding. To search for one in Paris was like looking for a needle in a haystack, and to enquire for one was to court suspicion; but he was prepared to risk that, as it seemed the only means by which he might succeed. Yet on setting about it he found himself up against a brick wall; his Revolutionary colleagues gave him queer looks and wanted to know what had got into him, while such respectable citizens as he accosted in the Granvilliers Section shook their heads and hurried away from him as soon as they could. Most reluctantly, he reached the infuriating conclusion that he might go on asking different people for days and get no further, as those who did know where a priest was hidden would not tell him.

Late in the afternoon he had the sudden inspiration that the Blanchards might be able to help; so he hurried to *La Belle Étoile*, but Mère Blanchard told him that their curé had fled months before, and she knew of no other. Much depressed, he went out to Passy, and, after dining with Amanda, told her about his fruitless search.

"But, Roger," she exclaimed at once, "M. de Batz's private chaplain has remained in hiding all this time at Neuilly. He is a deeply religious man and would, I am sure, consider it his Christian duty to take any risk himself in order to perform the last rites for the Queen."

Roger looked up quickly. "In that case I pray you go to Neuilly first thing tomorrow, and arrange for him to come into Paris and meet me. You may tell him that I anticipate little difficulty in smuggling him into the prison and getting him out again; but as the hour at which the Queen will be taken back from the Tribunal to her cell is uncertain, we must arrange a place where he can wait for me and I can collect him at any time that circumstances may dictate."

As they talked the matter over, Roger decided that in a case such as this he must give away his other hideout; so it was agreed that the priest should ask for Dan at *La Belle Étoile*, and wait there with Dan until Roger came to take him to the Conciergerie.

Next morning Roger waited at Passy while Amanda went on her mission. She returned at midday to say that Father Jerome had expressed himself proud and honoured to be called on to serve this office. He had often gone into Paris on similar missions at the request of the Baron; so he should have no difficulty in passing the barrier, and would be at *La Belle Étoile* at eight o'clock the following evening.

With a considerably lighter heart, Roger went into the city, saw Dan and arranged with him to receive the priest, also to have a one-horse coach ready in the yard of the inn from ten o'clock, which he was later to drive himself. Next, he went to Thellusson's and drew out a further supply of de Batz's gold, having it first made up in several packets for easy distribution about his person. Then he began to look for Goret. After drawing a few blanks, he ran the Commissioner to earth at one of the cafés he frequented, passed him one of the packets of gold and told him what he intended to do that night. To his consternation Goret handed the packet back; but after a moment he smiled, and said, "In this I require no payment to aid you."

It was one more instance of the way in which the feelings of all decent people had changed from hate to sympathy for the Queen, owing to the manner in which she was being persecuted. With a closer bond between them than they had ever had before, they drank a bottle of wine together; then, to kill time, went to the Hôtel de Ville, and attended a session of the Commune.

Shortly before ten they left the Chamber and crossed the river to the Conciergerie. There they learned that the trial was still in progress, and did not look like finishing for some hours. At midnight prospects were no better; so, thinking the Court would soon decide to rise and meet again for a final session on the following day, Roger left Goret and went to *La Belle Étoile* to fetch the priest.

When he arrived there, Dan was patiently waiting for him in the shadow of the side doorway. After a word with Roger that all was well, he slipped upstairs to his room and a few minutes later emerged with Father Jerome. The priest, a short, very fat man, was sensibly taking every precaution against being recognized, as he was muffled in a heavy cloak, had the lower part of his face buried in a high white stock, and wore a broad-brimmed beaver hat pulled well down over his eyes. Roger greeted him politely, and the three of them walked quickly round to the stables.

The horse Dan had chosen was standing in its stall already harnessed, so they had only to put it between the shafts of the coach. Father Jerome and Roger got in, Dan mounted the box, and they were off.

The drive was a short one, so there was little time for conversation, even had Roger wished to make it; but his thoughts were too fully occupied with the tricky business in hand for him to do more than reassure the priest that there was no great danger of his being caught.

Father Jerome's few words in reply came in rather a thin voice, partially muffled by his stock. For a few minutes the only sound was the clicking of the horse's hooves on the cobbles; then the coach turned off the Pont Neuf and, as Roger had instructed Dan, pulled up in the shadow of some buildings about three hundred yards short of the entrance to the Conciergerie. As Roger got out, he said in a low voice:

"I want you to wait here, Father, until I return. I may be a considerable time, as if they decide to finish tonight the Court may sit for another couple of hours or more. Should anyone want to know what you are waiting here for, say that it is to take me home when the Court rises. If they don't believe you, drive on to the Palais de Justice entrance, and tell them to go in and look for me; I shall be somewhere about. But in no circumstances go away, for if sentence is passed tonight the execution will take place tomorrow; so this is our last chance."

When he rejoined Goret in a passage leading to the Court he was thankful that he had taken the precaution to tell Father Jerome that his wait might be a long one, as the Tribunal was still sitting, and word was going round that it did not mean to rise until the case was over.

After a while one o'clock chimed from the steeple of the Saint Chapelle, then, hour by hour, two, three, four. Cold, stiff, weary and anxious, Roger and Goret waited with a little crowd of other people in the broad passageway. At last the doors were thrown open and the journalists came running out. The Widow Capet had been found guilty on all charges; she was to take a peep through the "little window" and be given "a shave with the national razor".

Ten minutes later the Court was clear, but Roger allowed three-quarters of an hour for things to settle down. At about ten to five, he and Goret walked to the coach and told Father Jerome that the death sentence had been pronounced; then they drove in it up to the entrance of the Conciergerie.

No difficulty was made about the two Commissioners going in and taking a third man with them. A turnkey unlocked gate after gate for them: at each the guards drew back and saluted with the sort of cringing fear that all simple folk now displayed towards these terrible Commissars. But the two gendarmes in the Queen's cell were under orders not to leave her. While Goret and Father Jerome waited outside, Roger went in and said to them calmly:

"Citizens, I have a man here who has paid me a good whack to have a few words with the Widow. Here's your share, and it's enough to buy you a comfortable cottage apiece. Now come outside and let him get on with it."

As he spoke he handed each of them one of his packets of gold. On feeling their weight, they swiftly realized their value, glanced at each other, nodded and left the cell. He beckoned Father Jerome in, then followed the gendarmes out.

Roger, Goret and the two men stood in the passage and began to talk about the trial, but in less than two minutes Father Jerome came out again. Roger looked at him in surprise, and said:

"Surely you have not yet done what you came for?"

The priest nodded, bowed his head, made a gesture like the sign of the cross, then with short quick steps started off down the corridor. With a hasty good night to the guards, Roger and Goret caught him up, summoned the waiting turnkey from a room near by, and repassed the many wickets. As soon as they were safely out in the street, and the prison gates had shut behind them, Roger said:

"What happened, Father? Surely you could not have confessed her in so short a time? What happened? Did she refuse your ministrations? I can hardly believe that possible."

Suddenly the priest burst into tears, and in his thin, rather high voice sobbed, "She wouldn't . . . she wouldn't. She refused to change clothes with me."

An awful suspicion leapt into Roger's mind. Seizing Father Jerome by the arm, he gave him a violent shake and exclaimed:

"What are you? I don't believe you're a priest at all! I—— By God, I believe you're Lady Atkyns!"

"Yes," sobbed the pseudo priest, "I . . . I am. I wanted her to change clothes with me, but she wouldn't."

"Let's chuck the bitch in the Seine," snarled Goret. "If her crazy idea had come off it would have cost us both our heads. The difference in their figures would have given the game away at the first gate we had to go through. And if we had got the other woman out, what the hell did this lump of folly think we could do then, with no preparations made to hide her or get her out of the city, and every street kid knowing her features as well as his own backside?"

Roger was equally furious. He could not help admiring the courage that had inspired Lady Atkyns to make this eleventh-hour attempt to change places with the Queen; but he knew that Goret was right, and that by her foolhardiness she would certainly have brought disaster on them and herself, and not even have saved the Queen, had her plan succeeded. For a second he wondered if Amanda had been a party to this criminally dangerous deception, but could not believe that even her sense of the romantic would have led her to allow him to run such an awful risk unknowingly. After a moment he asked:

"What of the real Father Jerome? Is he a party to this wicked fraud, or did he know nothing of your intentions?"

"He . . . he was coming himself," came the half-stifled reply, "but . . . but I locked him in his . . . his bedroom."

That cleared Amanda, but it made even worse the frightful thing that this stupid woman had done to the Queen. Roger felt that she needed a lesson, and proceeded to give it her.

"Madame," he said harshly, "at this awful hour Her Majesty must be in more need of a priest than anything she has wished for in all her life; yet you have taken it upon yourself to deprive her of that last consolation. My coach will take you back to the inn and you may pass the night there. Tomorrow you will set about leaving France. My colleague and I are too well-placed for anything you may say about us to be taken seriously; so if I learn that you are not gone from Neuilly within forty-eight hours I shall denounce you."

Still weeping, but without a word, Lady Atkyns climbed into the coach and Dan drove her away.

Roger and Goret remained staring glumly at one another about twenty yards from the silent prison gates, through which Marie Antoinette was to pass in a few hours on her way to execution. At last Roger spoke:

"Oh, the wickedness of that woman! To think that out of vanity and a desire for self-glorification at any price she has deprived the Queen of what must mean so much to her. I would give my right hand could I but find a priest, and now it is too late."

Yet an inscrutable Providence decreed that it should not be too late. Dawn had not yet come. At that moment a tall, lean figure detached itself from the shadows of the wall some distance away, and walked up to them.

"Citizens," said the stranger in a low voice, "from your hats I judge you to be high officers of the Republic. I am the Abbé Maguin and I am willing to surrender myself to you as a non-juring priest. I came here tonight voluntarily for this purpose, believing upon Jesus Christ our Saviour that He would soften the hearts of those to whom I surrendered myself, so that they would grant me the favour of taking me into the prison to perform the last rites of the Church for our unhappy Queen before I, too, am taken to execution."

Goret instinctively crossed himself. Roger removed his hat, and said, "Father, God has sent you to us; be pleased to follow me."

Inside the prison, more gold greased ready palms. Half an hour later the three of them came out into the grey dawn. The brave Abbé Maguin gave his two companions his blessing, then walked quietly away. Roger and Goret silently shook hands, then made separately for their lodgings.

Roger was very tired, and slept through most of the day. When he awoke in his bed at the Cushion and Keys, Marie Antoinette had already been dead for several hours. To the last her courage and dignity never faltered; but once the spectacle was over things soon returned to normal. There were a thousand more important things to think of than that the once most beautiful neck in France had, at half-past seven that morning, been severed by a knife, and that later a painfully thin body had been thrown into quicklime. The work of the Revolution, as decreed by the *Comité*, must go on.

That evening Roger had a meeting of his Section; so he went as usual. On such nights he never went out to Passy, as the meetings were rarely over before twelve o'clock, and sometimes lasted well into the early hours of the morning. On this occasion the meeting ended soon after midnight and, having slept most of the day, he was still wakeful. He was also terribly depressed, and when in such moods he always turned, if it were possible, to Amanda. She would be going home in a few days' time now, as there was no longer any reason for her to remain in France, although he did not wish to hurry her unduly, as he had decided to refuse to let her make the journey with the unpredictable Lady Atkyns, and, instead, to send her home with Dan. She, too, he felt, would be frightfully depressed at the news of the Queen's death; so perhaps they could cheer each other up a little, and over a picnic supper in their bedroom he would tell her about last night's happenings.

After he had walked a little way, he hailed a night-hawk coach and drove out to Passy. The house was in darkness; but he had expected that, and quietly let himself in with the key that he had carried since Amanda had been living there. Taking off his boots in the hall, he went softly upstairs and opened the bedroom door a crack. No sound came, so she was evidently fast asleep. He tiptoed over to the big bed and, in the faint moonlight that percolated between the curtains, could just make out her curled-up form. Bending over her, he touched her cheek with his lips to lightly rouse her. She murmured something and turned over; so he kissed her again.

Suddenly she started up, shook back her hair, flung her arms round his neck, and cried in French, "Oh, Rojé, Rojé, you are back; and I had given up hoping for you till tomorrow!"

He was instantly transfixed, as though suddenly rendered incapable of movement by some witch's spell. The woman in his wife's bed was Athénaïs.

CHAPTER XXIII

BARREN VICTORY

FOR the space of three heartbeats Roger remained rigid. His mind told him that he positively must be dreaming, or seeing a ghost; although the soft, warm arms that clasped him were anything but ghostly. Could his ears have played him a trick? No; he might have been momentarily deceived in the semi-darkness, but the fervid, hungry kiss that closed his mouth told him it must be Athénaïs whom he was embracing.

A moment later his last doubts were resolved. Jerking her head back, she looked up at him and sighed, "Oh, Rojé, how heavenly to be with you once more! Did you worry greatly over what had become of me?"

"I was utterly distraught," he cried; then, in his relief at knowing her to be alive, he embraced her again with a violence equalling her own, and covered her face with kisses.

When they drew apart they were breathless and trembling; but already, for him, the joy of their reunion was troubled by wild speculations about Amanda, and he stammered, "But how . . . what . . . what happened?"

"I was caught," she replied. "I was anxious to know what had become of my friend Marguerite de Damville; so on my way to Paris I decided to go to her *château* and find out. It lies a few leagues to the south of Evreux. The *château* had been sacked, but she was living with her children in a farm near by. She had been there unmolested for nearly a year, and I should have been quite safe there too, had it not been for the civil war. General Wimpffen's headquarters were at Evreux, and when the Federalists were defeated we hid some of their officers in the barn. The Reds found them and took us all off to Mantes. Marguerite and I were shut up with a lot of other women in a convent there, and she, alas, is still a prisoner; but a young National Guard fell in love with me and smuggled me out in an empty hamper. That was the night before last, and I fear the poor boy was much disappointed when he failed to find me at his lodgings. Naturally, the moment I was free to do so I came straight here."

"Yes," muttered Roger, "yes. I feared you dead; or, if not,

certainly a prisoner. But when you got here? What . . . what happened then?"

Athénaïs gave a hard little laugh. "Why, what do you expect? Finding another woman in my husband's house, I threw her out."

Roger could feel the blood draining from his face. "You do not mean that?" he gasped.

"Not literally. As we were both persons of breeding, the matter was conducted with perfect decorum."

"But . . . but you cannot have realized——"

"What? That she was your English wife? Oh yes; but we are in France, and you cannot have forgotten our understanding. Here, as your French wife, I considered myself entitled to act as she would have done had we been in England."

At the thought of the shock his poor Amanda must have sustained, and this callous treatment of her, Roger was seized with a cold fury. Controlling himself with an effort, he said, "I pray you tell me exactly what took place."

Athénaïs shrugged her bare shoulders. "I judge from your voice that you are annoyed; but I assure you I did not go out of my way to be unpleasant to her. Since you brought her to live here, while knowing that if I was still alive I should come here as soon as I could, things could hardly have happened otherwise. If her pride is hurt, you have only yourself to blame."

"Yes, yes, I am well aware of that; but tell me what occurred between you."

"Very well, then. The door was opened to me by the old manservant. I told him that I was your wife and asked for you. He looked somewhat disconcerted and said you were from home, then suggested that I should leave a message and call again tomorrow. I said that by arrangement with you I was to join you here, but that my arrival had been delayed, and that I would like to be shown to my room at once. By then he was obviously much embarrassed, and asked me to wait for a few moments in the hall.

"After leaving me for a while, he returned to say that Madame Godfrey wished a word with me in the drawing-room. At that, coupled with the poor old man's obvious perturbation, I naturally jumped to the conclusion that, thinking me lost to you for good, you had installed a mistress here to console you. When I entered the drawing-room your wife was standing in front of the fire. I thought her a fine creature, if somewhat on the large side, and I have never been partial to red hair, even of that subdued shade.

Her teeth, too, are a little prominent, and, although I did not know her to be English at the time, from that and her big feet I might have——"

"Pray spare me these trivialities!" Roger burst out; "I desire to know what took place."

"And you shall," Athénaïs replied a trifle tartly. "This encounter was entirely due to your mismanagement, and I have no wish whatever to conceal my part in it. As she did not invite me to be seated, I bobbed her a curtsy, then sat down without being asked, and said:

"'Madame, I must apologize for arriving unannounced; but it seems that M. de Breuc has done us both the discourtesy of neglecting to inform you that he has been expecting me to join him here since early August.'

"'Indeed, Madame,' she replied, 'this is the first I have heard of it: and I am still at a loss to understand why he should have done so, or by what right you claim to bear his name.'

"'Then, Madame,' said I, 'allow me to enlighten you. It is because I am his wife.'

"At that her eyes grew round as berries; but she was quick to recover herself, and exclaimed somewhat sarcastically, 'How very peculiar! In that case one of us must be sadly deluded; for I was under the impression that he is married to me.'

"By then her accent and attitude had given me more than a suspicion of her identity, but I had no intention of giving you up to her; so I remarked, 'Your impression can hardly have been a very strong one, seeing that he does not permit you to use his name, and that you are living here with him as Madame Godfrey.'"

Roger dug his nails into the palms of his hands. Internally he was fuming; but his anxiety to know the worst checked his impulse to interrupt, and Athénaïs went on:

"That upset her somewhat, and she launched forth on a rather muddled explanation about using her maiden name in France for special reasons; then she insisted that she had been married to you for over three years, and that I must be either wrong in the head or the victim of a cruel deception. It was upon the last I took her up and, I fear, caused her some distress: but I saw no other way to end the matter.

"'Madame,' said I, 'it would be discourteous in me to disbelieve you, so mayhap we have both been deceived; but it seems that your case is the more deserving of condolence, for I at least have been told about you, whereas it appears that you were unaware of my existence. I feel sure you must be the lady with whom my—perhaps I should say our—husband lives at Richmond when he is in England. You speak of three years, but I can go back ten. I knew Rojé when he was a young lawyer's clerk in Rennes, and when I was of an age to marry we lived in my father's house in Paris. Later, a cruel fate separated us for several years; but, on our meeting again some months ago, both of us realized that the loves we have known since are of no moment compared with the passion of our youth, and we swiftly renewed our vows.' "

"Do I gather that you caused Amanda to believe that you and I were actually married?" asked Roger hoarsely.

In the faint light to which his eyes were now accustomed he saw the lovely curving shoulders shrug again. "She took it that way, and I'll not deny that I meant her to. Why should I not use such ingenuity as God has given me to defend the thing you gave me by your oath? I then played my final card and said, 'Should you doubt me, Madame, let us both remain here until our gay deceiver arrives upon the scene, and see which of us he prefers to retain.'

"As I expected, she refused the challenge, and exclaimed, 'Nay, I'll not stay to suffer any such indignity.'

"On that I administered the *coup de grâce*. Standing up, I opened the door, curtsied to her, and said, 'You have my sympathy, Madame, in that you lack the prior claim. I pray you be at your leisure in collecting your belongings; but the coach that brought me is still at the door, and when you are ready it can take you wherever you desire.' "

"And where did it take her?" asked Roger quickly.

"How should I know?" replied Athénaïs. "All that concerned me was that she departed bag and baggage twenty minutes later."

"You devilish jade!" roared Roger, now losing all control of himself. "How dare you put such a cheat upon my wife? How dare you make me appear a bigamist? Have you no sense of decency? Do the accepted canons of well-bred behaviour mean nothing to you?"

"Who should know better than I how to behave *à la grande dame*?" Athénaïs flared, jerking herself bolt upright in the bed. "Did you expect me to slink from the house like a serving-wench who had been caught seducing the master's son? For shame, Monsieur! 'Tis you who should grovel for having placed a woman of my birth in such an intolerable position. On that I have yet to listen to your excuses. I warned you, though, that first night at Bécherel, that did your wife ever cross my path I would fight her for you. Well, owing to your bungling, she has done so. Although much provoked by this unforeseen encounter, I treated her with perfect civility. I kept both my dignity and my head, and used only my wits to triumph over her."

"So be it, Madame!" Roger snapped back. "But allow me to inform you that you have scored a barren victory, for I'll be no party to this shameful deceit."

"Rojé!" she gasped, falling back upon her pillows as though he had struck her. "Surely . . . no, I cannot believe that you love her better than myself."

"It is no question of love, but of honour, decency, right feeling. Were she the veriest drab whom I'd married while drunk in a brothel, I'd still stand by her in this."

"You should have thought of that before you swore your oath to me. In any case, 'tis useless now, for she is gone."

"Not so far that I cannot overtake her."

"No, Rojé! No!" Athénaïs stretched out her arms. "You cannot mean that because I have driven her away you intend to pursue her, instead of remaining here with me?"

"That is exactly what I mean! 'Tis not the fact, but the way in which you did it. Be pleased to remain here as long as it suits your convenience, but do not expect to see me again." Turning on his heel, he blundered out of the room and slammed the door behind him.

Down in the hall a lamp had been lit. Their voices had roused Antoine and, wrapped in a dressing-gown, he was patiently standing there. As Roger descended the stairs the old butler picked up a silver salver on which there was a letter, proffered it with a bow, and said, "Madame Godfrey asked me to give you this, Monsieur le Chevalier."

Roger ripped the letter open and read:

My mind is still in a turmoil. I do not yet know what to believe. Only one thing is clear—the reason that you have been so anxious to be rid of me ever since early August. Well, now you have your wish; and should I not receive your prompt assurance that I have been told a tissue of lies, it will be for good.

Amanda.

"Thank you, Antoine," he said. "At what time did Madame leave?"

"Soon after four o'clock, Monsieur."

"Did she say whither she was going?"

"No, Monsieur. She was clearly much upset, and seemed in a great hurry to be off. As Monsieur knows, she had little baggage. When she came downstairs she sent me for my wife and gave her a diamond brooch; then . . . then she kissed me on the cheek, snatched up her bundle, ran out to the coach and drove away." A tear ran down the old man's cheek as he added, "Monsieur will permit me to say that my wife and I were greatly distressed: we had become much attached to Madame Godfrey."

"And I," said Roger bitterly, giving Antoine's arm a sympathetic squeeze. Then he went on, "With regard to Madame . . . Madame de Breuc—she will be here for a while, but I think she will soon decide to return to Brittany. For her journey she will probably need money, so I wish you to offer her on my behalf the hundred *louis d'or* that I asked you to keep here for me against an emergency. I shall not return as long as she is here, but will send Dan out in a few days' time to learn from you if she has departed, or is about to do so. In the meantime, I am sure I may count on you and Marie to show her every civility."

Antoine bowed. "Monsieur le Chevalier may rely upon us, as always."

It was now nearly three in the morning and very chilly. Going into the dining-room, Roger poured himself a wineglassful of old brandy and tipped it down his throat. He gasped, shuddered and shook himself, then the mellow spirit began to do its work; as its warmth coursed through his veins, he thought glumly how typical of Amanda her departure had been.

In her brief note she had said that her mind was in a turmoil; yet she had not forgotten to take leave of the Velots fittingly, and to reward them for their loyal service. On the other hand, while the note amounted to a declaration that she was leaving him for good unless she received a prompt assurance that she was his legal wife, she had left no address or indication how he could communicate with her. And the devil of it was that, although it was a hundred to one that she had gone to Lady Atkyns, he had not the faintest idea whereabouts de Batz's house at Neuilly was situated.

After a few moments' thought, he decided that he would not

get very far with the type of enquiries he wished to make at Neuilly as long as he was dressed as a Commissioner; so he went out to the stable, saddled a horse that he always kept there, and rode back to Paris. The city was not yet astir; so he had to knock up the Cushion and Keys. By the time he had done so, his first fury had worn off; but he felt terribly tired, jaded and depressed, and, knowing that he had a long day before him, he ordered a hot bath to be prepared up in his room. At times of stress that was a luxury in which he permitted himself to indulge; so the staff had become used to this eccentricity of his, and, seeing the black mood he was in, hastened to obey him without their usual jocular comments.

While he was bathing he had a meal cooked and brought up, ploughed through it without noticing what he was eating, then dressed himself in civilian clothes and rode out to Neuilly. It was a fashionable suburb on the Seine to the west of Paris, a few miles north of St. Cloud. In happier times hundreds of well-to-do families had either lived there, or owned villas with pleasant gardens which they occupied during the summer months; so the task of finding the house in which de Batz had lodged Lady Atkyns was an extremely difficult one. It was quite certain that the wily Baron would never have contemplated taking the Queen to a property associated with his own name, or one suspected by the local Municipals of harbouring Royalists; and such loyalists as knew of it would, with equal certainty, not give its location away to a stranger.

After stabling his horse at an inn called *Le Cheval Pie*, Roger went for a walk round the little town, as experience had taught him that when he had no definite plan such an open approach sometimes brought him inspiration; but it did not prove so that morning. By half-past eight he was back at the inn with no more promising idea than to go from house to house enquiring for a mythical personage in the hope that Amanda would see him from one of the windows and come out to listen to any explanations he had to offer. Mounting his horse again, he rode up the drives of every worthwhile-looking property along the river bank and, instead of dismounting at their doors, remained in his saddle, shouting until somebody came, in order to attract as much attention to himself as possible. In the afternoon he continued the same wearisome business in the environs to the north of the Seine, but with no success and with ever-increasing despondency, since innumerable small properties, any one of which might be the Baron's secret retreat, stretched away almost cheek by jowl to Puteaux, Courbevoie, La Garenne and Colombes.

He did not eat again till early evening, and it was over a meal at the inn that a new idea occurred to him. He had been morosely cogitating the infuriating fact that he possessed the power to turn out the local National Guard and have domiciliary visits paid that night to every house in the area, but positively dared not use it from fear of the ultimate consequences, when a thought came to him of a way in which he could use his authority. In view of his threat to Lady Atkyns, it seemed probable that she would leave for the coast with Amanda either that night or the next. If they headed direct for any Channel port they would have to pass the cross-roads between Puteaux and Courbevoie, and by posting himself there in his sash and feathers he could stop every vehicle that approached merely by lifting his hand; so he rode back to Paris, changed into uniform, packed a small valise, returned to *Le Cheval Pie*, took a room there, borrowed a lantern, and at half-past nine began his vigil.

In these days few conveyances left Paris after nightfall, as it meant getting a special permit to pass any of the gates; so Roger's task was more wearisome than arduous, and he had no luck. Half an hour after dawn he reluctantly abandoned his post, repaired to the inn and slept till midday. That afternoon restless anxiety drove him out to continue his bogus enquiries at properties further afield, and that night he again haunted the cross-roads with his lantern. By the morning of the third day, although he felt that little hope remained, he could not bring himself to abandon his endeavours to catch Amanda before she left for England; yet a further twenty-four hours of his dreary routine, with its long series of disappointments, brought him no better fortune.

When he woke early in the afternoon of the fourth day he decided that it was useless to persevere further. Amanda might have left by day or taken another road by night; or, if Lady Atkyns realized that he did not know where she was living, she might have made up her mind to defy him and stay on as long as it suited her. Mentally exhausted, and in a most evil temper, he returned to Paris.

While at Neuilly he had neither looked at a news-sheet nor talked with anyone, except to give abrupt orders for his requirements at the inn, and his morose manner had been so forbidding that no member of the staff had volunteered the news that had come in the previous day; but on entering the city he found it bedecked with flags and its open spaces crowded with patriots who were celebrating. The reason, as he soon learned, was that on the day of the Queen's execution the Republican Armies had gained two great victories.

In the north, Maubeuge was the last major fortress remaining to the French. The Allies, following their text-book policy of reducing all such strongholds before advancing on Paris, had laid siege to the town. Prince Coburg had surrounded the place with 25,000 men and disposed a further 45,000 in strong positions about the village of Wattignies to cover it. The able and energetic Carnot, now firmly in the saddle, had appointed General Jourdan as the new Commander of the French and sent him with 50,000 men to endeavour to raise the siege of the fortress. On the 16th of October Jourdan had given battle and inflicted a severe defeat upon the Allies. Maubeuge was relieved, and for the first time for many months the threat of invasion from the north had been dissipated.

The scene of the other victory was La Vendée. On the 1st of August the *Comité* had issued a savage decree that the districts in revolt should be depopulated and devastated. Westermann, Rossignol and other terrorist commanders had carried it out with such ruthlessness wherever their columns penetrated that the whole population joined in offering the most desperate resistance. All through September battle had succeeded battle in which no quarter was given on either side and the carnage had been appalling. In an action at Luçon the Royalists had left 6,000 dead upon the field, but on the 18th and the 22nd they had revenged themselves by inflicting equally severe defeats upon the Revolutionaries. Early in October the Royal and Catholic army had been weakened by the withdrawal of Charette to his own territory of the Marais; then, on the 16th, a pitched battle had been fought at Cholet. It had raged all day with varying success, until towards evening, in a last magnificent charge, the Royalist Generals, Bonchamps and d'Eblé, had both been mortally wounded. Panic had ensued among their followers, who had then been utterly defeated and dispersed; so that it was now believed in Paris that the Vendéen war was over.

This quelling of the revolt in the west was largely due to General Kléber and the seasoned troops he had brought from

Mayence. On the surrender of that fortress, and also of Valenciennes, towards the end of July, the Allies had granted the garrisons of both the honours of war, and they had been allowed to march out with their arms on condition that they were not to be employed again for a year. But this prohibition applied only to service against the external enemies of the Republic; so the Convention had at once directed these veterans against its internal foes, and while the army from Mayence had formed a backbone for the *sans-culotte* forces in La Vendée, that from Valenciennes had made a big contribution to the reduction of Lyons.

That great city was now suffering a martyrdom comparable with the levelling of Carthage by the Romans. On entering it Couthon had written to the *Comité*, "Lyons has three classes of inhabitants—(1) the guilty rich, (2) the selfish rich, (3) the ignorant who are of no party. The first should be guillotined, the second forced to contribute their whole fortune, and the third be dispersed so that a Republican colony can be planted here in their place."

The *Comité*, inspired by fear that some other great revolt might yet overwhelm them and result in their being called to account for their crimes, decided to make of Lyons a terrible example. They accepted Couthon's recommendations and further decreed that the city was to be destroyed. "No part of it shall be preserved," ran the order, "other than the manufactories and the public buildings. The city shall cease to be called Lyons. It shall be renamed 'Commune Affranchie', and on its ruins shall be erected a monument inscribed with the words 'LYONS MADE WAR UPON LIBERTY—LYONS IS NO MORE'."

So now, after a summer and autumn during which the life of the Convention had not appeared worth a month's purchase, it could at last breathe more freely. Toulon, now besieged by General Carteaux, alone remained to be reduced; and it needed only two more victories, on the Rhine and in the Pyrenees, for the Revolution to be triumphant everywhere.

When Roger reached the Cushion and Keys he found among the papers waiting for him a note from Dan, asking him to let him know as soon as he was back; but as there seemed nothing particularly urgent about it, he put it aside for the moment. In his absence his work had accumulated shockingly; so during the next two days he tried to put thoughts of Amanda out of his head by plunging into it and straightening out a score of matters that needed attention. It was not until the evening of the 22nd that he came across Dan's note again, and as six clear days had elapsed since Athénaïs's arrival at Passy, he felt that it would now be worth sending his henchman out there to see if she had left; so he sent a runner to fetch him.

As soon as they were alone, Dan's first remark was, "She do be a foine recruit what 'e sent we; but 'er's proper angry with I fer sayin' I dunno 'e's whereabouts. Bin naggin' at I summat awful she 'as these foive days gone for I to fetch 'e to 'er."

"What in thunder do you mean?" Roger asked with a frown.

Grinning broadly, Dan made the situation clear. It had slipped Roger's memory that he had told Athénaïs before leaving the Red Lobster that should she find the house at Passy in wrong hands she was to enquire for him at *La Belle Étoile*. The afternoon after he had left her she had gone there and, on asking for him, been referred to Dan. He had at once recognized her as the long lost "little wycountess wot 'e got out o' Rennes" and Athénaïs had told him a very plausible story. Roger, she said, had told her about the Rescue League and she had come to Paris to work for it. Her secret activities in Brittany had already given her excellent training for such work; so, after a talk with her, and believing it to be Roger's wish, Dan had taken her on without hesitation. He had installed her in Roger's room and procured for her a variety of disguises. She had soon proved herself to be a remarkably clever actress and as quickwitted as a monkey, and even in these few days had already executed several very tricky commissions successfully. The only trouble from Dan's point of view was that she refused to believe that he did not know where Roger was, and was perpetually badgering him to arrange a meeting between them.

Roger was much disturbed by this new situation; but, after a moment's thought, he decided that he must see her, otherwise she might become a danger to herself and everyone else concerned. So he told Dan that he would call at *La Belle Étoile* at three o'clock the following afternoon.

When he arrived upstairs in his old room he found Athénaïs dressed as a Normandy apple-seller, and very seductive she looked in her peasant costume. She made him no reproaches about not having been to see her before, but said at once:

"Your man tells me, Monsieur, that for some days you have been out of Paris. I assume that you went in pursuit of your wife. I trust that you caught her and made it up?"

"No," replied Roger drily; "I failed to discover whither she had gone."

"I regret to hear it," said Athénaïs quietly. "Believe me, I am not without sympathy towards her, as I can imagine how I would feel did a similar misfortune overtake myself."

"You succeeded most admirably in concealing such feelings at the time," Roger remarked acidly.

"Rojé, you are unfair!" she protested. "When I arrived at Passy I was newly escaped from a month in prison. I expected to find comfort and safety there, with you overjoyed to know that I was still alive; but what did I find? At a moment's notice I was called on to deal with a totally unexpected situation, and one which, had I not shown my mettle, would have resulted in my being thrown out into the gutter like a trollop. That the other woman happened to be your wife was most unfortunate; but that was no fault of mine. Either she or I had to vacate the field, and in France I regard the field as mine; so how can you blame me for driving her from it?"

Roger's face remained hard, as he said, "She too had recently been in prison. It was for that reason I could not rid myself of her before you arrived, although, in all conscience, I tried hard enough. There was nowhere safe to which I could make her go. Even so, the blame is entirely mine that the two of you should have come face to face without warning, as you did. For that I most humbly apologize, and I am far from insensible with regard to your feelings. That you should have felt yourself justified in endeavouring to dispossess her I understand, but it is the means you used to achieve your object that I cannot stomach. Your coming inflicted a distress upon her that you could hardly avoid, but to increase it tenfold by inferring that her marriage to myself had been naught but an empty sham I account abominable."

"It was a harsh measure, I admit; but what other line could I take? Had I simply announced that I was your mistress and desired her to give you up to me, do you think she would have agreed?"

"She might well have done so."

"Then she cannot love you very much. Had I allowed the cards to be dealt that way she would have held all the trumps, and would have been both weak and stupid had she allowed me to get the better of her."

"Perhaps; God knows!" Roger shrugged miserably. "The harm is done now. I can only hope that I may soon find an opportunity to repair it. I take it, Madame, that you wished to see me with regard to your future plans? Well, I am here, and at your service."

Athénaïs cast her eyes down and, clasping her hands, began to twist her fingers together. After a moment, she said, "I had hoped that after a week you might feel differently. I am truly sorry for the hurt that I inflicted on your wife. Will you not forgive me?"

He shook his head. "It is I who should ask your forgiveness for being the prime cause of our love having come to such a sorry pass. But I am so stricken in my conscience that I could no longer be happy in its continuance."

She sighed and stood up. "So be it then. As for myself, that splendid desperado of yours has already found a use for my small talents in fighting the fiends who now rule Paris. With your permission I will continue to occupy this room, and aid him in his work to the best of my ability."

Roger bowed. "Madame, you are welcome to remain here as long as you wish, and I shall pray that in the course of your endeavours no harm will befall you."

Turning away, he walked to the door, and his hand was already on the latch when she suddenly stepped forward with arms outstretched, and cried:

"Oh, Rojé, think again, I beg! That which I did was done only out of love for you. Do not be so harsh upon us both. You look so tired, so ill, that it breaks my heart to see you thus. Please, please let me comfort you, and nurse you back to happiness. In my arms you will forget all this. We are already agreed that neither of us is free from blame; yet we live now in a world where the unhappiness that we have brought upon your wife cannot compare with the awful sufferings that are inflicted upon thousands here in France every day. Since it is our portion to live in the centre of this earthly hell created by the Revolution, can we not face it together? Sooner or later one or both of us will be caught, and caught for good. If we must die so young, let us at least first draw strength and joy from our love."

Sadly, he shook his head again. "Nay, Athénaïs. Forgive me, but I could not do it. I would be haunted all the time by the thought of her misery."

Athénaïs flushed to the roots of her black-dyed hair, and when she spoke again her voice held cold, hard anger. "Am I to understand, then, that you love her better than myself?"

"I did not say that," he muttered unhappily. "You have played a far greater part in my life than she has, and I shall always love you."

"Yes," she said, "I think you will; and when your mind is less disturbed you will realize that my love for you is greater than your wife's. In England you have a saying that 'possession is nine points of the law'. Had our positions been reversed, do you think that I would have left that house? No! I would have defied her, and rather than have given you up without a struggle I would have risked any humiliation. She did not love you enough to gamble on your standing by her, but left without a word. Mayhap a time will come when you will regret that you should have sacrificed me for what you feel about her today. Should that prove so, I'll not risk suffering again what I am suffering now, but should require your whole allegiance. Go now, Rojé, please. May God have you in His keeping."

Still resentful on Amanda's account, but made miserable and much shaken by Athénaïs's arguments, Roger closed the door behind him. Then, just as he was about to go downstairs, it occurred to him that before leaving *La Belle Étoile* he ought to have a word with Mère Blanchard. Dan had told him that Athénaïs, evidently hoping that he would come to live with her, was using his name; and, while the Blanchards never showed curiosity about his doings, he felt that he could hardly let such a situation continue without making any mention of her. In circumstances such as the present it would never have crossed his mind to repudiate her claim to be his wife; but to acknowledge it, yet never come to see her, set him a pretty little problem in explanation.

However, after a pause on the landing for a few minutes' thought, he decided on a suitable story. It was to the effect that he and his wife had long been estranged owing to differences in their political opinions. She had now come to Paris in the hope of saving a relative of hers who was one of the Girondin deputies recently impeached, and had appealed to him to use his influence in the arrested man's favour. He had refused her request for what he considered to be very good reasons, but his refusal had still further increased the breach between them. Therefore, to avoid unpleasant scenes, he did not intend to visit *La Belle Étoile* as long as his wife remained there.

The good landlady listened to this with an expressionless face, but when he had done she snorted and said, "I never did hold with women mixing in politics; but she's a lovely young thing and 'tis a great pity you've quarrelled with her. You're looking as thin as if you'd been in the poorhouse for a month. Can you not persuade her to kiss and be friends, so that you can come back here to live and I can feed you up?"

"Bless you, I would that I could," he smiled, "but 'tis out of the question. Now that she has come to Paris, though, she talks of remaining for some time, and I would be grateful if you would do all you can to make her comfortable during her stay."

Having received Mère Blanchard's ready assent, he left the hostelry slightly less dissatisfied with himself from having, at least, dealt efficiently with this comparatively minor matter; for his invention about the Girondin deputy had been extremely plausible. Paris was on the eve of savouring a new excitement. Having witnessed the sacking of the Tuileries, the butchering of the Swiss, the massacres of September, the murder of the King, the Queen, and a great number of so-called "enemies of liberty", it was now to see the legalized slaughter of a group of men who were jointly more responsible than any others for these excesses; not from the criminal sadism of terrorists like Hébert, but from vanity, folly, self-seeking and lack of courage to stop them when they had had ample powers to do so.

Two days after Roger's interview with Athénaïs, twenty-one of the leading Girondins were brought before the Revolutionary Tribunal, Brissot, Vergniaud, Gensonné, Carra and Valazé among them. At their trial they ran true to form: instead of presenting a solid front, each made desperate efforts to save himself at the expense of his associates. The accusations that Fouquier-Tinville formulated against them were Machiavellian; they included such charges as that of having plotted the September massacres in the hope that the Provinces would be so alarmed by the course the Revolution was taking that they would rise and march on Paris, with the object of substituting a bourgeois tyranny for the Rule of the People.

Without dignity or courage, each Girondin endeavoured to prove that he had been in the front rank of those who had destroyed the Old Order, inspired and encouraged every excess of which the *sans-culottes* had been guilty, approved the execution of the King, and supported the policies of the Mountain.

In their fight for life they had lost none of their powers of oratory. After three days the Committee of Public Safety, wearied of their now pointless declamations, issued a new decree that no trial should last longer than forty-eight hours. On the evening of the 29th their defence was summarily terminated and all twenty-one were condemned to death.

On the 31st, the citizens of Paris turned out in force to be present at this new spectacle—the guillotining of a score of Revolutionaries. Once the condemned men realized there was no escape they regained their courage. Valazé committed suicide by stabbing himself in Court, and it was ordered that his dead body should be taken to be beheaded with the rest; but the others were permitted to hold a last supper in the Conciergerie. At it they joked, laughed, and discussed philosophy until dawn, then when the tumbrels came they went bravely to execution.

That same day Roger launched a project that he had long cherished in secret. Under the influence of Hébert, now the most powerful man in Paris with the one exception of Robespierre, the Commune had become ever more terrorist in character. Roger rarely spoke there, and knew that in recent months he had begun to be regarded as lukewarm. That was dangerous, and the time was already overdue for him to make some gesture which would reassure the extremists about the "purity of his patriotism". Having caught the President's eye at an afternoon session of the Commune, he denounced Citizen Égalité, formerly Philippe Duc d'Orléans, in a forceful, scathing speech.

Orléans had been arrested in Marseilles on the 7th of April and recently transferred to Paris. Above and beyond all men he was the creator of the Revolution. He had used the basest and most unscrupulous methods in an endeavour to have his cousin Louis XVI dethroned and himself made Regent. His vast fortune had enabled him to provoke famine riots by cornering grain; to defame Marie Antoinette by printing hundreds of thousands of obscene pamphlets describing her invented immoralities; to keep, finance and organize a private army of agitators and *agents provocateur* who had incited the people to rebellion; to import into Paris a legion of bandits, cut-throats and assassins from the Mediterranean ports whom he had plied with liquor and had sent out to pillage and murder. But now his bolt was shot; he had raised the whirlwind, but had failed to ride it. Robespierre, Hébert and their friends had never favoured the idea of a Constitutional Monarchy, however mild in form; but the Girondins had toyed with it, and Orléans was known by all to have been hand in glove with them.

After twenty minutes spent in recalling "His Royal Highness's" manipulation of the markets, boundless extravagance, and political treachery, Roger cried, "Those enemies of the People, the Girondin deputies, are this day meeting their just deserts. But why should they die while this scheming Prince—this tyrant's spawn in whose veins runs the vile Bourbon blood—this multi-millionaire who all his life has lived on the sweat of the workers—this arch-conspirator who inspired all their treacheries—be allowed to live? I demand the head of this traitor, who has brought indelible shame upon the glorious word '*Égalité*'."

His denunciation could not have been better timed, and it met with a great ovation. The Chamber rose to a man, cheering, stamping and shouting, "We want his head! We want Égalité's head!" A deputation was at once formed to go to the Convention, and at its bar Roger had to make his speech all over again. There, he received another ovation, and was decreed the honours of the sitting. Orléans's trial was ordered and the news ran round Paris. For a few days Roger was in the limelight, for his skilful move had served him well; not only had he regained the complete confidence of the *Comité* and the Hébertists, but also the adulation of the ordinary people of Paris who cheered him wherever he went, as they had gradually learned the truth about Orléans, and were delighted that he was to die.

On the 6th of November, the *ci-devant* Duke was sent to the guillotine. As the tumbrel in which he stood was drawn slowly through the streets by a heavy cart-horse, the mob howled its execrations. The people had not forgotten the part that he had played at the trial of his cousin, Louis XVI, the previous January; all along the mile-long route they mocked and derided him with his own words, "I vote for death! I vote for death!" So, one of the basest men in all history went to his doom.

Roger's triumph gave him little satisfaction. He was still too miserable about his own affairs. A fortnight had elapsed since his interview with Athénaïs, and it had shaken him badly. He had to admit to himself that, cruel as her conduct had at first appeared, it had from her point of view been fully justified; and the more he thought of the matter the more he came round to the view that

Amanda was largely responsible for bringing her present unhappy situation on herself. Had she remained to challenge him, as Athénaïs maintained she should have done, she would have emerged the victor. She was his wife, and, however great his passion for another, he knew that honour and decency would have compelled him to stand by her at that moment, whatever might have happened afterwards. She should, he felt, have had sufficient trust in him for that; but she had not. Without giving him the chance to say that he loved her best, which for all she knew might have been the case, or even to save her dignity and humbly beg her pardon, she had run away.

Yet he could not leave matters as they were; and, having failed to find her, his next thought had been to write to her and reassure her about the legal status of their marriage. That he had not done so yet was because he was in no position to have letters smuggled to England whenever he liked. He was dependent on the brave men of the League for that, and often a month or more elapsed between the occasions when one of them came into Paris. He had by these means sent off a long despatch to Mr. Pitt shortly before the Queen's execution, informing him about many political matters and predicting the early elimination of the Girondins. He was shortly due to compose another, but as yet there was nobody in Paris by whom he could send it; so he decided that, rather than keep Amanda in suspense any longer, he would use Dan as his messenger. Since his return to Paris in July, his share of the Commune plunder had amounted to over £4,000, most of which he had converted into bills of exchange on cities outside France; Dan could take the despatch, the letter for Amanda, and this handsome nest-egg safely out of the country at the same time.

When, early in the month, he had been checking up his plunder, he had decided to put his name down again for duty at the Temple. The poor Queen was now beyond rescue, but the boy remained. Since he had become King he was, potentially, a more valuable pawn than ever in the game of European politics; so still worth a hundred thousand pounds. During all the months Roger had been in France he had never lost sight of that, and although his three attempts to snatch him from his captors had, by force of circumstances, been made at long intervals and had all failed, he was very far from having given up the game.

He was listed to report at the Temple on the night of the 10th; and that morning saw another outstanding execution. For once, when the knife of the guillotine descended, a shorn neck spouted bile instead of blood. Only twenty-five days after Marie Antoinette, her inveterate enemy, Manon Roland, who had planned to have her murdered in the Tuileries, followed her to the scaffold.

The other Girondins were now being hunted through the length and breadth of France. News was coming in that one by one they had been caught and executed or, lacking the courage to defy their enemies at the end, had taken their own lives. Roland and Clavière stabbed themselves, Condorcet took poison, Rebecqui drowned himself, and Buzot put a bullet through his brain. The vile and treacherous Pétion had not even the courage to commit suicide, and tried to hide in a forest; but he met a fitting end—his body was discovered half devoured by wolves.

Madame Roland's execution early on the 10th served only as a *hors-d'œuvre* to the feast of base emotions provided for the *canaille* that day. Hébert, Chaumette, Rosnin and many other of the most violent members of the Commune were not content with having revolutionized the Catholic Church in France; they wished to abolish it altogether, and their endeavours were on the point of bearing fruit. Three days earlier Gobel—a priest who, on abjuring the Pope, had been made Archbishop of Paris—and a number of his fellow renegades had appeared at the bar of the Convention with red caps of Liberty on their heads, thrown down their mitres, crosses and rings, and formally abjured Christianity. Now Notre Dame was to be converted into a Temple of Reason.

No sooner had one of Citizen Executioner Sanson's assistants thrown Manon's body into a cart and pushed her head between her legs than the crowd turned its back upon the guillotine and streamed towards the great cathedral. In the square before it, to the raucous laughter of the mob, *sans-culottes* dressed in surplices and copes parodied the Mass, then sang the *ça ira* and danced the *carmagnole*.

In due course a solemn procession appeared: all the Sections of Paris were represented and Roger had no option but to attend with his fellow Commissioners. Borne aloft among them in an arm-chair placed on a litter was a beautiful young actress, who had been the mistress of several of the Commissars and was now the terrorist Momoro's wife. Robed in white, with a blue mantle and red Phrygian cap, she represented the Goddess of Reason; accompanying her as her handmaidens were a score of the prettiest prostitutes in Paris. With absurd parodies of religion, Chaumette,

Anacharis Clootz and other leading atheists installed her upon the altar; then they carried her to the Convention and back again, followed by all the deputies, who gave up further business for the day to participate in these profane rites.

Towards evening it became clear to Roger that the general junketing was about to degenerate into an orgy; so he was glad that his having to go on duty at the Temple provided him with an excuse to get away. He found that no material change had occurred there. The quiet routine of the saintly Princess Elizabeth and the young Madame Royale continued on the same lines as before the Queen had been taken from them. The Simons still had charge of the little King, and the only change in the boy was that signs of their "education" were beginning to appear in his face; for, instead of its former engaging beauty, it was acquiring a mean, sly look.

Now that sufficient time had elapsed since the scare caused by Michonis's arrest for things to settle down again, Roger hoped that he might win over Goret, or some other Commissar, to assist him in a revival of the plan to smuggle the little King out in the big birdcage; but in this he was disappointed. The birdcage was no longer there, and a casual enquiry about it to Simon produced the information that the musical box in its base had been broken, so it had been sent to be repaired. While up in the apartment, Roger scrutinized every other piece of furniture for a possible alternative, but could see nothing at all suitable; and, as he could think of no better plan, he decided that he would do well to wait until the birdcage was returned.

Among the Commissars on duty was one whose son had, the previous day, returned from Lyons; and he gave his colleagues an account of the latest developments in that unfortunate city. Apparently Couthon, although Robespierre's oldest collaborator and, like him, completely ruthless of human life, had thought it a senseless proceeding to destroy many hundred million *francs*' worth of property; so on the 29th of October he had been replaced by two other Representatives, Collot d'Herbois and Joseph Fouché. The first had been chosen by the Hébertists and, having as a small-part actor been hissed off the stage at Lyons, was peculiarly suited to exact vengeance on the city. The second, Roger's old enemy, was a Robespierrist, and had presumably been selected on account of the notoriety he had won by smashing up statues of saints, stained-glass windows and other Church ornaments wherever he went. Apparently these two beauties were having a high old time, killing and destroying to their hearts' content.

Roger took mental note of the latter appointment with satisfaction, as it meant that Fouché would be well out of the way for two or three months. After challenging recognition by him when he had first arrived in Paris as a deputy to the Convention, Roger had been fairly easy in his mind that the ex-oratorian teacher of mathematics was unlikely to remember him, provided they were not called on to work together; but any business that necessitated a renewal of their acquaintance might prove highly dangerous. That possibility, together with the fact that Michonis might give him away if brought to trial, was an ever-present menace to Roger's security, of which he never entirely lost sight; but it looked as if Michonis, having been imprisoned, had been forgotten, and it was comforting to learn that he had nothing to fear from Fouché for some time to come.

As he had little to occupy him while on duty in the Temple, he spent his second morning there composing a letter to Amanda. He found it by no means easy to write, as he did not wish to evade the blame for the distressing situation to which he had exposed her; but he did want to impress upon her that, had she had sufficient faith in him to wait at Passy until he arrived, she could have spared herself the far greater distress of returning to England in doubt as to the validity of their marriage. At length he succeeded in getting down a fair draft of what he wished to say, which, in essence, was: a frank admission that he had first loved Athénaïs when he was sixteen and that she still meant a great deal in his life; an apology that through his mismanagement they should have met; and an assurance that Amanda was both his legal wife and that she still held a special place in his heart which no one but herself could ever destroy.

Before going off duty on the night of the 12th he learned that another celebrated figure of the Revolution had been executed that day, in peculiarly revolting circumstances. Bailly—the renowned astronomer and great humanitarian, who understood what liberty and freedom meant in their best sense and had endeavoured to bring them to his countrymen; the first President of the National Assembly, and the first to take the famous oath of the Tennis Court, by which the deputies of the Third Estate had pledged themselves not to separate until France had a

Constitution; the elected Mayor of Paris who had laboured night and day for months on end to feed the capital when its poor were starving—had been victimized, at Hébert's instigation, in order to appease an old score that the *sans-culottes* had against him.

After the abortive flight of the Royal Family to Varennes in the summer of '91, the Club of the Cordeliers had at Danton's suggestion laid for signature on the Altar of the Nation in the Champs de Mars a petition calling for the King's deposition. This had led to a riot. The National Assembly, fearing to be attacked, had ordered Lafayette to call out the National Guard and disperse the people. Bailly, as Mayor, had accompanied Lafeyette and read the Riot Act. The mob had both stoned and shot at the troops. Without orders some of the troops had retaliated by firing on the mob. It was the sole instance throughout the whole Revolution of the forces of law and order using their arms against a riotous assembly. Only a handful of people were killed or wounded, but the mob dissolved as if by magic; which just went to show how easily Louis XVI could have restored order in his capital on a score of occasions had he only had the courage to do so instead of simply looking on while his loyal defenders were butchered. However, the Jacobins had seized upon the episode and made great capital out of it as an example of the way in which "the armed lackeys of the Tyrant" were used to enforce slavery upon the "People". Owing to their fulminations this affair of the 17th of July, '91 became known as "the massacre of the Champs de Mars".

Now, two and a half years later, as a result of the aged and honest Bailly's courageous refusal to testify against the Queen at her trial, it had been resurrected as an excuse to condemn him to death. In order that the *sans-culottes* might enjoy their vengeance to the utmost it had been decreed that for this day the guillotine should be removed to the Champs de Mars, where the "massacre" had occurred, and that instead of going in a tumbrel, Bailly should be made to walk there.

It was a cold, rainy day. Soaked through, chilled to the marrow, and with his arms tied behind his back, the poor old man had bravely walked two miles through a lane of jeering, hostile onlookers; yet that was not enough. When he reached the scaffold some depraved ape in human form raised the cry that the Field of the Nation was a place of honour; so it should not be polluted by the blood of such a "criminal". With acclamation, the assembled *canaille* agreed that the guillotine should be removed to a dung-heap on the banks of the Seine, then proceeded to dismantle and remove it. Three hours elapsed before it was re-erected, and during that time Bailly was made to run the gauntlet round and round the Champs de Mars while the "sacred People" pelted him with mud, beat him with sticks and kicked him. When finally executed, he was already half-dead.

When Roger heard of the episode he felt that there was some reason to doubt the justice of God; for why had He allowed Louis XVI to go comfortably in his own carriage to the scaffold with a Confessor, while He had let Marie Antoinette be reduced to a skeleton in a dungeon before she was taken in a cart to die, and had allowed a great soul like Bailly to be slowly beaten to death?

Two days later another perished for having refused to bear witness against the Queen: that strangest enigma of the whole Revolution—Manuel, the man who had known the inside of the Bastille as a prisoner—was condemned as a reactionary and executed.

Roger, meanwhile, had had a long talk with Dan. That born adventurer had been loath to give up his rescue work even for a fortnight, but at his master's wish he agreed to go to England. He was to take a despatch for Mr. Pitt, the letter to Amanda, and the £4,000 worth of securities, which he was to deliver to Droopy Ned for conversion into British Government funds. He asked a few days to arrange for the continuity of his work during his absence; then, on the 14th of November, he quietly disappeared from Paris.

Once Dan was on his way, Roger felt that honour was satisfied as far as Amanda was concerned. More and more he leaned to the view that, greatly as he was to blame, she had brought her worst troubles on herself, and more and more his thoughts gravitated towards Athénaïs. There he knew her to be, day after day, night after night, living less than a mile away from himself, alone and eminently desirable. He began to wonder if he had not been the most colossal prude and fool to reject her explanation and the advances she had made when he had been to see her at *La Belle Étoile*.

Again and again he caught himself thinking of what she had said of their living in a nightmare world of blood and death in which one or both of them must sooner or later be caught and sent to the scaffold; so why should they not take such joy of each other as they could while they still had the opportunity?

It was nine days after Dan had left Paris that an event occurred which placed Roger under the necessity of visiting Athénaïs again. His contribution to the work of the Rescue League was to supply the passports, permits, *cartes de civisme* and other papers necessary to get suspects away, and usually Dan let him know what was required; but sometimes he had advance information about people who were to be arrested, and took measures to save them himself. As it was of the utmost importance that the secret of where these papers came from should be kept, he never personally warned suspects of their peril, but always sent Dan with the papers required for them to leave Paris. Such a case now arose in his own Section. The young Doctor Guilhermy, whom he had reluctantly been compelled to browbeat on the famous night of the 10th of August, fifteen months before, had come under suspicion. If this brave and honest man's life was to be saved, Athénaïs must be used, since Dan was absent, to provide him with the means to flee while there was still time.

Next day, the 24th, Roger went to see her. In the quiet hours of the previous night he had already made up his mind to ask her to forget the harsh things he had said, and when they had finished arranging the Guilhermy business he opened the subject by saying:

"Athénaïs, I fear that during the past six weeks I have behaved like a great fool and treated you very badly. When we last met you were generous enough to say that you were sorry that you had seen no alternative to causing my wife such distress. I should have accepted that and begged your pardon there and then for having myself been the prime cause of the whole trouble. I can only say now that had your positions been reversed I should have felt just as strongly on your account as I did on hers; and that despite the anger I displayed, I have never ceased to love you. Will you forgive me?"

She smiled at him. "Dear Rojé, I am only too anxious to do so; but as I warned you when we last discussed this matter, I must ask you for some guarantee that a similar situation will not arise again."

"I will agree to anything that will ease your mind," he replied eagerly, "but what guarantee can I give you?"

"Would it be possible for you to take a few weeks' holiday?" she asked.

"For officials of the Revolution there are no such things as holidays," he said a little dubiously. Then, thinking she had in mind a renewal of their joyous honeymoon at the Red Lobster, he added, "Still, I suppose I could get away if I said that overwork has made me ill. After all, Danton has but just returned from a month's stay at a fine estate he bought with his ill-gotten gains at Arcis-sur-Aube; and with no better excuse than that he had just married a chit of seventeen."

"Very well, then; make your arrangements and take me for a week or two to your father's house at Lymington."

"What say you?" Roger exclaimed.

She laughed. "Do you not think the idea an excellent one? Such a change would do you an infinity of good, and would at the same time fulfil my own requirements. I am not, of course, suggesting that you should take me there as your wife, but as a refugee. There need be no scandal, but a notice would appear in the Hampshire papers that 'Mr. Roger Brook is recently arrived from France with Madame la Vicomtesse de la Tour d'Auvergne, whom he had saved from the guillotine.' Outwardly, at least, we would behave with all propriety, but your wife would read between the lines and understand that I hold first place in your affections."

"No!" said Roger. "No; you ask too much. I could not inflict such a further hurt on her."

"Why? By this time you must have written to her to let her know that my claim to be your wife has no foundation."

"Yes, naturally I did so, but——"

"Then honour is satisfied as far as she is concerned. She knows that she has a right to your name and is secure in her position. I count her exceedingly fortunate in that."

"Athénaïs, I beg you not to ask this of me."

"I would not, had you not given me cause to doubt your love. After what you have made me suffer you owe it to me to prove that you count me something more than a convenient plaything."

In vain Roger implored her to alter her mind. She would not, and nothing would have induced him to hurt Amanda further by doing what Athénaïs asked. So, twenty minutes later, angry and disappointed, he left her.

As it so happened, he would have found great difficulty in getting leave to absent himself from the activities of the Revolution, even had he been cowardly enough to agree, for, two days later, Carnot sent for him.

Roger knew well by sight the long face, high forehead and great, ugly, crooked Roman nose of the man who was now called France's "Organizer of Victories", but he had never had any dealings with him. Somewhat puzzled, he went to the offices of the Committee of Public Safety and sent in his name. He was not kept waiting long. When they were face to face, Lazare Carnot gave him a long, shrewd stare, asked him to sit down, then said briskly:

"Citizen Commissioner, from what I have heard of you, I have formed the impression that you have little taste for missions which entail enforcing the will of the Convention upon the civil population."

Fearing a trap, Roger replied with caution, "I have ever been averse to unnecessary slaughters which deprive France of men to produce food from her fields or serve in her armies, Citizen General; but where the safety of the Revolution is concerned, I should never hesitate to employ the guillotine or any other measure at my disposal."

Carnot nodded noncommittally, and went on, "On the other hand, I recall General Dumouriez telling me that you served him exceptionally well in restoring discipline among his troops, and for a civilian showed an excellent grasp of military matters. I require such a man to strengthen the army investing Toulon. General Dugommier is now in command there, and has with him several Citizen Representatives; but none of them have had any military experience, except Barras, and Fréron is one of those 'patriots' who can prove a serious menace with an army. The others are more of a hindrance than help; so I wish you to go there as a counterweight to these meddlers, and do your utmost to assist the General in wresting Toulon from the accursed English."

To fight against his own countrymen was one of the last things Roger wished, but he dared not refuse this new mission; so, half an hour later, he left Carnot's office with a packet of despatches under his arm and a new warrant giving him powers of life and death in his pocket.

As he was about to leave the building, a clerk called him back, and Robespierre emerged from a nearby room. In his hand he carried another packet. With his cat-like smile, he held it out to Roger, and said:

"I am told that my colleague is sending you to Toulon, Citizen. I have here an important despatch for Lyons, and you will be passing through that city. I wish you to deliver it personally—personally, you understand—to Citizen Representative Fouché."

CHAPTER XXIV

TWICE HOIST WITH HIS OWN PETARD

As Roger rode south next day he was by no means sorry to be leaving Paris. In the past three weeks, the craving for Athénaïs that he had felt in August when he had first feared her lost to him for good had begun to obsess him again. Only stubbornness and lack of an excuse to save his face had prevented his seeking a *rapprochement* with her even earlier than he had; but he had left it too late. Punishing her had brought punishment on himself, for her resentment had crystallized into a demand to which he could not possibly accede. Yet, knowing her to be recoverable at a price, he would have been constantly subjected to a base temptation had he remained near her; at least he had been spared that by Carnot's sending him away.

On consideration he thought himself lucky, too, in having been selected for this mission, when it might so easily have been another requiring him to take a portable guillotine as part of his baggage. Anything was preferable to a renewal of those two months of horror that he had lived through in the spring; and, although at first sight it had seemed a most repugnant task to have to help fight his own countrymen, he felt that if he kept his wits about him he might be able to find ways to aid them more than he injured them. That would be much more difficult without the resourceful Dan to assist him, and the absence of his jovial henchman was one of his worries; the other, a very much greater one, was that he dared not ignore the order he had received from Robespierre to deliver his despatch to Joseph Fouché personally.

The precept "know thy enemy" being to Roger's mind a sound one, he had been to considerable trouble to find out all he could about the Deputy for Nantes. He was the son of a moderately wealthy merchant captain, had inherited some plantations in the West Indies, and it was as a representative of bourgeois trading interests that he had been sent to Paris. Yet, for a long time past, he had had associations with the extremists. At one period the Oratorians had sent him to teach physics at their school in Arras, and it was there that he had met Robespierre, who was the local legal adviser to the Order. As Fouché was only a lay brother he had taken no vows to prevent his marrying, and he had paid his attentions to Robespierre's elderly sister Charlotte. Nothing had come of the matter, but he had remained a close friend of the family and had lent Robespierre money to enable him to support himself in Versailles when he had been elected to the States-General. Then, on his return to Nantes, Fouché had become one of the earliest members of the Jacobin Club there, and, as soon as he could, had dissociated himself from his religious connections. Nevertheless, he had taken his seat in the Convention pledged to protect property and all established institutions, and for his first few months as a deputy had acted the part of a cautious moderate.

The King's trial had proved the turning point in his political career, as every deputy, in giving his verdict, had been forced to show his colours. Most men in his position did so only half-heartedly, but, shrewdly assessing future trends, Fouché had nailed his to the mast. Not only did he vote for death, but at once joined the Mountain, and with supreme effrontery issued a circular to his electorate, seeking to justify his conduct by using the very arguments that he had himself publicly contested only a few days before. It was his first, but by no means last, great betrayal.

Since then he had risen rapidly in the esteem of the *Comité*. In March they had sent him to La Vendée, then in June transferred him to Troyes and Nevers. In the latter town he made a name for himself, emerging there as an arch-enemy of the Church which, during his early life, had provided him with his living. He had not long been married to a very plain but handsomely-dowried girl, and at this juncture she presented him with a daughter. Instead of having the child baptized, as was still usual, by a priest who had taken the oath to the Revolution, he set a new fashion; parading the Municipal and National Guards round an Altar to the Nation in the market square, he christened the child himself, giving her the name of Nièvre after her birthplace. He went further, by commandeering a church in order to hold a Republican banquet in it; then, with Chaumette of the Commune, who had been sent to him as a colleague, he set about plundering churches and *châteaux*. During September and October they had sent over 50,000 pounds *weight* in gold and seventeen packing-cases full of chalices and chasubles to the Convention. Many people wondered how much loot had stuck to the fingers of the pair; at all events it was known that the frugal Robespierre had made some very caustic remarks about the enormous bills they had put in for entertaining. And now Fouché had been given a job in Lyons after his own heart, with another even more ferocious partner, Collot d'Herbois; Roger could only pray that when he came face to face with his old enemy he would continue to escape recognition.

When in Nevers during the summer, Fouché had issued a decree that no religious emblem, cross or image of any kind was to be allowed in any public place, and now the Convention had adopted this policy officially as a part of the Revolution. On the 24th of November, five days before Roger had left Paris, the Commune had followed up the desecration of Notre Dame by closing every place of worship in the capital; and, within twenty days from that date, 2,436 French churches were converted into "Temples of Reason".

On that date, too, the new Revolutionary calendar had been introduced. Owing to the mania of the new masters for changing everything, this fresh means of creating an upheaval in the nation's way of life had long been under discussion; so long that when it was at last put into operation people found themselves in the Year II of the Republic. The new Era, it was finally decided, should date from the 22nd of September, 1792, the day on which Louis XVI had formally been deposed. In the Republican year there were 12 months, each of 30 days, and named appropriately to the seasons, as the months of Rain, Germination, Flowering, Harvest, etc. The week was abolished, and each month instead contained three periods of 10 days called *décades*; at the end of each year, 5 days called *sans-culottides* were added, and for Leap Year a sixth, to be called *le jour de la Révolution*.

Roger, however, preferred to continue to think in terms of the Gregorian calendar; so for him it was the 2nd of December, 1793, when, with the plumes waving from his hat and his escort of cavalry clanking behind him, but extremely uneasy in his mind, he entered the tragic city of Lyons.

From several miles away he had heard the sound of detonations, and now he saw that both explosives and fire were being used to speed up the demolition. Bellecourt Square, designed by Mansard and the finest piece of architecture in the city, had already been reduced to rubble, as had many of the rich people's houses that stood in their own gardens. Under the supervision of National Guards, the thousands of silk-workers who had been thrown out of employment by the Revolution were now being driven to execute its stupidest command; in nearly every street gangs of them were mining under houses and shops or burning down isolated buildings.

At the Hôtel de Ville, Roger expected to find the two Proconsuls charged with the enforcement of all this destruction; but he was directed to a house some way from the centre of the town which, when he reached it, had the appearance of a military command post. A full company of troops were on duty as sentries all round it, the garden walls had been reinforced with sandbags, and there were cannon in the courtyard with their gun-teams lounging round them. These precautions against an already cowed population struck Roger as somewhat redundant, but he was far too concerned about what might happen to himself during the next hour to think of much else. After he had shown his papers to four people and waited for some minutes in an ante-room, he was shown in to Citizen Fouché.

The Representative was seated at a desk covered with papers. It was there, filling the inexhaustible crevices of his mind with facts about people which he might later use to his advantage, that he was in his element. It was that extraordinary capacity for absorbing information and applying it unscrupulously which was, later, to make him invaluable to Napoleon as Chief of Police, earn him a dukedom, and enable him to pile up a fortune running into tens of millions; but to look at, no one would ever have suspected his unrivalled powers for work, or his age—which was only thirty-three. His bony face was so lean and pallid that it might have belonged to a week-old corpse; his hair was sparse, his eyebrows reddish, his heavily-lidded eyes green and fish-like. He suffered from a perpetual cold; so was always sniffling; and the hand that he extended to Roger was as limp as that of a drowned man who had just been fished out of a pond.

The acquiring of secret information being Roger's special business, he had been greatly tempted to learn the contents of Robespierre's despatch before delivering it; but now he thanked his stars that he had heeded the instinct which had warned him to refrain, as Fouché, apparently quite unconcerned by the rudeness of the act, took up a powerful magnifying glass from his desk and examined the seals of the despatch very carefully, to make certain they had not been tampered with.

He had not once looked Roger directly in the face; but having glanced through the despatch he laid it down, and said, "Have we not met before, Citizen Colleague?"

Roger's blood seemed to freeze in his veins, but he replied quite casually, "Not to converse, Citizen Colleague; but we often passed within a few feet of one another in the halls of the Convention before you left Paris to perform your splendid cleansing of Nevers."

Fouché ignored the compliment, and persisted, "It is not your face alone that is familiar to me, but also your voice. What part of France do you come from?"

"From Strasbourg," lied Roger promptly.

"Ah! That, then, accounts for the suggestion of heaviness in your accent."

Outwardly, Roger remained impassive; inwardly, he breathed a sigh of relief, as Fouché, apparently satisfied, made no further enquiry, but said, "It is too late for you to continue your journey tonight; so I will order accommodation to be provided for you and your escort here."

"I thank you, Citizen Colleague," Roger replied, quickly rising to his feet, "but pray do not put yourself to that trouble; I can easily find quarters at a hostelry."

"No; this accursed city is being taught a lesson, and there are many ill-disposed persons still at large. We patriots must take care of ourselves, and I cannot allow you to run such a risk."

As he spoke, Fouché jangled a bell on his desk; and Roger, feeling that it might excite suspicion if he refused the proffered hospitality, had to stand unhappily by while orders were given to an underling to provide him with a room and all he required.

His uneasiness was redoubled when, just as he was about to follow his guide, Fouché added with a thin-lipped smile, "Supper will be served in half an hour, Citizen Colleague. Over the meal perhaps we shall remember where we met before."

Upstairs, Roger contemplated feigning illness to escape this fresh ordeal; but he decided it would look too much like running away, and his chances of laying the dangerous ghost that haunted Fouché's mind would be better if he continued to put on a bold front. So, after a horrid interval, during which he suffered from an acute attack of nerves, he pulled himself together and went down to supper.

His apprehension was somewhat allayed by finding that, instead of having to spend the evening in intimate talk with the two Proconsuls, some twenty people had assembled for the meal;

and soon he was fully occupied giving them news of Paris while they told him about their work of "purifying" Lyons.

As a start they had elevated Challier, the Revolutionary who had been executed by the reactionaries, to the status of a saint. He had not been a villainous person at all, but was an ex-priest who, out of genuine sympathy for the misery of the slum-dwellers, had exchanged Christianity for Communism. His activities had inevitably caused riots; so as soon as the Federalists had gained control of the city they clapped him into jail. Some months earlier, Paris had sent Lyons a guillotine, which had been left unused out in a yard; then, when the Federalists had broken finally with the Convention, they had decided to make a cynical gesture of defiance by christening the instrument with Challier. As the executioner of Lyons had never before operated a guillotine and its blade had been allowed to become rusty, a horrifying bungle had ensued. After the axe had been hauled up and dropped three times on poor Challier's neck, the awful business had had to be finished with a sword. Even so, Roger was inclined to doubt if the martyr would have approved the acts that were now being committed in his honour.

On the arrival of Fouché and Collot, every church in the city had been despoiled of its crucifix, and a bust of Challier set up on the altar in its place. To initiate this measure the two Proconsuls had organized a solemn procession in which a donkey had played the leading rôle, a bishop's mitre having been strapped on its head, and a crucifix and Bible tied to its tail. On reaching the Altar to the Nation in the principal square, the Representatives had gone on their knees in the dust before Challier's bust, the donkey had been given a drink out of a chalice and communion wafers to eat, and a great bonfire had been made of all the Bibles, crosses and other religious symbols that could be found. The gentlemen from Paris had then set about their congenial work of avenging Challier's death in earnest.

When the company sat down, Roger was given the place of honour between Fouché and Collot, and he was thankful to find that the latter did most of the talking; yet, his danger from Fouché apart, he found it a great strain to show the lively interest in the conversation that was expected of him. The ex-comedian took a ghoulish delight in describing the harrowing scenes which were daily taking place before the Revolutionary Tribunal and on the scaffold. He and Fouché were sentencing scores of people to death at every sitting, sometimes trying and condemning them *en bloc* in groups of a dozen or more; the prisons were now crammed to suffocation, and, as Fouché cut in to remark, "Our trouble is that the guillotine works too slowly."

They were, however, making plans to rectify this, and they described to Roger a new procedure they intended to introduce in two days' time. Two parallel trenches were to be dug across the field of Brotteaux, on the far side of the Rhône. A number of prisoners were to be ferried across tied up in couples back to back, so that they could not run away. They were to be placed standing up in a long line between the trenches, and cannon loaded with grape-shot fired at them. They would then fall into one or other of the trenches which, after their bodies had been stripped, would only require to be filled in.

Roger pointed out that the bodies of those nearest the cannon would protect the rest; so many might only be wounded or temporarily escape injury altogether, with the result that a most horrible scene must ensue. But Fouché only shrugged, and Collot remarked cheerfully:

"Oh, a few musket-shots will soon finish off the remainder; and I assure you this method will be much more humane than the guillotine. When about to embrace 'Madame', the last in a queue of twenty dies nineteen times by anticipation, whereas in our *mitraillades* all will be dead within a few moments of each other."

While carp and roast pike were followed by capons, partridges and venison, which in turn gave place to tarts, jellies, ice creams and custards, these gruesome topics continued to hold the interest of all present; with the one exception of Roger, who gave only his outward attention to the respective merits of beheading and shooting. He knew that he was sitting on a powder mine; so he drank sparingly of the fine Burgundies and *Châteauneuf du Pape* that were put before him, and carefully chose every word he said, lest he should inadvertently start some chain of thought in his enemy's mind that would lead to his recognition. Fouché, too, seemed even more dangerous towards the end of the evening, as he was one of the few in the party who kept sober; but at last it began to break up, and with nothing further said about a previous meeting he went off to bed.

Within a few minutes Roger followed him, but could not sleep. Again and again in his mind he saw the sidelong glance of those merciless fish-like eyes, and with every creak of the house he reached for his pistol, fearing that it must be Fouché coming to denounce him as an Englishman and a spy.

At last dawn came. Hurriedly he dressed, descended to the dining-room and bolted a cup of hot coffee that was being served there, then went out and cursed his escort into greater activity. By half-past seven, with a sense of having escaped from the clutches of the devil himself, he was on the road south once more, yet he did not feel really safe until he had left the tragic city several leagues behind him.

On the afternoon of the 6th, Roger presented himself at the headquarters of General Dugommier outside Toulon. The General proved to be a fine, soldierly-looking man, with nothing of the Revolutionary about him; but he received his new *Représentant en mission* with becoming deference and, after reading the despatches brought by him, proceeded to explain the military situation.

From the heights of Six-Fours to the west of the town, on which the Republican headquarters were situated, the whole scene of operations lay spread out in a panorama. France's greatest naval base consisted of two bays, the inner of which was almost landlocked by two jutting promontories. Below them, some three miles away, lay the western one, on which stood Fort Mulgrave. Two miles to the north-east of it, across the inner harbour, rose the spires of the city. Beyond them the ground sloped up to a long ridge—the *Montagne de Faron*—held by the Allies. To the south lay another great promontory, and to both south and north of it were scattered the tall ships of the Allied Fleet.

Vice-Admiral Lord Hood had appeared off Toulon in July with 21 ships of the line, to blockade the port and contain the 17 French warships that lay within it. Towards the end of August the Federalists in Toulon had placed their city under the protection of the Admiral. Shortly afterwards 17 Spanish ships of the line had appeared, followed by contingents of Neapolitans and Sardinians. All these naval forces had landed sailors and marines to reinforce the small French Royalist-Federalist garrison which had felt itself too weak to hold the port alone; but the Austrians had failed to fulfil their promise to send 5,000 regular troops from Italy.

On the other hand, after the fall of Lyons and the defeat of the Piedmontese in the Nice area, the Republic had been able to divert more and more troops to the investment of its recalcitrant naval base. Ollioules, five miles to the north-west, had been captured in mid-September, and the three-quarter circle about it closed to the line La Valette-La Garde in the north-east. Since then the Republicans had succeeded in advancing their lines to within a kilometre of Fort Mulgrave, their forces had increased to some 37,000 as opposed to a garrison of about 17,000 and, during a sally from the fort on the 30th of November, they had captured General O'Hara, who had commanded the few British troops that could be spared from Gibraltar.

The fort, and the promontory it covered, known as "Little Gibraltar", were, as General Dugommier pointed out to Roger, the key to the whole position, because if they could be captured the inner harbour could be closed, and the town compelled to surrender.

That night Roger met four of the Citizen Representatives who had now, as the result of the merging before Toulon of several Republican armies, congregated at Dugommier's headquarters. They were Fréron, a forceful terrorist, whose influence Carnot had been anxious he should counteract; Ricord, a nonentity; Augustin Robespierre, who would have been another nonentity but for the prestige of his elder brother Maximilien; and Salicetti, the deputy for Corsica. None of these people knew the first thing about war, or had the natural flair for it of a Dubois-Crancé or a Rewbell. After they had been talking for a while, the General drew Roger aside and said:

"You see how handicapped I am by all these men who think they know best, and to whose opinions I must accord a certain degree of respect. Citizen Carnot tells me that you were of great assistance to General Dumouriez; so I pray you make your own assessment of the situation as soon as you can, and see if you cannot support me in my plan to concentrate everything against the Little Gibraltar; otherwise I shall be forced into senseless and wasteful attacks from a dozen different directions."

Roger promised to take stock of things for himself, and next morning set out on a tour of the thirty-mile-long Republican perimeter. That night he slept at a second headquarters at La Valette, from which the forces to the east of the town were commanded. He found it very different from that in the west, and soon realized that this was due to the presence of Citizen Representative Barras. Here there was none of the spartan simplicity that he had met with on the previous night, but a dinner cooked by a *chef* of the *ancien régime* and a dozen pretty young ladies to help eat it.

Paul Barras was a *ci-devant* Count who had seen military service in India, and gone over early to the Revolution. His views were radical, but his tastes were still luxurious and women were his ruling passion. Nevertheless, he was a power to be reckoned with, as he had more intelligence and personality than all four of the other Representatives put together. Roger found him easy to get on with, but too wrapped up in his own pleasures to prosecute the siege with vigour.

On the night of the 8th, Roger was back with Dugommier, and on the 9th he accompanied him on a tour of inspection to the south-west, where the Republicans were driving their saps toward Fort Mulgrave. The greater part of the Republican artillery was also concentrated there and the General introduced him to its Commander. He was a short, thin, seedy-looking individual with a sharp, slightly-hooked nose and lank hair, whose dark eyes were his best features. He was about Roger's own age, and his name was Buonaparte. With those dark eyes of his flashing in his sallow face, he explained to them his reasons for the siting of each of his batteries, one of which he had pushed so close up to the fort that it was under a continuous fusillade. So many of his gunners had become casualties there that to overcome the reluctance of others to take their places he had christened it the "Battery of the Fearless", and now it was considered an honour to have served at it. That the expenditure of men was justified there could be no doubt, as from its forward position the battery could fire right into the fort, and was doing terrific execution.

When they had left him the General remarked, "That young man has been a godsend to us. At the taking of Ollioules in September our only capable artillery officer was killed, and this little Captain happened to come up from Aix, where he was kicking his heels in charge of the artillery park. We gave him Lieutenant-Colonel's rank, and ever since he has worked like a Trojan. We had less than a dozen cannon at that time, but he despatched people in all directions to collect pieces from the forts along the coast, found gunners from God knows where to man them, and animated his men with tireless ardour. He is never absent from his batteries, yet somehow finds time to organize his own supplies. He is having 5,000 gabions a day made at Marseilles, and at Ollioules has established his own shot foundry with eighty workers. Unfortunately, though, he is an incredibly self-opinionated man and extremely temperamental; so unless he is careful he will break himself by running counter to one of his superiors."

On the 11th a council of war was held, and Roger found himself in a position of some difficulty. He shared Dugommier's views entirely—that the capture of the Little Gibraltar would bring about the fall of the city, and should be given priority over all else; but as that was obviously contrary to British interests, he was most loath to lend his support to it. As it transpired, he had little option, for the General had already won over most of the others to his plan, and the fiery little Artillery Commander scathingly silenced the only murmurs of opposition. Although he was the junior officer present, he hammered the table with his clenched fist, and appeared ready to fight anyone who attempted to contradict him; so the matter was soon settled, and it was agreed that all the forces that could be collected from the other sectors should be concentrated for an all-out night assault on Fort Mulgrave on the 16th.

Roger had learned that Buonaparte was a Corsican; so as the thin figure in the threadbare uniform stalked away from the meeting he said to the Corsican deputy, Salicetti, "That young countryman of yours certainly knows his own mind; he should go far."

Salicetti gave him a doubtful look. "Perhaps; if he does not over-reach himself. He has ambition enough for ten and is a born intriguer, but at any time he may take one chance too many and come a cropper. Four times in the past three years he has gone to Corsica and remained there for long periods without leave, because he hoped to do better for himself in the Corsican National Guard than in the regular army. For the past year or more he should have been serving with his regiment in Northern France; so he is at least technically guilty of desertion. In normal times he would long since have been cashiered, but owing to the unsettled state of things his neglect of his proper duties has been overlooked. He has the fact of his being a good Jacobin to thank for that, and recently he was clever enough to work himself into the good books of the Convention by writing an anti-Federalist pamphlet called 'The Supper of Beaucaire'."

"I think I saw it," Roger remarked, "but I did not recall the name of its author. Was it not about five travellers who met at an inn? The soldier of the party, who I take it was supposed to be Buonaparte himself, argues the other four around to the view that patriotism must be placed before internal politics, and that everyone should support the Convention in the war against foreign enemies?"

"That is so. The Convention liked it so much that they ordered several thousand copies of it to be printed and distributed. If he keeps to those lines he will do well. Personally, I admire his forthrightness; but I fear he is likely to make many enemies."

Now that the plan of attack and its date was settled, Roger began to cudgel his wits for a way in which he could help his own countrymen to resist it. This was just the kind of occasion on which Dan would have been invaluable to him, as the bilingual ex-smuggler would have found no difficulty at all in slipping through the lines at night to convey a warning; but for Roger to do so himself was out of the question, as it was impossible for anyone in his position to disappear from headquarters for more than a few hours without his absence being noticed. After much thought he decided that he must allow himself to be captured; but how to do it without serious risk of being killed presented a knotty problem.

It was at Fort Mulgrave that nearly all the English forces had been concentrated; so next day he rode down there again and spent several hours studying its defences through a telescope. To the north of the Fort lay the village of La Seyne, and outside it was a small redoubt. To suggest that its capture before the general assault would facilitate the major action seemed plausible enough, and it did not appear to be strongly defended; so a surprise attack should secure it, at all events temporarily. *Représentants en mission* always went into battle with the armies to which they were attached, and frequently took command in local actions, so it would not be thought at all strange if he proposed to lead an attack on the redoubt himself. Some risk had to be run, but if he escaped injury in the first rush the rest should be easy. Under cover of darkness he could become separated from his men and allow himself to be captured. As a prisoner of importance, he would at once be taken before the senior British officer, and if he said he would talk only to Lord Hood they would send him aboard the Flagship. To the Admiral, in private, he was prepared to disclose his true identity, as a guarantee that he was telling the truth about the Revolutionaries' plans. It was possible that he might even see his father, as, when he had last heard of him, Rear-Admiral Brook had been serving in the Mediterranean.

There was, too, a special bonus to this plan, if only he could pull it off; for a Citizen Representant ranked as a Major-General, and he felt confident that Lord Hood would have no difficulty in arranging for him to be exchanged under a flag of truce for General O'Hara. This idea for getting back quickly to his own work and at the same time rescuing a British General from captivity greatly appealed to his sense of humour, and as he snapped his telescope shut he was grinning broadly.

That night the talk in the headquarters mess was all of Lyons, as a courier from that city had arrived that afternoon. From the 4th Fouché and Collot had been putting into practice their new idea for disposing of reactionaries in large batches, and on the first day they had liquidated sixty. As Roger had foreseen, it had proved a horrible business; only about fifteen had been killed by the discharge of the cannon, and half the remaining pairs had had legs or arms blown off, while the rest had suffered no injury. As the still living staggered about with corpses or wounded tied to their backs, the troops had been ordered to shoot them down, but several fusillades of musketry had failed to still the writhing of this screaming, tormented mass of humanity; so eventually the gendarmes had had to go in with their sabres and finish them off.

This horror had been repeated on the following days at the rate of 200 victims a day, until the corpses had become too numerous for trenches across the field of Brotteaux to hold them; so the bodies were now being stripped and thrown into the Rhône, with the idea that they would be carried down the river to Toulon, and show the inhabitants of that city what was in store for them. Citizens Fouché and Collot sent fraternal greetings to their colleagues with the army.

General Dugommier declared that he would permit no such barbarities in his command; but he was roughly taken to task by Citizen Representative Fréron, who declared that once Toulon had fallen the civil authorities would do as they thought proper, and he meant to see to it that not a single rebel was left alive.

Later in the evening Roger got the General on his own, and put to him the project of capturing the redoubt at La Seyne. Dugommier remembered the little fortification, but said that he would not like to give an opinion on the matter before viewing it again, so it was agreed that they should ride down to within half a mile of it on the following afternoon.

The younger Robespierre and several staff officers went with them on this small expedition, and the ubiquitous Buonaparte joined them for the actual reconnaissance. It was agreed by all that the capture of the redoubt previous to the main attack would aid the major operation, and that a company of infantry should be sufficient for the task; but the young Corsican pointed out that it would be a waste of effort to carry out the venture until a few hours before the main attack was launched, as if given time the enemy would counter-attack and retake the redoubt.

Much alarmed, Roger hastily argued that once captured it could be held; but Buonaparte replied that if the enemy counter-attacked heavily it could not. Roger said it could be reinforced, but at that the Corsican replied scathingly:

"Why do you not stick to your pen, Citizen Representative, and leave fighting to people who understand it? Do you not see that if one side plays that game the other may follow suit? Then we should either have to give the place up in the end, after losing a lot of our men to little purpose, or involve ourselves in a major action for it, which is the last thing we desire."

It was Roger's first clash with the future Emperor Napoleon, and it was not to be his last. On this occasion the Corsican came off best, as everyone else agreed with him; and it was decided that Roger should attack the redoubt at dusk on the 16th.

No arrangement could conceivably have been more prejudicial to the carrying out of his secret designs, and he was hard put to it to conceal his anger. It meant that, as he was to be deprived of the cover of darkness, it would be exceedingly difficult to let himself be captured without any of his men suspecting that he had played the traitor; that if he was captured, by the time he was taken before a senior officer it would be too late for the British to reinforce Fort Mulgrave from their ships; and that by having to carry out the attack while it was still light he would stand a much greater chance of being killed or wounded. So the project had become a highly dangerous enterprise by which nothing was to be gained; yet he could not possibly brand himself as a coward by backing out.

During the next three days he managed to behave as though he had not a care in the world, but inwardly he felt like a man who has challenged a far finer swordsman than himself to a duel *à l'outrance.* In vain he racked his brain for a way of passing advance information to the British of the impending assault-in-force, and of wriggling out of his own mess; but, short of making a bolt for it, he could think of nothing; and if he did that he would be finished as far as the Committee of Public Safety was concerned. As he was convinced that Toulon must fall within a few weeks, anyhow, he considered his own position in Revolutionary France too high a price to pay to give the city a short respite; so he saw no alternative to going through with the now highly-frightening affair he had planned. His only consolation was that if he could get himself captured it might give the garrison of Fort Mulgrave an hour's warning, and he would still be able to score off the Revolutionaries by having General O'Hara exchanged for himself.

On the afternoon of the 16th, as the December light was failing, his Citizen Colleagues and a number of officers escorted him as far as a group of trees from which the redoubt could be observed. A sap had been dug from it some way across open ground, and a company of Fusiliers were already waiting for him to take command of them. Buonaparte had, of course, appeared to watch the fun with the little crowd from headquarters. All of them shook Roger warmly by the hand and several of the civilians encouraged him with speeches about the honour of France and the glory of the Revolution.

He had intended to delay his start for as long as he could, in order to gain an increased degree of darkness, but the shabby, efficient, lean little Corsican kept shuffling his feet impatiently and saying it was time to go; so Roger had no option but to get his men together. After a few words with the officers, he signed to them to follow him, and led the way down into the trench.

Stooping, so as to keep his head below ground level, he sloshed his way through the muddy puddles until he reached the end of the sap. From there he could see the redoubt quite plainly. It was a small earthwork, about five feet high and fifty feet across, with two black cannon muzzles poking out of square ports. As he crawled over the edge of the trench he kept his eyes fixed on the redoubt for signs of sudden activity; but evidently the sentry was not doing his duty, as no sign of alarm was to be seen. With a beating heart Roger waited until most of his men were out of the trench. Then he stood up, but he did not draw his sword. He had no intention of having British blood on his conscience. Instead, he took off his feathered hat, waved it high in the air, gave a shout, and ran at the fort as fast as his long legs would carry him.

What happened after that he never remembered very clearly. A single musket-shot cracked like a whip in the chilly air. The redoubt became alive with flashes. Bullets whistled past his head. Someone near him screamed and fell. Before the first cannon belched fire and smoke he had scaled the turf rampart and jumped down on its far side. Next second, to his utter consternation, he heard one of its defenders shout something in Spanish. No sooner had his mind registered the fact that he had botched the whole affair, and could no longer hope to be captured by his own countrymen, than a huge Spanish gunner aimed a mighty swipe at him with a cannon ramrod. In vain he threw up his arm. The end of the five-foot-long pole descended full on his bare head. His knees gave under him and he slumped unconscious to the ground.

When he came to, he had no idea where he was. His head ached intolerably and he was lying on a straw palliasse with a rough blanket over him. Neither his eyes nor his brain would focus. After a time he faded into unconsciousness again. The second time he came to he knew that he was in semi-darkness and in a small, confined space. He could not make out the ceiling above his head, but it seemed to press down upon him. For a few terrifying moments he was seized with the idea that he had been buried alive. It was only by a great effort of will to reassure himself that he managed to raise his head. As he lifted it the pain struck him with a blinding ferocity and he fainted. When he came out of his faint he was conscious of an awful thirst, but he was too weak to call out, and lay there feebly passing his tongue round his dry mouth for what seemed a long time; then he dropped into an uneasy sleep.

He was woken by the sound of a terrific explosion. It was pitch dark now, but in part he had regained the use of his senses. He could feel a slight rolling motion and could smell a mixed odour of tar and bilge water. He knew then that he must be somewhere down in the bowels of a ship, but how he had got there his brain still refused to tell him. As he listened he could hear guns, another deafening explosion, and distant shouting; but the noise made his head ache afresh. It hurt still more when he tried to think; so he gave up the effort, and eventually dozed off.

When he awoke again there was enough light to see by, and

two men were standing beside him. One was feeling his pulse and after a moment gave him a drink of water, then one of them spoke to the other in Spanish. That unlocked the cells of Roger's brain and he muttered a question; but they would not let him talk, and, after giving him another drink, left him.

Now he remembered the attack on the redoubt and all that had led up to it. Grimly he realized that he was a prisoner in a Spanish man-o'-war. But his head still pained him badly and he was terribly weak from loss of blood; so he still could not concentrate for long, even on his wretched situation.

He had learnt a little Spanish from Isabella d'Aranda, and twenty-four hours later he was sufficiently recovered to put a few questions to his captors. It was the 21st of December; Fort Mulgrave had been stormed on the night of the 16th, and on the 17th the Allies had decided to abandon Toulon. He was in the Flagship of Admiral Langara, and they were on the way to Majorca.

Later he heard the story of the four days during most of which he had been unconscious. The fall of the Little Gibraltar had immediately been followed by Buonaparte advancing his batteries to the point of the promontory, from which they could bombard both the town and all ships passing the narrows. Short of stores and with few reliable troops at his disposal, Admiral Lord Hood had taken the only possible course, and ordered the Allied forces to withdraw to their ships. Fear of the vengeance of the Revolutionaries had caused a terrible panic in the city. As many as possible of the French Royalists had been taken off, but the crush of people on the wharfs, trying to escape in anything that would float, had been so great that hundreds of them had been forced into the harbour and drowned. At such short notice it had been found impossible to man and withdraw more than half the ships of the captured French fleet; so on the 19th wrecking parties had been sent in to scuttle or burn the remainder, and to destroy the naval stores in the dockyard. The two great explosions that Roger had heard had been the blowing up by the Spaniards of two French powder ships, the detonations of which had shaken the earth for miles around. Toulon, the last foothold of the Allies in France, was now once more in the hands of the Revolutionaries. Roger's only consolation was that he had escaped being compelled to witness Citizen Representative Fréron and his butchers exact their terrible vengeance.

On the 22nd of December the Flagship dropped anchor in the roads of Palma, and Roger was carried up on deck. It was crammed with Royalist refugees, crouching there haggard, listless and brooding in the pale winter sunshine. Suddenly a group of them came to life. They had caught sight of Roger's *tricolore* sash. With yells of hate, and murder in their eyes, they pressed towards him. For a moment he feared that he was about to be torn to pieces, but the Spanish soldiers used their muskets to drive the angry crowd back, and bore him safely aft under the poop into a big state cabin.

Several officers were there, among them one resplendent figure who Roger guessed must be Admiral Langara. They greeted him with chill civility, and he had no doubt at all that these Spanish aristocrats loathed everything he appeared to represent almost as much as did the French refugees out on deck; but for the Dons the laws of war were sacred, and demanded that they should treat him with the courtesy due to a high officer of an enemy Power. It was not the first time in the past few days that Roger thanked his stars he had been wearing the uniform of a Citizen Representative when captured, as he knew that otherwise he would most probably have been thrown into the hold and left there to die.

One of the Dons questioned him in French; but his examination was purely formal as, the Allies having given up Toulon, there was no useful information he could give them, even had he been willing. He was still very weak but now fully *compos mentis*, and had been trying to think of a way in which he could get himself handed over to the British; so he asked if there was an English officer in the port with whom he could speak.

The Spaniard replied with a shrug that he did not know, but that the prisoner could enquire of the Governor of the fortress to which he was being sent. Roger was then taken out and, half-deafened by the howls of execration from the refugees, lowered into a boat; an hour later he was helped into bed in a cell of the fortress that dominated the harbour.

That evening the Governor, a lean, sallow-faced gentleman named Don Miguel de Gamba, paid him a formal visit; and he too barely veiled under traditional Spanish politeness the repugnance that Roger's *tricolore* sash aroused in him. Roger knew that the Spaniards would never give up an important prisoner to their Allies, except for some very special reason; so unless he could find a way to communicate with a British Captain, his prospects were that he would remain a captive, perhaps for many months, until the Spaniards chose to exchange him for some officer of their own who had been taken prisoner by the French. So, direct application being useless, he told the Governor that he had an important personal message for Rear-Admiral Christopher Brook from his son, Roger, and wished to see a British naval officer in order to pass it on. Don Miguel said coldly that he would see what could be done, and left him.

Apart from his anxiety that he might be held indefinitely by the Spaniards, Roger was not uncomfortable. The cell was actually a fair-sized room with a barred window that gave a good view of the harbour. The food was quite passable and he was given a soldier-servant to wait on him. The wound in his head was mending nicely and by Christmas Day he was able to get up for the first time, but so far there had been no news of a British officer coming to see him; so he sent a request that the Governor would pay him another visit.

Twenty-four hours elapsed before his request was granted, and then the interview gave him little satisfaction. With true Spanish indolence, Don Miguel said that such matters could not be arranged in a hurry; but he had the decency to suggest that now Roger was on his feet again he might like to take the air on the battlements for an hour or two every morning.

Roger gladly availed himself of this privilege, although for the first few days he was not strong enough to mount the spiral stone staircase without an arm to lean on. Gradually he regained his strength, but as the days passed he became more and more worried by his situation. On several occasions British men-of-war had visited the harbour, to water and revictual; but, in spite of repeated requests, the Governor proved either unwilling or too lazy to put him in touch with an English Captain.

By the end of the first week in January, Roger came to the conclusion that, for some reason best known to himself, his captor had no intention of carrying out his request, and the thought depressed him terribly, as in his weak state all idea of escape was out of the question. He was extremely loath to commit anything about himself to paper; but had begun to contemplate writing a very guarded letter to Lord Hood, when another idea occurred to him, which he decided to try out first. Controlling his impatience as best he could, he waited until the British flag should again appear in the harbour. On the afternoon of the 10th of January, three ships of the line and a frigate dropped anchor in the roads.

Next morning he went up for his walk on the battlements as usual, and stood watching the ships until one of them sent off a boat. As it came nearer he felt a thrill of hope, for he could see that it was a smart white gig; the officer in the sternsheets must be a Captain, and with luck he might get a message directly to him. Thanking his gods that his father had taught him as a small boy how to semaphore, he threw up his arms and swiftly sent the signal, "Help—I am British—son of Chris Brook."

In an agony of suspense he stared at the boat, praying that one of its occupants would look in his direction. He had sent the signal three times before the coxswain caught sight of his flailing arms and drew the officer's attention to him. At that moment the sentry tapped him on the back and said gruffly in Spanish:

"What are you up to, Señor?"

Swinging round, Roger gave him a quick smile and replied, "Sending my love to a lady." Then, turning back, he sent his signal for the fourth time.

An acknowledgment came from the gig, which was now almost below him, and he heaved a sigh of relief. He felt sure that the abbreviation of his father's name from Christopher to Chris would prove a talisman to any British Naval Captain, and he was not disappointed. That afternoon he was taken down to the Governor's office, where, seated with the Spaniard, was the officer from the boat.

He was a delicate-looking man with a firm, thin-lipped mouth but a kindly look in his bright blue eyes and, as he soon showed, a quick, discreet mind. Instead of demanding to know, as Roger had feared he might, what a British Admiral's son was doing in a Spanish prison dressed as a French Citizen Representative, he introduced himself as Captain Joshua Lightfoot, and said in careful French:

"Monsieur, Admiral Lord Hood charged me, while in this port, to put a few questions to you; and His Excellency here has kindly agreed to let me interview you alone."

Don Miguel smiled, and, after all three of them had exchanged bows, left the room. When he had gone, Roger whispered his thanks to the Captain for his tactful intervention, then, in a low voice, told him how he came to be there. He had little difficulty in convincing his visitor that he was Rear-Admiral Brook's son, and learned with delight that his father was actually with the main Fleet blockading the French coast.

Captain Lightfoot said that he would be rejoining Lord Hood's flag in a few days' time, and would inform Roger's father of his position at the first opportunity. He added that the Dons were so dilatory in all matters of business that the prisoner might have to exercise considerable patience, but he had no doubt that in view of his special activities his transfer to British hands could be arranged without the disclosure of his identity.

Much comforted, Roger shook his rescuer warmly by the hand, and was shortly afterwards led back to his cell; but he had to exercise his patience for a further ten days before there were any developments. It was the 18th of January when another two British warships put in to Palma, and on the 20th Roger was again taken down to the Governor's office. A Lieutenant Jenkins was there, and Don Miguel informed Roger that on the previous evening arrangements had been made for him to be handed over to the British. Jenkins then gave him a portmanteau, and requested him in French to change into the civilian clothes it contained, in order to avoid the hostility of the Royalist refugees as they went down through the town. A little under an hour later Roger ran up the ladder of a British seventy-four, and to his joy found his father waiting on the quarter-deck to welcome him.

Christopher Brook was a bigger man than Roger. He had a full, brick-red face, slightly protruding blue eyes and a bluff, hearty manner. It was over two years since they had met, so they had a thousand things to tell each other, and it was a great reunion. The Admiral was not in his own ship, but declared it to be a most welcome excuse for snatching a short spell from the dreary winter blockade to have come down in the first vessel due to water at Majorca in order to arrange personally for Roger's transfer. They dined alone in the Captain's cabin, disposing of two bottles of Rioja and two of port while Roger told the long tale of his adventures. When at last he had finished, he said to his father:

"Now tell me, sir, how soon do you think Lord Hood can get me exchanged for a British officer, so that I can continue my work in France?"

The Admiral shook his head. "No, my boy, you're not fit to go back to that damned country yet awhile. That good fellow Lightfoot told me you looked like death warmed up, and the ten days since he saw you have done little to improve your appearance. You're due for leave, and this will be sick-leave at that. I'm sending you back to England."

With the rescue of the little King in mind, Roger protested that he still had a very important job to do in Paris; but his protest lacked real vigour. For nineteen months he had been living under a constant strain, which at times had been appalling, and he knew that his father was the last man to divert him from his duty without an adequate reason.

Ignoring his protest, his father went on firmly, "Our consort, the frigate *Audacious*, is sailing for home with despatches tomorrow, and you are going in her. As she goes up Channel, I'd like you to drop off at Lymington. You'll probably recall that after your mother died I installed Mrs. Hapgood as housekeeper; so you'll find Grove open and can stay there for a night or two on your way to London." The Admiral fumbled with his port glass, refilled it, blinked a little and continued:

"While watering ship from Syracuse last October, I happened on a Greek urn. Stone's a bit worn, of course, but there's something rather good about it. I thought it would look nice on your mother's grave. It's got a pattern of birds carved round its middle, and your mother was always fond of birds. I'll have it lifted from the hold tomorrow and transferred to *Audacious*. Glad if you'd see Banks, the stonemason, and have him erect it for me."

This request clinched the argument. Roger's sense of duty, his passion for Athénaïs and his desire to earn a huge reward that would make him independent for life all called him back to France; but for the time being he was mentally and physically exhausted, and beyond all things he yearned for a few months' peace and quiet with his dear Amanda in their home at Richmond. He nodded. "Indeed, sir, you're right that I need a spell, and I'll execute your commission with every care."

So, on the 21st of January, '94, Roger sailed in *Audacious* for Portsmouth. He was not a bad sailor, but far from a good one, and the winter passage in a frigate proved a gruelling experience. The confined quarters, the stench, the unappetizing food, and the unceasing motion of the ship, which at times increased to a violent plunge and roll, combined to make him thank his gods that he had resisted his father's wish that he should adopt the sea as a profession. He managed to weather the greater part of the voyage with a fair show of equanimity; but he suffered two bouts of appalling sea-sickness and was incredibly thankful when, after twenty days at sea, the frigate passed the Needles light and lowered a boat to take him in to Lymington.

Darkness still shrouded the Isle of Wight when the boat's crew were piped away, and the February dawn was only just breaking as they pulled in to the wharf. No one was yet about; so when the sailors had landed the crate containing the Greek urn, Roger gave them a cheery farewell and set off up the slight rise on his ten minutes' walk to his old home. In spite of the discomforts of the voyage he felt the better for it, and the chill air of the early morning stimulated his brain to a swift review of his situation.

His interests in France now seemed remote to him. He was more than ever convinced that, since Athénaïs had asked a price he could never pay, he was lucky to be so far removed from temptation. It was most unlikely that any harm would befall the little King, as it was to everybody's interest to keep him alive; so the golden prize for his rescue would continue to be attainable for many months to come. In the meantime, Dan would have banked the £4,000 with Droopy, and Amanda's fears about the legality of their marriage would have been set at rest by his letter. He did not think it likely that her resentment about Athénaïs's arrival at Passy would now be very difficult to overcome, and two nights hence he hoped to be with her at Richmond with all forgiven and forgotten. Then he would settle down to a good two months' rest, and become really strong again before returning to France on a new bid to rescue that now-horrible child from the Temple.

Striding up the avenue of lime trees to the east of the house, he reached the postern gate in the tall wall, but found it locked; so he walked round to the main entrance, then took a side path that wound through a shrubbery and served as a short cut to the front door. The path ended in a narrow archway cut in a thick yew hedge. As he reached the opening he stopped dead in his tracks.

The door was open, and a man and woman stood framed between the stone pillars of the Adams porch. It was still only half light, but the porch was barely fifty feet from where Roger was standing, and it was light enough for him to have seen at first glance that the man of the pair was not a servant. He was wearing a cloak and a high-crowned hat. The Admiral had said nothing about having lent the house to anyone, and it was Roger's wondering who could possibly be using it that had caused him to pull up.

As he watched, the man kissed the woman's hand, turned,

and with the jaunty step of a gallant who has passed a happy night with his mistress walked down the drive. Roger stepped softly backwards so that he should not be seen, then his eyes almost popped out of his head. The man was the Baron de Batz.

Roger's glance swivelled towards the woman, who was still standing in the open doorway. She had on only a chamber-robe, and her hair fell in curls about her shoulders. She blew a kiss after the retreating figure of the plump little Baron. Roger stared at her in fury and amazement. She was his "dear" Amanda.

CHAPTER XXV

HOME, SWEET (?) HOME

ROGER's fists clenched spasmodically and his teeth closed with a vicious snap. It was all he could do to restrain himself from striding after de Batz, boxing his ears and kicking him into the road; but for so long he had had to guard even his words for fear of his life, that it had become a habit with him to think twice before giving way to an impulse.

Any assault on the Baron must inevitably be followed by a duel. To have run him through would have afforded Roger great satisfaction, but the laws against duelling were now being enforced very strictly in England. If he killed his man he would be charged with murder, unless he fled abroad and remained there at least two years to give the matter time to blow over. No doubt he would meet de Batz again in due course on the Continent, and he could then spit this French turkey-cock on a yard of good Toledo steel without fear of legal repercussions.

But what of Amanda? Roger itched to stalk into the house, call her a faithless jade, and create hell's delight; but again he fought down the impulse. There would be tears and recriminations, then he would either have to forgive her or stalk out again. The servants must be getting up by this time; a row could not be carried on in whispers, and they would be certain to hear it. If his first act on returning after a long absence was to quarrel violently with his wife, and if de Batz had been visiting her frequently in the day-time, they would be bound to suspect its cause; then, whether he forgave Amanda or not, the scandal would be all over the town before nightfall. The only alternative was to swallow his rage and pretend to know nothing—for the moment anyhow. But that would mean getting into a bed still warm from the body of that plump Frog; and Roger decided that he would be damned first.

Suddenly it struck him that if he stood there much longer old Jim Button or one of the gardeners would be starting work and would probably run into him. Then, nothing could stop his return becoming generally known. If that happened he would be faced with having either to leave without explanation, and setting tongues wagging, or to play the part of the happy husband home from the wars, and allow Amanda to believe her infidelity to be undiscovered. Next second, he realized that he would be faced with the same alternatives if he allowed himself to be seen in the town; he was so well known there that he could not possibly hope to escape recognition if he went to the Angel Inn to wait for the London coach, and the same applied if he returned to the harbour in the hope of finding a salt barge due to leave that morning for Southampton.

Nevertheless he continued of the opinion that he would be damned rather than crawl into bed with Amanda within an hour of the Baron having played lover to her, and it added no little to his fury that the only alternative was to walk all the way to Lyndhurst.

Quickly, now his mind was made up, he tiptoed back down the path and out into the road, crossed it diagonally, climbed a stile giving on to Fairfield meadows, and set off at a swift pace to work his way round the town on to the London road. One small consolation was that he had no baggage which might have given away his arrival at the port. Since leaving Majorca he had acquired only a razor and a few oddments from ships' stores, and those he was already carrying in a small bundle. The crate containing the urn for his mother's grave was fortunately labelled with his father's name, and might have been dropped off from any homecoming naval vessel; the harbour people would find and deliver it, and later he could send written instructions about it.

It was nine miles to Lyndhurst, mainly across deserted heaths and the woodland glades of the New Forest; so his chances of a lift were poor, and he did not manage to get one until a farmer's gig overtook him a mile outside the town. He would have ridden sixty miles in a day and thought nothing of it, but he was not used to walking, and his eight-mile tramp had done Amanda's case no good at all.

He knew well enough that she could cite Athénaïs's arrival at Passy against him, but he now took the view that she had brought that entirely on herself. In the first place she should never have come to France with that meddlesome old fool, Lady Atkyns; in the second she should have left Passy when he had asked her to. Then she had gone off without giving him the option of standing by her, and gone without even leaving the address to which she was going; thus causing him endless trouble and anxiety. Lastly, it was in order to spare her feelings that he had sacrificed Athénaïs and himself. It was that beyond all else which made him seethe with anger. The thought of his wife having taken a lover in his own home town, and under his father's roof, while he had denied himself the embraces of a mistress who, for years, had aroused in him stronger emotions than had any other living woman, caused him to come near bursting a blood-vessel.

Owing to his having landed at Lymington so early, he managed to reach the cross-roads beyond Lyndhurst in time to catch the Poole coach, which set him down at the Swan With Two Necks in Lad Lane soon after seven in the evening. As it was just on two months since he had left France he was in no position to give Mr. Pitt anything but stale news; and in his present mood he did not feel that he could face even his good friend Droopy Ned. In fact, there was only one person in the world to whom he was prepared to admit he had been cuckolded, and that was his beloved Georgina. Each was an only child and, as neighbours for several years in their teens, they had been like brother and sister; then, on that now distant day when he had run away from home, she had given to him both her jewels and herself. Four years later, during one mad winter, they had been lovers; and they were friends to that high degree in which either would at any time have given his or her fortune or life for the other. He knew that if he fell in love or married a dozen times no woman could ever replace Georgina in his innermost heart; and he knew too that she felt the same way about him. In his present anger and misery she was the only person who could possibly bring him comfort and help him to straighten out his life.

He could only pray that she was not wintering abroad; but it seemed probable that, at this time of the year, she would be at her husband's country seat near Northampton. Having booked himself a room at the Swan, and ordered supper there, he sent a runner to the St. Ermins' town house in Berkeley Square to enquire her ladyship's whereabouts. At half-past eight the man returned to report that the Earl was abroad and his Countess was at White Knights Park.

Next morning Roger went early to his tailor and collected a trunkful of clothes that he always kept there; then at ten o'clock he caught a Manchester coach which dropped him off at Northampton at six that evening. There, he hired a post-chaise and at a little after seven it entered the mile-long drive. Ten minutes later he alighted at the broad central steps in the west front of the great grey stone mansion. An under-butler and two footmen ran out to take his things, and as he entered the lofty pillared hall, with its marble staircase, crystal chandelier, statuary, tapestries, bowls of hothouse flowers and two roaring wood fires, it struck him that he might be on a different planet from that of the squalor and misery in which he had been living for so long.

The sound of the chaise driving up had brought Georgina to a window, and now, surprised but delighted at his unexpected appearance, in a flurry of silk skirts, she came running into the hall to greet him. Her dark eyes shining, she kissed him fondly; then sent him upstairs and urged him to change his clothes swiftly so that she might hear his news the sooner.

When he came down he found to his relief that she had only a Mrs. Rafferty, who was a widowed aunt of her husband's, staying with her. As soon as he had been presented, they went in to supper; again he was strongly conscious of the contrast between the taverns in which he had taken most of his meals for so many months and this—the rich mahogany, the silver and cut-glass, the soft glow of the candles lighting Georgina's lovely face, the portraits of past St. Ermins looking down from the walls, and the silent servants who handed the food and wine.

While they ate, Roger pulled himself together sufficiently to tell the two ladies something of the terrible state of affairs in France; then, a moment after they had left him to his port, Georgina returned to collect a comfit box she had purposely forgotten. As she picked it up she whispered with a smile:

"We'll not be long in the drawing-room, but to preserve the proprieties I shall go up with Aunt Sarah. Give us ten minutes, then come to my boudoir."

In the drawing-room they spent barely half an hour, then Georgina yawned and took her aunt off to bed. Roger watched the clock until the ten minutes was up, put out the candles and went quietly upstairs.

Georgina was not in the boudoir when he reached it, but she came in from her bedroom a moment later. She had freed her raven hair from its pins and changed into a chamber-robe. She was a little over a year older than he, but did not look it. Her skin was flawless, her big black eyes moist and shining, her rich, full mouth a perfect setting for her fine white teeth. Her mother's hot gipsy blood, that had made her by nature wanton, gave her both her splendid colouring and her tremendous vitality; her father had contributed her good brain and ready wit. As Roger looked at her, he thought, not for the first time, that her very presence was as heady as drinking a great vintage wine. But as she looked at him, the smile faded from her lips, and she said softly:

"Roger, my sweet, what in the world has happened to you? Even your long sojourn in Revolutionary France, and your having been seriously wounded, can scarce be enough to have made you this sad-faced ghost of the man you used to be."

Side by side they sat down on a sofa. Then, staring into the glowing wood fire, he began with the morning in Rennes when Athénaïs had been brought before him as a prisoner, and told the story of his tangled love affairs.

Georgina was a good listener; she did not once interrupt, but let him unburden himself to the very end. When he had described how he had come on the Baron and Amanda he fell silent. After a moment, as she made no comment, he turned to look at her. To his surprise, her eyes were dancing with amusement, and, suddenly throwing herself back among her cushions, she gave way to a gale of laughter.

"I see no cause for mirth in this," he said acidly.

"Then . . ." she burbled, "then, dear man . . . you've lost your sense of humour as well as your looks."

He shrugged. "Were it a stage play, the fact that Amanda had *trompéd* me in the very place that Athénaïs wished me to *trompér* her would be an amusing twist. But since this has happened to myself, I think your laughter most unkind."

She stopped at once, and asked, "Well; what mean you to do?"

"I have had ample time to think matters over these past two days. Amanda showed her lack of faith in me by running away, and has since revenged herself by taking a lover in my father's house. In a small place like Lymington it is too much to hope that news of this intrigue of hers will not have got about. In fact, it is now plain to me that must have been her intention, and her choice of the scene of her adultery been deliberate——"

"Lud, Roger, 'the scene of her adultery' indeed! How pompous you are become. Had you and I a diamond apiece for the times we've committed the act, we'd be rich as nabobs. And you were not wont to use so ugly a word when you took your pleasure in my first husband's bed."

"Oh come; that was very different! We observed all possible

discretion, whereas Amanda has done the exact opposite. It is my father's wish that she should go down to Grove once in a while to see that all is well there; but it is the very last place to which she should have taken a lover."

"Since he left her at dawn, he cannot be living there."

"No, not in the house; but he must have a lodging near by, and no doubt dances attendance on her in the daytime. I am convinced that her intent was to make me the laughing-stock of the neighbourhood."

"Well, what mean you to do?"

"I shall send de Batz a challenge to meet me on the Continent, and divorce Amanda on his account."

For a moment Georgina did not reply. Her first loyalty was to Roger; but Amanda was also her friend, and she was greatly distressed that their marriage was in imminent danger of breaking up. No one knew better than herself how easily passion could temporarily blind one's judgment, and she was convinced that they were at bottom deeply attached to one another; so she was determined to do all she could to heal the breach. But she saw that with Roger in his present mood it would be worse than useless to take up the cudgels on Amanda's behalf; she would be able to do that far more effectively when she had heard from Amanda her version of this unhappy story. So she said:

"I well understand, m'dear, how incensed you must feel at the possibility of all your friends in South Hampshire being privy to Amanda's affair with the Baron; although 'tis not yet known that they are. Still, she certainly behaved like a fool in running away from you; and I cannot help but admire the audacity of this French woman. She must be mightily smitten with you to go to such lengths to take you from your wife, and 'tis a true enough old saying that all's fair in love and war. From all I recall of what you told me of her when you returned from France in '87, she seems greatly changed, though; I formed the impression that she was a beautiful but quite brainless little baggage."

He nodded. "Yes, apart from her looks, she has changed almost beyond recognition. Tragedy has given her great character and courage. She has developed into an extraordinarily fine and fascinating woman."

"After your divorce, do you intend to marry her?"

"No. It was the fact that neither of us could bring ourselves to change our religions that prevented us running away together seven years ago. That insurmountable barrier still makes marriage impossible."

"Then I pray you, Roger, take no steps to divorce Amanda for the moment. Matters may not be as bad as you think. You have both erred, and despite popular prejudice I believe you are just enough not to count that a greater crime in a woman than in a man. If she has indeed deliberately sullied your name, you would be right to put her from you, but should it prove otherwise you are so well suited to one another that you might later regret it if you took any hasty action now."

Without waiting for him to reply, she pointed to a bottle of champagne that was standing in an ice-bucket on a table against the wall, and added, "Now, m'dear, let's take a glass of wine, and talk of happier things."

Roger opened the bottle, and he was soon smiling again as they revived old memories. An hour went quickly by while they discussed their friends and the doings of the wicked world; then Georgina stretched and asked casually:

"Will you shortly be rejoining Athénaïs in France?"

He shook his head. "Not yet awhile. In view of Amanda's behaviour I'll bring Athénaïs to London and flaunt her openly if she wishes; but that must wait. This business has upset me greatly; besides, I'm devilish tired and not yet fully recovered from my wound, so should make but a poor lover. I need a little time to regain my serenity of mind and the sort of gaiety without which a love affair can so easily become only a sordid intrigue."

"My poor Roger." She took his hand and leaned a little towards him. "How badly you need comforting."

Without her saying more he knew that she was offering to let him sleep with her, and he would have given a lot to find solace in her generous arms; but after a moment he replied with an apparently casual question:

"How fares your marriage with the good Charles?"

She pouted. "Well enough; I still dote on him and have so far remained a faithful wife, if that is what you mean. But do not let that concern you. For me you have always been a man apart, and long ago I told you that you would never lack a bed wherever I might be."

His heart began to thump as he put an arm round her shoulders and whispered, "My sweet, I know it; and count it the greatest blessing God ever bestowed on me."

"To be truthful," she murmured, "I think it about time that I *trompéd* Charles; and although I would not normally regard spending a night with you as having taken a lover, 'twill serve most admirably to restore my *amour-propre*."

"Why so? Is he being flagrantly unfaithful to you?"

"I have no proof of it, and not even a suspicion who the woman may be; but I am convinced that he is having a serious *affaire* with someone."

"Has his ardour for you, then, cooled so greatly?"

"Nay; he is as attentive as any wife could wish, and a lusty enough bedfellow when we are together; but for near a year now he has taken to leaving me every few weeks, for sometimes as long as ten days at a stretch, on all sorts of trumped-up excuses that I know to be lies. What other explanation can there be, but that he is mad about some chit whom he is keeping somewhere in secret?"

Roger withdrew his arm, and smiled. "My sweet Georgina, I believe that you are thinking ill of Charles without the least warrant. Has he told you nothing of his work in France?"

Georgina's big eyes opened to their widest extent, as she exclaimed, "In France? I had not a notion that he'd been there since we were in Paris together three summers ago."

"Well, he has; I saw him myself in Brittany last June. He is one of a league of gallant Englishmen who go there in disguise to rescue some of these unhappy French Royalists from the guillotine. Naturally, such work is highly secret; but, no doubt, his reason for not telling you of it is because he does not wish you to worry, whenever he is away, over his having gone into danger."

"Oh, Roger, how truly marvellous! And how wicked of me to think the worst of him."

Roger leant forward and kissed her lightly on the cheek. "Now that you do know, I trust that you'll continue faithful to him."

"Indeed I will; but . . ." she turned her lovely face up to his, "but this makes no difference between us two. I am still yours if you need me."

He smiled down at her. "I never needed you more. That is the truth, and you know that I have never lied to you. But as long as things remain as they are between you and Charles, I'll not take advantage of your generosity."

They came to their feet together, and she put her arms round his neck. "Dear Roger! Dear, dear Roger! I would have let you love me gladly; but I value more this perfect expression of your tender regard for me. You are indeed the only man who I shall ever love with all my mind as well as all my heart."

"You speak for both of us, my sweet." He gave her a long kiss on the mouth. As they drew apart both of them were trembling, but with a smile they wished each other good night.

Although Roger remained on at White Knights Park, he did not again visit Georgina at night in her boudoir; and quite naturally they resumed their relations of the past three years as dear friends. On the fourth day of his stay, Charles returned, and it delighted Roger to see the warmth of affection between his host and hostess. He had a private word with Charles and persuaded him to tell Georgina the reason for his absences; after which, when Aunt Sarah was not about, all three of them frequently talked of the work of the League. Little more was said regarding Amanda; but Georgina had written to her, inviting her to come up and stay for a while towards the end of the month, and it became tacitly understood that Roger should not start divorce proceedings until Georgina had heard what Amanda had to say.

After ten days in such congenial company, surrounded by the comfort, elegance and happiness of which he had been deprived for so long, Roger felt a different man. He was still young enough to be swiftly resilient to ill health and misfortune, and Georgina's coddling of him seemed to have worked a miracle by the time he decided that he ought to attend to his affairs in London. Having settled on the 23rd of February for his departure, he asked Georgina on his last afternoon at White Knights to tell his fortune.

Recalling the gallows that she had once seen for both of them in the glass, she was loath to do so; but after some persuading she agreed, and they sat down at a small table holding hands, with a crystal goblet full of water between them. On this occasion her gipsy's mystic art seemed almost to have forsaken her. For a long time she could see nothing, then only choppy wavelets; but after a while she said:

"I see you in a boat . . . in a rowing-boat. There is a child with you . . . a boy, I think, but I cannot be certain. A woman, too, is in the scene. How prodigious strange! She seems to walk upon the water. The picture fades; 'tis gone." In vain they sat there for a further twenty minutes; the picture would not come again, nor would any other.

On arriving in London, he went straight to Arlington House;

but to his annoyance he found that Droopy was out of town. However, he was expected back in two days' time; so Roger, not wishing to go out to Richmond in case Amanda was there, took up the old bachelor quarters which were always kept available for him in his friend's suite.

He spent the evening at his Club. There was always good company to be found at White's, and it was another pleasant link with a happier past to become really merry once again with a few men friends who believed, as he did himself, in God, the King and England.

Next day he got up late, then went out to do some shopping. That was another joy after the dreary or bankrupt shops of Paris. Swinging his tall Malacca cane in one hand, and toying with his quizzing-glass in the other, he sauntered down Bond Street, delighting in the wealth of fine fabrics, porcelains, silverware, weapons and furs displayed to tempt the rich from all parts of the Island Kingdom. For the past twenty months he had had little time to devote to art; but his interest in it had not lessened, and he was examining a Fragonard in a picture dealers' when a soft voice addressed him in French:

"Is it not Monsieur le Chevalier de Breuc?"

Turning, he found himself looking into the lovely face of the Comtesse de Flahaut.

"Indeed, Madame," he smiled, sweeping off his sickle-shaped hat and flattening it over his heart, "and what a pleasure it is to see you in London."

"It is thanks to you, Monsieur, that I am here," she said seriously. "Had it not been for those passports which you obtained for Monsieur de Talleyrand and myself, both our heads would have fallen beneath the guillotine ere this."

He made an airy gesture. "Believe me, it was a happiness to render that small service. What of the dear Bishop; he is well, I trust?"

She made a pretty grimance. "Poor man, he is on his way to those barbarous United States. Your Government recently made a new law for the expulsion of undesirable aliens, as they are called; and, alas, it dubbed him one. So he had no alternative but to depart; and, I confess, for a time I was left quite desolate."

Her big blue eyes held Roger's, and after a moment she went on, "All we unfortunate French are now living in most straitened circumstances; but I have a tiny house in Chelsea. Should you care to visit me there, it would be a most pleasant relief to my loneliness."

Roger at once expressed himself as charmed, and suggested that he should wait upon her that very afternoon. Smilingly she agreed and gave him her card, then bobbed him a curtsy and turned away. Lifting his quizzing-glass in the manner of the exquisite he had once more become, he watched her with admiration as she walked down the street towards Piccadilly. Her tiny hat perched on a mass of golden curls was typically French, and the sway of her hips beneath her full skirts he found quite entrancing.

At four o'clock he presented himself at the little house in Chelsea, carrying a box of fondants as big as a tea-tray. Adèle de Flahaut received him most graciously, and again asserted that she owed her life to him. He enquired after her son, Charles, and learned that a generous nobleman had secured the boy a foundation at a good school in the country; then they settled down to talk.

About her own set of refugees she was most amusing. As they were all Liberals and had contributed to the Revolution of '89, they found themselves more detested by the Royalists, who had escaped to England before them, than if they had been *sans-culottes*; but what they lacked in numbers they made up for in wit. On innumerable occasions de Talleyrand and his brilliant circle had made the stiff-necked diehards of the *ancien régime* look a set of fools. They were all desperately hard up for money, but pooled what they had, and in the previous spring a number of them had shared a house called Juniper Hall, down in Surrey; Madame de Staël, Mathieu de Montmorency, Louis de Narbonne, Madame de la Châtre, Jaucourt, Lally-Tollendal and the Princess d'Henin had all been of the party. Fending for themselves had been a new experience, but they had all thoroughly enjoyed it, and their English neighbours had proved kindness personified.

There had, however, been one unfortunate *contretemps*. Near-by, there lived a Mrs. Phillips and her sister, Miss Fanny Burney. Attracted by the irrepressible gaiety of this little French colony, Miss Burney had become a daily visitor there; but one sad day some fool had opened her eyes to the fact that all the ladies at Juniper Hall were living in sin with the men, and so shocked had poor Miss Burney been that she could never bring herself to call there again.

At six o'clock, Roger declared that he was enjoying himself so much that he could not bear to leave, and tactfully begged permission to go round to a local hostelry to order some supper to be sent in. To this suggestion Adèle made no objection whatever; so an hour later they were disposing of four dozen oysters washed down by champagne, with a fine game pie and salad to follow.

By the time they were half-way through the second bottle they were laughing about his having first met her in her bath, and the ruthless way in which she had converted him into a *sans-culotte.* He had long since ceased to wonder how sufficient wit, charm and beauty to hold simultaneously two such brilliant men as de Talleyrand and Gouverneur Morris could be combined in one woman; and soon afterwards it became plain to him that she had a highly honourable desire to make him some recompense for having saved her life.

As she could afford only a daily woman to come in and do the rough work of the house, they were now alone there, and had no need to resort to any subterfuge. When she had duly rebuked him several times for kissing her, while provocatively opening her mouth for more, he told her that he would do something to her that neither of her lame lovers could do. Then, with a gay laugh, he picked her up, swung her, kicking and gurgling with mirth, over his shoulder, and carried her upstairs. In her bedroom a glowing fire was burning, and its warm light was just sufficient for him to appreciate the beauty of her figure when he had unlaced her corset and teased her with a hundred kisses into undressing before him.

When he let himself out of the house at six o'clock next morning, and set off westward with a jaunty step, he had had ample proof that his good friend, the wicked Bishop of Autun, was a veritable master of the art of love, for none other than a great master could have produced so apt a pupil as the fair Adèle.

On waking in his bed at Arlington House soon after midday, he took stock of his situation. In the past twenty months he had lived through hell. The only real relief he had known from dirt, squalor, horror, anxiety and fear had been during his two brief visits to England, and those halcyon weeks spent with Athénaïs at the Red Lobster. Georgina's stately home, with its ease, comfort and perfect service in beautifully furnished, lofty, well-proportioned rooms; the free talk with men of his own kidney over good wine at White's; the display of all the gracious amenities of life in the shops of Bond Street and Piccadilly; a night of sophisticated, carefree love-making with the charming Adèle—all these brought crowding in upon him a world the existence of which he had almost forgotten.

Why, he asked himself, should he go back to France at all? He was still drawn to Athénaïs; but it was now nearly seven months since he had lived with her, and in the interim he had seen her only three times during brief, unhappy interviews; so the memory of their joy together had become a little blurred. There was, too, the possibility that as he had tried her patience for so long she might refuse to take him back; far grimmer thought, she might have been caught at her dangerous work and by now be dead.

There remained the little King. Upon his rescue there still hung a fortune. It seemed madness to throw away the chance to earn enough to make one rich and secure for life. Yet real security lay here in London; not over there in Paris, constantly rubbing shoulders with a gang of ruthless cut-throats. Any day something might click in Fouché's memory, or Michonis, brought face to face with death, might talk. To return was to sit again upon a powder barrel with two lighted fuses of unknown length, either of which, at any time, might blow him sky-high.

One thought continued to worry him. He had given his solemn oath to Marie Antoinette that he would restore her son to her. The vow had been made in circumstances which had led him to suppose that he would be able to fulfil it, and the fact that she had since died had rendered fulfilment impossible. Yet he could not escape a feeling that the spirit, rather than the wording, of the oath still placed him under a moral obligation to do his utmost to rescue the boy. For some time he considered the matter as dispassionately as he could, and at length decided that such a view was stretching too long a bow; for even if he did succeed in freeing the little prisoner, it could now mean nothing to the poor Queen.

Having set his mind at rest on that, his final conclusion was that he would be mad to risk his life again in France. His bank balance must be over £5,000, which would keep him in comfort for a long time to come; and he could send a message by a member of the League, recalling Dan. He had served Mr. Pitt well with his reports; so he had every reason to expect from him another mission, to a country less dangerous than France, when he felt like going abroad again.

In the meantime it would soon be spring, and he had acquired a new mistress. He knew that he would never feel the passion for her that he had for Athénaïs; indeed, he was perfectly well aware that Adèle was a strumpet at heart, and had not suddenly fallen in love with him any more than he had with her, but that did not affect the fact that she was a beautiful and witty woman whom anyone might envy him. Her charming companionship would do a lot to fill the gap that Amanda had left in his life, although he would miss Amanda terribly—he knew that now. All the way from Majorca he had been looking forward to making up their quarrel and enjoying a good spell at home with her. But, after all, for seventeen months out of the past twenty they had been forced to live separate lives; so he would manage to get on without her. Whether he actually divorced her would largely depend on how bad a scandal she had created at Lymington; but Georgina would find out and could be depended on to tell him the full truth about that. Meanwhile no scruples on Amanda's account need prevent his openly living with Adèle in London.

Droopy Ned arrived home at seven o'clock, and the two friends settled themselves in his sitting-room with their usual delight at seeing each other. Roger had few secrets from Droopy, and, now that his own mind was more settled, he told him about Amanda. His lordship did not laugh, as Georgina had done; but at the implications of the affair he was as greatly distressed as she had been, and took the same view.

Peering at Roger with his shortsighted blue eyes, he said, " 'Tis a wretched business, but I beg you to do nothing in a hurry. Lymington has become a headquarters for the French *émigrés*, who use the port to keep in touch with the Royalists in La Vendée; so 'tis full of them and de Batz's presence there will not have been remarked upon by your neighbours, as it would have been had he taken lodgings to be near her in some small Midland town. You've no proof yet that she has brought disgrace upon your name, or ever had any intent to do so; and few couples that I know are better suited to one another. For a woman, divorce is a terrible disgrace, and you owe it to your past fondness for her to think most seriously before branding her with such a stigma."

Roger nodded. "Yes, I realize that, and have no wish to be unduly harsh; but if there is a scandal it will be entirely her fault; so even if I don't divorce her I doubt if I'll take her back to live with me. Meanwhile, as I have ample funds and have got me a pretty mistress overnight, I do not mean to return to France. Instead, I'm looking forward now to a gay time in London."

"You'll certainly not lack the means to buy her gewgaws," Droopy grinned. "The packet you sent over in October came safely to my hands, and your investments lying at Hoars must now be worth close on £6,000. But what of that man of yours; did you succeed in getting him out of prison?"

"Man!" Roger started forward. "You . . . you can't mean Dan Izzard?"

"Why, yes; who else? Your packet reached me by way of a member of the League. He told me they had been surprised one night when they were taking some refugees off from a beach near Boulogne. There was a fight with the National Guards and several on both sides were killed or injured. Our people were greatly outnumbered. They already had some women in the boat, and all would have been captured had they not pushed off when they did. Izzard was among the wounded and had to be abandoned, but he managed to throw your packet into the boat."

"God's death! Poor Dan in prison all this time, and I knowing nothing of it."

Droopy spread out his elegant hands with a helpless gesture. "I had believed you knew all this and would have long since acted on it. There was naught the League could do but send a message to you in Paris, and my informant told me that was already being done. It was assumed that with your influence you would have no great difficulty in securing Izzard's release."

"He left Paris in mid-November and I left there myself on the 27th; so there would scarce have been time for a message to reach me. Was he badly wounded?"

"That I do not know."

"What of my despatch to Mr. Pitt, and a letter I sent by him for Amanda?"

"There was but one packet, as far as I am aware, and neither were in that handed to me."

Roger groaned. Gone at a stroke were all his fine plans, made only that morning, for forgetting his troubles and having a gay time with Adèle in London. To leave Dan a prisoner in the hands of the Revolutionaries was unthinkable. He must return to France at the earliest possible moment.

The League could put him over there secretly; but they might not be able to do so for ten days or more, and would have to land him at some prearranged rendezvous, which might be in Brittany or even further down the coast. Unquestionably, the swiftest way to reach the scene of action was to be dropped off by some naval vessel which could be ordered to take him to a spot chosen by himself. That meant making a personal request to Mr. Pitt.

Until a combination of Georgina's gracious home, carefree London and the charming Adèle had caused Roger to think again, it had been his intention to take a two months' holiday, then return to France; so there had seemed no great urgency about reporting his presence in England to the Prime Minister. Now, he realized that if he did not mean to resume his work in Paris, he owed it to his master to tell him so without delay.

His future hung upon Mr. Pitt's goodwill, so he could not possibly afford to quarrel with him. With fresh dismay, he saw that he could hardly ask for special transport on his own affairs, and at the same time refuse to compile another report on the latest developments of the Revolution. Mr. Pitt would have a right to expect that of him. Moreover, he would have to go to Paris in any case. As a private individual he stood no better chance of getting Dan out of prison than an ordinary member of the League would have had; to procure his release he must get back his old position and authority. Alas for the dreams he had cherished only that afternoon!

Half an hour later he was at No. 10, Downing Street. There, he learned that the Prime Minister was at Walmer Castle and was not expected to return to London for some days. But Walmer was only a few miles from Dover; so little time would be lost by going there on the way to France. Roger at once decided to take the night mail down into Kent, then hurried back to Arlington Street.

Not knowing at what hour Droopy would be home, he had made no appointment with Adèle for that night; but he had arranged to call on her again the following afternoon. Now, he quickly scribbled a note, telling her that quite unexpectedly most urgent business necessitated his going abroad at once, and it was probable that he would be away for some time. He went on to say —although he did not really feel it—that the sweet sensibility he had found in her would prove a greater spur to hasten his return than any other he could imagine; and he added that, having no time to buy a trinket for her, he wished her to buy one for herself, so that she might have some trifle which would call him to mind while he was away.

This last was an excuse to send her some money, as she had made no secret of the fact that she was hard put to it to make ends meet. Droopy willingly agreed to act as his banker, and promised to see that the note was delivered by a safe hand, together with a nice little rouleau of twenty guineas.

As the hour was now getting late, they had time to sup only lightly off a lobster and a duck, and to consume only a single bottle of *Château Lafite*; so Droopy, much concerned that his friend should have to face a night journey on such an ill-lined stomach, insisted that Roger should take with him a bottle of Madeira to drink in the coach. The February night certainly justified this sensible precaution, for it was cold, windy and raining; the rich wine both warmed him and, by the time the coach rumbled through Sidcup, sent him off to sleep.

Next morning he hired a barouche to take him from Dover over to Walmer, where, right on the beach, stood the great round castle of which Mr. Pitt enjoyed the tenure by virtue of his office as Lord Warden of the Cinque Ports, and where, having taken a fancy to the place, he now lived, often for quite lengthy periods. It was eleven o'clock when Roger sent in his name, and, after a wait of about only ten minutes, he was led up to the battlements, where he found the Prime Minister, muffled in a greatcoat, taking the sea air.

To Roger's bow the tall, austere, autocratic Premier returned only a chilly nod, and said, "I have wondered on several occasions during the past few months what has become of you; but no doubt you have been too occupied chasing some young woman half round Europe to give any time to my affairs."

The reference was to certain deviations from the strict path of duty of which Roger had been guilty in the past, but it annoyed him that the Prime Minister should, apparently, not even have considered the possibility that his dangerous work might have landed him in prison or even in a grave; so he replied with some asperity:

"Nay, sir, you overrate my intelligence. This time I was fool enough to get myself half-killed and thrown into a Spanish jail, through an attempt to enable my Lord Hood to prolong the defence of Toulon."

A faint smile twitched the Prime Minister's thin lips. "You

ever had a ready answer, Mr. Brook. Let us go down into the warm and you shall tell me of it."

As they settled themselves in front of a roaring fire with a decanter of port between them, Roger asked when his master had received his last despatch, and learned that it was one he had sent early in October. That was extremely disturbing, for it meant that the one carried by Dan had not arrived; so it might have fallen into wrong hands. If so, a third and even more dangerous fuse had been lit beneath the powder barrel on which he must sit directly he set foot in France; but it was no time to have a fit of nerves about that now, and he proceeded to give an outline of his activities for the past four and a half months.

When he had finished, Mr. Pitt shook his head, and murmured: " 'Twas a sad pity that we had to abandon Toulon. We could have had no better sally port on the Mediterranean, and had the Austrians not failed us in their promise to send 5,000 men from Tuscany we might by this time have overrun the whole South of France."

Roger looked at him in amazement. "It surprises me, sir, that you should think so. I fear you greatly underrate the numbers and determination of our enemy."

"Oh come, they are but a rabble!" replied the Prime Minister airily. "The successes they have achieved so far are due only to the incompetence of our Allies' Commanders, and to unfortunate jealousies between their Governments. The Austrians failed to support the Prussians, as they should have done, upon the Rhine; then the Prussians in turn excused themselves from sending the 30,000 troops they had promised to Coburg, to aid him in his campaign in the Low Countries. We came to the rescue there by diverting the forces of His Highness of York from Holland to his assistance; but we cannot be everywhere, as we would wish, owing to the smallness of our army."

"Surely," said Roger, "we would do better, sir, were our forces concentrated in one place, rather than scattered about in ha'p'orths as they are at present?"

"Some people advise me so, Mr. Brook, but they fail to appreciate the many demands that policy makes upon us. As you will be aware, the Habsburgs have long cherished a project of exchanging the Austrian Netherlands for the Electorate of Bavaria. That would not suit our book at all, and our best way of preventing it is to help to secure them in their present Belgian possessions: hence it is vital that we should maintain forces to operate with them. A similar argument applies to the Dutch. Then there are the West Indies. At least, while at peace, I was able to ensure for us the command of the seas in the event of war; but when war came, not unnaturally, the monied interests of the city of London pressed me to use our sea power to seize the valuable islands in the West Indies that still belonged to France. That project is well under way, but it has taken a large percentage of our troops."

"Speaking as one who has seen the other side, sir, I can vouch for it that one brigade thrown into La Vendée last summer would have brought us nearer victory than will the capture of all the Sugar Islands that litter the Caribbean Sea."

"That was His Grace of Richmond's opinion, and he pressed me strongly to it; but we had not the troops to spare. At the outbreak of war we had only eighty-one battalions, and near half of them were on foreign service in India, the Indies and elsewhere. 'Twas for that reason that when war came I had to send the Brigade of Guards to Holland, as the only force readily available. However, we shall soon be in better trim, for this autumn I have raised eight new regiments."

Roger forbore to comment. Eight regiments! What could such an infinitesimal force do against the terrible concentration of power that Carnot's terrific energy was creating in Paris? He was mobilizing fourteen armies.

After a moment, the Prime Minister said, "The measure of my annoyance, Mr. Brook, at having heard nothing from you for these past four months is, by contrast, the measure of my appreciation of the reports you sent me before misfortune overtook you. I found them invaluable, and your predictions about future political happenings in Paris were almost invariably correct."

Roger bowed. "I am happy to hear that, sir, for I badly need a rest."

Mr. Pitt's eyebrows went up. "Indeed! But you are fully recovered from your wound, and it is now three months since you left Paris; I sincerely trust you have not come here to tell me that I may no longer count you as in my service?"

Mentally, Roger groaned. Matters were going just as he had feared, and he replied, "No, sir, I have in any case to return in order to procure the release of a friend; so I will willingly furnish you with another up-to-date report. But, that done, would you not consider allowing me a few months' leisure, then employing me elsewhere?"

The Prime Minister's glance was not unkind; but he was by nature hard on himself, and was similarly hard on others where the nation's business was concerned.

He shook his head. "With the years, Mr. Brook, you grow in my esteem, and you may count upon me to have a good care for your future; but for the present you are too valuable to me in Paris for me to think of giving you other employment. There is, too, a matter that we have spoken of several times before. I considered your efforts to rescue King Louis and his Queen most audacious, and deserving of better fortune. In view of the initiative and courage you displayed, I believe that if you set your mind to the task you might yet rescue the Dauphin. I confess that your reports about the change in the boy positively made me shudder; but, nonetheless, the possession of his person would still be of incalculable value to us."

Roger gave a wry smile. "I had not forgotten the matter, sir, and will make a new investigation of the prospects of getting him away." Then, as his last despatch had never arrived, he described the final efforts to rescue the Queen from the Conciergerie and the hideous misery in which the Convention had condemned her to drag out the last seven weeks of her life. When he had told how he managed to get a confessor to her, he added, "Her health having been so sadly undermined, she had been suffering from serious haemorrhages for some time. Wishing to go decently to her death, she asked the guards to withdraw while she put on a clean shift, but they would not; so she had no alternative but to strip with only the cook-girl, Rosalie, standing between them and her. That, sir, may give you some idea of the brutishness and malice of these Revolutionaries."

"Such barbarity sounds almost incredible," Mr. Pitt sighed, "and what you tell me of these massacres in Lyons makes me almost sick with horror. In time this terrible madness must burn itself out, but is there no way in which its end could be hastened?"

"Lacking half a dozen Charlotte Cordays, I see none, sir; unless . . . yes, unless it could be done by setting these fiends at one another's throats."

The Prime Minister gave Roger a sharp glance. "That idea has but this moment occurred to you; am I not right? But it is a good one; I beg you do anything that may be possible to that end."

For a time they talked about the war. Everything that Mr. Pitt said about it showed him to be lacking in military knowledge, muddled in his strategy and hopelessly unrealistic about the problems involved. As Roger already knew, the Prime Minister's genius lay in the arts of peace, and he was so aloof and certain of himself that he would listen to no one except the few intimates who thought as he did. He was a financial wizard, a skilful reformer and a brilliant diplomat; with Dundas and Grenville to assist him he had performed miracles, but not one of them knew the first thing about war. They were determined and courageous, and had more integrity than all the statesmen on the Continent put together; but they had not the least idea how to grapple with the hydra-headed monster that now menaced the established order in every country in Europe, or even an inkling of its frightful power. The three of them, with the backing of the King, now dominated the nation absolutely; and the only other Minister who, as Secretary of the Admiralty, might have influenced their decisions was Pitt's pompous, incompetent elder brother, Lord Chatham. For Britain it was a tragic situation and one far beyond Roger's powers to alter.

An hour later he left the castle, with his master's blessing and an order on the Admiral commanding at Dover to place a sloop at his disposal for special service. He was greatly depressed, both by what he had now learned for himself about the mismanagement of the war, and by his own future prospects. He was now fully committed again, and the thought of the lost despatch caused him acute anxiety. The information it contained covered such a wide range that a careful analysis of it must lead to his identification as its writer; so if it had reached either the Great Committee or that of the *Sûreté* he would receive short shrift on his arrival in Paris.

Dinner with some naval officers in Dover cheered him up a little, then in the small hours of the morning the sloop put to sea. All day she beat down-Channel, and a little before dawn on the 1st of March he was landed from a boat outside Dieppe.

Shuddering, he dipped himself fully dressed in the icy surf, in order to give colour to a story that he had swum ashore; then he ran along the beach to warm himself up, but his teeth were chattering as he walked through the streets of the town to the Hôtel de Ville. There he announced himself as a Commissioner of the Commune of Paris, and the Mayor hastened out to greet him with oily servility. He told the official that he had been taken prisoner at Toulon, but had managed to make his escape from a ship that in the darkness had come close in to the French coast while carrying him to England. Then he demanded a hot bath, fresh clothes, and facilities for getting to Paris as soon as possible.

Everything was provided for him without demur, and by ten o'clock he was on his way. He had chosen to land near Dieppe as it offered the shortest overland journey to the capital; but, even so, the frightful state of the roads and the wretched weather made the going infuriatingly slow, so he did not reach Paris until four o'clock the following afternoon.

He was greatly tempted to find out if all was well with Athénaïs, but had decided that he must not bring suspicion on her or the Blanchards by going to *La Belle Étoile* as long as there was a possibility that he might shortly be under arrest. He would also have liked to have a talk with Citizen Oysé and learnt something of the state of things in Paris, before walking into the lions' den; but he knew that to do so was only to put off the dread interview which he must nerve himself to face. No minor official would know anything about the lost despatch. If it had been found and filed against him as a death warrant, only the members of the two Committees and a few of their intimates would be aware of the fact. To make certain, he must gamble his neck against the full restoration of his powers as a Commissioner and the ability to procure Dan's release.

From the coach station he walked slowly to the offices of the *Comité*. As it was Carnot who had sent him on his mission he should, properly, have reported to the General; but, if he was listed as a traitor, whichever member of the *Comité* he reported to would order his arrest. In the pocket of his greatcoat he was carrying a small, double-barrelled pistol, and if he were arrested he meant to use it on whoever gave the order. To assassinate Carnot would be to strike a valuable blow for the Allies, but he was not an evil man; there were others who deserved to die infinitely more, and whose deaths were much more likely to prove a serious check to the Revolution.

Roger's mouth was a little dry, and the palms of his hands were sweating, as he smiled at the clerk who enquired his business and boldly asked for Citizen Robespierre.

CHAPTER XXVI

THE GREAT TERROR

THE half hour that followed was for Roger the longest he had ever spent in his life. There was no clock in the dreary little waiting-room, and his dip in the surf off Dieppe had stopped his watch; so he had no means of measuring time. He dared not make any protest at being kept waiting, as the little lawyer from Arras had become as self-important as an Emperor, and, if all was still well, it would be crazy to antagonize him by an apparent lack of respect.

For four years Roger had watched his shifty, furtive, squirming, wriggling rise to power; so he had no illusions about him. Maximilien Robespierre was as slimy as a toad, as suspicious as a weasel, as dangerous as a tiger and as vain as a peacock. Now he had reached the top he was obsessed with fear; he was hag-ridden by the thought that just as he had sent the King, the Monarchists, the Moderates and the Girondins to the guillotine, so, if he relaxed for one moment, some group of enemies would rise up and fling him into the tumbrel. Constantly on the alert to protect his life, he watched for the least sign among colleagues and subordinates that might indicate hidden animosity, or resentment at the airs he could not refrain from giving himself; then, without warning, as soon as a suitable opportunity offered, he struck down those whom he suspected. Even the most powerful of his associates now realized the danger they ran if they failed to fawn on him; so Roger knew that even if he was kept there all night, he must not show impatience.

At a guess, he would have said that he had been sitting there for two hours, instead of thirty minutes, when he was at last summoned to the presence. Passing his tongue round his dry mouth, he straightened himself and followed the clerk who had been sent to fetch him. A moment later he was looking again into that wary, cat-like face with the broad, receding forehead and tip-tilted nose. The "Incorruptible" was today dressed in a suit of striped blue and white silk; not a hair of his flat head was out of place and his goffered frills were irreproachable. His nervous twitch seemed worse than ever, but he received Roger with cautious affability.

Encouraged by this reception, Roger explained about his having been taken prisoner and his recent escape. The green eyes regarded him quizzically and the thin mouth continued to smile; then the feline terrorist began to talk about Toulon, and Roger formed the horrifying impression that he was being played with as a cat plays with a mouse. Robespierre's younger brother, Augustin, had been one of the Citizen Representatives who had witnessed the attack on the redoubt, and, it transpired, had described Roger's gallantry in leading that first charge in the operation which had brought about the fall of the port.

Later that evening, apparently a frightful storm had arisen, so that the main attack had had to be launched in torrents of rain and a tearing wind. Whole companies had gone astray in the darkness; Colonel Buonaparte, who since the writings of his pamphlet Robespierre considered one of his young protégés, had had his horse shot under him; Victor, later to be one of Napoleon's Marshals, had led a picked column of 2,000 against Fort Mulgrave, and had only just managed to break through its defences. The confusion and carnage had been terrible, and the dead so many that friends and foes had had to be shovelled willy-nilly into common graves. Several survivors of the attack on the redoubt had seen Roger struck down by the Spanish gunner before they had been driven off. They had had to re-form and attack again later in darkness to achieve its capture. As the discovery of Roger's body had not been reported, it had been assumed that a coating of mud and blood had rendered his sash unrecognizable, and that the prisoners who dug the graves had pushed him into one of them.

On tenterhooks, Roger listened to all this, wondering with acute apprehension what was to come later. For a while he humbly accepted a few compliments that were slightly barbed with malice, their implication being that bravery in the service of the Republic was to be commended, but not quite so highly as were the brains that directed the course of the Revolution. Then came a dissertation upon Robespierre's own devotion to duty, his burdens, his sacrifices, his inflexible determination to maintain the pure principles which had animated Cato and Brutus, and the interesting fact that he was the one and only man who really understood the French people and the form of government most suited to them.

Doubtfully at first, but with increasing certainty, Roger became aware that he was not suspect. This callous, conceited little fiend knew nothing of the lost despatch; Fouché had not remembered; Michonis had not talked. For the time being he was still safe. Even so, not until he had actually closed the door of the office behind him did his brain really register the fact that, now, he had only to say to his old associates, "I have seen Citizen Robespierre, who knows the reason for my long absence, and was good enough to remark that I have deserved well of the nation," for all the power and prestige that he had formerly enjoyed to be restored to him.

With an assurance he had been very far from feeling an hour earlier, he asked another clerk to take his name in to Citizen Carnot. Ten minutes later the crooked-nose General rose from his desk, clasped him by the hand and greeted him effusively. He, too, knew all about the opening phase of the attack on the Little Gibraltar. With cynical amusement Roger learned that his leading the assault waving his feathered hat instead of a sword, because he did not wish to injure a fellow countryman, had been taken by the French as an action of the greatest gallantry. Carnot assured him that he was a hero and that his name would long be honoured in the Republican Army.

After they had talked for a while of his imprisonment and escape, Roger said, "Having been away from Paris for so long, I am anxious now to remain here for some time in order to re-assume full control over my Section; but before settling to that there is one mission of short duration that I should like to carry out for you."

"Please tell me of it," Carnot replied with quick interest.

"It concerns Boulogne, Citizen General. While exercising on the deck of the frigate which brought me round from the Mediterranean, I overheard some officers talking. You will be aware that the English have never fully reconciled themselves to the loss of Calais. These officers were discussing the possibility of its recapture. They considered that a direct assault upon the port would prove most costly and would probably fail; but it was suggested that if they could seize Boulogne, which is less well fortified, it might then be possible to capture Calais from the landward side. Mayhap this was mere speculation, but, as a precautionary measure, I feel that the Boulogne defences should be inspected and, if necessary, strengthened."

Carnot nodded. "You are right, Citizen Commissioner, and I thank you for your zeal. If you will call here tomorrow, I will have particulars of the Boulogne garrison ready for you, and an authorization to order such measures there as you think requisite."

A few minutes later Roger left the offices of the *Comité* with a great load off his shoulders, and well pleased at the success of his stratagem for getting swiftly to Boulogne. With quick firm steps he made his way through the spring dusk to *La Belle Étoile*. There, he learnt that Mère Blanchard was in bed with severe bronchitis, and that Maître Blanchard and Athénaïs were both out. Greatly relieved to learn that no ill fortune had overtaken Athénaïs in his absence, he decided to go up and wait for her in her room.

Instinctively, as he waited there, he began to examine the few simple possessions with which she had adorned it, and some clothes that she had left lying about. Her things called up a host of sentimental memories, and now that his mind was temporarily free of fear he was seized with unhappy misgivings about her possible reception of him. He had no intention of telling her about Amanda's infidelity, but meant to make it plain that, if she was willing to overlook the four months' unhappiness that his priggishness had caused her, he was prepared to do everything in his power to make amends. But would that belated concession prove enough, or would she by this time have hardened her heart against him beyond his power to melt it?

He had had little proper sleep during the past few days, and his anxiety about the reception he might meet with in Paris had taken a lot out of him; so, having looked round the room, he lay down on the bed to rest. The shadows lengthened; it was almost dark when he heard a light footfall on the landing.

As he sat up, Athénaïs opened the door; the light was still sufficient for her to see his silhouette outlined against the window. For a second she remained, as though frozen, in the doorway. Her left hand flew to her mouth to stifle a scream; with her right she swiftly crossed herself.

"I am no ghost!" he exclaimed, standing up. "Athénaïs, be not frightened. It is I, Rojé."

With a little whimper of fear merging with joy, she stumbled forward. Next moment he caught her in his arms, and she was murmuring:

"This can't be true! They told me you were dead. Oh, blessed

Virgin, I have not prayed to you in vain!" Then her voice dissolved into a passion of weeping, and Roger held her tightly to him.

It was several moments before she could again speak coherently, and even then it was only to mutter endearments, while covering his face with feverish kisses.

Greatly moved, he picked her up and laid her on the bed, then knelt down beside it and, clasping her two hands in his, said in a hoarse whisper, "Athénaïs, I realize now that I have behaved like a fool, and have caused you much distress through my ill-considered notions of chivalrous behaviour. I beg you to forgive me, for I am willing to make all possible reparation. I am told that Dan is in prison in the neighbourhood of Boulogne. My first duty is to free him. But the moment that is done, I will, if you wish, take you to Bath or London."

She turned over towards him and threw an arm round his neck. "*Chéri*, think no more of that. When I suggested our crossing to Lymington for two weeks or so, it was but to test the depths of your feeling for me. Had you agreed I would never have pressed you to it. Your work and mine lies here. Later, if we are spared and you wish to take me with you to England, that would be different; but I ask no promise for the future, only that we should waste no more of our lives apart in the present."

Brought face to face with Athénaïs's passion for him, Roger felt ashamed now that he should ever have contemplated remaining in London, and, his cheek pressed to hers, he murmured, "You are too generous to me."

"Nay," she smiled, "it is that I have learnt my lesson. It was I who, out of pride, erected a barrier to our reunion some days before you left for Toulon. When I believed you dead it seemed like a judgment upon me that I should have deprived myself of the happy memories I might have had of our last hours together. Now that the Holy Virgin has restored you to me, no act of mine shall ever again come between us."

As she spoke she drew him up on to the bed beside her. For a long time they lay there, tightly embraced, moving only to caress one another gently and speaking only in occasional whispers. The night lay before them and they both knew that in due course renewed passion would shake them to the roots of their beings, but for a while they were content to savour the profound bliss of lying almost still, with the knowledge that neither death nor the shadow of any third person came between them any longer.

It was now quite dark, and nearly two hours must have elapsed since Athénaïs's return when a soft knock came on the door.

"Who is it?" she called, quickly sitting up.

"It is Candalous," came a man's voice in reply. "Not having seen you at supper, *Citoyenne*, I feared you might be ill; I wondered if you would like me to bring you up something to eat on a tray."

"No!" Athénaïs called back. "Thank you; but I am quite well, and require nothing."

"Who was that?" Roger asked, as the man's footsteps retreated.

"Pierre Candalous." Athénaïs's voice held a faint note of distaste. "He is an ex-schoolmaster and one of the deputies for Mayenne. Some three weeks ago he came to live here, and he occupies the room on the far side of the landing."

"Mayenne! Why, that Department borders on Ille et Vilaine, in which Rennes and Bécherel are situated! I pray God there is no likelihood of his recognizing you?"

Athénaïs shrugged. " 'Tis most improbable that we should have met before the Revolution, and had we done so more recently one of us would have remembered it ere this. Yet on another score he has caused me some disquiet. Since the report of your death reached Paris towards the end of December, I have been looked on here as a widow, and Citizen Candalous has made no secret of his desire to console me."

"Damn his impudence!" exclaimed Roger. "Should he knock on your door again, kindly tell him that do I catch him at it I will give him a caning he will long remember."

"Oh, Rojé," she laughed, "what a child you are! I am well capable of looking after myself, and your arm would grow prodigious tired did you give a caning to every man who casts sheep's eyes at me."

He kissed her. "Yes, I am a fool; seeing your beauty, how could it be otherwise? Still, while living on your own, to have an unwelcome admirer pressing his attentions from across the landing may well prove annoying for you: so, with your permission, I will move in here."

"Rojé, that would be heavenly! But I thought your position compelled you to live in the Granvilliers Section?"

"To retain a room there will be sufficient for official purposes. Citizen Candalous's designs upon you apart, having obtained your forgiveness, I could now no longer bear to be separated from you."

"He has reminded us of one thing. We have not supped, and after your long journey you must be monstrous hungry."

Again he pulled her to him. "Your kisses had driven all thought of food from my mind, but I should have remembered that you might be hungry. In any case, I owe it to good Maître Blanchard to shake him by the hand and let him know that I mean to take up my quarters here. So one more kiss, then we'll go down."

The residents and regulars of the hostelry had all finished their evening meal, but Maître Blanchard took their order himself and fetched up a special bottle of Burgundy for them. He was overjoyed to see Roger alive, and, when they had finished supper, insisted that they should join him in his parlour for a glass of his *Vieux Calvados*, where they received his formal compliments on their reunion and talked with him for a while. Madame Blanchard was better, he told them, and would be delighted to hear that she was to have them both under her roof.

At eleven o'clock they went hand in hand upstairs to bed, both a little awed by the thought of the magical change wrought in their situations by a divine Providence since they had awoken that morning. Lonely, bitter and depressed, Athénaïs had risen to face another day, believing him to be dead; while he, in the discomfort of the coach, had roused up to wonder grimly if he would survive for more than a few days after reporting himself to the *Comité*, and, if he did, whether he would then find that she had either been caught and guillotined, or was now determined never to forgive him. She could still hardly credit that she was not living in a dream, and, every few moments, clenched his fingers hard between her own in a new endeavour to assure herself of his reality. He looked deep into her starry eyes, now lit by the moonlight; and, knowing as he did that Paris had become more than ever a city of dreariness and terror, he still could not understand how the joys and security of London, or the easy conquest of Adèle, had tempted him to remain away from her for a single hour longer than he could help.

Next morning he bought himself a new uniform, feathered hat and sash, then repaired to the Hôtel de Ville. His fellow Commissioners of the Commune were amazed to see him; but a number of them gave him a hearty welcome, and, on learning the particulars of his escape, congratulated him upon it. It was no more than he had expected from Goret, Daujon, Oysé and several others whom he knew to be decent fellows at heart, but he was somewhat surprised when Hébert and Chaumette, the two terrorists who dominated the Commune and with whom he had never been at all intimate, hurried up to shake him by the hand.

There proved to be no more trouble about his resuming his seat than if he had left only the previous day, as no general election of the Paris Municipality had been held during his absence, and in the event of the death of a member it was not the practice to hold a by-election. The same principle was followed in the Convention, to which in September '92 750 members had been elected. Since then, owing to death, imprisonment, proscription and fear, attendance there, even on special occasions, had fallen to less than 250; but the *Comité* had this rump so well in hand that it would never have agreed to any measure for the replacement of members who had fallen by the wayside, and the same ideas governed the policy of Hébert and his friends with regard to the Commune.

Early in the afternoon Roger accompanied Oysé back to the Cushion and Keys. He had a long talk there with the shrewd, dark little Provençal on the affairs of the Section, and on political developments in Paris during his three months' absence. Afterwards, he no longer wondered why both Robespierre and the two principal officials of the Commune should have received him so affably. Unknown to the general public, a desperate three-cornered fight for power was now taking place, and each faction was bidding for the support of every man in Paris who had any influence or personality. The leaders of these factions were Danton, Hébert and Robespierre.

Danton's return from his prolonged honeymoon with his seventeen-year-old bride, late in the previous autumn, had shortly been followed by the triumph of the Revolutionary armies on all fronts. Therefore, with the coming of the New Year, he had urged that as the Revolution was no longer in danger it was unnecessary to continue to intimidate the nation by terror, and that a greater degree of support for the Central Government could be obtained by granting amnesties in the revolted districts, by reducing the powers of the Revolutionary Tribunals, and by restoring the security of property to its owners.

Hébert was directly opposed to this policy of clemency. He was a pervert and sadist by nature, and his paper, *Le Père Duchesne*, pandered to the basest instincts of the *sans-culottes*. It was on their shoulders that he had risen to power, and to remain there it was essential that he should protect the licence they now enjoyed all over France to plunder, desecrate and massacre. He knew that if Danton had his way law and order would soon be restored, socialism would be substituted for communism, and he and his associates would be in grave danger of being sent to the guillotine on account of the excesses they had sponsored.

Robespierre stood half-way between them, swinging like the pendulum of a clock, first to one side, then to the other. He was completely ruthless, utterly indifferent to human misery, and governed only by a determination not to be caught on the losing side. He was not religious, but was strongly superstitious, and was therefore opposed to the outright atheism of the Hébertists; he also feared that if he lost Danton's support these ultra-terrorists of the Commune might overthrow the *Comité* and himself. On the other hand, his ice-cold nature kept him immune from all fleshly lusts. He lived very simply, and used women only to feed his vanity, as by occasionally having a pretty prisoner brought to him for the pleasure of witnessing her tears and pleas for mercy before sending her to die; so his own inhibitions provoked in him a jealous hatred of the Dantonists, with their wholesale plundering for enjoyment's sake and full-blooded debaucheries. Yet he feared them, too, for he knew how strongly they resented his strictures on their venality, and, if he sided with them, they might turn upon him, the "Incorruptible", once they had overcome the Hébertists, and use the excuse of one of his many treacheries to rid themselves of him.

After the fall of the Monarchy, the government of the country had become vested in the National Convention; but the Commune of Paris, dominated by Hébert, had consistently terrorized it and frequently usurped its powers. It was to protect the national authority from the weakness it displayed under these attacks that Danton had concentrated the strength of the Convention in the first Committee of Public Safety. For a time the Commune had lost ground; but, on the reconstruction of the Committee, Robespierre had forced Danton off it and had shortly afterwards eliminated his influence in it altogether, although only at the price of replacing Danton's remaining friends on the Committee by the two Hébertists, Collot d'Herbois and Billaud-Varennes.

Robespierre had then realized that the price he had paid to get rid of Danton had been too high; so he had re-allied himself with his old colleague in an attack on the Hébertists. Danton had pushed a measure through the Convention placing all local authorities under the control of the Committee, thus seriously curtailing the powers of the Commune. Their next step had been to encourage Danton's principal lieutenant, Camille Desmoulins, to attack the extremists. With their approval the famous journalist had begun the publication of a new paper called the *Vieux Cordelier*, in which he had denounced the Tribunals as having become mere organs of butchery that disgraced the Revolution. His appeals for a restoration of justice and mercy had met with wide approval, but had also aroused a storm of menaces from the Commune. A few of the minor Hébertists had been arrested, then Robespierre had become too frightened to go any further. Collot, fresh from the massacres in Lyons, had at that juncture returned to Paris, and his influence had proved decisive. Robespierre had agreed to a continuation of the Terror, and publicly recanted in the Jacobin Club by apologizing for his "weakness" in approving Desmoulins's pleas for moderation.

Yet the two warring factions still continued to be fairly evenly matched, as Collot and Billaud had recently tended to draw away from Hébert, not from any lessening in their appetite for terror, but because they wished to see all power concentrated in the hands of the Committee, of which they were members. So the Committee now formed a solid *bloc* behind Robespierre; frightened, but alert, dangerous, and terribly aware that to preserve itself it might soon be compelled to give battle to one or both of these powerful groups that regarded it with equal hate, distrust and envy.

Roger listened to all this with great interest and carefully-concealed pleasure. It seemed that just such a situation was developing as he had envisaged when suggesting to Mr. Pitt that an end to anarchy in France might be hastened if the terrorists could be induced to cut one another's throats.

Had the choice lain with him, he would have selected Robespierre as the first victim of this internecine strife, then left the others to fight it out between themselves until only a rump of the Dantonists was left, with his old friend, the hotheaded but honest Camille Desmoulins, to restore order. But he did not think things would go that way. The cold, calculating ruthlessness, which made Robespierre the most evil of them all, would protect him from both the excitable, venomous attacks of the snake-like Hébert and the thunderous charges of the bull-like Danton.

Between the prospects of the last two there seemed little to choose. Although Danton had lost much of his former power, he was still a tremendous figure in the eyes of the nation. Many of the early terrorists, men such as Fabre d'Églantine, Chabot and Philippeaux, as well as Desmoulins, still adhered to him; and obviously every decent person in France must now pin their hopes upon the triumph of his Party. But, unfortunately, decent people were like blades of grass, innumerable but voiceless. Hébert controlled the Commune, and with it the *sans-culottes*—that awful raucous monster that screamed incessantly for blood and death, and was capable of overawing a thousand times its own numbers.

On leaving Oysé, Roger went to the office of the *Comité* and collected his authority as Citizen Representative *en mission* to Boulogne; then he returned to *La Belle Étoile*. All through the evening and far into the night he and Athénaïs talked of their doings during the months they had been separated, and endeavoured to make up for them a little by the fervour of their caresses. She was terribly distressed at having to lose him again so soon, but would have been the last to suggest that he should postpone his enquiries about their good friend Dan. He was, too, able to assure her that he was not going into any danger, and promised to be back in Paris within a week. In the morning they took a passionate farewell of each other, and by nine o'clock he was on the road north with an escort of Hussars clattering behind him.

At midday on the 6th he entered Boulogne, and, going straight to the *Mairie*, presented his papers. The local "patriots" received him with all the nervous servility to which he had long been accustomed. Coldly acknowledging their protests of loyalty to the Convention, he sent at once for the Commandant of the garrison and the chief turnkey of the prison. With the first he arranged a full inspection for the following day; to the second, he said:

"You either have, or had, in your keeping a Citizen Izzard, who was taken in an affray with some English on a beach near here last November. What has become of him?"

"We have him still, Citizen Representative," replied the man to Roger's great relief; "he was badly wounded, and is still not properly recovered, otherwise he would have been taken before the Tribunal ere this. I fear his case must have slipped the Public Prosecutor's memory, but at a word from you he can soon be dealt with."

"On the contrary." Roger shook his head. "I am glad no steps against him have yet been taken, as I know the man and have a special use for him. He is an ex-smuggler and speaks English. Set a thief to catch a thief, eh? I've not a doubt that as the price of his freedom he'll prove willing enough to serve us at a place along the coast that I have in mind. I bid you bring him to me, and if he agrees I will give you an order for his release."

An hour later Dan was brought to Roger at the hostelry where he had taken up his quarters, and, dismissing the escort, he took his old friend into a small room looking out on the stable yard, where they could be alone.

Poor Dan was in a sad state; he had been shot through the ribs and only his fine constitution had saved his life. The cold and squalor of the prison had nearly finished him, but a stoic determination to live, and a positive conviction that sooner or later Roger would learn of his plight and come to his rescue, had pulled him through. He was bent, thin as a lath, lice-ridden, and shivering from jail fever; yet as soon as they were alone his fine teeth flashed in their old jovial smile.

Roger quickly explained how it was that he had learned of his capture only nine days ago, then asked anxiously about the despatch.

" 'E need fear naught on that score," Dan grinned. "The big packet were weighty enough for I to throw in the boat. T'others bein' too light, I scooped a hole in sand and buried they afore I were collared. 'Twere at low tide when they caught we, an' I were lying well below tide mark. They two letters o' yourn be washed out to sea come mornin'."

"You dear old rascal!" Roger grinned back. "I might have known you'd find some way of keeping them from falling into the hands of the enemy. Thank God, too, the big packet reached Lord Edward safely. There is a thousand pounds in the bank for you at home, Dan, so you can retire now, if you wish; but I hope you'll stay on at Richmond. The immediate question is, though, do you know a way of getting back, and if so do you feel strong enough to make the journey on your own?"

At first Dan protested that he would soon be fit enough to take up his old work in Paris; but Roger would not hear of it. He insisted that if Dan's health were not to be wrecked for good, he must spend six months at home, where he could be properly looked after. With a sigh Dan agreed; then he said that after a few days' rest and decent food at an inn he would be able to get about quite well, and that he knew several places down the coast where old friends of his still put in with illicit cargoes; so he would have no difficulty in getting back to England.

When they had talked together for an hour Roger said that, in view of the excuse he had used to get Dan out of prison, it would not look right if they remained longer together; then he gave him ample money for his journey, and, with great reluctance, watched him walk slowly out into the street.

Soon after dawn next day Roger began his inspection of the garrison and defences of Boulogne. Actually he thought them adequate, and had an attack on the port really been contemplated he would have left matters as they were, but as it was not he could afford to display his Revolutionary zeal. That evening he addressed the senior officers, ordered longer parade hours with intensive training, surprise calls to arms at night at least twice a week, and the calling up of all National Guards in the area up to the age of sixty. By midday on the 11th of March he was back in Paris, and in the afternoon made his report to Carnot, who was well pleased by the speed and efficiency with which he had executed his self-appointed mission.

Athénaïs received him with open arms, doubly relieved to have him safely back and to learn that Dan, although shockingly ill, was alive and now on his way to England. Later that evening she told Roger casually of a brush she had had during his absence with Citizen Candalous. Two nights previously he had knocked on her door at a late hour on the plea that he was ill and needed assistance; on her opening to him it had soon transpired that he was only pretending. After sitting in a chair holding his head for a few minutes, he had declared himself better, then said that since they were already neighbours how much nicer it would be if they could live together. Apparently he had found out that during the previous autumn although Roger had been in Paris he had lived apart from his wife, coming to see her only occasionally, so supposed that, after his recent two nights' visit, he had again left her for an indefinite period. Athénaïs had disabused him of that idea, and assured him that her differences with her husband were made up. He had nevertheless endeavoured to kiss her, and she had only succeeded in frightening him off by jabbing a hatpin through his arm, then telling him that if he paid her any more midnight visits she would ask Roger to stick a sword through his middle.

The manner in which Athénaïs related the episode made it sound amusing, but Roger was none the less annoyed that she had been molested, and he at once decided to take steps to prevent a recurrence of the incident should he have to leave her again.

Next day he had the offending deputy pointed out to him in the coffee-room, and walked purposefully up to his table. At his approach Candalous stood up. He was a tallish man of about forty and not bad-looking, except for a rather fleshy nose and lips.

"Citizen," said Roger, "I am told that you are interested in politics."

"Why, er—yes, Citizen," replied the ex-schoolmaster rather warily; "naturally so, as I am a deputy."

"Exactly!" Roger's blue eyes were icy. "Would it not, therefore, be a good thing if you found yourself a lodging nearer to the Convention?"

"I . . . I don't quite understand. . . ."

"Then let me be more explicit. On my return tonight, should I find you in the room upstairs opposite to that occupied by my wife it is my intention to throw you out of the window."

Having delivered this ultimatum, Roger turned his back and stalked away. Duels were no longer considered to be the inevitable outcome of a quarrel in Revolutionary Paris, as many of the most prominent personalities were incapable of handling a sword or of shooting straight with a pistol; but evidently the deputy from Mayenne was not prepared to risk a rough handling, as by evening he was gone, bag and baggage.

Athénaïs enjoyed a hearty laugh over his discomfiture, and the prompt way in which Roger had dealt with the matter brought her special pleasure, as it gave colour, more than anything else could have done, to the illusion she persisted in building up in her mind that she really was his wife. Now, too, that the first glorious excitement of their reunion had had time to die down a little, they entered on a period of wonderful joy and contentment in one another. During the day they went about their work in a half-famished city, drab from lack of paint, and populated by furtive, frightened people; but, although they were often unable to meet until late at night, when they did they would not have exchanged their room for a palace, luxury and safety, had that meant separation. There, they shut out fear, gloom and dread forebodings, drawing from each embrace fresh strength to meet the uncertainties of the morrow.

Roger was soon back in the swing of things, and learnt that the guillotine had claimed many of his old acquaintances while he had been away—among them Barnave, Dupont and Rabaut, all of whom had been dragged from retirement to execution although they had championed the People's cause in the days of the Third Estate. The Revolution, too, had proved equally ruthless towards the first Generals to lead its armies; Custine, Luckner, Houchard and the Duc de Biron had all paid the price of failure or suspicion on the scaffold.

For the last of these Roger felt no shadow of pity. The Duc de Lauzun, as Biron had been before inheriting the senior title, had in the old days been the handsomest man at Court. Rich, gay, beloved of all the women, he had graced the Queen's intimate circle at Trianon and Versailles. She had showered favours upon him, and, while still a girl, risked scandal by openly displaying a tender, if innocent, passion in response to his advances; yet he had proved base enough to serve the Revolution.

It was Danton who had been responsible for the appointment of these *ci-devant* nobles as Generals, in the belief that only officers who had held high command were capable of waging war efficiently; and their failures had contributed considerably to his own loss of prestige. Yet, as far as Roger could judge, he seemed to be holding his own in his deadly subterranean struggle against the Hébertists.

One evidence of that was the recall of Carrier from Nantes, as Carrier had surpassed every other terrorist in the scale of his atrocities. In spite of the annihilating defeat inflicted on the Royalists of La Vendée in mid-October, they had risen, as though from the dead, and fought on in wild desperation for a further two months. The last of their Generals, the twenty-one-year-old Marquis de le Rochejaquelein, had led them with a sagacity far beyond his years and a bravery that has rarely been equalled, but by the end of December they had been finally overwhelmed. Carrier had already been sent as Citizen Representative to Nantes, and he then proceeded to wreak his vengeance on the prisoners of war and all who had given the Royalists aid while in the field.

Having recruited a special terrorist brigade of negroes and half-castes from the West Indies shipping in the docks, he let them loose upon the city to pillage and rape, and to cram the prisons to overflowing with every man, woman and child who could not prove themselves to be a *sans-culotte*. On finding that the guillotine could account for his victims only at the rate of 200 a day, he had conceived the idea of drowning them in batches. As an experiment he had holes bored below the water-line in one of the big Loire barges, plugged the holes with wooden spigots, loaded ninety priests into the barge, had the hatches nailed down and the barge towed out into the river, then knocked the spigots out. To his delight it foundered so slowly that the despairing cries of its human cargo could be heard for half an hour before they were finally stifled by the water swirling across the barge's deck. From then on these *Noyades*, as they were called, took place every day.

Yet even this was not enough to slake his demoniacal lust for slaughter. Soon he was having his victims taken out on the decks of the barges as well, and thrown off with their hands tied behind them, so that he could watch them drown. Then he invented his triumph in iniquity, to which he gave the name of "Republican Marriages". He had the negroes strip the prisoners naked and bind them in couples, man and woman, face to face. For his Satanic amusement, the men were then beaten until they violated the women to whom they were bound, after which these couples too were thrown into the river. This fiend showed no mercy to white-haired men, the blind, or pregnant women, and babies of a few months old were torn from their mothers' breasts to be hurled into the water before them. In four months Carrier had murdered 32,000 people.

His recall to Paris to give an account of his Proconsulship suggested that, through him, a severe blow was to be struck at the Hébertists, although no one could be certain of that, as the *Comité's* order for his return had not been couched in terms implying censure of his acts. Moreover, Saint-Just made it clear by a speech in the Convention that the *Comité* regarded both factions as equally dangerous to the successful prosecution of the Revolution: first the *exagérés*, who by their atheism and excesses raised up fresh enemies for the Republic within and without; secondly the *indulgents*, who urged a policy of clemency because they were bribed to do so by foreigners, and were planning to sacrifice the Republic in order to obtain money for their debaucheries.

It seemed that Robespierre, as usual, was playing a waiting game, to make a final assessment of the strength of the two parties before he decided which to break; but in the Commune the general impression gained strength that if he hesitated much longer he might be broken himself. By the middle of the month, political Paris was in an unprecedented ferment. Carrier was openly stirring up the Cordeliers to insurrection, and they veiled with crêpe the tablet in the Club on which was inscribed the Declaration of the Rights of Man; a sinister step that in previous instances had signified the temporary abolition of Law, while the "People" reimposed their "Will" upon the nation by violent means. Meanwhile Ronsin, the Hébertist General, was known to be planning another massacre in the prisons as an opening move, to rouse the blood-lust of the *sans-culottes* before leading them in an attack upon the Government. On the other hand, Collot and Billaud had now definitely aligned themselves with Robespierre, and his old stronghold, the Jacobins, continued to declare themselves loyal to the *Comité*.

With intense interest Roger followed every move in the struggle, expecting civil war to break out at almost any hour; but at the height of the crisis he was compelled, temporarily, to give his attention to another matter. Soon after his return from Boulogne he had offered himself for duty at the Temple, and had learned then that, volunteers having become so few, an alphabetical roster had been instituted; but his name was inserted in it and, it so happened, his turn came quite quickly. He was detailed to report on the 16th, and that evening he entered the gloomy precincts of the prison for the first time in four months.

He had already heard about a major change that had taken place in the arrangements there. On the 3rd of January a new law had been passed that no official of the Republic might hold two posts simultaneously. For Citizen Simon this meant that he must either resign his "tutorship" of "young Capet", or give up his Commissionership of the Commune. He had elected to sacrifice the former post; so he was no longer at the Temple. But he had not been replaced; instead, the little King had been confined much more rigorously.

Roger had not been on duty long before, in casual conversation with various people, he secured details of what had transpired. On the 5th of January Simon had officially resigned. He had stayed on until the 14th, and had then left; but he had returned on the 19th, formally handed his charge over to the four Commissars on duty, then gone for good. Apparently Hébert and Chaumette had been greatly upset by the new decree which prevented their fanatically loyal henchman from continuing as watchdog over their invaluable hostage, and could think of no one with similar qualifications to take his place; so they had decided to substitute a material barrier to the boy's escape for the departed human one. With almost unbelievable cruelty they had issued an order that he should be walled-up; and this had been done on the 21st of January.

Later, Roger had ample opportunity to examine the situation for himself. He found it only too true that this wretched child of nine had been shut up in Cléry's old room and entirely cut off from communication with his fellow human beings. The door to his room had been both nailed and screwed up, and a cunningly-devised revolving iron hatch had been fixed in it, by which food and water could be passed in; but anyone outside was prevented from catching even a glimpse of the prisoner, or speaking to him except by raising the voice to a shout.

The boy had now been buried alive in this fashion for eight weeks, and one thing which struck Roger as strange about the matter was that, from the very beginning, he had, apparently, made no protest. With his volatile nature one would have expected him periodically to attack the door, cursing, screaming and endeavouring to kick it in, but not once had he been heard even to cry out. Yet there could be no doubt about his being alive, as he took in his food from the revolving hatch quite regularly.

Another change of which Roger had heard was the reduction in the scale of the meals served to the prisoners. During the autumn Hébert had raised in the Commune the question of their cost to the nation, and had declared that, as many good "patriots" had to make do on a cup of *bouillon* a day, it was an extravagance to feed the "spawn of the tyrants" better. Now, as Roger stood by, a silent witness, while the evening meal was served to the two Princesses, he saw that the former plenty and amenities of their table had both been entirely abolished; they were given only one course served on iron platters, and leaden forks with which to eat it.

Next morning, the 17th of March, a buzz of excited rumours ran through the prison. During the previous night the *Comité* had struck; Hébert, Vincent, Ronsin and seventeen of their associates had been arrested. When the news was confirmed Roger's colleagues became grey-faced and anxious. He had little to fear, as he had never been responsible for any excesses, and could count on the protection, probably, of Robespierre and, certainly, of Carnot; but for them the crisis was fraught with frightful possibilities. Never had Louis XVI, his Ministers or any group of deputies dared to cross swords with the Commune; but now that Ark of the Revolution had been attacked and its most sacred "Champions of Liberty" had been dragged off to prison with no more ceremony than if they had been "filthy aristocrats", what was to prevent a swift and horrid fate overtaking the smaller fry who had fawned upon Hébert and done his bidding for so long? Fervently they prayed that the *sans-culottes* would rise, demand the release of its protectors and submerge the reactionaries under a wave of murderous fury.

Too late, they realized that the *Comité*, in this instance under the skilful guidance of Saint-Just, had outwitted them. During the early part of the year Robespierre's pale, fanatical, young colleague had been on a mission to the armies; but when he returned, towards the end of February, he had put through a decree that the property of "suspects" should be confiscated for the benefits of the poor "patriots". At this the fickle mob had swiftly but imperceptibly turned their backs upon their old patrons of the Commune and gravitated towards the *Comité* as a new dispenser of easy plunder. Only now did the *volte-face* of the *sans-culottes* become apparent. In vain Carrier raved at the Cordeliers, inciting them to insurrection; he could achieve no more than a half-hearted demonstration.

It was five years, all but four months, since the mob had stormed the Bastille, and in all that time every successive government had proved incapable of standing up to it; but the *Comité* had performed the remarkable feat of first drugging its body, then cutting off its head. Within a week its power, and that of the Commune, had been broken for good.

On the 18th Chaumette was arrested, to be dragged with the others before the Revolutionary Tribunal. Strange as it sounded to many people, they were accused of plotting to restore the Monarchy with little Capet as King and themselves as a Council of Regency; but one charge was as good as another once the Committee of Public Safety had decided that for its own safety certain people must be put out of the way. Without dignity or courage these Neroes of the gutter strove to save themselves, but in vain. On the 24th Hébert was carried screaming and kicking to the guillotine; Ronsin alone showed bravery, and the atheist Clootz indifference; Vincent, Momoro and the rest died to the jeers of the mob with abject cowardice. Meanwhile, before the Tribunal had even had time to condemn its leaders, the headless body of the Commune had proceeded in solemn procession to the Convention and humbly thanked the Chamber for having purged it of its undesirable elements. The triumph of the *Comité* was complete.

For a few days a wave of infinite relief surged outward from Paris to every extremity of France. The long-suffering nation believed that with the death of these monsters the Terror was over, and that at long last it was to enjoy without further fear of death and despoliation the freedoms that the abolition of the *ancien régime* had brought about.

It was soon undeceived. The hands of Robespierre, Couthon, Saint-Just, Collot and Billaud were too deeply steeped in blood for them to dare adopt a policy of mercy, which must in time have led to reaction and their own downfall. The last two had abandoned Hébert only because he had become a menace to their own power, and on condition that the Terror should continue. Moreover, the fanatical purist, Saint-Just, was determined to purge the Revolution of those leaders who had used it to acquire fortunes and had disgraced it by their profligacies. On the 30th of March he struck, tabling a long report on the *incivisme* of the Dantonists for which the "Incorruptible" had himself provided the notes. That night, Danton and his friends were arrested.

On the 2nd of April the trial began. Camille Desmoulins, Lacroix, Philippeaux, Hérault de Sechelles, Fabre d'Églantine and Chabot were the most prominent of Danton's supporters who were brought with him before the Revolutionary Tribunal. The political charges, based on a complete distortion of their careers, were almost entirely false; those connected with their private lives were mainly true. Fabre and Chabot had been financed by the Baron de Batz to rig the money market; Hérault, a distinguished lawyer who had played a prominent part in formulating the Constitution, was living with a *ci-devant* Countess whom he had saved from the guillotine. He and Desmoulins alone were honest; the others, Danton beyond all, had practised extortion, accepted huge bribes and stolen state funds to live in opulence and indulge their vices.

For some time past Danton had been conscious of his danger, but had proved too lazy to take any vigorous steps to avert it. Now, instead of answering his accusers, he roused himself in a great effort to win back his former popularity with the people. During the whole of the 3rd of April his mighty voice boomed out in sonorous phrases well calculated to bring the mob to his rescue. In consternation, the *Comité* saw that popular clamour might easily bring about his acquittal; so, on the 4th, even this travesty of a trial was abruptly terminated, and the furious Danton was dragged away to rave incoherently through the bars of his prison.

By the following evening he had resigned himself, and when the three scarlet-painted tumbrels came to take him and his associates to the scaffold, he said with a shrug, "What matter if I die? I have well enjoyed myself in the Revolution: I have spent well, caroused well, and caressed many women."

Camille Desmoulins, by contrast, displayed pitiable weakness. In his despair he had so torn his clothes that the upper part of his body was half naked. He was with Danton in the leading tumbrel, and as it passed down the Rue St. Honoré he vainly appealed to the mob to rescue him, screaming out, "People, it is your servants who are being sacrificed! It was I who in 1789 called you to arms! It was I who uttered the first cry of liberty!"

The crowd only mocked him, and Danton, now too near death to bother any longer to disguise what he really thought of the "Sacred People", said with a derisive smile, "Be quiet, Camille! Do not demean yourself by pleading with that vile scum."

So perished what might be termed the Left Wing Socialists of the Revolution; the Right Wing Socialists had preceded them with the fall of the Gironde; the Liberals had either, like Talleyrand, fled abroad, or, like Barnave, been dragged from retirement to execution; the leading Anarchists had been despatched with Hébert and his murderous crew twelve days earlier. There remained only a crowd of powerless, terrified, sheep-like politicians and 24,000,000 French people, all of whom were now completely at the mercy of the six Communists who dominated the *Comité*.

Yet the killing did not stop. On the contrary, the great witch-hunt continued with increased fury. Anybody who at any time had expressed sympathy with the King, the Queen, the Constitutionalists, the Girondins, the Dantonists or the Hébertists was liable to be seized, imprisoned and executed; in consequence the entire nation was under suspicion, and it needed only a word from an enemy to send anyone to the scaffold. The number of victims sent to the guillotine in February was nearly doubled in March; the March figure was more than doubled in April; the April figure was increased by nearly fifty per cent in May, and the May figure more than doubled in June.

Day after day, week after week, the number of tumbrels in the dread procession increased; they were no longer a spectacle of interest, but rather an awful reminder to all who saw them that they too might soon be taking that free ride with their hands bound behind them. Rarely now was an aristocrat to be seen among the victims; they were minor politicians who really believed in liberty and at one time or another had been rash enough to say so, officials who had not passed on to their superiors a big enough proportion of the bribes they had taken; milliners, jewellers, lace-makers and tailors who lamented the ruin of their businesses owing to the passing of the *ancien régime*; officers who had shown mercy to prisoners in La Vendée; speculators in *assignats*; shop-keepers who had charged more than the maximum, and even housewives who had been heard to grumble at the meat ration having recently been reduced to half a pound per family for five days.

The agents of the *Comité de Sûreté Générale*, second only in power to the great *Comité*, were everywhere; and reinforced still further by the *Comités de Surveillance* in each Section. Hundreds of domiciliary visits were paid each night, and in the cafés no one any longer dared to talk above a whisper. The rump of the Convention, now reduced to a bare 200 attendants, slavishly agreed to every measure placed before it; the once powerful Commune dared debate politics no more.

In all Paris laughter was now heard regularly only in one place, and that was the fiendish laughter of the depraved harpies who gathered each morning at the foot of the guillotine. These *tricoteuses*, as they were called, prided themselves on having become veteran critics of the grim sport provided by the executioner. Every day they took their knitting and sat in rows on the chairs round the scaffold which, provided by a thoughtful Government, could be hired for a small sum. There they taunted the victims, exchanged bawdy jests with the executioners' assistants, booed, mocked, chuckled and drooled like wild beasts at the sight of the blood spurting from the necks of the still-twitching bodies.

Roger and Athénaïs continued their strange unnatural existence. As it became more and more difficult for members of the League to penetrate Paris, she found less to do, and spent much of her time in their room reading, or simply brooding over the horrors which she could not stop and to which she could see no end. He now trod more warily than ever among his colleagues, hardly daring to utter an opinion lest it should land him in trouble —and trouble these days meant death within a week. By night they took one another fiercely, ever conscious that each time might be the last, and striving to forget in a fury of passion that one slip next day, a chance meeting with someone they had known in the past, an unguarded impulse towards pity or a sudden giving way to anger, and never again would they lie embraced mingling happy sighs with breathless kisses.

As long as Roger remained in Paris he was now liable for duty at the Temple approximately once a month; so, although he felt it to be a waste of time, he had no option but to report there in mid-April, and again in mid-May. On both occasions, knowing how even small luxuries were now denied to the prisoners, he took with him a big packet of sweets which he surreptitiously gave to Madame Royale.

She was now a well-grown girl of fifteen and a half, with the typical Bourbon nose, and the rather parrot-like good looks, that often favoured the family before their features grew too heavy to be pleasing. Her manner was naturally subdued, although, considering her age and the awful experiences through which she had passed, she showed remarkable fortitude and self-possession. On his visit in May, Roger found her, as he expected, greatly depressed, as only a few days previously her aunt had been taken from her and, although she did not know it, executed on the 10th. She was, therefore, now entirely alone, her brother and herself being the only prisoners remaining in the Temple, each upon a separate floor and prohibited from communicating in any way.

No sound other than a faint shuffling was ever heard from the room in which the little King remained walled-up, and the possibility of his rescue now seemed more remote than ever. To break a way in to him would have necessitated the use of a saw or axe, and the resulting noise would inevitably have brought a score of National Guards running up from the floor below; moreover, now that an alphabetical duty roster had been instituted, Roger could no longer arrange for Goret, or some other well-disposed colleague, to take duty with him. Back in March he had realized that as long as the new system was maintained there was not the faintest hope of carrying the child off, and at the first opportunity he had informed Mr. Pitt accordingly.

Having made a martyr of Princess Elizabeth on the 10th of May, Robespierre set about preparing to make himself a High Priest. In the *Comité* he could count permanently only on his *alter ego*, the semi-paralysed Couthon, and his fiery young disciple, Saint-Just. Carnot and the four other members who devoted themselves to waging the foreign war maintained their unwritten pact of not interfering with him as long as he did not interfere with them, but he knew that none of them would lift a finger to save him if he were attacked. There remained Collot, Billaud and Barère. All three had allied themselves with him only as a measure of expediency, had only contempt for his fanatical incorruptibility, and were still Hébertists at heart. In seeking a way to destroy them he formed the conclusion that this could best be done through their atheism. The bulk of the French nation clearly felt the loss of the Church and craved for some form of religious expression, which the doctrine of Reason had failed to provide. Egged on by his own streak of mysticism and with the object of gaining popular support for an attack on his three secret enemies, he propounded and advocated, early in May, the general adoption of a new faith; the belief in immortality was to be restored, coupled with the worship of a "Supreme Being", and an inaugural fête in honour of the new deity was fixed for the 8th of June.

This announcement met with a most mixed reception. In the Convention the men of the Plain, now utterly cowed by Robespierre, slavishly applauded his proposals, but many of his old colleagues of the Mountain showed a stony disapproval. The very idea of religion was anathema to most of the terrorists, and it was equally lacking in appeal to the unscrupulous voluptuaries who had escaped being purged with the Dantonists. Nevertheless, so great had Robespierre's ascendancy become that the measure was adopted, and the whole Convention turned out "by order" to attend this new Church Parade.

The day was one of glorious sunshine, and the first part of the *Fête de l'Être Suprême* was held in the Tuileries gardens. A group of huge wooden statues had been erected, representing Atheism surrounded by Vices and Folly and threatened by Wisdom. In gala attire the deputies, commissars, generals and officials all arrived with their ladies and took their places before a high rostrum. After a prolonged and much criticized delay Robespierre appeared, immaculate in a coat of violet silk with snowy ruffles, and carrying a bouquet; from the rostrum he made a long Rousseauesque oration, then set fire to the statue of Atheism, after which the whole assembly removed to the Champs de Mars, where hymns were sung and a salvo of artillery was fired to complete the celebration.

The Great Terror had had the effect of destroying almost all social life in Paris, as the old rich who had so far escaped arrest no longer dared draw attention to themselves by entertaining, while the new masters mostly lived in lodgings and spent their evenings at the political clubs. The fête, therefore, proved something of an occasion, as the principal participants had all been bidden to bring their womenfolk to it.

Roger and Athénaïs naturally lived as quietly as possible, but since his return to Paris they had been unable to prevent their "marriage" becoming known to a number of people; so they agreed that it would be dangerous for him not to take her to the fête with him. During it and after it he introduced her to a number of his acquaintances, and the ladies, most of whom had not met before, showed the liveliest interest in one another.

Few such gatherings can ever have included so great a variety of the female species as the companions of the most important males. Robespierre lodged with the family of a carpenter named Duplaix, and brought the carpenter's wife and three daughters; the mother was one of the infamous *tricoteuses* who daily screamed insults at the dying as they mounted the steps of the guillotine. At the other end of the scale was the beautiful Madame Tallien, the daughter of a millionaire and widow of a nobleman, who had become known as the "Angel of Bordeaux". Tallien, Roger's old colleague of the 10th of August, had been sent as *Représentant en mission* to purge Bordeaux after its Federalist rising. He had begun his task with the same ruthless energy as had been displayed by the Proconsuls sent to Lyons, Toulon and Nantes, but, on this statuesque and quite exceptionally lovely lady being brought before him as a prisoner, he had fallen in love with her, and they had married. At her supplication he had changed his policy for one of mercy, and she had been responsible for saving thousands of lives. Between these two extremes, there were many like the pimply little Madame Fouché, the daughter of well-to-do bourgeois parents, and pretty prostitutes who had been lifted to outward respectability by marrying deputies.

Roger was careful to keep his opinions of the new worship to himself; but he listened with much interest to those of others, and many were scathing. Great resentment was felt at the way Robespierre had put himself above his colleagues, kept everyone waiting, and then taken the lead of the procession fifty paces ahead of the rest. The livery Billaud was openly quoting sinister tags of Latin about Caesar and Brutus; Collot condemned the proceedings with his usual foul oaths; Barras, who had returned from Toulon early in the year, laughed derisively at their "new Pope" and poked fun at the embarrassed Fouché, who, snivelling as ever from his perpetual cold, would now have given anything short of his corpse-like head for everyone to forget that only a few months ago he had been the leading exponent of Atheism. However, the multitude, ever optimistic but easily misled, rejoiced in the summer sunshine, taking this public acknowledgment of the Deity as a new sign that the Terror was to be brought to an end.

How utterly mistaken they were was soon made apparent. Only two days later Robespierre produced the most infamous of all his decrees, which, by its date in the Revolutionary calendar, became known as the Law of 22nd Prairial. Its object was to eliminate the necessity of hearing witnesses who might speak in favour of the accused before the Revolutionary Tribunal, and to increase its scope so that a far greater number of victims could be brought before it. The Tribunal was split into four sections, with twelve judges and fifty permanent jurors all personally selected by Robespierre; secret denunciations were to be encouraged, and henceforth anyone accused could be condemned on written evidence, thus relieving his accuser from having to appear in court, and there was to be one penalty only—death.

Day by day the Terror grew. The Law of 22nd Prairial brought denunciations pouring into Fouquier-Tinville's letter-box. Officials denounced their seniors to usurp their places; creditors denounced their debtors; women whose lovers had been unfaithful denounced their rivals; heirs to property denounced their relatives; husbands denounced wives who had become a burden to them; school-children denounced their teachers. Apart from the most prominent Revolutionaries, no one any longer dare be seen in decent clothes; men went about unshaven, and women with their hair uncombed, rather than risk drawing attention to themselves; but no one went out now at all unless compelled to do so. People distrusted even their dearest friends and avoided talking to them. Business was at a standstill and Paris was near starvation. Scores of children were born prematurely owing to the shock caused to mothers whose husbands were torn from their arms. Sometimes, driven to distraction by often baseless fears, weak-minded individuals ran amok crying, "*Vive le Roi!*" in order to bring a swift end to their nightmares. Hundreds, worn out from weeks of apprehension, committed suicide. By night the streets were empty, yet people hardly dare sleep; the sound of a marching squad outside, or a knock on the door, aroused everyone within to agonizing suspense. No one was safe, and once arrested there could be no hope of mercy. A woman in the Conciergerie whose name was called from the list for execution pleaded the last stages of pregnancy; her plea was ignored; she gave birth to a child in the gateway of the prison, was thrown into the tumbrel, and guillotined half an hour afterwards. Seven thousand people were crammed into the prisons of Paris and more buildings were being converted into prisons. In France over 200,000 people were held in prison awaiting death. In the Place St. Antoine, to which the guillotine had now been removed, a great conduit had to be dug to carry away the blood, and four men were needed to clean the channel daily so that this river of gore should not clot, but flow freely to the sewer.

On the 28th of June Carnot again sent for Roger, and charged him with a new mission. The General had received information that the English contemplated a descent on Cherbourg, and he said:

"Although your fears of an attack on Boulogne last March proved groundless, the measures you took there were most efficient; I wish you now to take similar steps at Cherbourg. News has just reached me that General Jourdan secured a great victory over Prince Coburg at Fleurus on the 25th, and the situation on our other battle-fronts is well in hand, but naturally I do not wish to withdraw troops from any of them to reinforce the Cherbourg area unless you consider it necessary. Make the best arrangements you can and remain there for some days to see that your orders are properly carried out, then return and report to me."

Reluctant as Roger was to leave Athénaïs, this new mission at least offered a means of easing his mind on one matter that had been worrying him. It was now over six weeks since a member of the League had been in Paris; so the transmission of a despatch to

Mr. Pitt was considerably overdue. At no great distance off the direct road to Cherbourg lay the little fishing village of Grandcamp, and an inn near by used as a depôt by the League. It would be easy for him to arrange matters so that he halted for the last night of his journey at Bayeux, gave his escort the slip, rode over to Grandcamp, and put his despatch into safe hands for early forwarding to England.

Next morning, having assured Athénaïs that he would be back within a fortnight, he took a fond farewell of her, and set out for Normandy. The weather was perfect, and the one thing the Revolution had not been able to destroy was the beauty of the countryside; so before he had been long on his way he felt as though ten years of his age had dropped from him. His only regret was that he had not been able to take his beautiful mistress with him, so that she too might enjoy for a while release from the awful fear that hung like an invisible pall over the sultry capital.

From Bayeaux he had no difficulty in making his midnight trip to Grandcamp and back unknown to any member of his escort, and the following evening, the 2nd of July, he arrived in Cherbourg. Having carried out a similar series of inspections to those he had conducted in Boulogne, and also visited the ships of the French squadron which was held there by the British blockade. The land defences proved fairly satisfactory, but the condition of the Fleet was deplorable. Nine-tenths of the officers who had served under the Monarchy in both the Army and Navy had been swept away by the Revolution, and while it had been possible to make new Army officers out of brave, intelligent men with reasonable rapidity, the Navy had presented a very different problem, as a lifetime of experience was needed for a man to be capable of sailing and fighting the bulging wooden fortresses carrying acres of canvas. In consequence, the officers jumped up by the Revolution, realizing their inefficiency, lacked firmness and confidence, and their crews, knowing that, were semi-mutinous.

Naturally, believing that the port might be attacked by the British Navy, Roger made a great deal of noise, but actually took no measures, other than those he could scarcely avoid, to strengthen its defences, and even managed to replace a few of the best officers by bad ones. On the 8th of July he set out on his return to Paris, arriving there on the evening of the 13th.

His change had made him feel wonderfully well, and he was

looking forward immensely to seeing Athénaïs again. In the hallway of *La Belle Étoile* he ran into Mère Blanchard, and, after greeting her gaily, he asked if his wife was in.

The good dame stared at him, her eyes going round with surprise, then she clapped a hand over her mouth.

"What ails you?" he cried in quick alarm; "there is naught wrong, I trust?"

"Monsieur," she stammered, "oh, Monsieur, did you not know? Your poor Madame was guillotined three days ago."

CHAPTER XXVII

DEATH TO THE TYRANT

ROGER lay face down on the bed which for most of the past four months he had shared with Athénaïs. He was dry-eyed but mentally stunned, and as yet not fully capable of realizing his loss. Here, while fear stalked the streets outside, they had lain secure and happy; sometimes laughing and teasing, sometimes talking of that now dead world of beauty, grace and culture that they had known when young, sometimes exciting each other to new heights of voluptuous bliss, then snuggling close and lying utterly still in the supreme contentment of mutually satisfied passion.

His face was buried in her pillow, on which there still lingered the scent that she dared to use only here, and then sparingly, in case it provoked comment by contrast with the simple, shabby clothes she always wore when going out. In his mental ear he could hear her soft, rich laugh while relating how she had fooled some stupid official, as she had so often done during her many months of courageous work with the League; in his mind's eye he could see the graceful curve of her lithe body as she stooped to draw on a stocking. It seemed impossible, intolerable, unbearable, that her laugh should have been for ever silenced, her body for ever stilled, and her decapitated trunk carried away in a blood-spattered cart, with her lovely head thrust between her legs.

For months past, arrests, tragedies, deaths had been taking place daily in every quarter of Paris, and she had often said that sooner or later their turn must come. Roger had never really believed that it would—yet now it had. How, he was not yet clear, except on the bare facts which placed her death beyond all doubt. Mère Blanchard knew only that Athénaïs had killed the Citizen Deputy Candalous, then given herself up for his murder. Even in Paris, satiated as it was with crime and violence, the assassination of a deputy had caused quite a sensation. That explained why Athénaïs had been brought before the Tribunal and sentenced without delay, instead of being left to wait her turn for a few weeks in prison; and the publicity given to the case left no vestige of hope that Mère Blanchard had been misled by some muddled rumour.

Refusing all consolation, Roger had begged her in no circumstances to disturb him, and had fled upstairs to writhe alone under the lightning blow that the evil powers had dealt him. Dusty, dishevelled and still in his riding-clothes, he had flung himself down on the bed. For over four hours he had lain there almost without moving, telling himself over and over again that he was not suffering from a nightmare but was wide awake, and that he must face the awful, shocking, agonizing truth—his beautiful Athénaïs was dead and he would never hold her in his arms again.

The summer night had fallen by the time he roused himself sufficiently to wonder how this frightful thing had come about. It occurred to him then that, through no fault of hers, something might have come out at her trial which made him suspect, and that possibly there was a warrant out for him. Since she had been passing as his wife that was highly likely. Now that the first shock was over his instincts urged him to get to the bottom of the matter, and he thought it probable that she had left some message for him.

Sitting up, he lit a candle, then knelt down, reached under the bed and prised up a loose piece of floorboard. They used the hollow under it as a cache, in which to keep a reserve of money and leave notes for one another if some business was likely to prevent them from returning until later than usual. As that thought crossed his mind, with its heartrending sequel—that from the last business on which she had gone she would never return—tears started to his eyes and ran down his cheeks.

He could feel some papers in the cache. Drawing them out, he wiped his eyes and peered at them through the wet mist that now bedewed his long lashes. They were several loose sheets covered with Athénaïs's fine angular hand. She had written:

Roger, my heart, we are undone. This morning, on going out, not far down the street, Pierre Candalous waylaid me. He addressed me ironically as Madame la Vicomtesse and asked me to accompany him to a café. Seeing that he had discovered the secret of my identity it was pointless to refuse to hear what he had to say. He told me that yesterday he had been walking with a friend recently arrived from Rennes, and that they had chanced to see me cross the Place du

Louvre. The friend recognized me at once. He was in the old days our apothecary, and when I was Mademoiselle de Rochambeau I often bought from him scents, soaps and essences. He knew, too, of my trial last summer, and how, having condemned me to death, you stayed my execution because, so it was said, I had promised you some information about the risings in La Vendée. He had supposed that you had carried me off to Nantes and that I was still a prisoner there, or more probably one of Carrier's victims; but he and Candalous soon put two and two together. They are, fortunately, unaware that we had ever met before, but assume that, having taken a fancy to me, you brought me to Paris as your mistress. You can guess what followed; Candalous requires me to come to live with him as the price of his silence, otherwise he threatens to denounce us both—myself as an aristocrat already condemned to death, and you for having given me your protection while knowing full well that I was a condemned enemy of the Revolution. I temporized with him; reluctantly he consented to give me until tomorrow, but he holds me on a chain. He told me that should I seek to escape him by flight he will denounce you on your return, and reminded me that Hérault de Sechelles was sent to the guillotine for the same crime as that of which you will stand accused. Roger, I am in despair. I know not what to do.

Miserably, Roger went on to another passage, evidently written later:

Roger, my heart, I have lain awake all night and I see but one way out of the snare into which we are fallen. Since that wonderful night in the ruins of Bécherel I have kept my vows to you. Even when you deserted me, even when you were abroad and I believed you dead, I remained faithful to you, although I was desperately lonely and much pressed by more than one gallant gentleman of the League. Yet could I save you I would give myself to a sans-culotte*; but in this, for me to submit to Candalous's embraces is no solution—or only a temporary one at best. He is of a mean, vindictive personality, and will never forgive you for the humiliation you put upon him when you forced him to vacate his lodging here. I have seen enough of these swinish revolutionaries to know how their minds work. Having made all the decencies of life illegal, they are determined to drag everyone down to their own level of the gutter, and delight in any excuse to destroy those who resist. They have no sense of honour, no chivalry, no mercy, and no constancy to the women whom they force to gratify* *their lusts. Did I give way to him, therefore, as soon as he had tired of me he would throw us both to the executioner.*

There is only one way by which I can save you and spare myself from degradation, and I am resolved upon it. I shall go to him to-night and take with me my poignard. *You have seen me use a dagger so you may be certain that I shall not fail in my purpose. I shall lead this lecherous rat to expect the utmost, then watch the triumph in his eyes turn to agony and despair as I seal his lips for ever.*

When the deed is accomplished I shall give myself up to the police at once, in my own name. I shall say that Candalous was one of the men responsible for the death of my poor children, and that on meeting him again I resolved to be revenged upon him. Your only danger will then lie in Baudin, the Rennes apothecary; but trials are now reduced to such a farce that they occupy only a few moments, and the odds are that even if he volunteers to give evidence they will not trouble themselves to hear him. Why should they, if I confess my deed? As I recall him, he was a quiet, elderly man of good disposition. My death should prove sufficient satisfaction to him for the killing of his friend, and as you will not be in Paris at the time he cannot suppose that you had any hand in it; so I count it most unlikely that he will go out of his way to denounce you.

Yet should he do so, I have also thought of a way to protect you from that. Regarding yourself, my story will be that I escaped from Nantes and met you again in Paris last October, and that I lied to you about my past. When you remarked on my great likeness to the Vicomtesse de la Tour d'Auvergne, whom you had handed over to the Revolutionary authorities in Nantes early in July, I accounted for that by telling you that I was an illegitimate daughter of M. de Rochambeau by a merchant's wife, and so the Vicomtesse's half-sister. You believed me, took me as your mistress and allowed me to use your name only as a convenience. If you are questioned and confirm what I shall say, how can anyone prove that it was otherwise? But I have little fear that you will be called on to use this story, except to satisfy such acquaintances of yours in Paris who may suspect you of having known me to be an aristocrat—and they can know nothing of your having first condemned, then saved me, in Rennes.

Oh, Roger, how I thank you for all the love that you have given me both in the distant past and in these recent nightmare months. Do you remember, dear Miller's youngest son, how I saved you from your pursuers by taking you into my coach that night long ago in Rennes? I was but a child then and carried an ugly doll that I called "my

Englishman". Do you remember our first kiss?—how in a passion I had struck you across the face with my whip, and as a punishment you kissed me? I thought I had been raped and threatened to have you branded; then in revenge I made you kiss me again when my face was all blotched with smallpox. Dear God, how vile a creature I must have been! What you can have seen to love in me then defeats my imagination. The thought that I have been able to repay your great love for me a little in this past year brings me some consolation, yet even now I know myself to be base and unworthy of it. Out of my selfish passion for you I treated your poor wife abominably. For that I humbly crave both your pardon and hers, and beg you to ask it of her when you return to England. If she too has erred I beg you to forgive her for my sake. Such is my wicked nature still that I cannot bring myself to hope that you will ever love her more than you have myself; yet it would ease my conscience could I have your promise before I go that you will do your utmost to become reconciled to her.

Think of me sometimes, Roger, my heart, but only to recall our happy hours together. Do not brood upon my death, for I am not afraid to die; and at the end I shall raise my voice to cry "Vive le Roi!" *May the Good God show mercy to our poor France, and have you always in His holy keeping.*

Athénaïs Hermonaie de Breuc.

Roger let the last sheet fall from his fingers and buried his face in his hands. She wrote of his love for her, but what of hers for him? There had been nothing to stop her leaving Paris; instead, she had remained and gone to the guillotine rather than allow him to be denounced.

Again he remained for a long time half stunned by grief; then there came a gentle knock on the door. Although he did not reply, it was opened and Maître Blanchard came in carrying a tray. As he set it down, he said:

"I ask pardon, Monsieur le Chevalier, for disregarding your wish not to be disturbed; but you must endeavour to eat something to keep up your strength. Look now, my wife has cooked this young pullet for you in your favourite cream sauce, and here is a bottle of *Clos Vougeot* from my own special reserve."

Roger shook his head. "It is most kind of you. A glass of wine perhaps, but more than that I could not swallow."

"Ah, come, Monsieur; Madame la Vicomtesse would be much annoyed if she thought you were starving yourself."

"You . . . you knew her real name, then?" stammered Roger, in surprise.

The landlord shrugged his broad shoulders. "Why, yes, Monsieur. Did she not live when a young demoiselle in her father's great mansion just round the corner, and was it not then that you first became one of my patrons? The famous duel that you fought on her behalf was the talk of all Paris, and despite her dyed hair I would have known her again anywhere. But there are many things known to my wife and myself of which we do not talk. It is sufficient for us that instead of living comfortably in England, you risk your life here month after month secretly fighting the great evil. There is, alas, so little that poor folk like us can do, and we count it a privilege to serve you in small matters while keeping still tongues in our heads."

Tears again sprang to Roger's eyes as he took the stalwart Norman by the hand, and murmured, "How blessed I am to have such loyal friends as you and your wife; it makes it all the harder for me to forgo your kindly care of me, as I must for a while. The whole house will remind me too poignantly of her until I am a little accustomed to her loss. But keep my room, for I shall return as soon as I feel I can bear to do so."

"I understand, Monsieur; and now please to attempt to eat a little supper before you go. I will have a coach waiting for you in twenty minutes."

Obediently, Roger sat down, ate some of the chicken and drank two-thirds of the wine, then drove in the coach to the Cushion and Keys. It was now past eleven o'clock, but Citizen Oysé was still up, and welcomed him in a subdued manner which showed that he knew about Madame Breuc's execution, but did not like to make any mention of it. Roger went straight to bed, and, after tossing miserably for a while, woke to find to his surprise that it was morning.

By the time he was dressed his grief had crystallized into a cold, hard rage against the state of things which had led to Athénaïs's death. The sights he had been compelled to witness during the past two years had given him cause enough to hate everything connected with the monstrous upheaval which had for so long crucified France, but his personal loss was like the turning of a knife in a wound, making him mad with the urge to strike out blindly at the system which had inflicted it. Had Candalous not already been dead he would have sought him out to exact a bloody vengeance, regardless of the consequences, but as it was he could only grope in his mind for some other means of slaking his agonized distress.

Fortunately, his long training in caution once again got the better of his impulse to take immediate action; yet all the same, as he was going to report to Carnot at the offices of the *Comité*, he decided that it would be wisest to leave his pocket pistol behind in case he ran into Robespierre there and could not overcome the temptation to shoot him.

When he had made his report, Carnot gravely commiserated with him on the loss he had sustained during his absence, and he had the sense to realize that this was the perfect opportunity for conveying to the *Comité* his ignorance of the fact that the woman with whom he had been living was an aristocrat. As he lied glibly about Athénaïs having told him that she was an illegitimate child, he felt like St. Peter when the cock crowed thrice; but to have done otherwise was to risk her self-sacrifice having been made in vain, and Carnot shrugged the matter off by saying that in times such as the present a man could count himself lucky if he even knew the private political convictions of his own mother, let alone his wife.

That afternoon Roger went for a long walk in the Bois. A single morning in Paris had been enough to bring home to him with renewed force the now desperate condition of its inhabitants. Four out of every five shops were closed; lined up before every baker's, butcher's and grocer's were long queues of lean, grimly silent people. The streets were almost empty of traffic. Even the uniforms of the National Guards were now in rags. Every passer-by had a furtive, hunted look. A prolonged glance was enough to send any of them scuttling round the nearest corner. Their eyes were ringed with black circles of sleeplessness and hunger, their faces were grey with fear. The squads of soldiers no longer sang the *ça ira* or the *Marseillaise* as they marched. The shouting mobs bent on demonstrating, so long a feature of the city, had disappeared. Even the *sans-culottes* were cowed.

Roger wondered if it would be possible for him to organize an insurrection, and decided that the chances of stirring up one of sufficient magnitude to overthrow the *Comité* were very slender. He was convinced that ninety-nine out of every hundred people would be overjoyed to see an end put to the Revolution, but the spirit had gone out of them. In the past month attempts had been made on the lives of both Collot and Robespierre, yet those exceptions only proved the rule. The people were desperate, but too terrified of betrayal to combine openly against their oppressors. If the thing were to be done at all it must be done from outside. There was plenty of secret opposition to Robespierre in high places; his antics as High Priest to the Supreme Being had done him great damage with nearly all his most powerful associates. The problem was which of them had sufficient resolution to gamble their lives in an attempt to bring about his downfall; how could their divergent aims temporarily be reconciled and their jealousies lulled long enough to prevent them betraying one another before the deed was done?

After a two-hour walk Roger returned to the city; his mind was made up. How could he better avenge Athénaïs than by organizing a *coup d'état* to end the Terror? How could he serve his own country, the wretched people of France, the whole of humanity, better than by bringing down in ruins the whole awful structure of the Revolution? The odds were that the attempt would fail and cost him his life, but he now felt that he had little left to live for. Even so, to get himself sent to the guillotine would be synonymous with failure; so he meant to go to work with the utmost caution and devote several days to an intensive study of the men best suited to his purpose before taking the first of several steps, any one of which might land him on the scaffold.

Collot, Billaud and Barère were the obvious choice for a combination against Robespierre, but Roger rejected them at once because they were all dyed-in-the-wool terrorists, and to exchange the present régime for one dominated by them would be to jump out of the frying-pan into the fire. Carnot was waging the war which kept France's many enemies at bay and Roger felt certain that he would not be willing to jeopardize the safety of the country by risking his own neck in a political conspiracy.

Outside the great *Comité* a score of possible names offered themselves. The men on the lesser *Comité de Sûreté Générale*, which controlled the police, were, unfortunately, mostly Robespierrists, and all the judges on the Revolutionary Tribunal had been appointed by him; there remained the men who had made great names for themselves as *Représentants en mission*.

During the next two days Roger sought out and, apparently by chance, ran into a number of the most prominent of these, to whom he talked for a while, cautiously sounding their opinions. The question of the worship of the Supreme Being served admirably as a hare to bring the conversation round to the Incorruptible. Almost without exception they expressed the view that Robespierre's vanity had affected his brain. He was not even bothering now to consult his colleagues on the *Comité*, but was issuing new measures simply signed "By the order of Robespierre". All agreed that it would not be long before he openly declared himself Dictator, and several hinted darkly that if France were to remain a Republic it was high time that the nation produced a Brutus; but none of them was bold enough to hint that he would be willing to play the part.

By the 16th of July Roger had chosen his men. As the risk of immediate denunciation would be doubled, trebled, quadrupled, and so on by each person to whom he put his proposals openly, he dare risk approaching only a very limited number; but he meant to approach those chosen few together, thereby taking the one big gamble that they would either unite in denouncing him or would all commit themselves in the presence of each other. His choice was governed not so much by apparent animosity to Robespierre as by an endeavour to secure a balanced group in which each member would contribute some source of power that the others lacked.

He selected Barras as a good leader, because the *ci-devant* noble was bold, unscrupulous, an able military commander, and a man whose scandalous debaucheries must soon bring him under the axe of the Incorruptible, unless he struck first. But Barras was a poor speaker and of only mediocre intelligence; so Roger's second choice was Dubois-Crancé, a deputy who had great influence in the Convention, possessed a first-class brain, and bore a deadly hatred for Robespierre's *alter ego*, Couthon, who had recently threatened to impeach him for having allowed a Royalist force to escape from Lyons. His third choice was Tallien, because he knew that unless he had one of the old school terrorists in the party its basis would not be broad enough to keep the *sans-culottes* from rising, should an outcry occur that the People's liberties were being threatened by a counter-Revolution; yet Tallien, although it was not known to the Paris mob, had fallen under the influence of his beautiful wife, who could be counted on to moderate his terrorist leanings should he become one of the new masters; while the fact that she had recently been arrested and imprisoned as a suspect should make him eager to join any movement for the overthrow of the *Comité*, as offering the best means of saving her.

Having decided with whom he would risk his neck, Roger invited the three of them to dine with him on the 17th at *La Belle Étoile*, although he had no intention of entertaining them there. When he woke on that day he was much relieved to see that it promised to be fine, apart from the possibility of July thunderstorms. Going straight to *La Belle Étoile*, he asked Maître Blanchard to prepare the finest picnic lunch for four persons that he could provide, and enquired whether he would then be willing to drive one of his hire coaches himself to take the party to the Bois.

The good Norman, realizing that secrecy was the object of his being asked to act as coachman, at once agreed, and when Roger returned at three o'clock in the afternoon he found all in readiness. As each of his guests arrived he popped them swiftly into the waiting coach, and immediately they were all assembled it set off.

The moment it got under way, Dubois-Crancé said to him, "I had no idea this was to be a party, and thought myself bidden to dine with you at your inn. Where are you taking us?"

"To enjoy a little air and sunshine," Roger replied lightly. "Paris stinks too much of blood for my liking these days, and I thought it would be a pleasant change for us all to eat a meal in God's country, sitting on the grass."

Barras gave a great guffaw of laughter. "God's country, say you? Have a care! 'Tis your blood that will be stinking soon, unless you refer to it as the Supreme Being's country—or Citizen Robespierre's."

Roger's reference to "God" had been deliberate, and he was much encouraged that his first shaft had found so ready a mark; but Dubois-Crancé's serious reply, a second later, was even more to his liking.

"How right you are about Paris stinking with blood," he said; "the smell of it and death have begun to pollute the very atmosphere we breathe. Had I my way I would lop off another hundred heads, then make an end of this madness."

Tallien's small, dark eyes glittered. "Then, Citizen, your head would certainly be the hundred-and-first to roll into the basket. The guillotine must be kept moving for our own preservation. Our trouble is that too many, and mostly the wrong, heads are falling at the moment."

Well content with the way the party had started, Roger thought it undiplomatic to pursue the conversation further for the time being; so he tactfully changed the subject. When they reached the Bois, Maître Blanchard followed the instructions Roger had already given him, and drove on until they came opposite the opening of a glade that led into the densest part of the wood. They alighted there and carried the hampers along to a small clearing which was hidden from the track, while Blanchard drove on a little way, hobbled his horse, and returned to keep watch at the entrance of the glade.

As they spread out a tablecloth and unpacked from the hampers the cold viands and a big wine-cooler full of bottles wedged into chopped ice, it suddenly struck Roger that it was in just such a place that he had intended to conceal the Royal Family for the day nearly two years earlier. Since then—exclusive of France's losses in her campaigns against foreign enemies—by the annihilation of the population of La Vendée, the civil war against the Federalists and the massacres in the cities, it was now estimated that over a million people had perished. It was too, he reflected, at this very hour of the day that the ever-lengthening line of tumbrels would be carting another company of victims to the guillotine.

None of his companions appeared to be entertaining such grim thoughts. On the contrary, as they sprawled in the sunshine, the peace and charm of their surroundings, by contrast with the dusty, fear-ridden streets of Paris, made them behave with the lightheartedness of schoolboys out on a spree. It was not until they had all eaten and drunk well that Dubois-Crancé remarked:

"Did anyone come upon us here, they might well take us for conspirators."

"We are, or must soon become so," Roger replied, "otherwise all four of us will shortly lose our heads."

Tallien gave him a sharp glance. "Was it with that in mind you brought us out here?"

"Yes. The city swarms with agents of the *Sûreté*, and every other person in it is become an informer. Here, we are free to speak our thoughts without fear of eavesdroppers; there, even the whisper that four men such as ourselves had met behind locked doors would be enough to make us suspect."

"We are suspect already," Dubois-Crancé said bitterly. "You, because until recently you were living with an aristocrat; Barras, on account of his extravagance; Tallien, for his choice of a wife;

myself, because I refused to incur unnecessary casualties among my troops by sending them in to massacre two thousand poor wretches who, although defeated, still had weapons in their hands. And who is not now suspect? Desmoulins was right when he wrote in his *Vieux Cordelier* that if people opened their mouths they were abusing the *Comité*, if they kept them shut they were manifesting discontent, if they went out they were inciting to insurrection, and if they stayed at home they were plotting in secret."

"*Mort Dieu!* Then let us plot!" cried Barras. "For our host is right. If we do not, in a month from now we'll have nothing left to plot with." He looked at Tallien and added brusquely, "Are you with us, Citizen, or against us?"

"I must know what is intended before I answer that," Tallien rapped back. "As a good Republican I have no stomach for dictators. Providing our aim and end is to be Robespierre's downfall, I am with you. But should you have thoughts of establishing a Reactionary Government over his dead body, then you must count me among your enemies. Even with the hope of securing my wife's release from prison I would never lend myself to such a project."

"It would be futile to replace one group of man-eating tigers with another," argued Dubois-Crancé.

"Perhaps, Citizen, you regard me——" Tallien began angrily, but Roger cut him short.

"Be not so touchy; nothing personal was meant. All of us here have shed blood in the cause of the Revolution, and it is in the interests of all of us that the Revolution should continue."

"To what extent?" asked Tallien cautiously.

"To the full enjoyment by the people of the liberties they have secured by law, but are at present deprived of by tyranny."

"How would you ensure that?"

"By abolishing the *Comité* and holding a general election, then restoring to the Convention the supreme authority of which it has been deprived."

This suggestion was met by a chorus of protest, and even Dubois-Crancé pointed out that a general election would mean them all being swept away to be replaced by a Convention overwhelmingly reactionary.

"Very well, then," said Roger, seeing that he had gone too far; "let us retain the present Convention."

Tallien shook his head. "That would serve as no guarantee to us. We of the Mountain are outnumbered by the men of the Plain. Once they were free of their shackles they would serve us as we intend to serve Robespierre."

"Yes," Barras nodded, "we must retain the *Comité*, or some form of governing body, through which we can keep control of the situation."

"To that I agree," said Dubois-Crancé, "but I think Citizen Breuc is right in principle. Whatever form of machinery we may use, it should be our object to restore true liberty to the people."

"That is not practicable—at all events as yet." Tallien objected. "It would have the same disastrous result as allowing a starving man to gorge himself. I tell you, the Terror *must* be continued."

"To what degree?" enquired Roger.

"To a degree sufficient to prevent any reactionary movement among the people spreading to dangerous proportions, and to protect ourselves from our enemies in high places."

Barras laughed. "That suits me!" And, after a moment, Dubois-Crancé said:

"I see your point. Clemency has for so long been foreign to our affairs that it would be accounted weakness did we show it."

Roger, knowing that Tallien's participation was vital to their success, and feeling that half a loaf was better than no bread, decided that he must be given his way, so he said with a shrug, "So be it, then. Let us agree that to ensure the continuance of the Revolution and to protect the new government from the machinations of unscrupulous men, a moderated Terror should be maintained. How are we to set about ridding ourselves of the Dictator?"

"We four are not strong enough to bring about his downfall," Tallien remarked thoughtfully. "Consider the forces he commands—Couthon and Saint-Just on the *Comité*; a majority on the *Comité de Sûreté Générale*; Dumas, the President of the Revolutionary Tribunal, with all the judges and jurors under him; Hanriot, who commands the National Guard; Fleuriot, the Mayor, and Payen, the National Agent, who between them control the Commune; the Plain gives him a majority in the Convention and the Jacobins are his devoted slaves."

"He is none too secure in the *Comité*," countered Barras.

"Billaud, Collot and Barère are all secretly his enemies and would, I am convinced, join in an attack upon him."

"Even so, I believe we would find ourselves in the Conciergerie within the hour did we approach them," said Roger quickly.

Dubois-Crancé nodded. "I, for one, am not prepared to risk it; but valuable help is not far to seek. Bourdon of the Oise, Cambon and Legendre are all of our mind upon this matter, as are many less prominent deputies. It is only for us to decide in whom we should confide, and we can quickly form a powerful following in the Convention."

"They would prove an asset," Tallien conceded; "but it is my belief that there is only one man capable of meeting Robespierre on his own ground of subterranean intrigue."

"You must refer to the Abbé Sieyès," said Barras; "no man can have had more experience in such matters."

"No, I mean Joseph Fouché," came the prompt reply. "Fouché has more reason for immediate fears than any of us. He knows that he will never be forgiven by the Pontiff for his atheistic activities, and he has already been expelled from the Jacobins for excusing himself from appearing before them to explain his conduct while in Lyons. For the past ten days he has neither dared to enter the Convention nor sleep in his own house. He has become a lone wolf; but he is none the less dangerous for that, and I am convinced that we should do well to consult him."

For a further hour they discussed numerous possible allies; at length it was decided that, as next day was a Decadi, and there was no sitting of the Convention, they should meet again at Dubois-Crancé's house in the evening under cover of attending a card party. In the meantime they would sound several of the men of whom they had been talking and, if satisfied of their reliability, would invite them too. Madame Dubois-Crancé would entertain the wives of her husband's friends while they met together round a table and decided on a plan.

When Roger had dropped his fellow conspirators at various points in central Paris and was free to think matters over, he felt that he had good reason to be pleased with himself. Not one of his chosen first echelon had refused to participate, and circumstances now seemed propitious for the attempt. Saint-Just had recently gone on a mission to the Army, and for some weeks past Robespierre had tended more and more to withdraw himself from the *Comité*. Couthon continued to keep an argus eye on the interests of the Triumvirate by attending every sitting, but apparently Robespierre's overwhelming vanity had led him into the belief that it was a waste of his invaluable time to argue with Billaud and Collot. His vanity was also obscuring his judgment in other matters. He had left his humble lodging with the Duplaix family and moved to a fine country seat at Maisons Alfort, about three miles from Paris, where he now held a little court every evening of Fleuriot, Payen, Hanriot, Dumas, Coffinhal and his other toadies, and now seldom came into Paris except to attend meetings of the Jacobin Club. The fact that the Incorruptible was no longer behaving as though he were incorruptible was having a disturbing effect upon those minor fanatics in the Convention who had always previously supported him, right or wrong, solely from a conviction of the purity of his motives; and his absence from the *Comité* was enabling Billaud, Collot and Barère to undermine his influence. Yet it could not be disputed that he was still by far the most powerful man in France and that, although he had not yet openly proclaimed himself Dictator, he wielded an authority far exceeding that enjoyed by any Bourbon monarch.

The following evening at Dubois-Crancé's a party of eleven men and six women assembled. His wife received them and for a while entertained them with refreshments and conversation. In due course their host suggested that the men might like a game of cards and, leaving the ladies to gossip in the drawing-room, they withdrew to another room that had been prepared for the purpose. Seating themselves round a big baize-covered table, they distributed the counters and dealt a hand of Faro, so that should some unexpected visitor arrive they could at once, by starting to play, disguise the fact that they had been deliberating.

Barras had brought with him the mean, cunning Abbé Sieyès, whose bitter hatred of the Monarchy, nobility and his own order had contributed so much to the first Revolution. He had had a finger in every pie, and had betrayed in turn each group of politicians with which he had been associated, yet with extraordinary skill had managed to survive every purge that had taken place. Roger disliked and distrusted him hardly less than he did Fouché, who was also present. In addition to the arch-atheist, Tallien had produced Fréron, evidently from a feeling that he would require the support of at least two well-proved terrorists to ensure the adoption of his own policy. However, Bourdon of the Oise, Legendre, Cambon and Lacoste, all moderates by comparison with Tallien's friends, were there at the invitation of Dubois-Crancé; so Roger hoped that, if the group did succeed in seizing power, the Terror would at least be greatly lessened.

At Dubois-Crancé's invitation, Barras took the chair, thus assuming the leadership of the Party; and Roger was pleased enough for him to do so, as he was now quite content to remain in the background. After ascertaining that everyone present was willing to risk his head in an attempt to overthrow the tyrant, Barras said that the sooner they got to work the better, and asked for suggestions upon the form the attack should take.

The general opinion was that on the next occasion that Robespierre appeared in the Convention he should be accused of conspiring to become Dictator, and Tallien, spurred on by the hope of securing his wife's release, strongly supported Barras in his contention that action should be taken at the first possible opportunity.

However, the wily Fouché did not at all agree to this. He pointed out that their number was very small and they could at present count only on themselves, whereas, if they waited until Robespierre attempted a purge, it was quite certain that many other names would be included on his list besides their own, which would automatically secure them the support of all those he attacked with them. They would also be in the much stronger position of men not only defending themselves, but resisting an arbitrary decree which, if allowed to go unchallenged, would menace by precedent every member of the Convention.

Tactically, he was obviously right, and the only sound argument against his counsel was that if action were delayed too long the fact that a conspiracy was brewing might leak out, and several of the conspirators be arrested in their own homes before they had a chance to strike.

To decrease this danger, Fouché then suggested that some lesser action should be taken, with the object of angering the tyrant and inciting him to come out into the open sooner than he otherwise would have done; and the idea met with general approval.

After several rather unsatisfactory proposals for bringing this about had been put forward, Elie Lacoste, who was a member of the *Comité de Sûreté Générale*, said, "I think the desired situation might be achieved by striking at some of Robespierre's protégés on the Revolutionary Tribunal. Charges have recently been laid with my Committee against the jurors Vilate and Naulin. Normally we should take no action, but I could arrange for them to be arrested; that would be certain to arouse the tiger's fury."

"*Sang du diable*, yes!" exclaimed Barras; " 'tis a fine way to twist his tail." The others agreeing, it was settled that this step should be taken without delay and, if necessary, followed up with other pinpricks until Robespierre was goaded into striking at the deputies he believed to be opposed to him. After some further discussion, the question of another meeting was raised, and it was felt that it would be running a considerable risk for so many of them to come together with any frequency; so Roger offered to act as liaison between his three original co-conspirators, and suggested that they should keep their respective friends informed. This suited everyone; so they then rejoined the ladies and partook of a bowl of brandy punch, after which the party broke up.

During the days that followed Roger could have been employed in no way better calculated to keep him from agonized brooding over Athénaïs. From early morning until far into the night he was on the move about Paris, from the Hôtel de Ville to the Jacobins, from the Cordeliers to the Convention, and from one to another of a dozen different cafés and restaurants. No one, other than his fellow conspirators, had any reason to suspect his intense activity, as he was careful never to give the appearance of hurrying and whenever he was with people he always seemed to have ample leisure, but he managed to put up a show of coping with his own work and at the same time keep his new associates informed of the latest developments in a dozen different political circles.

Vilate and Naulin were arrested on the 19th, with the result that a special joint meeting of the two *Comités* was called for the following day. Receiving no satisfaction from the meeting, the enraged Robespierre called another for the 22nd, with the intention of condescending to attend in person. By that time Saint-Just, brought back from the Front to support his leader, was able to be present and made a speech urging the necessity of dictatorship. It then appeared that the arrests had had the desired result, as the Great Committee authorized him to draw up a report on the subject, and it began to be whispered that a long list of proscriptions was being prepared.

When Roger heard this he decided to take precautions against being caught napping; so he moved out to Passy. He had twice visited the Velots since his return to Paris in March and, now that

Lady Atkyns was out of the way, Talleyrand's house once again provided a retreat for him, the secret of which was known to nobody. Old Antoine and his wife were glad to have him there, as even the few hours he spent in the house made a pleasant stir in their somnolent routine, and during these nerve-racking days it made an enormous difference to him to be able to go to bed at night without fear of arrest.

On the 23rd it emerged that there was serious trouble in the *Comité*. Collot and Billaud had not taken at all kindly to Saint-Just's announcement that France needed a Dictator, and were preparing to fight Robespierre on the issue. In fact they were now looking round for allies to support an attack upon him, but hesitated to approach the Mountain in the belief that, having aided them to eliminate him, it would then eliminate them. Roger was much worried by this new development, as he feared that Tallien, Fouché and Fréron might now be tempted to ally themselves with Billaud and Collot; but that evening Tallien indirectly reassured him by saying:

"The crisis is approaching and I think this dissension in the *Comité* should prove a great help to us. I gather, too, that the whole lot of them are at sixes and sevens, as Robespierre intends to censure Carnot for ordering sixteen thousand men to be detached from Jourdan's army for the support of our coastal operations towards the Dutch Netherlands. On the representations of the Generals, Saint-Just cancelled the order, and the fact that the men on the spot asked him to do so has given the tyrant a fine stick with which to beat poor Carnot."

"If we could win Carnot over to us he would be an immense asset," said Roger quickly.

Tallien nodded. "I would that we could; but I am in no position to do so. How about yourself? He has entrusted you with several missions, has he not?"

"Yes; but I can hardly think that my influence with him amounts to much."

"Even so, if you feel that you could approach him without sticking your head right in a noose, it would be well worth attempting. Our task would be rendered far less hazardous if there were fewer National Guards in Paris, and Carnot is the only man who can get rid of them."

Having thought the matter over very carefully, Roger went to see Carnot next morning. After a few minutes' polite conversation, he said, "I am told, Citizen General, that Citizen Saint-Just saw fit to cancel the reinforcements you had designed for the support of Admiral Venstabel in the island of Walcheren. I am come to propose to you a measure which might fill that gap."

"Indeed!" replied Carnot with swift sarcasm. "On occasions it brightens my day to hear civilians express their views on military matters; pray do not be bashful in expressing yours."

"It is," said Roger quietly, "that although the Law requires you to keep certain troops in Paris, I see no reason why a battery of artillery should remain kicking their heels in every one of the forty-eight Sections. Would it not be a sound move to send half of them to the Front?"

Carnot knew, and Roger knew, that in every insurrection for the past five years it had always been the gunners who had displayed the most violent sentiments, and led the other troops to participate in anarchy and terrorism. Under the thin but adequate cover of military operations, Roger had suggested that Paris should be made safer for an anti-terrorist *coup d'état*.

Lazare Carnot rubbed his crooked nose thoughtfully, and said, "I feel, Citizen, that the value of such a measure against the Dutch is highly debatable, but it might well be justified on other grounds."

Emboldened by this reaction, Roger murmured, "France cannot afford to lose a man like yourself in a political purge, Citizen General; and those who appreciate your great qualities might fail in their efforts to protect you if there were too many gunners about." Then, without waiting for a reply, he turned and walked out of the office.

He spent the rest of the day in great suspense, fearful that he might have overstepped the mark; but by evening he was able to breathe freely again. Loath as Carnot was to interfere in domestic affairs, he had seen the red light; the fifteen batteries of artillery in the most dangerous Sections had been ordered to leave Paris that night.

The move instantly aroused the suspicions of the Robespierrists. Next day the Jacobins sent a deputation to protest to the Convention that the departure of these "patriot" troops threatened the people's liberties. Then Couthon rose and hinted darkly that drastic steps must be taken against "intrigues". Dubois-Crancé followed him and flung down a challenge by demanding a full investigation into his own conduct. Barère intervened to read a long report; but it was now clear that the explosion could not be long delayed.

The following morning Roger drew from Thellussons' Bank the remainder of the gold that de Batz had left there at his disposal, and took most of it out to Passy. He also bought from an apothecary a bottle of opium pellets, as he thought he might need these, as well as a large sum of money, for a private *coup* he was planning.

This last week of July coincided in the Revolutionary calendar with the first decade of Thermidor, the month of heat, and Paris now lay grilling under a brazen sun. Through the dust and stench of the unswept streets the tumbrels continued to rumble with their cargoes for the guillotine. Among the latest victims was the great gutter-born courtesan, Madame du Barry. Her crime was that three years earlier, learning that the Queen was in difficulties for money, she had nobly ignored the many slights Marie Antoinette had put upon her, and had written to offer her a million *francs'* worth of jewels, with the words, "All I have I owe to the Royal Family, Madame; so it is only right that now they are needed I should return them." Another was Lavoisier, France's greatest scientist. He had asked that his execution might be postponed for a fortnight to enable him to complete an important experiment. Coffinhal, the Vice-President of the Tribunal, had replied, "The Republic has no need for scholars or chemists," and sent him to die. The executions in July had already far exceeded those of June, but this was not enough; arrangements were being made to double the number in the coming month.

Everyone was now aware that a coalition was forming against Robespierre; but his power was immense and he was received with a hushed silence when, next day, he appeared in the Convention to make his will known. He complained first that his great work for the Revolution was being hampered by lack of support in both *Comités*, then made a scathing survey of all the Government Departments, belittling Carnot's contribution to the victories of the Army, and castigating Cambon's handling of the finances.

Cambon rose to defend himself, and cried boldly, "It is high time the whole truth was told. Is it I who deserve to be accused of having made myself master in any way? No—the man who has made himself master of everything, the man who paralyses your will, is the man who has just spoken—Robespierre!"

Greatly disconcerted, Robespierre replied that he came there only to unveil abuses, and not to accuse any particular person. At this there arose angry cries of "Name the individuals! Speak the truth! Name those whose heads you are planning to take from them!"

The uproar was quelled by the President, and a violent argument ensued whether Robespierre's speech should be printed, as was customary with all important declarations; but on this occasion the vote went against it, which amounted to a flagrant insult. For the first time since the fall of the Girondins, the Convention had rebelled against its master.

Robespierre and his friends hastened to their stronghold, the Jacobin Club, where they received a great ovation. He read his speech again to thunderous applause, and Couthon proposed the immediate proscription of all the deputies who had voted against Robespierre that evening. Dumas, Coffinhal and Payen surrounded him, urging him to assert his authority by force of arms, while Hanriot declared himself ready to lead the National Guard against the Convention; but Robespierre, ever timorous when it came to taking drastic action, could not bring himself to accept their counsel.

During the day, Barère, realizing the danger in which the whole *Comité* stood, had made a desperate attempt to reconcile its members, and so bring Collot and Billaud to Robespierre's support; but they would not listen to him. The gloomy Billaud held aloof, while Collot showed signs of going over to the rebels. Collot now appeared at the Jacobins, boldly thrust his way in, and attempted to speak; but the members, having got wind of his treachery, howled him down and threatened him with their knives. He was lucky to escape with his life.

At length it was decided that Robespierre should go to the Convention again next day, the Jacobins should assemble in their Hall, the Commune should hold a session at the Hôtel de Ville, and Hanriot should order out the National Guard; so that all three bodies would be ready to aid the "Father of the Country" if a further attack was made upon him.

During the night the *Comité* was in session. Saint-Just was due to present his report next day; Collot, fresh from his rough handling at the Jacobins, demanded that the report should be read. Saint-Just said he had not got it on him and a violent scene took place, in which Collot declared that the report had for its object the murder of them all. To pacify him, Saint-Just promised to read it to the

Comité the following morning, before submitting it to the Convention.

The 9th Thermidor dawned with promise of stifling heat. Through the sultry streets the deputies made their way to the Convention; from fear of arrest few of the prominent ones had slept in their own apartments. Roger, ignoring his duty to the Commune, also went to the Convention, where he learned that several of his secret associates had spent most of the previous night calling on deputies of the Plain in an attempt to win them over. In the entrance hall he found Tallien haranguing a group; he promised to make the first attack and urged them to stand by him.

At half-past eleven Saint-Just entered. On seeing him, Tallien exclaimed to his friends, "This is the moment!" They all crowded into the Chamber, and Roger went to the Municipal box, where he found a number of his own colleagues who had also ignored the summons to the Hôtel de Ville in order to witness the coming battle. Saint-Just had not, as he had promised, read his report to the two *Comités*, which was hardly to be wondered at, for as he now read it from the tribune, it proved to be a denunciation of them. Before he could finish it, Tallien interrupted him on a point of order, seized the tribune and shouted that the time had come for the representatives of the People to get at the real truth.

This provoked a roar of applause. It chanced that it had fallen to Collot's turn to act as President that day; still smarting from the Robespierrists' treatment of him at the Jacobins the previous night, he refused to let Saint-Just continue. There followed a long wrangle, during which a dozen people tried to speak at once.

At about one o'clock, Billaud, who had been waiting about at the *Comité's* office to hear the promised private reading of Saint-Just's report, came hurrying in; Collot promptly gave his colleague the tribune. Billaud then accused the Jacobins of holding seditious meetings with intent to slaughter the Convention. Shouts of indignation rent the air. Continuing, Billaud openly accused Robespierre of conspiring to become Dictator.

Robespierre, who had been sitting with his brother, Le Bas, and Couthon, now left his seat and, livid with rage, endeavoured to mount the tribune. At the sight of him cries came from all parts of the hall, "Down with the tyrant! Down with the tyrant!"

Tallien rushed forward again, brandished a dagger before Robespierre's face and cried, "Last night at the Jacobins I saw the

Army of this new Cromwell formed. Unless this assembly has the courage to pass a decree of accusation against him, I will slay him myself."

His last words were almost drowned by a tempest of cheering, and, wild with excitement, more than half the deputies were now on their feet.

At length Barère obtained a hearing, and made a speech that occupied much of the afternoon. The arch-trimmer, assessing that the battle was going against Robespierre, attacked him, but only indirectly, by ending with a proposal that, as Hanriot had threatened the Convention, he should be deprived of his command of the National Guard. A vote was taken and this was agreed. Then Robespierre again endeavoured to get a hearing, and looked like succeeding.

Seeing this, Roger was quick to realize the danger. Robespierre had dominated the Convention for so long that three-quarters of its members had formed the habit of subservience to him from fear of their lives; if he were allowed to address them there was an awful risk that a majority would wilt under the lash of his tongue and that he might still emerge triumphant. Leaning forward from the box, Roger yelled:

"Don't let him speak! Don't let him speak!"

The cry was taken up by Bourdon, Merlin, Légendre, Guffory, Fréron, Rovère and a dozen others. Then it changed to "Accusation! Arrest! Accusation! Arrest! Accusation! Arrest!"

Had Robespierre, Couthon or Saint-Just been a Danton, they might yet have saved their party; but all three were physical weaklings, and Robespierre's naturally thin, shrill voice could not be heard among the clamour. A deputy named Louchet bawled above the din, "I accuse Robespierre! Who will second me?"

"I will!" replied a chorus of a hundred voices.

Amidst a tremendous uproar the vote was taken. By an overwhelming majority Robespierre's arrest was decreed, together with that of Couthon, Saint-Just, Le Bas and the younger Robespierre—the last two owing to their own courageous decision to share the fate of their leader. Yet the ushers were so thunderstruck that they could not bring themselves to lay hands on the accused, until scores of shouting members demanded that they be brought to the bar of the house.

Saint-Just's report, the speeches of Billaud and Barère, the constant interruptions, the voting and the fights to get possession of the tribune, had eaten up the day; so it was five o'clock before the prisoners were taken into custody. They were marched away to the sound of shouts, jeers and most frantic excitement; then the President decreed a two-hour break, in order that the deputies might recover a little of their calm before proceeding to further business.

Roger watched the sitting break up in alarm, as he felt that with the Commune, the Jacobins and the National Guard all standing by to assist Robespierre, the crisis was far from over. With several of his companions in the Municipal box, he hurried to the Hôtel de Ville to see what was going on there. The Commune, having been sitting all day, had also just decreed a recess; but by six o'clock the news of the arrests was all over the city, and a number of the Commissioners came hurrying back into the hall, filled with consternation. The sitting reopened with furious demands for an attack on the Convention; an order was given for the tocsin to be rung and the Sections raised to rescue the champions of liberty.

The tocsin had hardly begun to clang when it was learned that the triumvirate were in no need of rescue. Either through stupidity or treachery they had been taken to the *Mairie*, which was an adjunct of the Hôtel de Ville; so, in effect, they were prisoners no longer, but were among friends. On hearing this, Roger slipped quickly out of the building. He had compromised himself so deeply at the Convention that, now it seemed certain that Robespierre was coming out on top, any of the Municipals who had been with him in the box might, at any moment, attempt to save their own skins by denouncing him.

In the streets, he found everything in confusion. The National Guard were temporarily leaderless, as Hanriot had been arrested. The men were holding meetings, some passionately arguing for one side, some for the other. While the evening light lingered Roger moved from group to group, attempting to assess popular feeling, and it seemed to be about fifty-fifty.

At nine o'clock he returned to the Convention, where he learned to his dismay that, half an hour earlier, Hanriot had escaped from custody. On the other hand the deputies, now realizing that their lives were at stake, were determined to make a fight for it. Barras was appointed commander of the armed forces, and with twelve others sent to raise the loyal Sections. At eleven o'clock it was learned that Robespierre and his friends had left the

Mairie and gone to the Hôtel de Ville. By so doing they had broken their arrest; so a decree was at once passed declaring them outlaws.

No sooner had this been done than a man burst into the Chamber with the news that Hanriot was advancing against it with his National Guards, and that cannon were being trained on the Convention. The brutal Collot then showed great bravery. Seating himself at the end of the hall which would receive the first shots, he cried, "Representatives, the moment has come for us to die at our posts!"

Many of the deputies followed his example; but others, with more practical sense, ran out of the building to the Place du Carrousel, where the battery was drawn up. In impassioned terms they argued with the gunners; the gunners gave way, and when Hanriot ordered them to fire they refused to do so. Hanriot, abandoned by his men, turned his horse about and galloped back to seek shelter in the Hôtel de Ville.

All central Paris was now in turmoil and confusion; so Roger decided to go to his own Section and raise a score or so men he could rely on. By one o'clock in the morning he was back with them at one of the approaches to the Hôtel de Ville, but the whole square before it was blocked by a crowd, mainly composed of *sans-culottes*, who were shouting, "Down with the Convention!"

As his uniform of a Commissioner protected him from attack, he squeezed his way through them, and found that all the other approaches to the square were now jammed with partisans of the Convention, who had been raised and brought there by Barras and the deputies who had been nominated to aid him. No fighting had yet broken out, but on all sides the most furious arguments were in progress. Eventually the affair was decided by Barras bringing up the gunners who had deserted Hanriot, and persuading them to turn their pieces on the Hôtel de Ville. The crowd dissolved, and the partisans of the Convention rushed towards its entrances.

Roger, knowing the building so well, led his party through a side door. Dashing upstairs, they burst into the great Chamber. Robespierre was standing by the dais with his friends grouped about him. Had he acted with decision a few hours earlier the Convention could not possibly have survived, and the dawn of the 28th of July would have found him the absolute master of France. As it was, he had let the fateful night slip by, inveighling against his enemies and making vain boasts of the vengeance he would take on them. Many of his supporters had been stricken with terror on learning that the Convention had passed a decree outlawing him and his associates. Only forty members of the Commune had remained to stand by him to the last; the rest had gone over to the Convention on first learning of his arrest, or had since slipped away to go into hiding.

As Roger entered by one door Hanriot dashed in at another; he had just been down to the main entrance and found his own gunners aiming their pieces at the building. To keep up his courage he had been drinking heavily. Lurching forward, he cried, "All is lost! Even the *sans-culottes* have betrayed us!"

Owing to the warmth of the night the lower sashes of the big windows were open. With a scream of fury Coffinhal seized Hanriot round the waist and yelled, "Villain! It is to your stupidity we owe this!" and, lifting him up, hurled him out of one of the windows. At the same moment Augustin Robespierre threw himself out of another.

Hard on Hanriot's heels, Barras's men streamed into the Chamber and joined with Roger's party in seizing the Robespierrists. Couthon was dragged from beneath a table. Le Bas drew a pistol and blew out his brains. A second shot sounded. Robespierre had also attempted to take his life but lacked the courage to hold the pistol steady; the bullet partially shattered his jaw, leaving him in agony but still fully conscious. For a few moments the Chamber was a scene of wild confusion, but no serious resistance was offered; by three o'clock in the morning the triumph of the Convention was complete.

Hanriot and the younger Robespierre had both landed on a muckheap, so although badly injured they were still alive. The former had crawled away and endeavoured to hide himself in a sewer; but some soldiers had dragged him out, half naked and covered with filth. With the rest of the principal prisoners they were taken to the offices of the *Comité* and placed under strong guard there.

The Convention was still in session; delirious with excitement and relief, the deputies were congratulating one another, weeping, laughing, and swearing eternal friendship. Roger was as relieved as any of them to think that his own life was safe; but he still had work to do, and had returned there not to rejoice, but for a very definite purpose. At last, after having had to participate in mutual handshakes and back-slapping for over an hour, he managed to get hold of Barras.

He knew quite well that Barras had been far too occupied during the night to think of anything other than the work in hand, but, drawing him aside, he said in a swift whisper:

"What precautions have you taken with regard to little Capet?"

"Why, none!" exclaimed Barras.

"Then we must not lose a moment," said Roger urgently. "Don't you realize that he is in the hands of the Commune? If the Commissioners on duty at the Temple tonight are Robespierrists, they may kill him, or make off with him."

"*Mort dieu!* You are right; and as a hostage he is invaluable."

"Exactly! Should we ever wish to make peace we can demand our lives for his, and a fortune each into the bargain. You had better give me an order to secure his person."

Without hesitation Barras went to the nearest desk, seized pen and paper and wrote:

By order of the Convention.

Charles Louis Capet, prisoner in the Temple, is to be handed over forthwith to the custody of the bearer, Citizen Commissioner Breuc.

Paul Barras.
Military Governor of Paris,
10th Thermidor, Année II.

Sanding the paper, he shook it, then handed it over; Roger took it, gave a swift nod, and hurried away. Once outside the doors of the Convention he drew in a deep breath of the early morning air, with more joy than if it had been a draught of rare wine. He had just lived through a great twenty-four hours. He did not believe that, in spite of anything that Tallien or Fouché might attempt, the Convention would allow the Terror to be renewed. Far too many of the deputies had nearly lost their own lives through it. The lesson would not be lost on them, and they would fight tooth and nail before they allowed themselves to be manœuvred into a position of such risk again. He had avenged Athénaïs's death, and had now as good as accomplished the thing which, through two long years of innumerable disappointments, he had come to regard as almost impossible. In his hand he held a paper that it needed only a little luck and energy to convert into a draft on the Bank of England for a hundred thousand pounds.

With swift steps he walked to *La Belle Étoile.* In this matter, he felt no qualms about involving his old friend Maître Blanchard; the reward was so great that he could well afford to give a share of it to the honest Norman, who, in the event of a Restoration, would be certain also to receive a patent of nobility if he took part in the little King's rescue.

At the hostelry he got Maître Blanchard out of bed, gave him the great news about Robespierre's final overthrow, then told him that he wanted him to drive a light coach; but did not disclose the business they were going upon. While he hurried into his clothes, Roger ran to his old room, pulled up the loose floorboard under the bed, and collected his reserve of money. Beneath the little bags of gold coins his fingers fumbled on a flat packet that he had not realized was there when last he had gone to the cache. Evidently it was something that Athénaïs had hidden some time before. Pulling it out he carried it to the window. Dawn had come and the light was sufficient for him to see that it was a letter addressed to him in Georgina's round, vigorous hand; but now was not the time to read it. Stuffing it in his pocket he ran downstairs. In the yard he helped Blanchard harness a horse, and five minutes later the landlord was driving him to the Temple.

He had already decided that the more openly he set about the business the less likely he was to arouse obstruction or suspicion. The keynote to strike was that anyone who attempted to argue with him did so at their peril. On arriving he stalked into the court-yard, tall, grim-faced, tight-lipped, his blue eyes hard as sapphires. Snapping an order at the sentry, he had the guard turned out and sent for the four Commissioners on duty. To them he showed his authority, then took over the keys of the tower and led the way up to its second floor. Hammers, saws and axes were brought. While Roger stood with folded arms the turnkeys broke down the door of the room in which little Capet had been confined for half a year.

When the door was down Roger waved the others aside and went in. He was almost overcome with the stench. It was now just on six o'clock and the light was sufficient to see the state of the room. It was unbelievably filthy. Some rats scuttled away in a corner. The big bed was empty, but a figure lay hunched up in a large cradle. Roger walked over to it and looked down; the boy was awake but did not move. He was dressed in a pair of trousers and an old grey jacket. Roger's first thought was that he had grown a lot. Then with a shudder of disgust he saw the lice moving in the child's hair. His face was very puffy and covered with sores.

Suddenly Roger bent lower and peered into it. A spasm of rage twitched his mouth, and the blood seemed to rush to his head. He almost choked with the violence of his fury, shock and disappointment. Someone had played a devilish trick on the Convention—and on him. The boy in the cradle was *not* the son of Marie Antoinette!

CHAPTER XXVIII

THE MYSTERY OF THE TEMPLE[1]

ROGER's brain was racing. This, then, was the reason why the little prisoner had been walled-up—not in order to make his rescue impossible, but so that no one should see him and realize that a substitution had taken place. When had the real little Capet been removed? Who was the poor wretched child whom some monster had condemned to suffer this awful solitary confinement in his place? Where was little Capet now?

The walling-up of the prisoner made it clear that the substitution had not been carried out by a Royalist. Some powerful Revolutionary must have decided to seize the little King as a personal hostage for himself. The odds were, then, that he was still in Paris, or somewhere near-by. But who had taken him?—Hébert? Chaumette? Danton? Robespierre? Simon? Not Simon, as he had never possessed the power to order the walling-up; and the others, except Robespierre, were dead. Surely they would have endeavoured to buy their lives by offering to disclose little Capet's whereabouts; and the fact that they had not done so proved that it was not one of them. Perhaps Collot, Billaud or Barère had him.

In any case the attempt to trace and secure him must be made at once, for never again would an opportunity occur when any of the leading Terrorists could be put under such great pressure to disclose their secrets.

Simon had handed the child over on the 19th of January, and he had been walled up on the 21st; so the natural assumption was that the substitution had taken place on the night of the 20th, although it was just possible that the walling-up might originally have been a precaution against rescue. If not, as Hébert and Chaumette had been responsible for the prisoner up to the time of their arrest in March, they must have known of the substitution, even if they were not responsible for

[1] Note: In this chapter the state in which the substitute child was found by Barras (actually at 6 a.m.), Madame Royale's midnight experience, Robespierre's action, the particulars of the postern door of the Temple, of the Simons' removal and their lodgings, of Simon's execution, of the laundry basket, and of the mysterious imprisonment of Tison, are all historically correct in every detail.

it; so why had they refrained from charging their enemies with it before they died? Perhaps, then, it had been made since. In an endeavour to settle the point, Roger said to the boy:

"You poor little chap! Cheer up; we'll soon make things much pleasanter for you. How long is it since you were brought here?"

"A long time," came the reply, evidently spoken with great difficulty. "A long time, Monsieur."

"Was it in the winter?"

For some moments the boy did not reply; then he feebly shook his head and murmured, "They brought me back from the country. I . . . I think it was in May."

"Do you know the name of the man who brought you here? Can you describe him?"

Again the boy shook his head; and now he wearily closed his eyes. He was obviously very ill and it did not seem likely that much more could be learnt from him for the present. Desperately Roger sought in his mind for a way to get further information. Evidently the substitution had taken place after Hébert and Chaumette were dead. In that case, to effect it the door must have been broken down. Some of the Temple staff must either have helped in that or heard it being done by men who had been brought for the purpose. He might be able to force them to talk, but it would take time to examine them all, and time was precious.

Suddenly an idea occurred to him. Leaving the room he, posted the Commandant of the National Guards on the door with orders that in no circumstances was anyone to enter; then he swiftly mounted to the third floor. There were sounds of movement in Madame Royale's bedroom; so she was evidently getting up. He knocked on her door and she opened it. Recognizing him as the Commissioner who had surreptitiously brought her sweets, she gave him a friendly smile and wished him "Good morning."

In a low voice he said, "Madame, can you keep a secret?"

She nodded, and he went on, "Then I have good news for you; but you must not mention it to anyone. Robespierre has fallen and the worst of the Terror is over; so I feel sure that in future you can expect better treatment. Now, with regard to your brother—for him this is very important. Do you recall a night when you heard a noise of hammering on the floor below?"

"Yes, Monsieur," she replied at once; "it was about two months ago—to be exact, on the night of the 22nd of May. So little happens to disturb my dull routine that I recall it perfectly, and the fright I had while it was going on, because a strange man came up here and demanded to see me."

"Did he give his name? What was he like?" asked Roger eagerly.

"He was a small man, very neatly dressed. His head seemed too big for his body, and he suffered from a nervous twitch. Not a word did he say, but stared at me impudently for a few moments. From the descriptions I have heard, I formed the impression that he was Citizen Robespierre."

"Thank you, Madame! I beg you to say nothing of this to anyone else; and I pray that when we meet again I may see you in much more fortunate circumstances." With a quick smile, Roger left her, relocked the door to her floor behind him, and hurried down the spiral staircase.

As he came round the last bend on to the little landing of the second floor he nearly collided with a man who was just emerging from the last bend on the way up to it. The light was poor but there seemed something familiar about the tall, lean figure. Hearing their approach, one of the Commissioners pulled open the iron door giving on to the ante-room. Next second, to Roger's consternation, he recognized the man opposite him as Joseph Fouché.

Fouché recognized him at the same moment, gave him a sharp glance and said, "I take it, Citizen Colleague, that, like myself, you have come here to make certain that our hostages are safe?"

"Yes; Barras sent me," Roger replied, striving to keep the annoyance out of his voice. So far he had had no chance to consider the repercussions of the entirely unexpected substitution; but, whatever they might be, he felt that Fouché's presence would prove a serious handicap to his own activities.

As they entered the ante-room together he was thinking, "This substitution of another child for the little Capet cannot be long concealed . . . as soon as it becomes known an intensive hunt for the real little Capet will begin . . . the hunt will be secret because they will do everything possible to prevent it becoming generally known that they have lost their precious hostage . . . my one advantage is that I now know where to start looking for him. . . . I must make the utmost of the lead I have . . . the longer they take in finding out the truth the longer my lead will be. . . . I must prevent Fouché from seeing the child . . . but wait—Fouché did not arrive in Paris until after the Royal Family had been imprisoned, and no deputies have ever been on duty here; so it is a hundred to one that he will not know the difference . . . but Barras may, and I must not yet jeopardize my standing with him. . . . So I must do what I can to protect the secret . . . that will be to my own advantage as a universal hue and cry would make things much more difficult for me."

Turning to Fouché, he said, "Citizen Colleague, the girl is in good health, but the boy is far from being so. He is in fact in such poor shape that I think a doctor should be called; yet I am averse to letting anyone enter his room until it has been formally inspected by a Commission. Would you oblige me by taking over here while I return to Barras and find out his wishes?"

Fouché at once expressed his readiness to accept responsibility; so, with a word of thanks, Roger left him and ran down the remaining stairs. As he crossed the courtyard he was chuckling to himself to think how well he had succeeded in turning his old enemy's appearance on the scene from a liability to an asset. The cadaverous atheist might go in and look at the boy himself; but he would prevent anyone else from doing so, which rendered it unlikely that the substitution would now be discovered during the next two or three hours.

On reaching the coach Roger asked Maître Blanchard to drive him to Maisons-Alfort as quickly as possible. It lay beyond Charenton to the south-east of Paris, and consisted only of a cross-roads with an inn and a few cottages on the fringe of the woods that stretched north to Vincennes. An ostler at the inn directed them to the property that Robespierre had recently acquired, and soon after seven they were driving up to a medium-sized house set in a pleasant private park.

The front door stood open, but Roger pulled the bell and waited in the porch. After a few moments a middle-aged woman crossed the hall to him and asked him what he wanted. She had close-set eyes, a somewhat Spanish look, and was dressed in black bombasine. Summing her up in a glance, he asked:

"*Citoyenne*, are you the housekeeper here?"

At her nod, he could hardly keep the excited tremble out of his voice, as he said, "I have come for the boy; be good enough to take me to him."

Her heavy black eyebrows went up. "To what boy does the Citizen refer? There is no boy in this house."

"Oh yes there is!" Roger grasped her arm and stared at her menacingly. "Come, now. Today is very different from yesterday. The Citizen Robespierre is a prisoner and within a few hours will be dead. I have been sent to get the child. If you thwart me it will be the worse for you."

She paled, but shook her head. "The Citizen is mistaken. He may search the house if he wishes, but there is no child here."

Feeling positive that she was bluffing, Roger snapped, "Very well, then; we will search. And for every five minutes you delay me in finding what I come to seek, you shall spend a month in prison."

Half pushing her ahead of him, he hurried from room to room, looking eagerly in each one for traces of the little King; and as they progressed upstairs he could not help observing a singular feature of this bachelor establishment.

For several weeks past there had been strange rumours about Robespierre. Until that summer it had been generally believed that he was sexually incapable. Cornelia Duplaix, the eldest daughter of the carpenter with whom he had lodged for so long, had endeavoured to persuade him to marry her and, having failed in that, had given out that she was his mistress; but few people believed her. Yet, after his removal to the country, it had become known that men like Hanriot, Le Bas and Coffinhal were not the only companions of his leisure hours. It was whispered that on summer nights the inventor of the Supreme Being was driven by his vanity to posture in his park while a bevy of nude beauties did their utmost to distract his mind from the cares of State. On the upper floor of the house Roger found evidence in support of such stories, for several of the bedrooms were still littered with the clothes and toilet preparations of women. The beds had been slept in that night and obviously their occupants had fled in a panic, no doubt upon news arriving with the dawn that morning from Paris of the "Incorruptible's" downfall. The servants too had fled. The black-browed housekeeper was the only person remaining in the mansion; even the horses were gone from its stables.

After touring the building from its attics to its cellars and visiting all its stables and outhouses, Roger brought the woman back to the front hall. He was bitterly disappointed, as he had confidently expected to drive away with the living equivalent to a hundred thousand pounds, and he had not even come upon any evidence that the boy had ever been there. It was possible that he had been taken from the Temple to some other hiding-place, yet it seemed most unlikely that Robespierre would have kept his precious prize anywhere but at Maisons-Alfort; as here, in his own residence, was the only place he could be reasonably certain of not having it stolen from him. There remained the possibility that the prisoner had been hurriedly carried off that morning, and that the housekeeper had since hidden all his things. Pulling one of his small bags of gold out of his pocket, Roger threw it with a clink upon a marquetry table, then said to her:

"Take your choice. Your protector is already as good as dead, and there are a hundred *louis* there, which will keep you in comfort for some time. Answer me truthfully and the money is yours. The alternative is that I take you back with me to the Conciergerie and charge you with aiding Robespierre to conspire against the Republic. I am convinced that he brought a boy of nine here during the last week in May. What has been done with him?"

The woman stretched out a claw-like hand for the gold and, her voice sharp with malice, replied, "Had you made your meaning plain earlier, and made it worth my while to talk, Citizen, you might have saved yourself much time. A boy was brought here towards the end of May, but one I would put at eleven at the least. It may be, though, that he had far outgrown his strength, for he was a poor sickly child of low intelligence and verminous from neglect. He was brought to the house by night and spent but one day here; the following night the Citizen Robespierre took him away again. That is all I know of the matter, and I cannot tell you more for all the threats or all the gold in the world."

In a flash Roger saw what must have happened. While the child was being smuggled swiftly and secretly out of the Temple in the middle of the night, it had never occurred to anyone to identify him. Not until he had arrived at Maisons-Alfort, or perhaps the next day, had Robespierre had a chance to examine him closely; only then had he realized that someone had been before him in removing the real little Capet. The substitute had no value whatever as a personal hostage to barter in an emergency, but, walled-up once more, his presence in the Temple could still be used to support the general belief that the Republican Government held the King of France prisoner; so, on discovering how he had been fooled, Robespierre had taken the wretched child back.

To Roger, the boy's own words, "They brought me *back* from

the country," now held a new significance. His immature and clouded brain had been thinking of the *last* time he had been cast into grim solitude, not the *first*. The woman was not lying; she knew no more than she had said. With a muttered word he left her, and crossed the gravel to the waiting coach.

He had intended to drive hell for leather to the coast; now he must return to Paris—and quickly. The clue to little Capet's disappearance must lie somewhere in the Temple. He had left Fouché on guard there, with the excuse that he was going to report to Barras, but having no intention of ever again seeing either of them. By this time Fouché would be wondering what the devil had happened to him. To still suspicion in that dangerous mind he must now act exactly as if he had, all along, intended to return. That was the only way to secure a free field for new enquiries at the Temple.

Roger's first cast was the offices of the *Comité*, and his choice proved a lucky one; Barras, Tallien and several others had installed themselves there. Its entrance hall was now a centre of gruesome interest. Robespierre, his fractured jaw bound up, lay on a table in its centre; Hanriot, who had had an eye gouged out by a bayonet-thrust when the soldiers had dragged him from the sewer, was slumped in an armchair; the younger Robespierre, several of whose ribs had been broken by his fall, was slumped in another. As many guards and citizens as could crowd into the place stood gloating over the fallen despots. Forcing a way through them, Roger gained access to Barras, and, after a few moments, succeeded by urgent signals in detaching him from two deputies with whom he was talking.

During the drive back, Roger had realized that, for all practical purposes, he had now lost his lead in the hunt for little Capet. His investigations at the Temple might take him days, and during that time, unless special precautions were taken, it would become generally known that a substitution had been effected. Therefore, it was now to his interest to let the cat out of the bag himself, and at least gain the esteem of Barras for enabling him to take steps in time to prevent the secret becoming public.

Having drawn Barras into a corner Roger said in a low voice, "The child is extremely ill and urgently needs the attention of a doctor."

"*Sacré bleu!* Then get him one!" exclaimed the harassed Barras impatiently.

"No; not till you have seen him." Roger cast an anxious glance at the men standing within a few feet of them, and added, "I can say no more here; but there are special reasons why you should return with me to . . . to the place whence I came."

"I am positively overwhelmed with work," Barras protested. But on Roger's insisting, he promised to follow him as soon as he could.

Back at the Temple, Roger thanked Maître Blanchard for his help, and sent him home; then he mounted to the second floor of the tower to be met by Fouché, who complained querulously of his long absence.

It was now a little before nine, so Roger had been away for just over two and a quarter hours. He shrugged the matter off by saying that it had taken him some time to locate Barras, and that he had then had great difficulty in reaching him. Having described the turmoil at the offices of the *Comité* and pacified Fouché, he ordered some breakfast to be sent up to him.

To his annoyance, Fouché, instead of going now that he had been relieved, declared that he also would have some breakfast; although when, twenty minutes later, a jug of coffee and a big ham omelette were brought up, he did scant justice to his portion. With his infallible instinct he had sensed that some mystery was afoot, and sat watching Roger beneath half-lowered lids. Roger would have given a great deal to be rid of him, but it was beyond his powers to order him to leave. In spite of his companion's disconcerting glance, however, Roger made a hearty meal, and had hardly swallowed the last mouthful when he caught the ring of spurred boots taking the stairs two at a time. Next moment Barras came striding into the room.

Pushing his plate aside, Roger beckoned him over to the broken-down doorway. Fouché uncrossed his long legs, stood up and followed them inside. The boy still lay hunched up in the big cradle, just as Roger had left him; he was now sound asleep.

Barras looked down at the puffy, dirt-encrusted face, swore, then glanced across at Roger. "It is years since I saw the Dauphin, but this boy bears no resemblance to the child as I remember him."

Roger nodded. "Nor does he to the boy who was in Simon's care when I was last on duty here, nine months ago. That is why I insisted on your coming to see him for yourself."

"A substitution has taken place," snuffled Fouché; "I felt

convinced of that the moment I set eyes on him. This youngster must be twelve years of age at least."

"What the hell are we to do?" Barras cried, in sudden consternation.

Fouché blew his nose. " 'Tis simple enough. We must wall this one up again, so that the secret of our loss does not leak out."

"Nay, that I'll not allow," said Barras angrily. "This poor little brute shall at least receive medical attention and in future be cared for properly. However, regarding policy you are right. The secret must be kept while we endeavour to trace young Capet. He must still be somewhere in France, for if the Royalists had got him out of the country we should certainly have heard of it ere this."

As he spoke he shook the boy awake and began to question him; but his replies were slow and sometimes meaningless. He complained of pains in his knees, which they found much swollen, as also were his wrists and ankles. Seeing that they could get little sense out of him, they gave up trying, and began to consult about his future. After some argument Fouché persuaded Barras to refrain in the interests of security from calling a doctor in for the time being. Barras asked Roger if he would remain in command at the Temple until a reliable man could be found to take charge of the unfortunate little prisoner, and as that was precisely the invitation that Roger had been angling for, he made no difficulty about accepting.

Between them they carried the child into Louis XVI's old bedroom, so that the one he had been occupying could be cleaned of its filth without anyone seeing him. Barras and Fouché then departed. Roger locked the door of the new prison, pocketed the key, and sent for cleaners; then, having been up for twenty-seven exhausting hours, he lay down on one of the camp-beds in the ante-room to snatch some badly needed sleep.

Before lying down he had given orders that he was to be roused at one o'clock with a meal for the prisoner and himself. When he was called the three hours seemed to have gone in a moment, but, after he had drunk a glass of wine, he felt all the better for them. Carrying the tray of food in to his charge, he fed him with some minced chicken and fruit, sponged his face, then locked him up again.

Now that a few hours of oblivion had refreshed Roger's brain, he felt that he must not lose another moment of this unique opportunity to get to the bottom of little Capet's disappearance;

so he went down to the ground-floor room of the tower, ordered the whole of the Temple's permanent staff to be paraded outside, and had them in for examination one by one.

As Robespierre had been fooled, it now seemed extremely unlikely that the exchange of prisoners had taken place since the walling-up on the 21st of January; further, it was quite definite that it could not have occurred before the 11th of November, as on that night Roger had been on duty at the Temple and had himself seen little Capet there. The inference was that he had been removed at the time of Simon's departure; so nearly all Roger's questions were aimed at finding out everything he could about the change in régime.

The permanent staff of thirty that had been employed during the early months of the Royal Family's captivity had been progressively reduced to fourteen by the end of the preceding December, and five of these were at present off duty. In an hour and a quarter Roger concluded a preliminary examination of the remaining nine, and while few of them could tell him more than the bare facts which he already knew, he managed to glean sufficient data to convince him that Simon was at the bottom of the substitution.

He had resigned on the 5th of January but had not moved out until the 14th; and he had not moved far then, as he and his wife had taken lodgings in a mews just off the street behind the Temple, and were believed to be still living there. In this connection an interesting fact emerged: there was a postern gate that gave on to this street which, at times, was used by members of the staff as a convenience. No sentry was stationed there; so they could come and go without showing their passes, and on their return they knocked on the door with a large stone that lay outside for the janitor to let them in. Apparently the Simons had often used this door, and on numerous occasions after their move had come in by it to visit their old friends among the permanent employees. When they had moved out on the 14th they had left by the front gate, and their possessions had been subjected to the usual inspection; but during the next few days they had returned to collect various belongings they had left behind, among them their clean washing. For the latter purpose they had brought in a big laundry basket by the postern gate on the evening of the 19th. At nine o'clock they had ascended to the second floor and Simon had officially handed his prisoner over to the four Commissioners. The couple had then left again some hours later, going out into the dark and foggy night by the back door, carrying their big laundry basket between them.

When Roger had finished his questioning he had little doubt that the laundry basket had been used to smuggle one child in and the other out, and he decided not to lose a moment in forcing a confession out of Simon.

The four Commissioners who had come on duty on the night of the 8th Thermidor should have been relieved, but the *coup d'état* had prevented that; and as the Commune had been a Robespierrist stronghold, they were glad enough to keep out of trouble by remaining where they were. From the moment Roger had arrived soon after dawn armed with his authorization from Barras, they had shown a scared eagerness to win his goodwill and protection; so he felt confident that he could rely on their obedience during his absence. Having sent for them, and for the Commandant of the Guard, he informed them that he had to go out on an urgent matter and could not say for certain at what time he would return; in the meantime double guards were to be posted, and in no circumstances was anyone to be allowed to enter any of the rooms on the second floor of the tower.

Five minutes later, he left by the postern door. As he shut it behind him he hoped that he would not have to return, for if Simon was hiding the boy he meant to get him out to Passy with the least possible delay; but if another disappointment awaited him, and he had to come back, he had done all he could to ensure that the secret of the substitution was protected in his absence.

He found Simon's number in the mews without difficulty, but, to his chagrin, repeated hammerings on the door brought no reply. A moment later a window above the next stable was thrown up and a slatternly woman poked out her head.

"It's no use knocking," she called down, "there's no one there. They only come here to collect their letters, and for a few hours now and then."

Roger heard this revelation with rising excitement. He had hardly dared to hope that he would find little Capet within a stone's-throw of the Temple, as it had seemed improbable that Simon would keep him prisoner in the first place in which he would be looked for should the substitution be discovered; but the fact that he had another address, at which he actually lived, suggested that he still had the boy, instead of having passed him on to Hébert or Chaumette, as Roger had feared would now prove to be the case.

Eagerly he questioned the woman. She could give him no information and did not think her neighbours could either, as the Simons kept themselves very much to themselves, and where they got to for most of the day and at nights had long been a matter for speculation in the mews. However, at Roger's pressing, she suggested that he might try Citizen Sauret, who owned the drinking-shop on the corner, as he was an old crony of Simon's.

Citizen Sauret proved to be a typical dark-browed, middle-aged *sans-culotte*, and Roger wasted no time in mincing matters. Having decided that a firm bluff would be the most likely policy to produce swift results, he told him he had definite information that he knew Simon's other address.

With a surly scowl the man denied it; so Roger drew a pistol from his sash, pointed it at him, and said, "Heads are rolling fast today, Citizen, and a different type of heads from those which fell yesterday. Either you give me the information I require, or I place you under arrest, and I'll see to it that yours goes into the basket before the end of the week."

Sauret collapsed under the threat, and admitted to knowing that the Simons had rooms in the former Convent of the Franciscans.

Roger told him that should he find that he had lied he would return and have him hauled off to prison, then he hurried back through the postern door and crossed the Temple garden to its stables. The Convent lay in the Rue Marat, a mile and a half away on the far side of the Seine; so he had decided to ride there. It was a little after three o'clock when, having borrowed the charger of one of the officers of the guard, he rode out of the front gate, now, once more, in high hopes that within half an hour he would be well on the way to earning a hundred thousand pounds.

As he rode southward the narrow streets became more and more crowded. No trial was needed to condemn Robespierre and his friends, as they, together with those members of the Commune who had stood by them to the last, had all been outlawed the previous night. The Convention had only to decide which of them were to die and have them formally identified; so the execution had been fixed for four o'clock that afternoon. For it, the guillotine had been moved back from the Porte St. Antoine to its old position in front of the Tuileries, so that the maximum number of citizens might enjoy the spectacle of the Terrorists being brought to book for their heinous crimes. During recent months the great mass of the people had become too sickened by the daily slaughter to watch executions any longer, but today they had come out in their thousands, and their cheerful faces as they streamed westward showed their delight at the downfall of the tyrant.

At every corner the throngs of people crossing Roger's route impeded his progress; so it took him nearly half an hour to reach the Convent. Leaving his horse to be held by a lad, he went in, and soon found the two rooms occupied by the Simons. In the living-room a grey-haired woman was sitting crying with her face buried in her apron, and two others were endeavouring to console her. At the sound of his entry she lowered her apron, and he at once recognized her as Madame Simon. Saying that he wished to speak with her, he abruptly ordered the other two from the room.

While they were shuffling past him, it struck him as fortunate that Simon was not there, as, if they had the boy hidden away in a cellar or an attic, it should be easier to force the truth out of the woman on her own. As soon as the door had closed, he said:

"*Citoyenne*, I must warn you that your position is serious. It is known to us that on leaving your post at the Temple, you and your husband removed Charles Capet in a laundry basket. Only immediate obedience can save you. Take me to him."

She stared at Roger with tear-dimmed eyes and shook her head; but she did not seek to deny it, and muttered after a moment, "I cannot, Citizen. Alas! You ask more than I can perform."

Her words had such a ring of truth that they instantly dashed Roger's hopes; but his fresh disappointment was submerged in a sudden wave of alarm, for there was something about the phrase she used which suggested that the boy was dead.

Striding forward, he seized her by the shoulders and cried, "What, woman! Do you mean that it was not enough for the two of you to poison that child's mind, and that you allowed him to die whilst in your hands?"

"No, Citizen, no!" she protested shrilly. "We were both fond of little Charles, and would have done him no harm. We did only as we were told. We would have liked to keep him with us, but we dared not refuse to obey the orders we were given."

Greatly relieved, Roger said in a kinder tone, "Tell me exactly what happened, and I will not deal harshly with you."

"He spent the first night with us in the mews," she sniffed. "Then, when it was dark next evening, we brought him here. The night after that Simon took him to the country."

"To whom? And where?"

"I do not know, Citizen; Simon has always refused to tell me."

"How long was Simon away from Paris?"

"Well above three weeks."

Her reply suggested that Simon had taken the boy on a considerable journey; but it was possible that the whole time had not been employed in travelling, and that having delivered his charge Simon had remained at the new hiding-place for a while to see him well settled in before returning. After a moment Roger asked:

"Do you know who gave Simon his orders?"

She nodded. "It was the Citizen Procureur Chaumette."

"Very well," said Roger. "The Citizen Chaumette is dead; so he cannot help us; but no doubt Simon can be persuaded of the wisdom of answering our questions, and if he does I will deal leniently with him. Where is he?"

Her eyes grew round and her mouth opened as if to emit a scream. With an effort she checked it and whimpered, "Do you not know, Citizen? He . . . he has always been a patriot. He . . . lived only for his duty. He was at the Commune last night when Robespierre was taken. They are going to . . . to guillotine him this afternoon with the others."

Throwing her apron over her head she again burst into tears. Roger, electrified by her words, ran from the room, shouted to her friends who were lurking outside the door to go in to her, and dashed out of the building to reclaim his horse.

As he mounted and turned its head northwards, his thoughts were chaotic. Simon was no terrorist, except in that he fully subscribed to the principles that had led to the Terror, but he had been the confidant of Hebert and Chaumette, and had for so long represented the Commune as chief jailer of the Royal Family that his name was known to everyone; so it was not surprising that he had been selected as one of the Commissars whose death was designed to signalize the downfall of the Red Municipality of Paris. That he deserved death there was no question; for the way in which he had warped, poisoned and befouled the little King's mind, Roger would have sent Simon to die without the least qualm. But if he died within the next half hour he would carry with him to the grave the secret of where he had taken little Capet.

Roger realized that in order to save Simon he would have to disclose to Barras all that he had so far found out about the substitution; but what was the alternative if he refrained? The boy might be living in a slum of some provincial town or on an isolated farm; his present keepers might not have been trusted with the secret of his identity, and might regard as childish romanticizing his statements that he was the King of France. Even if they knew who he was, fear of consequences might restrain them from ever acknowledging it; and as the years passed his memories of the days when he had worn a little sword and been addressed as *Monseigneur*, and even of the Temple, would fade until he came to believe them no more than dreams. So, if Simon died without disclosing what he knew, all trace of Louis XVII might be lost for ever.

As Roger urged his mount forward, he decided that rather than risk that he must make Barras a present of the result of his investigations. If he played his cards well Barras might commission him to recover little Capet. At least he would share in hearing Simon's disclosures; so would stand a good chance of carrying off the hundred-thousand-pound prize before anyone else could reach it. But would he be in time to save Simon?

He had spent less than ten minutes at the Convent; so there were still twenty minutes to go before the hour of execution. At any moment, though, the tumbrels would be leaving the Conciergerie. The streets on the south side of the river were now almost empty, but from several turnings trickles of people converged at the entrance to the Pont Neuf. The crowd grew thicker as he crossed the bridge. On the Quai de Louvre it was dense. In vain he shouted at the people to make way for him. They were too numerous to fear that he would ride them down, and angrily threatened to pull him from his horse. A quarter of an hour had gone before he came abreast of the Tuileries, and there he became finally stuck. He could move neither forward nor backward, and knew that all hope of saving Simon was gone.

His mount was a docile animal, and stood quietly in the midst of a sea of people. Over their heads, in the distance, he could see the guillotine. On all sides the crowd stretched away as far as the eye could reach; every window in sight and every roof for a mile around was packed. All Paris had turned out to witness the end of the men who had held the city under a pall of terror for so long. Waves of cheering were pierced by hoarse cries of execration as the tumbrels advanced. Down the faces of many people tears of joy were falling at the thought that by this day's work their friends and relatives in the prisons were being reprieved from certain death. Never had twenty-one men been brought to die in the face of such universal hatred and condemnation.

Couthon, Saint-Just, Hanriot, Dumas, Simon and the rest ascended the scaffold one by one. As each head fell the roar of cheering was like the thunder of a heavy sea. Robespierre was kept until last. To free his neck for the knife the executioner tore away the bandage round his head. His broken lower jaw fell forward on his chest, and he let out a scream so piercing that it could be heard a mile away. Next moment he was thrown upon the plank, the slanting blade flashed down, the executioner stooped towards the basket, then held the gaping, gory head aloft for all to see.

It was the end of the Terror. Men like Tallien and Fouché might consider its continuation on modified lines necessary as a policy, but as Roger looked about him he felt certain that they would no longer dare to press it in the face of this overwhelming demonstration; for to do so now would be to risk their own necks. The people had gone crazy with excitement; weeping, cheering, embracing, shouting, they called aloud on God to witness their joy, and fell on their knees to thank Him for their deliverance.

The press continued to be so great that it took Roger over an hour to get back to the Temple. The Commissioners reported all well and that no one of importance had called; so Roger had good hopes that Barras would never learn that during the afternoon he had absented himself from his post. Having thrice since dawn that day believed himself to be within an ace of securing the little King, and having thrice been cheated of his expectations, he felt grievously ill-used by Fate; but it was not in his nature to give up so long as he was capable of making a further effort, and on his slow progress back from the Place de la Revolution a new idea had occurred to him.

In the Commissioners' room on the ground floor of the tower a great book was kept. From the first day of the imprisonment of the Royal Family every circumstance connected with their captivity had been entered in it. Every Commissioner signed it on coming on duty and, having entered his personal report in it, signed it again before going off. In it were registered the engagement and dismissal of all members of the permanent staff, and every visit made to the prisoners by doctors, seamstresses, tradesmen and officials. By going carefully through the entries for the last months of 1793 Roger thought there was just a chance of his coming on some clue which might give him a lead to where little Capet had been taken. Having carried the book up to the second floor, he sat down at a table in the ante-room to study it.

After an hour's reading he was struck by one thing. From mid-September onwards there appeared to have been a deliberate movement to get rid of all the servants who had been there for a year or more. Le Baron, the turnkey; Cailleux, the administrator; Mauduit, the treasurer; Mathey, the steward; the three waiters, the two pantry-men and the two wood carriers; all had been sacked.

It was just before the beginning of this purge that the Commune had issued a decree, at Hébert's instigation, ordering a reduction of the Temple staff on the grounds of economy; but that did not explain the matter entirely as, although a reduction had been made, nearly half the dismissed men had been replaced by others. It occurred to Roger that possibly the walling-up of a child had not been part of the original substitution plan. Perhaps the purge had been initiated with a view to getting rid of all the servants who had come to know little Capet well by sight, so that if a boy resembling him could be found the substitution could be effected without the newcomers noticing the difference; and that only when the plotters had failed to find a child sufficiently like him had walling-up been resorted to.

On checking through the list of the original employees Roger found that one of them, Citizen Tison, had not been dismissed but imprisoned, at Simon's order, on the vague charge of "being too familiar with the prisoners". That seemed most curious in view of Tison's history, as Roger knew it.

In August, '92, a few days after the Royal Family had been brought to the Temple, the King had asked that a couple should be engaged to spare his valets the rough work of the household. The Commune had nominated the Tisons for this task. They were middle-aged and were proved Revolutionaries—the man acrimonious by disposition and the woman a sloven. On the removal of the Royal Family from the Little to the Big Tower in October, the Tisons had been installed in a room on the Queen's floor, where they were well situated to spy on her. The following April, Tison had laid information that certain of the Commissars were plotting with the Queen, and had made his wife give evidence that the loyal waiter, Turgy, was holding secret communication with the prisoners. It was this which had led to Turgy's dismissal, and the suspension of Toulan and Lepître from further duty at the Temple, thus rendering abortive one of the numerous attempts at rescue that had been planned. Madame Tison's part in the denunciation had so preyed on her mind that she believed herself to be responsible for the decision to remove little Capet from his mother, and that this was to be followed by their deaths. By the end of June her brooding had become a mania, followed by complete madness and violence, so that it had taken eight men to remove her to the Hôtel Dieu. But Tison had remained on, and, since he had so plainly demonstrated his loyalty to the Commune, it seemed quite extraordinary that in September he should have been imprisoned for "being too familiar with the prisoners". More extraordinary still, he had not been removed to one of the ordinary prisons, but confined in the Little Tower of the Temple itself.

Feeling certain that he had noticed a later entry about Tison, Roger flicked through the huge book until he came to December. Apparently a Commissar named Godard had raised the question of this mysterious prisoner, and proposed that since there was no proper charge or evidence against him he should be liberated; but this had resulted only in an official order that Tison was to remain where he was, and continue to be debarred from communicating with anyone.

That was the last entry about Tison; so it appeared that for many months past there had been not one, but two, prisoners walled up in the Temple. What could the wretched man have done, or heard, or seen, to receive such treatment? It could not be because he had witnessed the substitution of the child, as that had not occurred until three months after his own incarceration. But the date of his imprisonment tallied with the beginning of the dismissals of the other old employees, which suggested that preparations for the substitution were already under way, so he might know something of the plot. Trembling with excitement, Roger closed the book and went downstairs to the little room occupied by the turnkey.

On the man's confirming that Tison was still imprisoned in the Little Tower, Roger demanded his keys, then went up to the second story. There he found that Tison was confined in the east bedroom, adjacent to the water-closet. Its old door had been removed and a new one of stout oak substituted, in which was a revolving wicket, similar to that used for the child up in the Big Tower, by which food could be passed in without the jailer being able to see the prisoner. Unlocking the door, Roger went in.

Tison was sitting on his bed in a dejected attitude. His hair and beard had grown so long that he had the appearance of a shaggy animal. As Roger entered he came to his feet, stumbled forward and cried in a hoarse voice, "Let me out! Let me out! Why do you keep me here?"

Roger waved him back and said kindly, "Easy, man; it is about your release I have come. I think you may expect it soon if you answer my questions properly. What did you do to cause them to lock you up?"

"Nothing, Citizen, nothing! I have always been a good Revolutionary; I swear it. All was well one day, and I was locked in here the next. It has near driven me mad wondering why I should have been kept here all these months. For God's sake take pity on me!"

"Come; there must have been some reason. You quarrelled with Simon, did you not? Well, you need have no more fear of him, for he was guillotined this afternoon."

"Simon guillotined! *Sacré bleu*, for what?"

"That is no concern of yours. Answer my question!"

Tison shook his shaggy head. "I had no quarrel with Simon. I did always as I was told. I am a good patriot; I proved it by denouncing the widow Capet for her plots."

"I am aware of that; but what else did you find out besides her plots? Did you know aught of one to remove the little Capet and substitute another child for him?"

"No, Citizen, no! How should I? The boy was always in Simon's care, and on the floor below me. I scarcely saw him."

"But you might have heard Simon talking with someone about such a project."

"I did not, Citizen; I swear it."

"Listen," Roger said patiently. "I am convinced that Simon had you locked up because he believed that you had stumbled upon some secret that might prove dangerous to him. Try to remember anything unusual that happened to you on the day before they confined you here."

For a few moments Tison remained silent, then he shook his head again. "It is useless, Citizen; I can think of nothing. I carried out my duties as on any other day."

It seemed that they had reached an impasse, and as Roger looked at the hairy, dishevelled figure in front of him, it flashed through his mind that he might well have been participating in a scene enacted in the bad old days of the Bastille. Here, under the vaunted reign of "Liberty, Equality and Fraternity", was a poor wretch who had been imprisoned and denied all communication with the outside world for nearly a year, without trial, or without even having the faintest idea of what he was accused. After a moment he tried another line.

"Do you recall any special visitors coming to the Temple on that day? Citizens Hébert or Chaumette, for example?"

"Ah!" exclaimed Tison. "Citizen Chaumette came, and had a talk with Simon."

Roger's blue eyes lit up. "Did you hear any part of their conversation?"

"Yes; they stood for a few moments in the doorway of Cléry's old bedroom while I was cleaning out the lavatory at the end of the passage. I did not see them, but recognized them by their voices, and it is possible that they did not realize I was there. But they spoke of nothing of importance. Citizen Chaumette said that he had heard from his cousin with the farm at Divonne, and that he could do with someone to look after the pigs. At that they both laughed and Chaumette added, 'He must wait, though, until we can find someone suitable to play the other rôle.' "

Striving to keep the excitement out of his voice, Roger asked, "And then? What else? What else did they say?"

"I don't remember," replied Tison with a sigh; "I wasn't listening particularly. That bit stuck in my memory because my old woman came from the Jura and I've heard her talk of a village there called Divonne; but their talk of farms and pigs meant nothing to me."

To Roger it meant everything. Obviously, too, Simon must have later seen the cleaner come out of the lavatory, and, believing that he had overheard enough to understand the whole plot, had him locked up as the best means of making certain that he did not betray it. To Tison he said:

"Now I will give you a piece of news and some sound advice. Today Robespierre was executed, and the Terror is over. The robbery, imprisonment and murder of innocent people under the guise of 'patriotism' is no longer in fashion; so if you are wise you will not boast too much about your deeds when you are next questioned. Observe caution about that and I think you will soon be released. If I have the opportunity I will put in a word for you."

"Don't go, Citizen! Don't lock me up again!" pleaded Tison, stumbling forward. But Roger pushed him back, pulled open the door, slipped outside, then slammed and locked it.

On the lower floor the good library of M. Barthélemy, who had been dispossessed overnight to provide accommodation for the Royal Family, remained undisturbed; so Roger went straight to it and took out an atlas. He had no difficulty in locating Divonne, and a rough calculation showed that it lay about two hundred and ninety miles by road from Paris. In winter a coach would not average much more than twenty-five miles a day, and at that rate the journey there and back would have taken twenty-four days. That tallied perfectly with Madame Simon's "well above three weeks", and relieved Roger of the apprehension that Chaumette might have been referring to some other village elsewhere with a similar name.

Its situation, too, could not have been better suited to Chaumette's plan, for it lay almost in sight of Lake Geneva and only a few miles from the frontier. He would have had only to go there and take little Capet over into Switzerland to hold a truly Royal Flush. From Geneva he could have bartered with any of the Allies for protection and a fortune, or, if Revolutionary France had proved willing to give him an amnesty and a greater sum, sold the boy back into captivity. As it was, both he and Simon had been caught napping by overnight arrest, and had evidently decided that talking at the last moment would not save them from their treacherous enemies; so it was better to die silent and enjoy the revenge of having deprived them of the stolen prize.

Slamming the atlas shut, Roger gave its cover a triumphant smack with the flat of his hand. He had, after all, succeeded in solving the riddle of where little Capet had been taken. In addition, as though to make up to him for the many blows dealt him during the day, Fortune had decreed that the boy should be hidden within an hour's ride of the frontier, thus saving him from having to solve the awful problem of how to get that wilful, vicious, unpredictable child half-way across France without being detected.

It was now close on eight o'clock; so he went downstairs and ordered supper to be sent up for himself and his captive. While it was being prepared he went in to the boy, washed him, combed his hair, and made him as comfortable as possible; then when the food arrived, he fed him on tit-bits.

Having locked the prisoner's door again, he sat down to his own supper in the ante-room. As he ate it he joyfully made his plans. It was most unlikely that anyone else would get on little Capet's track for a considerable time to come; so he felt that he had secured a first-class lead and now had no need to hurry. For that he was profoundly thankful, as he had had only three hours' sleep in the past thirty-eight. He would get in a good long night, then in the morning send a message to Barras asking to be relieved. According to when his relief arrived, he would disappear from Paris either the next afternoon or the following morning. Four days later, unless he was the most unlucky of men, he would collect from the world's lottery his ticket for one hundred thousand pounds.

By the time he had finished eating he was feeling sleepy, and his thoughts began to wander a little over the incredible suspense and excitement to which he had been subjected during the past day. With a start, he suddenly recalled the letter from Georgina that he had found in his cache at *La Belle Étoile* early that morning. Wide awake again now, he pulled it from his pocket.

On its back, evidently with the same pen she had used to write her last letter, Athénaïs had scrawled, *Forgive me, Roger, for keeping this from you. It was brought over in March by a member of the League, and seeing it to be in a woman's hand I opened it. I could not bear the thought that news of your wife should come between us.*

In the last paragraph of Athénaïs's letter she had urged him to forgive his wife. As he had not told her of Amanda's infidelity the passage had vaguely puzzled him, but at the time he had been too distraught to think very much about it. Evidently this explained how she had learned that his marriage was on the point of breaking up.

Taking the letter from its envelope, Roger read it through. Georgina had discussed matters very thoroughly with Amanda. She counted herself fully justified in what she had done. Her attitude was that she had never received his letter by Dan, and that even had she done so her conduct would have been no more than tit for tat. Further, she pointed out that Roger had been abroad a great while and that, envisaging such absences before they married, they had agreed to count themselves free at such times if they wished. As to malicious intent, she was amazed that he could think so ill of her. It was, indeed, for the very purpose of protecting his name that she had removed to Lymington. Had she remained at Richmond, undesirable comment upon de Batz's visits to her would certainly have been made; but Lymington being the headquarters of the French *émigrés*, he passed there as one of the crowd. Lady Atkyns had been living in the house and provided admirable chaperonage for her as a grass widow, and they had entertained a score of French exiles there, both ladies and gentlemen, almost constantly. De Batz, she said, was intelligent and discreet; they had many interests in common and he had provided her with a most pleasant diversion, but meant no more to her than that. Finally, she took a firm stand on the point that she required no forgiveness. If Roger wished to resume their life where it had been broken off, that would make her truly happy; but it must be on their original understanding that, when he went abroad for long periods, they would both be free to indulge in transitory affairs should they feel so inclined.

Roger laid the letter down with a sigh. It was a considerable relief to him that he would still be able to visit his old home without fear of being the object of malicious laughter, and he felt that he owed Amanda an apology for ever having thought that she would place him deliberately in such a situation. He realized now what it was that had so warped his judgment in the whole unhappy business. Had they stuck to their original bargain neither of them would have suffered from sore hearts. It was their having unconsciously gone back on it and, unlike most of their contemporaries, enjoyed two years of faithfulness and perfect amity. Yet he would not have had that otherwise, as it would always be a mental treasure to recall with joy. It was the sort of experience which would bind a couple together later in life, when their blood had cooled a little and their minds dominated their matter, so that they had come to realize the folly of dissipating themselves in pursuit of things that could have no permanent value. All the same, he was not prepared to crawl back to Amanda. . . .

He had got only so far in his ruminations when the iron door to the stairway swung open and the tall figure of Joseph Fouché appeared. Roger hastily thrust the letter into his pocket and stood up.

"Good evening, Citizen," Fouché said without looking at him. "I have come to enquire about the progress of your investigations into little Capet's disappearance."

"I fail to understand you, Citizen," Roger replied in apparent surprise, but his pulses began to quicken in alarm.

"I think you do." Fouché's voice was soft and insinuating. "This morning, the moment you set eyes on our present prisoner you realized that he was a substitute. Yet you did not share your discovery with me. Instead, on the excuse of reporting to Barras, you dashed off to make enquires at Maisons-Alfort."

"What of it?" Roger shrugged; "I am not accountable to you for my actions. It crossed my mind that Robespierre might have made off with the little Capet."

"Quite so; and finding he had not, this afternoon you decided to devote your attention to the Simons."

"It seems that you have been following me!" Roger now allowed his voice to show a hint of anger. "But what if I have done as you say? It is of the first importance that we should recover the missing child."

Fouché's corpse-like face remained quite expressionless. "Indeed it is, Citizen. But is that your business? And is Barras aware that you deserted your post here for above two hours?"

"What the hell has all this to do with you?" Roger burst out.

"A lot!" Fouché's tone suddenly became sharp. "As a member of the Convention, I am entitled to question your intentions. Just now I learnt that on your return here you spent a long time examining the Temple book, then put the prisoner Tison through a private investigation. Why did you do that?"

"Because it is obvious that a commission will be appointed to go into the whole matter; and having nothing to do here I thought to save them time by making some preliminary investigations."

"I do not believe you; I believe that the frantic efforts you have been making all day to trace little Capet were inspired by a private motive. I believe that had you found him, it was your intention——"

Suddenly Fouché broke off. For once his shifty, fish-like eyes had ceased to flicker and had come to rest. Roger followed his glance and saw that they were riveted on the table. The sight of the thing they were now both staring at made his heart contract with dismay. It was the envelope of Georgina's letter; and it was not addressed to *Citizen Breuc*, but to Monsieur Brook.

Next second, Fouché's voice came in a snarl, "At last I recall where we met! You are the English Admiral's son! So you *did* mean to steal little Capet!"

As he spoke, he sprang backwards and pulled a small pistol from his pocket. Levelling it at Roger, he cried:

"Hands up, you accursed spy!"

CHAPTER XXIX

ROGER BROOK *versus* THE FRENCH REPUBLIC

As Fouché's dull eyes lit with triumph and he sprang away, Roger instinctively took a pace forward. There was still barely four feet between them, and less still from the point of the pistol to Roger's heart.

His brain was working with lightning speed. On the verge of victory he was faced with utter destruction. It was all or nothing. Once Fouché had got the upper hand there could be no escape. The loss of a split second would mean the loss of life and fortune. Before Fouché had time to cock the weapon, Roger hurled himself upon him.

At the same instant Fouché took another pace back, but the pistol was knocked from his outstretched hand. Grabbing at one another, they closed. Fouché was taller than Roger and his lean figure concealed surprising strength. He locked his arms round Roger's middle and pressed his chin down into his left shoulder. In vain Roger strove to force his enemy's head up and get a grip on his throat. For thirty seconds, sixty seconds, ninety seconds, their feet planted firmly, they strove silently for mastery.

The strain on the small of Roger's back became so frightful that he thought his spinal column would snap. Frantically he beat at the sides of Fouché's head with his fists; but the agony increased to such a degree that he could bear it no longer. With a groan he let his knees buckle and went over backwards.

The back of his head struck the floor heavily. A blinding pain seared through it. At the same second, but as though at a great distance, he heard Fouché give a howl of agony. All the strength seemed to seep from Roger's limbs; but Fouché, too, was temporarily disabled. As they fell his right wrist had been twisted violently beneath Roger's body. With a groan he pulled it out, knowing now that, crippled, he would not be able finally to overcome Roger. Instantly his mind reverted to his fallen pistol. Even if, left-handed, he missed with it, the sound of the shot would rouse the guard on the floor below. Twisting over, he wriggled swiftly towards the weapon.

Still half dazed, Roger sat up. For a moment his eyes refused to focus; then he saw Fouché's intention. With a great effort he flung himself forward, sprawling over Fouché and checking his progress. Turning on his side, Fouché kicked out savagely, but Roger got in a blow under his chin. His head jerked up and he rolled over on his back. Roger smashed his fist down into his enemy's stomach. Fouché's knees lifted as he doubled up with pain. Seizing his advantage, Roger sprang upon him and got both hands round his throat. In vain Fouché strove to claw Roger's hands away. His eyes began to bulge from his head; gradually his kicking and writhing grew weaker. At last he lay still, unconscious.

Gasping, Roger stumbled to his feet and wiped the sweat from his face. As he fought to get his breath back he listened anxiously for sounds of people approaching; but the fight had been short and sharp, and it seemed that no one below had heard it. His head was paining him frightfully, but he forced himself to think. Gone were his plans for a long night's sleep. At this vital eleventh hour Fouché had recognized him. It was now Roger Brook *versus* the French Republic. He must not waste a second if he were to escape from France alive.

Pulling himself together, he tied Fouché's ankles with his sash and his wrists with his cravat, then gagged him with a table napkin. Unlocking the door of the prisoner's room, he dragged his still unconscious enemy inside and locked him in there. With sudden elation he realized that he had not yet returned the turnkey's bunch of keys, so before going downstairs he was able to lock behind him the iron door to the ante-room.

At the bottom of the stairs he opened the door of the Commissioners' room and saw that they, and the officers of the guard, were about to sit down to supper. Without entering the room he told them that Citizen Representative Fouché was going to spend the night with him upstairs, and that as they had both been up for many hours they did not wish to be disturbed until nine o'clock next morning. He then slipped out into the garden, crossed it, and let himself out of the postern door.

Twenty minutes' quick walk brought him to *La Belle Étoile*. It had only just gone nine o'clock, and the main taproom of the hostelry was crammed with people. Money had never been so scarce in Paris, but that night everybody had managed to find a few *francs* with which to drink damnation to Robespierre. From a doorway in the hall Roger managed to attract Maître Blanchard's attention, and the landlord came out to him. He told his old friend that he had at last been unmasked; so had to leave Paris with the utmost urgency and wanted the best horse in his stables. Blanchard took him out to the yard, selected a bay mare and helped him saddle up. Roger then insisted that he should accept a hundred *louis* for the animal, and added that for the friendship of himself and his wife the crown jewels of France could not be a sufficient price.

Soon after ten o'clock Roger was stabling his mount at Passy. He would have liked to ride through the night, but knew that it would be penny wise, pound foolish, to attempt it. He would have fallen asleep in the saddle and come to grief on the roadside. The level-headedness and courage which now decided him to snatch a few hours' sleep, instead of making a panicky attempt to race as far as possible from the area of danger, was one of the secrets of his success as a secret agent; and now, quite unconsciously, he followed this natural prompting of his nature.

The Velots were up. They too were celebrating. Marie had cooked a special supper, after which they were enjoying, as they knew would be M. de Talleyrand's wish, a bottle of his best *Y'Quem*. They begged Roger to do them the honour of joining them, which he did willingly to the extent of one small glass, but told them that he must get some sleep, then make the dust of the French roads fly beneath his horse's hooves. To this faithful couple he gave 200 *louis*, which he thought should keep them going until things had quietened down sufficiently for de Talleyrand to return.

At three o'clock in the morning old Antoine called him; by half-past he was mounted and on his way. Owing to the orders he had given at the Temple no one would attempt to enter the second floor of the tower until nine. When there was no response to the guards' knocking it would take them at least two hours to prise the iron door off its hinges, and Fouché would need another hour before he could possibly be ready to leave Paris. That gave Roger an eight-hour start, but he knew that once the hunt was up it would be fast and inexorable; and he was under no illusion that his enemy would not know in which direction he had gone. The moment Fouché was free he would go down to Tison and make him repeat everything said to him and by him the previous evening; then Fouché would take express post for Divonne, and travel night and day. Roger, too, meant to travel post for the latter stages of his journey, as he dared not lose even an hour of his lead in sleep; but for as long as he could keep the saddle horseback would be faster, and he hoped to have increased his lead to eleven or twelve hours by that night.

It was still dark when he passed through Corbeil. At Melun he ate a swift breakfast then rode on through the forest of Fontainebleau. At Sens he dined. By the time he reached Joigny he was very tired and his mare was flagging. The next stretch on to Auxerre was agony, but he entered the town at six o'clock, having covered a hundred and five miles in under fifteen hours.

At Auxerre he sold his mare to the postmaster and hired a light four-horse coach. As it clattered out of the town he stretched his aching limbs and, in spite of the bumping, soon fell into an exhausted sleep.

He was woken by being flung violently sideways, and heard the crash of shattered glass. Crawling out, he found to his fury that through careless driving the near fore-wheel of the coach had caught an outcrop of jutting rock on the roadside and been wrenched off. Still worse, the fore-axle had broken under the shock.

It was pitch dark and they were in the middle of a forest. His postillions told him that Lucy le Bois was the nearest village and that it lay about two miles behind them. He could not bear the thought of going back and there was only an off-chance of securing another vehicle there; so he decided to take one of the saddle horses and ride on to Avallon. The postillions protested, but he used his authority as a Commissar and cursed them into silence.

The accident to the coach had occurred about half-past ten. An hour's ride should have brought him into Avallon. By midnight there was still no sign of the town, and he realized with dismay that in the darkness he must have lost his way. The road was little better than a track, and when he came to another that crossed it, using the stars as a guide, he turned northward. Two miles further on it curved away to the west; after another mile he felt sure he had gone wrong again, and took another that branched off it. By one o'clock in the morning he knew that he was hopelessly lost.

Hour after hour he kicked the post-horse into a trot along bridle-paths and down forest glades. He could have wept with rage and desperation, but it was not until half an hour after dawn that he came upon a solitary farm at which he could enquire. There, he learnt that he was further from Avallon than he had been when the coach had broken down. His mount was spent and the people at the farm had no riding horse they could sell him. It was nine o'clock before, utterly exhausted, he entered Avallon at a sorry amble.

While another light coach was being prepared for him, he drank a pint of wine and munched a piece of cake. Then he climbed into the vehicle, collapsed on its back seat as it drove out of the yard, and slept like a log.

He did not wake until well into the afternoon. His first thought was to turn and peer out of the little window at the back of the coach. His terrible misadventure the previous night had cost him ten hours, and that was the whole of the lead he had dared count upon. At the most Fouché could not be more than an hour behind him. He had promised his postillions treble pay for maximum speed, but Fouché too would make his men drive like Jehu in the hope of yet snatching the stupendous prize.

Roger reached Châlons at nine in the evening. He had not eaten all day, but did not now dare to stop for a proper meal. Taking food and wine into the coach with him he set off again, now to the eastward, as a great detour had to be made to pass to the north of the Jura mountains. The country here was much more hilly and the going slower; but all night they jogged on, changing horses every few hours while Roger slept fitfully.

At eight in the morning the coach clattered into Lons-le-Saunier. From there the road ran north for twenty miles to Poligny, whence by a hairpin bend one could come south by east on the far side of the mountains down another stretch of forty miles to Divonne; but there were by-ways across the mountains which would reduce the distance by a third; so Roger decided to transfer from the coach to a horse. In addition to the animal he bought from the landlord of the inn a good map, and fortified himself with a substantial breakfast before setting off. By ten he was out of the town, and heading up the first gradient into the foothills of the Jura.

Half an hour later, on breasting the summit of the slope, he looked back. As he had feared might be the case, a little cloud of dust just beyond the town was being thrown up by a fast-driven coach, approaching along the flat road by which he had entered it. In such sparsely populated districts of France as this, now that the wealthy were dead or had fled abroad, such conveyances were rarely to be seen; so it could hardly be anyone other than Fouché.

At the inn he would learn that his quarry had taken to horse; so he would follow suit. He would not follow alone, either. Now that he was on the last lap of the chase, he would order out a troop of hussars or gendarmes from the local barracks. Grimly Roger turned away and rode on up into the mountains.

His route was not difficult to follow, as it passed through several villages, the names of which he had been given; and from the map he was able to pick out various peaks that gave him his direction. Until well into the afternoon he was winding his way upwards into the Morez pass, and it was not until four o'clock that he emerged from it to see a wonderful panorama of the Lake of Geneva spread below him. Another two hours down steeper hairpin bends brought him to Divonne.

On enquiring at the inn for a farmer named Chaumette, he held his breath. All along he had realized that the Terrorist's cousin might have a different name. If so, long before he could hope to have questioned enough people to run the farmer to earth Fouché would come riding into the town. Only by going into hiding could he then hope to save his life, and while he sweated with frustration in some haystack his enemy would carry off his hundred thousand pounds.

His luck was in; Farmer Chaumette lived about three miles up the slope on the far side of the green valley in which Divonne lay. Shaking his tired horse into a trot, Roger pressed forward up the hill.

He was now about to come face to face with another problem that no amount of thought could have solved in advance—what was he going to do if Farmer Chaumette refused to give little Capet up? Had he not been pursued he could have simply made a reconnaissance, then returned at night and kidnapped the child; but he knew that his time margin was far too short for that. He could, if orders, pleading, threats and gold all failed, shoot the farmer; but it was now the supper hour so he would probably have one or two labourers as well as his family with him. Single-handed, it was going to be no easy matter to overcome them all, and at the same time secure a boy who might be unwilling to come away.

Roger had had no time to prepare a fake document authorizing him to collect the child, and his mind was so absorbed in speculating on what sort of reception his demand for him would receive that when he drew level with the farm he could hardly believe his eyes. In the glow of the sunset there was a small boy swinging on a gate. Fortune at the last had served him truly well. The child's underlip had grown thicker and his Bourbon nose more prominent; his fair hair was matted with dirt, he was barefoot and clad in rags; his eyes were shifty and his expression vicious; but Roger knew him beyond all doubt to be His Most Christian Majesty Louis XVII, King of France and Navarre.

There was no one else about, and the gate led into a barnyard from which only the chimney of the farmhouse was visible. Dismounting, Roger tied up his horse and said:

"Good evening, Monsieur Charles; I don't suppose you remember me, but I am an old friend of your mother."

The boy gave him an appraising stare, then nodded. "Yes; even with those bristles on your chin you have the look of an *aristo*! I suppose by friend you mean you were one of the old whore's lovers." With a sudden grin he added, "Perhaps you're my real father."

Inwardly Roger shuddered. Evidently Farmer Chaumette had proved a worthy successor to Simon as "tutor" to the little Capet. In their determination to root out from his mind any lingering thought of kingship, they had gone to the length of telling him that he was illegitimate. But this was no time to attempt to purge his poisoned mind of such beliefs, so Roger raised a smile and replied:

"Let's not talk of that. I wish, though, to act the part of father to you for the next week or so. I've come to take you away."

"Does old Chaumette know that?" came the cautious question.

"Not yet. Where is he?"

"Inside with the old bitch, and Louis and Jean. They're having their supper."

"Why are you not with them?"

Little Capet nodded towards a wooden platter lying on the ground. "I've had mine. They send me out to feed with the pigs, but I often eat at the gate here."

"You'll not be sorry to leave the farm, then?"

Again the suspicious look crept into the boy's eyes, and he asked, "Where are you taking me?"

"Where would you like to go?" Roger asked, not yet wishing to disclose his plans.

"To Paris!" The reply was instantaneous. "I want to see them cutting off real people's heads with the guillotine."

Roger was terribly conscious that with every moment Fouché

must be drawing nearer. He dared not waste an unnecessary minute in argument. He lied without hesitation:

"So be it; I'll take you to Paris, then. But we must leave at once. You'll have to ride in front of me. Come along!"

Instead of climbing over to Roger's side of the gate, the boy jumped down and turned away. As he ran off he cried over his shoulder, "I won't keep you a minute, but I've got to fetch something."

In an agony of apprehension Roger watched him, fearing that he meant to go into the house and might bring the Chaumette family on the scene; but he dived into a barn, and reappeared lugging a wooden and iron contraption half as big as himself. It proved to be another model guillotine, very roughly made, but much larger than his former toy. Panting, he pushed it across the top of the gate and cried with shining eyes:

"Isn't it a fine one? It does mice with ease, but I had much trouble with a mole; the knife would not cut through the brute's fur."

Roger was not listening. He had caught the sound of horses' hooves clicking against the stones of the track. Untying his horse, he jumped into the saddle. He could now see down into the valley. A group of some twenty horsemen were trotting up the hill. They were no more than a mile away, and at their head rode the tall, grey-coated figure of Joseph Fouché.

Knocking aside the model guillotine that little Capet was holding up to him, Roger seized the boy by the collar of his ragged jacket. With a heave he pulled him up and lay him face down, like a sack of potatoes, across the pommel of his saddle. Turning his horse he rowelled it, and it leapt forward up the track. A distant cry echoed through the valley. His pursuers had spotted him. With a cheer they broke into a gallop.

"My guillotine!" yelled little Capet; "I'll not go without my guillotine!"

"Be silent!" snapped Roger. "Or you'll be guillotined yourself."

For answer the King of France bit him in the soft part of the thigh.

With an oath Roger dealt him a heavy clout on the ear, and he began to bellow with some reason.

In a ten-minute gallop Roger reached the crest of the ridge. It was, he knew, the frontier, but no immediate safety for him lay on its other side. There were no frontier guards or barriers in these sparsely populated mountains, and Fouché would not hesitate to follow him a dozen miles into Switzerland. Below him he could again see the lake. The sun had gone down behind the mountains and the broad sheet of water was now misty in the evening light, but on its shore some eight miles distant he could just make out the spires of the little town of Nyon. If he could reach it there would be Swiss magistrates and police there, who would give him protection.

Half a mile down the slope there was a wood. In it lay the best hope of throwing off his pursuers. Leaving the track, he cantered across a stony meadow towards it. As he reached the fringe of the wood Fouché and his men appeared on the skyline behind him; he could hear them shouting as they urged their horses forward.

Plunging in amongst the trees, he guided his mount as well as he could, crouching low over little Capet's body. Every instant he expected a big branch to crack his skull and sweep him from the saddle. Small branches, twigs and leaves whipped against his face, half blinding him, and falling night now made it so dark under the trees that it was difficult to see more than a few yards ahead. His precious burden was screaming like a maniac with fear and anger. The slope was steep, and the wood over two miles in depth, but by a miracle they slithered from level to level without mishap and emerged safely on its other side.

Twilight had dimmed the scene. Roger could no longer see Nyon, but knew that to reach it he still had some five miles to cover. Turning his jaded mount's head half left, he spurred it to a fresh effort; but the going was bad, as the low-lying grassland between the wood and the lake was soft and spongy. He was only half-way across it when, one by one, his pursuers broke from the wood, shouting to one another as they caught sight of him.

Twenty yards from the shore he struck the lakeside track. On the firmer ground his horse seemed to take new courage. For a time he managed to increase his lead, but after he had covered another half mile his pursuers had also gained the firmer ground. Every few moments he glanced back at the bunch of shadowy figures in his rear. His mount had done as hard a day as theirs and now had the extra weight of little Capet to carry. Gradually they crept up on him. Another half mile and, with bitter, blinding fury, he knew that he would never reach the town with his invaluable cargo. He must either drop the boy or be captured and hauled back to Paris to die.

For a few moments the awful choice he now had to make caused wild agitation in his tired brain. If he thrust the child from his saddle at the speed he was riding the fall might break his neck or do him some serious injury, but he had only to swerve on to the grass for the fall to be soft, and children's bones are much less liable to sustain permanent harm from an accident than are those of grown-ups; so if he threw the boy off feet first the risk would not be great. His own life depended on it. He knew that for certain now. The sound of the pounding hooves behind was becoming louder and louder. Yet, after all he had gone through to win his splendid prize, he could not bring himself to surrender it.

Suddenly that strange, mysterious link which had served him more than once before functioned again in this emergency. Georgina's voice came to him out of the shadows, as plainly as if she were shouting in his ear:

"Roger, you fool! The boat! The boat! Do you not see it?"

His eyes had been fixed on the dim track ahead. As his glance switched towards the lake, he saw a tumbledown shack on the foreshore, and lying near it a rowing-boat with its stern just in the water.

Swerving his mount violently, he plunged down the bank towards it. As he drew rein the foaming horse let its head fall forward and stood with its legs splayed apart. Slipping from the saddle he lifted little Capet down and bundled him into the boat.

A chorus of furious yells came from Fouché and his men. One of them fired a pistol and the bullet whined over Roger's head. Another pistol cracked; but Fouché, fearful that little Capet might be killed, cried:

"Don't shoot! Don't shoot!"

Roger had his shoulder to the prow of the boat. As the horsemen left the track, he gave a great heave and it slid into the water. He leapt in, pushed the bewildered little Capet towards the stern, seized an oar and shoved off.

Shouting and cursing, the pursuers came galloping down to the beach. When they reached the water's edge the boat was already twelve feet out. Roger now had both oars in the rowlocks and was pulling with all his might. Darkness was closing in and the boat was drawing rapidly away from the shore; but Fouché would not accept defeat. Forcing his horse into the water up to its saddle girths, he drew a pistol and screamed:

"Halt or we will riddle you with bullets! In the name of the Republic, I swear to protect you if you return. Proceed and you die!"

For a moment Roger ceased rowing, and with a laugh of triumph yelled back, "To Hell with the Republic! I hold the King!"

EPILOGUE

In England it was exceptionally warm that August. Out at Richmond, one night towards the end of the month, Amanda, when about to undress for bed, pulled back the curtain of her window to let in more air. Above the trees of the park hung a sickle moon that lit the silent scene with a pale, unearthly radiance. A slight sound below her caused her to look down. A man was standing there in the garden. She would have known that tall figure anywhere. Leaning out, she breathed the one word: "Roger!"

He did not reply; but he turned his face up, and in the moonlight she saw that its fine features were thin and drawn.

"Wait but a moment," she cried joyfully, "and I'll be down to let you in."

Running down the stairs, she pulled back the bolts of the garden door and threw it open. He was not, as she had expected, on the doorstep, but was still standing several paces away, where she had first seen him. Going out to him, she said with a catch in her voice:

"So you've come home at last."

"I don't yet know," he replied after a moment. "That depends on yourself."

"My dear," she said gently, "I beg of you put from your heart any malice you may still bear me, for I bear you none. In more than two years we have spent scarce three months together. We expected too much of each other for young people during so long a separation."

He nodded. "Georgina told me, in a letter, of your feelings; and you were right. We should have stood by our original bargain. For my part, I bear no malice either. I want you back, and more than I have ever done before. It is not that which prevents me taking you in my arms."

"What then?" she exclaimed in bewilderment. "You speak so strangely, Roger. What has come over you?"

"I escaped from France by way of Switzerland near a month ago. I have been back in England this past week living in solitude at an inn down in Greenwich, where no one would know me."

"But why? What have you done?"

"Ah!" he sighed. "What have I done? That is just it. I have done something which may for ever make a barrier between us. It lies so heavy on my conscience that I could not return to you unless you knew of it and considered that I acted for the best. This evening I decided to come out here and tell you of it, and you must be my judge. If, having heard what I have to say, you can take me back, my faith in myself will be restored. But should you thrust me from you with loathing, I shall not blame you, and I will arrange for you to have your freedom to marry again. Come! Let us go over to the summerhouse, so that we can sit down."

In silence they walked side by side across the moonlit lawn. When they had settled themselves he began a toneless monologue. After telling her how he had found that another child had been substituted for little Capet in the Temple, and of all that had followed up to his escape in the boat, he went on:

"Realizing that we were about to get away, Fouché and his men did their utmost to kill us. They sent a hail of pistol bullets at the boat, but by a miracle neither the child nor I were hit. A few more strokes of the oars and we were out of range. Night was coming on and soon we were hidden by the darkness. At first I pulled northward for a while towards Nyon, then I realized that a strong current was running against me; so, being by that time well out on the lake, I shipped the oars and let the boat drift. Second thoughts told me that was all to the good, as fifteen miles away at the south end of the lake lay Geneva. With a little rowing now and then I should drift there by the morning, and once there I could take little Capet straight to the British Minister, Sir Francis Drake. That would have ensured the prevention of any attempt by Fouché to recover the child; and, the Legation being British soil, I could have counted the delivery of him there as a successful conclusion to my mission.

"Frightened by the bullets he had stopped his yelling, and had, at first, taken refuge on the bottom boards in the stern of the boat. When we were safe he emerged and sat staring at me for a time; then he asked me where we were going.

"Having got him away I saw no reason why I should not tell him something of the truth. I said that whatever Simon and other people might have told him, there was no doubt at all about his being the rightful King of France; that I was taking him to a place where he would receive affection, good food, fine clothes, live in every comfort, and be treated with the respect due to his rank; that he would be taught to hunt and shoot as well as receive a proper education, and that I thought that in a few years' time he would be restored to his throne to reign over a great people.

"He considered what I said for a while, then replied to me in a manner that was beyond belief horrifying. He said he was glad I thought he would become a real king, because kings did what they liked. If there were another Revolution, he would know how to put it down. Someone had told him about Carrier ordering mass drownings at Nantes. He said they must have been a fine sight, and that he would like to have seen them. It would be a good way to deal with rebellious subjects if they were too many for the guillotine; but that would be more fun, as he proposed to play the part of executioner himself. If there were no rebellion, he could start a war, and would use his guillotine to execute some of the prisoners. He would have women too: a lot of women, as he had been told his great-grandfather had had; and when they ceased to please him he would chop off their heads.

"I attempted to reason with him. I explained that, while a king naturally enjoyed many privileges and great riches, it was, in exchange for them, his duty to devote himself to the welfare of his people and set a high example by leading a good life. He only sneered at me, and went on to describe further crimes that his imagination conjured up as possible for him to commit if he had the power of a king.

"Feeling that I could support such a conversation no longer, I took out some opium pellets I had with me. I had bought them when planning to carry him off from the Temple, for use if it proved necessary to keep him quiet during a long journey across France. Catching hold of him, I forced him to swallow a couple, and a quarter of an hour later he fell asleep.

"It was now fully dark and for a long time I sat there brooding about the boy. I was by then convinced that a whole year of the tuition which had been ordered for him by those evil men of the Commune could never be eradicated. He had received it at the most receptive age; so his relatives might dress him up and give him a veneer of manners, but that abominable lust for cruelty would remain with him beneath the surface all his life. It must have been there from the beginning. After all, he was of the same blood as Louis XV, who was such a heartless debauchee, and as Louis XIV, who ordered the terrible persecution of the

Huguenots. Had he continued in his mother's care that horrible streak in his nature might have lain dormant; but having been brought to the surface and deliberately fostered, he would always be subject to hideous urges beyond his power to control.

"I wondered about his future. At best he would be a Prince living in exile, but provided with money by fellow monarchs and protected by his high birth from all ordinary laws. He would know few restraints; so would practise bestial cruelties on animals and on every human being who was unfortunate enough to fall into his power. At worst he would be crowned Louis XVII, King of France, in Rheims Cathedral. That was the most likely possibility; for I think it certain that, now a reaction has set in, it will be only a matter of time before the French people demand a restitution of the Monarchy, just as we did by recalling Charles II after the Great Rebellion. Then he would provoke a second Revolution, which might cost the lives of another million of his subjects; or perhaps start another war which might engulf all Europe. I realized then that I had with me in the boat, not only a hundred thousand pounds, but the most terrible menace to human happiness that existed in the whole world.

"I was desperately tired, and at length decided to snatch a little sleep; but it occurred to me that the vicious little brute might wake in the night, steal my knife, and do me an injury. So I took out my opium pellets again and opened his mouth. He did not even stir, but I knew two more would do him no serious harm; so I slipped a couple down his throat.

"When I awoke it was morning; and I was alone in the boat."

Amanda drew a sharp breath. "Oh, Roger! Then it was God's will that he should wake, and, while still dazed from the drug, fall out?"

Roger shook his head. "Nay, it was not like that. I do not recall falling asleep. I was still sitting staring at him when I heard a soft voice calling to me. I looked up, and there, walking on the water towards me, was Marie Antoinette.

"She was not as I last saw her, haggard and grey, but radiantly beautiful, just as I first set eyes on her when a boy; and she was holding out her arms to me.

" 'Monsieur de Breuc,' she said in that sweet voice of hers, 'my poor child's mind is sick, and nothing but my love can cure it. What he has become is through no fault of his; but only the ending of his life while young can now save his soul. When I was in the Temple you gave me your oath that naught but God's intervention should prevent you from restoring my son to me. I beg you do so now.'

"I knew without her saying more how she wished me to act. Picking the boy up, I laid him gently in the water at her feet. In that moment he too seemed to have regained his innocent look and former beauty. As he went under, he never stirred; but he was still alive. So, you see, I killed the King."

Tears were running down Amanda's cheeks as she drew Roger's head on to her shoulder, and murmured, "Oh, my poor sweet! How you must have suffered while carrying this dread secret for these past weeks. But suffer no more. You gave up a great fortune, and assumed a terrible burden to do what you knew to be right; and I shall never cease to love you for it."